DARK HORDE RISING

DARK HORDE RISING

IAIN HOPE

Copyright © 2015 Iain Hope
All rights reserved.

ISBN: 1519412045
ISBN 13: 9781519412041
Library of Congress Control Number: 2015919417
CreateSpace Independent Publishing Platform
North Charleston, South Carolina

CONTENTS

	Wildlands of Darylor	ix
Prologue	Flight from the north	xi
Part One	**Old Friends and New Allies (Blessed Year 1346)**	
Chapter 1	Danger on the road	3
Chapter 2	A meeting of friends	16
Chapter 3	Arrangements	23
Chapter 4	At the college	33
Chapter 5	Returning to Shandrilos	40
Chapter 6	Druid and mage	50
Chapter 7	A Chance Encounter	58
Chapter 8	The cost of failure	72
Chapter 9	The Conclave of Magi	82
Chapter 10	Assassin	95
Chapter 11	The Grand Council of the Wilds	100
Chapter 12	The goblin threat	107
Chapter 13	The catacombs	116
Chapter 14	Trapped	122
Chapter 15	Of Elves, Dwarves and Men	126
Chapter 16	The Conclave divided	138
Chapter 17	Decisions	147
Chapter 18	A duel	158
Chapter 19	The battle	170

Chapter 20	In the dark	177
Chapter 21	Into the unknown	187
Chapter 22	Descent into darkness	195
Chapter 23	Return from the depths	209
Chapter 24	A threat revealed	216
Chapter 25	The tale of Nossi Bee	230
Chapter 26	Rumours	237
Chapter 27	Magical revelations	244
Chapter 28	The group divided	257
Chapter 29	Dark thoughts	267
Chapter 30	Dangers in the dark	284
Chapter 31	Murder in the College	293
Chapter 32	The rising threat	308
Chapter 33	To the surface	315
Chapter 34	Escape from the dark	322
Chapter 35	Revelations	332
Part Two	**New Heroes and Old Enemies**	
Chapter 36	Dreams and Decisions	343
Chapter 37	The Lore King	357
Chapter 38	Guardian of the Elves	363
Chapter 39	Legends and Lore	375
Chapter 40	Death and Rebirth	386
Chapter 41	A hidden sanctuary	391
Chapter 42	The merging	396
Chapter 43	Prophecy and decision	405
Chapter 44	Visitors	416
Chapter 45	Relics of the dead	433
Chapter 46	Between a rock and a hard place	452
Chapter 47	Captivity	464
Chapter 48	A discovery beneath the ground	477
Chapter 49	Searches	487
Chapter 50	Deadly plans	501
Chapter 51	The fate of Nossi Bee	514
Chapter 52	The Ninth Kingdom	528
Chapter 53	Trials and tragedies	551
Chapter 54	Before the storm	563
Chapter 55	The coming storm	576

Chapter 56	Demon and mage	590
Chapter 57	At the Waygate	605
Chapter 58	The calm before the storm	619
Chapter 59	The storm strikes	634
Chapter 60	Last defense	648
Chapter 61	The Great Temple	669
Chapter 62	Defeat	683
Chapter 63	Sacrifice	692
Chapter 64	The Lifestone	708
Chapter 65	Aftermath	718
Epilogue	A farewell	727
Appendix 1	Cast of Characters	733
Appendix 2	Chronology of Darylor	739
	Dark Horde Rising	745

WILDLANDS OF DARYLOR

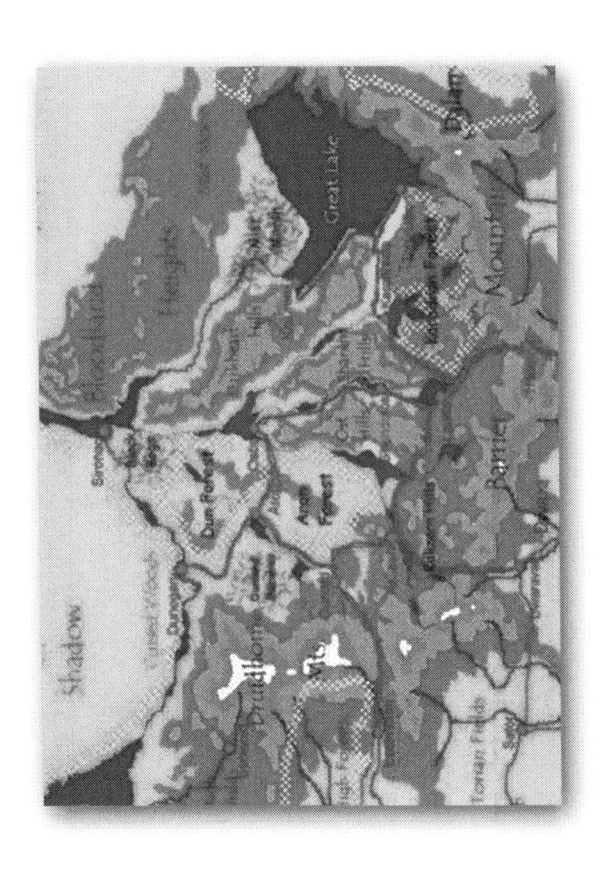

Prologue

FLIGHT FROM THE NORTH

Of the destruction of the Elder Kingdoms, little is now known, only that almost a thousand years ago some great calamity overtook them. Once it is said the vast northlands were the home to a great civilisation, yet how this was lost, along with its great wealth of knowledge is a mystery. Tales of the wonders of the Elder abound and tales of their demise too. They talk of a vast war, or of disease, or of demons, or of all these. Few can verify any of this now, the last descendants of the Elder who remain either hide away or have lost all knowledge... and the northlands themselves are lost to us too; they are now the domain of monstrous creatures that kill men on sight!

From 'The nature of the Elder' by Melkor Erin, Archmage of Shandrilos, Blessed Year (BY)1303

He thundered through the narrow canyon at such a reckless speed that the first wave of arrows missed him. He hit the line of goblin skirmishers before they were fully formed; his sturdy chestnut mare hammering the slim, rangy goblins aside. The grey skinned creatures screamed their anger, their sharp toothed mouths wide. Quickly, they drew more arrows, but by the time the second wave of arrows came raining down, Gael Pemarson had already thrown up a warding spell. The poorly made arrows shattered.

Frantically, he kicked his horse to further exertion. The brave mare gave a burst of speed that opened up a gap between him and his pursuers and once more he thanked all the gods of earth, sea and sky that goblins did not ride.

After a score of minutes, Gael was forced to slow his tiring mare to a walk. The goblins, although fast, would not be able to close the gap and it would give his mount time to regain her wind. However, Gael knew that he would have to push her hard if he were to give himself any chance of reaching Sironac territory. Thankfully, troll warriors could not move fast enough to be a threat or he would not have passed that last line; a group of heavily built trolls could have knocked his horse from its feet even at a full charge, yeti would have been even worse! Hopefully, he had left such terrifying creatures far behind.

How any of the foul creatures had got ahead of him again, he didn't know. It was almost like they knew exactly where he would be, which route he would take.

He had been riding hard for the past two days, heading south and west for the isolated town of Sironac. He had eaten his meals in the saddle and only rested the mare and himself for no more than three or four hours over the last two days. The goblins could never have run for long enough or fast enough to overtake him. They must have been sending messages ahead somehow, in an effort to cut him off. It seemed that they were desperate to prevent him from reporting what he had seen, but how could they know exactly where he would be?

Gael had been sent into the northlands by his master, the Archmage of Shandrilos. He had been working directly for the Archmage for almost eight years now and had become one of the best explorers the College had. Of course, only the Archmage and one or two other archivists and scholars knew of his activities. Gael knew that many of his fellow fighter mages at the college now thought him dead in the unknown North, he had been gone so long.

It suddenly occurred to him that they could well be proved right!

'No', he thought savagely, gritting his teeth. He would not fail. Too much was riding on this. As he rode on his mind was drawn inevitably back to what he had seen just a couple of days ago.

———

Gael had originally come to the northlands to explore. Once the Elder races had dwelt in these lands; there were ruins to be investigated and lost magics to be rediscovered. Gael had sought out lore and artifacts and had discovered much that he had passed on to his colleagues at the College of Magic in Shandrilos. It was fascinating work and that was why Gael had stayed so long away from family and friends.

However, he was also here now because of the goblin threat. The grey skinned creatures were the main enemy of mankind. They were cunning and greedy; intent on raiding and killing to take what they wanted and drive humans from the north. The Archmage had thought it important to maintain a watch on them, to give warning of potential trouble and Gael had agreed.

Over the years, he had scouted a large area of the uncharted northlands. He had searched out rumours of alliances and petty warlords and even built up trading relations with some of the friendlier goblin tribes. He had learned something of their language and culture. What he had also learned was that things in the northlands were changing.

Goblins had always lived throughout these vast lands in tribal groups led by a chieftain or 'Gul'. In themselves these tribes were not a large threat numbering in the hundreds. However, from time to time, a warlord or 'Gul Dor' would arise, conquer and unify tribes. The last time had been almost thirty years ago and had taken all the forces of the Wildlands to stop a goblin horde many thousands strong as they rampaged south. Thankfully, for the Wildland provinces this unity amongst the tribes happened rarely, and usually broke up after a few seasons; goblins were too wild and when faced with any real resistance or hardship, their own vicious, and self preserving natures inevitably broke them. True discipline was rare except amongst the elite braves of the tribes. Even a 'Gul Dor' could not hold them together for long.

At least that was what all previous wisdom had said.

Gael Pemarson had learnt over the last few years that this was no longer true.

In the Bloodland Heights, on the edge of the true north, the goblins were slowly being unified. They were being forged into a nation! Goblins spoke in hushed whispers of a legendary figure known as Marog or 'Strongheart'. Gael had reported this to the Archmage, as had others, but so far no one had been able to get close enough to verify that he truly existed and if he did, what his plans were.

That was why Gael and his apprentices had come.

Gael had believed he had finally tracked down this elusive unifier, this great Gul Dor. Gael needed to take this opportunity to find out more and return to the Archmage with unquestionable evidence.

Gael and his apprentices had stumbled on a huge encampment almost by accident and quickly hidden themselves on a high ridge to see what was going on. They had not been prepared for what they saw!

They had lain on the high ridge overlooking an encampment of not just goblins, but also trolls, kobolds and yeti; all enemies of mankind. A gathering that was, by all he knew, impossible. Savagery, brutality and hatred were a way of life for these creatures and they hated one another as fiercely as they hated men. Nothing he'd known could possibly bring them together.

As he had slowly got past his shock, Gael had begun to realise the true magnitude of what he was seeing. He had watched and scouted among these creatures for nearly a decade. He had studied them for twice that length of time; there was no one who knew these creatures and their ways better. True, no one really knew anything of the secretive trolls save they hated all outsiders and killed on sight. However, the yeti and kobolds he knew were so primitive there wasn't even a concept of unity beyond the family or pack, and all outsiders were generally seen as food. Yet here they all were, along with goblins under a single banner, that of Gul Dor Marog!

As Gael and his apprentices had watched carefully hidden, the chieftains and warlords of the different races had come together in the centre of the huge clearing below. Gael had seen them all clearly: the huge rangy yeti; the lumbering powerful trolls; the slim, cunning goblins; and the dog-like kobolds. They had moved to their allotted places as if guided by some hidden hand. They formed a large circle, all regarding each other with a mixture of distrust, fear and… something else, something akin to excitement. Gael noticed a powerful goblin, large and dominant at the fore. Marog!

Suddenly, Gael had felt magic called into being and within that sense came a feeling of such dread that he had almost turned and fled. Only his sharp whispered command had stopped his apprentices.

Down in the clearing, a grey wall had shimmered into being and Gael had recognised a portal opening. From within came a swarm of creatures Gael had never seen before; creatures that made even the monstrous denizens of the northlands look... ordinary. Giant insect-like creatures poured from the portal, hurtling across the hard ground of the clearing to freeze, insect limbs held ready, facing the circle of chieftains; then monstrous brutes that made even the trolls and yeti look small, followed with black skinned goblins coming next; armed and armoured better than any tribal warriors of which Gael had ever heard tell. Finally, into the centre of all, gliding shadows moved, hooded and cloaked. They were the size of men, but no man moved as they!

The portal had then vanished and silence had fallen. Gael had shared a disbelieving look with his two apprentices. Not only were these creatures he had never seen, but the magic they could feel was of a power they had never experienced and evil seemed to lie on them like a cloak. Gael had never felt such malice, it made his stomach roil and his heart pound. Gael sensed power thrumming around the hooded figures, and the being in the centre almost blinded his mystic senses. Not even the Grand Abbot and the Archmage, the two most powerful magic users he knew, had approached this being's power. The creature was evil. Gael knew no other way to describe the feeling of horror that seemed to pulse from the dark hooded figure. This went beyond Marog and the goblin unification, far beyond.

The figure had begun to speak.

It spoke of the Lords of the Night, the Dark Gods; those whom all the denizens of the North both worshipped and feared.

The figure's message was simple but powerful. He was the disciple of the Lords of Night and he had come to unite all the servants of darkness in a divine war of conquest, a war of retribution to slaughter all their enemies, and to return the Ata'Gon. The chieftains and leaders, led by the now undeniable Gul Dor Marog had prostrated themselves ecstatically, swearing allegiance with a religious fervour Gael had never seen. They had chanted the name over and over.

'Ata'Gon, Ata'Gon, Ata'Gon...'

The feeling of cold and dread had washed over Gael anew. He had no idea what he was seeing... sensing... feeling. The Ata'Gon. He recognised the name. It was the name used by the goblins for the Dark One. According to the old tales the Dark One was the most powerful of all the demon lords of old.

Gael's mind had been momentarily overwhelmed with questions and, for a moment, he'd not been able to think clearly.

Where had these new foul creatures come from? Who were they? If they were supporting Marog, what was their goal? Were the Wildlands in danger? Could this Ata'Gon be a threat?

No, the Ata'Gon was a legend. Whoever the hooded creature was down there, he was using the beliefs of the goblins and the others to control them. Gael wasn't sure who these new creatures and their leader could be, but he was sure of one thing. The danger to the Wildlands was no longer that of a goblin invasion, but of something far worse. The unified goblins alone could have called together an army greater than all the forces of the Wildlands combined, but the leaders represented down there could call together a force many times that. If they were pointed south...

Gael had prayed silently to the gods, and slowly he had regained control of his thoughts. They had been misled. The Archmage believed the Wildlands faced a threat from some simple goblin warlord. A very serious danger, but he had no idea of the truth. Who could?

Whoever or whatever these creatures and their Lord were, or what their intentions, the Archmage must know of them. All the Wildlands must know!

Gael and his apprentices had made their escape, unseen, undiscovered... or so they had thought.

They had sensed no pursuit, seen no pursuers and yet there they were, suddenly, waiting! Only hasty magic had saved them, allowed them to slip away. Gael had then reluctantly ordered them to split up and head for Sironac by different routes; it would increase the chances of one of them making it home to tell what they had seen. He feared for his apprentices, but they were tough and well trained. It should have worked, yet Gael knew one of his apprentices was quickly tracked and killed, though the enemy could not have known which way he had headed. The link he'd had with young Hignar had snapped. They had not been separated long enough for it to have been distance that broke their connection. No, Hignar had paid the price they all had known might be the cost of coming to the northlands. Gael had grieved nonetheless, even as his horse had galloped onwards. He would not turn to avenge his apprentice, much as he had so burned to do. His duty to his people was more important. He hoped that his other apprentice, Tallan would make it. Tallan was the elder of his two apprentices, a full adept and a seasoned soldier.

Two days on and Gael was seriously starting to doubt if he himself would make it. However, he was now sure that he had at least left the last lot of pursuing goblins behind, but where would the next ambush be?

He had left the grassy plains yesterday and had now entered the Bloodland Heights. The land had risen around him. He knew that these ravines had been carved by ancient rivers that had flowed from the northern mountainous edge of the Heights. They had flowed down to the plains to merge with the great river Elder that wound through these lands into the unknown north. He had been riding through these steep sided canyons with dead ends and switch backs for almost a day now and he knew an ambush could be anywhere. However, what was most galling was that this confusing land should have worked in his favour, yet the goblin braves had found him four times already with relative ease! Gael knew they could not be getting ahead of him. Perhaps they were signaling.

Suddenly it hit him. The portal! If they had the power to create such portals then they could send warriors ahead of him with ease. As he strained both his normal and his mystical senses to their limit, seeking out any signs of life ahead, he frowned. That couldn't be right. Using Portals still did not explain how they knew where to find him. This land was vast and he could have been anywhere. He had long ago developed the skill and discipline to hide his presence to magical scrying. He was an acknowledged grandmaster at the college. Still there was much they did not know of magic.

Abruptly, a noise came to him from behind. He turned and cast his senses back along the narrow ravines.

Pursuers, so soon, but not goblins, these felt different. Echoes started to reach his ears and he kicked his mount on, still looking to the rear. What were they? He looked ahead. The ravine split up into three smaller steep sided canyons. His mare began to toss her head and he saw her nostrils flare in alarm, her ears laid back. She cried out suddenly in fear. Gael saw in the distance ahead, down the two canyons on his left, dust clouds rising as if a small army were galloping down both. They were trying to cut him off!

Gael's senses screamed and he looked back to see the terrifying, gigantic insect creatures from the meeting he had observed, hurtle into view along the ravine. Their limbs pumped and whirled as they came on at a gallop. His mare bolted in terror for the last canyon ahead and Gael did not try to stop her.

A split second before it appeared, Gael sensed a portal. He threw up a shield of energy around himself and his mare just as the portal appeared. A dark cloaked figure stepped out, even as Gael yanked his horse to the left. Energy swirled into focus around the shadowy creature and fire crackled around Gael. Acting on instinct, he cast his best fireball in riposte, but didn't look to see its results as he desperately kicked his mount forward. More fiery energy slammed into him as he fled, but his shield held... just! Behind him, the strange chittering noise of insect limbs filled the ravine and he risked a look back. From the other ravines, insects appeared and turned to join those who had followed him. There must have been fifty of the things and they were spread along the canyon floor like a carpet of seething limbs, their shining insect eyes implacable. They were gaining. His brave mare might have just outrun them had she been fresh, but she had been carrying him with barely a rest for two days and had recently run hard to out distance the goblin braves. He knew he wasn't going to make it.

'Damn it!' he silently cursed. He drove his heels into his mount again, using the pain to spur her to new heights of exertion, hating himself even as he did it. He glanced back again. The giant insects were closer, but they were thinning out as he stretched them. Maybe there was a chance if he got far enough. He snarled at his mount and kicked harder. He knew he was pushing her beyond her limits, but more than his own life and his mount's were at stake.

Looking ahead, he saw with dismay that the canyon ended in a scree slope and then a sheer wall of rock, maybe half a mile away. It was maybe ten metres high. He was trapped!

'No...no,' he thought 'not trapped. This could be what he needed. If he could make it to the rock face he might be able to get up and out of the canyon before those insect fiends reached him! That might free him from this trap.'

He looked back. Yes, the insects were tiring. Only the fastest and strongest were still gaining on him. He was almost to the scree slope.

With a coughing scream, blood burst from his mount's mouth and nose and she stumbled. Gael knew she had given her last. He silently saluted her effort and blessed her. As her front legs gave way, her brave head ploughed into the dry earth and Gael was flung from her back. He let himself be hurled forward and then rolled and came up running, hitting the scree slope at a sprint. He was lightly armoured and his blades were strapped to his back. Nevertheless, he could not match his horse's speed and felt like he was running through molasses. He pulled his blades even as he glanced over his shoulder. The insects rushed towards him with ferocious speed. Around half a dozen led the chase.

He turned to face them as he reached the cliff wall. He blasted the two leading insects with a prepared Stormburst spell and grunted in satisfaction as they were hurled back into three more. Muttering the keyword, he triggered the enchantment on his blades and saw the blue flames run along their length. Two more insects flung themselves at him, razor sharp jagged forearms raised to dismember him. He dodged the first, which crashed into the cliff face, and lopped the other's arms off. A whistling scream almost deafened him as it reared back and he nearly lost his head to the first creature he had dodged as it threw itself back at him. He desperately parried its frenzied hacking arms as its partner slumped back down the slope. He backed away and then reversed his stride and sprang forward, blocking an inrushing arm and beheading the creature. Its shiny armoured head cracked as it hit the cliff face and bounced down.

With the skill of a practised master, Gael muttered the release cantrip for a telekinesis spell. He ignored the mass of insects that were heading for him and turned to face the cliff. He looked up, jumped and at the same time thrust down with a telekinetic burst. He shot up and forward, just clearing the ten metre sheer cliff. He landed hard, rolled and clattered wearily into an outcropping. 'I can't keep this pace up,' he thought, knowing his magical reserves were starting to run dry.

Gael stumbled to his feet and risked a glance over the cliff edge. The mass of insects were flailing at the cliff, trying to climb, but finding no purchase. Gael smiled. 'You might just make it,' he told himself. He turned. A figure stood not twenty feet from him, regarding him like a child does a bug just caught in a bottle; head tilted, inquisitive. It was in full jet black armour, a shield with a screaming female of some kind was on one arm, a slim dark sword was in the other. Behind the figure stood more warriors in similar armour and Gael stopped in stunned amazement. It was a wonder indeed to find their kind here. Few humans ever saw them, they were so reclusive. His hopes rose. He started forward, his hand raised in greeting. It was then he noticed the two creatures in black hooded cloaks and stumbled to a halt! Gael glanced from one to another. It couldn't be! These two could not be working together. It went against everything Gael knew. It made no sense!

Gael came to an abrupt halt. "You've got to be jesting!" he gasped in agonised disbelief, as the reality of his plight hit him. They were part of this, and they were here waiting for him. It was suddenly clear to him: if he got past the insects, these warriors were here to finish him.

Gael did not want to die, but there was nowhere to run. He clenched his hands tightly on his blades and defeat settled on him; he knew the reputation of the people before him.

"So be it." he snarled, but he would not go easily.

He screamed a battle cry and attacked, hoping by all the gods that his apprentice Tallan had fared better than he.

PART ONE
OLD FRIENDS AND NEW ALLIES
(BLESSED YEAR 1346)

Chapter 1

DANGER ON THE ROAD

The Nordic are characterised by pale skin and great height, the men often standing over six feet tall. Their hair can often be pale, golden or even red in hue, and their eyes are as often blue or green, as they are dark. They are also unfailingly savage and uncouth, favouring battle and contest over more refined pastimes. However, there are indications that their art and culture were once far greater than they are today.

Except from 'A discourse on the myths of the people of the Empire and beyond' by the historian, Casinian. BY456.

The big man heeled his horse forward, forcing the stream of people to part for him as he headed for the town's north gate. People crowded the main north road into the city of Lauria as they headed for the market in the great square. There may well have been a couple of hundred farmers and merchants hemmed in on the narrow street. All had wares and goods in hand carts or pulled by slow moving oxen or pack horses that sweated in the sunshine. They were all heading into the city. The main problem for Jon Madraig was that he wanted to get out!

From his vantage point atop his warhorse, the big warrior could see that the mass of people crowded the road all the way to the gates up ahead. He knew that once beyond that gate the crowding would ease on the larger open roads and fields outside the city walls, but it was going to be slow going until then. Thankfully, the crowd parted more easily for him than for the few others who shared his plight. The impressive sight of Atrell, his powerfully built stallion marching proudly, high kneed, chomping at the bit, tended to give people an incentive to get out of the way. It was obvious that only Jon's strong hands on the keen stallion's reins stopped the warhorse from charging headlong into the throng as if into battle.

Occasionally, some burly farmer or proud merchant would be forced to scramble out of the way and would look up at the big warrior, a curse on their lips, but it would die unspoken. It would be a foolish peasant or pedlar who would risk the displeasure of a Nordic warrior, especially one so obviously well armed!

Jon was a descendant of a strong house of warriors from the highlands of Calon. They had settled in the Wildlands to the north, near the frontier city of Ostia. His family held lands, but amongst the poorer Nordic people this was very different to the wealth and privilege of an Olmec noble. Jon was also a younger son and so had no title or land of his own. The only benefit his family's land and title had really given him was an education and this did separate him from most of those around him.

There was one other obvious difference between himself and the vast majority of the people around him and that was his skin; he was pale, while the Olmecs around him had coppery skin. There were other differences, less clear to define, but it was this difference that marked him clearly as an outsider in Lauria.

Looking around, Jon Madraig could read wariness in many of the eyes of the farmers and merchants who passed him. As he forged on towards the north gate into the teeth of the human tide, there were few who looked at him without suspicion. To these people, Jon and his Nordic kin were uncouth, savage heathens who believed in old strange gods. These common farmers believed Jon's people were wild and uncivilised, worshipping strange, dark gods, and sacrificed animals or even people!

Jon smiled wryly.

While it was true that they believed in the old gods of earth and sky, and that they gave offerings, it was nothing more than one would offer at a feast to an honoured guest. The idea of human sacrifice was ridiculous. However, his own people were no better, they had just as many preconceptions about the Olmec.

The Nordic were a warrior race, but they had to be in the harsh north with all manner of creatures and wild beasts roaming the lands. For the Nordic, glory in battle was the ultimate honour. They believed that the Olmecs were a soft people who valued money and soft pleasures over honour and strength. Yet Jon conceded that these people, migrants from the empire, were anything but soft. It was true that they had developed a culture that was concerned primarily with wealth, prosperity and comfortable living, but then life was easier in the rich, fertile lands from which they came. Yet such lands were always desired, and the Olmecs had been invaded time and again. Eventually, they had developed their own armies and for them it was not honoured battle they fought, but a ruthless war of survival. They had developed a system of warfare that was far more sophisticated than those of the people around them. The Olmec armies were disciplined and soon came to realise that in order to keep their lands safe they must attack first. It had not been long before they had begun to dominate. Eventually, this process led to the famed Carnacian Legions; well trained, well armoured and well disciplined, and all driven by the religious zeal of their Albanite priests. The rest was history; the Carnacians had united the Olmec people and had then conquered most of the known world from farthest Tanzabar to the deserts of Etosha. Even his own fierce ancestors had fallen to the Legions for a time.

Looking around at the rough and worn coppery faces of the farmers, Jon knew that few of these would appreciate this history; they were the lowest strata of society and had no education. What they knew would be bound up with superstition and myths. It was almost an irony that here he was, a Nordic barbarian amongst the civilised Olmec, and it was he who was the educated man.

His blue eyes danced at the thought, and his face, stonily set, cracked into a wide smile. He laughed aloud. Something he rarely did. The Olmec farmers around looked at Jon in fear, unsure of his sudden change. To these lowly farmers he must have seemed fearsome indeed, armed and armoured as he was; his bald, scarred head and broken nose clear in the light of the sunny morning. Neither was Jon a small man on a large horse; on foot he would stand over six and a half feet tall, at least a foot taller than most Olmecs. He was a large man even for his own people; he had broad, powerful shoulders and a wide flat-browed face that rarely changed from its sombre set. Many people mistook his flat, implacable look for melancholy or anger, but in truth Jon was rarely either, he was just also rarely so happy that it was obvious to others. It was a shame that such was not true of his anger. When angry, he was almost uncontrollable, a fact of which he was always aware. It was partly the reason why Jon had such a strong control on his emotions and consequently had a fairly placid temperament. He could not afford to lose his temper, he was no longer the young fool who drank to excess and fought so recklessly, now he was a respected tutor at the new Guild of Magi here in Lauria and he could not afford anything he did to reflect badly on the guild. It had been incredible that the Olmec leaders of the province had allowed the guild to set up in Lauria at all!

Jon came to the end of the crowded street and pushed forward into the shadows of the towered gates. He moved towards the guards who were checking the people entering town. Several men, labourers by the look of their well-patched tunic and hose, cursed as they were forced to stumble from Jon's path. They desperately clutched their large cloth sacks of wares. Jon quickly showed his papers to the guard on duty and with a wary look, the guard waved him through. Jon urged his stallion on into the sunlight, past the line of people, carts and animals, and out of the tight archway of the north gate. As soon as he reached the widened hard, dirt track of the north road he gave his eager mount his head. The fine stallion leapt forward and Jon enjoyed the feel of the wind in his face as he cantered north along the dark brown strip that separated the fields of wheat on either side of him.

After a few minutes, he slowed Atrell to a walk and the stallion seemed more content. The brief run had taken the edge of his mood after the long time spent in the guild hall's stables.

Thinking of the guild made him think of the look that had flashed across the guard's face at the gate. The guard had seen who he was, or more importantly, what he was. This time it was not just that he was Nordic that was an issue, it was the fact that he was a mage! Most of the time few would think such of him, he hardly looked the part, but then he was one of those rare mages who allied his mystical knowledge with his fighting skills. Indeed, that was why he was here in Lauria; to teach his particular brand of magic allied to swordcraft. However, to Olmecs, magic was the province of the Albanite church. In the Empire, magic users like Jon were classed as witches or warlocks and hunted down for their use of 'unholy' powers.

Thankfully, this was not the Empire and more tolerant views prevailed. Still to allow the Mages's Guild to set up a hall in an Olmec province was an amazing feat.

The Albanite priesthood in the Empire dominated the use of magic. It condemned to death those people who used magic outside of the priesthood. Luckily, that was a belief that was not so strongly held, here far to the north of the Olmec heartlands. Here in the Wildlands of Darylor, the Olmecs had settled without their Alban Priests. The only followers of Alba that had penetrated this far north were of the acetic missionary brotherhoods whose tolerance was far greater than that of the main church. Even so, the less educated Olmecs still held that magic was to be used by the followers of Alba or not at all. That was why it was such a feat that the Magic Users' Guild had actually managed to set up a school to train young mages here in the largest Olmec city in Darylor.

Jon rode on along the north road, his mind drifting in the still heat of the day. He drank in the views of the rolling green downs that sloped down in the north towards the green swathe of the Laur Forest. In the east was the great lake on whose north shores the town of Lauria stood. The lake was a deep, cool blue and the lightest of breezes seemed to stir the waters, but nothing more. Jon could see the white sails of half a dozen boats as they headed up or down the lake. To the northwest, in the distance, Jon could see the thin ribbon of blue where the lake funneled into the river Shandri that headed north. Jon knew that the river continued north into the great Shandri valley and in that valley was his destination, the city of Shandrilos, home to the College of Magic.

Shandrilos was famous in the Wildlands of Darylor and beyond. The College of Magic was unique as far as Jon knew; nowhere else had magic users come together to share their knowledge in such a way, and definitely nowhere else had conflicting priesthoods; the Nordic Druids and the Alban Monks been brought together!

Of course, Jon would not be heading directly to the city and college. First he had to meet Darin.

A few hours later and Jon was coming out of the downs country towards the Laur forest and his mind had turned to the meeting ahead. Hopefully,

Darin would be waiting for him at the crossroads where the north road met the east from Karodracia. However, Jon knew it was unlikely his oldest friend would be there waiting on time, yet he refused to arrive late himself, it was just something that didn't sit well with him. This was not a problem for Darin, though his friend assured him that since he had joined the Karodracian Knights he was a reformed character. However, Jon would believe it when he saw it.

Darin of Kenarth was Jon's oldest friend. They had grown up together. Both their fathers were large landowners, but where Jon's father had already been an established laird, Darin's father had made his fortune as a mercenary and had bought his title and land.

Jon and Darin had played together as their fathers' lands bordered one another. Later, They had both been sent to the court of Ostia for their education. The old High Lord of Ostia had been a visionary. He had encouraged academics of all kinds to come to his court as well as soldiers and gladiators from the empire to train his men. It was also the High Lord's idea to spread the influence of the College of Magic. He had studied there and had set up the first Guild Hall for mages outside of Shandrilos. It was so successful that others were set up later in other Nordic provinces of the Wildlands. The latest and most remarkable being the one Jon now taught at in Lauria.

Jon and Darin had been sent to Ostia to be trained as young lairds, to learn to read and write, to learn to fight and command, and to learn about the world. However, few knew the depth or nature of the education those youngsters at court would receive. Their teachers were mages, druids, Alban monks and fighter mages, they were gladiators and soldiers, academics and adventurers. The range of ideas and philosophies that were taught, discussed and practised gave the young members of the court a vast wealth of knowledge and an understanding of varied religious ideas. This, in turn, gave them a rather unique view of the world.

There had been about thirty children at court when Jon and Darin had arrived. From that group many had now become influential lords, successful merchants, prominent soldiers and promising mages. Jon had been one of the last group. However, Darin had shown only a minor talent for magic and an even more minor interest in it. Darin's interest was in fighting and he had shown a rare aptitude for the blade. He was now widely acknowledged as one of the finest master swordsman in the Wildlands and had gained fame as a champion with the Knights of Saint Karodra.

Jon, on the other hand, had been torn for he had also been pushed towards being a warrior. His father had been a swordsman and hero of the last Goblin Wars. Jon's family were Calonian highlanders and so it was expected that he would be a warrior too. As a boy, Jon was already a formidable size and he had also shown speed and good skill with a blade. He had enjoyed the contest and few his age could hold their own against him, yet he had always sought to avoid real conflict. He discovered his real joys at the court in Ostia; magic and ancient lore. At the court of Ostia, he had also happily realised he could learn to be both a warrior and a mage, and satisfy both his father and himself.

Up ahead, the north road entered the wall of trees that marked the edge of the Laur forest. Jon paused to make sure his shield was secure on his arm and that nothing blocked his sword from being freed from its scabbard if he needed it. With a light click of his tongue and rap of his heels, he moved Atrell into the shadowed track of the north road. The Laur forest was not known for being as dangerous as the larger, thicker forests that covered huge areas of the Wildlands; it had no known bands of outlaws, the Karodracian Knights and the Laurian Guards saw to that, but more importantly there were no non-humans dwelling within it! Jon knew that to the north and west in the Darkheart Hills were forests where the goblin tribes and troll clans made any travel life threatening. Then, to the west, were the vast green forests of Karodra where any trespass into the deep woods was fatal it was said because of the elves who still retained their hold on those ancient forests. The wild elves of the forests would kill anyone not of their kind instantly. Most would not even see any trace of their killers before their sudden deaths! So as forests went, the Laur was safe and bright and airy. Nevertheless, Jon would be careful. There were always still small bands of opportunist outlaws in these woods who could cause trouble for a lone rider.

The Laurians, keen to protect trade through this stretch of forest, had cleared the trees back from the road, so that for twenty feet on either side there was clear ground, but nature soon fought back and in places bushes and young trees narrowed that gap. Jon kept his shield high and used all of his senses, both ordinary and mystical to determine if anyone hid in ambush as he rode steadily onwards.

The tall archer waited. Their first target would be along soon, so she had been told. It would be a lone rider, armed and dangerous; a man who had committed several murders in Ostia and the Shandri Vale.

For the second target they would move up the road to wait. It was the first man's partner, a man who masqueraded as a knight.

As she waited, the archer wondered again how she had got to this point. She was by no means an innocent, she had indulged in some smuggling and a little tomb robbing for Elder artifacts, but she had not been hurting anyone save the greedy merchants of Ostia. The tombs had been ruins of the long dead Elder and the treasures were there to be taken by those bold enough and clever enough to find them. Yet how had she gone from that to this; standing, waiting to kill yet another stranger?

She knew the answer. It was the fire! She had lost everything and so had leapt at the chance of good money. She was widely known as an excellent tracker and marksman and the man had sought her out. It was only when she found out what she would be hunting that things got difficult. The tall, raven haired huntress was intelligent and though she was not unfamiliar with violence, she had never sought it. The thought of shooting someone was not an issue; she had done her share of fighting in border skirmishes and with goblin raiders. However, that had been about defending people. Shooting someone from undercover who never knew she was there was something she never thought she would do, but then feeding her children had forced her to do a number of things of which she was not proud.

For weeks, she had resisted the job offers before things got so dire that she could not even get enough to feed her family then she had been willing to listen. The job was in essence bounty hunting. She was to hunt wanted men; criminals and murderers who had evaded justice. However, she worried. She was not to apprehend them or tell others where they could be found, she was to kill them!

Was she not then an assassin?

It had felt like she would be. So despite the job paying well, she had not told her family. Her mother would not approve and her children were too young to understand. Even inside her, there had been a lingering sense of unease at what she was doing.

That had all changed after her first hunt.

That first man she remembered, she had hunted reluctantly. She had convinced herself that the man knew he was hunted and this would be a contest of her skill in the hunt with the other's skill in evasion. When she had finally tracked her quarry to an isolated cabin in the Ost hills, she had deliberately stopped and waited, observed and judged, just to make sure the man was all she had been told he would be. The huntress had known her target was travelling with a young girl, barely into her teens, a niece or something.

She had waited, watching the cabin intently. Was this man a cold blooded murderer? The archer had not been sure, she had been told so by those who had hired her, but what if they had been wrong, or this was the wrong man? She knew that innocents had been hunted for murder before. Another nagging doubt had been the fact that she had been hired to hunt this warrior down because the local guards had not connected the man to the murders. It was the mysterious mage who had hired her who assured her that this was a person responsible for a number of murders. So the huntress had waited, her mind full of questions. She was not sure why she was waiting. It was not like the word 'murderer' would be emblazoned on the stranger's forehead. No, she had waited because she couldn't bring herself to kill without making any kind of judgement of the man for herself. She almost wanted to see her target's evil, to know for sure that killing him was the right thing to do.

As she had sat there silently debating, the man had kicked open the door of the cabin and almost casually tossed out the young girl onto the hard rocks outside. Bonelessly, she had hit the ground and rolled, lifeless, her clothes torn and a look of horror on her young features! The archer remembered the devastation that had hit her. The murderer had taken this girl, abused her and killed her! She was no niece, he must have kidnapped her! She remembered the anger that had thundered through her then as she had leapt from the shelter of the trees. She knew that if she had moved in immediately the girl would probably have still been alive. Her hesitation had led to the girl's death!

It had been a heedless attack that followed and when the murderer lay dead, his body pinned to the door by the force of the clothyard arrows from her powerful longbow, she had felt some sense of justice, though regretfully she had buried the girl in the woods. The next murderer she hunted had died not even knowing she was there!

The archer crouched down in the shade, her back against the trunk of a huge old oak. She could see the road clearly, but she herself would be virtually invisible to anyone on the road against the background of the forest. Still she would need to be wary; this target apparently had the use of magic. However, the experienced huntress had grown up around mages, she knew that unless the man had specifically cast a scrying spell his mystical senses would not have the range to sense her this far back into the trees. This would have made it difficult for an archer to hit the target at such a distance, but she knew with her height, strength and training, her longbow was capable of punching through armour even at this distance. She would at least take the man from his horse. It would then be up to the other two to finish him, while she covered them.

She looked around for her partners and saw one of them some fifty or more yards away through the trees. There was no point looking for the other; he would be on the other side of the road. Both of her partners were well armed and armoured. They would take one shot with their crossbows from each side of the road and then move in with swords to finish the rider off.

The archer let her mind wander for a moment; her target was not due for a good few minutes yet. Thinking about this a frown returned. The last few jobs she had taken had been different somehow from those first few. The money was more for a start, but something was... different. She had not been told at first who she would kill, merely where they would be and when! More details had followed only at the last minute.

Her frown deepened as a thought occurred. If they knew when and where a person would be, why did they not say who they were and what they had done. She had not considered it before. For her last target she had only found out details after she had killed, and only then when she had asked questions. The answers to those questions had not totally satisfied her at the time but she had dismissed them.

The last target's name had been Tallan. He had been some kind of soldier, part of a small group led by a killer by the name of Gael... or so the shadowy mage had informed her. However, this Tallan, still prayed on her mind. Something didn't feel right.

The hunt had been in the far north on the edges of Sironac province. This Tallan, had sought shelter in the wilds. When she found him, the man was young and haggard and deeply tired. He had seemed no less savage than many the archer had hunted, but there was something more determined in him, more driven than the others, like he had some kind of mission. Even when the huntress had taken him down, he had still striven to get himself up and keep moving. He had cried in agony, not so much it seemed, at the horrific wound in his side, but more at not being able to do something or finish something. However, before the archer could get to the man, his partners had moved in and finished things off. When she had asked questions, her partners' answers were vague. They knew little more than she. The agent for the mage had said it was probably simple desperation. Still, it had greatly troubled her. This man, Tallan had not seemed a ruthless killer; he had seemed like a soldier given an important mission, knowing he had failed.

The last few jobs with her new partners, partners her mysterious employer had insisted accompany her, to help 'keep her safe', had not seemed so clear cut as those first jobs. Nowhere else did she hear of the crimes of which these men were accused, only from the mage. There were no rumours or reports of murders that the archer could find, but then she had to admit that many murders and injustices went unreported in the wilds, and people were often reticent about talking to strangers.

Her revelations were interrupted by the signal, a bird's trill, once, twice, thrice. She shook her head. 'Don't be a fool,' she thought as the face of that first murdered girl returned to her mind. With new determination, she stood and hefted her longbow. She would have no more innocents on her conscience.

She took three arrows from the long quiver across her back and stabbed them into the ground. One she then took and strung ready. Looking to the road, she heard the dull thud of a horse's hooves on the hard mud. She drew and stood, steadying her breathing and relaxing. It was over fifty yards to the road and it would be a difficult shot, nevertheless she was confident of the outcome. Slowly the rider came into view. First the huntress could see the dark head of a large powerful stallion and then the prodigiously sized rider atop its back. She breathed in, took aim and... froze!

Recognition hit her like a blow to the stomach.

13

No, her mind wouldn't accept what she could see at first and then certainty followed. The man before her was no cold hearted killer, he was not evil. The archer's eyes widened as she realised just what she had been about to do and then an involuntary gasp escaped her lips as the truth came crashing home, not just about this job, but also about those others she had taken recently. The faces of men she had killed appeared in her mind. They had not been killers, not the last few. It was she and her new partners who were the killers. She had been deceived and turned into a killer of innocents. The knowledge was shattering.

Abruptly another thought struck her and she turned to see her partner fifty yards off in the trees, waiting for the archer's arrow to strike. If she didn't fire, would they attack? The huntress was certain of the answer. They would kill without remorse. They suffered no qualms. Anger blazed within her, 'Bastards,' she thought.

Viciously she swung her bow, took aim and fired. Her partner was hammered down soundlessly as the three foot long arrow punched through his throat.

A sound like the ringing of a bell resounded across from the road and the huntress spun to see her other partner on the opposite side of the road. The man had dropped the crossbow he had fired and drawn his swords. The huntress quickly looked to the big man on the horse and saw him still reeling back from the blow of the crossbow bolt on his shield. The bolt had obviously screeched across his shield, leaving a jagged scar on the plain surface and had then ricocheted up to slash across his forehead. Blood was already flowing, but the huge man merely snarled and then roared his anger. The powerfully built warrior pulled his sword and frantically sought to turn his horse to face his attacker, using his thighs to control the warhorse. It was clear to the huntress that the burly warrior on the horse was still a little confused, but it seemed her partner was not. Confronted by a large, ferocious Nordic warrior, armed and armoured, and with the support he had expected not materialising, his decision was clear. He turned and bolted into the trees, heading for the thicker undergrowth where the horseman would not be able to follow.

The horseman swore savagely and pushed his horse to pursue the man, but it was clear to the huntress that it would be futile. In that part of the forest the advantage would be to a man on foot. The horseman clearly agreed as he quickly pulled his horse to a stop and bellowed in pure rage about what he would do to his attacker when he got his hands on him. The huntress smiled for a moment and then the guilt and shame returned at what she had almost done, and what she had surely done over the last few months. The horseman looked around vainly for an enemy to attack and the huntress crouched back into the undergrowth, burning shame and anger almost choking her.

She couldn't let this stand, she had to make it better somehow. Resolve to atone burned in her chest. Her partner might well escape on foot into the forest, but the tall huntress vowed he would not leave that forest alive. That was a killing she would gladly undertake for free. With that thought she grabbed her arrows from the ground and silently crept off into the forest. She knew where her former, and soon to be dead, partner would go.

Chapter 2

A MEETING OF FRIENDS

There are many calendars used but the most prevalent is that of the Holy Alban Empire that was in turn inherited from the Carnacian Imperium. This may well have been an adaptation of an even earlier Olmec calendar now lost to history. The Albanite Calendar tracks years from the founding of the Holy City on the site of the tomb of the great prophet Alba. Historians now use the letters BY or Blessed Year before a date to denote years since the death of the prophet and the founding of the Holy City. Events prior to this are given no letters, though some historians have started using the letters PA or Pre-Alba.

From a treatise on Chronology by the scholar, Gregorin of Tarsus. BY1132

Sir Darin of Kenarth forced his mount on at a gallop; he was already half a day late. He always seemed to be hurrying to meetings. A smile touched his face at the thought of the look he knew would be on Bear's face. Bear's brows would be drawn down in a gruff harsh look.

Darin would always think of Jon Madraig as Bear, no matter that he was now some fancy mage in Lauria. The nickname had been gained while they were still teenagers in Ostia and virtually everyone who knew Jon from that time called him Bear.

Darin pushed his horse on; ignoring the rubbing of the thick plate armour through his leathers as he bounced along on his warhorse, as well as the occasional clank against his back from the long handle of his great sword. He was not a natural rider, but he needed to get to the crossing point where he had agreed to meet Bear. The sun was starting to set and soon the forest road would be in darkness. Had he been on time, he would have arrived well before the sun went down.

He continued to push his tiring mount along at a gallop.

He thought about the young woman who had delayed him. The three men who were intent on robbing her of both her money and her virtue had been of little challenge to a knight, especially one of his skills. Darin knew he was one of the finest swordsmen in the Wildlands but the robbers had fled at the mere sight of him and his blade. The young woman had been overcome with gratitude. Darin should really have left it at that. His holy order only sought to protect travellers, and while he was only a knight and not a monk, he should have moved on, but it was clear the woman was smitten.

'And why shouldn't she be?' he thought.

Darin smiled. He knew he was considered handsome with his dark hair, boyish smile and twinkling blue eyes... or at least so he had been told by the ladies of Karodracia.

His smile grew wider. There had been nothing in his vows about chastity.

He rode on, thinking about the young woman and her... charms, but this was interrupted by the thought of how the monks and masters of the order would look on such behaviour. He frowned and then turned his attentions to the road. He gently kicked his horse on.

It seemed an age before he could see firelight glinting in the distance along the twilight road. Bear must already be there waiting and had set up camp for the night.

Sure enough, as Darin allowed his mount to slow to a canter and then a trot, he could see a large, 'bear-like' frame hunched over a small fire set back from the road. A horse was tethered nearby and the smell of meat cooking reached Darin's nose. He trotted his horse into the circle of light and the man at the fire looked up.

"'Bout time you got yourself here," muttered Jon 'Bear' Madraig.

"Good to see you too, Bear," Darin responded cheerfully, getting off his horse stiffly, "Is my dinner ready yet?" he asked, glancing impishly at the rabbit cooking on a rough wooden spit over the fire.

"Cheeky sod," Bear snapped back, "I've been sat here waiting for hours."

"Well, you know how it is with us hero type knights," Darin remarked flippantly as he tethered his horse by Bear's, "You've just got to stop for a damsel in distress."

"Was she in distress before you arrived or after?" Bear laughed.

Darin moved over to the fire and sat down on a convenient rock beside Bear. "Well I suppose you could say she was a damsel in desire beforehand and in distress when she found out I had to leave so suddenly." Darin reached out to take a piece of meat from the cooking rabbit and Bear slapped his hand away.

"Yeah, right," Bear responded harshly, but with a half smile on his lips. "Go and see to your horse properly. He's tired and you need to get that tack off him and clean and brush him."

Darin looked at Bear in mock annoyance, "Won't you do it my old friend? I know how much you love your horses."

Bear laughed in spite of himself, "If you spent even a tenth of the time looking after your horse as you do looking after yourself and the women of Karodracia, he'd be the best horse in the whole of the Wildlands."

Darin put on the hurt look he so loved to do, but Bear just growled at him, "See to your horse, Darin."

Darin moved to stand and only then did he notice the bloody scar on Bear's forehead that had been covered by the shadows in the twilight. He frowned at Bear.

The big man noticed his look and said, "Some bloody thief tried to kill me in the woods on the way here. I took the crossbow bolt on my shield but it bounced up and nearly took my head off." Bear grumbled. "I should have had my bloody helm on. I'll make sure I have it on next time. This cut is giving me a vicious headache."

Darin looked closer at the cut, "One to add to your collection," he murmured. "Doesn't look too bad. Did you get the thief?"

"No, the little swine ran off into the forest," Bear snarled in annoyance.

Darin nodded seriously, "You were right not to try and follow."

Bear nodded in agreement though it was clear he wasn't happy. Darin was sure he would not want to have been that thief had Bear caught up with him.

Darin moved off and saw to his horse. He didn't even have a name for his mount. Darin had never really cared for horses, not since he was a lad.

Still it was a necessity in his order. The knights of Saint Karodra were a holy order of warriors, though Darin was not what you would call a model knight. However, he believed in protecting the weak and could pay lip service to the Alban faith. He could then protect travellers in the Wilds as the fabled founder of the order, Saint Karodra had done so long ago. However, to do this, horses were indispensable.

By the time Darin returned to the fire, Bear had served the rabbit onto two wooden platters, along with a small vegetable broth he had boiled up.

"Thanks," Darin said and tucked into the food, sitting in comfortable silence with his friend.

Night fell quickly and soon only the light of the camp fire could be seen and the sounds of the forest heard. Darin finished his food and then got out his blankets and laid them on the ground. He carefully laid himself down and put his arms behind his head. Bear still sat by the fire. Darin looked up and saw the vast array of stars that had silently come out. The sky was filled with them, no clouds obscured the breath-taking view and Darin settled back, calm seeping into him as he took in the cool air. It would be a dry fine night by the looks of it.

Bear's voice broke the stillness, "Did you manage to get a message to the others?"

"I've heard nothing from Marcus. Nobody has heard anything from him in years. He could be dead. Stefan is off down in the empire somewhere from what I heard, travelling the world as he always wanted."Darin paused, turned onto his side and propped his head up on one elbow, "Rebba got a message back to me... as did Zara."

Bear's face went stoney. "Saying...?"

"Well, Zara said she will be there, guaranteed. She'd not miss out on some drinks and thought it would be a great laugh for us all to meet up again," Darin watched as a range of emotions crossed the big man's face.

"So we can't get Marcus and Stefan but the Whore of Ostia can come. Marvellous!" Bear muttered.

"You know she doesn't like that name..."

"It fits her." Bear interrupted.

Darin sighed. "You have to let this go. Move on."

A dangerous look had entered Bear's eyes. "I have."

Darin stared at his friend for a moment and then decided to change subject, "I must admit I never thought Rebba would come, she's over there

19

in some wilderness in the west, druiding or whatever it is druids do! I think she's got some man over there, but she'll be coming too."

"It's her thirtieth birthday in a few days," Bear answered, his mind still clearly occupied with the past, "She'd want to be there. We all promised we'd meet up."

Darin nodded and then added, "Rebba also got in touch with Garon Vale up in Sironac and he's coming."

"Garon!" Bear exclaimed, focusing fully on Darin again, "Gods, I haven't seen Garon in years. Not since he found religion, anyway."

"Aros and Dunstan can make it, but will be several days late... ". Darin thought for a moment "Oh, and Arkadi has got himself free of organising for the Grand Council of the Wildlands," Darin put in, "so he can set everything up for us for when we all meet in Shandrilos. He's also got Nat Bero to come."

Bear raised an eyebrow, "Really? I'd heard about Karis' death... the inn his father left them burning down, Karis caught inside... I didn't think she would leave the children."

"Yeah," Darin agreed, "but the kids are with her mother, I'd heard, and she was working off in the wilds earning some good money. Trying to rebuild."

"Poor Karis. I wouldn't wish that kind of death on anyone." Bear said sombrely.

Darin nodded. Karis had been a strange man at times, quiet and shy. It had been a bit of a shock years ago when he and Nat had got together. She was humorous and outgoing, he was shy and quiet. She was tall where he was short, dark where he was fair, confident where he was unsure; the big boned huntress and the small, wiry merchant's boy. Perhaps opposites did attract.

Silence fell as the two of them thought of the past.

Finally, Bear looked at Darin and in the shadowy light Darin saw Bear smile fully for the first time. "Gods, Darin. You know I actually didn't think anyone would come. Even with the promise. It's been years! Everyone's got their own lives now, their own problems, and we all live so far apart."

"Well, when we split up the band after Daggerdale, we always said that we would have to meet up if we were still alive and kicking. This meeting of the Council of the Wildlands has given us all the excuse to get ourselves together in Shandrilos."

"Yeah," Bear replied happily, "it's going to be great, even if we're missing a few of the band. Who knows what might happen?" he speculated.

"Well let's just hope Arkadi gets things sorted or we might find ourselves sleeping on the streets and I don't know about you, Bear but I think I'm getting too old for that, after all I'm nearly thirty myself," said Darin wryly.

"And still acting like a fifteen year old," Bear interjected.

Darin put on his best hurt look again and Bear laughed loudly. Darin managed to hold the look for a few seconds before dissolving into laughter himself.

⌒⌒⌒

Off in the trees some hundred yards away stood the huntress. Tears dried on her cheeks where she had cried silently as they talked of Karis and the inn. She smiled though as she heard their laughter. However, the smile quickly faded as she thought of what had happened today. She had almost helped to murder two of her oldest friends; men she knew were not murderers and all because she needed money. She had blinded herself to the truth about those last men she had hunted and who she had worked with and for.

She had finally caught up with the man who not long ago had been her partner. The man would have been easy to track, even without knowing where he had been heading. Careful not to kill him straight away, she had stalked him. She wanted information first and then he could die. Once she might have been a little more squeamish about that idea, but not this time. This man deserved it... as did his master.

Torture was not something she was good at, but strangely she had not really got the opportunity. The man, she took down with a shot through the thigh and had then easily disarmed him as he writhed in agony. Quickly, she had pinned him down and jammed her hunting knife under his jaw and begun asking her questions, but the man had just taunted her, gambling that the huntress did not have the guts to torture him. She had managed finally to convince him otherwise with some judicious cuts here and there on the man's body, but then the strange thing happened. He had begun to talk, but just as he was about to tell the huntress the name of their mysterious employer he had twitched violently and blood had gushed from his eyes, nose and mouth and he had died almost instantly!

She had known exactly what had happened... magic! Somehow magic had been used on this man to kill him if he divulged any information about his master. Suddenly, the stakes seemed much higher and the huntress knew she was in deep. It took strong magic to cast such an enchantment. She knew that from her teachings as a youth in Ostia. Whoever this mage was, he was a powerful master!

Gathering her resolve, the huntress had determined to return to find this mage and get to the bottom of what had happened, why she had been manipulated and why two of her friends were such a danger to an obviously powerful mage. She just wasn't sure how she could manage it.

First though, she had to get to Shandrilos, she was due to meet up with her friends there. She was sorely tempted to go out and sit with Darin and Bear but that would raise questions she wasn't sure she was prepared enough to evade at this time. She didn't really want to lie to them and she certainly couldn't tell them the truth, at least not yet, not until she had some answers. No, it would be better to go on ahead and meet them and the others up in Shandrilos as arranged. Luckily, the city of magic was the same place her 'employer' would be, along with the answer to her questions.

With that Nat Bero, turned and loped off into the trees

Chapter 3

ARRANGEMENTS

There are five methods for powering a spell construct, each with its own dangers and weaknesses. The most common is that of Evocation where the energy for the spell is drawn from within. This is the quickest but also the weakest as the spell caster must draw from their own energy. Invocation is the drawing of ambient energy from the environment around the caster, from consummation of materials. This is slower but can provide much more energy. The other three methods are either far less reliable or far less moral. Adjuration or Supplication is energy from communion with higher powers; Sublimation is energy drawn willingly from other living things, and Subsumption is the devouring of another's life energy.

From 'The Art of Spell Craft' by Grandmaster Bruenor Brae of Shandrilos, BY1312

He moved gracefully as he worked. Slowly, he etched the protection symbols on the grey stone floor, whispering incantations. He moved carefully around the chamber that was his inner sanctum. From time to time his thick robes caught beneath his feet; from time to time sweat rolled down into his eyes; from time to time his long, deep sleeves slipped over his hands, but nothing could shift the attention of his eyes and mind as he imbued the sulphurous compound lines with protective energy. He was meticulous.

Finally, circle and pentagram were complete. The hooded mage stretched himself to his feet and slowly shrugged and stretched his shoulders beneath the heavy robe. He glanced slowly around the room, making sure no obstacles touched, or could fall to cross, the lines of his design. It was not the summons itself that was the danger; he was not trying to reach another plane where dangerous energies could easily consume the unwary, he was merely opening a gateway to another place.

'Merely', he thought wryly, 'there were few here at the *great* College of Magic who could open such a portal.' Sarcasm laced his thinking. It was a tricky undertaking for most, but one he knew was well within the scope of his talent and knowledge. Most could open a portal to another place in this world, but as the distance increased so too did the difficulty. The difficulty also increased with the size of the portal and the time it remained open. Holding a portal open took a degree of mental stamina that took most adepts of the unseen arts many years to acquire. His stamina was prodigious. He would only open the portal for a few minutes and only make it large enough for a single being to communicate through. The difficulty would be in the distance. He was not sure how much distance exactly, that knowledge was forbidden to him, but he knew it was far outside the Wildlands.

He turned his thoughts to the one he would summon; his master! Oh how he resented that title; that he should have to call another his master. His face twisted in the shadows of his cowl. He tolerated that humiliation because it was necessary. At first it had been necessary to preserve his life, later it became necessary in order to expand his knowledge, now it was necessary to allow him to gain the magical might he longed for in order to fulfil his dream. Any humiliation was necessary to achieve that.

He had stumbled upon this particular gateway by accident. He had been young, unwary and reckless, and had used an enchanted stave found decades ago in the ruins of the ancient elven city that the College was built on. How could those that founded this place of magical research have ignored such a potent tool, such an opportunity to learn? None had the courage, he had felt, to use it.

He did.

At first he had regretted bitterly that summoning. He had been smashed to the floor by an unseen force of immense power. He had tried all in his considerable repertoire to shift it, had cast spell after spell at his captor only to see them torn apart with a skill that was breathtaking. He was held still and helpless by the creature he would come to call master. He had known death was close as he had lain there, exhausted and afraid, but instead an offer was made, an offer he could hardly refuse.

Desperation had prompted that first prostration to the ancient being, resentment followed it. Soon he realised how poorly he had been prepared for such a summons. How young and foolish he had been. He had settled himself down to watch and wait and over time his power and knowledge grew.

The creature... his master... at first wanted knowledge. It seemed he knew little of the Wildlands or of the people who lived there. His questions gave insights to the mage that he stored away. Later he was given assignments. He knew there was some reason behind the assignments, but he could not fathom it; to bribe a man here or to hinder someone there. Killings he was required to perform; however, he had no qualms about those; he had killed before to get what he wanted. Over the years since, he had gained more and more information about his so-called master, over the years his powers and talent had grown as his master was forced to teach his new minion skills and spells in order to complete his assignments. He knew he was still no match for his master, yet he knew too that his master still searched for something and whatever it was, it was powerful indeed! The plan that had formed in the mage's mind had been simple, take what his master desired and use it, ally it to his own burgeoning talent and knowledge and turn master into slave!

Oh, but if he could achieve that his dream would be so much easier. With a power of that magnitude, and resources behind him, he could unite these hopelessly divided provinces into a cohesive kingdom. He could unify all of Darylor behind him as its first ruler. His new nation would not be based on the old systems. He had grown up and seen the injustice of the world, the unfairness of riches and rule given to fools who had little more talent than to have been born to the right parents. No, his new kingdom would be based upon the rule of the strong. The more able his subjects the higher they would rise... within reason of course, they would not be allowed to challenge his rule.

A smile came to his face. He had prepared himself well tonight. Even his master would not break his defences easily. Not that he would know they were there. That foul creature had not physically crossed through the gateway since that first terrible summons. No, he would communicate, but not come through. The communication would be through a telepathic link, a link that revealed little. However, the mage had garnered some interesting information through it. He knew far more than his master presumed. He had stitched together images, stray thoughts and had matched them to knowledge gained from those, and about those, in which his master had taken an interest. There was danger in the course he had chosen, hence the magical defences he had constructed, but his master had little regard for humans and his arrogance gave the mage room to plot. Thus, it was unlikely his defences would be needed, yet the mage always ran the risk of his master gleaning some suspicion in their communications and the mage was not yet ready to die. Not when he was so close. If he were discovered, he meant to put up a much more effective fight than he had that first day so long ago.

Just lately his master had become somewhat predictable in his needs. It was killings he needed. Men who needed to die and the mage would arrange their deaths. By now the mage had a number of connections to mercenaries and assassins in a number of different cities who would do his bidding. Often his master would not even know who it was who needed killing; he would only give information about where they would be and when. The mage knew enough about scrying and the art of the seer to know that his master was using foresight to deal with people who might be a problem to him; a prodigious use of magic!

On a number of occasions the mage had deliberately disobeyed his master's orders and had the person who was to be killed watched instead in order to see what threat they might pose, but more often than not the person would eventually die anyway later and thus the mage had become aware that he was not the only servant his master had in these lands. The mage had then begun tracking down those other servants and had managed to have a number of them killed. He wanted no competitors.

The mage had recently sent some of his best hunters to kill a pair of men in the south but he had heard no word yet on their success. He made a mental note to try to find out. They had just recently dispatched a young warrior in the north, near Sironac. That had been a killing of great urgency to his master and the mage had been careful to send his best. Failure in such a task would not be tolerated and his master's displeasure could be painful. Still that would be as nothing to the prospect of his master finding out about his own plans. The thought made his heart pound.

With an effort he calmed himself and slowly brought his mind into focus on the ensorcelment he had to craft. He could afford no distractions and put all thoughts and worries out of his mind. He paused to calm and focus on the patterns required to bring together the forces needed to weave the intricate portal to his master. Slowly, slowly he began to gather energy from the world around him. He no longer needed the enchanted stave he had once used so recklessly save as a marker, his powers had grown much over the years.

The mage stepped to the centre of his guarding ward and stood up straight as magical energy straightened his back and made his eyes widen. He thrived on magic. It gave him a joy he could find in no other way. Rapture took him and he released his spell. The reality that was the air in front of his featureless wall shimmered and began to part. With a mental effort he opened the gateway.

It appeared as a grey line hanging in the air. It neither touched nor was actually part of the air rather it was a tear in the reality that was the air. It stretched and split and pulsing white energy could be seen for a moment before a scene revealed itself where the wall had been. In place of the wall a figure stood waiting, tall but slim, draped in a rich, long robe that reached to the floor. It was split wide and hung on the shoulders of the figure. Blood red armour could be glimpsed where the deep, velvet black robe swayed as if in a light breeze. The deeply crimson armour covered the shoulders, chest and abdomen of the figure. It was intricately decorated with whirls and wild patterns. At first the figure seemed indistinct as though seen through a mist but slowly it came into focus. It was then that the features of his master were revealed.

The mage hated those alien, black eyes that showed no whites. He hated the long, upswept brows and the thin savage mouth. He hated the twisted hair thin scar that ghosted from brow to jaw, marring the inhuman beauty. He had hated that face since it had laid terror and torture upon him that first, hellish night. The face itself was wide, strong and handsome; nevertheless, the mage hated those cold features. He knew they hid a monster!

"Master what is thy need," the mage whispered.

<hr />

Some time later the mage wearily stumbled across the unused patterns on the floor, his slippered feet dragging across the lines heedless of the time and energy used to construct them. They were not needed now. His master had suspected nothing. The audience had only lasted minutes yet fatigue wracked his body. The mage grasped the tall back of his stout wooden chair, and sat himself heavily in its firm embrace. The audience had been hard. He could still hear the echoes of that melodic voice in his mind. The telepathic link was invasive and hard to bare. The strain came from keeping some of his thoughts guarded while maintaining the façade of obedience. It was a tightrope that he walked. One slip could, and would, be his death. He had no doubts of that. His master would eradicate him without a thought. Human life meant less than nothing to him. Still the effort had been worth it. This time he knew what it was his master desired, and more importantly, where it was.

His master desired a key but not just any key. His master had not said anything more, but the mage had picked up a stray image from his master's mind and he knew its meaning instantly. This particular key had been sought by mages for decades. It was the lost key to the ancient Ways, the permanent gateways that myth said the Elder races had used to travel leagues with but a step. The Ways had linked up their whole civilisation according to the druids. No one knew who had built them. They were old even by the Elder race's standards. Legend also held that the Ways connected to other worlds and even to the legendary City of the Gods! The mage gave little credit to this. However, he was sure that the Ways led to the ancient cities of the Elder, lost centuries ago. The mage was also sure that those cities still held secrets despite war, destruction and the passage of time. Secrets of power and knowledge lay hidden in those ruined glories of the Elder races, secrets that could be his!

His mind spun through possibilities. Of course he had to be careful. His master had revealed little, but his thoughts had betrayed his desire for the power that this key could bring, and so the mage wanted it too... and now he knew where it was, where it must be or his master would never have asked for the catacombs to be kept clear.

To think it was here, beneath his very feet!

He sat up straighter, some of his exhaustion leaving him as he thought of the power he could claim. Really it made perfect sense for a key to be here. The city of Shandrilos, and the College of Magic in particular, were built upon the ruins of an ancient elven city. Some of the scholars here, who had spent years studying it, even claimed this was the site of the capital city of the elven kingdom of Dah'Ryllah that had once encompassed these Wildlands. Dah'Ryllah had disappeared centuries ago according to Nordic mythology and had been one of the lesser kingdoms of the Elder races, yet nevertheless the ruins showed signs that the city would have been able to house around a hundred thousand! Such an important site would have been a prime place for a Waygate. Perhaps he should search for that too. With the key and a gate of his own he could quickly search out the ruins of legendary El'Yaris or Hy'Deeria, or...

He stopped. He needed to be careful and quick. Timing was of the essence. The key itself would not give him the edge he needed to overcome his dark master. He needed to do things carefully. His master could not suspect that he had the key or an attack would come instantly. It was already clear the College was no safe haven. The mage was sure his master still had other servants here and in the other Wildland provinces. Yet if he were quick enough and secret enough he could keep himself above suspicion.

An idea occurred to him. He could spread rumours about the catacombs to get every adventurous spirit in the region to hunt them while playing the part of trying to keep people out. Yes, and one of those groups could be his own, with a clear guidance for where to look plucked from his master's own thoughts. He felt a deep humour and fierce excitement rising in his belly and began to shake in exultation, glee dancing in his eyes.

He turned and dragged the heavy chair across the short distance to his large oaken table. The table held an orderly array of bottles of all shapes, along with thick sheaves of paper bearing hastily scribbled notes. Excitement was bringing his energy back. First things first, he thought, we must acquire that key and quickly before his master suspected. Grasping a quill, he hastily dipped it in the open ink pot and drew a thin sheet of paper to him. He began to write. Preparations must be made, he needed resources and he needed men.

⌒ᛉ⌒

Four hours later the mage stood in the secret passage he had created some years earlier. One more step would take him through the gateway he had crafted and perfected himself. It was a long term portal, a triumph and yet another benefit of his unwilling alliance with his dark master. Its range was modest. It would transport him barely a few hundred feet to the house he owned just outside the College compound; nevertheless it gave him the perfect means to move unseen in and out of the College.

The rumours and false maps had been easy to get underway; people would know of the catacombs supposed new treasures by morning. However, it had taken longer than he had wanted and more explanation than he felt it needed to get the precious items he carried. He hefted the pack that he had brought. The school of Enchanters had worked long and hard to craft these. The items represented a fortune in gold and in magical effort. Inside were all twelve of the shadow cloaks that the Enchanters had worked for five months to craft for the High Lord of Ostia. Lord Elgon had commissioned the camouflaging cloaks for his new elite Huntmasters. These men were not responsible for hunting as the name suggested or at least not for hunting animals. These men were to be hunters of information and people; assassins and spymasters! Alongside these the mage had purloined some seeker stones. Seeker stones were relatively easy to craft for a competent Enchanter and of little use to a mage. Seeker stones could sense, and with a series of pulses on the correct symbol of the rock, guide the holder to any magical sources. The stones were crude and could not differentiate between sources or identify their potential risks; a mage could use his own magical senses far more accurately but these would aid his men in finding the key in the lower labyrinth while he kept the upper catacombs full of other visitors.

He still had a few hours before his master had required him to begin keeping the catacombs clear, but in that day he anticipated his men would have the key and have brought it to him. He had already communicated with the innkeeper whose inn stood atop an unguarded entrance to the catacombs. Few would find it difficult to enter the underground maze. Thus his master would find nothing below save humans intent on making their fortune. His own men would have enough time to search out the key. His master would never suspect anything; there had been some doubt in the creature's mind that the key would be found here at all, yet if it were to be found, the mage was determined it would be found by him.

Holding the pack of enchanted cloaks and stones in one hand, he used his other to quickly draw up his hood to hide his face deep in shadow. He kept his identity hidden and a glamour here and there usually kept people's minds unclear about his appearance. He had no desire for even his hired hands to know his true identity. That could lead to problems. A man in his position could not be connected to scum like Koros and his henchmen!

He had sent out a summons for Koros as one of the first things he did. Koros would gather his men. They were now a well trained and provisioned group that had proved itself many times for him. Koros himself was a skilled thief and warrior who could find a needle in a haystack given the right incentive. However, he was hardly the sort with which descent people should be seen consorting. It could damage his reputation.

The mage was not keen on the need for such men in this enterprise, but he had little choice, his master's other instructions meant he had to organise things for the Grand Council of the Wildlands, the day after tomorrow. The council was to be kept from any closer alliance. His master wanted the Wildlands of Darylor weak and divided. The mage could not disappear for a whole day; he was required to meet the High Lords and First Ministers as they arrived, not to mention the other duties of his position. Shaking his head at the distractions and the need for such meetings, he stepped through the portal and out into the room beyond.

In the near dark on the other side he stepped sharply around the furniture and moved silently into the next room. This room was small and nearly empty. It was dominated by the four doors that stood in each wall. He could see some light under the door directly ahead of him and stopped briefly to listen. He could hear the light scuffing of feet on the wooden floor and the occasional clink of metal from armour or weapon.

'Good, they were already here,' he thought.

Taking a breath, he slowly took a hold of the handle to the thin wood panel door and quickly twisted and pushed through. He was pleased to see the men in the room jerk in surprise at his sudden entrance. Some yanked weapons, surging to their feet; others, stood staring, wide eyed at the dark apparition that had burst in.

"Sit gentlemen," he said firmly, "we have much to discuss."

Chapter 4

AT THE COLLEGE

The history of the land that has now come to be known as the Wildlands of Darylor is a fragmented one. It was settled over time by Nordic people from the Kingdoms of Calonia and Tutonia in the west, and Olmec people from the Empire in the south. Each province has its own particular history of how it was founded. The oldest of which is that of Lauria which traces its settlement back over four hundred years.

Excerpt from 'A strange land; the Wildlands of Darylor' by Grand Abbot Alinus Quan Sirona, BY1320

"Master Talcost," called the novice urgently. "Can you help me please? I can't seem to get this divination to work at all."

Arkadi Talcost looked sternly at the novice. 'Why did so many of these novices have to be either careless fools or arrogant ones?' he asked himself, looking out across his class at the brightly clad novices. They all wore the rainbow striped robes of the novices of the College of Magic. Their robes were designed to bear the colours of each of the eight schools of magic here at the college. This showed that the novices had not yet chosen the school that they would join, though really most of those in Arkadi's class would know by now for which school they were destined. This particular class was one of three made up of students who had passed their level three examinations and were just now practising for their trials which would see them either made Adepts, the lowest level of mage, or return to studying and preparing to take the trials again. In theory a novice could attempt the trials as many times as he wished, though in reality three failures would consign the novice to looking for an assistant's position or leaving the college to make whatever future for themselves that they could.

A number of the people in the class had taken the trials before, a few had taken it twice before. Fion Runan fell into the latter group rather than the former and Arkadi was fairly convinced he would be applying for an assistant's role soon. Arkadi moved over to help the young man.

The divination spell Arkadi had the class practising was a relatively simple one in terms of conceptualisation, but with some interesting difficulties in terms of stability. It was the sort of spell that would cause the careless to miscast and the arrogant to lose control. So far most of Arkadi's class were doing a fantastic job of failing in one way or another, but then part of what Arkadi deemed his job in teaching spellcraft was to make the caster both careful with the skills they had learnt and humble before the might of what they sought to control.

Divination was the area of the mysteries concerned with sensory magic of the mind, body and spirit and this particular spell would allow a caster to actually perceive the emotional emanations from those around them. The effect produced was at once stimulating and beguiling. It often confused many novices. For those who became too arrogant with this spell, the effects could be surprising. Often the unwary would go beyond actual 'visual' perception of the emotions of those around them to actual 'mental' perception. So the caster would actually begin to feel the emotions of those around them. The results could be humbling for the caster as their mind was bombarded with emotions that heightened their own. Before now, Arkadi had sent out classes of wailing, tearful, ecstatic and even terrified students. The effects did not last long, but they did serve as a fairly safe way of reminding the novices of the cost of losing control. It was a tactic he had copied from Master Brae, the eccentric, old tutor who had taught him. Master Brae was now so old that he had taught most of the students who had come through the College in its sixty year history.

Half an hour later, Arkadi Talcost dismissed his class amid tears, fears, joy and confusion. Once more many of the students had failed. Surprisingly, Fion Runan had managed the spell once he had been told it several times. Arkadi was impressed by the serious manner in which the novice was approaching his last trials. He might just make it after all.

Arkadi wondered what school Fion would apply to if he did pass. The boy was not particularly suited to be either a druid or a monk, both were religious orders; one dealing with the physical realms and the other with the spiritual. Neither was the somewhat clumsy boy suitable for the Enchanters who crafted items of magic, or for the Wizards who dealt with elemental forces of incredible danger. A single error in either of these schools could rapidly cause destruction. He was neither a fighter nor had he shown talent in a number of areas of magic so both the school of Fighter Magi, and of the Magi, were out of the question. That left only the Seers school that focused on seeing the past, present and future or the Sorcerors who dealt with dimensional magic of space and time. Perhaps the Seers would be best; the boy had shown a quiet patience with the divination spell.

Arkadi collected together his teaching materials, his scrolls and his spell books and headed out of the large instruction room and down the dim hall towards his office. Arkadi was the current Master Tutor from the School of the Magi. He had only risen to being a full master around two years ago and had been the second youngest mage ever to pass the masters' trials. He knew he was well thought of in the College and was a rising star. He had heard that some had named him as a potential head of his school in years to come, a prospect with which Arkadi fully concurred. In fact, he had just realised the first step on his climb to greatness. He had just been given the position of Tower Warden for the School of Magi. The School of Magi was the largest and most powerful in the college and the new role would make him an officer and give him a seat on the council of the school as well as control of the administration of the Magi Tower itself.

Arkadi moved into the office he had shared for the past few years and moved over to the window. The window was not actually made of glass or even open to the air with shutters, it was in fact made from a perfectly transparent piece of rock. This rock merged seamlessly with the black rock from which the central mammoth building of the college was made. Arkadi never ceased to be amazed at the massive black building. The Black Hall as it was known, was the largest single building in the whole of the Wildlands, possibly even in the whole of the northern lands. The building was huge and rectangular in shape at the base. It was several hundred feet long and nearly as wide, and it rose up straight for four floors to an almost flat roof. Rising from this for another sixty feet, and one hundred and twenty feet in diameter, was a huge dome in which there were three floors. The building also had two basements and could easily house over a thousand people. During the Grand Council it would have to! The Grand Council was when all the rulers of the major provinces came together to discuss trade and the future of the Wildlands.

However, even this huge, black edifice was not the whole of the College of Magic. The college was also made up of a series of towers and buildings that were the centres for each of the college's schools. Only the newest school, the school of the Seers did not have its own tower yet. They had their own section in the Black Hall itself for the moment.

Looking out from his window Arkadi could not see the tower for his own school, he could actually only see the recently finished keep-like tower of the School of Sorcerors and the gigantic, ancient white dome occupied by the Cleric's school. Arkadi had actually seen the completion of the Sorceror's tower only ten years ago when he was just a novice himself. However, no one knew when the Clerics dome had been built. The dome like the slim and delicate Wizards tower, the stepped pyramid of the Druids and the Black Hall itself had all been here long before humans arrived to take up occupation. It was believed that this site had been the ancient capital of one of the lost kingdoms of the Elder, destroyed or abandoned centuries ago when the Elder kingdoms vanished. Indeed it was true that below the college, and below much of the town of Shandrilos, were catacombs that were thought to have been part of that city. Much was still unexplored and very mysterious, despite what the people of the town believed. Arkadi had often heard masters talk of the unusual magical emanations and fields in the deep catacombs and had always thought one day he might go down there and search out some clues to the powers of the Elder. It was widely acknowledged that the ancient races had known great magics and had performed wonders with them; the construction of this majestic building being one of them. Mages had often sought out the surviving remnants of those races who even now dwelt in the deep forests and high places of the Wildlands. They had found that the wild elves and the hill dwarves were not their ancestors. From those rare individuals who had gained an understanding with the hill dwarves it had become clear that these descendants of the Elder who survived, while still wielders of natural magic, retained only a fraction of their ancient knowledge and power. They were a wild fragment of the glorious kingdoms of old.

Arkadi stood still, wondering and thinking about those ancient magics, that lost lore, and wishing he might uncover some of the secrets of old as many of the grandmasters at the college; the finest magic users, were in the process of trying to do through research, exploration and experimentation.

A polite knock on the door brought Arkadi from his reverie and he turned to face the stout oaken door as he called for whomever to enter. The door swung gently open and in walked a mage wearing blue robes etched with silver crescent moons along their hem. These marked the wearer as a master of sorcery. In the tall, slim man's hand was a long, blue staff bearing a crescent moon on top that marked him as the head of that school!

Sorceror Supreme, Xameran Uth Altor was an impressive sight. He was not overly tall or even powerfully built in physical terms, but he had deep blue eyes that burned with a passion and you could feel the power and magic exuding from him. He had a handsome face that was welcoming with its broad smile. Arkadi often felt a little dowdy and plain in his grey robes before the splendour of the Lord of Sorcery. It didn't help that Arkadi was a head shorter than the Sorceror Supreme and somewhat in awe of what the man had achieved.

Arkadi stood and gave a short bow before politely gesturing for the sorceror lord to take a seat.

Xameran Uth Altor's smile grew even wider as Arkadi stood staring.

"Come now Arkadi we do not need to stand on ceremony. Please sit." The sorceror lord laughed good-naturedly, as he moved to take the seat opposite Arkadi. "I merely came to congratulate you on your recent appointment."

Arkadi flushed a little, "It was a surprise that they gave it to me, I am still only young to get such a responsibility."

"Nonsense, my friend, the responsibility is what you need to develop yourself. It will give you the experience you need in administering a school in order to run it. It is the next logical step for you and you're definitely ready for it." Xameran enthused. "I have not seen anyone with your talent, skill and drive since..." he paused and winked at Arkadi, "Well since me." he finished with a laugh.

Arkadi smiled and nodded his thanks at the compliment, but then frowned at Xameran.

"You are wondering at the formal robes for an informal visit, yes?" the sorceror responded in answer to Arkadi's silent question.

Arkadi nodded.

"The Archmage has called the Conclave to discuss the last details for the Grand Council." Xameran shrugged and looked a little irritated by the need for another meeting. "It's only three days away now, but still we meet." He signed and then leaned forward conspiratorially. "Between you and me I feel that the Archmage and his Moderates are planning something, hmm?" he questioned, referring to the loose groupings of masters in the assembly that favoured the Archmage and his slow reforms of the college.

Arkadi frowned, "The Archmage's staff has been unusually busy and secretive of late, and particularly those close to the Archmage, but other than that I have heard nothing."

Xameran Uth Altor just stared at Arkadi for a moment, his eyes searching and then shrugged, "Perhaps it's nothing, but we need to be vigilant. We need to see that we keep the process of change stimulating the college lest it stagnate. The Archmage can't be allowed to move towards the Traditionalist's view."

Arkadi nodded sharply. He agreed firmly with the sorceror lord. As soon as he had become a master and gained a seat on the college's governing body, the Assembly of Masters, Arkadi had joined the Progressive party led by Xameran Uth Altor. The Assembly was made up of the masters and grandmasters of the college and was roughly split into four groups, the most powerful being the Moderates and the Progressives. However, there were also the Traditionalists who believed in stability and adherence to the beliefs that had founded the college over sixty years ago. The fourth group was not really a group at all but consisted of all those masters who had no real affiliations to the other groups or existed in small groups based on friendship ties or research groups. They had their own small agendas to push. Often these Independents as they had become known could hold the sway on major decisions though they were few in number.

Arkadi stood as the sorceror lord rose to his feet to leave.

Xameran began to turn and then paused. He looked at Arkadi thoughtfully, "Are you going to be around for the Grand Council, Arkadi?"

"No, my lord, I have taken the time off. Once I have moved my things from my rooms here to my new rooms in the tower of the Magi I shall be off teaching duty for a week." Arkadi replied.

Xameran raised an eyebrow in surprise. "Going somewhere are we Master Talcost?" he asked in mock seriousness.

"I will still be around, but I am meeting up with old friends in the town and am planning on enjoying myself for a while. I haven't actually taken a break over the last two years or more and I need one."

"The novices wearing you down?" Xameran smiled and then turned serious again. "Don't be gone too long Arkadi. We need you around."

Arkadi was gratified by the sorceror lord's words.

"I have a feeling that important matters are afoot. Change is in the air." Xameran hinted and nodded at Arkadi. "I will need your support in the days to come."

Arkadi frowned and opened his mouth to ask a question, but the sorceror lord held up his hand to prevent him and said, "Don't ask me for more, just keep your eyes and ears open."

With that the Lord of Sorcery swept out of his room and Arkadi carefully sat himself into his comfortable chair wondering what was to come. He shook his head. He couldn't worry about that at the moment. He needed to organise the rooms for the others. His friends would be arriving tomorrow and he needed to have moved all his things to his new more spacious quarters. He relished the idea of not having to share with anyone anymore. He smiled for a moment, but then reminded himself that he needed to get moving, he also had to book the rooms at the inn for his friends. If he wasn't careful there would be none left. With the people coming from all over the Wildlands for the Grand Council, rooms in town were going fast. Rebba of course could stay in the spare room that Arkadi would now have in the suite given to him as Tower Warden, but he would need at least five more rooms in Shandrilos for the others.

Arkadi Talcost moved over to the chest he had begun packing earlier and began to take the last of his precious books and scrolls from the shelves and put them into the heavy, reinforced chest. If he quickly finished this chest he would then go and book rooms.

Chapter 5

RETURNING TO SHANDRILOS

The Wildlands of Darylor are divided into independent city states. These cities claim dominance over a province containing many smaller towns and settlements. The lands within the province claimed are often not fully controlled and the line is blurred between what is governed by the central city state and what is 'wild land'. Added to this, there are large areas of land that even the city states do not claim. These are the domain of the non-humans, many of whom kill any who enter their lands without warning, pity or remorse.

Excerpt from 'A strange land; the Wildlands of Darylor' by Grand Abbot Alinus Quan Sirona. BY1320

Garon Vale sat still and quiet in the prow of the boat. It had been years since he had last been in Shandrilos. He was looking forward to seeing the College of Magic. He had spent five wonderful years studying there and had not seen the city in nearly twice that long.

The lake boat, he and his fellow monks rode on, was long and wide. Its sides were well rounded and it had only a single mast with a wide square sail that billowed out smoothly. Along the sides of the boat there were benches and oars, though they were empty and the oars were stored and fastened tight. The boat was moving at a good speed, pushed along by a strong breeze from the north. Ordinarily going up river would only be possible using oars, but the Shandri River was unusual in that it generally had a prevailing breeze that moved against the current. This allowed a strong trade along the valley all the way from Ostia up through Shandrilos to Lauria in the highlands. Traders could let the current take them down river and use the winds to move against the current to come back. It was this natural coincidence that was now allowing trade to go even further down river past Ostia and on to Garon's adopted home of Sironac.

Garon had spent the last seven years of his life in that harsh frontier town. It was now his home as much as Ostia where he had grown up. Sironac was a small city of only around three thousand people, though there were a number of smaller towns and villages nearby that were dependent on it. The town itself was dominated by the great monastery that Grand Abbot Alinus had begun building fifty years ago. The monastery's main buildings were finished, although the grand chapel would probably take another decade or more. The monastery was the heart of a group of communities that had grown up on the eastern shores of the Great Serpent Lake. The town had been founded by the Grand Abbot who had begun his new Sironacian Order at the same time. The entire town's existence was based upon the order of monks. The town was defended by them and was also fortified with a huge stone wall to hold out against the goblin tribes of the region. They had constantly raided in the early years after the exiled priests, monks and followers had arrived there. The monastic order had been forced to take on a more martial role; all monks were trained with weapons to defend themselves and their community. They had combined their clerical magic and strength of arms with such success that they had not only held off the goblins, but beaten them back. Soon the goblins became wary of the 'white witches' as they ironically called the monks. Eventually, a large area of land was secured and people had begun to settle in greater numbers. Long years later, some of the goblin tribes had actually even begun to trade with Sironac, but it was the links that were formed with the dwarves that really secured the town. With their support and trade, Sironac had flourished.

Years after, Garon had gone to study at the College in Shandrilos. There, he had been attracted to the monks and their gentle ways and healing. It was their influence that took him away from the heavy drinking and self pity that had plagued him. He had joined the clerics' school after passing his trials and had dedicated himself to the teachings of the Sironacian order and of the Prophet Alba.

Garon had always desired to help people and while he knew his magical talent was not great, his desire to do something for those around him was. His friends had not fully understood his need to believe in a gentle god who would help and guide him and allow him to do the same for others, but for Garon finding the order had been his fate. He had been brought up to pay lip service to the old gods of his Nordic forefathers but those gods had always seemed so selfish and small, concerned with little other than themselves. The great God shown to the world by Alba seemed so large and caring. The teachings of the Sironacian order had opened Garon's eyes to how people should be; how they should treat one another; and how they should strive to lead good lives and deny evil. Over the last ten years Garon had put those teachings into practice and had fought and healed and lived a good life. He had put behind him his wasted life and now he felt at peace and ready to face the world outside Sironac again. He was looking forward to meeting up with his old friends. They had organised to meet in Shandrilos this very afternoon.

Garon turned his scrutiny outward and looked again over the prow of the boat. The view had changed somewhat in the last few minutes. He could now make out the low-hilled island in the lake upon which the town of Shandrilos stood. Soon they would move around the west side of the isle and be able to see the town itself just hidden by the small hills. Sitting back, Garon took in the whole view of the valley ahead. On either side of the grey waters of Shandri Lake, hills could be seen rising up to the harsh forests of the heights. On the eastern shore the hills rose sharply and cliffs and scree slopes could be seen against the green hillside. On the western side, small villages dotted the shore and the land rose more slowly so that neat farmland could be seen on the lower slopes with specks of white on the higher hills where sheep grazed. Beyond that the dark forests covered the highest slopes and heights like a blanket.

'This is a beautiful land,' Garon thought. 'I have missed it.'

Less than an hour later, Garon found himself waiting to disembark. The boat had found little problem moving into the huge docks of the town. The docks had been a stroke of luck for the first settlement of mages. Almost a century ago, the mages had to move back and forth between the villages on the shore more and more as their community grew. The docks had been discovered by accident when the mages were looking for a good place to tie their boats. Instead of the wooden jetties they had planned, they discovered a vast stone, deep water dock, built with incredible skill. As it was slowly uncovered it became clear that this ancient construction was capable of docking dozens of craft easily four or five times the size of their little twenty foot fishing boats. Later, this beautifully crafted harbour became the focal point for the building of the town of Shandrilos.

However, the focal point for the College of Magic had always been the impressive ruins of the elven city that had lain hidden in the light forest around a mile back from the shore. The forest had grown over the centuries to cover the ancient city and most of it had succumbed to the earth and forest and had been completely covered, but even back then there were some buildings that just simply were too big to cover. The greatest of these was the huge black rock building that became known simply as the Black Hall.

Initially, the town had been separate from the college itself. However, that had been almost a century ago. Later, as the settlement grew, it stretched to meet the college. It was hard to believe that this had been little more than a dozen buildings built to house the mages as they resurrected the ancient shell of the elven ruins. Now, Garon could see warehouses, shops and inns lining the entire curve of the great stone harbour. What had once been the hideout for a couple of dozen disenchanted magi was now a bustling city of over seven thousand people.

However, Garon's eyes were inevitably drawn to the imposing structure that was the College of Magic. The great midnight Black Hall still housed most of the college, but other towers and buildings had either been repaired or built over the last half century to give the schools their own space for living quarters and research. They now rose above the rooftops of the town, a collection of spires, towers and domes, the least of which was still twice the height of the highest roof in the city. The towers and domes were made of beautifully crafted colourful marble and night black rock. The great slim spire of the Wizards was made of some kind of purple quartz and was a legacy of the Elder race, while the squat dark, castle like tower of the Fighter magi had been built thirty years ago by dwarven engineers from the local Swiftaxe Clan who had strong ties with the Archmage. There, also, he could see the shining white dome of his own school that contrasted so sharply with the midnight black of the great central building. All of the eight schools had their own buildings.

Garon was snatched back from the view as the lakeboat thumped against the stone wall of the dock. Lines were thrown down from the dockside by weathered men in rough, dirt stained clothing. Garon watched as the sailors aboard moored the boat securely. From the large cabin that dominated the rear of the boat, came some of his brethren robed as he in white with the black rock symbol of the order on their chest. They were both younger than he, but more muscular and carried large two handed great maces. They were part of the martial arm of the order and were here, along with others to act as personal bodyguards for the Grand Abbot. There were also a dozen soldiers of Sironac to help safeguard their holy leader. These same numbers of troops, along with other members of his order, were in the two lakeboats that had moored ahead of them. Garon was not sure how much the Grand Abbot needed this amount of protection; to those with talent the Grand Abbot practically thrummed with power. Alinus often seemed an ancient to others, but he was still a force in his own right.

Garon had pushed hard to come along on the journey and Abbot Marius had allowed him to come along to act as one of his aides. Ten years of dedicated service had gained Garon some influence in his order. He had been told he was well thought of and he had progressed quickly to be a senior monk. His unstinting service had also given him the chance to come along on this important mission merely as an observer. Officially, he was a scribe to Prior Astinus but really he was here to 'test his faith' as Abbot Marius had grandly put it; 'To pit his discipline against the ills of his past.'

Garon noticed that Prior Astinus followed the two warrior monks out of the cabin. The prior quickly pushed past them onto shore and began looking around for the senior monks in charge of the other boats. Garon could see soldiers of Sironac in their white livery boiling up from the crowded common room below deck. They moved quickly to the wharf side where Garon could see the monks and sergeants had begun readying the other troops and monks for an escort to the College.

It took only a few minutes to organise the men and Garon was unsure if he was supposed to be part of the escort or would be allowed to head off to meet his friends. From the rear cabin he saw two more monks appear, quickly followed by the white bearded Abbot Marius. He spotted Garon and signalled for him to come over. Garon walked carefully across the boat and up the stone carved stairs to the wharf. Immediately at the top, the Abbot halted and called for Prior Astinus. He issued a number of commands before turning to look at Garon. For a moment he just stared Garon in the eye, his watery blue eyes seeming to search for something.

"There is much about you that is still unsure of itself, brother Garon," he began. "You must be wary of losing yourself to the worries of the past. You are a strong person now. Hold to your convictions, your teachings and your faith. Alba will guide you."

Garon was a little taken aback at the formality of the address. He was only going to meet old friends. The temptations of alcoholism and his feelings of self pity and inadequacy were long past. Those had been the weaknesses of Garon Vale the loser, the wastrel. That man was long gone. Garon the healer and shield of the weak had replaced him.

Abbot Marius seemed to read something of his thought. "An important time is approaching. The Holy Father has seen a dark time ahead. How dark I do not know, nor can our master see through to the truth."

Garon felt his eyebrows rise.

"We will all be tested physically, mentally and spiritually. The Grand Abbot had words for you."

Garon knew his face now showed outright shock.

Marius put a weathered hand on Garon's shoulder and sighed as if weary before continuing. "He has said that you, Garon, must trust in your abilities and strengths, even when it seems all have failed you." With that the old monk firmly turned Garon in the direction of the main street and gave him a light push.

Garon walked into the crowded street as if in a daze, his feet moving while his mind seemed frozen. So it was he did not see the figure that fell in behind him.

'She was a rogue,' she thought darkly. 'She thieved, she smuggled and she hunted, she was good at it! Her recent employer had been generous with his rewards, very generous.' Her thoughts were dangerous now and violent. 'She had become a hunter of men and her favoured method was to kill from a distance. It was an efficient way to kill, no looking in the eye, no anger or recriminations. Of course this would not be possible in these streets; killing would have to be done up close and personal.'

She lengthened her stride. She could see the tall, rounded figure ahead of her. She recognised the white monk's robe and cloak that covered a chain mail shirt. The man's ears stuck out slightly from the side of his head even through his short wavy brown hair. She knew the man's face was dominated by a pair of slightly protruding teeth giving him a comical look. They had been prominent when the monk had spoken to the older man at the wharf.

'Not the prettiest of faces,' she thought with a tight smile.

She quickened her pace, lengthening her stride yet again. She was barely a couple of steps behind the barrel shaped monk. The man was walking heedlessly through the street, occasionally bumping into others and ignoring the annoyed glances they threw his way.

What was the matter with the man?

He was close enough now that she could see the monk shaking his head slightly as if arguing with himself.

'Now was her chance' she thought, and she moved right up behind her unsuspecting prey. Deftly, she drew her short, skinning knife and grasped the monk's unblemished white cloak. She pulled. The man stumbled backwards a little, just enough for her to wrap her long arm around the monk and pin his arms. The other arm jammed the hidden knife up under the man's wide mouthed jaw and she hissed, "Going somewhere, Garon."

Garon Vale's light brown eyes widened in horror and he spluttered, "You!"

She smiled and pulled in close and gave him a kiss on the cheek. "Yes me. Surprised to see me after so long?" She asked, smirking.

With a gruff snort the monk heaved and broke her grip. "Get that out of my face," he yelled, shoving the knife from under his chin.

Nat Bero threw her head back and laughed. She then bent double, a hand on her bow stave keeping her from falling over. She laughed and laughed. People stopped and stared at the tall huntress as she laughed.

She looked up at Garon's outraged face and pointed with the small skinning knife, "You should have seen your face!"

The monk was having trouble with his composure. His face alternated between outraged anger and worry. Finally he snapped, "You shouldn't sneak up on people like that."

Nat's laughter became a little strained. Garon's words had reminded her of recent events.

Slowly the huntress stood up straight. This was the first light relief Nat had had in weeks. She had needed it badly, but now it seemed to her that the joke was no longer funny. Her actions mocked her own shame.

"You shouldn't have let me get that close," she muttered seriously. "What was the matter with you?"

Garon's face went flat and darkened. The archer could see her old friend had things on his mind too.

The monk was attempting to get his dignity back. "I was... That is I...." he mumbled before finally snapping, "It's none of your business, Nat."

Nat held up her hands and replied in genuine apology. "Sorry Gar."

Garon looked at her askance and then frowned. She could see that the sensitive monk had realised something important was bothering her and she got a grip of her feelings.

"Fine, just don't do that again." The rotund monk took a hold of his cloak and straightened it, along with his composure, with a sharp tug. He then looked hard at Nat Bero.

Nat fought to settle her features. She had always enjoyed the lighter side of life, little given to dark moods, yet she knew that the year had changed her. Her face must now seem careworn and hard to her old friend. She was finding it hard to hide her emotions. Her ill use at the hands of the unknown mage still filled her with anger, and the killings still filled her with shame. Nat could see that her friend was curious. She quickly switched the subject before the black feelings she had could rise up and swamp her again.

"I saw Bear and Darin disembark just before you at the dock."

Garon looked hard at her for a moment. He seemed to see her reticence to speak and let it go.

"You didn't get a chance to talk to them?" Garon asked as he turned and began to walk down the street.

47

Nat fell into step beside him, sheathing her knife. "No, they... didn't see me..." She paused a little painfully and then added. "Zara is already here, I spoke to the dockmaster and she remembered seeing her. 'Beautiful as an angel with an attitude like a demon,' I think were his words."

An almost surprised guffaw burst from Garon's lips. Nat was glad to see her friend had not become a complete misery during his time as a monk. Living in a monastery would surely make anyone miserable. Not that most people would think she was the life and soul of the party just lately. This trip to meet her friends was as much for her sanity as for anything else now. She needed a little joy back in her life; her friends knew how to enjoy themselves, and she could talk to them about Karis... and the fire... and other things.

After some time with her friends, she knew she could then face tracking this mage though she still wasn't sure whether to tell Darin and Bear, or what exactly she would say. She also still wasn't sure how she was going to deal with an obviously powerful mage. She was realistic enough to know that she did not have the skill to face the mage or his men directly, she was no warrior, but there were few who could match her skill with the bow. Her immediate plan had been to stick an arrow in him, even a mage couldn't always protect against that, but first she needed information. This mage had been clever in hiding himself... or herself? Nat had a number of contacts from her smuggling days that could maybe help... then maybe her friends; she had no doubt that Darin and Bear would be eager.

Nat realised that Garon was looking at her askance, a frown on his honest face. She forced a smile and enthusiastically slapped Garon on the shoulder, "It's good to see you Gar."

Garon seemed genuinely pleased at her words and smiled back warmly. "Yeah, it's good to see you too, even if you did almost give me heart failure."

The two of them walked on in companionable silence before Garon said, "Well it's a good few hours until we're supposed to meet the others at the Lucky Star. I was going to visit the Green Dragon." he said, looking at Nat questioningly.

She shrugged and said, "Sounds good to me, though I do need to do some business of my own between now and then as well."

The two friends walked on for a few more minutes, turning down side streets with Nat following Garon's lead.

"Did you hear that there are rumours of lost tunnels under the town with elven riches down there?" Nat asked, trying to keep her mind from dwelling on recent events.

"Elven riches?" Garon questioned in disbelief, "I suppose it's possible, but I'd have thought the college explored the tunnels long ago when they first excavated the ruins. All artifacts were collected." He looked at Nat as they turned onto a narrow street. "Who did you hear that from?"

"Apparently some mercenary groups have been heading down since last night. That seems to be where the rumours started," Nat replied vaguely.

Garon said nothing and just looked puzzled.

"It would be nice to have some riches again." The huntress mumbled.

Garon did look at her then, a question on his ruddy cheeked face.

Nat shrugged. She found she had a sudden need to confide in someone. "I've had a few problems lately and something has just changed things for the worse... I have done some terrible things, Gar!"

Garon's face took on a look of serious concern. "The Green Dragon's just two doors down," he said nodding in that direction, "we can talk in there."

Chapter 6

DRUID AND MAGE

Each of the cities of the wilds has a different story for how it came to be. Kalizern was founded by a rogue general from the empire. He had marched his legion north from the empire and deserted. He, his men and camp followers founded a camp that later grew to be the city of Kalizern. Shandrilos was a hidden retreat formed to protect those who used magic from all persecution. Later, under the leadership of Melkor Erin, it grew into the college and city it is today.

Excerpt from 'A strange land; the Wildlands of Darylor' by Grand Abbot Alinus Quan Sirona, BY1320

"No, I will not entertain the officials from Lauria or anywhere else." stormed Arkadi Talcost, "I organised this break months ago."

Arkadi's brows were drawn down tight over his dark eyes. They seemed to flash in the light from the tall arched window as he spoke. Rebba watched him point at the grey robed mage before him as his irritation grew.

"You were aware it was the Grand Council and had plenty of time to organise some of the senior students to take that role. I have a prior engagement that I cannot miss!" Arkadi finished with a slash of his hand, cutting the man off as he began to protest.

The poor mage was spluttering like a fish out of water. There was something definitely fish-like about the man, in Rebba's opinion, or maybe eel-like. He was an oily, political creature, who Rebba instinctively felt she could not trust. He would wriggle free of any agreement. 'Well not this time,' Rebba thought, 'Arkadi was not a person to enter into a debate with, especially when he thought he was right!' The wily mage had a mind like quicksilver to back his equally swift tongue. Rebba knew of few who were his equal intellectually.

The man tried to speak and Arkadi deliberately glared at him and then turned away and walked across towards Rebba. Behind him, Rebba could see that the man's face was flushed with pent up frustration. He spun on his heel and stomped to the door, flung it open, and left without closing it. Rebba glanced back to Arkadi. The mage was grinning.

"Don't worry about him," Arkadi said with a nod in the direction the pompous mage had disappeared. "He's a jumped up fool who's more interested in gaining favour than with doing his job properly." Arkadi smiled mischievously before adding, "I think that should stop him bothering me again." Arkadi placed his hand on Rebba's and turned her towards the still open door. "Let's get out of the offices. I want to show you my new rooms!" He said excitedly, "We can then get a bit of food. You must be starving."

Rebba nodded, smiling at Arkadi's obvious excitement. She fell into step beside her oldest friend and they headed out of the office. They entered a long dark corridor with numerous identical doorways regularly spaced in the walls on both sides. The passageway had no windows and was lit by torches high up on the walls, magically attached to the immutable black stone of the college. Arkadi paused to pull his door shut behind him and locked it with a bright brass key he produced from inside the grey robes he wore. The grey robes marked him as a member of the School of Magi, the school concerned with the general theory of spellcraft rather than any particular speciality. Rebba was wearing her green robes that marked her as a member of the School of Druids, those dedicated to the magic of nature and preservation, and to the worship of the Nordic gods.

They walked on and then down the steep stairs at the end. They were heading for the rear of the Black Hall where the general offices of the administration of the college and province were held. At the bottom of the stairs, they turned and walked down another passageway nearly identical to the one they had left save it had long slim windows on one side that gave it a much more airy and pleasant atmosphere. At the far end they came out into a hall that dominated the rear entrance to the huge black building in which they walked. The Lower Hall, as it was known, had a flat roof that was supported by tall thick columns with intricately carved patterns that made them look like great stone trees, branching off into the roof thirty feet above. It was carved with such intricacy that it looked like the trees were alive. It was yet another marvel of the college.

The whole of the Black Hall was a marvel of Elder construction, though none now knew what it had been used for, it was clear that magic had been used in its construction; there were no joins in the building as if it was carved of one block; it maintained a steady heat in some unknown way; and the windows gave light, but were invisible from outside no matter their size. Even the black stone of the hall itself was of an unknown substance that could withstand all but the most potent spells without showing even a scratch! Only the fixtures such as the doors, or the dividing walls that the mages had added were vulnerable. It was a mystery what this building, along with the underground catacombs and the adjoining structures, had been for. Yet the greatest mystery was that even the most powerful mages couldn't sense anything magical about the structure. This went against all known magic. The massive building should have shone like a beacon to the senses of all those who had any talent in the mysteries. Why it did not was a conundrum that had occupied the finest minds for over a century.

As Rebba and Arkadi reached the Lower Hall, Rebba noted the heightened activity. Officials of the province and the college, and magic users from all the schools, stood in groups talking or moving hurriedly on their various errands. This was a very busy time as the Grand Council of the Wildlands was to begin tomorrow morning and many preparations had to be made to house and entertain the various contingents from the provinces.

The council had been the idea of the Archmage, Baden Erin to help bring all the Wildlands of Darylor together and each of the major provinces had hosted it.

Thinking about the leaders of the provinces, Rebba looked up. She knew there was a hall above this that would be a hot bed of political discussions and bargaining over the next few days. The province leaders themselves would sit in council in the high, round room above that, in the huge dome atop the Black Hall.

As they moved down the steps to the floor, Arkadi leaned in and said conspiratorially, "Did you hear that the Enchanters have managed to lose the cloaks they crafted for Elgon of Ostia?"

Rebba looked at him blankly.

"It seems the Enchanters had spent months on special cloaks that would allow men to almost disappear into the background, making them excellent for spy work." Arkadi looked at Rebba and grinned mischievously, "and it seems that they managed to misplace the whole lot." Arkadi sniggered wickedly. "You could hear the screams from the other side of the College."

Rebba looked at him. "They were stolen?" she asked disbelievingly.

"Well that's just it. The tower of the Enchanters is the most secure place in the College." Arkadi put in.

As the two of them moved across the Lower Hall, Rebba noticed eyes turning her way. In her time in the forests of the west, she had forgotten what it was like being around so many people. Her long coppery gold hair always caught people's attention, and she knew that many considered her pretty, but she had never courted the looks. She was not like Zara who dominated a room with her brash confidence, and who wore some of the most revealing clothes Rebba, and most of polite Nordic society, had seen! Rebba had actively sought to make herself look plain, wear heavy robes, and leave her hair unkempt, but this didn't seem to work. In some cases it seemed to make things worse! Eventually she had learned to ignore the looks, but as the two of them pushed past a group of officials from the southern province of Lauria, she felt herself blush slightly at the admiring looks. Arkadi seemed to notice and he drew her through the group to the high double doors that led out onto the rear plaza of the college.

Looking out in relief across the neatly trimmed lawns and gardens, Rebba smiled as she took in the beauty of the gardens, maintained by her own school. She noticed a group of students sat cross-legged like children in the shade of a particularly old oak tree. In the shadows beneath the oak's branches was a grey robed master who spun and gesticulated wildly as he spoke in what Rebba was sure was an impassioned voice even though she could not hear, but then Rebba still remembered mad old Master Burion Brae, still remembered his ruffled, stained and battered old robes and his equally scruffy appearance. His sparse hair would always end up pointed in all directions. Rebba wondered when the College would finally retire the old man from teaching. It certainly didn't approve of his manner, dress or methods. However, none could dispute his results; the students he taught always achieved highly in exams and testing, and all the students loved his lively, irreverent and unorthodox teaching. Nevertheless, the man was mad as a March hare and possibly the oldest mage in the college.

Rebba caught Arkadi's eye and nodded in the old mage's direction. Arkadi smiled and shook his head before continuing with his story.

"There is no way that those cloaks could have been moved except with the permission of the High Enchanter himself, or the Archmage." Arkadi gave Rebba a meaningful look. "Neither of those has said anything, but the rumour is that the other Enchanters know nothing and are on the warpath. They had intended to give those cloaks to Lord Elgon tomorrow when all the Wildlands' leaders attend the feast in their honour."

"What do you think happened?" Rebba asked. She was not really that upset at the Enchanter's problems. They were far too secretive and money grabbing in her opinion and she thought they needed taking down a peg or two.

"I think the Archmage may have had a hand in it."

Rebba was genuinely shocked at this and almost tripped on the stairs down from the rear plaza.

The stairs ran down gently towards the grey stone tower-like structure that was the home of the School of Magi where Arkadi now had his rooms.

Arkadi noticed his friend's surprise and added, "The Archmage has been acting very strangely of late you know." He nodded at Rebba and raised his eyebrows. "He's been disappearing at odd times and no one knows where or how, but he's never seen going or returning. He's been organising his personal staff and sending them off on secret errands. Not one of his people would tell me a thing, not even a hint."

Rebba was surprised at the Archmage being seen as involved, but not at Arkadi being blanked by his staff. Arkadi was too inquisitive and generally wanted to know everything. He was also politically aligned against the Archmage.

"Why would they tell you anything, you're a teacher for the college, not a part of the Archmage's staff. They are just doing their duty and not letting an overly clever mage poke his nose into affairs that are nothing to do with him."

Arkadi looked genuinely hurt for a moment. Rebba stopped, put her hand on her hips and stared levelly at Arkadi until the sneaky mage's face split into a grin.

He held up his hands and said, "I'm just trying to get a grip on what's happening. It's just so much more interesting than teaching arrogant fools who think they know all there is to know just because they are in their final year." His face twisted in mock boredom briefly and then quickly switched to excitement. "Besides, I'm on to something…"

Rebba cut him off. "Oh no! Don't be telling me. You've dragged me into your little nefarious schemes before. I don't want anything to do with this… whatever this is." With that she pointed to the entrance to the Magi's tower that gave access to the private quarters inside.

Arkadi huffed, "You're just no fun anymore. Those years in the woods out in the middle of nowhere have made you as dull as ditch water." He headed to the door and produced a key from a hidden pocket in his robe and quickly unlocked and opened the thick reinforced door.

Arkadi would never understand Rebba's fondness for the wilds. Arkadi was in love with the intrigues of the college and loved the hustle and bustle of the town. Rebba hated crowds and loved the quiet peace of the wilds, whether it be forest, moors or hills, though forests were her favourite. Upon completing her training at the college, Rebba had asked to be sent to work with a group of forest communities in Aron Vale to the west and had spent all her time there helping to heal the people and the lands, caring for the spiritual and physical well being of the small communities who still held to the old beliefs in the gods of earth, sky and sea. Out there in the wilderness, Rebba had put the magic she had practised to its proper uses and had developed her skills and knowledge. Arkadi on the other hand had stayed on at the college and become a member of the teaching staff. He had risen high, but then Arkadi was a superb magic user, talented and skilful. His recent promotion to Warden of the Tower of the Magi reflected his talent and drive.

They entered the grey stone tower, Arkadi leading the way. Rebba could tell he was keen to show off his new spacious rooms. After only a brief time, they stood outside the sturdy door to the apartments of the Warden of the Tower. Arkadi swung the door open and with a proud wave of his hand, gestured for Rebba to enter.

"I now have two bedrooms, a study, and even my own heated bath in the room over there," he gestured to a smaller arched door off to the side, " and..." he began.

Rebba cut him off, "A heated bath!" She was already heading for the smaller door. "Would you be a dear, Arkadi and have my things sent here from the gate house?"

"What about seeing my study? You should see my library..."

"Oh I will, Arkadi... later." Rebba mumbled, already opening the door to the small bathhouse. She paused and looked back at Arkadi, "I just have to get a bath. I've been travelling for days."

Arkadi's shoulders slumped a little, but he smiled wryly, "I'll have your things put into the spare room."

Rebba smiled dreamily and ducked into the marbled room with the heated bath. She did miss civilisation sometimes.

A few hours later, Rebba sat, relaxed and refreshed, picking at the food on the table. Arkadi went into his sleeping chamber to change into his travelling robes.

"You know there's something odd going on in town." Arkadi called from the other room. "There are all kinds of rumours about the old catacombs."

Rebba looked over to where Arkadi's voice emanated from the open doorway, interested.

"Just between you and me, the college has done nothing about them for years, few have ever really spent time exploring them fully." Arkadi continued. "You know there's all kind of vague magical resonances from down there. We have little idea what they are or even exactly where they come from. The most talented of the seers are sure they are making headway in terms of sensing the Elder magic and that there are areas of huge magical energy, but they cannot deduce their nature or even fully locate them."

Arkadi appeared at the door in his black travel robes and Rebba replied, "Vast knowledge about magic was lost when the Elder kingdoms were destroyed."

Arkadi nodded in agreement and a faraway look entered his eyes. "Can you imagine what they could do back then? It would be amazing to discover some of that lost knowledge." He had a fierce look in his eyes.

"Dangerous though." Rebba warned.

"Oh you're far too timid, Rebba. You need to be more adventurous, more forceful." He moved over to sit at the table and pull a leg from the cold, half eaten chicken on the table.

Rebba just gave him a flat stare.

"Anyway," Arkadi went on, "aren't you supposed to be getting changed and ready to go meet the others. They'll be waiting at the Lucky Star for us."

"I thought we weren't meeting until sundown." Rebba said sitting up.

Well that's only half an hour or so away," Arkadi responded in his lecturer's tone, "and we have got to get across town yet."

Rebba quickly rose and headed off towards her room where her pack and things were now waiting. More adventurous, she thought wryly, we'll have all the adventure we need if Zara, Bear and Darin are in Shandrilos.

Chapter 7

A CHANCE ENCOUNTER

The city of Karodracia was founded by Saint Karodra and his followers. Saint Karodra was a great Knight Templar who was famed for breaking from tradition when he had a vision that said he should protect the lost and poor. He travelled the empire protecting the roads, travellers and village folk. He gained many followers and in his wake many shrines grew. It is believed a vision took him into the northern wilds to found a settlement, but the reality is much more prosaic. He had come to the attention of powerful members of the church who had grown to dislike his influence with the common people. The church drove him from the empire.

Excerpt from 'A strange land; the Wildlands of Darylor' by Grand Abbot Alinus Quan Sirona, BY1320

Zara Halven glided passed the men at the entrance and into the Lucky Star Inn, noting the speculative glances she got. Looking around, it seemed an unusually clean little tavern, nowhere near as large as the one she owned in Ostia; hers was far more vibrant, lively and... Interesting. This was the typical sort of place that the pompous little mage, Arkadi would opt to book; a place to gamble but a safe one. Respectable.

Zara sneered at the thought. She looked around.

The Lucky Star was given over to quiet drinking and gambling. It had aromatic smoking candles that hung in iron-wrought lanterns from new oak beams that had barely had time to age before being chopped and stripped for the two storey structure. The ceilings were low and its walls were white daubed in the Nordic style with shuttered windows that could be opened on a warm night to let air into the close area of the bar. It had numerous little rooms off to the sides and back that were used for the gambling side of the business.

Zara had heard of the owner. He was an unusual man in that he had travelled widely in the south. It was said he had ventured to lands even beyond the empire and had returned with many new and interesting ways to gamble money away.

Gambling of all kinds was a great source of interest to Zara, but not in such an environment. Where was the danger? Without that, the gambling didn't seem worth it.

Looking at no one in particular, Zara threw back her floor length cloak to show her extravagant tunic and trousers, and her beautifully decorated thick, leather belt and calf high boots. All were designed to show off her lithe athletic form. The rich colours of her clothes she knew complimented her dark eyes and shoulder length black hair. Zara always liked to be seen in her finery when she could, why else work so hard for the riches if not to show them off? Appreciative eyes looked her way, but she realised with annoyance, none that she recognised. Where were they?

She languidly strutted across the room, all confidence. Eyes followed her and she smiled. She was enjoying the effect she had, but strutting like this did also draw fools and thieves like flies. She was an expert on those and never failed to make sure any admirers saw the daggers and short swords that hung at her waist. She smiled to no one in particular, enjoying herself. She needed to cheer herself up a little. Her fortunes were not what they had once been, but she would bounce back. She always did. Once she'd been one of the richest people in Ostia, someone to whom even nobles showed respect.

Zara grimaced slightly at the thought of how that had changed, but the smile came back an instant later. She had to keep up appearances, stay positive.

'Where was everyone?' she thought again with a little annoyance. 'I get the best tip off of the year and they are nowhere to be found!'

To think that right beneath their feet there might be Elder artifacts that could set her fortunes back on track.

One of the benefits of her mercenary work was that she had developed a network of contacts who could keep her in touch with everything that was going on in the Wildlands. Vatris, a merchant contact here in Shandrilos, was sure of the rumour of new tunnels discovered and likely Elder treasures even if Zara had been skeptical.

Why now? The mages had searched the tunnels many times over the years, yet Vatris was adamant. These tunnels were new. Recently found.

It was perfect really, the timing of this discovery and meeting up with the old band. Plundering ancient Elder ruins had practically been their speciality. Year ago, it had earned them all enough gold to give themselves a good start in life. It had almost got them all killed too, but that was part of the risk and the excitement. She had never fully understood why the others had wanted to quit. Without the band, she'd had to find other ways to earn money and fund her rise to power. This had forced her down less savoury avenues for money making opportunities.

She moved casually around the inn.

Vatris had said that he had heard only recently of the discovery and that the mages of the college had tried to cover it up. Zara had to act fast, mercenaries and bounty hunters like Tathgar and Alrin of Katurem were already heading down into the tunnels. She had almost panicked when she had heard this and gone down alone, but then Vatris had produced a map that no one else had, copied from one held by the mages themselves. He wouldn't say how he got it? The map showed the extent of the catacombs and a way down from the very inn at which she and her friends would be staying!

It was fate! The gods were pointing the way.

Zara knew her friends would help her. It would only take a little bit of persuasion. For a group with their knowledge and experience of Elder relics, their knowledge of magic and their fighting expertise, it would be easy money.

A thought suddenly made her frown. Her friends wouldn't try the dice tables would they? Not with the monk and druid along surely! However, Darin and Arkadi did enjoy a roll of the dice.

'Damn!' she thought as she deftly wove her way between the tightly packed tables. She headed for the thick, oaken doors to the back rooms, off to the side of the bar where the gaming tables would be.

As she approached, two men, hidden from her view, rose and moved to block the door. Neither was particularly tall yet they were both big and broad, bull necked and wearing thick, rough woolen cloaks that Zara knew covered padded mail and an array of weapons. The two bouncers could have been brothers, but for one being of Nordic blood and the other clearly having the coppery skin of an Olmec.

"I'm looking for some friends of mine." She said haughtily.

Noting both men's blank looks, Zara huffed in exasperation. "Four men, two women, a couple of them mages," she hinted.

"Red headed women?" One of the men grunted. The two men looked at each other and smiled.

Zara barely hid her annoyance. 'Of course they'd remember Rebba Korran!' Men were so predictable.

"Yes," she said through clenched teeth. Hiding her irritation.

"They headed to the private room at the back." The other man grunted.

Zara smiled her most charming smile as she contemplated sticking knives in the pair. 'Not worth it,' she thought 'these two have the combined intelligence of the sheep whose wool their wearing. It would be like picking a fight with livestock.' She had no doubt she could kill both before either could draw a weapon, but such things tended to cause trouble with guards and she didn't need that at the moment.

Zara spun on her well-crafted heel and headed back to the common area at the front of the bar to find the innkeeper and the private rooms. Her mood was steadily declining.

As she headed towards the far side of the inn, she noticed a huge, thick set man with a shining bald head ordering drinks at the side of the bar.

'At last,' Zara thought, recognising Bear's unmistakable form… Abruptly, she hesitated. Zara couldn't wait to share the good news, but seeing Bear made her pause. They had parted on such bad terms. Bear had always been the one man she could rely on, the one who had stayed with her, the one who knew her best. When he had left her, it had hurt more than she would ever admit. She knew she had hurt him too… but who was he to tell her how to live her life.

Some of the old anger returned as she remembered the argument all those years ago.

Distracted, she didn't notice the three shadows that seemed to appear before her until they were on top of her. They slammed into her, but even as she went down, her lightning reflexes allowed her to roll, catch the first man's weight on her knees and draw a blade. She found herself staring into the startled eyes of a face she vaguely seemed to recognise. She frowned even as she thrust the man up away from her. He was a big man, strong and heavy and weighted with armour. Zara found she couldn't get free.

Suddenly, the man seemed to fly up into the air as he was wrenched off her and Zara heard Bear's gruff voice saying angrily "Why don't you look where you're going." It was a statement not a question.

Zara swiftly rolled herself back to her feet. Upon standing up, she saw the leader of the three men shove at Bear savagely trying to free himself from the big man's grip. He pulled a long, wickedly thin dagger.

"Get off me!" he snapped.

Bear let go and held his hand up warily, though his other hand, Zara noted, was ready and clenched into a fist.

Zara stepped forward angrily. "Try it and I'll feed that knife to you..."

She was cut off as Bear pulled her back sharply and glared at her.

"Whatever you say friend," Bear replied slowly, "we don't want any trouble."

"Like hell we..." She began.

Bear growled at her.

What was the matter with him?

Bear's eyes flicked to the two other men who were now standing with swords drawn, their peculiar cloaks thrown back to show full armour underneath.

Bear stepped back and pulled Zara with him, leaving the way to the door open.

The three men glanced once at Bear, then at Zara and then turned and headed for the door as if a dragon were on their tail. Zara reflexively glanced towards where they had come from, half expecting to see some monster chasing them. When she looked back, the men were gone. A strong hand fell onto Zara's shoulder and she quickly looked up to see Bear's icy blue eyes glaring down at her.

"Could you try to look where you are going!" The giant warrior snapped in annoyance. "That could easily have turned bloody."

Zara angrily slapped his large hand from her shoulder and brushed at her cloak in mock worry for the material. "I *was* looking where I was going but the light in here..."

"Yeah, the light and your poor eyes," Bear interrupted mockingly, "maybe you're getting old." he finished with a snort.

Zara snapped back, "Older maybe but not fatter like some." She pointedly looked at the big man's midriff.

Bear glared and then turned and headed back to the bar.

Zara stood for a moment, wanting to say more. To be fair the big man looked better than he had seven years ago, but he had started the insults. It was only then she realised what she held in her hand.

She smiled and called out to Bear. "And besides I'm not that old."

Bear turned and looked at her. With that she held up a large money pouch.

Bear's brow came down sharply and he hissed, "You robbed him?"

Zara felt the answer was obvious so she refrained from responding.

"Bloody typical. Still got the morals of a sewer rat, I see!"

Zara deftly slipped the hefty bag into one of her cloak's inner pockets as Bear stalked off towards a small room in the far corner of the inn. Things weren't exactly getting off to a great start. Suddenly, she remembered her news.

"Damn it, Jon Madraig, you big lump!" she snarled. "Wait."

⌒⌒

An hour later and the long limbed huntress, Nat Bero was almost dancing around the table in excitement while the others laughed at her obvious enthusiasm. "I'll get those packs I brought over earlier. I stashed them in the rooms upstairs." The tall huntress had a huge smile on her broad face. She strode off to get the packs. Her joy was excessive, but infectious and even the dour faced Bear was smiling his half smile.

Not so Rebba Korran. Something seemed to be bothering the sensitive druid. "What? We're just going to leap up now and head off?" Rebba said in surprise.

"Well I have organised with the innkeeper for us to use his cellar to get into the tunnels; we have the map showing us where the treasures lie; and we haven't had too much to drink." Zara said, as she came back into the room. "Can you think of a better time?"

Rebba's mouth opened like a fish out of water, but before she could gather her thoughts, Zara continued.

"All of us are together, we have our weapons and armour, though we shouldn't need them, Nat's getting some supplies and the entrance is in the next room." she insisted. "The gods are showing us the way."

"Since when did you believe in the gods, Zara? Or in anything for that matter. You are reckless and don't really care what happens so long as you get what you want!" snapped Rebba in irritation.

Zara couldn't deny Rebba's comments. She had lied, cheated and stolen, even killed to get what she wanted, and though her friends didn't know the full extent of her deeds, they knew enough. She was also certainly a skeptic when it came to gods of any kind. She believed whatever suited her needs at the time.

As this went through her head, she felt her smile drop as she looked at the druid. "You really don't want to go?" She looked around her and then back to the annoyingly pretty druid. "Fine, stay here." Zara snapped. "You were always a waste...".

"Back off, Zara!" Bear growled.

She turned and shot him a vicious look. "Oh, look if it isn't the big brave Bear. What are you going to do? Run off again."

Bear rose to his feet, his head almost touching the roof beams. His large form blocking the light so that the room noticeably darkened.

"Run off. I didn't run anywhere. I left. My choice. But, like everything that happens to you, it's always the other person who is wrong, isn't it? Never you! Never Zara Halven! Maybe if you took a look at yourself, really looked, you'd understand why everyone leaves."

Silence fell on the room. Moments passed. Zara glared at Bear, who glared back.

"Oh, do I detect a change in the mood?" Darin asked sweetly, the knight's tone laced with sarcasm and a sudden grin on his face.

A slightly drunk, Arkadi sniggered. Garon Vale gave a startled guffaw! The white clad monk had stayed very quiet so far, watching everything.

The tension seemed to drain away. Bear looked away and then sat back down. Zara took a deep breath. Why could he still get to her? She switched her gaze from Bear, ignored the looks from the others and smiled thinly at Darin. She turned back to face the fiery haired druid. It was time to change tack.

"Come on, Rebba," Zara said smoothly as if the last few moments had not happened, "it'll be fun; just like old times, and we might even find something."

Arkadi nodded a little drunkenly and added, "It's true those catacombs have been entered before, there's no danger and if there are new tunnels there is a chance someone has missed some hidden cache."

"What about those magical emanations down there? Even the Grandmasters couldn't find what they were or even where they came from." Rebba shot back at the mage. "Added to which we are forbidden to go down there."

"I am a master now, Rebba." Arkadi asserted. "I have permission to go where I need to." The mage took a long swig from his mug. Arkadi was clearly enjoying more alcohol than he'd had in a long time.

Darin of Kenarth leaned over and thumped the druid on the shoulder playfully. "See nothing to worry about, Rebba. Arkadi's a master." he said, then rolled his eyes, "Master of what, we aren't sure... Not of buying a round in." Darin rattled his now empty mug at the mage who frowned and pointed at himself, a questioning look on his face.

Rebba ignored Darin and Arkadi.

"I've had an odd feeling; a nagging sensation at the back of my mind. It has been growing all day. The prospect of going into the catacombs has brought the feeling more to the fore."

Rebba glanced at Bear who Zara could see was clearly still angry, but who was also the only one who didn't seem that eager to go down into the tunnels, not that the giant warrior-mage ever seemed eager about anything.

"What do you think, Bear?" Rebba asked.

The heavily built Bear, looked at the druid, his anger fading. He thought briefly and then announced, "I trust your feelings Rebba. You were always the one whose senses were most attuned to the mysteries, but your feelings could be nothing more than being back in Shandrilos, or related to us all being together."

"Why are we even talking about her feelings?" Zara demanded angrily. "So she has a bad feeling. By the gods, it is probably indigestion!"

"She has been right before..." Arkadi put in.

"And she has been wrong!" Zara snapped back.

She looked around and could see she needed to change tack.

"Look, think about Nat. She could really do with this. Finding some Elder artifacts could mean some serious money. You lot might not need it but she does!"

She neglected to add that it would do her a lot of good too. All her money was tied up in the inn. She looked around and could see that her point had had an effect. Only Bear eyed her suspiciously.

Rebba still looked troubled. "I am still not sure. I haven't felt anything this strong before..." She trailed off.

Interestingly, Garon was now starting to look worried. Gods! All she needed now was for the fat monk to chime in.

"Right, are we decided then?" She prompted quickly.

"Let's vote on it." Bear rumbled.

"Vote, you big oaf!" Zara snapped, "We don't need to..." She trailed off at the glare from Bear. She threw up her arms. "Fine!" she muttered. "Let's see then, raise your hand if you want to go."

All hands save Rebba's and Bear's went up, though Zara suspected this was partly to make Rebba feel better and partly to annoy her.

At that moment, Nat Bero returned, a grin stretching her weathered features as she struggled in with a mixed group of packs.

"What's this?" she asked looking at her friends with their hands high, "Is the ceiling about to fall on us?" She smiled at her own joke.

Zara stood smoothly, swept up her pack and leaned in close to Nat, smirking, "No, we were just voting on who was going to have to baby sit you down in the tunnels." She laughed and then moved past the lanky huntress towards the back room door which led to the cellar.

The rest of the group began to rise and Nat looked at the four people who'd had their hands up, frowned for a moment as they began to take their packs, then suddenly she smiled again, "Well it seems I am popular at least."

"No, those are the people who wanted to be as far from you as possible." Zara laughed from the doorway.

Nat spun, a retort on her lips, but a firm thump on the back from Darin as he grabbed his pack made Nat gag on the smart comment she was about to make.

"Come on Nat," Darin called, chortling, "I thought you wanted to go hunt some treasure."

Nat grabbed her pack and then pushed past the laughing Darin with a muttered curse that only made the tall knight laugh more.

⁓⁓⁓

Rebba retrieved the last of the packs, but she couldn't shake the feeling that something was out of place. She hesitated and then realised the others had all gone on, except Bear, who was frowning worriedly at her.

"Don't worry Bear," she responded to Bear's unspoken question, "I'm fine."

Bear stared at her a moment in concern. He seemed about to ask something when Zara Halven's voice called from the back room, "Come on, laggards. Get a move on."

Bear face went rigid, but he nodded at Rebba and then headed for the back room.

Rebba Korran followed, unsure of what she was feeling. She reached the back room and watched as the others headed off to get their armour and weapons. Arkadi stayed with her. The two of them had no need to change, they were wearing their travel robes and had their leathers on underneath. They had what they needed.

As they waited, Arkadi was content to sit quietly and drink water as he tried to sober up a bit. She brooded over what she was feeling. There seemed something strange here, something she couldn't quite put her finger on. It wasn't like she was afraid of going underground. She was a druid, in tune with nature; her mystical senses could tell her exactly where she was even in the deep underground so what was it?

She thought back.

The feeling had really begun to nag at her when first they had all come together in the inn. It was something at once elusive and yet... she struggled to define it... something charged...! It was as if something important was about to happen! There was something important about them all being together again, about going down into the catacombs!

"Come on, Rebba," Bear called, disturbing her thoughts.

The big man had now donned his armour and had his shield slung on his arm.

Rebba grimaced and hoisted her pack to her back, deep in thought. She crossed to the back room, hugging her staff for comfort. Arkadi somewhat unsteadily got up and followed.

The room they entered was small and had a set of rough stairs going up to the second floor, but at the side of the stairs was a trapdoor in an area that had clearly been a space used for storage. The boxes that had obviously been there had been shoved aside to partly block the stairs. The trapdoor in the floor had been swung open and Darin was shouting down to the others who must already have headed down.

Bear waved Arkadi forward and then disappearing down through the trapdoor himself. Darin helped Arkadi negotiate the steps, a smile on his face, and then gestured for Rebba to hurry. She quickly moved to the trapdoor and started down the steep, narrow steps. She descended into a stone walled cellar that smelt of earth and alcohol. It seemed like it was rarely used these days as the casks and boxes down here were covered in dust, though there were signs of lots of footprints on the floor. People had been in here recently. She wondered who, but the strange nagging feeling was making it hard to think.

Loud curses distracted her. Off in the far corner, Nat and Zara were clearly having difficulty prising open a large iron grate. The others were making small comments and laughing quietly at them, their mood light.

While she waited for Nat and Zara to open the ancient looking grate, Rebba again considered the feelings that plagued her. She thought back to when she had first experienced such feelings. It was years ago now, back when she was an apprentice at the college. They had scared her when they wouldn't go away and the masters had been unable to define them. One of the seers had suggested that it might be a talent for sensing the unknown or even a touch of prophecy, that rarest of gifts.

For a time Rebba had been excited by the idea, but nothing had come of the feelings and she had pushed them aside as unreliable. Instead, Rebba had focused on her druidic senses and magic; however, her odd feelings had come and gone over the years and at times they had predicted important events for her. Now it seemed the coming together of her friends had prompted the feelings to return again. Could she rely on them this time? She had certainly never known them so strong.

She looked at the people around her. Could it just be them?

Rebba had always considered her friends special, even Zara. In some ways it was obvious that they were all different from the vast majority of people in the Wildlands; there were few who were so well educated, so different to one another and yet so free from prejudice and superstition.

However, it also had always seemed to Rebba that many of her friends were destined for great things, some of them had already made names for themselves; Darin was already a swordsman of renown; Arkadi was one of the most promising magic users of his generation and a future leader at the college: and none could deny that Zara, who was not so much famed as infamous, was a hugely talented warrior and mercenary, as well as a unique character.

Even the others, though lacking in fame, were remarkable; Bear had the ability to be a formidable fighter or mage, but few knew that he was also one of the foremost scholars on the Elder; Nat Bero was a superb tracker and the only women to have ever won the Golden Arrow, the foremost archery contest in the Wildlands. Garon Vale and herself were perhaps the least of the group, but they were both very competent magic users and excellent healers. This was not even taking into account the friends who either couldn't come or hadn't arrived yet.

However, none of this really explained the sudden inexplicable feelings she was having. She had always felt this way about her friends. Why had these feelings resurfaced now?

A great dull thump snapped Rebba from her reverie.

She looked up and saw that Zara and Nat had moved aside to allow Bear to use his huge strength to wrench the large grate aside. Zara was standing, brushing dirt and rust from her hands while Nat Bero, ever the scout, had already grabbed a flaming torch and leapt into the dark hole that had been uncovered. Soon all of the friends followed and they found themselves in a large earthen tunnel that angled slightly downwards. To Rebba, it seemed that the walls had once been much more solid, but they were obviously not Elder in origin.

It wasn't long before the group erupted through another more easily shifted iron grate into the lower cellars of the college. Rebba recognised them from the black rock and swirling patterns on the far wall that covered all of the Black Hall, even its foundations. The many rooms down here had been added by the mages in the door-like gaps in the Black Hall's foundations. They were only used to store long term supplies.

Nat Bero led them on through to another room and then paused. She glanced at a piece of parchment that Zara offered her. She held it to the light of the torch and the two of them conferred. Nat then began to search the back wall of the small, cluttered room. It wasn't long before the wily tracker discovered a small partially hidden niche and slipped her hand inside. There was an audible click and then Nat strained and pulled. A large section of the wall swung open with startling ease. Arkadi muttered something about counter balances to a startled looking Darin.

Zara Halven turned to everyone and laughed delightedly. "Let's go and find some treasure."

Everyone looked at everyone else for a moment, then, caught up in Zara's joy, they all smiled or laughed. Even Rebba was affected by the mood. The sensitive mage could sense Zara's excitement. Rebba knew her well enough to know this kind of adventure was intoxicating to her. The dark haired warrior was making the most of this reunion, as she did of most things in life. No one could deny that about Zara Halven.

Was that what the strange feelings were? Was she sensing the strong feelings of her friends, together again after so long?

Once, they had all been together at the court of the High Lord of Ostia, children of Lairds, merchants or court officials. Years later, as they came of age, a dozen of them had decided to stay together, to explore the world, to get out and experience life. For Darin, Marcus, Aros and Bear, younger sons of Lairds, this was easy. They had no pressing needs. For her Garon, Arkadi and Dunstan, this meant missing time from their magical studies and training. However, for Nat, Karis, Stefan and Zara, it had been more serious. This was their start in life. This was to be their opportunity to earn money and fortune. Their parents were staff at court, they had no family wealth to rely on.

For a couple of years the band of friends had moved around the Wildlands, in the first months earning coin by guarding merchant convoys and hunting goblin raiders. They had become a kind of mercenary band but had then moved more to fortune hunting; exploring and raiding Elder sites for treasures. They had used their unique combination of knowledge of the Elder, of the lands, and of magic. They had earned well and had started to earn a reputation for themselves. Yet it couldn't last. The Wildlands were dangerous and unpredictable.

Problems had inevitably developed; Bear had been terribly injured, he had nearly died and consequently became dour and bitter, Garon had fallen to drink and Marcus and Zara had become more and more reckless. Arkadi, Dunstan and herself had then decided to leave to continue their training at Shandrilos. There were the inevitable arguments over this; when Zara was involved there were always arguments. It got so bad that Aros and Stefan had decided to go off on their own and explore the world... away from Zara. Marcus had left without any warning; there one day, gone the next. He had never been the most stable of individuals. Darin too, headed off. He said he was just bored; not enough challenge and battle. He joined the Knights of Saint Karodra to train with their sword masters and fight.

Eventually, only Zara, Bear, Karis and Nat had been left. They had carried on for a couple more years. However, even the ever loyal Bear had finally fallen out with Zara and left to finish his training at the College in Shandrilos. Without his knowledge of the Elder and magic, the others could not go on. Karis and Nat had settled down, married and started a family. As for Zara, she became... notorious; a fighter, smuggler, courtesan, assassin, merchant... Rebba had heard them all. She was not sure what was truth and what was fiction.

Abruptly, Rebba stumbled and fell with a curse in the low light. She angrily thrust her thoughts aside and focused on where she was heading, but as she descended into the ancient Elder city, the inexplicable feelings continued to gnaw at her.

Chapter 8

THE COST OF FAILURE

The relative power of a magic user is determined by three factors; experience, talent and mastery (though the actual intelligence of the magic user is the fourth, unspoken factor). Experience is the amount of time the magic user has using magic, constructing spell forms, researching, and using magic. Experience notably leads to increased speed of casting and a greater array of castings known. Talent is the inborn, strength of the magic user and this factor is set at birth and is an affinity for magic. It is this that affects the strength of the magic and the stamina of the magic user. Mastery is the factor that is least understood as this would seem to be linked to experience, but it is actually more about perception and manipulation; it is about the basic abilities in magic. Advancement in this area takes both experience and talent.

From 'The Art of Spell Craft' by Grandmaster Bruenor Brae of Shandrilos, BY1312

The mage was livid. 'How could the fool have lost it? He had it, the key. It had been in his belt pouch and he lost it!'

As the mage stared hard at Koros, his anger grew. With an almost incoherent scream, he reacted with instinctive fury. A combat spell flew from his lips and slammed into Koros, lifting him and hurling him between his two startled henchmen through the air to slam with a bone crunching thump into the stone wall some ten feet behind. The mage pushed on with his telekinetic attack and caught Koros as his sagging weight bounced off the wall and began to fall. With a gesture, the mage lifted his body and pinned it to the wall all limbs splayed in a star-like shape. The mage walked forwards between the two hulking henchmen, paying them no heed as they stood frozen in terror and surprise by the unseen force that thrummed in the room. Their eyes followed the mage as he passed, but neither would look directly at his face. As the dark robed figure moved behind them, they looked at one another and twitched in the first move to make a silent break for the door to their left.

The mage's cold hissed voice stopped them in their tracks. "Don't move gentlemen. You would find it hard to live out your lives if I am forced to remove your feet!"

Both froze. Neither knew whether this was just an empty threat, but both knew the power of the mage and didn't want to risk it.

"Turn around gentlemen and give me your full attention." the mage's grave cold voice continued, "You will only leave when I give you permission... if I give you permission!"

The tone was devoid of feeling and yet both of the men could feel the anger emanating from the shadowy cloaked figure. The two turned on the spot, almost rigid with fear and looked to where their leader was transfixed to the wall by some unseen hand. This had not been the best day of their lives.

It had begun well enough with the search of the labyrinthine tunnels beneath the town finally yielding its hidden treasure, though it had seemed disappointingly ordinary, little more than a dull grey rock with markings intricately carved upon it. The rock had been clasped in the skeletal hand of some long dead warrior in black armour. He had been hidden away in some kind of secret room and they had to pry open some doors with their weapons. Many had broken and blunted. Still, they were getting well paid for it.

 However, from then on things had gone from bad to very much worse. Giant insect creatures had appeared from nowhere and sliced two of their companions to pieces before the others could drive them off; then had begun the nightmare dash through the dark tunnels! More of the insect creatures had burst upon them as they ran this way and that seeking escape. Two more of their fellows had fallen, hamstrung from behind and then torn apart in a mad frenzy of limbs by the hideous creatures. For a while they had thought they had escaped and had begun to relax. They had been ambushed yet again. It had been a scene from a nightmare. There seemed to be brutal giants, shadowy creatures, black faced goblins and more of those insects everywhere. They had panicked, yet had still fought hard in sheer terror and desperation, but they were outnumbered. It was Koros who smashed his way through and found a way out. They had followed, the screams of their comrades echoing down the corridor behind them, followed by the skittering sound of chitinous insect feet in pursuit. None of them thought to turn and help the others; it was every man for himself. It was the cloaks that the mage gave them that finally saved them, hid them, allowed them to slip by the next ambush and flee up to the surface, through the inn's cellar.

    Once on the streets they had relaxed and the terror had begun to ebb. They were all shaking from the deaths, but Koros had laughed and said that since there were only three of them that meant more money each! Feeling better they hurried to meet the mage in the old house by the college's high wall. Things had seemed like they were all going to end well for them. They'd have more money than they could have earned in twenty years of guarding merchants and their caravans and they could get as far from Shandrilos and its magic as possible. All that had ended the moment Koros had reached to give the mage the key; the stone tucked away nice and safe in his belt pouch.

    The shock had registered first on their leader's face. The look was the same look a man would have on his face if he had been stabbed in the gut. His hands had frantically searched his clothes, he had looked down and then up in a frantic search. His eyes had found those of their dark cloaked employer to see curiosity had appeared on the shadowed face. Koros had slowly straightened like a man who had just accepted a sentence of hanging. He realised he did not have the stone, nor his pouch. The look on the dark mage's face turned from curiosity to a frown. Koros's consequent confession had hit the mage like a blow. He had reeled back and snarled.

Now the fear they had thought left in the tunnels with the nightmarish creatures was back, only this time it was inspired by the mage and their now helpless leader. This time they fervently hoped at least two of them would survive.

<hr />

The mage's fury was subsiding, being replaced by a cold, calculating need driven by a fear of its own. He could not afford failure, he needed that stone, but more importantly he could not allow others to know of his failure. His own savage master had eyes and ears where you least expected it.

The mage approached his unconscious prey. Koros had been knocked out when he was hammered into the wall and now sagged into his bonds. The mage studied the thief he had hired. He was a powerfully built man, though still lean. He was a highly skilled thief and warrior and so a valued servant, but the mage was uncertain whether to kill him as a sign of displeasure to the others and to prevent any possibility of his actions getting back to his master, or to merely impress upon Koros the cost of his failure. He raised a hand to his chin and tapped it thoughtfully.

First he needed to know all that had transpired below. He made his decision and wove a glamour that would allow him to read the recent events from Koros' mind even as he spoke of them It would wake Koros from his stupor while ensuring that he spoke nothing but the truth to his master. He, and his hidden ally, would see into Koros' mind as he spoke. This was a difficult spell, one that would require a great deal of strain to link minds. Weaving his hands through the intricate postulation that encouraged his mental summoning of energies, he cast the glamour and the unconscious thief snapped awake. He looked around dazedly, not sure what to make of where he was. The mage gave him a few moments to recall what had happened and where he was and then spoke.

"Tell me all that has happened since you last left me," he commanded and the mercenary spoke.

It was an almost incoherent babble to those listening yet the mage understood clearly. He was witnessing events through the mercenary chief's eyes. Eventually, the babble ceased and the mage stood thoughtfully trying to make sense of all that he had seen, his eyes distant. Abruptly, he focused on the man before him.

"You have disappointed me, Koros. I thought you a skilled thief and a man to be trusted to succeed. Obviously I was in error."

"Master," he called painfully.

It was unusual for the man to use such a title, normally the proud mercenary referred to his employer as 'mage' or at best 'my lord'.

"I will retrieve the stone." he finished desperately.

"Are you telling me you know where it is?" the mage asked, though he suspected an attempt by Koros to escape the fate that awaited him for he had seen nothing in Koros' mind that would indicate where he had lost the key. It was clear that he had retrieved the key, but it must have been lost in the mad escape through the catacombs.

Koros was nodding even as the mage asked. The mage was unsure.

"I think you are trying to deceive me, to escape my anger, thief." the mage hissed, seeking the tiniest sign of guilt. There was none.

"I know where I must have lost it." Koros answered without hesitation, "It was that damned bitch that got in my way at the inn."

The mage frowned slightly, he remembered the woman from Koros' memories but he had not noticed anything being taken. However, he was seeing as Koros had, and the mercenary had noticed nothing. The woman had been with a group of friends. Koros had got a quick glance at them as he had passed them leaving the cellar of the inn.

Koros forged on quickly. "She looked familiar and now I know where I have seen her before. It was Zara Halven. She pretends to be some kind of lady in Ostia, dresses all in finery, but she's also a ruthless little bitch, a mercenary and thief. We've even used her ourselves for getting rid of people. She's good; a master with shortswords and daggers. She would have had no problems lifting my pouch when we fell," the mercenary finished angrily.

"The one they call the Whore of Ostia?" the mage asked warily. The woman had appeared ornately clothed, but she had moved with startling speed.

The scarred features of the mercenary leader twisted in fury as he nodded. He was thinking of what he wanted to do to the woman. Koros was a vicious man.

The mage paused. He could use the mercenary to retrieve the key. Koros was obviously well motivated to get even with the thieving woman and he had proved a resourceful man in the past. Also, if the mage were to kill Koros, he would lose his best connection with the underbelly of the Wildlands. It would take time to find another trusted link, not that there were not others, but Koros was well regarded and could draw upon a wealth of connections to draw men and resources to the mage's call. However, he could not afford to let Koros think he was too important or that the mage needed him. He needed to demonstrate to the burly mercenary the consequences that failure would bring to him should he fail to retrieve the key again.

The mage studied the mercenary held before him for a moment and then he moved in close to the helpless man's face, his dark eyes locked on Koros's blue, and his face twisted with malice. "You have failed me once Koros, you will not fail me again, will you?"

The warrior shook his head, a quick certain movement.

"Failure cannot go unpunished." the mage snapped and began a savage incantation. He saw the fear in Koros's eyes grow. All who had no use of magic feared it, feared the unseen power that could be unleashed.

"Master..." Koros began pleading.

Suddenly, the mage spun and flung out his hands, fingers splayed and slashes of terrible light like an incandescent web swept out from his fingers at the two startled henchmen. They had remained still and rigid in place, hoping to avoid the mage's notice. They had only a fraction of a second to twitch before the lethal web hit them. At first it seemed nothing had happened. Koros' eyes were transfixed on his hapless men and the mage knew that Koros was wondering whether the mage's spell had failed. The look of surprise on his men's face never changed. The mage smiled as the lines that criss-crossed the henchmen's armour and flesh where the magical web touched them turned red. Blood began to flow and then suddenly the men's bodies just slid apart along the lines with a sickening, sucking noise and spurts of blood. As slabs of meat and metal the two men's bodies slapped to the stony floor. Blood rapidly pooling around the meat as it pumped free of the bodies. What had been two living, breathing men moments before now resembled a slaughter house floor. Where the web of light had struck, the two men had been sliced through keener than any knife. Through his link, the mage felt Koros' stomach heave as the warrior vomited the little he had in his stomach down his front.

The mage turned a cold stare on Koros and smiled at the mercenary without humour. "This is the consequence of failure," he whispered. "If you fail me again you will wish for such a speedy death."

With a slight gesture, the mage freed Koros who fell heavily to land on his hands and knees, still retching. The mage waited. Koros got control of himself and looked up to meet the mage's dark scrutiny.

"I expect you to find this Halven woman quickly and retrieve the key. Do whatever is needed. I shall add an extra tenth to your payment for the added trouble and I will also expect you to contact Sardyk Andar and send him to meet me here tonight at midnight. I have need of his services."

Koros nodded weakly.

"I have faith in your skills and I expect you not to be bested by some whoring smuggler again." The mage saw the flash of anger in Koros's eyes and smiled. "Now, go. I will expect to hear from you, in the usual way, by tomorrow night.

Koros again nodded. He wearily stood and limped across to retrieve his helm. He pointedly walked around the mess staining the floor, avoiding looking at it. He snatched his helm and hurried to the door which he almost ripped open before disappearing into the gloom beyond. The mage smiled. Koros now had a double incentive to find the woman, but it wasn't prudent to put all your eggs in one basket, as his dear mother had always said. He turned and called lightly.

The side door to the room opened and in walked a man robed in a grubby grey robe. The figure was powerfully built, and although he looked short he was in fact almost the height of the mage. It was the fact that he was almost as broad as two men that made him look short. The figure raised callused and savagely thick hands to throw back his deep hood. The face that was revealed was flat, hard and cruel. A scraggly, balding scalp and thick jaws dominated the head. The eyes were small and sheltered beneath a thick brow in shadow where they could not be read.

"You saw it all?" The mage questioned.

A grunted acknowledgment followed.

"You will recognise this woman and her friends?"

Again, the grunted agreement.

"Follow Koros. Make sure he does as I ask. If not kill him!" the mage commanded.

The thick limbed man smiled then and the smile did not lessen his fearsome features. His teeth were blackened, where he had any, the lips were cracked and thin, and the face twisted when he smiled. However, the voice that emanated from the apelike form always surprised those who met him.

A cultured, soft, clear Olmec voice replied, "With pleasure, my lord. Am I free to make it as prolonged as possible?"

The mage looked at his servant hard. When he said it would be a pleasure, the mage was sure he meant just that. Ivello enjoyed killing. He didn't enjoy death more the act of taking life and he had become something of an expert at it. Ivello was also completely loyal. Once he had been a monk of the Karodracian order, but his vices had led him astray. He had been discovered with the dismembered body of a young girl. The small monastery was shocked! Soon further discoveries were made and Ivello was put on trial. The result was a foregone conclusion. Ivello was unrepentant. He was accused of being in league with the dark powers and was sentenced to burn at the stake. The mage had by chance been passing through and had seen an opportunity. He arranged for Ivello to escape his captors and the twisted monk had pledged himself to the mage.

Over the years, Ivello had proven himself a fine servant. His priestly gifts and clerical magic were easily perverted and made to serve their cause, also his immense strength and joy in slaughter were put to good use, along with his surprising intellect and knowledge; a hidden blessing. Ivello's apish appearance hid the fact that he was in fact a scholar. His only failing intellectually was a lack of imagination and a devout belief in his given word as his bond. Thus the mage had no fear over Ivello's loyalty. He was irrevocably bound to the mage.

All this passed through the mage's mind as he stared at his bestial looking servant. "So long as you are careful to conceal all evidence, my friend, and do not kill him unless it is absolutely necessary. Koros may still prove useful."

Ivello nodded his heavy head.

"Oh, and this lot needs clearing away." said the mage, pointing at the mess of human remains amidst its blood red pool. "I have not the time to do so, I must meet with the Conclave. See to it." the mage ordered.

Sharply, the mage turned on his heel and left.

The hulking grey robed monk smiled as he looked at the pile of meat, bone and armour that lay on the stone tiled floor. He was hungry and there was nothing in the house. The mage had not said how he wanted the bodies disposed!

The mage hurried back to his chambers, his hood drawn up and his mood dark. His mind whirled as his feet took him forward. He was seeing again what he had plucked from the mercenary thief's head, but refrained from commenting on to the warrior. Koros had seen strange creatures; giant insects, black faced goblins, giant brutish creatures and, standing out above all the others for the mage – creatures like his master! There was no doubt that the forces in the deep tunnels were his.

The mage was fascinated with the creatures his master had sent to retrieve the key. It gave him a chill to think that the infernal creature had access to such fearsome servants. Shaking his head he turned his attention to the immediate problem ahead; the Conclave of Magi.

It took considerable skill on the mage's part to manipulate the Conclave. They were the leaders of the schools of magic and had all reached that position through skill and ambition.

The mage entered his apartments and hurriedly changed into his robes of office, all the time thinking. His master would be getting more desperate soon. Once his infernal lord realised his creatures had failed to gain the key, he would quickly bring his scrutiny to bear fully on Shandrilos and so it was inevitable his scrutiny would turn the mage's way. What the mage would have to do was to plant his master's suspicion elsewhere, perhaps onto a member of the Conclave, or one of the High Lords. The mage smiled to himself then suddenly frowned. The difficulty would be in convincing his master. The prospect of that made the mage decidedly uneasy.

The mage abruptly realised he had been stood still, so hard had he been thinking. He would never make it to the Conclave on time at this rate.

The mage stopped before the door to his chambers and made a conscious effort to calm himself. He realised the loss of the key and the demands of his master had thrown his usual calm equilibrium. It was getting to the point where he was finding it hard to maintain both his own schemes and those of his master. Yet he needed to continue both, at least until he had the key and the chance to exploit it. He was not ready yet to face his master, but with time… Perhaps that was what had thrown him off balance, the fact that he was so close to true power and had built himself up. He needed to keep his feet on the ground and be calm. Only when he was calm could he juggle all the balls he had thrown into the air.

Taking a deep breath he pushed open his door and hurried to the upper chambers and the small hall where the Conclave of Magi would be gathering.

Chapter 9

THE CONCLAVE OF MAGI

The Empire is dominated by the Olmec peoples. Only the provinces on the extreme west, south and east have populations dominated by other ethnic groups. The eastern provinces have sizeable populations of Hanite descent, while in the far south and west, the desert races of the Tanzabari, Kishians and Dashani dominate. In the northwest, it is the Nordic who have sizeable populations in the Kilimarian provinces.

From 'The Holy Lands of Alba' by Arch Prelate Jorus Enarius Florian, BY1180

The Archmage sat and waited and brooded. He didn't know how this meeting would go, but he needed the support of his fellows before he could go to the Grand Council of the Wilds.

The Archmage had been the first into the hall and he now watched as each head of the schools of magic arrived. There were eight magi for the eight schools of magic and four now moved to sit to either side of the Archmage. They were organised in a rough circle that followed the table. They would take their places in the heavy chairs carved with the symbols of their school. There was a gap at the far end of the table that allowed access to the central area inside the circle of the table.

The Archmage studied each of his fellow magi in turn not sure how to begin and seeking to steady his understanding of the men and women who headed the schools – some he had known for years, others he had taught, still others were less well known to him save from this Conclave.

Farthest left from the Archmage sat Chief Druid Marillia Aronis, head of the school of the druids. She was pale skinned and tall, taller than most men. Her tawny hair cascaded down to her waist in wild abandon. She was stern looking, solidly handsome and seeming in her middle years though she was easily past sixty; sensible use of magic slowed the ageing process. She wore the green robes of the druids with the oak leaf symbol of her office as her clasp. This symbol was mirrored atop her gnarled and twisted oak staff. The path of the druid was one dedicated to serving all living creatures and aiding nature in all its guises. The druids worshipped the old Nordic gods and spirits of the world and had agreed to join the College of Magic on the condition that their beliefs were respected, and knowledge of their gods be taught to the apprentices regardless of the school they intended to join when they became adepts. The Archmage knew that Marillia would be sure to give him wholehearted support against any danger to her beloved Wildlands. Protection of the land and its people was an integral part of the role of the druid.

Next to her sat the Sorceror Supreme, Xameran Uth Altar, head of the school of sorcery, a school of magic dedicated to understanding the nature of time, and of the world and the planes beyond it. He was still young to be the head of a school, only in his late forties. Yet he had reached the position through skill and intellect and was widely regarded as one of the most brilliant magic-users at the college. He had a perpetually happy look, like a man who was enjoying himself immensely. Sorcerors were usually mistrusted, but Xameran was well liked. The Sorceror lord turned and whispered something merrily to his companion on his right who frowned disapprovingly at him.

This was the High Enchanter, Atholl Dorard, dour head of the school of magic responsible for creating permanent magics in items, potions and the like. Enchanters were a very secretive lot and the smallest school in terms of numbers while being the most popular with the common people.

Everyone wanted an enchanted sword, magical wand or a potion though enchanters generally hated this popular view of their craft. Atholl Dorard was dressed in his crumpled enchanter's red robes and clutched his red gemstone-topped metal staff. He was famous for his miserable nature and harsh punishments of the apprentices. No one could recall when last he had smiled - and he had been around a long time! He had been a founding member of the College and it was believed he was past a hundred years old. He was bald as an egg and pale to the point of looking ghostlike. His age showed in his deeply lined face and rheumy eyes. He had a beard which was unkempt and seemed to grow in clumps on his face rather than all over. The hair was still dark, though shot through deeply with grey.

Atholl Dorard made a strange contrast to the smiling Xameran, and the Archmage had no idea how either man would react to the revelations he had. He suspected they would vacillate; neither was overly fond of visions and portents and treated both with suspicion.

On the other side of the High Enchanter sat the rather demure and petite figured, Eliantha Shamass, the Mage-Master. She was the rather unlikely head of the school of Mages, the school of magic dedicated to knowledge of all areas of magic; his own school. Apprentices who did not want to specialise in one field or another joined this school of general spell craft. Eliantha was an unusual member of the Conclave; she was timid and quiet and sat looking down at the table in front of her, her coppery skinned, heart shaped face, framed by neck length wavy, dark hair. She was small built, bird boned and had the face of a young girl lost amongst her seniors, though she was, in fact, in her sixties. This timid persona was how she was generally perceived, yet it was well known to the Archmage that she was one of the most knowledgeable people on the nature of magic in the entire school and was fierce in pursuit of that knowledge. She held very strong beliefs about how magic should be used for the people. The Archmage knew he could rely on her support, they had known one another almost their whole lives and she was his closest ally.

The Archmage turned his attention to the people on the opposite side of him, to the giant Magus-General. Here was one who would say little; he much preferred action over discussion. This monster of a man was hugely built, broad shouldered yet slim of waist. When standing he towered over most, only a few inches less than seven feet. What also stood out about this man was that he was not Nordic, nor even Olmec, though his stature tended to rule the latter out. He was of Tanzabari stock and hailed from that far distant land beyond the deserts of the Juub Ali. He had the dark skin and hair of Tanzabar, with green eyes that stood out like shards of jade. He wore the coppery brown robes and armour of his school with the flame symbol atop his ritual blade. Few knew why Jammu Quadai Pendi had come to this land. It was a secret he kept secure behind his buttress-like forehead. When asked, his huge arms would fold across his equally huge chest and he would stare angrily until the offending individual either moved on or apologised. The Archmage knew little more than any other about the formidable giant, he had arrived at the College only a decade ago, already an accomplished warrior and mage and had proceeded to rise through the ranks of the Fighter-Magi at an astonishing rate. One thing the Archmage did know about him was that he would welcome the chance to test his fighters. They were few in number compared to guardsmen, but Jammu had great pride in their skills and saw them as the future protectors of the province.

The last three members of the Conclave sat with their heads together discussing something urgently. The Archmage was fairly sure these too would support him.

The three were the large and rounded Allseer, Arimenes Corvindar, an Olmec man who had fled the Alban lands some twenty years ago. He was head of the seer's guild another small school and the newest in the College's brief history. He had been one of the first to see the portents in the north. He was whispering as he leaned across, the skeletal-thin, grey haired Zarina Agroda, First Wizard. He was speaking to Abbess Izonda, head of the monastic school of magic. The school set up by the Sironacian monks to teach the worship of the One God and the spiritual magic of the Alban clerics.

Even from across the table, the Archmage could catch some of what was being said, Allseer Corvindar was insisting that there was real danger and that a party should be sent below to see what was going on. The Archmage understood what they were discussing. The Abbess vaguely replied that she could not feel any evil directed at the college and certainly nothing immediate.

The Allseer was practically turning purple with the intensity of what he was saying, an interesting combination with his golden robes, the Archmage thought. It was at that point that the First Wizard said she had felt disturbances deep below, but it was difficult to pinpoint and, just as Corvindar was about to pounce on this, the stately old First Wizard snapped that the discussion could wait. She had glanced at the Archmage and seen his eyes on them. She then turned a fierce glare at Corvindar who had been about to continue. Instead he sat back into his chair.

"Thank you for agreeing to this hurried meeting, my friends." the Archmage began, "I thought it best to call you here to discuss things before the council tonight." He paused and met the eyes of all as they turned to look his way. "I have spoken to you before, both in this meeting and individually, about my concerns for the future of our lands however, recent events have given more urgency to my concerns and changed intangible omens into a real threat." Again he looked around at his fellow magi and noted their frowns and puzzlement. "It is my belief that..." he hesitated over his words. Now when it came to naming his fears, his tongue found it hard to form the words. All eyes looked at him. "It is my belief," he repeated, forcing the words out, "that someone, some force is seeking to unify the goblins in the north and not just a few tribes, but a whole nation!"

The Archmage watched keenly the response to his words even as he sat back into his tall chair. It was immediate and ranged from sudden understanding on the faces of the Allseer and the Abbess, to outright disbelief on the face of the gruff old High Enchanter. They all looked from one to another.

"Of course!" the Allseer exclaimed, "That explains many of the visions of my seers." He stood and looked around anxiously at the others. "My most gifted seers, soothsayers and dreamspeakers have been seeing a dark cloud over the northlands for these last few years. The seers have seen faceless multitudes marching in savage glory. They have seen wild, blood-faced creatures and huge beasts attacking and killing!"

"Bah! These are just dreams and visions, they are not proof. They are the fears of the mad and the timid. A goblin nation? The goblins are vicious animals, they could never hold together long. They are a nuisance not a threat!" snorted the bluff faced High Enchanter. Turning away from the others, he muttered, "Why are we even wasting our time with such talk?"

Arimenes Corvindar's jaw hung down. He was speechless at the complete disregard of his school's magical discipline, but then the High

Enchanter was a man of the old school of magic. He had seen the College grow from nothing and had always opposed the creation of a school of magic dedicated to what he saw as unreliable and of little practical use.

Marillia Aronis snapped in support of the stunned Allseer. "Shame on you Atholl. You know as well as the rest of us that such visions hold true portents of the future."

The diminutive and ragged looking enchanter shrugged his shoulders and refused to look at the tall, stern figure of the Chief Druid.

Instead it was Xameran, the lord of sorcery who replied. "I think what my learned friend is trying to say, and doing it in his less than diplomatic way, is that such visions and dreams are unreliable. They give no clear indication of time or of the nature of the danger. These visions may relate to some danger a year from now or a century from now, they may relate to a threat of war or merely represent some forces as a kind of visual metaphor for some other event. We cannot plan our future policies on such visions."

The Allseer had slumped back into his chair as the sorcerer lord spoke. However, the formidable head of the druids was not so easily cowed. "Your argument is known and appreciated, Xameran, and were it the only portent then I would be tempted to agree, not..." she hastily added for the Allseer's benefit, "that I think these visions are not clear in their meaning. When so many see such images it is clear the danger is near and important." She paused and looked around the table, "However, my own druids have seen portents of such dangers in the lands. The Gods of earth and sky are warning us..."

She was interrupted by the Abbess Izonda, "The monks of my order too have also seen grave portents of dangers to come."

Marillia nodded to the stately head of the monks of Alba here in Shandrilos, showing great restraint at the interruption by the Abbess. The two had conflicting theologies, but had managed to keep that out of their councils.

Marillia continued. "If it is something more tangible you need, Lord Enchanter, I will also say that the druids of my order who live in the wild forests and hills north of here, have reported seeing large groups of goblins heading northwards."

"So what!" The High Enchanter almost yelled, cutting the druid off. "You worry when our enemies flee our lands?" he asked almost incredulously. "Foolishness!" he cried, throwing up his small callused hands.

"Foolishness!" The Chief Druid snapped in response. "You are the only fool I see here, Atholl. You are so set in your ways you cannot tell the difference between enemies fleeing in terror and those hurrying to unite!"

Both the High Enchanter and the Chief Druid seemed about to continue when the Archmage stood and slapped his hand on the table. "Enough!" he barked. "We are here to discuss not argue."

Yes indeed, my lord Archmage," Xameran Uth Altor, said into the silence that followed the Archmage's reprimand, "and there are things to discuss, like the breach of security in our college and the dangers from beneath our feet." he exclaimed.

The Archmage looked at him in consternation. That was not what he had wanted to discuss, but before he could switch the subject back, the already agitated High Enchanter leapt onto the comment.

"Yes, that is far more important. A dozen camouflaging cloaks were stolen from my school. We had toiled and crafted at them for months, and they were taken." He snapped his fingers. "Something must be done. Those cloaks were worth much and they must have been stolen by someone with at least a master's level of ability in the art, no one of lesser ability could have penetrated our defences!"

He was almost shouting by this point and it was clear to the Archmage that he would need to deal with this.

"Thieves within our own ranks!" Atholl Dorard hissed to the Conclave and all looked shocked.

"Perhaps our Magus General should investigate this, as well as the disturbances we have all felt from the catacombs below?" put in Xameran, adding another issue to the debate.

All looked towards the mountainous man beside the Archmage who had said nothing throughout the proceedings. He just stared back at them, his green eyes and dark features giving nothing away. He then turned and looked at the Archmage who, standing up, was little taller than the Magus General sat down. The Archmage was glad of the big man's deferment to him in this. The debate was moving in the wrong direction and he needed to get it back on course.

"The Magus General and his Fighter Magi will be needed for more important tasks in the time ahead. I feel others could resolve the very serious issue of theft within the college and also look into the brief disturbances in the old Elder tunnels." He took a breath and looked around at his fellows.

The thievery was disturbing them as were the troubles underground. Throughout the entire life of the college there had been regular intruders into the catacombs hunting treasure or the like but it would not do for the College to sit by and do nothing; the tunnels were part of their domain and people needed to know that if only for their own protection. The problem was an investigation should be performed by the Archmage and his staff, yet he had other, much more pressing and important tasks to complete. He needed to push this back on to one of them. That left him with a dilemma. Who to head the investigation?

All this passed through his mind as his eyes scanned his fellow magi. Chief Druid Marillia and Abbess Izonda would not be able to carry out a full investigation. Although both heads had shown clear understanding and toleration of the other's religion and beliefs, at the lower levels many monks and druids still were vehemently opposed to one another. In other lands each had been deadly enemies and part of that opposition still existed in the Wildlands of Darylor. No, if he chose either, the other school would resent and even oppose such a choice. Neither could he choose the Magus-General or the High Enchanter, both would be crucial for what was to come; one to help fight and the other to provide the weapons and armour. The Allseer would be a poor choice, his authority was the least of those assembled while Eliantha Shamass, the head of the magi would be a fine choice but for the fact that she was already heavily burdened with running the teaching in the college and with its general administration. Neither could be neglected or the whole college would cease to function! That left just Zarina Agroda, the First Wizard and Xameran Uth Altor, the Sorceror Supreme.

In the moments that the Archmage had been thinking, Atholl Dorard had become increasingly impatient. The Archmage could see his features darkening in anger. The Archmage made his decision. "Xameran, would you look into the theft and the disturbances in the catacombs?" He asked looking at the head of the school of sorcery.

The head of sorcery looked puzzled. "Should this not be carried out by your staff?"

"My staff are stretched at the moment with the Council," he said firmly.

"It may be difficult to pursue this thoroughly without the authority of the Archmage." Xameran replied carefully.

"I will see that it is known you have my full backing." The Archmage insisted, impatient to proceed.

"Then, so long as there are no objections I would be glad to look into these matters and hopefully get to the bottom of them speedily." The sorcerer responded.

"Good," the Archmage began as he retook his seat and clasped his hands together in front of him firmly. "We have discussed the portents and omens of a possible danger ahead and some of you have expressed your doubts, but I have recently received some information that makes these possible dangers more real whether you believe in a threat from the goblins or not." The Archmage noticed frowns on many of the faces of the assembled magi. "For many years it has been no secret that I have sought to unite this land into a strong whole, into a new nation. Many of you have shown your support for this ideal," he noticed heads nodding, "while others of you have pointed out the difficulties and problems." He looked at the High Enchanter who sat with his stocky arms crossed and his rough features set like stone. "In doing so, I have also sought to always be vigilant for conflicts or issues that could threaten this land and its recent stability." He now had the attention of all within the room, though the High Enchanter sought to hide it and the stoic Magus General's dark face gave little away. "I have, as some of you have suspected, built up a large network of 'friends' who agree with my ideals in all corners of these lands. Thus, it has come to my attention that the goblin tribes of the northlands *are* uniting."

The Archmage saw Xameran about to speak and held up his hand to forestall him. "Please let me finish, my lord of sorcery." he insisted. "I have been observing, in particular, the goblin tribes of the Bloodland Heights and the Mist Moors just beyond the northern borders of what is considered to be our Wildlands. Under a strong young chieftain they have been uniting. I am sure you are all somewhat familiar with the hierarchy within goblin society." The Archmage asked not really wanting a reply though he did hear Marillia, the Chief Druid mutter something along the lines of 'what society!'

"Most tribes both in and around the Wildlands that we know of are commanded by a 'Gul' or chieftain, and the tribal numbers can vary from five hundred to five thousand with up to a third of those being warriors. Larger tribes could, and have, proved highly dangerous to the people of the Wildlands, but for the most part internal divisions have always led to the tribe being split from within amongst the 'Hobs' or lesser chiefs." The Archmage looked around his colleagues like a teacher to his students.

Unexpectedly, the deep, sombre voice of the Magus General interrupted, "Also, these dangers have always been successfully dealt with," he said firmly, the Tanzabari inflections clear in his use of the common tongue, "because even the larger tribes, when united, have little grasp of strategy, less discipline and are poorly armed. The soldiers of our provinces have always been able to confidently face two or three times their own number or more, and so the goblins pose no real threat to the Wildlands as a whole, my lord Archmage." he finished, a question clear in his tone.

The Archmage could see others silently agreeing with the giant fighter magus.

"You are quite right, my friend, on what we know of the goblins so far, but over the past ten years one 'Gul' in particular, a young and dynamic warlord by the name of Marog has successfully managed to unite almost all of the tribes of the Bloodland Heights." The Archmage paused to let this sink in.

The Bloodland heights were a huge area of land almost a third the size of the whole Wildlands and partly occupied by the Ironcleaver dwarves, the largest of the hill dwarf clans. It contained a dozen or more large goblin tribes and had, with their sporadic raids and alliances with the goblin tribes within the Wildlands, always been the bane of peace within the provinces.

"This Marog has named himself 'Guldor', High Chieftain of the Bloodland nation, as he styles it, and by my estimation now rules over forty thousand goblins and could field some ten to fifteen thousand warriors!"

There was an immediate reaction amongst the conclave, eyes widened and involuntary gasps escaped lips. That was more than double the number who had invaded a generation ago.

Before anyone could say anything, the Archmage pushed home his point.

"What's more this Guldor Marog is acting as something of a magnet to goblins all throughout the Darkheart Hills and the Mist Moors. As Marillia," he nodded in the direction of the Chief Druid, "has pointed out, goblins flock to join him. It is also just a matter of time before other tribes declare for him and make no mistake about this creature; he is no ordinary goblin, he has shown clear military talent in defeating his rivals in pitched battles and has begun to actually train a core of his warriors and arm them

91

with the best weapons and armour he can gather. He seems almost blessed with good luck..."

Voices called out, but the head of the sorcerors got in first and loudest. "How do you know this, my lord? Where did your information come from?" Xameran asked, "Surely we would have gained some inkling of goblins uniting on such a scale from those who have ventured north in the last few years?" There were calls of agreement from the High Enchanter, Magus General and First Wizard.

"My sources are many." the Archmage responded firmly, thinking of men like Gael Pemarson, "and some are... secret." He added, thinking of the source he could not mention. "I have been awaiting further information though it has not yet come. Nevertheless, you have heard from Marillia, and there have been clues that have filtered through from adventurers and from Grand Abbot Alinus of Sironac in the north. Individually they are little but taken together all the clues are there," the Archmage insisted and then leaned forward and met the conclaves stares one by one. "However, this Guldor Marog has been doubly clever." He warned. "He knows that the lords of the Wildlands would be a threat to his designs and see any unification of the goblins as a danger. With this thought foremost, this Guldor has made sure that adventurers to the north learn nothing of these events and has tried to make sure that those who venture into the north, his neighbours in Sironac, and even the dwarves, see as little conflict as possible. Now, this goblin subterfuge, I believe, is a clear sign that this Marog means to eventually aim his warriors at us!"

Most of the conclave were clearly shocked by their leader's revelations, though not the irascible, old head of the enchanters who snapped, "These are goblins we are talking about, they have no more brains than a dog and you expect me to believe that they are raising a nation, hiding their schemes! Nonsense," he laughed, "you have been duped, my lord Archmage. You are building a house of cards based on hearsay and exaggeration. I suggest you check your source isn't some drunken treasure hunter inventing tales for a willing audience." The enchanter ignored the obvious indignation building in the Archmage's face. "These dreams and visions have warped your perceptions, boy." he snapped derisively.

The rest of the conclave was taken aback at the attack on their leader, as was the Archmage himself.

"Do you think old man," he retorted, "that I would be fool enough to trust one source and a poor one at that." He took a deep calming breath, but his dark eyes burned, "I have verified this information from more than a score of independent sources over the past year. I only await final confirmation from a master who has ventured to the territory himself. You may be the most senior member of this conclave and a founder too, but you will not insult my intelligence. Such foolish remarks make it seem to me that perhaps it is time for you to retire and let someone more open to new ideas and less likely to spout ill-thought accusations, take your place!" the Archmage thundered, glaring at the balding, rough faced enchanter who was giving an equally furious glare in return.

"Now, now my lords," the ever courteous Xameran interjected, his hands raised in a gesture of peace, "there is no need for such disagreements. We are all sure that the Archmage would not have brought such a serious matter to our attention without first having verified it as thoroughly as he can. We should be thinking about what to do about such tidings." The sorcerer looked around at all the assembled magi and added in a calm voice. "Since this is such a serious threat I propose that we send a party representative of all our schools to look into this matter. What say you all?"

Before anyone could reply, the Archmage almost snarled, "There is not time for such. I can assure you that what I am telling you is the truth. What we must agree is to take this to the Grand Council and discuss it there."

Xameran smiled at the Archmage gently and insisted, "The lords of the provinces will treat such news with the same skepticism as the Lord Enchanter, my lord. Surely we need to approach this serious matter carefully?"

"Would you have us wait until this threat is on our doorstep and beyond our abilities to stop, my lord of sorcery?" the Archmage asked savagely. "I agree that serious matters must be investigated fully, yet if we delay when the risk is so severe, we risk all. Surely, my friends," the Archmage said passionately, "it is better to begin preparations to face this threat now and have it turn out to be nothing than do nothing and have the problem turn out to be our doom?"

A number of heads nodded reluctantly at his argument though others still looked unconvinced.

"Yes, let us send a party to investigate, but let us also take this to the Grand Council now!"

The Archmage forced his point and called for a vote. Silently he counted the hands, two against and five for, with only one undecided.

"Thank you." he said with true feeling. "I shall see you all within the hour at the Grand Council."

He sat wearily, watching as the conclave came to their feet and slowly filed out. He had not expected it to be so difficult. He had felt sure that even the gruff old Atholl Dorard would be able to put aside his near perpetual bad humour to see the danger. Perhaps the loss of the cloaks had riled the High Enchanter up into such a temper that he could no longer reason clearly. He had seen it before. If Atholl Dorard wasn't such a talented enchanter he would probably have been replaced long ago.

Chapter 10

ASSASSIN

Here in the Wildlands of Darylor, the halflings are a rare sight, but not so much as they once were. Here, halflings are not viewed as animals as they are in the Empire. The wilds are full of strange creature so halflings are no oddity. In the Empire they are kept as house slaves and their non-human nature means they can never be anything else. In recent times, halflings who have managed to escape, head north where they know they can live free in the wilds. This has led to small communities of halflings growing up in isolated areas of Darylor.

Excerpt from 'A strange land; the Wildlands of Darylor' by Grand Abbot Alinus Quan Sirona, BY1320

The mage hurried back to his chambers. He worried over it. Was this all part of his master's plan, this goblin threat? He would never have thought so yet amongst the creatures sent by his master, that had attacked Koros and his men in the catacombs, were goblins. The mage would never have believed that goblins would be creatures of his master, but he knew so little of his nature and people, even with what he had gleaned. Admittedly, the goblins in the catacombs had been black skinned rather than grey like those he was familiar with, but then no one really knew what hid in the vast northlands beyond humanities reach. His master might well be connected to this goblin unification, black goblins might well be from some unknown tribes in the north.

Certainly, his master wanted the Wildlands split and divided and it followed then that this would allow a much easier conquest, but why conquer the Wildlands? His master had never given any indication that such was his desire. It made little sense. The Wildlands were not rich or even particularly good for farming or settling. Unless, his master's eyes were looking beyond the Wildlands to the rich southlands of the empire!

The mage shook his head as he walked. No, he thought, an army of hundreds of thousands would be needed for that; the Imperial Legions were the finest solders in the world and the Empire could field around a quarter of a million men, even with the rebellion of the Kilimarian provinces. No goblin army could ever threaten such a force.

The mage was confused. He wasn't sure where he was heading with this line of thought. Perhaps his master was not connected at all to this goblin threat; perhaps it was just a coincidence.

He found himself outside his chambers with no real recollection of how he had got there. He quickly unlocked the heavy door and pushed inside. He marched through his comfortable main chamber and into his large study. He was half way across to his desk before he realised he was not alone.

Spinning on his heel, he began a silent combat cantrip. The spell slipped almost soundlessly from his lips as he brought his staff of office up to defend from any physical attack. The cantrip was to paralyse any intruder. Indeed, with his skill it was powerful enough to have frozen half a dozen men in place. Even as he released it, the mage was calling up a second more potent spell. It fell from his lips unformed as he recognised the intruder fixed helplessly in place.

He frowned as he approached the small statue that was his captive. "How did you get in here?" he asked.

The diminutive man just looked up at him, unable even to blink. His eyes were starting to water.

With a muttered oath, the mage spoke the counter cantrip and the captive stumbled forwards, blinking heavily. He dexterously caught himself from falling.

The little man shrugged his shoulders, stretching his arms slowly before looking up at the robed mage.

"Well?" the mage spoke impatiently.

The man smiled inanely and said in a light tone, "You sent for me and I came, my lord."

"You were not to meet me here. You may have been seen." hissed the mage angrily as he spun and marched to his desk. His flowing robes of office swung out behind him.

Turning the heavy, high backed chair slightly, he carefully folded his thick robes and sat himself at his desk, placing his staff in the holder specially designed for it. He then turned his attention back to the small figure standing lightly across the room. He rested his elbows on the thick padded arms of the chair and steepled his fingers in front of his chest. The mage then beckoned.

With a light bound, the little man soundlessly crossed the distance to the mage and then squatted down before him like a child before its parent. The little man's slim arms dangled down before him. He looked totally relaxed in a position the mage would have quickly found painful.

"No one saw me, my lord. All these mages are so obsessed with their magical wardings that they make their ordinary wards and locks so easy to pick, a child could get in."

The mage doubted it was that simple, but it was true that the college relied on magical protection too much and neglected the mundane. "And how did you avoid the magical wards, might I ask?"

Again the small man smiled and his eyes seemed to dance with delight as he replied, "Ah, well, I used a combination of my native ingenuity, paranoia..." he paused dramatically, "and this!" he exclaimed bringing forth a seeker stone.

The mage was impressed. Even with the seeker stone, it would have only allowed him to sense the magical wards and traps; it would not have got him passed them. The man would have had to have climbed every wall and roof in the unlikeliest of places, slipped through windows and squeezed through light shafts. It was extraordinary.

However, the person before him was not ordinary, nor even human. He was a halfling, a diminutive race that, in most ways, resembled human children, save for their pointed ears and large effeminate eyes; very much like an elf's it was said, though there were few who had seen that secretive race. Also, though halflings were small, no bigger than the size of a human child of ten when full grown, they were slim limbed, and lithe and agile beyond most humans. It was believed by some that halflings were distantly related to the Elder and had a natural affinity for magic if not a natural talent for it. That might explain his ability to avoid the magical wards.

The mage made a mental note about testing halflings and their senses. However, there were very few halflings in this area of the Wildlands. They were fugitives or descendants of fugitives from the Empire where they were used as house slaves. Luckily, quite a few in the Wildlands were the same and so they fit in. The mage had no idea whether the halflings were native to some distant part of the Empire and had no real desire to know. What he did know was that the halfling before him was far more dangerous than his easy smile and child-like appearance suggested. He was no normal halfling.

His name was Sardyk Andar and he was one of the most talented and ruthless killers the mage had ever come across. To look at him, squatting easily, without a care in the world, you would not think he could kill without a thought. Yet he took child-like pleasure in killing, not the same dark joy and savage ecstasy that Ivello felt while killing, just a kind of pure joy in seeing what happened when people died! The halfling was insane. He gave no thought to the value of life, even his own. He was reckless and this often gave him an edge. He seemed to believe that life was just a game and he was going to enjoy it to the full. The mage had never seen the smile leave his face for more than a few seconds and that was usually when he was talking.

Along with Ivello the monk, Sardyk Andar was the mage's most valued servant.

As if reading his thoughts, the halfling said, "I bumped into the mouldy monk as he left the safe house. He said you had a job for me." The halfling tilted his head quizzically and let his long pony tail of brown hair sway behind him.

"I did not expect you so quickly." the mage responded and the halfling shrugged his thin shoulders unconcerned.

"I may have need of your unique services here in the college, though it will need subtle methods." the mage warned.

The halfling's pretty nut brown eyes lit up. "What, kill a mage? How wonderful!" he cried clapping his hands in glee.

appeared to move and swirl as if alive. Elgon was not sure if this was some magic ingrained into the wood or a trick of the bright light that shone through the clear crystal of the roof around the circular hall. He was sure he could sense nothing of magic in the table and yet... the table was an artifact of the Elder.

This would be the twelfth annual Grand Council of the Wilds. It had begun as a meeting between the council of the magi of Shandrilos and its nearest neighbouring provinces, Lauria and his own city of Ostia. It had been an idea of the Archmage to prevent border clashes and improve trade. It had been such a success for Lauria, Ostia and Shandrilos, that others had been drawn into the council. This would be the seventh council to which all nine of the major provinces of the Wildlands had come and yet there was still an air of edginess about the room, but then men who practised trade or war were sometimes ill at ease in this place. This was the heart of a building where the unseen powers were used, where powers beyond the ken of ordinary men were practised. This would always upset men whose lives were based upon the certainties of what they could see, buy or cut.

Elgon noted Sir Arleas Di Mardul, Grandmaster of the Knights of Karodra and ruler of Karodracia, take his seat flanked by monks of his order. He was a tall, thin man in his late forties, clean shaven and square jawed. His eyes seemed small and dark in his gaunt face and his frame seemed slight, but Elgon knew he was a deadly swordsmen and lancer. His slight frame hid a wiry strength and his dark eyes hid an almost zealous love of combat.

Elgon liked Sir Arleas, there was no guile in him only a straight forward honesty. He was sometimes overly blunt, but at least you knew where you stood. The only drawback for Elgon to a strong friendship with Sir Arleas was his religious attitude. He was not a zealot, but he was 'Alban' minded, influenced by the current beliefs of the mother church in the Empire, and often found it difficult to see a middle ground with non-believers. However, Sir Arleas and the Karodran knights were a strong force for good in the wilds, they had been formed to protect travellers and they continued to keep the roads of the southern Wildlands safe for all.

Sir Arleas caught Elgon's eye on him and smiled politely his way. Returning the smile briefly, Elgon turned his attention to the men taking their seats between himself and the ruler of Karodracia. They were dressed all in white robes and had the black rock of the tomb of Blessed Alba on their chests. One was a man who appeared to be in his eighties though Elgon knew he was much older, preserved by his faith in Alba and his strong magical talent. The man was tall and rake thin even in his thick woolen robes. His red skinned Olmec face was impressively wrinkled and his head was balding with wisps of long white hair trailing down the sides and back of his head. These merged seamlessly into his long white beard and moustache which fell down his chest almost to the plain hemp rope belt tied around his spare waist. His body reminded Elgon somewhat of a proud old stork, long limbed and awkward as he sat in the high-backed chair. Elgon knew this man's name; he was something of a legend in these lands.

He was Alinus Quan-Sirona, founder of the order of Sironacian monks and of the isolated province of Sironac. Elgon, like most in the Wildlands, knew something of his history, but not all. It was said that he was now well over a hundred years old and had once been a high ranking member of the church of Alba, close to the Holy Emperor myself! Whether that was true or not, few knew. What was known was that some seventy years ago, he and a number of other priests and monks of Alba, had come to the Wildlands. Quan-Sirona preached radical ideas about Alba and the church, heretical definitely to the main Alban Church in a time of religious intolerance. He claimed that the church had been corrupted and had changed the teachings of the prophet over time, perverting the beliefs of his followers.

Quan-Sirona and his new followers had spent a number of years recruiting people to their cause and joining forces with the new fledgling College of Magic in Shandrilos. Quan-Sirona then headed into the north to found a new settlement, Sironac. Elgon knew the Grand Abbot sought unity in the Wildlands, partly due to his beliefs and partly to gain aid for his people in the bitter north against the constant goblin raids. They were keen to see an alliance of provinces that went beyond trade to a full formal alliance of mutual defence.

This view was mirrored by the men taking their seats opposite Elgon on the vast table. Elgon could see that the High Lords of the Nordic provinces of the Wildlands were taking their seats together with no advisors with them. All were warriors and ruled by strength of arms and strength of will. Elgon noticed that the High Lords of Dunard and Arondar followed the lead of Raban 'Ironhand' Machaig, High Lord of Dunegan.

Opposite the Nordic lords sat the rulers of the southern and eastern provinces that were dominated by descendents of men from the Empire. Unlike the Nordic rulers who brought no advisors, each of the rulers of the provinces had two ministers as advisors. This reflected their method of government. In the Olmec provinces, rule was by council and the council was formed of leading merchants and landowners. It was elected by the citizens, at least the citizens that could afford to vote, and the council then elected a first minister who would hold the title for two years or more if he was re-elected. The first minister was usually the richest merchant or largest landowner. Elgon knew three of the four First Ministers well; the last was newly come to power.

The most powerful of the four was the man taking the middle seat between his two near identical short, rounded and soft looking advisors. He was Korlin Di-Vorseck, First Minister of Lauria, the largest and richest province in the Wildlands. The other Olmec leaders would look to his lead as always.

Elgon believed that Di-Vorseck was secretly in favour of uniting the Wildland provinces to a greater degree, but was wary of committing his own province to anything other than a trading alliance for fear of alienating his own supporters and the other Olmec provinces that were open in their opposition to anything other than a trade alliance.

Elgon took a moment to sweep his eyes across the whole arc of the great table. He spotted the group from Katurem. He leaned back trying to get a good look around the curve of the table. There were three men. Two he knew, but the third was new. He was young and brightly clad. He sat where the High Lord of Katurem should have.

Who was the he?

Previously, the High Lord of Katurem, Adzem Ithill had always sent representatives. Perhaps the newcomer was Zeras Ithill, the son of the ruthless ruler of Katurem.

Whoever the man was, all the rulers of the provinces were now present, all save the rulers of Shandrilos.

Elgon looked towards the rear doors. He noticed out of the corner of his eye that Raban Ironhand of Dunegan was looking impatiently the same way. Elgon turned his head and found others inspecting those doors.

We are all eager to begin, Elgon thought. The agenda for this year's council had made sure of that. Baden Erin, Archmage of Shandrilos had been putting forward the idea of closer unity ever since the council had begun. That had, in a way, been the reason for the council in the first place, but this year the quietly spoken Archmage had insisted in his missives that closer ties were now imperative. All here were well aware that Baden Erin was not a frivolous man and not one prone to dramatics. Consequently, Elgon had spent much of his time while journeying south from Ostia, contemplating what it might be that would prompt the Archmage to be so forthright and explicit.

It was a puzzle, to which he believed he knew the answer.

Goblins!

The Archmage had shared his concerns over the threat of a large tribal invasion before, but Elgon had always dismissed the idea. Goblins were a rabble and they had always done so much damage in the past because they had fallen on the provinces without warning. All the northern provinces now kept an eye on the larger tribes. His own sources would have informed him if any were gathering, yet they had gone strangely quiet. It was a worry.

Elgon's ruminations were interrupted by the muffled noise of spears slamming to the ground as guards came to attention. This was promptly followed by the faint clank of a latch being released before the double doors on which all had been so intent, swung silently open. Elgon heard someone mutter 'finally' in an exasperated tone as men and women in long robes began to enter the room. The Conclave of Magi, Elgon thought, the rulers of Shandrilos and heads of the schools of magic.

Elgon drank in the sight of them as he had done so many years before as a newly accepted apprentice at the college. Then he had stood in the great hall with its vast marble pillars and arched roof lost in the shadows above, the light even from the tall windows not reaching that mighty vault. He had been awed by the Conclave and still was impressed by them all these years later.

Things had changed though, both with himself and with the Conclave. When he had arrived as a bright eyed youth he had thought these men beyond gods with their awe inspiring knowledge and immense magical might. The legendary Melkor Erin had been Archmage. Golthair Nairn had been the Magus General, head of the school of the Fighter-Magi. Elgon had joined that school when his apprenticeship ended. He had spent a further three years at the school as an adept before returning to his father to take up his responsibilities as heir to the High Lordship of Ostia. Now, several decades later, Elgon still knew all of the heads of the schools, though they had changed a number of times since his tenure as a student. These men were now colleagues and friends, and Baden Erin was now Archmage.

Elgon watched as the Archmage took his seat. His robes were deepest black, save for their colourful hem, and he carried the shining staff of his office, the Staff of Melkor that bore the silver circle and hand. His face was implacable and gave nothing of his feelings away and his eyes were black pits in his pale face. Clean shaven, he appeared much younger than he was. Elgon knew the Archmage had a fierce intelligence allied to a magical talent that could almost be felt by people not trained in the mysteries, and though he always appeared placid and calm there was an intensity whenever he spoke of things he held dear. He was a man of great vision who had begun to unite the people of the wilds as no one had before, and not with swords and battles. Baden Erin's battleground was the mind and the discourse of the council table, an arena where Elgon had yet to see his equal.

The rest of the conclave moved to stand behind their chairs before taking their seats around the Archmage, having waited respectfully for their leader to sit.

"By the circle of wisdom and the hand of power" the Archmage began in ritual, "welcome to this council my lords and ministers." He paused and looked around the table opposite him. All of the rulers of the provinces sat around the opposite curve of the table to him. There was a gap of at least a half dozen chairs on either side of the Conclave that separated them from the assembled leaders.

"It is good to see you all here in peace and fellowship." he smiled gently, but then his face turned serious and he continued in a tone that was heavy with feeling. "I must beg your indulgence at the beginning of this Grand Council. Usually this first evening's meeting is little more than a formality to agree our agenda for the coming days, but I find that I am forced to change this in order to introduce a grave matter for your immediate attention." He paused and looked around the wide table to gauge the lord's reactions.

"Over the last generation, our peoples have enjoyed peace that our predecessors in this harsh land never thought possible. There has been no major border skirmish or incursion in almost twenty years and trade has increased tenfold. There has not been a major war with the goblin tribes in almost thirty years and their raids have grown rarer as the years have passed." The Archmage took a deep breath then and spread his arms slightly in welcome. "We live gentlemen in an era of peace and plenty compared to our forebears." He smiled and looked at the assembled lords.

Elgon was unsure where the Archmage was going with this speech and so the next words hit him almost like a blow.

"An era that will soon come to an end!"

Chapter 12

THE GOBLIN THREAT

Of the Elder there is much debate. It is said that the word Elder is used for the ancient races we now know as dwarves, elves, pixie and others. It is interesting to note that in some instances the feared races of trolls and goblins are included within this term implying they too were once greater than they are now. Certainly the remnants of the dwarven and elven people who inhabit the wild forests and hills are a pale shadow of their forebears.

From 'The nature of the Elder' by Melkor Erin, Archmage of Shandrilos, BY1303

Suddenly, there was a cacophony of voices echoing in the lofty chamber. Ministers sought their lords' attention while lords called out in puzzlement. Elgon's gaze was fixed on the Archmage.

"Please, my lords, I know you have many questions and I know that many of you will have even more once I have finished, but please allow me to continue."

The noise in the room quickly faded and the Archmage began again. With care and obvious deliberation over his words, the Archmage spoke at length.

Elgon listened almost spellbound at the Archmage's words. Questions leapt to his mind and fears arose and contested with doubts at the revelations the Archmage spoke of with obvious conviction.

Minutes later, as the Archmage finished, a stunned silence settled on the gathering. Elgon sat back in near amazement. 'Was it possible' he asked himself, 'that a powerful 'Gul' had arisen amongst the goblins of the Bloodland Heights?'

It would not be new. 'Guls' came and went in the incessant battles that raged amongst the tribes in and around the Wildlands. That a 'Gul Dor' had arisen amongst the tribes was incredible, that he had managed to unite so many tribes so quickly and amass such a large army was an evil revelation indeed!'

"Are you certain of the size of this goblin force, my lord Archmage?" asked Sir Arleas of Karodracia, incredulously.

Before the Archmage could answer a dozen questions were called out from lords all around the great table.

"My Lords," the Archmage began forcefully and the questions turned from calls to mutters, "allow me to try to address some of the concerns I know you will have and at the same time answer some of your questions."

The muttering halted.

"I am sure many of you are wondering why you have not had any information on this new Guldor... this Marog. Well, he is no ordinary goblin. To even have united so many tribes that is obvious. However, he is more than all others before him and he is aware of our scrutiny. He knows we must seek to destroy him and so he has striven hard to hide his rise from us, to keep us unsuspecting and vulnerable until he is secure. He shows signs of clear intelligence and strategic understanding and has succeeded in uniting the tribes on an unprecedented scale. In this, I think you will agree, he presents a greater danger than any before faced by the Wildlands."

The Archmage met the eyes of those around the table. Elgon could only agree. He had known of many goblins who were cunning and wily, that was their nature, but it was unheard of for a goblin to organise and control his subjects so thoroughly that he could prevent knowledge of his rise filtering into Darylor!

Before questions could be asked, the Archmage forged on. "Many of you will also be wondering how I have perceived this threat when you have not." The black robed mage lord looked down at the table. He was leaning on the table with both fists firmly planted on the shining wooden surface and he seemed to be debating with himself. Abruptly, his head came up and his dark eyes looked distant. "I occupy a rather unique position in these lands in that I can draw upon the mundane sources that you yourselves have used and also I have at my disposal other... rarer means of obtaining information and a way of knowing where to look." The Archmage turned to look to his left and gestured towards the conclave members there. "From amongst the school of seers we have received many grave visions and omens. Thankfully we have perceptive seers such as my friend the Allseer...", a rather surprised looking Arimenes Corvindar was a little abashed at the attention he was given as all eyes swung towards him, "who have given me vital clues as to where to look for approaching dangers. It was a number of years ago that this threat was first brought to my attention and I turned my scrutiny northwards. The visions were clear about the extent of the danger, in fact they showed danger on a scale that not even a goblin invasion such as we have seen before would present, but nevertheless, there were clear hints as to the origin of the most immediate danger and so I turned all my attention to the Bloodland Heights and used every craft at my disposal to discover the true danger."

Here the Archmage paused and Elgon saw that he seemed hesitant over how next to proceed. His eyes searched the far wall seemingly in an effort to resolve some unspoken dilemma. Slowly his eyes focused on those around him. "Recently, I have received information that has further shaken me. It seems there is more at work here than the rise of a Guldor of unheard of skills in the Bloodland Heights. Beyond those forbidding lands are the true northlands, vast and unexplored. We know very little about those lands, not even who or what dwells there. From my sources I have learnt something of those lands, something that turned my blood cold."

Elgon noticed that a number of the other magi around the Archmage were looking at their leader in growing alarm. This was new to them too.

With a tone that was heavy and filled with doom, the Archmage continued, "Those lands are inhabited by trolls, yeti, kobold and all manner of foul creatures, but prime amongst them are the goblin tribes whose numbers are beyond my ability to grasp." With eyes cold and filled with certainty, the powerful figure finished, "Suffice it to say, my lords, that their numbers are legion... and they too are uniting!"

Bedlam erupted amongst the council members. The Olmecs, almost to a man were on their feet and shouting questions or calling their disbelief. The three Nordic lords were snarling and banging the table trying to get the attention of the council. Even the other magi were filled with emotions ranging from alarm to outright disbelief. Elgon himself was not sure what to think. He was overwhelmed by the Archmage's revelations.

Elgon heard Sir Arleas's strong voice rise above those of the other lords as he called for calm. Many of the lords seemed to realise they were behaving like a rabble and seated themselves at the Lord of Karodracia's call. Slowly, lords took their seats, reluctant and angry and silence once more fell on the assemblage. Only the Archmage remained on his feet, stern and unbending before the human gale, his pale features rigid.

A cough sounded and Elgon looked to his right. Grand Abbot Alinus Quan Sirona calmly nodded at the Archmage, "I too have seen these portents of which you speak and I have lately suspected such a leader among the goblins had arisen. Indeed, I have seen more of what you speak though I have been unable to verify it. However," the white bearded ancient continued, "beyond my northern borders there have been rumours of battles amongst the tribes of that vast den of evil known as the Shadowed Forest and of a Warlord who has arisen there too."

Elgon was beginning to feel like his whole world was being up ended. The Shadowed Forest was to the north west of the Wildlands and few who entered there ever left. That a Warlord had arisen there was as bad as within the Bloodland Heights, the Shadowed Forest was thought to be as big, if not bigger in size, and would no doubt hold thousands of goblin warriors.

"Aye, I too have heard this rumour," put in the burly Raban Ironhand of Dunegan, another province that shared a border with the treacherous Forests of Shadow, "I had not mentioned it before because it was so unbelievable and I could not find any concrete evidence. There too perhaps knowledge has specifically been denied us."

Elgon knew Raban's reputation as a fearless warrior and skilled commander and was further troubled by the worry he saw written in his ice blue eyes. Raban was not a man easily perturbed.

The strong voice of the Archmage again echoed around the beautiful council chamber. "Many of you will know the legends of these lands and of the Elder races who once ruled here."

The Nordic lords were nodding, as was Elgon himself. He was familiar with the stories, but as he looked to the Olmecs he could see skeptical looks cross their faces. They would find it hard to admit that such legends had any truth to them. As far as many followers of Alba were concerned, and the Olmecs were all worshippers of the great prophet, the Elder races were seen as mythical, as children's tales. Even in the wilds, the Olmecs saw the remnants of the Elder as something less than human and certainly not civilised. The arrogant Olmecs still held to the belief that theirs was the first civilisation and still the greatest. To give credence to the idea that some great civilisation existed hundreds if not thousands of years before their own was near impossible.

"In legend, the goblins were once united under a dark king and the old stories tell us that only an alliance of the Elder and men succeeded in defeating it. Now, whether you believe in such legends or not is irrelevant, but the reality is that the goblins are uniting and on a scale not heard of in recorded history. Whether we shall face it all or only a portion is unclear. What is clear is that we need to prepare ourselves to face such a threat for it seems clear that its focus will inevitably turn our way. We are its natural target, we have wealth, we are their sworn enemies and there is nowhere else for them to go except south. We need to unite, my lords, we need to forge an alliance that will give us a chance to defend against this foe." the Archmage warned.

"To what purpose, my lord Archmage?" interrupted Lord Del Aro of Torunsport sarcastically. The obese lord lifted his prodigious bulk from his chair, "From what you have said the force that will march on us would be more than we could ever face; a hundred thousand goblin warriors perhaps!" Lord Del Aro said somewhat disparagingly. "If you give credit to such fairy tales!"

He looked at the other lords around him almost mockingly.

"Even united our armies would only number around eight to ten thousand with perhaps twice that number in militia. The Nordic kingdoms or the Empire will not send forces to our aid. They will be impossible to persuade of such an unfounded danger and one so distant from their homes."

He paused to let his skepticism sink in. "They have their own problems and far more tangible ones at that."

He laughed harshly.

"If your goblin horde exists, do you expect us to face odds of ten to one? That is if this is not a ploy to further your dreams of unifying this land, no doubt under your divine leadership." he finished with a snort of derision as he slumped into his chair which groaned audibly under his weight.

Sir Arleas of Karodracia snapped to his feet, "Although I do not agree with all that my Lord of Torunsport has said," the warrior lord began, "I feel he has a point. If these goblins are as organised as you have said then we have little chance against them even if we do unite. We should be looking to buy in mercenaries…"

"We do not have the money for mercenaries on that scale nor can we trust them to stand and fight when their lives are on the line." Di Vorseck of Lauria calmly stated from where he sat.

Elgon saw the young Serales of Kalizern, another of the Olmec lords, push himself to his feet.

"Pardon me, my lords, but it seems to me we are discussing something of which we have only scant evidence. Other than from the Archmage, we have only unsubstantiated rumours of these goblin armies and no evidence at all that they are aimed at us. They could be uniting in response to each other, intent on only themselves and the destruction of their kin." He looked around and saw heads nodding in agreement with him, "Forgive me, my lord Archmage, I am new to this council and I do not know you as others here do, but why should we trust your word that there are armies out there. What or who are these shadowy sources you speak of that only you have access to, and how do they know so much of goings on in the northlands that are still such a mystery to the rest of us after four centuries in these lands?"

Elgon was impressed with the young man, he was little more than eighteen from his looks, but he could already speak persuasively and had a point about the lack of evidence. Even though Elgon himself was inclined to believe the Archmage, he could see that others would not be so easily convinced.

The young Olmec lord spurred on by his success finished, "Where are your witnesses? Bring them before us so that we may question them and be convinced."

Voices from among the Olmec ministers and lord's rose in agreement and began muttering, "Yes, bring them before us."

Elgon looked back at the Archmage who seemed to have grown stiller and more forbidding. His jaw visibly twitched as the calls continued. Suddenly, he seemed to sag slightly as he sighed in resignation, like a man faced with a choice he had long ago known he would have to face, but had finally come to the point of decision.

"You still find what I and others have said hard to believe and wonder at the truth of these rumours and whispers from the far north?" The Archmage was looking at the rulers and ministers from the Olmec cities of the south, obviously saddened by their disbelief, yet seeming to expect it.

The polite and diplomatic Lord of Lauria was an old ally and friend of the Archmage and he climbed slowly to his feet. "I think it is clear that we need to see the evidence for ourselves, my friend, listen to the rumours from the witnesses with our own ears."

Korlin Di Vorseck of Lauria looked around, seeking support and agreement.

"If they are not here or cannot be here before this council ends then I suggest, my lords that we go forward with the agenda as normal so as not to unduly upset our people and call another emergency council when we can examine the evidence. This would also allow us time to look into the threats ourselves, my lord Archmage."

When the ruler of the largest and most powerful province in the Wildlands finished, and when nothing was immediately forthcoming from the slump shouldered Archmage, he asked gently, "Well what say you, Baden?"

Slowly the Archmage straightened and spoke, "I do have the sources here within call and will call for them…" began the Archmage in a near whisper. It was obvious to all that he was reluctant to call them and yet, equally obvious, that he had been ready for such a call to have his sources so close, "but before that I must say that I agree with this council that we need to gain allies who can support us against this danger or we will fall before it. We do not have the forces to face this, so allies we can trust, who feel as we do about this land and will defend it without the offer of money, are imperative. I would ask you to keep that uppermost in your minds my lords!" the Archmage insisted.

With those words he signalled and the doors behind him that had closed silently and unnoticed some minutes before swung open again and out of the shadows of the hall beyond, from both sides of the doorway came a rush of people, weapons bristling and armour clanking. As they poured into the chamber, encircling the room and the men in it, all sprang to their feet in consternation. Elgon too had automatically pushed himself to his feet and knew that surprise etched his features as it did all the others in the room, including the other mages of the Conclave. Only the Archmage looked at ease. Elgon noticed the Nordic lords reaching for weapons that weren't there and the mages spinning to look around in all directions. Elgon was just as confused.

Elgon looked hard at the warriors who had surrounded the table standing back against the wall, weapons held ready. They were… short! He looked harder, they were covered head to foot in thick, steel, full plate armour of unusual design and carried heavy double bladed axes and round polished shields with hammers, axes, rocks and the like emblazoned on them. Spinning around he looked at the warriors behind his back and saw men of medium height in jet black armour that covered their upper bodies while their legs were covered in leather trousers of differing colours. They carried long staves and had short swords strapped to their thighs with quivers of arrows showing over their shoulders. Their heads were covered by dark winged helms with cheek guards that hid their features.

Elgon was completely floundering, his brain said there was something odd about the warriors he was seeing, but it was still trying to deal with the unusual sight of armed men in the hall of the Council.

Elgon heard gasps from the First ministers of the Olmec towns and frowned at them. He could see Di-Vorseck and Surtez, Lord of Hadek had their hands over their mouths and were looking at the open doorway in what could only be described as amazement. Elgon's head spun, his eyes following the direction of the other men's wide eyed gaze. More men had moved into the entrance behind the Archmage who had turned, seemingly to greet them. As the men moved from behind the mages into his view, he suddenly found himself back in his chair as his legs gave way. He heard Di-Vorseck gasp, "Elves!" while Sir Arleas shouted, "Have you betrayed us Baden?" and banged his fist on the table.

Suddenly, a voice boomed out, enhanced by magic, "SIT DOWN MY LORDS!!!"

The voice bounced around the room for a second and then silence fell. Everyone stood still staring at the rigid figure of the Archmage, whose face was alive with emotion. Slowly and then with gathering pace men began to sit themselves down, some hurriedly, others slumping back and some with bitter, anger radiating from every move they made.

"Now," the Archmage continued in an ordinary voice, "let me explain."

Chapter 13

THE CATACOMBS

It is said that many wonders were possible in ancient times; there are tales that the Elder races could travel leagues with but a step and fly through the air with their fabulous ships that sailed the skies! It was said that dragons were tamed and elemental creatures harnessed to serve. It was said that the power and knowledge of the Elder were beyond anything known to us today!

From 'A collection of Folktales' by Rogarin Draghar, Bard to the King of Tutonia, BY1107

'How did we get ourselves into this mess?'
Looking around him, he could see the worry on his friend's faces in the poor light of the subterranean room. The stillness was only broken by the jangle of armour and clink of Zara's blades. She was muttering to herself angrily.

Jon Madraig noted Darin's exhaustion from the way he leaned on his great two handed sword, the point hard against the floor to support him. It was cold, cold enough that Jon could see clouds billowing forth from his friend's mouths and nostrils from their exertions.

Jon glanced again at the small doorway to what seemed now to be their cell and possibly their tomb! It stood open and it seemed almost as if nothing could prevent their exit. Nothing that is, unless you happened to glance at the blood-wet ground and let your gaze carry across the wide corridor to the opposite wall where the slumped bodies of the creatures lay!

The creatures were in no way human and the nearest Jon could come to an easy comparison was to an insect, save these insects were much bigger, about the size of a small pony! They appeared to have two 'arms' with savage pincers on the end, and four longer 'legs'. Jon knew from bitter experience that they could move at an astonishing speed, their four long, spindly limbs churning and their arms weaving like some wild, dwarven engine from myth. They were a dark brown colour, like wet sand, and were covered in thick armour save at their narrow joints. Their armour was alternately smooth and jagged. This was not by coincidence either it seemed. The creatures had used their wickedly serrated forearms and legs like weapons to tear and slash. Several of the company bore slashes only limited from being serious by their own armour. The creatures would be devastating against ordinary people.

The creatures' bodies were split into three sections; as Jon knew all insects were from his studies, studies he had undertaken in the college that now stood far above them. They had a long, thin abdomen that they carried out behind them, almost like a tail for balance, while their middle section was large and bulbous. Six limbs sprouted from it. The head was long and thin, with two large, shiny, jewel-like eyes and two antennae that resembled stalks of wheat protruding from their otherwise featureless heads. As Zara Halven had pointed out acerbically a few moments earlier, they were balder than he was!

One other feature they did have on their heads; where a man's chin would be they had a dark slash from which serrated pincers snapped out, whether in anger or excitement, Jon did not know.

Of course, the tangles of arms and legs that lay on the floor of the corridor were missing this third section of their bodies. Their heads had bounced out of sight when Darin and Zara had desperately hacked them off as the group had been forced to stop running and fight here in this dead end room.

Jon grimaced. Things were bad, yet it had all started so well.

Barely a couple of hours ago they had been walking into the catacombs looking forward to a night of easy comradeship; a safe jaunt to relive old adventures and maybe even some treasure, though he had not been convinced of that. The company had gone down laughing and joking; spirits high.

None of them could have predicted they would end up cornered in a bare stone chamber by a small army of creatures out of nightmare with little hope of escaping alive!

The room in which they had taken refuge was a small antechamber off a short, wide corridor. Down that corridor was a large main chamber. Now the way stood in gloom, the only light penetrating their hideout filtered down from the main room where *they* were!

Jon heard Zara snarl in frustration. "Well, what by Ishara's icy tits, do we do?" she hissed into the silence.

Bear saw Rebba wince at Zara's vicious blasphemy. One did not name the death goddess lightly in a situation like this and certainly not to insult her.

"Don't look at me," Nat Bero replied in near panic, though Zara had not been looking her way, "We should have bolted back to the surface as soon as we saw those…" her pale mouth twisted slightly and her brow knotted as she tried to put a name or easy description to the creatures they had faced, "…things!"

"Not a very productive comment." Arkadi snapped.

Jon knew the mage had seen some strange sights in his time, but the creatures and their allies made the mage more nervous than Jon had ever seen him. Arkadi was nearly invisible against the back wall where his thick black cloak merged seamlessly with the dark that crowded the back of the room, but his unease was obvious.

"We are here now and can't really change what's been done. Can we?" Arkadi finished harshly.

Nat's head turned slowly. Her hunter's hood was thrown back and her long dark hair seemed almost to shine in the half light. She gave Arkadi a wild look, but said nothing.

"What do you think, Bear?" Darin asked carefully, catching his breath and levering himself off his father's sword. He stood up straight and tall. He was whip-lean yet strong; his shoulders wide, his waist thin. He was every inch the swordsman and knight in his full plate armour. His breastplate gleamed and carried the red dragon symbol of his family. He carried no shield. His motto was 'the best form of defence is attack' and that was partly why all of them still stood here now. His thick armour had been proof against the creatures and he had withstood the initial onslaught to allow them all to flee. He was also the only one that fear had not touched, but then Darin was a little crazy that way, always had been.

Jon considered things carefully as all eyes turned to him. He felt like spitting out a flippant panicky remark like Nat Bero had, but quickly squashed the urge. It was pointless, as Arkadi had already pointed out.

'What to do?' he thought. 'Be objective, think things through. That's what his old mentor had always said, 'reason is the greatest of weapons'.'

Jon slowly looked at each of his friends in turn. Darin, knight of Saint Karodra, now possibly the finest swordsman in the north, heavily armed and armoured. He was also cool and clear headed in a fight. Zara Halven, was a highly skilled duelist who possessed explosive speed and a near unnatural agility. She was savage and would stop at nothing. She was a survivor.

He turned. Nat Bero was a competent fighter close up, but a superb archer at distance; while Garon Vale's magic and mace allied to his strong arm made the portly monk very useful in a fight, but it was clear that both he and the tall huntress were on the verge of panic; their eyes wide and darting. They needed a boost.

Jon turned to squint at those behind him, towards the back of the room. Behind his left shoulder was the shadowy form of Arkadi. He would definitely prove useful. When they had been young his magic had been little more than an aid to his practical jokes and quick tongue. Then jibes and dodges had been his primary weapon. Long years of study had changed that; his magic could be devastating. The quick witted mage would prove useful.

This brought Jon's gaze to the last of their company.

Rebba Korran was a sensitive soul and it seemed now that her strange feelings earlier had been well warranted. Now she was as afraid as he'd ever seen her. Her nature was to heal not to hurt, but even she could defend herself and, like Arkadi, Rebba's burgeoning control of the elements would be of use in this ancient labyrinth of earth and rock.

All in all, this was a formidable group. If he were able to choose a group to stand with him in danger, there were few he could pick better. The thought was a good one, the first he had had in the last hour.

Jon then turned his mind to what faced them even as he turned to face the entrance to their trap. *They* were out there he knew, seemingly as wary

119

of entering as he and his friends were of leaving. "How many do you think we face, Arkadi?" he called quietly over his shoulder.

"Hard to say, Bear, I saw at least three of those black robed creatures along with at least twice that number of those freakish looking goblins!" Arkadi said thoughtfully.

"No, there were more than three of those dark robed bastards." Zara spat, "There was at least twice that. Move like ghosts they do. Give me the shivers." Zara gave a slight shudder.

"So, how many of those 'bugs' do we think there are?" Jon muttered.

The whole party seemed to look at each other before Darin said, "Well we've killed four of the things."

"That doesn't really tell us how many are left." Arkadi quipped sarcastically.

"Yeah, alright, Talcost," Darin snapped back, "I don't see you leaping up with a ready answer. Where's all your superior intelligence?"

Arkadi's lips moved to respond, but Rebba's whispered voice cut across the room, "We must stay focused on the enemy."

All looked to the earnest druid in surprise at her sudden calm. One by one they nodded. All eyes turned to the doorway, hands gripping weapons and Jon felt his heart race.

He was about to speak when suddenly an alien voice tore the stillness.

"Humans...? Can you hear me...? Do you understand us...?"

The voice was soft, each word slowly, deliberately and sweetly formed, almost like a man whispering to his lover. The voice had a musical quality that no human could produce. It was compelling.

The company stood mute. Jon looked at Darin and then Zara. Each shrugged in the gloom, neither knew what to do. Jon felt a movement behind him as Arkadi pushed forward.

"Some sort of magic is being used," he whispered intensely, "in the translation I think."

He glanced at Jon who could now make out his large, dark eyes.

"They do not speak our tongue." Arkadi finished, moving back.

Jon paused thoughtfully. 'Not much help really,' he thought dismally.

He noticed everyone looking at him expectantly. 'Why was everyone looking to him all of a sudden?' He had a real urge to just go to the back of the room and sit down.

'Damn it' he thought recklessly snapping to the other extreme. He took a deep breath and called, "We understand you."

His rough voice was laced with the fear he felt. He cursed quietly under his breath and steadied himself as the others looked his way in alarm.

"What is it you want of us?" he shouted, this time happy to hear only anger in his voice.

He noticed Zara and Nat looking at him as if to say 'What are you doing?' He moved his shield up his arm and held up his hand, waving them to stay quiet.

They all waited. Jon was angry with himself. He should not have shown his fear. Neither should he have let his anger make him shout before he thought things through carefully. Why everyone was suddenly following his lead, he didn't know. Earlier, they had argued like fools about even which direction to go down here. Now suddenly he was the leader.

'Swines,' he thought bitterly.

Chapter 14

TRAPPED

There are many dangers in the Wildlands of Darylor, first amongst them is that of the non-human races; an idea thought ridiculous to those in the Empire. To the people of the Empire, creatures such as elves, dwarves, goblins and trolls are seen as fiction, stories to frighten children, or, if they are acknowledged at all, they are seen as demons. However, here in the wilds, they are very real and very dangerous, yet are they demons? The Nordic have very different beliefs about the elves in particular, and the dwarves are valued highly for their trade.

Excerpt from 'A strange land; the Wildlands of Darylor' by Grand Abbot Alinus Quan Sirona, BY1320

Darin of Kenarth, knight of Karodra and self confessed ladies man was beginning to get bored with the silence. He stretched the muscles in his arms and sides slowly and carefully. His ribs still smarted where that bug had caught him with its last attack. He had let it come in close so that he could hack at its head, but it had been quicker than he'd expected and had scuttled forward with the speed of a startled cat, slamming its serrated forearms into his side as he took its head off with his great sword.

Plate armour was always a good idea, he thought, even though Zara always said he waddled around like a turtle with it on. Better that than gutted by some freakish giant insect!

Again, the soft voice echoed down the corridor.

"We seem to have a problem." the tinkling voice called.

Darin's brow crinkled as he thought, 'Problem? They have a problem?' He looked to Bear to see an equally puzzled expression on his oldest friend's wide, pale face. Bear chewed thoughtfully on his lip.

"You want to get out of this place and we want what you carry."

Darin's eyes had been on Bear the whole time and now he saw real puzzlement. He heard several gasps come from the others as they too reacted to the eerie words. Darin looked to Zara, Arkadi and Bear, his adrenalin starting to pump again. He realised with a little surprise that he was actually enjoying himself.

This was like the good old days when they had gone out adventuring, looking for action and gold. He realised now that he missed it.

His training with the Knights of Karodra had been wonderful. He had learnt all manner of useful skills, though he still hated the jousting. It wasn't the jousting itself, it was the damned horses. He had always hated horses. When he had joined the Blessed Order of Saint Karodra, patron saint of travellers and Shield of the Weak, he had already been an accomplished swordsmen and eager to learn more. The order had done that quickly and had given him the discipline he needed to hone his talents. Now there were few who could match him in a duel or in the melee. However, the day to day role of a knight of Karodra was one of travelling the roads and wilds of the lands, protecting merchants and travellers, aiding families and villages. It could be rewarding work, but it could be boring as hell too. Darin knew that he needed action to keep his interest; battle and adventure. Both had been a near constant with his friends in the early days. Later things had got difficult and there had been arguing. He had no desire for that and had left. He shook his head in regret and admitted to himself, he'd missed the camaraderie.

He noticed that Bear, Zara and Arkadi were whispering together and brought himself back to the present. Another thing he always found difficult was thinking hard on one thing for any length of time. He wasn't stupid, but the idea of worrying over something, debating, or talking just got a little boring very quickly for him. He preferred to just jump in and see how things went. He was glad Bear had called out earlier. He had definitely been getting edgy and he hated that.

We need to do something, he thought almost exactly as he heard Bear say the same thing to Zara and Arkadi. He knew Bear liked to debate and consider things carefully, but he also knew his old friend found it hard to control his temper in a tight spot. That wasn't to say that Bear always got angry. No, Darin had rarely seen his friend really angry, that was a definite time to avoid him! Darin believed that Bear existed in a near permanent state of irritation if there was such a condition, but it was a good natured irritation.

Darin smiled to himself. This was, in fact, part of the reason for his nick-name. Zara had always said he had the disposition of a grizzly bear ready for hibernation, although this just added to the real reason which was the extensive amount of hair that covered his thick body.

Looking at Bear, Darin contemplated his friend's face in more detail. He actually thought Bear's large head had a character all of its own, the broken nose and scars and lumps gave him a distinctly savage look. That was one of the strange things about Bear, Darin thought, most people looked at Bear and thought 'big bruiser', dumb and dangerous. He had the disposition and the looks to back this, yet few were ever perceptive enough to see the fierce intelligence and the sensitive man underneath. Few that were except his students, Darin knew. He had seen Bear work with them. Out went the harsh demeanor and volatile temper and in came the patient understanding and sense of humour. It was hard for many to believe that Jon the Bear, warrior and bar room brawler, was now Master Jon Madraig, fighter-mage and tutor!

"I think we should just attack," Zara was saying forcefully, "we could rush them and punch through, then make a dash for it." She punctuated her ideas by waving her beautifully crafted sabres at the entrance.

"Don't be stupid, we couldn't guarantee all of us would make it." Arkadi insisted. "They'd be ready to slaughter us as soon as we passed around the corner..."

"What about some magic to cover us?" Darin interjected and Zara nodded.

"Yeah, you could cover our attack, like you did with those Tavori scouts that time." Zara pressed, but Arkadi was already shaking his head.

"No, I couldn't," Arkadi began.

Zara went to interrupt, but Arkadi held his hand up with a firm look on his face, "Those were ordinary men, warriors, they did not know even this much magic," the small mage said as he held his hand up with thumb and forefinger only an inch apart. "To those creatures in black, magic is like air, they have a natural affinity to it." He pointed to the doorway as if he could see their enemy. "Those creatures are elves remember!"

Chapter 15

OF ELVES, DWARVES AND MEN

There were said to be many Elder Kingdoms but by far the most well known were those of the Elves. If tales are to be believed there were nine fabled kingdoms of Elvenkind that stretched the length and breadth of the uncharted northlands. We now know that the lands known as the Wildlands were once part of the ancient elven kingdom of Dah'Rhyllor. However most acknowledge that the greatest of the elven kingdoms was El'Yaris, seat of the Lore King of the Elves, Tal'Asin the Wise!

From 'The nature of the Elder' by Melkor Erin, Archmage of Shandrilos, BY1303

A dazed silence hung over the hall. Everyone's eyes were on the tall, dark, forbidding figure of the Archmage. His eyes were fierce.

His potent voice broke the silence. "You will have to forgive me my lords, I had hoped to introduce my guests in a more diplomatic way..." the Archmage began, power still evident in his voice, "but events and portents have forced me to other more precipitous methods."

Elgon glanced around at the faces of his fellow rulers and found all were still in shock. None had been able to gather their wits sufficiently to speak, but that would not last long. Already he could see the anger building again in the faces of Sir Arleas of Karodracia and the Olmec ministers. Glancing across, Elgon saw the Nordic's shock was giving way more to curiosity by the looks on their faces and the way they twisted and turned to get a better look at those around them. The men from Katurem were simply bemused, not knowing what to think, their leader was sitting back in his chair, a completely neutral look on his handsome features, but a sense of wonder in his face. Only Grand Abbot Alinus seemed composed and listening carefully.

Elgon turned his attention back to the Archmage who had turned to face his surprising guests. He was gesturing them to take the vacant seats on either side of the heads of the schools of magic. At first it seemed they would not move; their alien eyes scanned the assemblage before them, warily. There appeared to be some seven elves that stood clear and straight, but there were also five dwarves whose heads could only just be seen above the table's wooden expanse. As a group they all seemed to come to an agreement. Glancing at each other, they began to move around the table, the elves going to the left, towards Elgon's side of the table, and the dwarves headed for the chairs on the right. Elgon and, he had no doubt, everyone else in the room, studied the groups as they moved.

Elgon focused in on the elves. Dwarves were a rare sight though not unknown, but it was unheard of for elves to be seen outside of their forest strongholds! Elgon felt as if time was slowing; never before had he had the opportunity to study elves. He had seen them before, but only as darting flashes in the forest or as silhouettes on the hills, gliding along with long loping strides.

All of the elves shared the prominent, upswept, pointed and lobeless ears, but it was the eyes that held his attention. Their large, almond shaped eyes seemed to be of all one dazzling colour; there was no white to the eye and each elf seemed to have slightly different tones and hues. Their eyes were spellbinding. Elgon could understand the stories now of being held rapt simply by their stare and of how they could beguile.

Elgon pulled his eyes away quickly. He wasn't sure he believed the stories but he wouldn't chance it. He switched his focus. He noticed that although their eyes varied in colour their skin did not. They all had pale white skin with a strangely metallic shine that made it look silvery as the light played across it, but it wasn't just the strange colour of their skin that seemed so odd, it was the perfection of it. There were no blemishes or freckles, no hair or stubble. Their skin had the qualities of those of an unspoilt child's, smooth and soft. The absence of any lines or wrinkles made them all seem young. They were also all very slight by human standards with one or two of them looking so thin as to be emaciated, and all of the elves were wearing leathery clothing of intricate design, along with dark armour and cloaks of differing earthy colours from brown to green.

As the elves approached their chairs, Elgon noticed there was one woman amongst them who had incredible golden hair that cascaded down to her waste from a narrow line of hair on the top of her head. The sides of her head were shaven and showed light tattoos as Elgon had heard was the custom amongst wild even warriors from the few bits of knowledge he had gleaned. She was not the only warrior amongst the group by this indication.

Elgon was suddenly surprised to see one of the elves did appear older. He had been at the back and had come into view as the others glided around the table. His face was lightly creased and his back stooped slightly. In human terms this might have put him in his fifties or sixties, but Elgon realised that this elf must be very old indeed to show any signs of age, perhaps centuries old.

Elgon found his eyes drawn to the elf leading the group around the table; he seemed more powerful than the others, it seemed to exude from him. He too was a warrior with the warrior's part shaven head and tattoos. He stood out amongst the colourful array of alien features for his lack of colour. His hair was grey and settled on his head like threads of dust or thick spider's webs. His eyes were grey too, like thunder clouds. When this was combined with his kind's pale silvery skin, Elgon found himself wondering if this creature was merely an illusion or a spirit and not really there at all. He looked like a ghost as he glided round towards Elgon, a ghost in jet black armour and grey, his cloak the colour of his eyes.

Elgon watched as the elf lords took their seats, bending their thin limbs and sitting uncomfortably, aware of the eyes on them. Elgon had been so engrossed with the elves that he saw nothing of the dwarves. It was only as the Archmage began again to speak and his attention was broken from the elves that he realised they had taken their seats across the table. Most would have laughed at the ridiculous sight of the dwarves, sitting like children with their heads just above the table top. Of course, children didn't have the beards or the impressive breadth of shoulders. These dwarves were obviously powerful and looked like they could crack rocks with their fists. They were also obviously aware of how they looked at the table and were doing their best to glare angrily at all around them, daring anyone to comment or sneer. It was well known that dwarves were formidable warriors and not to be judged by their size. Their prodigious thickness of limb hinted at alarming strength.

Elgon realised he was not listening to the Archmage and snapped his attention back.

"... need to act like leaders and not let personal feelings cloud our judgement." The Archmage was saying. He paused and looked around the table at the lords and ministers, taking the measure of all. "My lords, I would like to introduce you to our fellow rulers of this land, the clan chiefs of the Elder races who have generously agreed to attend this meeting to discuss the threat that faces all of us."

Elgon heard a chair scrape the floor and turned in time to see Sir Arleas of Karodracia leap to his feet. "Fellow rulers!" he spluttered angrily, his spare frame rigid. "They are enemies who have preyed on our people and shot men down in cold blood." he snarled, hammering his fist on the table. "You have betrayed the trust of this council."

The rotund Lord Del Aro of Torunsport rose to his feet and yelled, "And what are these warriors doing surrounding us? Is this a peaceful meeting of leaders or an armed attack?" He waved a short sleeved arm at the warriors around them as he spoke and Elgon found himself captivated by the way the fat that hung from his upper arm wobbled as he gesticulated. First Minister Del Aro seemed to delight in opulence and wore brightly coloured silks and satins with overly large jewels sown into the materials to match the overly large gems that glinted on his pudgy hands. Del Aro was only interested in his own self interests and that of his city. Elgon knew he was the sort who would only commit to anything if he would get something in return. He was also primarily concerned with his own safety and it was clear he feared the Elder lords and their warriors. The man was a greedy coward.

Elgon turned his attention back to the Archmage to hear his response. Although he despised Del Aro, he had a point; armed men should not have been allowed in the council room. It smacked of a threat or coercion.

Before the Archmage could respond, the female elf, who the grey elf had been urgently whispering to, making placating gestures, shook her head viciously and leapt to her feet snarling, "You dare to call us, killers!" She pointed at Sir Arleas. "It is you who have trespassed on our lands, slain our people and driven us from our ancient forests." Her stunning blue eyes gleamed and her alien voice seemed to sing even as she cursed the tall knight.

   Suddenly it seemed that everyone was on their feet shouting or trying to calm things. The ghostlike elf was on his feet, his hand on the elven women's arm, whispering again into her ear and gesturing to the warriors behind him to remain still. Meanwhile Di Vorseck of Lauria, ever the peacemaker, was trying to calm his colleagues, the Nordics and the dwarves eyed each other warily, but kept their seats and Grand Abbot Alinus sat too, his head shaking gently. The Archmage merely stood, still, quiet, his hands folded into his voluminous sleeves and his face stiff and dark. His fellow magi knew their leader well and were keeping quiet. While he was not one to lose his temper, when he did it was a sight to see according to the few who had witnessed it.

   Slowly order was restored and all eyes turned again to the Archmage. Elgon could see his jaw muscles knot with the effort of containing himself. As he spoke his voice was calm and still but his eyes were fierce. "I realise there are some long standing enmities and land issues amongst some of us here and I realise that armed men in this hall is a violation of your trust, but surely the danger facing us outweighs any other concerns. It is imperative that we all unite to face what is to come." The Archmage was practically spitting out the words which were all the more savage for the fact his arms remained coiled inside his robe almost as if he could not trust himself to unfold his hands, and considering the power they could call forth, Elgon was glad of his restraint.

   Grand Abbot Alinus spoke into the stillness following the Archmage's impassioned speech. "I too know something of the true danger of which you have spoken, Baden." He began, using the Archmage's first name, "It is as grave as you paint it, but I have to agree with my Lord of Torunsport," he nodded down the table, "that these warriors around us seem unnecessary. Unless you suspect one of us is part of the danger?" he finished questioningly.

   Faces around the table seemed slightly confused and alarmed at this and the Archmage's eyes raked the assemblage before he replied, "These men here," he indicated the elven and dwarven lords, "have been the allies of Shandrilos for some time now. They have shared their knowledge of the goblin tribes with me and thus forewarned us. I invited them here, but I could not be sure of the response they would receive and they rightly felt that they would be at risk in our lands where they have not always been well received."

"And for good reason," Sir Arleas muttered.

The Archmage ignored the comment, but now he appeared to be talking at the knight from Karodracia, "The response they have received has so far, from some, not fallen far short of their expectations." He paused, "They came here in an effort to end any enmity between our races so that we might ally ourselves against a common foe and so protect our lands and people. If that is not the intention of this council then we are a poor group indeed." He paused again to look at all the lords before him. "I for one welcome these men and the possibilities their presence brings."

Elgon looked around the table in the somewhat subdued atmosphere of the room. The Nordic lords were looking to one another and nodding slightly while the Olmecs were huddled in their prospective groups, with ministers whispering furiously. Sir Arleas sat with his arms folded, unmoved. Elgon knew the Olmecs would be hard to persuade on this issue, they had little problem with the dwarves, but he knew that their Alban faith was somewhat dubious about the nature of elves and many saints past had said the elves were agents of evil or little more than beasts and to be treated as such. They had never allowed elves into their lands and had, as the elves had said, hunted them.

Elgon himself welcomed the possibility of an alliance; the Elder races could dramatically enhance the armies of the Wildlands in both numbers and expertise. The elves had always been a mystery yet they were famed for their knowledge and magical skills, while an alliance with the dwarves promised rich trade in metals and gems as well as weapons.

Suddenly, Elgon found himself on his feet. For a moment he was unsure why he had stood. All eyes turned to him and he took a moment to collect himself. He realised he did want this alliance, that, as the Archmage had said, this was the best chance for their people to survive an attack by the goblins. He realised as he stood there, looking around into the eyes of his fellow leaders that he could not sit back and let others dictate where this debate went, he had to make them understand that they could not let this chance pass.

As his eyes settled on the Olmec ministers he also realised that a call to history would not work. They had no history with the Elder races. No, the Olmecs would need a different approach, an approach that would appeal to their nature, really make them sit up and take notice.

"My lords and ministers, I find that I am deeply disturbed by the revelations I have heard. A goblin army massing in the north, dark dreams and visions from both the druids and the priests; these are grave tidings indeed." Elgon paused and then looked intensely at the Olmecs, "However, what I find more alarming is that what seems like our best chance to enhance our chances of survival, an alliance with people who value this land as much as we do, is being ignored in favour of bickering and old grievances." Elgon could see anger on the faces of several of the Olmec ministers, but he forged on, changing tack to keep the Olmecs off balance, "Shouldn't we be embracing this opportunity, after all it will cost us nothing and gain us troops that we desperately need." He looked at Sir Arleas of Karodracia and asked, "How much would it cost us to hire mercenaries to help us defend our lands, my lord?"

The thin lord knight was taken aback slightly at the direct question though he quickly rallied, "My friend it is not a question of mercenaries. How do we know we can trust…"

Elgon cut him off, "How much would it cost?"

Sir Arleas was even more taken aback by the steely insistence in Elgon's voice and struggled to respond, "It's hard to say…" he stuttered, "Calonian mercenaries will usually work for a couple of coppers a day…"

Before the Lord of Karodracia could add more, Elgon switched his attention to the shrewd banking lord of Lauria, "Perhaps you could do the calculations, my lord; say five thousand mercenaries at two coppers a day for a year?" Elgon mused.

The lord of Lauria looked at him, a thin smile on his face and his eyes hooded; non-committal. He didn't answer so Elgon answered for him. "Around forty thousand in gold?" He asked and the close-mouthed lord of Lauria nodded almost imperceptibly. Elgon looked around the table, his arms wide and a look of mock wonder on his face. "I don't know about the rest of you, but that is almost the revenue for my whole province for a year," Elgon could see the Nordic lords nodding and looking at one another in agreement, "and that's just the mercenaries pay." He continued, forcing the point, "I wouldn't even hazard a guess at how much it would cost to house, feed and keep equipped these men, and that's only for a single year!"

Slowly he turned back to face the Olmec ministers and he could see calculating looks on many faces. "Why," he pleaded, "pay all this when we have allies at hand, allies with formidable resources at their disposal." He could see his argument was having an effect. Now to force the point home. "Why, turn away these allies when we have so much to gain from them." He turned to First Minister Aristos Surtez, the wealthy lord of Hadek. He was dressed like a typical Olmec-style patrician, in white toga and sandals over an Etoshan cotton tunic and trousers. Elgon knew First Minister Surtez had little interest in an alliance only that trade remain strong. He was a merchant, shrewd faced, slim and slight of build and had one foot in Wildland affairs and one in the Empire's. His city of Hadek was on the border with the Empire and existed primarily as a stopping point for traders when crossing the Barrier Mountains. The city spanned a deep valley in the high pass, a logical stopping point for caravans. Elgon also knew that the city had also developed a close link with the hill dwarves who lived to the west of the pass in the high valleys. He also knew the trading benefits of this alliance had made them a rich city. "Some amongst us already benefit from an alliance." Elgon glanced meaningfully to the other Olmec lords before taking his seat. He knew they all were envious of the control on trade that the Hadek merchants had on dwarven-made goods that were so highly sought after throughout the Wildlands and the Empire to the south.

His little speech was met with whispers from the Olmecs while the Nordic lords slapped the table in agreement. Elgon could see that Aristos Surtez was angry, but he could not risk a retort without making it seem like he was going against an alliance in order to protect his unique trade. Such was not Sir Arleas' concern. He rose fluidly from his seat and leaned with his fists on the table. He took a deep breath and then looked up and to the side, addressing Elgon directly, his voice steely though restrained.

"I will not dispute that mercenaries will cost or that it will hurt our people to pay for such, but as you say this is a grave threat and we need to take grave measures to protect ourselves. I will also not dispute that an alliance with the dwarves would bring us a formidable ally both in terms of warriors and trade." He stopped to nod respectfully at the dwarf lords across the table, who sat in stony silence. They were still wary and unusually quiet.

Sir Arleas continued, "However, I do not understand how you can claim that these..." he gestured at the elven lords, who were also staying unusually quiet, "are somehow automatically trustworthy."

Out of the corner of his eye, Elgon saw the grey elf lay a calming hand on the fierce female, nothing else gave any indication that the elves even heard the whip lean lord of Karodracia.

Sir Arleas continued, "The dwarves have always dealt honourably with our people, but these 'elves' have been a constant threat to us. They hunt our people, they have sought no contact or understanding with us, nor have they ever proved they can do aught except ambush innocents from hiding."

Elgon could see that Sir Arleas' words were starting to have an effect on the elven lords and so it seemed could the Archmage who rose with a fierce frown on his pale face. "You go too far, my lord of Karodracia. You see things only from your own point of view."

"Go too far, Baden!" Sir Arleas barked. "I have not gone far enough. Our own saints tell us to beware these people and you expect us to ally with them?" The sharp faced knight shook his head and then looked straight at the Archmage, "How can you expect us to trust these people, Baden?" he asked earnestly. "They have shown us nothing but distrust and hatred."

Elgon looked at the knight lord who stood there almost rigid with emotion; his face looking almost like carved wood it was so angular and taut. Elgon realised that the knight was torn. He was an honourable man who wanted the best for his people, but he was also a man who had been raised with the rigid rule of Saint Karodra and had spent much of his life and that of his men patrolling the forest roads of the southern Wildlands, roads often dotted with the corpses of those who strayed too far off the forest trails. To the knights of Karodra the elves were little different to the goblins and trolls. Elgon wasn't sure how the Archmage would answer; he wasn't sure how he could. How do you convince a man that his beliefs and life experiences are wrong?

Surprisingly, it wasn't the Archmage who answered the knight; it was the grey elf lord. His voice drifted almost musically across the room, "Might I answer that, my lord Archmage?"

The Archmage's dark brows rose in surprise as he looked at the elf's implacable features. He nodded and gestured for the elf to rise while he retook his seat.

Elgon looked to Sir Arleas to see his response. Strangely, the fervent knight did not become angry, but he looked at the elf almost hungrily, like he needed understanding, needed to have his mind put at ease. Gently, Sir Arleas slid back into his seat and silence descended on the room.

The grey elflord rose smoothly and his smoke grey alien eyes swept the room. His face was almost serene and no emotion showed on the pale shimmering skin of his face.

"I have heard your arguments, your problems and your views. What I would like to add now are those of my people, for it seems many of you understand us little... and with good reason." He paused and looked to his own people sat around him seeming to silently seek their opinion, their agreement.

"We are a proud people, sometimes too proud. Once we were a great people. This land was ours and we were the land, we loved it and laboured to make it fruitful, we found magics and crafts that were wondrous and then..." he paused meaningfully, "it was all torn from us. An evil came to our lands and our people and visited such destruction on us that we could not recover from it. Even now, centuries later we are a tiny spark compared to the blazing fire our people once were, and that spark could be snuffed out in an instant no matter what my people may think." A pained look ghosted across his calm face and he passed his hand across his face in an unfamiliar gesture. "As I said we are a proud people. It is hard for us to admit that we are not what we once were. In fact we are a frightened people."

"For so long we have struggled against everyone, convinced we could survive against any odds without the need for others, but that is not the case. It is clear now that we cannot again let our pride allow us to make mistakes that could destroy us. That tiny spark, that is my people, is too precious and too fragile to risk. We risked once and almost lost everything." His fine, upswept grey brows came down in a frown. "Now we must change our ways, we must learn to trust." With a slight lowering of his head, he turned to look directly at the lord of Karodracia who sat seeming lost in thought, his eyes distant. "We have spent many years protecting what we saw as ours, we have savagely made no distinctions between those who come into our woods because we have trusted no one. We have defended and never sought to find understanding." He paused and again his alien grey eyes swept the room. "Perhaps now it is time we found that understanding before the evil is once again visited on all our people?"

Silence fell again as the slim, cloaked figure of the elf lord gracefully sat. No one moved, even the incessant chat of the Olmec advisors had stopped as all paused to take in what they had heard. In the end it was the saintly old Abbot who broke the quiet.

"I thank you, my lord" he said gravely to the elf and then he turned, "and I thank you, my lord Archmage for your forethought in this time, for having the vision to invite these Elder lords and for having the courage to see a way through the coming darkness."

The ancient monk took a deep breath and his spare-framed chest rose and fell beneath the carpet of his deep beard. He blinked his deep blue eyes and his sombre voice began again strongly, his feelings clear, but calm, "It is true that many of the ancient writings of the Books of the Saints condemn those who are not human as agents of evil yet if we look to the example of Blessed Alba himself, he never once condemned any race as evil nor did he say that evil existed purely in one creed or kind. Evil is shown by its deeds and although many people of our land have seen the elves as killers, never once did we consider our own actions in these lands."

The venerable abbot shifted his piercing gaze to the Olmec leaders. "If a man came into our home and claimed it as his own, would we not defend it? If a man threatened our family and our friends, would we not defend them?" He shook his head heavily and closed his eyes sadly. "Too long have we seen things only from our own selfish point of view. That must stop. That way leads to disaster and darkness. I have foreseen that without an alliance of all free peoples, we will fail and if we fail, a much darker future will follow; a future so dark that my heart and mind flee from it."

Sitting up straight and tall, Grand Abbot Alinus looked resolutely at the Olmec ministers. "I and my order welcome the elves and dwarves at our table in an effort to find peace and to make an alliance against the dark future I see ahead of us."

Elgon could see the faces of the Olmec leaders and ministers practically agog. The abbot was going against their beliefs and the religious traditions of his own faith yet such was the ancient holy man's reputation. He was not afraid of controversy or going against dogma. The problem for the Olmecs was that the Grand Abbot was the nearest thing to a head of the Alban religion in the Wildlands despite the influence of the Karodran order. An agreement from him completely undermined the Olmec provinces religious opposition to the elves, though Elgon had no doubt that the Karodrans would have something to say about it.

"However," the Grand Abbot continued, "I do not feel it is appropriate for these..." He waved his arm at the warriors on the wall opposite him, "to stay any longer." He looked at the Archmage, "They have served their purpose and your point was well made, but now we must try to form an alliance peaceably and the presence of these warriors will only jeopardise those efforts."

The Archmage looked at the lords who were nodding their agreement and then turned his attention to the dwarves who nodded firmly. The Archmage turned his attention to the elves on his right. Elgon watched them intently. He saw the ghost haired elf lord look to his fellows on his left and receive the slightest of nods. He then looked to his right where the elven woman sat. Her face was stony and for a moment she gave no indication before finally giving a stiff nod.

The grey elf rose to his feet and looked around the table, "We agree," he said calmly before turning to the warriors behind him. "Hironsar Tath'Delsis, please return to the corridor without and send half of our men back to the upper hall. Leave the rest in the corridor."

The elven warrior nodded.

Silently, the elven warriors turned and began to file out with little more than a whisper of cloth on stone. The grey elf lord turned smoothly and looked to the dwarves enquiringly. They nodded and, without turning, the small, scarred dwarf in the middle held up his hand and made a gesture while barking an abrupt command. With clear discipline, the dwarven warriors turned sharply, stamped their steel shod boots in unison and marched out of the hall, joining the elven warriors who seemed to glide in comparison to the clanging, stomping dwarves. Everyone else in the hall was silent. The giant doors swung to and abruptly the hall was completely silent.

Chapter 16

THE CONCLAVE DIVIDED

In ancient times there were said to have been three kingdoms of the dwarven people. These were named Findreth, Ezelchor and Azerl. However, these kingdoms were said to be so far into the north of the world that they were covered in ice and snow, and that the dwarves lived deep below the mountains of the north. The roads that connected them to the elven kingdoms ran far underground. Dwarves from these ancient kingdoms came south to work and eventually settled in the lands of the elves, adding their skill as artisans and engineers. This is the origin of the great schism in the dwarven race that split the hill dwarves who came south from the mountain dwarves of the north.

From 'The nature of the Elder' by Melkor Erin, Archmage of Shandrilos, BY1303

The mage watched the elven warriors leave. He was practically in a panic. The possibility of an alliance between the Elder races and the men of the Wildlands was impossible and yet here they were. The mage sat quietly, his mind racing. He paid little heed to the debate that was going on around him. He was hearing it and digesting it, but he could not stop his mind from imagining all kinds of scenarios, but foremost in all of them was that his own cruel master was an elf!

The mage could see himself rapidly becoming a real puppet to his elven overlord, and one that would soon be beyond use if this alliance was the prelude to the conquest that he suspected it was. The poor deluded Archmage; he believed these elves were here to help. He hadn't an inkling of what was really happening. The mage could see it clearly now. His master was obviously manipulating the goblins in the north to make the leaders of the Wildlands think they needed the elves as allies. What they were really doing was taking their enemy into their midst! The mage had to do something, but what?

He needed to be careful to hide his involvement in any opposition to the elves. He could not get directly involved in the talks anyway, save through the Archmage and that wasn't going to happen. The mage would have to wait until this initial council session was over and then try to undermine any alliance with the Elder races. The Olmecs, particularly the Karodracians, were the obvious weak point, but he could also make things difficult for the Archmage with his fellow members of the Conclave, none of them had agreed to the Elder races being invited to the council!

That was an excellent idea.

Perhaps he could even get one or more of the others to question the Archmage, let the others lead instead of himself. He needed to keep himself in the background. The Archmage would be focused on the Great Council; he wouldn't notice the mage enlisting others to his cause. He began to carefully scribe on the loose sheets of parchment he had been given for note taking.

'Yes,' he thought, as he wrote, 'there would be cracks to exploit. He just had to be patient. Again, the mage wondered briefly what his dark master's full intentions were. Would he kill all humans who it was clear he hated, or just take over? Either way it was not part of the mage's plans to be killed or enslaved. However, the mage had to be careful in how he split the council, he needed some unity if he was eventually to take control of the Wildlands himself and face his master!

Baden Erin was struggling to contain his elation. It was clear that he had been right in thinking the Elder races would not be easily received, but never could he have expected things to go so smoothly or Lord Elgon and Grand Abbot Alinus to be so eloquent. Nevertheless, he knew he couldn't relax now, the three races were at the same table, but that had to be maintained and there were so many other issues yet untouched upon. Baden wasn't sure whether the Lord of Karodracia would be swayed even by such a respected man as the Grand Abbot and, if he left the council, whether the other Olmec lords would follow on mass. Baden was fairly convinced that many of them were still unconvinced about the Elder lords. Now had to be the best time to push for an agreement, at least on the continued presence of the elves and dwarves at this council, a more formal alliance and an agreement on what direction such a new alliance would take could be thrashed out in the days ahead.

Baden quickly calculated. It was clear that of the leaders of the twelve provinces, his own vote, that of Elgon of Ostia, Grand Abbot Alinus, and the three Nordics lords would be in favour of the elder lords joining the council. However, that only made six of the twelve and a majority was needed for an agreement. He was sure that Sir Arleas was still unconvinced, it would take more than talk with him, it would take time. However, had Elgon's clever argument swayed the Olmec lords? Not Surtez of Hadek, he was sure, nor Del Aro of Torunsport, he was too much the coward to go with such a decision, but what of Di Vorseck of Lauria and the boy Serales of Kalizern, not to mention the young Zeras Ithill of Katurem. The last had said nothing throughout the proceedings. Would he be swayed? Baden was torn. He looked intently at the darkly handsome heir to the thieves' city. The boy looked impressed with the Elder races, wonder had flashed across his face and in no way had he looked angry or shocked by them. Could Baden risk throwing this to a vote now? If he delayed he might lose those that he already had.

It must be now, he thought, before the Olmecs gather their thoughts and their resistance. Alinus had thrown them, as had Elgon, yet if they collected their thoughts they could muddy the waters and obscure what Baden thought was now clear; a deadly threat was coming at them from the north and the Elder races were here in good faith willing to stand with them against that threat.

Quickly, Baden rose; a dark shadow, "I call for a vote. We must decide whether we will accept the clan chiefs of the Elder races into our councils in order to combat the growing threats from the north. What say you all?"

There were a few growls of dissent, but then Elgon of Ostia raised his hand, quickly followed by Grand Abbot Alinus. The others slowly cast their votes.

Silently, Baden counted, seven in favour, five against! Zeras Ithill had voted in favour! He could feel a smile starting to spread on his face, but this froze as he saw Borus Del Aro labour to his feet.

"My lords, I cannot say that I am happy with this situation." he sneered. "However, there are other considerations. By including…" he waved in the general direction of the elves, "these new members we have in effect doubled our numbers. Are we suggesting that they have an equal vote in our councils or merely one vote for all?" he questioned. "After all they do not represent as many as we do."

There were calls of agreement from the Olmecs. They would be prepared to argue now for the minor points of the agreement. They might have lost the initial battle, but they would make the aftermath difficult in the details. However, Baden knew that if he could take advantage of the late hour and push these issues back until after the great feast tomorrow that officially opened the Grand Council, much of these details could be thrashed out in small meetings and agreements behind the scenes.

"I agree my Lord of Torunsport that these matters need to be resolved and we must decide when." Baden could see the frown of consternation on the round face of Del Aro. "I believe that such a discussion should be first on our agenda for our next meeting." He smiled and took his seat as the lords turned their attention to the matters for discussion in the coming days. Many of the items were the mundane matters that had dominated previous meetings, but now that the threat from the north was clear, it needed little coaxing to make this a prime feature of the agenda. The Olmecs still pushed for more details, but the Elder were at the table and that was the main thing.

The elves and dwarves remained silent for the rest of the meeting and only spoke to make a formal withdrawal as the meeting broke up. Baden was sure that they would now go and have their own discussions on what had occurred here and Baden would seek them out later. He had much to discuss with them. He had not had the chance for more than a brief meeting before coming here and he needed to know the elves' minds and characters. What he knew of them came mainly from his friend Storlin, chief of the Swiftaxe Dwarves. He had known Storlin for many years, as had his father before him. Both of them had secretly used this friendship to forge greater understanding between Shandrilos and the dwarves; he and his father had been meeting with the dwarven leaders for many years. This had led to the connection with the elves, but he knew so little about them.

Could he trust them?

The dwarven lords believed so, but the elves were largely unknown even to them. Their contact was only sporadic and for trade; the elves had always resisted closer contact even with their ancient allies. That was why it had been such a surprise when they had initiated contact with the dwarves only two years ago about creating an alliance. Baden had convinced the dwarven lords already about the necessity of forging a true alliance with the provinces and had planned how to bring the dwarves into the Grand Council. It wouldn't be hard as the dwarves already had trading ties with the cities of Hadek and Sironac, and were positively viewed even by the Olmecs. The chance to include the elves had been too good an opportunity to miss, despite the added complications it could bring. Yet Baden had never spoken with the elves directly until they arrived in the College yesterday. They had arrived in utmost secrecy through paths only they knew. Baden and his most trusted staff had welcomed them and secreted them away until the Grand Council began. It was a massive risk, but one he felt worth it, considering the threat from the north.

As he sat thinking, Baden saw the Olmec lords move off as a group, Korlin Di Vorseck in an ardent discussion with Surtez of Hadek, while Zeras Ithill hovered; waiting it seemed for the golden haired Elgon and the white clad monks of Sironac. Baden had no doubt that the lesser halls and the corridors and apartments would quickly become a hive of political activity.

Behind him, he could hear Atholl Dorard whispering fiercely as he rose to his feet. Baden himself rose and turned to leave through the rear doors, but he found himself confronted by Xameran Uth Altor, Lord of Sorcery with the conniving Atholl Dorard at his shoulder. The other members of the conclave also stopped, caught by the swift urgency of Xameran's movements and the uncharacteristically fierce look on his usually amiable face.

"My lord Archmage, I must protest this... this..." he struggled for words, "betrayal of our trust! When did we agree to this alliance? When were we to become privy to your machinations?" His eyes were flashing and he held his crescent moon topped staff with a white knuckled hand.

Baden looked around and found old Atholl Dorard smiling and nodding his head with Xameran's sentiments.

"Are we not to be trusted, my lord, is that it? Are we agents of this evil of which you are so convinced? So quick you were to cast our vote in favour of this alliance when not once were we given the opportunity to decide on this matter!" stormed the blue robbed sorcerer.

This time more than just the harsh old Enchanter showed agreement with the young head of the school of sorcery.

The stately First Wizard added her voice. "It is true." she began sincerely. "It is not that I would not have been in favour of such an audacious move, it is that you took this decision alone." She frowned. "It was agreed at the very founding of our college that it was not to be led by one individual, that the potential in this college was a power too strong to be put in one person's hands. The Assembly of Masters and the Conclave were formed to give a voice to our members, to give a balanced and considered lead to our fellowship."

It was clear to Baden that Zarina Agroda agreed with the results of his decision, but not the manner in which it came about. Baden was on dangerous ground here. He had hoped to avoid this, had hoped that the results of this meeting would convince the Conclave of the necessity of his secrecy in setting this up. He was sure that most of the Conclave would understand that, but Xameran would not it seemed, nor would Atholl Dorard, the irascible old enchanter would be difficult simply out of spite. The lord of sorcerors might not be that petty, but he would not stand to be left out of any decisions. He was a man who loved his position and the power it brought. He would not allow that power to be ignored. Baden raised his hand in a placatory gesture. "Xameran, you must understand the nature of the threat, it was imperative I kept this secret..."

"Why..." the sorcerer lord interrupted, "because you knew we would not agree with you? Is that not the reason, because you did not trust our judgement?" He was fierce as he looked around briefly at his fellow masters including them in his argument. "We are too blind, too short sighted for our great leader it seems." He mocked. "We are just children to be led."

"Xameran, please?" Zarina pleaded. "This is not the time or the place."

The blue robbed sorcerer caught a hold of his emotion and the familiar smile returned to his features. "No, you are right, of course, my dear lady." He turned back to face Baden, "This is not the time or the place, but we must have the time soon. I will not allow this usurpation of our rights to go on in this most important of times. We must meet in formal session. We must call the Assembly of Masters…"

The Allseer interrupted, "We cannot do that now, most of the masters are involved in organising events here!"

"They can spare time for this!" Xameran snapped. "We will call the masters and we will debate properly the way we wish to go."

Baden's mind was racing. He knew he couldn't afford to lose the time organising and debating in a full council. He had delicate negotiations to make and orchestrate. The alliance would not succeed without the most careful guidance.

"Is this the will of you all?" Baden asked pulling himself up straight. He looked around him. Zarina Agroda, Atholl Dorard and, of course, Xameran Uth Altar were nodding and slowly the others, all save Eliantha Shamass who knew the extremes he had been to, began to nod. He could not blame them, he had acted alone, but then sometimes difficult decisions needed to be made alone, a leader could not always defer to his council, though this was not the time to point that out.

"Very well, we will have this assembly, but not until the Grand Council is over." he said firmly, though Xameran was already shaking his head.

"That is not acceptable, it must be before the next session, we need…"

Anger rose in the Archmage. He would not tolerate this now when things were so carefully balanced. Baden cut the sorcerer off, "Then you will have it without me and you will organise it yourself…" he stabbed a finger at the lord of sorcerors, "and you will use no member of my staff!" Baden finished with fury in his voice, and with that he swept past the others and out of the hall.

'Damn him!' The mage thought as he watched the Archmage leave. 'Damn him!' Without his agreement or staff, things would be virtually impossible to organise quickly. 'No,' he corrected himself, 'not impossible merely difficult.' If he kept manipulating the others to take this further they would push harder to make a speedy Assembly of Masters possible.

"Perhaps we should leave this until after the Council as he suggests," Zarina said into the silence.

The mage was thinking furiously, his mind whirling through scenarios.

Eliantha, the Mage Master, cut in. "Don't you see that he had to do things this way? Secrecy was imperative for all our safety!" she insisted.

Zarina Agroda responded gently, "We cannot allow him to abuse his position like this. The fundamental beliefs of this college are at stake. If we let him get away with it now, we give him a mandate to continue and where then could he lead us?" She looked at each of the leaders in turn. "We do not even have anything other than his word for this threat he speaks of, that and the word of one or two others who could easily have been misled. We also do not know these Elder lords or their intentions; we do not know of what the Elder races are capable."

"How do we know the Archmage is not manipulating us all to further his ambitions to unite this land!" the mage put in, "You'll notice his so-called sources of information for this dark threat have not been questioned. The Grand Council was too dazzled by who they were! Elves and dwarves, the Elder races come to save us!" the mage finished sarcastically.

The ever officious Zarina Agroda glanced at the mage in annoyance for a moment and then pushed on with her argument, though she could see some were still disbelieving. "We all know that he wants what is best, but if he succeeds in uniting this land, can we trust he will still defer to others around him... the Conclave... the Council itself? Is he becoming a man intent on ruling and ruling alone? He must show now that he will trust us and defer to the will of the Conclave or we must oppose him as a potential tyrant." Zarina looked at Eliantha and pleaded, "I have always known Baden Erin to have good intentions, but the road to damnation is paved with good intentions and people have been corrupted by power before."

"Nonsense, Zarina. You're mad if you think Baden would do such a thing. He is no man in love with power." the tall, tawny haired Chief Druid scoffed.

"And yet he refuses to answer to us. He refuses to see that he has abused his position." The mage let this hang in the air for a moment before continuing, knowing they could not refute his words. "We must call the Assembly. The Archmage must be held to account." He could see they were reluctant in their agreement, but an agreement was all he needed. "Will you all call your masters?" Again there were reluctant nods. "We will meet tomorrow morning before the ceremonies begin. Let us say three hours after dawn in the Assembly Hall."

"But what of the Archmage and his masters?" Zarina protested, shock on her noble face.

"We have given him the opportunity and he has scorned it. What more would you have us do?" the mage pressed back.

Zarina was at a loss. She firmly believed in the laws of the College and was scrupulously fair. To her the Archmage should be there, but he was unwilling. Zarina blinked her eyes and her lips moved, but then resignation took control of her features. "Then we will proceed," Zarina sighed, "and hope the Archmage sees sense."

The mage watched as the rest of the Conclave slowly left the hall, their faces serious. A smile spread slowly on his face. With a little luck the Archmage would ignore the Assembly, assume that they would simply chastise him. He would be too busy firming up the cracks in his new-born alliance to take things too seriously, the mage thought. Oh, but the Assembly would do more than merely chastise the Archmage. Oh no it would be more than a slap on the wrist that the mage would engineer, he would see the Archmage removed and a new, more suitable Archmage chosen. Oh, the mighty Baden Erin would not see that coming.

Of course such a decision would be impossible without more serious accusations against the Archmage, but those could be arranged, especially with investigations into the strange goings on in the college of late... as well as those that would happen tonight... as soon as he had arranged for them to happen that was.

A small laugh escaped his lips and echoed around the now silent and empty hall. The mage got a grip of himself. He would need help and he had to move swiftly. He could not let this opportunity pass. To think he had spent the last few years trying to engineer such a corner to back the Archmage into and now it had just dropped into his lap without effort.

It was indeed true, that all good things come to those who wait, he thought. Smiling, he left the hall.

Chapter 17

DECISIONS

For the Nordic, Elves are seen as kin to the gods. They are seen as masters of nature and its magic, in tune with the spirits of the elements. To some degree, all of the Elder races are seen in this way, even the races viewed by the Nordic as inherently evil. It is easy to see the dwarves are linked to the earth such is their knowledge of stone, metallurgy and alchemy. Even the goblin race show a knowledge of nature that is in advance of our own.

Excerpt from 'A strange land; the Wildlands of Darylor' by Grand Abbot Alinus Quan Sirona, BY1320

"All elves have an affinity with magic, but all elves can't know spell casting, Arkadi." Bear put in lightly and Arkadi looked at him darkly.

"Do you want to bet your life on the possibility that these ones don't!" he snapped.

"There is no reason to," came Rebba's call from the back where she had stood still and quiet. Her voice was thick with worry. "I have been trying to get a feel for these creatures. My senses are attuned to creatures close to the elements and all elves are such..." she finished softly.

Darin watched with amusement as Zara, Bear and Arkadi looked expectantly at Rebba for some moments, but the druid remained quiet.

"And..." Zara hissed finally, narrowly beating Arkadi to an exasperated response as the silence became too much.

Darin noticed Rebba's brow furrow slightly as she looked at Zara, the two had never been overly fond of one another, though Rebba would never really show it. Rebba was a warm-hearted woman, but she was sometimes prone to brooding and solitude. Zara was loud and brash and naturally tended to try to be the centre of attention and to dominate in most situations. This grated on the quiet druid who preferred to be less forthright and more introspective, but she was too polite to say anything.

"And...," Rebba emphasised strongly, "there are at least three elves out there who have a strong talent in the mysteries."

Everyone seemed interested now, though Nat Bero never took her eyes off the doorway. Arkadi made an impatient motion with his hand for Rebba to continue. It seemed to Darin that Arkadi was a little irritated, perhaps that his own senses could not match Rebba's.

"One is the leader, he is the one whose voice we have been hearing. He is talented but his talent is less than the two who stand with him. They have power as great if not more so than I sense in Arkadi here." she finished nodding at her old study partner.

"Well they should be a push over then," chortled Darin, "Arkadi struggled even to start a fire, the last time we were out in Redvale." He laughed quietly, a broad smile on his face.

Zara grunted something nasty under her breath.

No one else laughed.

Darin looked at Arkadi. He was surprised to see the mage was angry. It dawned on him that he had touched on the one thing that Arkadi was very sensitive about. He took his skills as a mage very seriously. The knight was about to say he was only joking; Arkadi had been very drunk, when Bear spoke.

"As I recall Darin, you were so drunk that night that you couldn't even tie your boot laces. You were finding it hard to put a sentence together let alone a spell!"

Arkadi smiled slightly at this. However, all turned serious as the voice called out again.

"Why don't we make a bargain?"

Zara, Bear and Arkadi looked at each other and then at Darin. He shrugged at them and gestured for Bear to continue. Bear looked a little peeved at this. Nevertheless, he spun to face the doorway and shouted.

"What kind of bargain?"

"Give us what we want and you can go free," was the quick response.

"How do we know we can trust you? You have attacked us without provocation." Bear replied quickly, though Darin was now a little confused as to what it was they wanted and he could see that Arkadi and Nat were thinking the same thing from their expressions. It was no doubt going through everyone else's mind too, though he could not see the others' faces.

"We only want what is ours. You took it and we then took you for common thieves." The voice paused, "Of course, you have my word as a *Hironsar* that we will not harm you."

"As a what?" Zara queried in a confused voice. She looked to Arkadi who shrugged.

Bear looked hard at Zara, his face saying clearly, 'Does it matter right now!'

Bear shouted "We need time to discuss this."

There was a pregnant silence and then the voice called "You have five…" it paused as if finding the words hard, "…minutes."

Bear turned back to face everybody, a worried look on his pale face. No one seemed ready to speak so Darin put in quietly, "The important question is what is it that they want?" He looked around casually at his friends. He had no idea himself, but he was genuinely surprised that no one else seemed to know. He had expected Arkadi or Bear to at least have an idea. Everyone began looking at everyone else, but blank looks and shrugs were all that were returned.

"Well, if what they're after is an idiot, they have their pick here!" Darin muttered, only half joking.

"We should probably send out the biggest idiot then Darin, so out you go!" Arkadi responded harshly.

"Owh, bitchy, bitchy!" mocked Darin in a high pitched voice and smiled. He then noticed Bear wasn't smiling.

"Would you just quit it, Darin. This is not the time to jest. We need to think!"

Darin was about to joke again, but took one look at Bear's twitching jaw muscles and savage frown and thought better of it.

"We cannot take this lightly." Bear snapped.

"Oh come on Bear, we have faced these kind of odds before." Darin said encouragingly, "Even three magic users isn't an obstacle, we've got

Arkadi, Rebba, Garon..." he paused to smile reassuringly at the broad frowning face of his friend, "not to mention you, yourself."

Bear looked at him like he was insane. Darin looked around. The others were regarding him with similar looks. Darin realised that the others perhaps weren't so optimistic about their chances.

"Yeah and what of those huge creatures," Bear suddenly whispered fiercely. "You remember?" He nodded at Darin, his eyebrows raised in question, "Looked like a troll only bigger." he hinted angrily.

Darin grunted in reluctant acknowledgement. He had forgotten about them. How you could forget about a creature the size of a small house he didn't know, but he had. 'Must have been all those bugs' he thought wryly.

"Bear is right, this is more serious than you think." put in Rebba forcefully, "I have been pushing my senses further." She paused to look around. "We are not only facing the enemies out there..." She stopped and looked at her friends hard.

"Your talent for the melodramatic pause is impressive, Rebba," snapped the usually patient Garon who had remained quiet throughout, "but for Alba's sake tell us what you sensed!"

It was now clear that the big monk was on the verge of panic.

"You were right Zara," Rebba continued, looking at the lithe chainmail clad warrior, "there are six elves out there," she looked to Arkadi, "along with a near equal number of goblins to whom they seem closely linked."

That was one of the weird things about this. Everyone knew that elves and goblins were mortal enemies; they slew one another whenever they met... and enjoyed it. At least that's what they did in the wilds that Darin knew about, but maybe these were not normal elves and goblins. Not that he knew what a normal elf was like. However, the goblins he had spent most of his time killing were grey, yellow or even green skinned not black as the night like these.

"There are two of those huge creatures," Rebba said looking now at Bear, "along with three of those insect-like creatures."

Rebba took a deep breath and an exasperated snort came from the impatient Zara at the delay. "Plus there are another five searching the tunnels leading here. They seem unaware that we have been found."

"Though the longer we wait the more chance there is of them finding that out." remarked Arkadi to Bear.

"Yes, two to one odds are bad but three to one is pretty much terminal." Garon muttered gloomily.

"We need a plan, Bear." Darin suggested, "Something to even the odds."

"Wait," called Rebba, "there is more!"

The others all turned to her and Darin saw the fear in the druid's eyes.

"This group is only one of at least three! I can sense others at the extremes of my range. There is a huge labyrinth down here and it would make sense that similar groups to these would be sent out to search them. If we do not get out of here soon we never will."

All of the group was as stunned as Darin at Rebba's revelations.

"Are you sure, Rebba?" Arkadi called out in alarm. "Can you sense so far accurately?"

"Rebba looked back at him, "The rock down here thrums with elemental energy, Arkadi. It makes my senses so much more potent. However, I could be wrong, but only on the details. Fifteen stand against us outside. It may only be smaller groups elsewhere, but I don't think so."

Abruptly, Bear snarled, "Marvelous, bloody marvellous!"

Darin could see the big man was angry now.

Bear turned to Nat and Zara and pointed savagely at them, "You said this was going to be simple," he hissed. "A lucky break it was finding that map" he mimicked Zara's words from earlier. "It will be quickly in, grab some old treasures and then quickly out; money in the bank!" Bear threw up his hands and wandered over to the wall, angrily kicking it. "What did we find down here?" he snapped, looking up at the ceiling, "Nothing, not a thing, except for hellish creatures who wish us dead!"

Nat Bero looked warily over to where Bear was taking out his aggression. She looked back at Zara, then Arkadi, then Darin, but said nothing.

"No one could know this was going to happen." Zara said defensively, "And we haven't had the chance to search properly."

Darin saw Bear spin around angrily and move towards Zara. He moved to block the angry Bear.

"Search properly! We've managed to find no treasure and plenty of trouble and you think that we are going to get the chance to search further?" Bear asked incredulously. "We'll be lucky if any of us get out of here alive!"

"Calm down, Bear" Darin said, putting his hand on Bear's broad chest."It was a good idea, Bear." He continued carefully, "It's just things haven't gone our way." Darin stared hard into Bear's angry eyes and saw the anger recede slightly.

"This is not helping," Rebba said worriedly, gnawing on her fingernails, a habit she had not exhibited since they were youngsters.

Arkadi nodded his agreement, along with Garon.

"We need a plan, and from what Rebba says, we need one quickly before the odds get even worse." Arkadi stated firmly.

Darin watched as Bear began to nod slowly. Darin could see the big man was now thinking hard. Bear sheathed his broad sword, took off his Nordic-style horned helm and rubbed his bald head anxiously. He began to pace up and down, his armoured boots rattling against the stone floor.

"We need to deal with those two troll-like creatures quickly, neutralise them or else they could do us serious damage. We also have no chance of getting out in a hurry with those brutes blocking the way" Bear mused aloud. He turning as he paced to look expectantly at Arkadi.

"I could possibly deal with them, though I'd be better suited to dealing with those elven magic users," he stated.

Just what we need, thought Darin, another debate.

Rebba cut across Darin's thoughts, "I can deal with those huge creatures."

Arkadi looked quizzically at Rebba who replied to the unspoken question a little shakily. "I'm not saying I could kill them both, but I can neutralise them for a while." she finished firmly.

Bear looked at Arkadi and then at the druid. "Are you sure, Rebba? This is not something with which we can afford to make a mistake."

Rebba looked angry for the first time as she responded, "I may not have Arkadi's knowledge or range of attacking spells, but I do have talent." She finished in a tone that brooked no denial, "I can hold those two long enough if the rest of you can finish the others?"

Bear seemed to measure Rebba's resolve and after a moment gave a satisfied nod, though Arkadi and Zara still seemed dubious.

"Perhaps I am missing something," Nat Bero, quietly put in.

"You usually do." Darin said smiling.

The huntress ignored his comment.

"Isn't anyone going to even ask them what it is they want?" said the archer, adjusting her longbow over her shoulder.

"We haven't picked anything up down here, Nat." responded Zara harshly. "We can't have what they want because we don't have anything we did not have when we set off. That is unless you think that they are after Garon's underwear for the unique scent it has now acquired." she finished nastily.

Darin sniggered, but Bear was looking penetratingly at Nat.

"We haven't picked anything up, have we, Nat?" He asked slowly, looking at the leather clad huntress. "You didn't find anything while you were scouting ahead did you?"

Everyone else was now looking at the long limbed archer. She seemed genuinely shocked at Bear's question.

"It's not something you have forgotten is it; something small or insignificant perhaps?"

Nat Bero was shaking her head at Bear's question. Bear looked hard at her and everyone else turned to look at her.

"Honestly," she cried, "I haven't picked anything up. I just thought... well, that is... I..." She stumbled to a halt and looked apologetically at the others.

Zara tuned away in disgust while Garon, seeking to help said, "Perhaps we should find out what it is they want?"

Arkadi said thoughtfully, "Although we would like to know what it is they want, if we show our ignorance of what they want by asking then surely we put ourselves at a severe disadvantage." Arkadi looked around at faces, looking for agreement.

Darin noticed that it was obvious Nat did not really understand. Darin did not want to admit he wasn't that sure either.

Arkadi went on. "One possibility is that they will think we are lying and trying to take what they want and so attack instantly or... think us fools for not knowing. Either way it does us no good to let them know of our ignorance." Arkadi looked around, finally focusing on Nat and nodded at her.

The tall archer nodded slowly.

"It's like gambling," Zara put in acerbically to the huntress, "you don't show your opponents your hand in order to win!"

Nat glared at Zara who ignored her.

"There is no point to this discussion," Zara snapped angrily. "Say we did know or find out what it is they want? Even if we gave it to them, they'll still kill us. They just want an easy fight. They'll probably have an ambush waiting for us as soon as we leave this room!" She smoothly sheathed both her blades across her back in one practised fluid motion and turned to Darin, Arkadi and Bear. "This is wasting time. Rebba says she can hold off the two large creatures, but what about those other bastards?" Without waiting for an answer Zara continued, "I suggest that you, Darin, and you," she pointed at Bear, "take out the three bug creatures as quickly as you can. That means that Nat can take out the goblins, or at least pin them down while I take the leader, with Arkadi and Garon taking the other two magic users."

"An interesting plan Zara, save it leaves several elves free…" Arkadi began.

Nat Bero cut him off "…and me to take out five!" The tall archer was obviously not happy with the odds.

"And that's if they aren't firing back" put in Garon somewhat subdued and shaky.

Nat Bero continued, "And what if those goblins decide to charge?"

"Oh, life is just full of these uncertainties." Zara snapped back, "We either get them or we don't," she finished firmly.

Zara was always a gambler and strangely it often worked out for her, thought Darin, but… he paused in thought, was that really true? Zara did have good luck, yet as Bear often pointed out, she seemed to use it all up on the little things and then all the big things would fall apart. Darin had thought this wasn't quite true; Zara continued to survive the fights and battles as a mercenary and had made a lot of money, but as Zara herself had said earlier at the inn, her life had been all up and down and her latest partner had just run off with her earnings from her last three ventures, leaving her finances severely dented. Added to this a previous lover had taken the town house she had bought in Ostia and another, the farmstead she'd bought in Redvale. Now she was currently reduced to her 'trading' business which was a front for a smuggling operation.

"You know chancing things on one role of the dice may be your best idea," Bear snapped, "but I'd prefer a more thorough plan."

"Bear, there is no other way. There are too few of us to take into account everybody." Zara insisted. "If you and Darin can take care of those bugs quickly enough then you can attack the goblins."

Bear did not look convinced.

"We can do it, Bear," Darin said happily, "those bugs are no match for us."

Bear still did not look convinced. "Is there any way you can neutralise a few of them in one attack, Arkadi?" Bear asked hopefully.

"There is, but that would leave me open to those elven mages," he answered bitterly, though he then looked up hopefully, "What about you, Bear?"

"I have a few tricks up my sleeve, but they are spells to cast on myself not on others, that takes much less concentration as you don't have to overcome your opponent's resistance."

Darin thought Bear, had slipped back into lecturing for a moment.

"Combat magic is tricky; attacking with sword and with strong magic at the same time is no easy task." Bear reminded Arkadi.

Arkadi nodded, though Darin himself was none the wiser. He understood the nature of magic like he understood the nature of women; both were a mystery, though one was of far greater interest than the other in his opinion. At least there was a clear benefit to understanding women. This he believed was a noble goal and one to which he could happily dedicate his life.

"There is another problem," Nat Bero put in thoughtfully. She silently moved up to the doorway. She glanced around the edge, quickly pulling her head back, wary of elven archers. "They are just sitting there ready and waiting," she whispered as she moved back from the entrance, "they will not let up their guard as we move out, they will be prepared and will no doubt get in a concerted attack first as we move down the corridor." She moved over to Zara and stretched up to her full height. She looked down angrily at Zara nearly half a foot shorter than she. "How do we get around that and then still take the odds you suggest? At least one or two of us must fall or be injured in that initial rush, unless Elisis, lady of luck, herself runs before us!"

Zara looked up at Nat, "Alright you long streak of piss, you tell me."

Nat Bero blinked warily back at Zara.

"See, all you seem to want to do is throw in problems. Where are your answers?" Zara squared up to her.

"I have an idea." Rebba whispered though no one took any notice as everyone concentrated on Zara and Nat. There was no chance of a fight,

Darin knew, it was all just nerves. Nat stood little chance against Zara and knew it. Added to which, Nat was a natural archer, she preferred to fight from a distance. Although Darin had to admit that took courage. Darin had seen Nat Bero stand firm and slowly take her aim while arrows whizzed around her!

"I have an idea," Rebba repeated again, a little louder.

"What?" asked Darin, taking his eyes of the two glaring women.

"I do actually have an idea of how to even things up." Rebba responded in her quiet voice.

"Really," Zara muttered, "this I have just got to hear." She sneered nastily in Nat's face and then looked at Rebba.

Everyone looked at Rebba.

The quiet druid quickly outlined her plan, and though Darin was dubious, Bear seemed to think it had merit. One of the company would challenge the elven leader to decide the fate of... well whatever it was they wanted. This would distract the elves and their company long enough to allow the rest of the group to get into position. At an agreed point the group would attack, roughly as Zara had outlined, taking the initiative and getting a strong attack in first.

"They'll not go for that!" Zara snorted. "We are not in some knightly tale of honour and justice."

"Elves do tend to have a strong sense of honour from what the old stories suggest," Nat snapped at Zara, obviously still angry.

Darin remembered that Nat had always loved anything to do with elves when they were growing up. She had avidly listened to all the old stories of them.

"Stories!" Zara exclaimed. "We can't rely on stories. We need to be sure."

"I think the leader will go for it Zara," Rebba said looking earnestly at the group. "He seems to have a strong sense of honour from what I can feel of him."

She looked to Arkadi for support, but he just looked at the fiery haired druid with an expression that seemed to say, 'You can sense that?'

"Let's try it," Zara said firmly, completely changing tack, "I like it, it's sneaky, and I think I can take him. There's few who could face me in a duel."

"Very modest of you," Nat Bero muttered.

"No, that would not be a good idea," Arkadi quickly put in, "If there is going to be anyone to fight, it should be Bear."

The mage look at Bear who looked startled.

"You're very quick to put me forward, Arkadi." he shot back. "Very brave of you, but I think Zara or Darin are more accomplished with a blade than me."

"Think, Bear," Arkadi insisted, moving right up to the big man, "This leader has talent. It is likely he would be proficient in using it in combat or he would not be leading this group."

From Bear's face, it was clear that he couldn't help but agreed, though it was also clear that he didn't want to do anything of the sort. Zara was also starting to look a little dubious at the thought of magic being involved.

Bear looked at Rebba, "What do you think? Is he right?"

The cloaked druid pushed her cloak back, showing her leather armour underneath as she clasped her gnarled wooden staff to her chest. She looked down thoughtfully at the floor and whispered, "It is impossible to say… though I would think it likely. He feels more of a man of action than the other two. He would probably be more of a fighter mage like you, Bear."

Zara began to look more uncomfortable. She rubbed her chin and grimaced before looking at Bear. Darin looked at him too and soon everyone was looking at him.

"Damn it!" Darin heard him whisper as he turned away.

Chapter 18

A DUEL

The Ancient Olmec believe that the Great Sky Mother, Ai gave birth to all things and first amongst them was Serris, the Sun God. He in turn created the other gods. Foremost amongst these were the seven greater gods. However, unknown to Serris, his light brought into being darkness where his divine light did not reach. This darkness took form and became Ubukul, the Moon God and for each God Serris created, Ubukul in secret created a dark mockery. This primitive belief system has similarities with that of the Nordic and Etoshans. Into this world of ignorance, Blessed Alba brought the true belief in the one God!

From the Book of Belminian, third book of the Divine Alban Scriptures, circa BY78

Hironsar Dar'Elthon Ath Totheariss was growing impatient, which was an unusual feeling for one of his kind. Elves lived long, but he felt that time was running out for him. His master would not be pleased if he did not complete his mission and quickly. Prince Uh'Ram had been explicit about this task and the prince had not gained the title 'Bloodfire' for being understanding and patient!

This task was imperative and so he had entrusted it to Dar'Elthon. His previous skill in handling delicate matters and his unfailing loyalty to his prince had got him this mission! Dar'Elthon would not have this, his most important task go awry simply because of some 'humans'! He would retrieve the Great Key and give control of the Ways to his prince.

Prince Uh'Ram Bloodfire was one of the most ancient and powerful of the race. He was beloved of the Lords of Night and a demon lord of renown. His knowledge and power were vast and he had planned long and hard to make sure their conquest was assured before it even began. Dar'Elthon was just a small part of that plan, but a crucial one. He knew he had the talent to rise high or he would not have been given this crucial mission. He was also ambitious and determined; one day he would be a *Parinsar* himself. He would be the right hand to Prince Uh'Ram, the Dark One's own grandson and *Kaldesar* of the Divine Avengers.

It was a fine ambition.

Dar'Elthon brought himself back to the here and now. He could not afford to indulge in dreams, especially when they had so nearly slipped away from him. He had lost the Great Key and the humans who carried it in a skirmish in the tunnels. He also knew that the magic users above in their pathetic city, built atop the ruins of a great elven one, might have sensed something was amiss. If so, they would soon be sending down scouts. He could not afford to be detected. His master had been clear that they were not to risk discovery. It was not yet time for open attack. Secrecy was necessary until Prince Uh'Ram had eradicated all possible opposition. He had other plans in motion for dealing with the humans above.

Dar'Elthon found himself striding cat-like up and down, his hands clasped behind his back. He had little time to wait, yet he refused to rush into that corridor and watch those humans slaughter a large section of his command. He could sense that they were not mere mercenaries. This group was well trained and there were also an unusual number of magic users amongst them.

Dar'Elthon himself had not been amongst the group that had battled those who stole the Great Key, but he knew they had magic about them. Magic was rare amongst the 'beast races' and made this group more dangerous. They were also well armed and armoured as *Sar* Gal'Tain had described. It was his error that had lost the group earlier. He would not make that mistake again; *Sar* Gal'Tain's only remains now were ashes on the floor of a chamber to the east. Failure of that kind could not be tolerated.

Dar'Elthon now had the company of thieving humans cornered and sending his own warriors in there would inevitably result in a victory, but a bloody one. Dar'Elthon was not yet ready for that. He had already lost eighteen of his Warparty and refused to lose more. He needed to impress and such a bloody victory against humans would not look good. It would not matter that these were more than ordinary humans. With two cousins pressing for his position in House Totheariss, he could well lose his command and then, soon after, his life as his allies deserted him. A quick and successful mission could see him made a *Gonhironsar*, a commander of a full Warband with a chance at real glory in the wars to come. His family name would rise again and his house would gain favour with Prince Uh'Ram.

House Totheariss had suffered in recent times under his brother's poor leadership. Once the lords of his house had held the title of; *Parinsar*, commander of a whole Battlegroup; and of *Parindar*, chief of a clan. Dar'Elthon believed he could quickly reclaim that eminence. This mission was the first step on his house's, and his own, rise to power.

Abruptly, he stopped as the rough, human voice called out of the darkness. He listened intently letting the translation glamour change the words to his own tongue. He could speak their language somewhat, but preferred to use the glamour. He let the human's words sink in.

What were these creatures up to? Were they stalling for time and help to arrive? Did they realise the full nature of what they carried?

It was possible, a number were adept in the mysteries. He noticed Kara'Tor, his Loremaster and Gal'Vortath, his Cleric watching him intently. They too had heard the human's words and were wary. He beckoned them over and the two magic-users glided smoothly across the floor in their thick robes. A Loremaster was responsible for the defensive and attacking magics that would aid his command in battle, while a Cleric provided the healing and guiding magics. Both were of his house yet he trusted neither fully, their allegiances had not yet been confirmed.

"Do you think they could know the nature of the key and its importance?" he asked the two advisers.

They did not speak immediately.

Kara'Tor was the first to break the silence, "It is a possibility, my lord. Certainly, there is one among them who has sufficient talent to… deduce its nature."

"But they have not had the time," Dar'Elthon snapped.

"I agree, my Lord," Gal'Vortath responded smoothly, "and neither do we. The *Parinsar* was specific that we could not be captured. There must be no clues left," the Cleric finished.

"Do not lecture me Vortath. I am well aware of what is required."

He thought carefully. Things were getting out of his control, but this proposed duel could allow him to quickly retrieve the key. He would not even have to kill the other humans, he could let the trap in the first hall do that. He had prepared it to slow down any scouts from above, yet if he had the key he could leave quickly and he was certain that none of the humans would survive.

Glaring at his two advisers, he said quietly, but with command thick in his voice, "I will accept this challenge." Noting the disbelieving looks he continued, "Do you believe any of these humans can stand against me?"

"Of course not," both advisers said in unison.

"But there is risk in any venture like this." Kara'Tor insisted."And these humans are more than we have seen before..."

Dar'Elthon silenced him with a sharp look. Still, Kara'Tor's arched, black brows drew together in worry. Dar'Elthon ignored this and continued, "You two will stay close to watch for any spells or treachery by the other humans." Dar'Elthon pulled his long sword from its scabbard on his hip and swung his shield from his back. It was decorated with the screaming banshee symbol of his house. "And tell our brothers to remain vigilant. The rest will draw back to the far wall of this chamber. The two ogres will guard the doors. No sudden charge will get past them."

"Sire we cannot trust these humans, I sense danger and something else...." Vortath insisted.

"Of course, there is danger, we are too close to the surface." Dar'Elthon quipped. "As for the humans, be prepared. I will take care of their champion quickly and snuff out any chance of treachery. We can then take the others too if they hesitate to hand over the key. They will be no match for us in the open," he finished firmly.

Turning to face the shadowed corridor, he listened as his men withdrew back towards the entrance to the now well-lit room. Dar'Elthon wondered if this room had once been filled with elves. There was no evidence left now to show what the room had been used for. Many centuries and countless human thieves had taken care of that.

He called out, his words translated from the beautiful language of his forefathers into the crude tongue of the humans by his spell. He then turned and took the measure of the area in the room.

It had a lofty roof, but that would play no part in this battle. The chamber was at least twenty feet wide and twice that in length. He walked casually back to stand in the middle of the room and let his mind relax. He was a skilled swordsman, but he also had the training of the Lorewardens.

Lorewardens were skilled fighter mages and the most feared warriors amongst his people. He had always wanted to walk the path of the Lorewarden, yet other concerns had pressed on him and turned his attention from rising amongst their ranks. He was, after all, a member of a ruling family and as such had other skills to master.

His sharp, upswept ears picked up the sounds of the humans as they moved out into the shadowy end of the corridor. They came out carefully; fear etched on their faces. They were obviously worried about attack. Dar'Elthon snorted in disgust. He had given his word, not that these animals would know what that meant.

He studied the humans as they came into the light. The first to come into view was a female human who carried a large bow. She was less beast-like than other humans he had seen. She was taller and thinner and moved almost like an elf. She also carried the favoured weapon of woodland elves and wore woodland coloured clothing An arrow was held low, but ready against the yew wood of her bow.

Dar'Elthon smiled, she was afraid, he could smell it.

Humans were such pathetic creatures to allow their emotions to be so obvious.

After the archer came two who were obviously warriors, one was tall, but broad and moved with balance even in his thick plate armour, the other was shorter, about the height of an elf. The second he suddenly realised was another female. She wore chain with some plate attached at the chest, shoulders and thighs. Both carried swords and both gave no sign of fear at all.

These two were dangerous.

Three more humans came forward and took up positions on the other side of the corridor entrance. The first was tall yet round as no elf could be. He wore a white cloak and carried a mace and shield, both white with a black rock symbol on his shield that seemed somehow familiar.

Dar'Elthon dismissed him, he was soft, fearful and of little interest, the talent Dar'Elthon sensed in him was limited.

The other two humans' faces were hidden within voluminous hoods, one black, one brown, and both carried staffs; one gnarled and twisted; the other straight, light and smooth. They were obviously more powerful. He could sense their talent more clearly, one of them might even surpass him in his talent, though he knew neither was his equal in their knowledge of the mysteries. Humans were ignorant of the higher mysteries. Nevertheless, these human lorewise would be dangerous. He was sure that both Kara'Tor and Gal'Vortath would have taken note of these.

Dar'Elthon's gaze was drawn from these as the last human stepped into the light. 'Ah,' he thought, 'so here is my opponent.'

The human's talent was clear to Dar'Elthon's senses though it was less than the cloaked pair. Dar'Elthon was tall for an elf, but this man was much taller and wider. He had a breadth of shoulder greater than any elf's and he was obviously strong for one of his kind. Looking at the creature, Dar'Elthon was reminded that humans were little more than upright apes. This one certainly bore a resemblance to his simian ancestors. Dar'Elthon silently allowed himself to appreciate the humour of the thought before continuing his scrutiny.

The human was armoured with plate mail at shoulder, chest, and back, and toughened leather underneath. From his waist to the top of his knee hung a thick kilt of hardened leather strips and below this were patterned plate greaves that covered his knees and shins. On his feet were armoured boots. Lastly, he carried a thick bladed sword in one hand and a round shield on his other arm. He moved well, balanced and ready.

He could see now why the humans had asked for the duel. This giant was impressive, but these humans did not know his people. Size would only matter if Dar'Elthon was slow and he was never that. Interestingly, Dar'Elthon could sense fear building in the man. Perhaps the humans had made a mistake with their choice. This would be short but pleasurable.

Dar'Elthon smiled, he had so missed single combat. He could still remember slamming his parrying dagger to the hilt up under the chin and into the brain of his dear brother. He remembered the near ecstasy that had come over him as he watched the surprise in his brother's eyes die as his life faded.

※

Jon 'Bear' Madraig was not ready for this. He was nervous to the point of bolting, though he hid it well. The only thing that kept him walking forward was he was more afraid of looking afraid, of being thought a coward by his friends. It was always like this when he fought. He could remember those mercenary battles he had fought all those years ago. Zara seemed to relish the fights. Jon had not. Each time, he would first have to win the battle with himself before he fought anyone else. He once again wondered whether he was cut out to be a warrior. He had realised long ago that it was his size and his temper that made him formidable. Like most others when angry, he seemed to lose control, yet unlike others this was just a loss of mental control, a freeing from inhibitions and worries. The problem for Jon was that he prised intelligence, learning and control above all other things. His experience as a child had taught him why it was so important to control his emotions.

A shudder passed through Jon and he stopped and looked towards his opponent. 'Need to concentrate on the here and now, Bear,' he thought to himself, using his familiar nick-name to bolster his courage. 'Come on, you are a better person now. You have reason to take pride in yourself.'

Jon looked into the face of his adversary. The bastard was smiling; it was faint, but it was there! Jon imagined he could see glee in the large, alien eyes.

Those eyes seemed all one midnight colour, though Jon quickly realised that in fact the elf's eyes had huge, near iridescent dark irises. Jon had heard that elves could see in the dark and realised that this might be true as eyes like those before him might well be able to adapt to tiny amounts of light.

A smile suddenly appeared on Jon's face as he realised that here he was thinking like a scholar when he was about to go into single combat! Zara would have been examining her enemy for weaknesses, looking at how he moved or what weapons he carried and here he was conducting an analysis of anatomy.

Jon noticed that his smile had provoked a tiny hint of uncertainty in his opponent.

"Are you ready?" asked the elven leader, his head tilting slightly. "Can we finish this?"

Was he in a hurry? Jon deliberately held up his hand, silently asking for a moment and twisted his head around to look at Rebba. "Are you sure?" he asked again repeating his question of earlier.

A slight dip of the brown hood was the only reply he got. Rebba was concentrating.

"Here we go," Jon said to no one in particular as he twisted back to face the elven commander. He could see that his delay had produced a tiny crease on the metallic skinned forehead of his opponent. He is impatient, thought Jon. Why? Surely a delay played into his hands as it brought more allies to him?

Jon now forced himself to study his opponent properly. It was hard, his heart was now thumping and his adrenalin pumping as he realised there was not going to be any double cross from the elf lord.

The duel was on!

Jon would have to fight on his own until he had maneuvered his opponent close to Darin and Zara who could then cut the elf down quickly. A tiny bit of guilt surfaced at the thought of this breach of honour, but he was enough of a realist to understand that sometimes survival meant bending the rules. That was the plan they had quickly sketched out after the elf had agreed to the duel. To be honest, Jon had not thought the elf would go for the idea, but Rebba had been right. Jon just hoped the druid was also right about being able to hold those two hulking brutes. He could see them standing almost ten feet tall over by the great doors to the chamber. Seeing them like this made it clear how bad their situation was.

'Study your opponent,' he thought angrily to himself.

The elf was thin, twig thin. He wore a kind of plate armour, but it was black and dull. It seemed to absorb light and covered him from the neck down. That should slow him down a little; elves were thought to be incredibly agile. On his head he wore a cap that covered the top of his head and had dark chain mail that hung down from it to cover the rest. Through a hole in the top of the helm came a knot of long, black hair that then cascaded down his back. The elf's weapon was a long, thin blade and he carried a shield with some sort of twisted female face on it. It seemed he and the elf were similarly armed, save the elf's weapons were slight in comparison to his.

"Well, ape man. Can we begin or does your courage desert you?" snapped the emaciated figure in black.

'Ape man! Skinny little swine,' thought Jon his mind racing. "I'm ready," he snarled.

As soon as the words left his mouth, the elf was attacking. Jon barely got his shield up as the elf was suddenly no longer ten feet away, but hammering at him with a swinging blow designed to end this fight by taking his head from his shoulders. Half stumbling back, he managed to get his armoured shoulder up to absorb the blow. Nevertheless, his whole arm seemed to go numb as the blade made a dull 'thwack' against his armour. The elf followed him back and Jon found himself desperately trying to block vicious blows, left and right with his shield.

'Tynast's fiery breath!' he cursed silently, using the God of Battle's name. 'Can't keep this up,' he thought, desperately retreating with each attack. Jon could now feel pins and needles down his arm and painfully hacked at his opponent, more in an effort to unbalance the creature than with any hope of hitting him. He quickly uttered a healing cantrip and immediately feeling rushed back into his arm.

The idea of maneuvering his opponent now seemed laughable. The elf was superb! Fear coursed through him at the terrible realisation that their plan wouldn't work, and more importantly he was probably going to die! Fear almost stopped him meeting the next attack.

Suddenly a savage fury arose in him like a black wave at the idea that he was afraid. 'Fight you coward' his mind yelled at him. Furiously, he thrust forward at the darting elf, smashing his shield into his opponent with a snarling growl and knocking him back.

The elven commander pirouetted away and to the side of Jon's attack to come at him from the side as he overstretched himself. Anger pulsed through Jon and he moved with a speed he wouldn't have thought possible had he been thinking, but now he was fighting on instinct. He was able to parry the elf's lunge and followed this by smashing him in the ribs with the rim of his shield, a move not often seen in a duel but straight from a bar-room brawl. A grunt escaped the elf's full lips as he leapt back with startling agility, his plate armour not slowing him at all.

Blind reaction saved Jon from the next attack. He felt it instinctively, the hair rising on his neck as a burst of unseen static charge rolled forth from the elven leader. By an immense stroke of luck he was very familiar with this form of attack. He had recently tutored his most talented student in its use. It was designed to temporarily paralyse and there were few who could manage it with the minimum of concentration needed in combat. Luckily, he had also spent time tutoring its counter and had spent hours going over it. Thus, it flew from him with almost no thought, his anger giving it potency.

Jon did not notice the slight widening of his adversary's fierce eyes as his sword rose to block the elf's mighty overhead swing. He did not know, but his enemy had developed a greater respect for his opponent. Jon only thought to kill!

Anger flooded through him, guiding him to form his next spell and release it with fury as he slid his sword from under his opponent's. Out to the side it went as he fiercely concentrated, and then in with wicked speed came his blade, preceded by crackling magical energy that would cut an armoured man in half.

The elven leader wrenched himself back from the blow, throwing his shield out. The energy and Jon's sword sliced through the shield, yet it was strong, strong enough to slow the big man's attack, allowing the lithe warrior to get his body out of its path. At the same time a fiery arrow of energy appeared to leap from his opponent's chest, as the elflord muttered a spell of his own. It sped straight for Jon's heart, but the big man had already sensed the spell forming and deduced its nature in an instant. Jon desperately threw up a shield of icy mist that barely intercepted the fiery missile as it hardened. The fiery arrow slammed into the ice shield. A sudden blast, as the two energies collided, forced Jon back, but also threw the more lightly built elf off balance.

Jon savagely pushed his advantage and thrust forward at the still reeling elf, forming one of his most powerful cantrips in his mind, one that would enhance his speed. He could feel his anger ebbing and knew he had to finish this quickly. Casting powerful spells sapped energy as much as did physical exertion. Doing both was incredibly draining. His anger would not maintain him for long and he felt instinctively that he could not manage another magical attack of this magnitude. He didn't want to find out if his enemy could. As the speed spell took effect, the world around him seemed to slow. The elf was quick though and had neatly caught his balance and already set himself, just in front of his two magic-users. Jon felt a powerful magical attack forming in the elven commander and moved to attack.

Suddenly, paralysing terror coursed through Jon's body turning his resolve to jelly. He heard a primal scream and realised it sprang from his own throat! As if moving through molasses he saw the elf's slim blade rise and saw the light of triumph glisten in the creature's ebon eyes. A smile of delight grew on the elf's lips. Up the sword swept and Jon felt his knees beginning to buckle beneath the crippling fear. Dread was taking control of him. He could feel his fingers loosening on the handle of his sword. The need to close his eyes and curl up into a ball in abject terror took hold of him. He could not fight, he was paralysed by panic. Unexpectedly, the thought of his friend's disappointment at his fear and failure hit him again. The old paranoia about cowardice tightened his gullet, years of fighting his inner demons gave him a fierce resolve and his suppressed aggression resurfaced in all its savage glory. Fear was an old adversary and one he had mastered before.

"Nooooo!" Jon screamed hoarsely, a cacophony of emotions bursting from his throat as his hand tightened again on his sword. He transformed his fall forward into a fevered lunge that ripped into the slow moving elven commander, splitting his beetle black armour at the chest and sliding smoothly, with barely a protest, into the slight chest beyond. Jon saw his opponent's expression change so slowly as the realisation, then the pain, and finally the shattering grasp of death, hammered into him.

Slowly, the elven lord collapsed into a mortal embrace with Jon, and over the slim, ebon shoulder Jon could see the two elven magic users' faces turning from stunned disbelief to savage fury. Their hands began to unfurl from their cloaks and dark energy began to form in the air around them. Jon was sure that Rebba, Arkadi and Garon would be doing the same behind him and realised that he had a chance to really turn the odds in their favour. His speed spell was already cast and although he had scant seconds left, he was within reach of the two powerful magi. He began twisting with the elven leader's body, moving his shield in front of him as he turned. His sword began to slide from the recently stilled chest, bubbling as it slid back on its fatal course. Spinning on one heel as his foe had bare seconds earlier, Jon let his momentum pull his sword free under the cover of his shield. He began a lighting quick arc, turning his back on the two dark robed figures as he spun. Lengthening his arm, his blade came round in a screaming circle. Goblins and elves blinked in slow reaction as their master's blood flew slowly through the air to splatter across their faces.

Jon did not see this; he was intent on his attack.

Jon's thick, steel blade hammered into the neck of the first cloaked elf, slicing effortlessly through material and across his throat, blood splashing leisurely across Jon's blade. The blow knocked the small boned elf into his companion. Crackling energy spat out at the ceiling in slow motion from the twisted hands of the second elf as he went down under his thrashing companion. Jon felt the preternatural speed leaving him and heard the thunderous crash as magical energy tore chunks of rock from above and the chamber seemed to rock. The body of the elflord collapsed to the floor at his side.

Swiftly, chaos seemed to erupt around him as an arrow whipped across the room, punching into a bug's head, knocking it back on it rear legs even as its fore legs collapsed. A dark faced goblin appeared to be hurled backwards as another arrow tore into its chest. Jon saw the two armour clad elves draw their swords as one and spring towards him. He looked back to where the second elven mage had fallen beneath his companion. He was desperately pushing his now blood-sodden choking companion from him, but Jon could see his concentration was also focused on calling up a second incantation. Jon ignored the rapidly approaching elven warriors and went for their more deadly kinsmen. He knew he would only have a brief moment to attack before the elven warriors' blades slammed into him. In the background, he heard booming guttural roars and wondered whether Rebba had failed to hold the giants. Hoping to dodge blades, Jon dived bodily at the kneeling mage, his sword point leading the way.

Chapter 19

THE BATTLE

In the beginning there was an eternal sea of chaos and from it sprang the All-Father, Allorn who rose up and created the first land. Upon this land he grew the first tree, Elai, the tree of life. However, also from the sea of chaos leapt Surtyn the Shadow and he desired the tree and the wondrous bounty that grew upon it. Allorn and Surtyn fought for eons until finally Allorn cast Surtyn back into the boiling sea to perish, he believed.

The Druidic story of creation as recorded by Falmin the Tuton, Prince of Bards, BY892

Arkadi had realised early on that the elven commander was far faster and more skilful with the blade than his friend. However, he had watched with something akin to awe as his friend grew in strength against his formidable opponent. Arkadi had wanted to shout him on.

However, what had also been immediately clear to the mage was that their plan wasn't going to work. They had desperately needed to rethink, yet he, like everyone else, hadn't been able to take his eyes off the duel. Bear fought the battle of his life. The elf lord had been amazing, but Bear had fought back and matched him spell for spell. It was incredible. However, Arkadi though, intimately knew the cost of spell casting. He had seen that the elf lord had far greater mystic reserves than Bear. He had begun his own spell.

It was at that point that he had seen Bear stumble under the onslaught of a powerful fear spell and realised that the big man had gambled on his speed cantrip and had no counter to his adversary's magical fear. Arkadi had noticed Darin and Zara's hands begin to pull their swords from their scabbards as they too sensed things go awry for Bear. Arkadi's own hand had twitched as he automatically began calling forth his power even as he realised he could never do so quickly enough to save his friend; he did not have Bear's skill with combat cantrips.

Somehow though, in a split second and with a primeval scream, Bear had smashed though the elf's powerful spell and killed him, spinning in an instant with preternatural speed to attack the two mages behind. Arkadi had been momentarily stunned by the sudden reversal and savage joy had filled him and given strength to his spell casting.

The others also sprang to action, following the plan. They were viciously attacking their shocked enemies. They had gained the initiative, but in that split second, Arkadi realised Jon was in trouble. The attack on the second elven mage was a step too far. He would not reach him without the other elves skewering him and he had no magical energy left!

Without thinking, Arkadi finished his most potent killing spell and hammered it recklessly at the sprinting elves.

Even as Arkadi saw another demon-faced goblin spin and go down with an arrow through his hip, his spell energy slammed into the leading elf and literally tore him apart, disintegrating him in an instant. The elf behind him was not so lucky, part of the blast tore into him and left smoking holes the size of fists through his upper body and arms and he hit the ground writhing as shock took the life from him. Unfortunately, the third elf was shielded from the spell by his kinsmen, though the force of the blast caused him to stumble sideways to his knees. For Arkadi this was enough. He saw a flying Bear slam into the rising mage. A feeble hand had come up as if to stop the huge man, and his sword sliced through the hand and on into the elven mage's body before Bear's massive frame, given extra momentum by the blast from Arkadi's spell, smashed the mage back. Both slid off into the shadows of a shallow alcove behind the blazing brazier with an audible crunch!

Arkadi surprised himself as a snigger slid through his lips at the image of the flying Bear. This ended very abruptly as he felt himself punched backward and a sharp pain sliced up his arm.

"Arhhh," he yelled as his back hit the wall behind him and his staff clattered to the floor.

He looked down. A feathered arrow had gone right through his cloaked sleeve, his arm and then out the other side. Alarmingly, he could see his own blood dripping from the steel head of the arrow. The arrow was wonderfully crafted he noted in morbid fascination and laughed lightly to himself in shock.

'Fool,' he thought half giddy with pain.

Arkadi looked up to see the last elf fall, slammed forward as it started to rise, one of Nat Bero's arrows protruding from its back. Quickly, Arkadi summoned up his will and gestured with his good arm, releasing a warding spell that would block any other arrows coming his way. Suddenly he noticed the crumpled, brown form of Rebba. She was flat out on the floor. Arkadi couldn't see her face as her large hood still covered her head. The only thing to tell there was flesh underneath was a glimpse of a tightly clenched fist poking from one voluminous sleeve scant inches from her oaken staff.

'The troll-like creatures!' Arkadi thought with trepidation even as he worried for his friend. Quickly, he threw back his hood and looked anxiously across the hall, scanning for the monstrous brutes. He could see that Darin had dispatched one insect creature as he had the one in the corridor earlier and was busily hacking at the other two. Zara was faced off against two bat-eared ebon goblins, her twin blades were weaving silvery arcs to block their short stabbing blades. Meanwhile, the last of the goblins was dancing around Garon, holding its bow and trying to pull its sword. The white clad monk was swinging his mace recklessly at the black faced beast and calling on Alba's help to make the creature stand still and fight.

An arrow whizzed across the room and into the gloom at the tall entrance doors to the chamber. Arkadi looked back at where the arrow had come from and saw the tall form of Nat Bero lining up a second shot, her dark eyebrows drawn down in concentration. Arkadi looked back and peered hard into the gloom.

Was there movement there?

Yes, something huge appeared to be struggling frantically by one of the tall thick wooden doors. In fact, now that he concentrated on it, it almost looked like the door was struggling back!

Gesturing quickly, Arkadi threw a light spell into the gloom, pushing it into the space between the doors with his will before igniting the tiny light spark into a glowing slash of illumination that lit up the entrance way. Suddenly, Arkadi knew what Rebba had meant by 'restraining' the huge creatures. Somehow the druid had animated the tall, oaken doors and moulded dozens of limbs from them. The hulking warriors must have been stood by the doors like guards for one door had grabbed each powerful creature and grasped it tightly before turning back to solid oak. In fact, it seemed parts of the solid rock walls had come alive and grasped the beasts.

'Impressive!' Arkadi thought. The druidic faith was dominated by the need to protect and preserve and so their spell craft was limited in its uses in battle so he was genuinely impressed by what Rebba had achieved. Animation of materials was amongst the most difficult areas in magic, even the temporary animation that Rebba had achieved.

Another arrow whipped across the hall to hit the giant figure on the left in the neck. Arkadi noticed that it already had five arrows sticking out of its thick torso. Its struggles were growing weak now as blood pumped down its body. However, its twin was struggling more frantically, spurred on no doubt by the fate of its brother. Arkadi realised that he could see a third figure, below the first, slapping at the door that held it by both legs and one arm. This figure was tiny though in comparison to its two neighbours and its features were shadowed by the thrashing form in front of it.

'So,' Arkadi thought, 'it seems Rebba caught three in her spell.'

The thought of Rebba brought his attention back to the fallen druid and he pushed himself painfully off the wall and stumbled over to the prone form, his hand dangling by his side. He quickly knelt, grimacing as he caught the arrow shaft sticking from his arm on his cloak. He reached out and pulled back Rebba's hood to reveal her long, wavy red-gold hair. It was matted with sweat and a trickle of blood flowed from beneath her cheek which was flat against the dusty floor. Arkadi put his hand to Rebba's neck, above her toughened leather armour. He was relieved to feel a pulse.

Two cries echoed around the hall in quick succession and Arkadi glanced around to see one goblin go down clutching vainly at its throat, the second was already slumped down at Zara's feet as she looked eagerly this way and that in search of another opponent. She had a trickle of blood running down her forehead. It also seemed that Darin had dispatched his foes as he hacked the legs off the last of the insect creatures.

Arkadi heard footsteps approaching and turned to see Garon hurrying towards him, the goblin he had been fighting was a crumpled heap behind him. A worried frown marred the monk's rounded face.

"Rebba's alive, but unconscious. I think she overstretched himself with her spell." Arkadi muttered wearily.

"Someone managed to stick an arrow in you as well, eh?" Garon smiled, his prominent front teeth showing. The worry was still there but his fear had subsided.

"Well, if you had managed to hit that goblin quicker, I wouldn't be in this mess would I?" Arkadi returned only slightly serious.

"Oh, my fault is it…?" Garon paused to look over at the inhuman cry that sounded as Darin finished the last bug. He looked back at Arkadi with a mocking expression, "If you actually paid attention to what you were doing, I wouldn't have to come clean you up." He went to kneel in front of Arkadi, but at that moment a huge cracking sound reverberated around the hall. Garon spun round and Arkadi stood up to see the second giant pull itself and the entire door off the wall and struggle forward into the room.

"Alba's tears!" Garon whispered in amazement. "That door must weigh a ton at least!" He exclaimed shifting his shield into place on his arm and reaching for the mace at his belt.

Arkadi heard Darin shout, "Karodra!" almost in glee as he charged across the hall towards the swaying brute who was screaming its defiance in return.

'Now there's a man in his element,' Arkadi thought. 'Utterly mad when it came to fighting!'

However, before Darin could get to the beast, an arrow plunged into the creature's bellowing maw and it reeled back, the huge door taking its balance and slamming it to the ground with a force that shook the whole hall and took a chunk out of the already battered roof. An instant later, Darin leapt onto the door and plunged his sword into the creature's chest. The creature arched in agony and Darin slammed his blade down with all his weight. The creature thrashed and then gasped as death took it.

Darin looked around eagerly, but was somewhat disappointed as he realised there were no other enemies.

A stillness fell across the room and swirling clouds of dust began to settle on what now looked like a slaughter house. Only the sound of heavy breathing could be heard.

Darin suddenly yelled fiercely, a huge smile on his face, "Ha, haaa! We did it! Told you we could take them."

Arkadi saw Zara smile. Tiredly, Nat and Garon smiled too.

Silence fell.

The stillness was broken half a minute later as Darin's voice snapped everyone back to life.

"What's this," he called, pointing with his sword at the small figure still bound to the standing door, "it looks like a dwarf, dwarf," he said and then laughed lightly at what he had said, "if there is such a thing."

He looked around at Zara who was marching towards him. "Get it?" he asked and repeated, "dwarf, dwarf? Small, dwarf?" he finished hopefully looking at Zara's bloodied face.

"Yeah, very funny, Darin. We're all bleeding to death and you're cracking jokes." Zara growled.

Darin smiled, completely un-phased by the rebuke.

"Don't kill it." Arkadi shouted and both Darin and Zara turned around to stare at him.

"I'm not a savage, Arkadi," Darin returned.

Zara looked questioningly his way. Arkadi could see she would have killed it in a second.

"I don't know about you, but I could do with some answers and this looks like the least of our foes." Arkadi called. "We could question him."

Nat Bero had walked to where Darin stood and leaned in. Arkadi saw the creature move back in alarm and into the light of his spell. Darin was right, it did look like a dwarf, short, stocky with blunt features yet it was smaller than any dwarf he had seen, and without a beard!

Nat reached out and lifted something Arkadi couldn't see.

"It seems our little friend is not altogether here at his own invitation." Nat called out. "He appears to have been manacled and chained to this great lump here." She finished pointing at the slumped giant still attached to the upright door.

"Has anyone seen Bear?" Garon called out, abruptly changing the subject.

Arkadi was snapped from his musings about the dwarven creature. He hadn't seen Bear since he had cast his disintegration spell.

Nat sprinted quickly over to the shadowed alcove as she called, "He disappeared over here."

Arkadi watched as Nat slowed and moved carefully into the shadows, pausing to let her eyes adjust to the gloom.

"I think you should take a look at this" came the archer's voice filled with uncertainty.

"What is it?" Zara called back in concern.

"Well, I've found Bear…" there was a short silence before Nat continued, "and he seems to have found a hidden passageway…" there was another pause until Nat finished, "with his head!

Chapter 20

IN THE DARK

Long Allorn contemplated. He created more lands and at the centre he raised up a mountain upon which he dwelt and thought, but he grew lonely. He decided he needed companions and so he went to the first tree and took from it five limbs. From these he shaped the gods; Banus, Elisis, Sarahiri, Ishara and Varinoth. These gods were great and could shape the chaos as the All-Father could, though they were confined in their creating. Banus created waters to compliment the earth, Elisis threw up the heavens and the stars, Sarahiri made the earth rich and fruitful and created trees to imitate their mother, Ishara created the great ice of the north and Varinoth the fires of the deep places, pushing back the chaos.

The Druidic story of creation as recorded by Falmin the Tuton, Prince of Bards, BY892

'His head?' Zara thought incredulously. 'What the hell was the lanky archer on about?'

Zara left the strange looking dwarf and clambered across the broken door with its monstrous dead captive. She began to walk across to where Nat Bero had entered the gloom behind the large pedestal upon which stood the brazier. She smoothly sheathed her double blades and examined the alcove as she approached. It was like a bite out of the wall much like the four others that stood at each corner of the large underground room they were in. No one had noticed anything unusual about the alcove, but then they'd had scant time to search with those bugs skittering along the corridors, searching them out like giant blood hounds.

Zara wiped the blood from her brow with the back of her hand where it threatened to spill into her eye and grimaced more at the red smear it left across her fist than the pain.

'Need to get that patched up' she thought, her gaze darting to where Garon had begun to gently examine the arrow in Arkadi's arm. He was busy and Zara knew that Rebba Korran would be no help either, unconscious as the druid was.

Zara approached the large pedestal that stood in the centre of the alcove and stopped to let her eyes adjust to the gloom. She noticed the scrape marks and blood on the floor, no doubt from the elf that Bear had hammered back along the floor.

She had to admit that she had been impressed with Bear, though she would never say it to the big man himself. The elf lord had been stunningly skilled. Zara thought she could have matched him, but there was no way she could have countered the magical attacks that, even to her untrained eye, seemed to whistle around the two. Bear had become much more powerful with his magic, there was no doubt about that. Zara knew from experience that Bear could be a fearsome opponent just from his size and strength, but the magic now made him formidable indeed.

Zara and he had fought side by side for years. There was a time when Bear had been closer to her than anyone had ever been in her life.

Her mind flashed back. It had started all those years ago when her mother and father died of the wasting disease. Zara's life had been shattered. She had been only seven years old, sent to the court in Ostia and passed onto her uncle...

She shuddered at that memory and drove it quickly from her mind.

However, it was at court that she had met her friends and made them her family, particularly Bear. Zara had not been close to anyone else save her friends. She had thrown herself into their company, relying on their friendship to keep her sane... and safe.

Those were the best times and the worst. Days of fun, nights of terror! There seemed to be few worries for the others and she clung to their innocence, even as hers was taken from her. Only Bear knew the truth of her uncle. Only he knew the real reason she had fought and fought, in the training arena, practised and practised her swordsmanship. She had got close to Darin and Marcus, but never as close as to the brooding Bear. He had his own demons and the two of them seemed to sense a kinship in the other. They had trained together, fought together and laughed together. The others were often away with family or focused on their other studies. Bear stayed.

Still the best of times had been when they'd all been together.

She shook her head, dismissing the memories. Life had changed her. Too much had happened. She had done too many things that she couldn't undo. Those times were gone.

She looked at the darkness where she could see the back of Nat's tall form. She hesitated. It had been obvious that Bear was injured from Nat's worried tone. Zara fell back into the comfort of her anger to prepare herself. True, she and Bear had been close, but those days were in the past. He was a bloody idiot to think he could take on so many.

Stepping carefully, Zara moved up alongside Nat Bero in the half dark and nearly tripped as her feet tangled with something on the floor. She crouched down and found herself looking at two pairs of legs, one obviously Bear's. What was surprising, and made her kneel down to make sure her eyes weren't playing tricks, was that both bodies seemed to have disappeared into the lower part of the wall and only their bodies from the mid rift down still showed. There was some rubble and it appeared that the two men had crashed head first through part of a thin stone façade that hid… well something! Crouching low she could see a room or corridor beyond that disappeared into darkness. She called this fact out, but no one replied.

She shook Bear's leg. No reaction.

'Damn it, Bear, don't you have killed yourself! She thought angrily.

"Grab Bear's legs" she snapped at Nat, who quickly crouched down and took a hold of the nearest armoured leg. Awkwardly, in the tight space, the two of them pulled. Bear had been wearing a helm and it appeared that the elf was further in than Bear and Zara hoped this meant that the elf had hit the wall first. It was definitely possible that slamming into even the thin section of the wall with force enough to shatter it could have caved in a person's skull or broken their neck. Zara hoped that Bear's horned helm and thick head had saved him.

Slowly the two of them backed out into the light where they found Darin waiting.

Nat Bero stood up, clearly not knowing what to do next and clearly not eager to see how bad Bear was. She had always been a bit squeamish around injuries. This was always a puzzle since she could, kill, skin and gut an animal without a thought.

Zara looked around at Darin who was trying to get past the huntress. He looked worried.

Darin lost his patience with the huntress. "Get out of the way. You're in the light and I can't see!"

Nat looked helplessly at Zara and tried to get out of the knight's way.

A thought came to Zara even as Darin struggled to push forward and take a look at Bear.

To Nat she said, "There are still those other groups of evil bastards out there. We need someone to scout around and keep an eye out, Nat."

Zara saw the dark haired archer nod in agreement. This was something she understood and would keep the squeamish idiot out from underfoot. Nat Bero headed off for the entrance as Zara began turning the heavy, limp body of Bear. Darin quickly leaned in to help and as soon as Bear slumped over, Darin quickly slipped off his armoured gauntlet and pushed his hand against Bear's throat.

"He's alive," the knight said in relief and then jumped as a short cry of pain came from Arkadi across the hall.

Zara looked and noticed that Garon was holding up a broken arrow and Arkadi was swearing at him. Zara smiled. Garon had snapped the arrow and pulled it out.

Arkadi was soft as always.

Zara stood, moved around and knelt by Bear's head. There was a huge dent in the top of the steel and both horns had snapped off. "Let's get this helm off and see what damage there is." She was a little afraid of how to start and grasped the padded rim of the helm gingerly. She could already feel stickiness as she began to pull. The helm slid off easily, slick with blood. Darin had pulled out a wad of cloth from his belt bag and placed this carefully under Bear's head. Casting the helm to the side, Zara wiped her own blood from her brow again and squinted at Bear's bloody scalp. "It looks bad" she said quietly.

Garon suddenly appeared. He placed a hand on Darin's shoulder and said firmly in his deep, slightly lisping voice, "Go and help Arkadi finish bandaging his arm." Darin hesitated. "Go. I'll sort this out." The knight moved off reluctantly.

This was the most commanding Zara had ever seen Garon. Maybe the fat sot had developed a backbone!

Garon had turned his attention to Bear. He motioned impatiently for Zara to move out of the way. "Shouldn't have removed the helm until I was here," he admonished.

Zara clenched her fist, but moved back and let the white clad monk take her place.

"We were worried. We needed to know if he was alive or dead." She snapped angrily.

She could see Garon was shaking his head even as he bent over to see the gashes on Bear's head. 'Arrogant, fat oaf! Who did he think he was?'

"Well go and worry elsewhere and let me work" Garon said, completely ignoring her tone. The monk pulled a small pack from under his white tabard where it had hung on his belt along with several others.

Zara was annoyed at the tone and it was a struggle to let it pass. She reminded herself there was no point in arguing with the monk over healing; it was Garon's area not hers.

She swallowed her angry retort and looked around the room. It struck her again how vulnerable they were. This hall was a dead end and, if what Rebba Korran had said were true, there were other bands of elves, goblins and whatever else out there. This hall could once again quickly turn into a death trap. They needed to get out of here; they could not withstand another attack. Only Bear's mad duel and luck had got them through the last one without any fatalities. As much as she liked to rely on a little luck now and again, Zara firmly believed in playing the odds and here the odds were well stacked against them.

Zara quickly moved over to the bodies of the elven leader and his kin. Might as well search them, she thought, they needed some more information on what was going on.

As she stared at the bodies, Zara was struck by how strange this whole encounter had been. First, was the fact that creatures out of nightmare had attacked them; giants and huge insects! These were creatures no one

181

had ever seen or heard of before, even Arkadi had said so and he'd studied such things. Second, there were goblins under the control of elves when everyone knew they were sworn enemies. Lastly, they had been attacked for something they didn't have, something they didn't even know about. It all made no sense! Why would elves attack them in the first place? Why were they here, now? They needed answers.

Zara quickly searched the bodies, but found little of interest; no pouches or scrolls, nothing to give any clues as to who they were or where they were from.

The elf lord's features were intriguing; so human and yet so alien. The skin seemed faintly metallic, the hair incredibly fine, the ears like those of a halfling, though larger and more pointed. This would be an interesting find for a scholar, but of little interest to her and less use. However, the elf lord was wearing some very interesting armour. Had Zara the time, she might have taken it off and took it with her, but time was pressing. She was just about to head over to the door when she noticed the sword and shield; they were easy enough to have a good look at. They seemed to be made of the same dark material as the armour. It seemed to almost absorb light. Zara reached out and lifted the slim bladed sword. It was incredibly light! It felt like it was made of wood. It did not feel like metal at all and yet Zara knew it was as strong as steel; it had withstood Bear's finely made steel blade.

Zara glanced around again. She was ignoring her own council, but the weapons and armour were fascinating. Something else caught her eye. She stood and moved towards the elven mage whose throat Bear had cut. He was lying in a pool of blood and Zara was careful not to step in it. She did not want to be leaving tracks even a blind man could follow.

The creature's robe was partially cut and through the gap something was shining. Zara pulled her belt knife and cut into the robe and then pulled it open. Inside there was an array of small pockets, each seemed to be full.

"I wouldn't if I were you, Zara," came Arkadi's voice from where he sat not far away. Darin was busy bandaging his arm. "…those are enchanted objects and spell ingredients. They may be dangerous."

Zara stopped. "Could we use any of it?" he called.

"Possibly," Arkadi replied, "I'd need to take a look."

Zara nodded and rose. There were no packs she realised. That was very interesting. They themselves had come down with only minimal packs; some food, water flasks and a few other small bits; just enough for a day or so, nothing more, but this group seemed to have nothing at all. Perhaps they existed on air.

No, it was more likely they had their packs elsewhere. This reminded her that they had left their own packs in the small antechamber. They would need them.

Turning around she noticed that Darin had finished helping Arkadi who was pulling down the sleeve of his dark robe to cover the white bandaging.

"Darin" she called, "you see if Nat has headed off. She should be scouting down the corridor for anymore of those bugs. Rebba said another five of them were nearby."

The heavily armoured knight simply nodded. Zara was surprised; Darin usually seemed to delight in making small jibes at the most inopportune moments. Still, Darin was no fool and probably realised as well as she that they mustn't get caught unawares or fenced in. Zara looked at Arkadi and saw the man grimace slightly as he tried to move his fingers. Zara smiled. Garon's magic would speed the healing, but it would still hurt for a while.

Before, Zara could suggest anything to Arkadi the slight mage frowned, obviously noting her amusement at his pain, "I'll see to Rebba. We need to wake her."

He turned and walked over to the prone druid.

Suit yourself, Zara thought.

Abruptly, she wondered about the dwarf-like creature. It had seemed practically paralysed with terror the last she had seen of it. Hopefully, the creature would stay that way, Zara thought, the less trouble the better.

Zara turned. Darin was sat busily fiddling with the lock to the small creature's chain and humming to himself. Zara strode over to him. She could see the creature was still cowering in the corner, but was also watching with interest what Darin was doing.

"What are you doing, Darin?" Zara asked, and then continued before he could reply, "You were supposed to be checking on Nat, and anyway, picking the lock is not going to free that thing, he's bound by more than just the chain." Zara stressed pointing at the wood that encircled his legs and arm.

"Nat is fine without me blundering around in my armour and I know this won't free him. I am not a complete idiot!" Darin looked balefully at Zara. "Now, sweet Zara" he began in a patronising tone, "I can't affect those bonds" he pointed at the oak that encased the small man's arm, "but I can undo this chain. Soon Rebba will be awake and will undo her spell and if I haven't undone this chain beforehand we still will have to do that unless you want to take that huge creature with us!" he said pointing at the troll-like creature attached to the door. "Or we could stay here to interrogate this creature," Darin paused and looked pointedly at Zara, "but time is an issue you know," he finished, sarcasm dripping from his tone.

Smiling, Zara snapped back. "Well, get on with it then."

She moved past Darin and into the corridor beyond. It was bright here; Arkadi's spell lit the place and the corridor could clearly be seen for thirty of forty feet, beyond that though nothing could be seen. They had not lit any braziers as they had moved along the corridors, indeed they hadn't found any. However, there were some rooms that were lit by a faint light, like the one they were in. How the ancient elves managed this she had no idea.

Earlier the group had walked quickly with torches that they had discarded as they hurried. The corridors were wide, ten feet across, and tall, probably about fifteen feet she had estimated. They were long too, a good hundred feet or more before turning off in a different direction. Doors had stood here and there in some corridors, some tall and wide, others little more than small doors at her height and a tight squeeze to get through. They had then wandered in and out of empty room after empty room, descended three different flights of stairs to find little more than dusty skeletons, cobwebbed bits of furniture and broken objects of which they didn't even know the purpose! They had traipsed about these halls, searching for a long time before running into those bugs.

It had been clear though from the tracks that others had been down here recently, very recently. Zara had assumed then that it was other searchers like themselves.

They had all still been enjoying the search at that point. They had been keen to discover something of value while enjoying each other's

184

company; after so long they had easily fallen back into their old patterns and routines. It was while wandering this lowest level that they had literally turned a corner and blundered into that first bug. Zara wasn't sure who was most surprised, Garon who had fallen half over its back, or the bug who found itself in the midst of a group of armed men, with one of them practically riding it!

The creature had obviously seen clearer than they in the dark, but had been momentarily blinded by their torches. Zara's memory of what exactly happened next was vague, torches were swinging around as the group pulled weapons and everyone was shouting out in surprise and fear. Garon was shouting almost hysterically as the bug shook violently, flinging him head first over it and onto the floor. The creature itself was making some kind of high pitched scream and thrashing savagely. Only the fact that Darin, Bear and Zara had thick armour on and had been at the front had prevented any real damage from the flailing creature's wild limbs.

The fight had been short and brutal with all of the company hacking at the creature in near panic at its fearsome appearance. It really shook everyone up. They had not really expected to meet anyone down here, least of all some creature out of a nightmare. They had been debating then what to do when more of the creatures had come screeching down the hall at them. It was then that they had begun to run.

Zara brought herself back to the present. She looked back into the hall and saw that Rebba was sitting up, her hood was down and she was shaking her head groggily. Garon was still intent on his work on Bear, and Darin was now pacing to and fro in obvious agitation, having finished the manacle.

The knight hated doing nothing. Zara saw him stop, his head coming up and swiftly he disappeared out of Zara's sight, striding past Garon who stilled worked on Bear.

Zara saw Arkadi sat by Rebba. She called out to the mage, "Is she alright?" She nodded to the bleary eyed Rebba who was just sitting up. Arkadi was helping the druid to her feet.

He called back, "She's just a little groggy, she'll be fine in a moment or two."

"Fine enough to undo her spell?" Zara responded hopefully "We could do with freeing the little fellow if we are going to take him with us."

"I can take care of that in a moment" Arkadi insisted. Rebba still looked a little pale. "Rebba will need an hour or two before she should attempt any magic." Arkadi finished firmly.

"Well as long as one of you can do it," Zara paused thoughtfully before continuing, "Oh, and can you get rid of that," she said pointing at the light, "It's like a beacon for any of those hell spawn that are down here."

Arkadi nodded and helped Rebba over to a wall with a small ledge where he left the ashen faced druid to sit.

Zara noted the look of confusion on Rebba's face as she looked around the room. Bodies still lay everywhere and the druid had missed the entire battle. Zara turned her attention back to the hall way, but was suddenly alarmed to hear a dull clanking thud and then another.

Arkadi must have seen his alarm and said with a wry smile, "I think Darin is intent on finding out what's behind that hidden panel."

"What is the matter with the..." she began but never finished as she saw Nat Bero burst into the light of the corridor, running for all she was worth.

She dashed up to Zara and hastily gasped, "There's more of them coming this way, maybe twenty or more by the sound! I could hear them in the corridors. They were searching carefully. I don't think they know about us but that will change in about five minutes. There is no way around them from here!" Nat was wide eyed in near panic.

Zara turned and was about to bark a command for everyone to get ready when she realised there was nothing they could do. They were trapped again!

Chapter 21

INTO THE UNKNOWN

Of these offspring, Sarahiri was the greatest and she became wife to the All-Father and gave him many children, the greatest of whom were her firstborn triplets; Tynast the Summer King, Lord of battle and the earth; Olwyn the Wise, keeper of the Book of Knowledge; and Malindar the Swift, Lord of the Winds.

The Druidic story of creation as recorded by Falmin the Tuton, Prince of Bards, BY892

"Damn!" Zara hissed in pure frustration, clenching her fists tight in an effort to contain her anger. "We should have sprinted out of here the moment the battle was over."

"I doubt we would have got far carrying Rebba and Bear," Arkadi commented, "unless you meant to leave them." His thick, dark brows drew down slightly in accusation.

"Yeah course I was, Arkadi," she sneered back sarcastically. "You'd like to believe that I would, wouldn't you, you arrogant prick!" she shouted, and took a threatening step towards the mage.

Arkadi brought his staff up protectively. She smiled harshly and shook her head. She turned away. The mage would always believe the worst of her. He hadn't changed.

"What do we do?" Nat Bero cried.

"First thing we need is time." She snapped firmly at the panicky huntress. "You," she said, "slow them down. Give them something to worry about. You know what I mean?" she asked and was pleased to see that the archer did.

They had used this tactic before. Shoot a couple of shots from cover and then retreat quickly, take cover and do it again. Whether you hit anyone or not it gave the enemy pause and made them move cautiously waiting for the next attack. That would hopefully slow their advance. As the dark haired huntress moved to go, she had a grim look on her face.

"Give them only two shots and then return straight here."

Nat nodded and took a deep calming breath before she headed off.

Zara turned to Arkadi who looked equally focused and said "I'll remove the light spell and Rebba's too if I can." He turned and then hesitated and looked back at Zara. "Unless you want me to help Darin?" He questioned, "That is where we are going to have to go isn't it?"

"Unless you have a better idea," she asked acerbically, knowing the mage did not. "Get rid of the spells."

Zara looked over at the small creature they had discovered. He had been freed from the chain to the door and stood meekly as if awaiting his execution. The chain hung like a leash for the pathetic looking creature.

"Darin!" she shouted. "Stop smashing that panel and get yourself under it and see where it goes... if anywhere." she finished miserably.

Zara moved into the hall as she heard Arkadi begin chanting. She saw Garon finishing up a bandage around Bear's head and noticed the big man was still unconscious. 'Bloody typical,' she thought wryly, 'we are up to our necks in it and he's sleeping on the job!'

"How is he, Garon?" she asked after a moment.

Garon finished packing his first aid pouch away and placed the small bag back onto his belt with the others. "He will be fine given time and rest." He pushed himself up from his knees and stood wearily. "Luckily the impact was mainly absorbed by the helm. He did fracture his skull in two places, but I have fixed those using a bone melding weave. He was very lucky; I don't think there is any damage to the brain." Garon looked at his bloodied hands and continued. "I used an herbal salve on the cuts in his scalp and then wrapped them." The monk muttered a quick prayer to Blessed Alba as he finished speaking.

Zara had kept up with most of what Garon was saying.

"So why is he still unconscious?"

"He needs rest and time to recover. Had I brought him back to consciousness he would have been too dizzy to stand and would likely have spent most of his time retching." Garon said authoritatively. "Now, from what I heard we are going to go through that secret passage." he said a question in his tone.

Zara merely nodded.

Garon looked beyond her and motioned with his hand for a weary looking Rebba Korran to come over. The druid had just returned with the packs from the other room. "I'll get these two through now; we want them through and with a good start before those foul, ungodly creatures arrive."

Zara nodded again and finished by muttering that Darin could help. She was actually impressed by the fat monk for once, though she wouldn't admit it.

She spun on her heel and headed back to the doorway. If she was honest, she was feeling guilty and that was making her cranky. It had been her idea to come down here and she was afraid she was going to get all of her friends killed. Added to which there was no one else to take charge, Bear was unconscious and the others were not experienced enough in command to lead. She realised that wasn't true. Arkadi or Darin were equally capable of taking charge when the situation warranted it, but Zara realised *she* wanted to get them out. She had got them into this and she would bloody well get them out!

She saw the light in the corridor wink out and saw too that the double door had given up its small prisoner who looked ready to bolt, save that Arkadi held his chain. Zara rushed over to take the chain, Arkadi looked a little awkward trying to cradle his staff and hold on to the chain with only one good hand. She didn't want the creature yanking free and escaping.

"Thanks" Arkadi said gruffly.

Zara ignored him. She frowned at the small creature attached. Whatever this little thing was it stood still and quiet. It had not even tried to speak.

She saw Arkadi take a firm grip on his staff and look down the corridor with worry etched on his dark features. Zara continued to stare at the little man they had captured.

He wore a dark woolen jerkin and trousers that were tucked into a sturdy pair of leather thigh-high boots. Zara had met a number of dwarves, they were not a common sight, but not unknown either in the Wildlands. They traded with the human towns and tended to travel often to visit their kin in other clans. Dwarves usually stood about five feet tall, were impressively thick limbed and powerful; they had bluff, round faces and well chiseled features with deep set eyes. They also almost always had thick beards and long braided hair like the Calonian highlanders. Dwarves were a bawdy lot, fond of good ale and an equally good fight; they seemed to love getting into brawls when they were in towns. None of these descriptions fit this little man. The creature was under four feet in height, not as broad or sturdy looking as a dwarf and had no weapons or armour. He looked soft and timid. The most telling difference was that he had no beard! As far as Zara had ever heard all adult dwarves had beards, it was some kind of status thing. Only a very young dwarf would not. The strange thing was this little creature did not look young. In fact, the creature looked quite aged, with deep folds creasing his careworn face. This was no youth.

Zara noticed the creature was in turn studying her and Arkadi, though he was trying to hide it. He seemed as puzzled about them as they were about him. He clearly reached a decision and began talking in a deep thick voice, gesturing this way and that with his hands in mounting urgency.

Arkadi said, "Suddenly, he is keen to communicate."

"Yeah, but can you understand what he is saying? It's no language I've ever heard." Zara responded.

The creature seemed to realise that both faces in front of it were staring blankly back at it and began speaking single words in what seemed to Zara to be a questioning way.

"I'd guess he is trying out other languages." Arkadi said and leaned in saying several words in a similar tone to the little man, none of which Zara could understand, but then she had only ever really needed the common tongue. She could also get by in Nordic and knew a spattering of words in a few of the goblin's crude dialects, but other than that she was lost.

"Perhaps you could use one of those translation spells like the elf lord did?" She suggested.

Arkadi seemed to be considering this when both heard muffled steps. Zara drew one of her blades and waited. The creature went mute and looked anxious.

A moment later Nat Bero appeared, sprinting out of the darkness, "I gave them a little to think about" she said, "even managed to take down one of those bug things." she boasted.

"Good. You're sure they didn't come pouring after you." Arkadi asked.

"I'm not a fool Arkadi. You stick to your magic and let me handle the archery. They were reforming and coming on at a crawl. It'll be a couple of minutes at least before they get here." Nat flung her longbow over her shoulder.

Zara noticed that the archer's hands were shaking slightly, but said nothing. "Right," Zara interrupted, "we are going to go down the hidden passage…"

"The one that Bear found?" Nat asked before Zara could continue.

Zara saw Arkadi roll his eyes and snapped, "Do you know of any others?" Nat looked a little sheepish. "We could do with you scouting that passage" she continued. The huntress perked up a bit at this. She did enjoy the need for her skills.

The tall green clad archer moved off, hurrying towards the hidden passage.

"I have another idea" Arkadi exclaimed a nasty look coming over his face. He snapped his fingers on his bad hand and grimaced fiercely as the pain reminded him of the wound he still had.

Zara smiled at his pain. Idiot mage! Still when he had an idea they were usually good.

"What have you got in mind?" She asked as she began heading for the hidden passageway. When Arkadi had a look like that it was for something nasty. It was a look he had worn whenever planning a practical joke when they were younger.

"It will be a surprise" he smiled mischievously and darted off ahead.

She jumped as a hand touched her shoulder, spun, drew a blade and almost took Darin's smiling head of, helm and all.

"My, we're getting jumpy aren't we?" he said in mock amazement.

Zara frowned at him disapprovingly.

"How was I to know you were so deaf you couldn't even hear a man in full plate armour approaching?" Darin finished tritely.

"What do you want?" Zara returned, ignoring Darin's jibe. Something made easier by the way the knight's earnest face smiled innocently at you whenever he joked. The fact that he had joked now, yet again proved his spectacularly bad timing.

"We are all ready back there." Darin looked down the corridor. "Are we leaving this party or what?" he asked. "Nat says they'll be on top of us anytime soon, fear of ambush or no."

Zara didn't answer she just pulled the strange silent little man by his chain and hurriedly pushed past Darin who was still looking down the corridor. The little creature offered no resistance; in fact he seemed as pleased as Zara to be moving. Darin turned and jogged into the room behind her.

Zara hurried after him into the shadows. She saw Darin practically dive at the gap in the wall, drag himself along the floor and disappear beyond. The knight had earlier made the gap wider and Zara hoped that it would still be well enough hidden in the shadows to at least delay pursuit. Quickly, she shoved the little man towards the hole and the creature clambered through eagerly on hands and knees. She followed. She panicked a little when her still sheathed sword handle got stuck on the stone panel above her. She could almost feel insect pincers grabbing at her. Angrily, she dismissed the thought and wriggled the sword free. She dragged herself through. Darin moved to help her up, but she thrust his hand away. Arkadi hurriedly began chanting and gesturing at the gap in the panel. This continued for a few moments and Darin disappeared up the corridor. Arkadi finished chanting and the hole they had just passed through vanished. The rock panel was whole again!

"Fantastic, Arkadi!"

"It isn't fixed. I have merely placed the illusion of an undamaged wall over the gap." Seeing Zara's delighted expression, he added grudgingly, "It is easily detected I'm afraid, but I have also added a small delayed explosive spell and interweaved it with the illusion."

Zara was non-plussed, "And that means…?"

"That means whoever dispels the illusion will also shatter this wall, take their head off and hopefully cause some serious damage. At the least it will prompt some more caution on our pursuers' part."

"Excellent!" Zara exclaimed, smiling and slapping the mage on the back.

Arkadi smiled back, then frowned all of a sudden, "It's a shame I didn't get a chance to look through those mages' robes."

Zara shook her head at the inquisitive mage and then the two of them headed after the others down the narrow passageway.

It took longer than expected to catch up and Zara realised that Garon and Rebba, dragging the hefty Bear between them, must have headed straight on as soon as they got the big man through the hole. Good thinking really since they would be the slowest of the group.

Zara noticed that the passage way was only five feet across and unlike those they had already travelled, was roughly hewn out of the rock. It was also heading down at quite a steep angle. Zara was at the back of the group and could only see the bobbing torch now carried by Nat Bero who she could see some distance ahead. Zara put her head down and walked, concentrating on not stepping on the diminutive chained figure that walked scant feet in front of her. She also kept an ear out for any signs of pursuit.

They had been walking for almost ten minutes when Zara realised that she could hear Garon saying something and looked up. The long striding Nat had stopped. Zara could see her getting closer as the group caught the huntress up. A moment later the passageway opened out into a natural cave easily fifty feet across and almost spherical save for a flat man-made floor, or perhaps elf-made if legend were true, she corrected. It suddenly became obvious why they had stopped. There was no exit, only the way they had come. They were trapped again, save this time they were further into the trap than they had been and with less chance of getting out.

"I don't understand" Nat Bero hissed in frustration, "Who makes a tunnel that leads to an empty cave? Why waste all that time digging?"

Nat answered her own question before anyone else could.

"There must be a hidden passage here." The archer began hunting around, scanning the walls and the floor and Darin joined her.

Garon and Rebba wearily dragged Bear over to a patch of wall less rough than the rest and then sat him down against it before slumping themselves next to him. Bear's armoured feet were starting to look a mess where they had dragged along the rock floor.

Garon muttered quietly "How can he weigh so much?"

Arkadi turned to Zara and looked at him worriedly. "There is another possibility" he stated quietly, "We could have missed a hidden passage along the way."

Damn, Zara swore to herself, that was a possibility, but no one had really expected someone to have a hidden passage in a hidden passage. That seemed almost too secretive. "Let's check here first" she said aloud, "we have a good few minutes unless your little surprise didn't work."

Zara was pleased to see Arkadi shaking his head, "It'll work, I hid that second weave well and I'll know when it's tripped." the mage responded.

Zara hoped he was right. They knew nothing of what these elves were capable. She moved over to where Garon and Rebba sat with Bear, Arkadi at her shoulder. She was about to hand over the chain of their captive when she heard Nat Bero yell excitedly.

"Here it is!" the huntress called and thrust her hand into some crevice on the opposite wall. Before anyone could say anything they all heard a loud click. Nat stood back and turned with a grin on her face.

Abruptly, an alarming creaking began where the crevice was and Nat spun back to face the wall and took a step backwards. The creak turned into a low rumble and the wall they all were now facing began to shake. Nat hurriedly backed up towards Zara. Darin also retreated. Zara suddenly saw that the entrance to the cave was sealing as a rock slid down silently from above too quickly for anyone to try to prevent it.

"It's a trap" Darin yelled over the din.

As abruptly as the rumbling and shaking had started, it stopped. Everyone looked around at everyone else. The silence was palpable. They were all now crowded near the side of the cave, opposite the wall where the shaking had begun. It was then that Arkadi noticed the cracks in the floor. They ran from the sealed entrance to the opposite wall in perfectly straight, parallel lines, maybe a foot apart, at least two dozen lines. This time everyone frowned first at the floor and then at each other.

"Wha..." Zara began.

It was then that the floor beneath them gave way.

Chapter 22

DESCENT INTO DARKNESS

Unknown to the gods, Surtyn the Shadow had watched the All-Father and grown jealous. He had not perished. In secret he crept upon the tree of life and stole from it branches to shape to his own will. Each would be the antipathy of the gods. Seven hateful creatures he created; Atrall the Fair, Lord of Mischief; Mayvan the Enchantress; Grav the great sea serpent; Yarvik the Warrior, Destroyer of Hope; Taythor the Fire Giant; Bearwan the Frost Queen; Jarmangard the Thief; and Alethvar the Stormhound.

The Druidic story of creation as recorded by Falmin the Tuton, Prince of Bards, BY892

Her eyes slowly opened, she could see faint light coming from a small torch, barely lit. A figure moved before her eyes and she realised she was lying on her back. Slowly the features of the figure came into focus as her mind tried to make sense of what it was she was seeing. It was the dwarf creature! It was saying something. She understood nothing and felt darkness creeping up on her again. With little resistance her eyes closed and her mind went black.

Again she awoke, this time fully. She coughed out dust and grit. Darkness encircled her and not the darkness of night; this was a thick inky darkness that swallowed all light. It was as if she still had her eyes shut; only she knew they were open. This was the darkness of the abyss.

Slowly she sat up, one hand bracing her while the other was held out questing in front. She did not know how long she had been unconscious, but she was sure it had not been long. She could still clearly remember the tumbling chaos as everyone plummeted and then bounced and rolled over and over down a steep and rugged incline. Flashes of images of flames, of faces and cloaks, packs and limbs had whirled passed her eyes as she fell. Then the light had disappeared and she saw only flashes of light as she slammed into hard surfaces and softer bodies. She did not remember when this had stopped. It felt like it had gone on for ever and yet had also been over in seconds.

She groaned as she sat up and moved her hand to rub at her head and neck that was now bare. Her helm was gone. She put both hands on the rough floor and began to feel around to the limits of her reach. Her hand found something hard and curved. She continued to search the object and realised with relief it was one of her swords, still in its sheath. It must have snapped from her back as she fell. Grasping the hilt with the familiarity of years of use, she slowly dragged the sabre to her. She winced at the noise of the blade as it scrapped along the ground, yet she needed it with her, it brought a sense of security. Suddenly, she became aware of other noises, the light creaking of leather and scraping of metal on stone, low moaning and deep breathing.

"Darin... Nat..." she whispered urgently, "Are you there?"

Her question was answered by an incoherent and pained sigh followed by the sound of a heavy movement.

"I'm here" Darin replied in a thin voice, "though I think there is someone sat on my chest!"

"Zara is that you?" came another voice, muffled and wet.

There was a spitting sound and then the voice came again.

"I think my staff hit me in the face"

The voice was Rebba's!

"Can you get us some light?" Zara asked quickly, "it blacker than a devil's heart in here... wherever here is."

There was a long pause then...

"I… I'm afraid not I'm finding it hard to even move." Rebba replied apologetically.

Zara was finding it hard to pinpoint exactly where the druid's voice was coming from. There was an echoing quality to their voices and she felt like she sat in a huge space. Fighting down panic, she called. "What about you, Darin?"

"Just a moment," he gasped, "let me get out from under whoever is atop me."

There was strain in his voice and Zara could hear a slow scuffing followed by metallic scraping and Zara guessed that Darin's armour was dragging on the floor. Abruptly there was a coughing protest and a muttered oath followed by a sudden scraping movement.

"Arghh. Who is shoving?" came a sharp protest.

"I am!" was Darin's quick response, "now get off me Garon."

"I can't, someone is on top of me!" The unseen monk responded angrily. It seemed he was unhurt. "Wait while I try to get my legs out."

There was a gasp and then a dull thump.

"Right," Garon snapped.

"About time!" Darin snapped back.

During this time Zara had slowly risen to her feet and then begun moving cautiously in what she hoped was the direction of the voices. She was feeling forwards with her foot and also began waving her scarbarded sword out in front of her as she went.

"Stop!"

Zara froze and Darin called out, "What?" alarm in his voice.

"Don't move any further Zara you are heading for a sharp drop." Rebba said softly. "I have been trying to sense where we are and there is a deep drop ahead of you."

Zara held still.

"Turn to your left and walk forward slowly and you will be approaching me. There is a body about five stops in front of you. I believe it is Arkadi."

Zara turned and began walking slowly. As she did so she called to the druid, "Is he alright?"

"I can't tell. I'm afraid my senses are a little dulled at the moment and my head is still a little fogged." Rebba answered, weariness evident in her voice.

Zara's foot bumped into something soft and she knelt down and began feeling around. The soft material certainly felt like a robe. As she probed some more there was a soft breath and then a light moan.

"Arkadi?" she called lightly. "Arkadi?" she repeated, shaking the body before her.

The mage roused himself quickly and before Zara could ask anything he ignited a ball of light that near blinded her. Both she and Darin cursed in unison at the sudden explosion of light in their eyes and all threw arms across their faces to block the brightness.

"Sorry," Arkadi mumbled, "automatic reaction." he insisted.

Zara's eyes quickly adjusted to the light and she glanced around her. The bodies of the others all lay nearby. Nat was the person who had obviously lain on both Garon and Darin, and she was already stirring. The chamber they were in was round and rough hewn, much like the one they had fallen from. Opposite each other in the room were two large arching doorways. One of which, Zara now realised the group had fallen through. Zara could see a set of large, wide stairs going up from the entrance and suddenly it dawned on her that they had tumbled and bounced down stairs not some pit for a trap. Another revelation struck her and she had to slap her head in exasperation at their stupidity. Those lines in the floor and the floor then giving way, it was to create a series of steps that led down. This then joined more steps that in turn led to this room! Had they just stayed on the other side of the room near the door they would have been able to simply walk down the steps instead of nearly breaking their necks!

She looked at Garon and Arkadi helping Nat to her feet while Rebba collected their things together.

Zara suddenly realised that not all her friends were there. Bear was nowhere to be seen! Spinning around she looked towards the second doorway that Rebba had assumed was another drop and began heading towards it in a panic. As she hastily approached, she caught sight of Bear. His still form was sprawled uncomfortably a few steps down on another wide staircase that dropped off into the darkness.

Zara was taken aback by the sight. He was still as death, lying on his back with his eyes closed as if he were asleep.

Without turning, she called out, "Bear's over here. He doesn't look good."

To be fair he hadn't looked good before the fall, but he seemed to have suffered more damage. Zara found she was afraid to go towards him. She knew from the battered look on the big man's face and head that he was no longer going to wake easily. For the first time in a long time she felt real concern for Bear. She had worked hard to drive out her feelings for him after their argument years ago. Seeing him again, she had steeled herself, and his lingering anger towards her had made it easier. Even when he had fought the elf lord, she had kept a tight hold on her feelings; kept her anger burning. It had been easier to do because deep down she had believed he could win. Bear was like two people in one body; the dominant one was kind and gentle and... weak; the other was strong, savage and exciting. She had loved that other side to him and yet despised his weak side. She had seen him cut his way through half a dozen attackers like they were wheat and he the scythe, yet she had also seen him scared to even stand up to a single man despite the fact he dwarfed the other. It was all about fear with Bear.

In the battle with the elf lord, it had been close and she had almost leapt to his aid as soon as she realised how good the elf lord was, but she had again clamped down on her emotions, knowing that once he was angry enough to let the real Bear out he would smash the elf down as he had her uncle all those years ago!

Images flashed in her mind, but she thrust them away and looked back at Bear. To see him now so still and helpless was... hard.

Garon shoved past her, disrupting her thoughts as he hurried towards Bear's still form, closely followed by a weary but concerned looking Rebba. Both carried bruises that were already swelling on their faces and both looked worried. She watched mutely as they knelt and carefully examined the big man. Garon glanced her way, his rounded face serious then looked to Rebba. She and Garon silently agreed and took a hold of Bear's shoulders and feet. Carefully they moved him up the steps and placed him gently on the rock hewn floor. Rebba kept a steady hold of his head while Garon hurriedly grabbed a nearby pack and thumped it to check it was soft before placing it beneath.

Zara found she couldn't watch anymore. Feelings and memories she had thought long buried were starting to resurface. She turned and looked back to where the others were pulling themselves together and sought to do the same with her emotions.

Nat Bero was now up. She was holding a thick wad of cloth torn from her tunic to her head above her eye, and blood was clear on the light coloured cloth.

Darin called to Zara and she moved over to where the tall knight was sitting up. Darin asked, "How's Bear?"

Zara looked at him for a second not sure what to say and Darin frowned at her.

"That bad eh?"

Zara shrugged and said warily, "I'm not sure. Garon doesn't look happy though."

"Garon should be happier than me; I broke his fall after all." Darin smirked sardonically.

Little seemed to dampen Darin's humour, though Zara could see the concern for Bear in his eyes. He was the only person who had been closer to Bear than she.

After a few minutes, Zara, Darin and Arkadi had collected together all their belongings and lit some torches to add to the light from Arkadi's spell which he then ended so as not to tax his strength. Nat had been up the stairs and reported that the stairs went up some fifty or more feet and did indeed end in the room from which they had fallen, but the entrance was still blocked by Elisis only knew how much rock in that thick heavy door. That took care of the pursuing elves and their minions at least.

Nat had been very subdued through all of this. It was clear her head pained her, but the careless way she had tripped the hidden trigger in the first place was obviously paining her too.

Arkadi suggested that the room they had been in was designed as a protection and that a trigger might be needed to reopen the door from down here.

The mage's theory about this place made sense, yet Nat had reported that she had hunted out another trigger and could find none. She wanted to keep looking, but as Darin pointed out, that way led back to those elves and their bug warriors.

Arkadi had also suggested that all of these triggers and hidden sections might be some sort of defence or security measure and that whatever was down here was important.

That was the only good news Zara had heard so far this evening. Important meant valuable and that meant a chance to at least make this whole thing partly worthwhile. The group just seemed to be plagued with misfortune. It seemed that the Lady of Luck was not smiling on them at all, something Zara was starting to get used to recently. It had been just another piece of ill luck that when they first triggered the steps they had been stood on the side of the room that the floor would drop down from to form the steps.

All this was going on while Garon and Rebba worked over Bear. They seemed to be alternatively feeding him mixtures that they debated over, forcing them down his throat, and waving their hands over him while they murmured what Zara took to be incantations. Considering the two were followers of religions that outside of the Wildlands at least, were enemies, they worked well together. Bear did not move the whole time they worked and he seemed terribly pale. The dried blood on his head was stark in contrast.

Eventually, both the brown robed druid and the white clad monk climbed to their feet and moved wearily over to throw themselves down beside the others. They looked at the ground, eyes dull and faces lax. Silence fell over the group.

It was Rebba who broke the silence. Without raising her head she said dully, "He remains unconscious and we cannot rouse him."

"The damage to his head has been compounded in the fall and has caused much more serious internal wounds." Garon interjected, now staring wearily at the torch that Nat held.

Rebba's head rose. Her usually rosy face seemed grey with fatigue. "Perhaps with rest I will be able to reach him, but at the moment his mind has fled deep within." She paused and little hope showed in her face. "For the moment we have begun the healing and have given him some herbs to stimulate his energies. There is little more we can do."

"What are you saying? Will he never wake?" Darin asked a deep frown heavy on his forehead. "Will he die?" he almost whispered at Rebba.

Rebba's eyes closed slowly and her face sagged even further with despair. "I do not know for sure, but both Garon and I are agreed that we have never seen anyone recover from such damage... though head injuries are the most difficult to treat or predict."

Anguish twisted in Zara's gut. Bear couldn't die!

Before she could react, Darin growled angrily, "But he has barely a few scratches on him."

"You know as well as we that damage to the head can be fatal even when there is no mark." Garon returned, pleading for understanding.

Darin was having none of it. He shook his head, stood and began pacing. Savagely, he slammed his armoured boot into an outcropping in the floor. The rest of the group glanced at each other in misery. Abruptly, Darin stopped and came over.

"What about the healers above… in Shandrilos? You know those high priests or whatever of yours…" he questioned of Garon, "or that Chief Druid of yours?" he prompted of Rebba. "Surely they could do more."

Garon looked at Rebba in uncertainty.

Rebba replied carefully, "Perhaps, though I have to be honest with you, I have seen others die of fewer injuries than he has sustained."

Darin did not seem to hear the clear message in the druid's tone.

"Then we move out and try to find a way back to the surface." Darin insisted.

The knight looked around at the group his eyes hard, his resolve certain. "Well, what are you waiting for? Let's get moving." He turned to look at Rebba. "You and I will carry Bear." he stated firmly.

Rebba looked Darin straight in the eye and said, completely earnest, "I must rest and sleep." Darin's brows fell even lower in anger and Rebba added, "I would not get a hundred steps before I'd collapse, Darin."

"But Bear…" Darin began, spluttering in fury.

"Bear should not be moved and I will be able to do more to aid him once I have rested!" the druid insisted and was backed by a firm nod from Garon.

Darin looked around. It was clear he was having difficulty believing what he was hearing, but then the Knight of Saint Karodra was more used to action and would find it hard to credit that doing nothing could be helping. Zara sympathised, she wanted to do something for Bear, but she understood they could do nothing until all had rested.

Zara moved over and put a hand on the tall knight's shoulder. "We have been wandering and fighting for several hours now. We seem to be safe at the moment behind that stone door. The evening is gone now, it's night up above. We all need to sleep."

For a second Darin looked like he was going to brush Zara aside, but Arkadi stepped up and added, "The rest would allow us to heal our wounds, we've all been hurt, Nat is still dizzy from the blow to her head, I only have the use of one arm," he emphasised, holding up his bandaged arm, "and Garon and Rebba are exhausted. If we bumped into those creatures again," he glanced up at the ceiling, "we would not last a minute. Do you think that would serve Bear, us all getting killed?"

Darin's jaw twitched as he ground his teeth in frustration. He knew they were right. Abruptly he spun away and walked over to the stairs leading up and sat heavily, his armour screeching briefly against the harsh stone.

The others looked at each other. Slowly each of them began getting packs and opening them, their hands leaden and their movements mechanical. Nat Bero had done well. She had made a point of pre-packing some key items before they had headed down. They had included the usual items for emergencies, some dried and cured food, water skins, blankets and the like, and had made a point of putting in plenty of tinder and torches for light. She had packed a backpack for everyone.

The group quickly decided to use some of their torch wood to light a small fire, more to provide light than warmth. The temperature in the room was quite warm. It was as they were getting their blankets in order and digging out dried strips of beef and a bit of bread and water that Arkadi discovered broken shackles under his pack and stood up in alarm, scanning the room and then looking towards the arched entrance that headed down into the depths. The rest of the group stared at Arkadi in surprise and then they noticed the shackles in his hand and involuntary gasps echoed around the chamber as it hit them all that they had forgotten the small creature who had tumbled down with them!

Zara leapt up and grabbed at the shackles in Arkadi's hand. "I saw him!" she exclaimed in realisation as the fading memory of the creature standing over her came back. "He was standing over me, looking at me." She strained to think. What was it the creature was doing?

Arkadi looked at her, a questioning look in his eye and his dark brows rose in enquiry. Zara waved him away as she tried to think. "He was holding a torch," she began, uncertain, "he was speaking… saying something." Zara shook her head. "He was free of the shackles."

"Well, he's gone now." Nat said and Arkadi looked at her in disgust. The huntress noticed this and insisted, "Well he is!"

"Your powers of observation are incredible, do you know that, Nat!" Arkadi snapped.

"What's more important," Rebba put in, "is that he left without causing us any harm."

Garon nodded, "Yes he had us at his mercy and did nothing. That speaks well of him."

Zara shook her head, "We don't know that for sure, he might have been disturbed by my waking and fled."

"Well, we know which way he went." Arkadi said walking over to stare into the dark hole that was the second stairwell.

"We'll need to post a guard; the creature does not seem too dangerous, but those elves and bugs could find a different way down."

Before anyone could volunteer, Darin stood up and said, "I'll take the first watch. I can't sleep at the moment." Everyone looked at the knight and none argued. He had sat unmoving the whole time that the others had been organising things, staring at the floor in front of him. Zara quickly volunteered for the second watch and Nat took the last.

Zara watched as Darin sat himself on the top steps again; pulling his huge sword from its sheath he placed it carefully by his leg in easy reach. The others quickly moved over to lie or sit on their blankets. Nat was clearly in pain and Garon gave her something to ease it from his belt pouch. Only Zara and Arkadi did not go right away to their blankets. Zara stood staring at Darin, trying to get a grip on what she was feeling, while Arkadi stared at the shackles, puzzlement evident in his swarthy features.

Obviously, reaching a decision, Arkadi moved over to Zara, pointed at the shackles and asked, "May I examine those? There is something not quite right about them."

Zara shrugged, "Of course," and handed over the shackles and chain.

Arkadi took them gently and walked over to his blankets, his gaze fixed.

Zara watched him go and then sighed heavily, thoughts of the past running through her mind. She realised as well that she was actually tired. With all the action, she had been running on adrenalin and now she could feel that ebbing to leave the bone deep weariness that came after combat. It was a feeling she had not felt in some months, not since the duel in the arena.

She walked over to her blanket and lay down. She moved around for a few moments trying to get comfortable, but quickly gave up; her armour would not let her get properly comfortable, but she was not going to remove it. She placed her hands behind her head for a pillow and stared up at the featureless, grey stone ceiling.

Where had things gone wrong? Was it when she and Bear had gone their separate ways all those years ago?

Things had been difficult after Bear left. Darin had become a knight, Karis and Nat got married and settled down. It had been difficult to be on her own with no stern giant to watch her back or to support her when things got tough. She had wandered for a while then used her money to buy a house in Ostia. She had also bought the Greatheart Inn and had enough left to set up a partnership with an Ostian spice merchant. This gave her a comfortable life. Eventually, though she had got bored and signed on with another mercenary band. Without Bear's morals holding her back, she had no qualms about joining a less than wholesome group. There had been some difficulties at first as some of the more vicious warriors had tried it on with her, but she had brutally shown that she was no easy target. She had learned quickly how things worked and used her charms and looks to gain allies to watch her back while using her blades to deal with competitors. It had been exciting and she had enjoyed the life and had risen and finally taken over, killing the band's chief in single combat. Once she had command, she used the band to further her fortunes and theirs, but something had always been missing. She could admit that now. It had been an exhilarating time, but she had not been able to show any weakness or to get really close to anyone. The mercenaries in her band were not the sort to ever really trust, not like Bear and Darin and the others.

The band did well under her leadership, their wealth had grown. Yet she had tired of leading the band so she had passed over control, took her money and looked for other challenges.

With her wealth invested in many businesses in Ostia, she had become a prominent citizen and had decided to reinvent herself as a lady and return to the court of the High Lord. She had adapted herself to the combat of court, but it had not been what she thought it would be; too many niceties and subtleties, not enough direct aggression. She found she missed the dangers and excitement of battle. Steadily, she had become more and more reckless, putting herself in positions where she knew she would be in danger; irritating powerful nobles. People turned on her and her business suffered, but she ignored it.

Only now could she see how self-destructive she had become, but there had been no one to check her. She indulged in whatever took her fancy, descended to depths of excess and lost herself. She poisoned, murdered and swindled the arrogant nobles until she was almost universally hated at court, but then she got careless.

Her businesses were suffering, her excesses were taking control and she was finally trapped by the nobles. The Whore of Ostia as they now named her was arrested and charged, framed by the noble houses.

It was the High Lord who had saved her. Secretly, he offered a way out. The High Lord's pardon in return for her working for him. He knew her skills. There was little choice; become his agent or be executed! She had agreed to serve. However, the High Lord warned her to clean herself up, she was no use to him drunk, drugged or as reckless as she had become. She worked at being the reputable merchant again, while the High Lord sent her off on his special 'errands'!

However, to the nobles of Ostia she was still the Whore! They hated her and wanted her gone. They made her life hell in Ostia but they could not act directly against her for fear of the High Lord.

It was then she met Evard

Now that she looked back on it she realised what a fool she had been. It was too convenient. Yet she had fallen for him. He was such a compellingly beautiful man; exotic coppery, Olmec complexion; lustrous, long raven black hair; and eyes almost as dark and absorbing. He was confident and brash, exciting and bold, and best of all, rich! She was convinced he was the man for her and she pursued him.

Oh, how the nobles must have laughed. If she ever found out which house was behind it all, she would hunt them to extinction!

Zara closed her eyes in pain as sharpness seemed to pierce her chest.

Even now, with the reality clear, her feelings for Evard still hurt, though she would admit that to no one. Evard had shared her interests, humour, desires and excesses and she became truly enamoured of him. Life became almost bearable again. She had even begun to believe him when he said he loved her. When he had proposed they leave Ostia, go south and start again, she had jumped at the idea; get away from the hateful nobles and get out from under the High Lord's control.

'Oh, why couldn't it have been true,' she thought, misery rising up in her again. 'But no, life could never be that simple for Zara Halven,' she thought bitterly. 'No happiness, only disappointment and loneliness.'

Her thoughts strayed back again to the duel in the arena. Evard had been waiting for her. He'd placed the bets and was sat next to the master of combat ready to collect the winnings and meet her in the pit stalls after the death match.

Evard had convinced her they needed one big score before they left to help set things up in the south. They planned the duel on the fact that few nobles knew the extent of her skills. It was still dangerous, but she was confident. She gathered all the wealth she could and pooled it with Evard's money to bet it all on a death match. Once the match was over they would leave the city. They would head south for Lauria and beyond into Kilimar where Zara had been investing with Evard's brother, a merchant in the very profitable spice trade to far off Tanzabar. They just needed the right target. Zara would have challenged one of the nobles, but Evard had pointed out that they would not accept and they would not get very good odds unless the opponent was sufficiently skilled and well known. There was only one target who would work; Lord Killilan, the High Lord's champion!

Zara had forced the confrontation with Lord Killilan, insulted him in front of the whole court. She had known the arrogant sword master couldn't tolerate the insult from her, the Whore of Ostia. The insult had resulted in the inevitable challenge being issued and the duel being set. The High Lord had been furious, but he could not step in for his champion, it would insult his honour, but it had not stopped him from pressuring her. She had avoided his agents and the duel was set. It had been high news in Ostia; a death match! The sword master had won more than a dozen duels. No one had even so much as scratched him; the Whore of Ostia stood no chance and the nobles were more than happy to bet against her!

Zara found herself blinking back tears and furiously wiped them away. It hurt to have been played so completely. She knew now that the High Lord had been trying to warn her, had even tried to have Evard killed, but she had foiled the assassination herself! At the time this had made her hate the High Lord even more and made her all the more determined to kill his champion.

Her mind returned to that triumph in the arena.

The swordmaster was yet she had cut him down in under five minutes.

The common folk in the crowd had cheered her name and she had basked in their adulation, adrenalin had sharpened her every sense to the extreme and her chest had swelled with pride and power. She had stridden off the sand like a god. Life was divine.

A scant hour later her life was in ruins. She was no longer a god, merely a fool. Evard had collected the bets they had placed, had collected the winnings from the master of combat, had collected their horses and belongings, and had… vanished!

At first, as she sat in the pit stalls, she had felt worried. She had wondered why he was late. What was taking so long.? An hour later, she was in a panic. Had he been attacked?

Gods, what a fool she had been!

Zara's concern had begun to change to suspicion; a suspicion that was later confirmed in a visit from the High Lord. Her heart turned to dust as he related what had happened and at the same time cut all ties with her. She was lucky he hadn't done worse. Evard had gone, many had seen him heading for the gates as fast as he could ride.

With Evard's departure, she lost a small fortune, but more than that she lost her pride and belief that anyone would ever care for her. Her heartache had quickly turned to anger, the familiar anger. She couldn't believe she had been so completely fooled. Zara had wanted too much for Evard to be real.

She had almost lost all grip on life at that point, had used what little she had left to drown her sorrows. She still had the inn and her house in Ostia, but nothing else. Slowly, she had sought to close the wound and repair her defences. She buried her feelings deep and stoked her anger and bitterness to armour herself, but it was hard. She had begun to contemplate ending it all. When the call to meet her old friends had come, she had seen it as a life line, a chance to go back to the way things were before Evard to a time when she had been happy. A chance perhaps for a new start.

What hurt most was that she had managed to ruin that too and possibly kill the only man who had truly felt anything for her.

She hadn't cried since she was twelve years old, but she drifted off to sleep with tears streaming down her cheeks.

Chapter 23

RETURN FROM THE DEPTHS

The Nordic believe that the All-Father created many worlds, among them; Kalathrond, realm of the gods; Nargathrond, the dark underworld; and Mithrond, our world. Connecting these worlds is a fiery bridge upon which Varinoth stands eternal guard. When a person dies they go to Kalathrond to Dorvath Kor, the Hall of Reckoning and are judged by Olwyn the Wise. The good go to Elithra, the land of eternal summer ruled by Tynast, and warriors get to feast in his hall, Stoba Kor! The evil go to Nargathrond, where Surtyn the Shadow holds sway and are taken there by cold Ishara the Doombringer who guides all of the souls of the dead.

From the Writings of the White Lady of Mundia, believed to date from around BY260-280

Darin of Kenarth watched the gloom in front of him. It had been hours since he had begun his watch. He knew he should have woken Zara for the second watch some time ago, but in truth he needed little sleep. He had spent all of yesterday and this morning resting in his order's Chapter House while Bear had been off meeting some old masters from the college.

He wasn't sure exactly how much time had passed since he had begun his watch; it was hard to tell in the permanent twilight from the small fire. He estimated it was the last hours of darkness before dawn. The fire had almost gone out, but he had fed it with a few bits of thin branches from the torches every so often. They would soon be running out of wood and would have to rely on Arkadi to light the way.

He stared at the gloom below where the steps disappeared into total darkness. However, he kept seeing Bear's pale face, slack, his head slashed and bloodstained. He couldn't shake the image no matter how much he tried. It seemed to return again as soon as he relaxed. It was not the injuries themselves but rather what Rebba had said. 'No one she knew had survived injuries like that.' Darin had not given up hope though. If anyone could prove Rebba wrong it was Bear. He was one of the strongest men Darin had known, not just physically, but mentally. Little more than a few hours ago he had watched in admiration as his friend fought the finest battle of his life.

'Hah,' that elf had looked really surprised when Bear's blade had spit him like a stuck pig! The elf had been so arrogant, so confident, and Bear cut him down to size as Darin had known he would. Others might not have believed Bear could beat the elf lord in those first moments; after all it had been clear that the elf was far more skilled than Bear and lightning fast, but Darin knew Bear better than anyone. Darin was a student of war and he had watched his oldest friend closely over the years and knew that once Bear entered combat he changed, he became a berserker-like warrior, his strength and speed increased, but also, unlike other berserkers, so too did his skill. He was unique in Darin's experience and so he had watched and waited. The magic had been a cause for concern and he had worried that the elf would do some real damage before Bear could get going, but just as things seemed to go badly, the berserker rage exploded out and he had torn through the elves. Darin just couldn't understand what had happened after that. His friend laid low by a blow to the head!

So intent had he been on his thoughts that he realised with a start that he was no longer seeing darkness down the steps ahead of him. Instead he was seeing light, or at least a lightening of the darkness. Suddenly he saw a flickering flame, tiny in the distance, but clear and heading this way. He strained his eyes to see, even as he grasped his sword and stood up. Was it a figure he could see below? Holding a torch?

"I see something!" he hissed intensely. He heard a rustle and scrapping sound as blades were drawn and his friends came to their feet at his urgent call. "There's something coming."

Suddenly, Nat and Zara were next to him. Peering down at the bobbing light below, shadows stretched and danced and threw monstrous images across the stone walls. The friends stood there for several moments, still and tense. Darin was eager for a fight, anything to take away this helplessness he was feeling.

'I'll take care of whatever needs taking care off.' He thought.

His hand tightened around the soft leather bound hilt of his great sword.

"What do you see Nat?" whispered Zara past Darin's ear, even as she slipped on her battered helm.

The lanky huntress had good eyes, but it wasn't the huntress who replied, it was Rebba. Her voice came from behind Darin.

"It is the dwarf creature. He is alone." the druid asserted firmly.

Darin trusted Rebba's senses, besides it was clear now that it was a single figure. Why was it coming back? It had made good its escape.

"Perhaps there is no way out down there and the creature has been forced back this way." Arkadi ventured in response to Darin's unspoken question.

Darin was unsure what to do and no one else seemed ready to do anything. They all just stood and watched as the figure got closer, marching steadily up the rock steps. Soon they could all make out its blunt features and slightly gaudy cloths. Its face was ruddy red like an apple and though its face seemed more suited to jollity, worry lines creased its brow and surrounded its tightly drawn mouth. When it was no more than a dozen steps from where the group stood huddled at the entrance to the chamber, it stopped with its arms by its side and a slightly puzzled look on its face. Its blue eyes scanned them, its head tilted slightly. The creature seemed to have a question that it didn't know how to ask. Its small mouth opened and it brought the hand up that was not holding the torch and opened its hand palm first. Then it began to speak. At least that's what Darin assumed it did, though he couldn't understand a word it said.

Abruptly, Rebba gasped, "What was that last bit? *'Galton ath di'*, did it say? Isn't that Elven for 'friend' or 'I am a friend' or some such?"

Darin knew the question was not for him, he knew nothing about elves save they were a people he would now happily avoid. It was a question for Arkadi, none of the others knew anything more than he so it was a surprise when Nat Bero answered.

"The phrase, '*Galton ath di*' means 'we can be friends'." the archer muttered, "He seems to want peace.

"Hardly surprising in his position." snorted Zara.

"Yes, but do any of us speak Elven?" Arkadi asked. "I know very little save some bits that I learnt by rote in my apprenticeship." He paused before adding, "Bear was the expert."

Zara snapped, "Is the expert!" She glared at the mage.

Arkadi grimaced and held up a hand in apology, nodding. "What about you Nat, do you speak any more?"

"That depends on what you want me to say, doesn't it. I have a few phrases, mostly picked up from Bear or from old stories."

Darin could almost see the frown on Zara's face at the archer's tone, but she did not take her eyes off the dwarven creature that seemed to have stopped and was straining to hear and see what reaction his words were having.

Darin listened for a moment while Arkadi, Zara and Rebba debated what it was they wanted to say and whether they should trust the creature.

"Why don't you use one of those translating spells, or whatever you called it… that the elf used to talk to us?" Darin interjected.

The debate stopped. Zara asked, "Do you know how to do that, Arkadi?"

There was a pause and Arkadi hummed. "The trick with translation spells is that you need to either link strongly with the mind you are communicating with or have some kind of highly adaptive sound interpreter for a language that is based on the sounds made and a low level empathic link that can decipher the patterns of the language and link the structure of the language with the empathic emanations." Arkadi took a breath to continue, but Zara spoke over him.

"By Tynast's fiery breath!" she exclaimed. "If I wanted to know all that I would have joined your bloody college myself. A simple yes or no, Arkadi."

"What I am saying Zara," Arkadi snapped back, "is I don't know. That elf managed it without any empathic link of which I know. I can't even speculate on how he did it. I, on the other hand, would have to have the creature's co-operation, or at least not have it bolt as soon as I start my spell!"

"The let's invite it up here," Darin put in quickly, anxious to get on with something, anything.

"Move back," he snapped not waiting for a reply. "We need to get it into the room."

Everyone began moving back as Zara snapped acerbically, "How are you going to invite it up? Send it a nicely scented letter, perhaps."

"No," Darin replied, "I am going to use simple body language." Darin put away his sword as he stepped back into the room. He waved for the others to do the same and then began to motion to the creature to come forward. The creature glanced at them all in turn, warily. It chewed its lip and then moved a few steps forward. Darin saw it hesitate and said, "Everyone sit down... near the fire. Try to look friendly." He lowered himself down to his knees and then sat. The others looked at Darin and then at each other. Rebba quickly sat, followed by Garon. The others followed suit. None of them could see the creature now, but they heard its foot falls on the steps and then its head came into view. Again, Darin beckoned to it and the creature responded. It slowly stepped up and into the room and moved to face the group who were sat in a rough semi-circle around the fire. Abruptly it sat. It lowered its torch which it then carefully added to the fire.

Arkadi then began his spell with a light chant under his breath. Darin only knew because he had expected it, but the creature seemed to know instantly. Its dark eyes fixed on the cross legged mage, they widened and it made as if to move backward, but it did not flee. Instead it seemed to be listening closely, trying to discern what the mage was saying. Arkadi's whispering spell came to an end with no discernible effect as far as Darin could see. Everyone was still; they didn't know what to do.

It was Nat Bero who broke the silence with a loud whisper to Arkadi, "He seems to know about magic." she said nodding at the creature who stood little taller than Darin when he was sat down.

Before Arkadi could respond the creature looked directly at the huntress and said in a clear voice, "Indeed I do, master, and though I am not familiar with that particular weaving, I sensed its purpose."

Nat Bero looked at the creature in alarm and gasped, "It can speak."

Arkadi frowned at Nat as if to say 'of course he can you idiot.' Nat realised her mistake and looked around the group a little sheepishly before grinning and shrugging.

Darin wondered about the title the creature had given to Nat automatically. It seemed clear that the creature was a slave or servant of some sort, but why had he been chained.

"You are familiar with magic, how? Earlier I sensed no talent in you, yet now I do. You are obviously trained or you would not have sensed my spell so quickly." Arkadi said in a calm, authoritative voice.

"You are wise, master." the creature began in its high piping voice before licking its lips a little nervously. "I do have talent and I have trained for many years, but my expertise is limited to a small field of magic at which I have..." The creature paused and seemed to sit straighter, "become *Uthsan'kal* to House *Totheariss*." He seemed a little dubious as he finished, as if he was no longer sure of himself.

"*Uthsan'kal...? Totheariss...?*" Arkadi questioned, looking over at Rebba and Garon, at a loss. "We are unfamiliar with these words."

"Ah, master. Forgive me. I had forgotten where I was." The creature swallowed and then began to speak slowly. "*Uthsan'kal*, is a title. It means that I am one of the craftsmen responsible for creating magical artifacts for my house. The name of my house is *Totheariss*. I have been told that in the ancient language of the Great Masters it refers to a fearsome ghostly woman."

"He's an enchanter!" Garon exclaimed, looking at Arkadi who nodded.

Darin knew that enchanters were one of the rarer types of magicuser. They specialised in creating items that retained a magical ability permanently.

"The Great Masters, who are they? The elves?" Arkadi speculated.

"Yes, master." was the quick reply.

"We know little of your Great Masters. We would like to know more." Arkadi hinted quietly but firmly.

Zara interrupted roughly, "Yeah, and what are they doing here? Why did they attack us?"

The small creature stood and took an involuntary step back at Zara's angry tone and Arkadi shot her a warning look. "Please, my friend. Sit down and join us." he said soothingly, pointing for the creature to sit down where he was stood. "We are very confused and could use your help."

The creature seemed appeased by Arkadi's tone and even seemed to perk up at the thought of helping. He was definitely a servant, Darin thought, and a well conditioned one at that.

As the creature carefully folded his legs and seemed to get even smaller, Rebba asked quietly, "First of all tell us your name. We don't even know what to call you."

The creature seemed uncertain and Darin guessed that the creature was unused to such familiarity with its former masters.

"My name is Nossi Bee, masters. I..." he hesitated, "I will try to answer your questions, but it is difficult, Masters, there is such a lot." The creature, Nossi seemed pained by his response.

"Please Nossi, you don't need to call us masters, my name is Rebba..." the druid put in, though Nat Bero muttered in a loud whisper, 'Speak for yourself, I like being called master.' but already the creature was shaking its head strongly.

"No, master, it would not be right." Nossi Bee replied firmly.

Rebba frowned.

Arkadi put in, "Start at the beginning, Nossi. Tell us how you ended up here."

Zara looked firmly at the black robed mage. "We need answers and quick, Arkadi, not the damn things life story."

"We aren't going anywhere at the moment, Zara. Bear can't be moved and Rebba and Garon need rest if they are to help him." Darin returned before Arkadi could.

Zara looked at him in defiance for a moment and then waved her hand for the creature to get on with it.

Darin turned and smiled at the strange little man. "Please, go on. We are all interested in your story, little friend."

215

Chapter 24

A THREAT REVEALED

The ancient Cumb'Rai, our ancestors, it seems inherited their beliefs and gods from the Elder races. The links between the gods of our people and those of the dwarves and elves is direct; the Elven Lord of Light, Estarn is associated with the earth, battle and duty, much as Tynast is for us, while Themone, Lady of Knowledge and Justice equates almost exactly with Ishara, our harsh goddess of Winter. This is also true of the Elven Lords of Darkness, the Demon Gods such as Eleora'Ashar the Plague-Bearer who equates with Mayvan the Enchantress, Queen of the Undead.

From the Writings of the White Lady of Mundia, believed to date from around BY260-280

The group of humans continued to look at him expectantly and Nossi was uncertain what they really wanted. It was such an easy thing to ask – to tell his tale - but such a hard thing to do. Nevertheless, it was obvious that he had little choice. Regardless of how these 'humans' – he rolled the word around in his mind, he had only heard it rarely – regardless of how these humans had accepted him to their fire, he knew they were a dangerous and unpredictable lot. They had managed to destroy the dark brothers, the mayax and the ogres, not an easy feat in itself, but they had also slain the Great Masters and the Lord of House Totheariss himself!

That was unheard of; only Great Masters could slay other Great Masters. He realised, even as he thought it that this was not completely true, the Great Masters were mortal just like all the other races, but they were powerful, long lived and deadly. They controlled all aspects of life and almost all of what Nossi knew came from the Great Masters, indeed all that any of the lesser races knew came from the Great Masters.

For his whole life Nossi had believed all that he had been told without doubt; instantly. That was until they took away his greatest treasure, his greatest love. Since then nothing had seemed to make sense. Doubt was a constant companion, doubt and hatred! These two things had led him here now, facing a group of savages. He knew some would quite happily do him harm without a thought while others he sensed, though controlled, were not far from violence. He was especially afraid of the female warrior with the swords strapped to her back and the dark robed mage who looked at him as the Great Masters had done; coldly, without feeling. To this creature he was a puzzle, a mystery to be unravelled, not a living thing. This one's power he could feel, he was strong in the Lore.

Looking into the hungry and curious eyes, Nossi was suddenly sure of where to begin. He knew little about them and they knew little of him and his kind. They had looked at him with curious eyes even as they fled down the tunnels. They had looked at him as if he were going to turn into something nasty at any moment and he had been afraid. The stories the Great Masters had told about the ape men, the 'humans' were horrific and yet they had done little so far to justify those stories. However, Nossi still wasn't sure of them. They were obviously powerful and well-trained killers. They had asked him for his story because they wanted to understand the threat they faced, but Nossi felt a need to tell them more; to make them understand his life and his choices, though why this suddenly seemed important he wasn't sure. Perhaps he just wanted to be accepted now that he had no one.

Nossi looked around him at this strange group who were his only hope in these alien lands. He was far from home, if home it had ever been; and he was far from being the person he had once been just a short time ago. His life had been shattered in the last few months and this seemed to be just the latest in a long string of harrowing upheavals. Those events leapt to mind and Nossi quickly pushed them back. It was painful to think about his past and his land. He looked again at those around him, hemming him in, and wondered if he had made the right decision.

He had realised quite quickly after the fall that he now had a chance to escape from the humans, and escape he had. Down the stairs he had fled, only pausing to take a torch. However, as he fled he began to wonder to where he was fleeing. If he returned to the Great Masters he would become their slave once more, something he once had not even realised he was. Also, if he managed to avoid his former masters, where then? He was in a strange land full of strange people of whom he knew nothing and the humans he had met were savage and strange.

However, what had finally made him turn around and return was the thought that the humans were the enemies of the Great Masters; the people who had destroyed all that he had loved. Also, these humans had proved themselves quite capable of killing them; something that Nossi in his wildest and most secret fantasies hadn't believed could be done.

It had been a hard decision; one that might see him killed and yet the prospect with the Great Masters was even more terrible to him now. He would rather die than be a slave again. He was better off with the humans, at least for the moment.

They were an odd race; tall like the Great Masters, but far thicker and heavier in build. They appeared stronger but cruder, like poor imitations. However, in a way, their features were kinder, more animated and alive. Emotions played across their faces far more easily, and their movements and features reminded him more of his own people than the cold Great Masters, though of course humans were far too big and cumbersome.

Nossi took a deep breath and then took a long look at the expectant faces around him. The tall one clad one in green; and the warrior with the two blades were quite obviously losing their patience.

"I am sorry, masters. Your question is a simple one, but not one so simply answered." He could see the brows of several of the more brutal looking humans fall and realised that this was not a good sign, he stuttered, "I will endeavour to give you a clear account of myself. However, before that you must understand something of my people and my land for they are far from what I know of yours."

Shifting his gaze to the small fire that gave off what little light there was in the stone chamber, he began. "My people are a small race by your standards. I am little more than average in height for a male and am better in health and strength than most due to my high status among the Lessers. As an *Uthsan'kal* I have privileges that others of my people would not. Most of my people are workers; we have great skill and dexterity and so tend to be craftsmen amongst the Lessers of the Great Houses. My people call themselves the '*Gnorman*' or 'earth people' for we have always been closely connected to it. To our masters we are more simply known as 'gnomes', a corruption, though one more easily pronounced by the ogres and mayax."

Nossi could see that a number of the humans were looking at one another with expressions that Nossi guessed meant confusion or lack of understanding and he added, "The ogres you have met. You slew two of those great creatures after using a mighty spell to imprison them in the living wood of the two great doors." Nossi saw the human's nod and some looked towards the fiery haired female and smiled.

'How easily they gave their emotions to one another,' Nossi thought. 'How unwise and yet how wonderful.' "As for the mayax…"

"Are they those giant insect-like creatures?" interrupted the tall female.

"Yes, those are the mayax, the most loyal servants of the Great Masters. They are the common workers and soldiers of the Great Houses." Nossi could see the dark robed loreman and the brown clad one were intrigued. "You see my people are but one of many different peoples who serve or are allied with the Great Masters. My own people have lived as Lessers of the Great Masters for as long as we can remember… though there are some who believe we were once our own people before the coming of the Great Masters, but that is just rumour. In truth no one knows whether we came with the Great Masters or whether we already dwelt in the homeland, though the *Gonkalder* might know." Nossi mused.

"The *Gonkalder*?" This was a question from the steel clad warrior with the sword that was taller than Nossi at full stretch.

"Yes, the princes of the Great Masters who rule the lands. You see the Great Masters, those whom you call elves, are not all equal, although even the lowliest is far above my kind. The Great House in which I was born is very clear in its structure; as are all of the Great Houses. At the bottom are the Lessers; the mayax, the skriegan, vilyarans and my own people, then come the citizen peoples, the ogres and the dark brothers…"

"You mean the dark skinned goblins?" the female warrior with the blades asked, her tone harsh.

Nossi was reminded of how precarious his position here amongst these creatures was, but he watched as a number of the others, the more dominant ones glared at the angry female warrior. It was puzzling with these creatures. There seemed to be no real leader among them, no clear line of leadership. It was so unlike the ordered society from which he came. Rank was known and most carefully adhered to; to break rank was to take an immense risk. The consequences would often prove fatal. "Yes I believe I do, though I do not understand the word that you use." Nossi quickly answered not wanting a dispute among the humans. "They are paired with the elves and totally loyal to their given Great Master."

"See this is what I don't understand!" the female with the twin swords snapped, not at Nossi, but now at the other humans. "Goblins hate elves and elves hate goblins!" She asserted."It is central to everything we know!"

"It's obvious that those are only the elves and goblins we know, Zara," responded the dark loreman, "not that we really know either of those races. What do we truly know of the elves? No one has ever really spoken to them as far as is known and the goblins come from the northlands and they are vast by all accounts. Who knows what might exist there?"

"Okay, okay, Arkadi, though it is good to hear you admit that you precious magi don't know everything." the warrior pointed out, firmly.

The dark robed loreman glared at the warrior.

Nossi wondered if this play for dominance among these two would end in combat, though Nossi did detect some undertone he was not familiar with in the warrior, Zara's tone, and he noticed too that some of the other humans were smiling.

Again Nossi was confused. These humans seemed to take delight in baiting one another, an act that would have produced an instant and probably fatal response from the masters of his land.

Nossi sat quietly as the two humans stared at each other, not daring to make a sound lest he set off something. Instead, the tall steel clad warrior with the huge sword, snapped, "Would you two just drop it and let us get on with this. You can debate who knows what all you want afterwards." The swordsman turned his blue eyed gaze onto Nossi again, as he had at the start and motioned with his large hand for Nossi to continue.

Nossi was a little flustered, but the kind eyed female in the brown robes reminded him where he had been up to, saying, 'dark brothers' questioningly.

Nossi nodded gratefully. "Those you term 'goblins' we call the dark brothers because they are joined in some unknown way to the Great Masters. For each Great Master, a dark brother is given to be his companion, his guardian and his most trusted servant. Dark brothers are utterly loyal." Nossi could still see that this just seemed to confound the warrior, Zara, but he pushed on. "Amongst the Great Masters themselves there are ranks, from the lowest workers and crafters to the lords of the houses and the princes of the realms, the *Gonkalder*. The Great Houses, the *'Athron'* are the basis of our society. All people must be members of a house or they are outcasts, renegades, with no rights or protections. The Great Houses are made up of a ruling family of Great Masters with many lesser families or Houses as part of the Great Houses. Below these are the citizen peoples and the Lessers. Houses vie for rank amongst each other with the greatest houses becoming heads of clans made up of many houses. These clans in turn are part of a province ruled by the princes of the realm. These are the greatest among the Great Masters and are the descendants of the *Ata'Gon*, the Great One himself!"

"Great One? An interesting sounding title." The white clad, rotund human muttered.

"The *Ata'Gon* is the Lord of All. He is the ruler of all people and the most powerful of all mortal creatures. He is the first servant and disciple of the Gods."

There was silence for a moment with all the humans thinking and looking uncertain.

The brown robed female loreman with the wild fiery hair looked to her dark robed companion, "Do any of you recognise anything of what he is saying? I have heard that name somewhere before, but the rest doesn't seem to tie in with the druid legends of the Elder races that I know."

"Bear would know." the harsh female muttered.

The loreman, Arkadi nodded and then looked around at the other humans. They all looked blank. The loreman looked at Nossi and asked quietly, "What is this 'Great One' like?" His scrutiny was intense.

Nossi opened his hands and shrugged, "I cannot say, master. I have never seen him, nor know of any who have. He has always been our leader and our guide for thousands of years."

"Thousands of years! That is not possible, even for an elf, surely." The dark robed loreman looked to his brown robbed companion and said quizzically, "A legend perhaps?"

"Or a prophet or holy man venerated still." The kind eyed female responded, receiving a nod from his dark robed companion.

Nossi wasn't sure what the two loremen meant, but did they think the Great One dead? Nossi was nervous at such blasphemy and looked around fearfully for a second wondering if the Gods would strike them all down. When he looked back, Nossi found both loremen were now looking at him. The dark robed Arkadi nodded and raised his brows, a sign, Nossi assumed, that meant he should go on.

"From the *Ata'Gon* are descended the great princes. There are many princes who vie for power, many of their names are famed throughout the lands for they are the holy leaders of the Great Masters and all very powerful. My province, clan and house are in the demesne of Prince Uh'Ram Bloodfire, said to be the most powerful of the princes, a great warrior and loremaster."

Nossi could see that many of the humans were now frowning at the strange names and titles and trying hard to understand what Nossi was telling them.

It was the white clad human who finally broke the silence. "This is all very interesting, but what are these ungodly creatures doing here?" He asked of the group, looking at several faces before all eyes began to turn to look at Nossi once again.

"How I or we got here is another question that is not quickly answered, masters." Nossi said meekly.

"We have plenty of time on our hands at the moment it seems." The warrior woman, Zara snapped abruptly before continuing in a more normal tone. "All this information is very interesting as my large monkish friend here has said…" Again Nossi detected that tone that he was unfamiliar with in the warrior's voice. "But how did you get here, why did you come, and more importantly why did you attack us?" she finished harshly.

The warrior frightened Nossi. He wanted to turn and flee, but he knew that the others, while more sympathetic, were as keen to get answers as the warrior and would pursue him in an instant were he to run. He had made his choice now and would have to stick with it. These humans were his best chance of survival, though why that mattered to him anymore he was not sure. He had little to live for, save his revenge, though he hardly dared even think of such a possibility.

"First of all," Nossi responded firmly, surprising himself, "let me say that I did not attack you, nor did I ever have any intention of attacking you. I was as much a victim as you yourselves."

"That we have seen, my little friend," responded the brown robed female kindly, "but we need to understand the motives of those who came with you and what they want. I have a feeling that this may be the most important information we have ever heard in our lives." The other humans looked at her and frowned, though they did not disagree.

Nossi was not sure of how to explain. The politics of the Great Masters were complicated and he was not someone privy to their machinations. However, he had picked up bits and pieces of information and had also been educated by the Great Masters as all the Lessers were; educated to know their places and to know who their masters were! Nossi took a deep breath to steady his nerves and then began.

"As I have said, the structure of our society is based upon the Great Houses. My house was Totheariss and the Lord of House Totheariss in my youth was Lord Vol'Dakor. He had successfully led his house to control many lesser houses and to take the leadership of all of Clan Ar'Karon. Now Lord Vol'Dakar was a very pious man, he believed strongly in seeking to find a way to take revenge and take back the land of plenty that they had been driven from. So it was that Lord Vol'Dakor came to the attention of Prince Uh'Ram and was rewarded for his beliefs by being given a place in the *Athel dra'sah Mandil Koh'Ran* and allowed the position of *Parinsar* in Prince Uh-Ram's own Warhost."

"Woh, woh!" cried the tall armoured swordsmen, "Hold on there." He held up his hand in apparent dismay.

Nossi frowned and looked from face to face in alarm. He almost got to his feet. Had he offended the swordsman?

"Sorry, my little friend but…" he looked around at his companions, "is it only me or are the rest of you losing what the hell he is saying and just not admitting it?"

"Well actually, I know exactly what he is talking about." snapped the tall dark haired woman with the bow, "Surely you've heard of the 'Atheldasamandiloran' Darin?" She asked in that tone of which Nossi was unsure.

The tall swordsman, Darin just snorted in derision at the woman while the dark loreman, Arkadi replied in a similar tone, "It was 'Athel drasa Mandil Koran' actually, and no," he said turning to the swordsman, Darin, "I have no idea what it all means." He turned his dark piercing eyes to Nossi and pinned him with his stare. "Nossi you are going a little too fast for us. We have never heard of these things of which you speak, despite…" and here his eyes looked briefly towards the woman in green, "what some of us have said. You must explain."

Nossi was still confounded by how these humans interacted, but although it was said in a polite tone, it was a command all the same.

"*Athel dra'sah Mandil Koh'Ran*, is from the old language of the Great Masters and it means…" Nossi paused thoughtfully, he knew only a little of the ancient dialect of the Great Masters and there were several possible translations, "the war or crusade of divine retribution, I think." He thought and then nodded. "Yes, that is about right and Prince Uh'Ram leads the *Mandilath Koh'Ran* or Divine Avengers, the Warhost responsible for avenging the Great Masters and taking back their ancient lands!"

"Yes, but what does that all mean?" the swordsman, Darin asked obviously no clearer on the subject. "War against whom? Avenge what?"

"I am sorry master." Nossi apologised, "but I do not know. Such history of the Great Masters is not permitted of the Lessers." Nossi noticed the faces of the humans once again darkening and hurriedly added, "However, there is a story amongst the Lessers, a forbidden story…" Nossi hesitated and shuddered, to be caught spreading this tale was fatal, but he had thrown his lot in with the humans now so he took a deep breath and forged on, "It is said that ages ago, a great war was fought by the Great Masters against an ancient enemy. The *Ata'Gon* formed the *Mandilath Koh'Ran* and his favoured heir, Prince Areng'Var was sent to strike back at the enemy. Little is known of what happened save that many died. It is even said…" Nossi whispered and leaned forward conspiratorially, "that the Prince was killed and the Great One himself somehow injured. He has not been seen outside of the Holy City since, though the Great Masters refute this and any caught uttering such blasphemy faces a swift death!" Nossi looked around fearfully. Would the dark gods strike him down? He was committed now and continued. "However, in my youth, it was said that another attempt was to be made against the Great Master's ancient enemy and Prince Uh'Ram was very keen to lead and take revenge. The lost prince, Areng'Var was his father!"

Nossi had not looked at the humans as he spoke, his eyes had been looking at the stone floor in front of his sturdy leather boots, his mind's eye intent on the faces that flashed past from his memory as he spoke, sticking on that most wonderful of faces; the face he would never forget. So as he looked up he was unprepared for the faces that looked back at him. Some of their faces were turned away, but all that he could see were astonished; alarm, curiosity, worry and fear were spread thick across their faces in equal measures. Nossi was at a loss for words for a moment. He gathered himself and asked, "Have I offended, masters?"

Eyes that had been looking off into the distance refocused on Nossi and he was afraid.

"Are you trying to tell us that we were attacked and almost killed because of some elf's desire for revenge for his father who died centuries ago?" snarled the warrior woman Zara in fury, her fist clenched in front of her.

Nossi just stared at the fearsome woman, unable to answer her anger.

The brown robed female loreman sat forward in sudden excitement, "Do you think this links to the legends of the destruction of the Elder?" The kindly woman stopped and frowned. "There is no mention of a divine leader of the elves in the legends and what is all this about vengeance… vengeance for what… against whom?"

"That's a large jump, Rebba and all very interesting, I agree…" the loreman, Arkadi snapped, "but none of that is what's really important!"

Nossi saw the brown robed woman look at the loreman in surprise.

The loreman, Arkadi continued, passion in his voice. "That is all in the past, Rebba. What's more important is that a powerful race that we know next to nothing about is here beneath the College searching for something and no one above even knows they are here." The human in black leaned over, staring the fiery haired woman in the eye. "Think, Rebba, no one has seen elves out of their forests in… well ever, and suddenly we bump into a group secretly searching here and attacking anyone who comes down. Something is wrong! What's more, we have only legends to rely on for what we know of the elves and that is centuries old. Certainly, the elves today are less than friendly towards us; they kill any who trespass on their lands whether they are goblins, trolls or humans. They make no distinction. For all we know the elves may see us as the enemy and if that is the case then they may be a threat. The college must know."

The brown cloaked loreman looked troubled, "I'm not sure I can believe that, but you could be right. We must tell the Archmage; that does seem vital."

The dark robed loreman nodded his head in firm agreement, as did the white clad one, but then added, "Rebba, we must get Nossi to the surface, to stand before the Archmage and tell his story otherwise none will believe such a fantastical story."

"I'm not sure I believe a word of it either!" muttered the tall woman with the bow to herself, in disgust.

The dark loreman suddenly snapped his fingers and his eyes opened wide in realisation. "If these elves want their homeland back, they may want it back from us. These lands used to be elven lands!"

Nossi had no idea what this, Arkadi was talking about, and from the looks of the humans' faces, most of them had no idea either.

"But everyone knows that the goblins are the enemy, Arkadi," the tall swordsman responded, a frown on his face, "the goblins over ran the northlands. Everyone knows that."

"That could be wrong though, Darin. What we know of that time is sketchy at best. We don't even fully understand the nature of the fall of the Elder kingdoms. Why not?" the loreman asked, obviously not wanting an answer. He continued, "We are told in stories from the druids, which in turn allegedly come from the elves, that some nameless evil destroyed the Elder civilisation. What was this evil? Why do we not know?" Before any of the other humans could voice an answer, the loreman, Arkadi again went on. "Don't you see?" He asked looking around. "We could all have been misled. Perhaps, the elves destroyed themselves, or perhaps we were not the allies of the Elder at the end, but their enemy? Perhaps alliances have changed and now we are the enemy? I don't know, but I do know that things just don't seem to fit. Also, what I do know is that the ancient elven lands are the northlands, but they are also the lands in which we now live. If they want these lands back too we could all be in grave danger. Perhaps this elven prince, Uh'Ram has been given the task of re-conquering our lands. This elven prince may now wish to turn his forces upon us. The elves we have faced here may be scouts for an invasion!"

All the humans sat in stunned silence. A range of emotions played across their faces in a way that Nossi had never seen on any Great Master.

"That does not sound good," the warrior, Zara finally muttered, "but perhaps this is getting blown out of proportion, Arkadi." She looked to the other humans for support. "You may be jumping to conclusions... and even if you were right, just how big a force are we talking about?" The warrior turned to look at Nossi questioningly.

"I am not sure master," Nossi replied hesitantly. The charged atmosphere was making him decidedly nervous now. However, he instantly saw his lack of knowledge was met with grim looks and he mused quickly, "I... er... know that the Great Masters... base their military, as all else, upon the sacred number nine." The warrior, Zara stared at Nossi and nodded and so Nossi continued, a slight lump in his throat. "There are nine warriors in a... er... basic group of warriors and nine of these to a... warparty, with... nine warparties to a warband." Nossi stopped and calculated, "That's...."

"Seven hundred and twenty nine warriors in a Warband," the loreman, Arkadi supplied instantly.

"Er... yes, master," Nossi nodded his head in thanks before continuing, "And there are nine warbands in a warhorde, and nine warhordes in a warhost!"

"By the cold heart of Ishara," the warrior Zara exclaimed fiercely and Nossi shrank back from her. "But that means there's..." she paused and looked up at the ceiling and frowned.

"Fifty nine thousand and forty nine warriors in a warhost!" supplied the loreman, Arkadi, coldly.

Nossi heard the tall swordsman whistle while the others sat back heavily in what seemed like amazement.

The warrior, Zara though, was shaking her head in complete disbelief. "No one has an army that size!" she spat. She then turned a savage gaze on Nossi. "Are you sure?"

Nossi nodded mutely. "Prince Uh'Ram has been bringing his Warhost to this land and others just to the north, but he has found this difficult as the power needed to create the magical portals and to move so many is enormous." Nossi could see the loremen of the group start in surprise at the mention of portals and then nod in understanding, "His full strength is split across these lands."

"So this elven prince cannot focus his full strength?" the warrior Zara questioned.

"Yet... Zara, yet," the dark loreman, Arkadi put in quickly. "And we have not even thought about the goblins and others. How many are there? How many follow this elven prince?"

"But elves hate goblins!" Zara snarled almost in a fury. "This does not make sense! It's all just guesses. You could be completely wrong."

The loreman in black nodded but replied, "Even if I am wrong, Zara, do you see now the importance of this?"

The warrior stared at the loreman for a moment and then finally nodded in mute acknowledgement.

"At worst we could face the greatest threat to the Wildlands since…, well, ever! At best we have elves, goblins and the gods only know what else plotting something that no one knows anything about!" the loreman, Arkadi insisted.

The humans looked one to another with a mixture of what Nossi thought must be disbelief and… fear?

The rounded, white clad man muttered fearfully. "If the forces are as little Nossi here suggests, we are talking of armies potentially greater than anything we know of in the north. We would need the might of the Imperial Legions to defeat such a force!"

Nossi had no idea what a 'legion' might be, but things didn't sound good.

"But only if it is as Arkadi says. If not then these elves may not be enemies at all. The legends say our peoples were allies!" The brown clad loreman insisted.

Nossi had never heard of such a thing from the Great Masters; they allied with no one!

Others amongst the humans were talking now and getting to their feet. Slowly, their voices rose. Nossi shied away from the angry noises and thought again about bolting for the door and trying his luck on his own. Suddenly, a peal of metal grinding against stone reverberated around the chamber and all looked to the swordsman, Darin sitting with quiet fury in his blue eyed gaze.

"Enough!" He yelled in terrible anger. "We will not panic over things we can only guess at, I don't deal in 'what ifs' and 'maybes'. What we will do is sit here and we will listen to the rest of what this little gnome creature has to say and…" the swordsman continued in a voice that was heavy with suppressed rage, "we will rest because our friend over there," he nodded with his head, "needs rest. So sit your arses back down and stop your blabbing! Understand!"

Everything stopped. Nossi had forgotten the large human who had faced his lord. The man still lay terribly still. The humans all looked at the rigid swordsman and although the dark loreman, Arkadi opened his mouth as if to protest, the words died in his throat when he met the swordsman's stare. Gently, the humans lowered themselves back down and sat once more.

After an uncomfortable silence, the loreman, Arkadi looked to his friend with a look of regret and sympathy on his face. "You are right, Darin there is no point rushing to any conclusions. We all need rest and we need to learn more from Nossi so that we know what threat we truly face. After all it may not be as bad as I have painted it… and we shouldn't forget that these elves were here looking for something, something that may be of importance."

Nossi saw the others settle back in agreement. The loreman then turned back to Nossi and again Nossi found the intensity of those dark eyes hard to bear.

"Now, my little friend, how did you get here and where do we and these catacombs fit into this great prince's plans… hmm? What is it he seeks here?"

Chapter 25

THE TALE OF NOSSI BEE

King Earondar Greatheart is the most renowned hero of the Nordic people. It is said that he united all the people of the North into a mighty Kingdom. All of the Kings of the Nordic claim some kind of descent from him. Of course Imperial scholars debate whether he really existed and if so in what form. It is more likely that he was some local chieftain or king around whom legends have grown. Legends also surround his death. Different tales abound. In some it is said he went to fight with the elves, in others to fight against the elves. In some tales he battles a horde of demons with his fabled Rainbow Guard. However, all these fanciful tales agree that he never returned.

Except from 'A Discussion on the Barbarian People of the North' by the historian, Erinius Pontius of Kilimar, Blessed Year (BY)734

"I… I…" Nossi Bee stuttered, "that is, I got here along with the others from my House who were ordered to attend my Lord Dar'Elthon to make up for the shame of my Lord Cal'Aron and my Lord Uh'Thraan's failures." Nossi saw that this information wasn't helping, it was only creating puzzled frowns.

"I believe you were talking about a Lord Vol'Dakor as the head of your House, is he related to these other lords?" the brown robed woman asked quietly.

Nossi took a breath and drew some strength from the kindly faced woman.

He nodded. "Yes, my Lord Vol'Dakor was very old when he accepted the honour of being a *Parinsar*, in the prince's Divine Avengers, and so his son and heir Lord Cal'Aron was sent in his place. Very soon after, Lord Vol'Dakor succumbed to age, but before Lord Cal'Aron could even be acknowledged Lord of House and Master of Clan, news came that he had been killed in battle and so his son, Lord Uh'Thraan became Lord and Master, much to the silent despair of many for he was one of the most harsh of the Great Masters, full of anger and cruelty."

"Immediately, Lord Uh'Thraan was commanded to join the prince's forces in preparing the way for the Divine Crusade. Uh'Thraan's father had let the prince down, it was believed, and the prince was angry. The prince is known as 'Bloodfire' because of his fiery temper and House Totheariss needed to regain the prince's goodwill. The prince had destroyed whole houses before that had displeased him. However, news soon came of Lord Uh'Thraan's incompetence and he was sent home in disgrace and House Totheariss was stripped of the leadership of the Clan to House Warah'Toris and barely avoided destruction." Nossi looked up at the ceiling as he remembered that time. "It was a time of great upheaval within the House, Uh'Thraan was unpopular and factions split amongst the ruling family." Nossi smiled in sudden memory.

Such a different time for him it had been, a time of love, a time when his heart had opened. With surprise he realised that this was the first time he had been able to remember the good times. So much of late he had only seen the black wall of his sorrow.

"Lord Uh'Thraan was challenged by his brother, Lord Dar'Elthon, who was well thought of as a warrior and lorewarden. Lord Dar'Elthon slew his brother, but his rulership was unsteady, there were others, cousins and uncles who were eager to rule. He had to prove himself and so he pleaded with the great prince for a part in the Divine Crusade and he took on a role far beneath that of a *Parinsar*, keen to prove he could regain his family's honour."

Nossi looked at the dark loreman, Arkadi and said, "You asked me how I came to be here, well..." Nossi began dully, his mood changing, "Lord Dar'Elthon was asked to provide a Warparty from his own house to repair the losses suffered under his brother. So 'volunteers' were called for because many of the House's best warriors had fallen in battle."

'Volunteers,' Nossi thought bitterly. He had refused to volunteer, but that had meant nothing to the Great Masters, he was required. When he refused, all he held dear was taken from him! His love flashed before him again and the pain flooded back, crushing him. He folded over and buried his head in his hands, fighting to hold back the tears. Why now, the tears, when he had thought them dried up and buried with his feelings. Over the last few months he had managed to wall those feelings away, but going over his life in this way had caused a breach in his defences. Nossi felt a hand on his shoulder. He looked up from between his thick fingers. It was the white clad, rounded human and his eyes were moist and full of shared pain as if he understood and could feel Nossi's heartache.

"Come my friend, let me help you." he said softly, the serious look was somehow at odds with his jolly face. The force tightening Nossi's chest eased and the pain of his memories began to recede, the images lost their potency and he pulled himself upright, even as he sealed the wall in his mind. He saw in surprise that several of the humans were looking at him with genuine sorrow. Perhaps these humans weren't so savage.

"This is a trial you must eventually face, my little friend. Each time you deny it, you die a little inside"

Nossi heard the white clad loreman's warning, as the man shifted his prodigious bulk back to his seat. He stared at the man in wonder. What strange and wondrous lore this man possessed. Nossi had not paid much attention to the rounded loreman. Even though the man had stood out well enough in his white garb, he had seemed so much less the warrior than the other warriors, and so much less the loreman than the other loremen. Yet, he possessed such wonderful strength! Nossi had sensed in that brief touch a faith that shone with power, not power in the mysteries, but power in its surety. Nossi had always shied away from the clerics from his own lands, the gods were stern and savage to the Lessers, completely ferocious to doubters. This man was obviously a different kind of cleric. The power of this man in white seemed more gentle and yet more subtle and more powerful than those of the Great Masters. It was yet another puzzle of which these humans seemed so full.

The warrior, Zara interrupted his thoughts, "So you were a volunteer and came along with this new lord to our lands? How did you get here? Did you come directly here, to these catacombs?"

The white clad cleric leaned across and put a gentle hand on the warrior's scarred arm. "Give him a moment to recover himself." Nossi heard him whisper firmly. The warrior woman cast a harsh look at the man, but waited.

Again, Nossi found the gentle eyes looking at him, seeming to offer silent support. Nossi nodded in gratitude to the cleric. After a moment or two he felt strong enough to continue.

"No, we came to these catacombs much later. First we were brought to a broken city in the far north. As to how I got there, I cannot tell you clearly other than to say that after we completed the long journey to the Holy City, we passed through a mighty portal, the earth, stone and buildings around which, thrummed with immense power. I cannot tell you more than that because everyone, other than the Great Masters and the dark brothers, were blindfolded before we entered the Holy City as decreed by holy law. The members of our warparty passed through the portal as easily as stepping from here to there." Nossi said pointing from the space before his feet to the other side of the fire where the warrior Zara crouched. Nossi saw the three loreman look at each other in wonder. "Yet I knew I had travelled far. All among my people possess a strong sense of the earth, of place and location, and my mind rebelled at the shift that had occurred in that single instant." Nossi paused in thought. "Neither can I tell you of what it was like on the other side, for the blindfolds were not removed until we had been marched for almost an hour, roped together, each following the other. I can tell you this though, it was hot when we arrived and closed in and I knew we were deep underground much as we are now, but it was like we stood within some huge space, the echoes chased around and confused our ears. It was only after a few moments wait and some hushed and hurried discussion amongst the Great Masters, that we had ascended."

"I can tell you that when the blindfolds were removed we were above ground, the air crisp and chill. Around us was a mighty city of tall, incredibly thin and graceful towers; mighty, luminous seeming domes; arches and pillars. Yet it was also a city that was broken and empty, its grace stolen here and there by nature winding its way through it, exploiting it and creating cracks and collapses. We did not pause for long, but continued to walk through this lost city and near the great wall that surrounded that place it was as if some huge forces had gouged out the flesh of the rock, scoured it and thrown it down in chaos. Beyond this destruction, I could see the city was surrounded by water, like a city on an island in a lake, and beyond that lake was a green teeming flat land of grasses that astonished me and even stunned the Great Masters."

"Within this city, hidden in its midst, were others of our people. It was there we met other warparties of Prince Uh'Ram. There were also other creatures there; large hulking creatures with thick skin and fearsome tusked features and huge, cruel weapons; and there were creatures like the dark brothers only somehow less than they and with sickly hued skin. There too, were smaller wiry creatures, swift and savage with mouths full of savage teeth and ears like a bat; and creatures as large as the ogres only thick with fur and claws."

Nossi could see the look of grave concern on Arkadi's face, and the look of hatred on several of the warriors' faces. Nossi noticed the woman Zara unconsciously grasp the hilt of one of her blades and squeeze.

"You know of these creatures?" Nossi asked quietly, knowing the answer.

"Trolls, goblins, kobolds and yeti," Zara snarled between clenched teeth. She turned to the loreman. "You are right Arkadi, this is serious."

"How many warriors were there, Nossi?" asked the tall, swordsman, Darin, quietly.

"I...am not sure, master." he stuttered. "Certainly, I did not see the whole of the prince's forces, but from what I had heard, they were intent on missions of their own. However, there must have been at least several warbands and an equal number of those other creatures."

"Tynast!" swore the woman, Zara angrily, "Even that's enough to match all of the forces of the Wildlands combined!" She smashed her armoured fist into the floor and the others cursed.

Nossi gulped.

"There may be other ways to oppose them." The dark clad loreman muttered. "Go on, Nossi," he urged. "We need to know about how and why you came here in particular."

Nossi gave a swift nod and continued, not wanting to make the humans any angrier. "The next months were a whirlwind of activity. We travelled a great distance through portals to seemingly endless plains; to lands with no sign of buildings or civilisation save huge mounds here and there that could have been the ruins of some lost race; to other cities, though not so grand as that we had left, but ruined too, their history hidden amidst their fractured towers. We were sent through dozens of portals held open by a hundred or more loreman under the prince's command to deal death and fear to green and yellow skinned dark brothers. We fought and conquered, slaughtered or subdued many of those creatures that I had seen in the ruined city on the plains so that their numbers amongst us swelled as we brought back survivors ready to swear allegiance." Nossi noticed the humans frown at this out of the corner of his eye and heard the warrior Zara mutter something about 'bringing the goblins into line', but Nossi continued, "the slaughter and savagery were horrifying." He shook in spite of himself. "I became numb to everything, apathetic and unwilling to craft and use my talents."

"Meanwhile, my lord Dar'Elthon had shown his skill and quickly become a favourite again of the prince. To consolidate this position, my lord put himself forward for a difficult yet crucial mission for the great prince; to go to the catacombs beneath a human city, and retrieve an artifact of great power… a key."

Nossi saw the humans react to this with puzzlement.

"There was to be left no sign of our search… and no witness. The humans above were known to be loreman and might perceive us. If so we were to leave the way we had come, activating the portal stone affixed where we arrived. If we were prevented from leaving we were to destroy ourselves. Nothing of our nature must be known to the humans." Nossi could see questions forming on several lips, but still he forged on. "I refused to go at first, but was coerced into it, shackled and whipped, though my shame was not public and so I was not slain. I was too valuable to slay outright." He laughed bitterly. "When we arrived we soon located the key, its resonance had been given to my lord and his cleric and loreman. However, there were others in the tunnels, humans! They took the key and fled. We pursued them, cornered them, killed some of them, but some escaped. We lost them!"

Nossi could see consternation on the humans' faces now.

"The resonance moved to the surface where we could not go and then… something strange happened. The resonance started to descend again! We split up and began the hunt anew. The resonance moved around haphazardly, but eventually we caught it… and you," said Nossi looking around at the group of humans, "or should I say, more particularly, you!" Nossi whispered pointing at the warrior woman, Zara.

235

All eyes turned to look at the woman who stood and stepped back in surprise, "Me!" she gasped, "What are you talking about? I haven't got any key." She looked at the eyes on her and almost snarled. "I haven't got any key! I swear."

Heads began to turn back towards Nossi, who shook his head and allowed himself a wry smile. "My lord was right. You truly do not know."

"Know what?" The warrior woman spat.

"If this key is so powerful, we would have sensed it with our talent." the dark cloaked, Arkadi insisted, though not fully convinced. "Magic cannot be shielded save by a guiding mind maintaining a warding spell."

"Of course it can." Nossi replied. "You simply invert the weave of the spell."

"You what?" the loreman said in surprise.

"Look," said the dark haired Zara stepping forward to stand almost over the fire, "sorry to interrupt your discussion of matters magical, but could we get this cleared up right here and now. I do not have any key, nor did I make those elves and their freakish allies attack us!" She pointed at Nossi. "Look you little …"

Nossi ignored the threatening tone from the warrior, he was so intent on his target. He stood up quickly and stepped forward. He yanked the warrior's large purse from her belt.

"Hey, what the… What do you think you're doing?"

"That's the purse you said you stole from those men you bumped into in the inn." said the loreman, Arkadi.

"I stole that fair and square…" the warrior woman began.

Nossi, oblivious to all, emptied the contents onto the floor. Coins scattered everywhere, but Nossi swiftly retrieved the item he wanted.

"Here it is… the Key!" he cried triumphantly.

The humans all leaned forward and looked at the object Nossi held, thrust out in his open hand. It was a grey, smooth rock about the size of a child's fist covered in small symbols and writing!

Chapter 26

RUMOURS

The people who inhabit the North and Northwest regions that border our glorious empire all claim kinship and name themselves Nordic while showing bitter hatred of one another. It is said that in ancient times they called themselves the Coomrii or Kumbran and were united as one until some calamity or strife split them. However, there is no historical evidence of this, yet there is no doubt that the same ethnic group comprises all the kingdoms of the North West from Mykadia in the south to Nornheim in the North and that they are very distinct from the Olmec people of the Empire. Only in the province of Kilimar, and the Wildlands to the north of there, do our people and theirs coexist happily.

Except from 'The Nordic Barbarians' by the historian, Antoninus Brolianus, Blessed Year (BY)1034

The labyrinthine corridors of the college's Black Hall always bothered Eliantha. She always wondered why the elves who had built the place so long ago couldn't seem to make the corridors more distinctive. They all seemed to look the same, with whirled patterns and carvings that seemed the same with no colour other than the unidentifiable black rock of the walls. Occasionally, her gaze was snatched from the architecture by the bows and nods of respect from passing magi, but she found it hard to pay attention. She was still wearing her formal silvery grey robes of office as Mage Master, hence the bows. She had been so beleaguered by formal requests for audiences with all kinds of people tonight that she had not had the chance to change since the meeting. The people's concerns ranged from the trivial day to day running of the College, that she had taken on to aid the Archmage's staff, to the more serious matters of masters and various politicians reactions to the rumours of elves and dwarves, along with mysterious goings on, both in the college and under it!

In fact, it was the rumours that concerned Eliantha most, particularly the sudden rise in rumours of all kinds relating to the Archmage.

She had known Baden Erin almost all her life and had secretly loved him for almost as long, though she would never have admitted it. Both she and the Archmage were of an age and had grown up together, studied together and taught together for over half a century now. No one knew of her love for the Archmage, not her closest friends and colleagues, not her family and certainly not the Archmage. It was something she would never have spoken of, not now. Her love for Baden Erin had begun when they were both teenagers, had begun as a respect developed from similar interests and ideas and had developed for her into a blossoming, all consuming love that for many years had almost destroyed her. In later years that burning passion had become an enduring flame.

When she was younger she had come close to admitting her feelings to Baden, but the mere idea had always sent her into a panic. She was an incredibly private person, shy and wary of hurt and Baden Erin was similarly a quiet person, though not so timid as she. She could never believe that he felt anything other than friendship towards her. Added to which, the time had always seemed wrong. In their younger years, Baden was away a lot, or he would be researching, or busy on his father's work and then later with his own. When he had finally met a young women on his travels, Eliantha had been crushed and had despaired and sought to expunge her secret love. It had not worked, but she had managed to gain control of her emotions enough to merely admire from afar. Baden's relationship had not lasted more than a few years, but by then, Eliantha was resigned to merely be a friend to Baden and held her love deep within.

Now she was worried for him. In everything Baden Erin had done, she had supported him, more than that she agreed with him; agreed with his vision and dream of uniting the Wildlands and creating a land fairer for all. It was that noble dream and his drive to achieve it that had originally been part of what made her love him. She understood his reasons for hiding the knowledge of the elves and dwarves from the Conclave and agreed with them. However, it was an undeniable fact that the Archmage had acted in a way that was against the founding beliefs of the College. He knew it and she did, though what he seemed to ignore was the strength of feeling of some of those on the Conclave. He believed that his motives, and the good that would come of his actions, was self evident and would convince all that the end justified the means. As he had said, 'It was only a slight bending of the College's rules and traditions.'

Eliantha shook her head. He refused to see that people like the High Enchanter, actually hated him, and that the Sorceror Supreme, was so ambitious he would use whatever he could to make his way to power. Ordinarily this would not have worried her so much; she knew that the Archmage had taken them into account, even if he didn't agree with Eliantha on the extent to which those two would go. However, tonight Eliantha had heard rumours that gave her a thick knot of worry in the pit of her stomach. Rumours were flying around that the Archmage was responsible for the theft of the camouflaging cloaks from the enchanters, a ridiculous idea, but one now being given credence because of other darker rumours. These spoke of the Archmage being in league with the elves to take over the Wildlands, to use them to help him force the other rulers of the provinces to do as he wished, that he had somehow made a pact with the Elder races and that these rumours of goblins uniting were merely lies told to force unity and to force them to make the Archmage their leader!

It would have been laughable, but for the fact that so many were whispering such nonsense.

Eliantha's resolve hardened as she thought things through. She turned and mounted the great steps that led up to the Archmage's personal rooms. The college guards ignored her as she moved between them, lost in thought. She drifted heedlessly into the small entrance hall. There she stopped and took a deep breath. Baden needed to know of these rumours, he had been so busy up here he had not had time to take stock of what the magi were thinking and planning.

She smiled at the young adept who was serving as the Archmage's doorward and asked to be announced.

The youth disappeared for a moment and then returned, opened the door wide and lightly called out her formal title and name as she moved through into the second hall beyond.

The second hall was the Archmage's official welcoming hall. It was here that he did a lot of the state functions that were a part of his duties both as Archmage and as ruler of the province of Shandrilos. The hall was semi-circular and high roofed with the same black, whirl-patterned walls, but this was broken up with colourful hangings, landscaped paintings and beautifully weaved tapestries. The floor was still the harsh unforgiving stone, yet here and there were plush Olmec style couches on which to recline and small tables for drinks. A few adepts of the college, serving on the Archmage's staff, stood by the walls ready to carry out any tasks for the guests who clustered in groups in the middle of the room.

Eliantha Shamass' eyes widened at the sight of elves, dwarves and men mixing freely, a sight she never thought she would have seen, another testament to Baden Erin's determination. Her eyes quickly found the Archmage, still in his dark robes. He was stood with Elgon of Ostia and Raban Ironhand of Dunegan, and was talking with one of the elf lords and one of the dwarven chieftains.

Eliantha quickly made her way across to the group, avoiding eye contact with all others. She moved up behind the Archmage, hoping to merely distract him with a touch and draw him away for a quiet discussion, but as she approached, the bear of a man that was Raban Ironhand bellowed a loud greeting and all turned to see her standing there almost foolishly with her arm half outstretched to touch the Archmage. She found herself blushing and sought to collect her dignity and ask the Archmage for a moment, but the gruff lord of Dunegan was already speaking.

"So what do you think of our new council members, Mage Master? Were you as stunned by their arrival as we or had the crafty Archmage here failed to pull the wool over your eyes too?" He chortled amiably.

"I am afraid I had... little..." she mumbled.

"Eliantha had my confidence, but did not know the details." Baden Erin put in, saving her. "Indeed, I, myself was not sure how things would go until the last moment. I wasn't even sure if my lords would even enter." he finished, nodding his head at the Elder lords, and smiling.

The elf and dwarf nodded, but did not smile.

"I am sorry, Eliantha. I have not formally introduced you to our guests." Baden added. "May I present, Chief Afindor of the Ironcleaver clan…" he paused to let Eliantha greet the dwarf chief and she nodded as gracefully as she could manage. Afindor had blood red hair and a beard that was platted. He was almost slightly built from what Eliantha had seen of dwarves, yet he seemed fearsome with burning green eyes and scars of all kinds crisscrossing his face.

"…And may I also present Lord Val'Ant, *Parindar* of the Suthantar." Baden finished.

Eliantha was not sure of the titles, she knew much less than the Archmage about the Elder. However, she did recognise the elflord instantly. Lord Val'Ant was the elf who looked almost like a ghost with his grey hair, eyes and silvery grey skin. She smiled politely, a little perturbed by the beautiful alien eyes.

Turning to face the Archmage, she said firmly, "Forgive me Archmage, but I must beg a moment of your time in private." She smiled again at the group and then turned and headed over to an empty corner of the room. She heard Baden make a polite withdrawal and then begin to follow.

"Is there something wrong Elie?" Baden whispered as he moved close.

Eliantha looked into the familiar dark eyes and had to stop herself from blushing. 'Pull yourself together,' she thought. "Yes, I am very concerned with what I am hearing from the masters about this business with the Grand Council."

Baden looked a little relieved and began to smile.

"You are not taking this seriously enough." she snapped, annoyed at his disregard of her concerns. "Xameran is determined to have this meeting of the Assembly and he will have it."

"Let him," Baden replied unconcerned, "he will no doubt have his moment to pontificate and discredit me and the Assembly might even vote to give me a formal chastisement, but nothing more."

Eliantha was already shaking her head. "No, no, you are taking this too lightly. I am convinced that Xameran and Atholl are up to more. They are looking to have you removed…"

"It won't happen," Baden interrupted firmly, "they might gain enough sympathy amongst the masters to have me reprimanded, but not removed."

The man was infuriating, Eliantha thought. He refused to listen. Gritting her teeth, she hissed back, "There is more going on than you know. Already it is widely believed that you stole the cloaks from the enchanters' hall and that you are in league with the elves to take control of the Wildlands, uniting them beneath your rule!"

The Archmage was shaking his head and he laughed harshly, "That's ridiculous. No one would believe such nonsense. They know I would unite the Wildlands, but not rule them."

"Then why have I been visited by no less than two dozen masters to ask me if it might be true? If it was so ridiculous, why do they even ask?"

Baden frowned. "So many…" then he shook his head. "No!" he finished not wanting to believe.

"Baden, there are maybe just under two hundred masters in the college at present and we both know that more than half will vote to have you reprimanded now because of Xameran's firm opposition. However, Atholl, Xameran or someone is now damning your name and seeking to link you to all kinds of rumours, ridiculous ones to us, but with weight and pressure you could face a vote on your very leadership of the college!"

"Not enough would believe such. A majority of the masters would be needed."

"Already, it is clear that both Xameran and Atholl have all of their masters from the schools of sorcery and enchantment behind them. With the fact that many amongst the clerics naturally distrust non-humans, most of them would vote against you, added to which the Magus General has a keen dislike of non-humans and will heavily influence the fighter magi. The wizards and my own magi are split. With things as they are, Xameran and Atholl are not far off a majority." Eliantha insisted.

Baden looked worried for the first time. "Perhaps you are right, I should take this more seriously, but I still will not believe that so many would vote to remove me!"

"Yes, but should anything else happen…"

"Okay, okay. You are right. I shall be careful and look into this, but I must cement ties with the elves and dwarves first. I do not know these elven lords and they are wary. I sense something is happening that they are hiding from me. I must allay their fears and doubts and show that they can trust us." The Archmage smiled at her reassuringly. He turned and moved back to speak to the Elder lords.

Eliantha had a bad feeling. These Elder were unknowns. Also, she knew Baden would do something about the rumours, but she worried that it wouldn't be good enough or quick enough; Baden was scrupulously fair and would play by the rules, something she knew Atholl, and perhaps Xameran too, would not.

Chapter 27

MAGICAL REVELATIONS

The oldest myths of the Nordic speak of how they came to the north of the world. It is said that they were a nomadic race of horsemen who travelled from the east. Their first king is given the name Cumb'Rai which is now the Nordic word for 'people'. The kingdom of Cumbra is thought to be a derivative of this and long ago it is thought all the Nordic were known as the 'people of Cumb'Rai. Interestingly, this could link with the legends of the 'Horselords of Koomra' who were said to plague the northern Olmec lands in pre-Alban times.

Except from 'A discourse on the people of the Empire and beyond' by the historian, Casinian. BY456.

"What, that?... That's the key?" Zara Halven laughed, "It's a bloody rock. It doesn't even look like a key!"

Zara was right, Arkadi thought, it is a rock, just a rock. There was no magical resonance to it. The familiar aura he had spent years developing the senses to perceive was missing and yet... What was it the little gnome creature had said, 'invert the weaves'? Arkadi knew from his own training that sensing magic was the first of the prime abilities magi developed, followed later by an ability to perceive the actual purpose of magic detected. A strong adept could decipher the patterns in the magic to identify the actual nature and function of the spell that created the magic, so long as he had seen it before or seen something similar. Masters, and he counted himself one of these, could detect and identify quickly and accurately the faintest auras and residues of magic and even decipher the most complex of spells cast. However, Arkadi had overheard discussions between some of the few Grandmasters at the college, that with long years of use and study, a magi could learn to not only detect and identify spells cast, but actually see into the magic, see the individual strands of forces and energies that made up the spell, and most worryingly, the term they used to describe the combinations of differing forces that made up a spell was 'weaves'! Could that be what the gnome was talking about? What then did 'inverting the weaves' possibly mean, turning them upside down, inside out? Arkadi shook his head.

Arkadi found himself walking away from the group, though he couldn't remember standing. He had his hand on his chin and his other arm tucked behind his back, a habit he had somehow picked up. He turned and found many of his friends looking at him. Arkadi felt out of his depth here and he hated that. He also hated feeling that others knew more than he did.

Deliberately, he turned away from the fire and his friends who had taken the key from the diminutive Nossi Bee and were passing it around, examining it. He heard Darin ask what it was the key did and also heard the wary response from the gnome that he did not know, that he only knew it was important to the prince and some great magic that would give the Great Masters a huge advantage.

Turning his mind back to the problem of the key itself and the revelations he had heard from the gnome about the nature of magic, Arkadi cast around for inspiration. From his knowledge of magical theory, Arkadi had heard that although the way to defend against a spell attack was to produce a counter spell that cancelled or protected against the attacking spell, there was also another way that an increasing number of Grandmasters were investigating. This method, he had heard whispered by friends who aided in the experiments, was to actually pull the attacking spell apart and thus negate it. What had made Arkadi think of this was the fact that how this negating spell worked was to slice through what the Grandmasters had termed the 'binding strand of the spell weave' and thus the spell construct of forces and energies fell apart. There had been some injuries in the resulting losing of said energies, but his friends had confirmed that the spells had been destroyed before they actually took effect, albeit at times the damage from destroying the spell was actually more devastating than the spell itself would have been! However, what Arkadi was again worried by was the weaving terms used again in this new field of study.

Arkadi turned and looked at the gnome, Nossi Bee. Arkadi could now clearly sense the magical talent in the creature. It was no novice. Its power was clear. The creature sensed his scrutiny and looked at him and gave him a tight nervous smile. However, it was not the creature's talent that worried him. You could have the most talented individual in the world, but if their spell craft was poor and undisciplined they would be no real threat. Arkadi was worried that this creature knew far more about magic than he, or even any of the Grandmasters, knew! It was widely believed that the elves had known far more of the nature of magic than humans now. Could this servant of elves know secrets of magic lost so long ago? The thought was mildly worrying, but also made Arkadi smile. The chance to discover such knowledge, to learn and expand his skill was an exciting thought.

Decisively, Arkadi marched back over to the fire and sat himself carefully down in front of the others, and in front of the gnome. He gestured to Zara who was looking hard at the keystone to hand it over and the puzzled warrior gave it up with a shrug. Arkadi turned to the timid gnome and asked with a little difficulty, "Can you... re-invert the weaves and show us, Nossi?"

Suddenly, the creature's ruddy, rounded face lit up in a smile of genuine happiness, probably at the thought of helping a master, Arkadi thought.

The small man-like creature took the stone from Arkadi's outstretched hand and set it down in his tiny lap and Arkadi watched intently, as he knew the others did, though only Rebba and Garon had any chance of actually seeing anything.

Arkadi watched as the gnome stared intently at the stone for long moments, occasionally moving his dexterous hand over and around it, almost caressing it. Arkadi realised the little man was making little sounds and noises, but quickly realised these were not part of any spell craft more a habit of deep thought like how the eccentric old Master Bureon Brae would 'hmmm' as he thought, and stroke the tip of his chin where the brush-like, thin beard stuck out in all directions. The comical image made him smile for a moment.

Abruptly, the little man looked up. "I am afraid I cannot do as you have asked, master." He said and Arkadi could tell he was afraid at the consequences of his admittance. "The weaves are very complex and beyond my skill to decipher which hold the inversion." Arkadi knew his face was darkening in frustration and he knew the gnome noticed this too as the creature hastily added and pointed, "Do you see here, at the apex of the grey spirit weaves where the green matter and red energy weaves intersect, the pattern is immensely dense and bound so closely with the blue force weave as to be very dangerous to alter without greater understanding." He looked at Arkadi as if expecting him to shed some light on the puzzle. Arkadi was unsure how to respond. It would be dangerous to admit their lack of knowledge to this little known creature…

Just as Arkadi was thinking this, Rebba said gently, "I am afraid we see nothing, Nossi, we have no perception of these 'weaves' and 'patterns'." Arkadi closed his eyes and held back from the acerbic comment he wanted to bark at his far too trusting friend.

The gnome's face was a bundle of confusion and then he snapped his fingers in revelation. "So that is why you did not know you carried the key. You not only did not know that the stone was shielded, but also could not detect the inversions!" The gnome beamed at them and started to chatter, "I can help with that at least." he said almost to himself, "It was very remise of your masters to withhold such knowledge, though it has been known for a master to keep certain knowledge secret in order to maintain control over his apprentices." The gnome shook his head and frowned as he said this. "If I cast the same glamour that the Venerable Loremaster cast on my Lord Dar'Elthon to locate the key you will be able to perceive the inversions yourselves." The gnome smiled again in his eagerness to please, "Of course I do not have the strength of the Venerable One, but the glamour should last long enough for you to see the problem." The gnome looked at Arkadi and then Rebba silently asking for permission to proceed.

The others were all quiet. Talk of magic was outside their understanding and so it was down to Arkadi. He gestured for Nossi to begin.

Arkadi stared hard at the gnome. The casting of magic surely could not differ much, but Arkadi wondered all the same. Spells were cast using certain methods either alone or, more often, in combination. The methods came to mind by rote, he had learnt and then taught them: meditation, incantation, postulation, and adjuration; more often these methods were known as 'will and word, symbol and prayer' to students. Meditation was the discipline of the mind, the routine of the thoughts; incantation was the rhythm of sounds, the pitch of voice; postulation was the movement of body, the gestures and symbols made; and adjuration was the calling to and connection with the greater powers, the gods and spirits. All of these methods had to be done perfectly in the correct way, order and degree or disaster could happen. It was known for spells to go awry and few could tell what the consequences might be. It was not unknown for magi to be killed!

The gnome cast swiftly and surely, a master in his control and posture, and Arkadi watched the spell come into being. He would not need the spell repeated, he would be sure to recognise it again. However, learning to cast the spell would require either a communing link with the gnome or a great deal longer with a lot of practice to acquire the discipline.

"Wow! Would you look at that beauty!" Arkadi heard Nat Bero exclaim. Arkadi had been so focused on the gnome he had not thought of the results of the spell. He looked at the keystone on the floor and could see it glowing like white hot metal. It shone to his new senses. He cast his gaze around and saw to his surprise that Rebba, Garon and the gnome were all aglow to differing levels, Rebba the brightest. He realised he was now actually seeing their talent not just sensing it. He could see the others looking now at him in wonder.

The gnome, Nossi caught Arkadi's attention and pointed to the stone, "Do you see now the difficulty? It is beyond my skills to unravel. Could you..." The gnome tailed off.

Arkadi stared at the keystone, but it was just a bright glow to his eyes. He began to shake his head then Rebba's hand on his shoulder stopped him.

"If you look really hard, it's almost like there are colours in it. I just can't seem to make out what..." Rebba looked pained as she spoke.

Arkadi looked back at the blazing stone. He squinted his eyes and concentrated on the stone. Were there colours there? Yes, he could just make out blues and reds and many other colours in differing hues, but they moved in and out of focus. There was no way he could make out any details. Angrily, he looked harder, his eyes began to water and slowly more details began to appear... He lost it! He needed to work at this. He was sure that if he concentrated hard enough he would be able to see more.

Rebba interrupted his thoughts. "Nossi I start to see colours vaguely… but little more. No pattern or weaves. Why is that?"

Nat Bero muttered, "Colours? I just see white glows."

The gnome grimaced, his smooth face crinkling and his merry eyes looking sad again as they had throughout most of his tale telling. "It takes long years to develop the skill of seeing the weaves. I had presumed you masters of lore with many years discipline, such was your skill and strength in spell craft, but your perceptions are weak. I cannot explain this."

"How long have you studied magic Nossi, since first you were tested?" Rebba asked.

"I was tested on my tenth birthday as is proper and I am now twenty years old." The gnome replied seriously, the puzzled expression still creasing his face.

"That makes little sense." Arkadi snapped and turned to look at Rebba. "Both you and I have studied since before we were sixteen and we are now almost thirty. We have studied longer?"

They looked at each other in puzzlement.

From the back of the group, Nat Bero voice called out, "I don't know if this has any relevance, but according to Bear, elven years are much longer than ours."

"He's not an elf!" Zara replied acidly.

'Could that be it?' Arkadi thought, 'he is not an elf, but he was raised under their rule.' "How many days are there in your year, my little friend? How many passings of the sun through the sky?" Arkadi said, looking again to the gnome.

"Days, master? Why there are one thousand four hundred and sixty one, as decreed in the ancient calendar of the Great Masters." the gnome replied as if stating the obvious.

"One thousand four hun…but that's…" Arkadi calculated, "…four years. So that means…" Again he paused to think, "…you are eighty years old!" He exclaimed to the uncomprehending Nossi Bee.

"It also means," Rebba added, "that he has been practising magic for around forty years!"

Arkadi was astounded. This creature had been practising magic for twice as long as he had, as long as most who made it to be Grandmasters! Obviously his race, like the elves and the dwarves lived much longer than humans. It was astonishing. This creature was not only a source of incredible information about a massive threat to the Wildlands, but also a source of lost lore about magic, lore they would need.

Arkadi felt a heavy hand on his shoulder and found Zara Halven's serious face close to his. "We need to talk… in private." She nodded with her head for Arkadi to move over to the far side of the chamber away from the others.

As he stood to follow the lithe warrior, he saw Darin rising smoothly to follow, despite his heavy armour and sword. Zara looked at the two of them as they approached, a look of deep concern on her tanned face.

"We're in some serious shit here," she began. "We need to sort out what we are going to do."

Darin nodded seriously, his handsome face solemn for once.

"The way I see it we need to get back to the surface, and get back as soon as we can. This place is rapidly starting to look like a tomb." Zara looked at Arkadi, "You're right in that the authorities… this Archmage and the like, need to be told about these elves and their creatures running around down here, but do we believe this gnome's tale of some great elven prince and his armies. A lot of what this gnome creature has said seems too incredible for me. I mean, that about these elves working with the goblins and the like in the northlands. It makes no sense. The goblin tribes would attack any elf on sight and no one can reason with the trolls, they have the brains of a rock!" She scratched her head, her muscled arm brushing the bound hilt of one of her sabres. "That lot about weaves and magic, I have no idea about, but this key must be the key to something. What do we do about that? Do we hunt for a little longer or just start heading back up and let the mages deal with it?"

"Don't forget Bear," Darin put in. "We still need to give him a chance. We can't write him off. He could still pull through."

Zara nodded, a pained looked crossing her face.

"I am inclined to believe the gnome's story. It may well be that some of what he has told us is false, but he believes it, I have no doubt of that. As for the magic, he is talking truly and what he has said and what he knows about magic are as important as his knowledge of these elves and the threat they may pose. The problem about heading back to the surface is first of all, how, and second, what will be waiting for us on the way." Arkadi replied thoughtfully.

Zara looked around not sure what to say. It was clear she was feeling somewhat responsible for what had happened, especially for Bear. If she cared for anyone other than herself, it was for him.

"We could search around up there a little more, give Nat a chance to have a good look for a hidden way of re-opening that doorway..." Zara began.

"Are you sure we want to let her near anything," Darin interrupted, "she's the one who found the last hidden mechanism and nearly killed us all!"

Zara let Darin's comment pass and then continued, "...but even if we open it, we can't be sure who or what will be on the other side."

Arkadi held up a hand for Zara to stop and said, "We can possibly find out more from the gnome. He would know more about what those left up there would do without their leader and the key, and he has also explored more of this place. Maybe he can tell us what's down those stairs." Arkadi finished gesturing to the second doorway where Darin had sat guard.

Arkadi spun around and looked back to the others to see most of them sitting quietly, their eyes on Zara, Darin and himself. "Nossi," he called, "What would those left of your warparty above do? Would they wait?"

Nossi answered without hesitation. "They would have no way of returning through the portal without one of the lorewise to activate it. They would be forced to wait and would probably try to find some way down here to retrieve the key and exact revenge. They would know that Prince Uh'Ram would be unforgiving of failure and would send others through to investigate if there was no word from my lord, Dar'Elthon."

Arkadi swung back to see frowns on Darin and Zara's faces, but he turned again to face Nossi before they could say anything and asked, "You have been below and travelled these catacombs, do you know of any other way to get down to us, other than through that hidden corridor?"

This time Nossi did not answer straight away, but thought hard for some moments, his small face serious. "The passage from this room descends for about a hundred metres and joins a large curving hallway that eventually goes around full circle. There are seven passageways such as the one we are in that come off the large curving corridor, including the one that descends from this room. They are evenly spaced along the circular hallway and are identical. I would surmise that each rises to the upper catacombs in an identical manner and meets a number of hidden entrances in the upper levels as there were a number of these that we detected as we passed. One of those passageways could give access to this chamber in a roundabout way from above."

Arkadi was about to turn away when Nossi continued, "The circular corridor below is strange. There is a great magic concealed down there. I could find no access, yet there is a huge hidden chamber inside the circle of that corridor that holds something potent. It is warded and the wards are inverted and of a complexity that I have never seen. They make this key," he pointed at the rock which still sat by the fire, close to the fiery haired Rebba, "look like an apprentice's spell!"

'Wonderful, more mysteries,' Arkadi thought, as he turned back to Zara and Darin. At any other time he would have been thrilled, but not now, not with those foul creatures out to kill them. "It would seem to me that it is possible for those we left above to reach us and that that way is also possibly our best chance of escaping these tunnels."

"It seems to me that our best chance of escaping is to know where any of those elves, bugs and other creatures are, and avoid them." Darin suggested in a resigned voice.

"That's only if we cannot find a way out above." Zara insisted.

Darin was already shaking his head, "No, even if we could return that way, if I were them I would leave some men to watch and raise an alarm."

Zara reluctantly agreed.

"So again, our problem is knowing where they are." Darin thumped his fist in frustration.

Arkadi leaned forward and said quietly, "I might have a way of doing just that." The two warriors were immediately attentive. "I have a scrying spell that would allow me to locate them. However, there are drawbacks." He quickly added seeing the others' eyes light up, "One, is that the spell will only allow me to locate them while the spell lasts and locating them may take the duration of the spell. The spell allows me to wander as a spirit through the rock, but at no greater speed than ordinary running at most. So I can only give you a snapshot of where they were at a given time. Secondly, it will take preparation and rest before I can accomplish such a complex spell."

Zara was shaking her head at this, but Darin was nodding and smiling. "That gives everybody time for some good rest and will give Rebba and Garon time to work on Bear." he said firmly.

Zara grumbled at this, though she did not disagree. "We still need to let Nat check the room above to see if there is a way through. Even if there is someone waiting, it is unlikely to be all of them and it is a point that we know and from which we can find our way. We should make sure that there is no way through before abandoning it." Zara looked to Darin and Arkadi who quickly agreed. "Also, if there is no way back up we need to move from this room as soon as possible, regardless of rest, at least down to that circular corridor the gnome mentioned."

Arkadi expected Darin to disagree, to insist that Bear should not be moved, but instead he nodded his understanding. It then hit Arkadi why the knight was so quick to agree. If there was no way out up the stairs then they were sitting in a dead end if the elves came up from below. They would have nowhere to go, but if they went down it would be much harder for the elves to trap them.

"So we are agreed then." Zara asked. Arkadi nodded, as did Darin.

Zara quickly moved off and grabbed Nat Bero to whom she began to talk quietly. Arkadi could not hear what she was saying, yet he was sure she was telling the huntress to investigate a way out upstairs. Regardless of her mistake earlier, she still had the best chance of finding any hidden locks or such.

Darin had also moved off and had begun packing things away. Arkadi was tempted to go over and ask the gnome some more questions, but he realised he was still quite tired and he needed to be fresh to cast that scrying spell. He moved over to his pack and blanket and laid himself down beside Garon and Rebba who were already back to their blankets trying to get some rest. He told Rebba to look after the keystone and watched as she slipped it into one of the hidden pockets in her robe. Something nagged at Arkadi's mind, but he couldn't put his finger on it. He looked around and noticed the gnome was sitting completely still. It was only then that he remembered the shackles that had once bound the gnome. He sat up. He realised why he had not sensed anything magical about them now; they had an inverted spell on them. He frowned. Was their purpose only to hide a person's talent then as it had Nossi's? That seemed a strange function and an even stranger object to choose to do it. There must be something more.

"Nossi, what about the shackles you were wearing? I can see now that they are magical and the magic is hidden by an inverted weave, but what else did the magic do?" Arkadi asked.

The gnome looked incredibly sad again, his big, round eyes, heavy with sorrow. "They were meant to prevent me using my talent and render me docile. They prevent anyone of talent from removing them themselves by imposing immense pain on you if you try to remove them or work magic." Arkadi found it hard to believe the gnome could be anything other than docile. "So how did you escape it?"

Nossi smiled a melancholy smile. "My father made those shackles, yet he was enough of a realist to understand that they might be used against him so he worked an interdict into the shackles' enchantment and he taught me the release cantrip."

Arkadi raised his eyebrows in surprise. He was impressed with the forethought and the bravery in making such a thing. An interdict was like a break in a chain for an enchantment and allowed the enchantment to be temporarily broken. An interdict could also be detected. Smiling at the audacity, Arkadi lay back down and stared at the roof of the stone chamber. He used a meditation exercise to allow his mind to drift off.

※

It didn't seem long before Nat Bero reappeared down the stairway. Arkadi had been dosing, but he watched as the long legged huntress moved over to Zara and spoke with her, shaking her head. 'No way out that way,' Arkadi thought.

To give truth to his thoughts, Zara quickly announced the dead end above. Quickly, everyone started to collect their last few things together and began grabbing the larger bundles of sticks from the fire to light the way. Bear would be difficult to move, but Arkadi realised that Darin had taken care of that and had used some of the longer bits of wood and some twine to make a support for the big warrior's head. Darin and Garon took hold of either end of the prodigiously sized Bear to carefully carry him down. 'It would be hard work,' Arkadi thought, and was glad he had a damaged arm. He grimaced guiltily at the thought as he remembered that Bear had carried him out of dangerous situations on at least two occasions.

Surprisingly quickly, the group got itself together and began moving out. Arkadi had to admit that even after many years they all still worked well together. Zara and Nat led the way and Arkadi brought up the rear.

It took about ten minutes before the group came out into the circular hallway Nossi had mentioned. It seemed more a curved narrow room than a corridor; it was easily as wide as the chamber they had just left. The group moved along the corridor a little way. Working as one, the group quickly got the fire going again. Torches were lit and Bear was laid down near the fire. Zara posted Nat by the entrance they had come down. The group camped by the next entrance along. It was identical to the one they had just come from and to the next one just visible around the curve of the inner wall. The rest of the group slumped down and took the opportunity to rest, Arkadi along with them.

Arkadi lay with his pack propping his head up, all the hard bits knocked to the sides and padded with his cloak. He was looking straight at the inner wall. As he stared he began to see something; a faint glow, and he realised he was actually seeing the inverted weave the gnome had described even without the aid of a spell. Admittedly, the glow was faint and the weave, from what the gnome had said, was incredibly powerful, but he was actually seeing it. He smiled. Perhaps he was not so weak in his perceptions after all. He closed his eyes.

He had always been a quick learner and a dedicated researcher. He had always wanted to learn everything he could about magic and had progressed rapidly in the college. Only the Sorceror Supreme, Xameran Uth Altor had progressed quicker in the college's history. Xameran was twenty years older than Arkadi, and had been one of the youngest heads of school ever after Syris Darvo, the previous Sorceror Supreme died.

Arkadi had modelled his rise on that of the Lord of Sorcerors; Xameran was something of a standard for him. He was flattered when Xameran spotted his talent and with the Grandmaster's guidance, Arkadi had risen quickly after his apprenticeship from Adept to High Adept and finally to Master a year ago, one of the youngest masters in the college's history. However, it was unlikely he would make Grandmaster by thirty nine as Xameran had, the most talented Masters could spend upwards of twenty years to attain that level of mastery, while most never made it at all! Xameran Uth Altor had managed to make it to Grandmaster in just ten years! No one had ever progressed so quickly save the Archmage himself!

As a master, Arkadi had joined Xameran's party in the Assembly of Masters, linking himself with the growing power of the Progressive Party. Arkadi dreamed of one day being acknowledged a Grandmaster, the real elite of the College practitioners, and then of being named Mage Master. He even wanted one day to become Archmage; a pipedream, but a pleasant one. He saw himself as succeeding Xameran Uth Altor as Archmage, for it was clear Xameran was the obvious choice to follow Baden Erin. The Lord of Sorcerors had an incredible grasp of magical theory and superb discipline and energy. Sorcery was a specialised field, but Xameran had an amazing breadth of knowledge as well as a genius for sorcery. Arkadi was sure that only his own head of school, the quiet Eliantha Shamass and the Archmage himself had as detailed a knowledge of the mysteries, and only the ghastly Lord Enchanter, Atholl Dorard had the same kind of genius for a particular field of magic.

Looking at the wall's faint glow, Arkadi began to wonder just what it was that was hidden beyond that wall. Although he might be imagining it, he thought he felt a strange throbbing, a presence in the ether that was impinging on his mind, but it was so faint.

His mind drifted off…

Chapter 28

THE GROUP DIVIDED

It was said that the ancient Druid Kings of the Cumb'Rai were guarded by seven princely warriors each wore armour of a different colour. This is believed to be where King Earondar, several hundred years later got the idea for his Rainbow Guard, a force of champions from all the lands of the Nordic. The Rainbow Guard consisted of seven orders each with its own purpose, colour and Lord Champion to command it.

Jontis SaTor, chief archivist of the Mykadian Academy, BY399

Startled, Arkadi Talcost sat up at the light touch on his shoulder. He was a little disorientated as he looked up into Nat Bero's pale face in the near dark. Waking up without the light of day was not something he wanted to do too often, he thought.

"Zara says it's time we were up and about and finding where those slanty eyed freaks are hiding. I think she is getting tired of standing watch; I know I am."

Nat Bero looked a little better than earlier. She seemed to have regained something of her colour. Nat was usually tanned from her time outdoors, but after the fall she had been ghostly white. Also, the circles beneath, and the pain within, her dark eyes had receded. Arkadi knew that much of that pain was not physical; Arkadi had been one of those who had visited Nat after the fire. Arkadi had never seen the roguish archer so utterly down; Nat had always been something of a joker, lighthearted and carefree.

Looking up, Arkadi noticed the huntress had combed her dark hair and brushed off her clothing and leather armour.

"How long was I sleeping?"

Nat stopped and thought, chewing her thin lips for a moment. "Maybe a few hours..." she muttered, "difficult to tell down here." The huntress walked away towards the entrance she had been watching.

Arkadi pulled himself together, stretched and slowly stood up. His arm had stopped throbbing and was probably well on its way to healing cleanly. Having a cleric and a druid along was a real benefit. Thinking about that brought his thoughts to Bear. He looked over and could see that Garon was already examining the big warrior, kneeling next to his still form. Rebba was on her way across too. Both of them looked fresher. Bear on the other hand seemed unchanged.

Arkadi reached into his pack and took out his lesser tome. This was his collection of spellcraft notes that he used when travelling light, as did most magi. It was a smaller book, only slightly larger than his hand and only contained a select group of notes on useful spells to aid his memory. His true spell books were locked away safely in his room and were large, thick, detailed treatises, notes and experiments of his own into spellcraft, but also notes on spells he had been taught and had acquired over the years. He would never have been able to carry those and they were far too precious to risk taking around with him.

Zara was walking towards him from the far entrance where she had obviously been standing guard. Arkadi focused on the armoured figured.

"You ready for that scrying you mentioned?" Zara asked as she got close, "I've already got Rebba and Garon getting ready to have another crack at Bear."

"Good." Arkadi nodded, "I'll get started in a minute or two, I need to wake my mind up fully and get myself ready before I begin."

Zara nodded and moved off to speak to Darin, who looked fresh and ready, before heading over to check the far stairs just around the bend of the corridor.

Zara took a quick look up the dark stairway and listened. There was nothing. She turned back to see what was happening with Bear. She couldn't see his face clearly from here as Garon's white clad bulk was blocking her view. She could see that Rebba had her hands floating around over the big man's chest. Zara had no idea what they were doing, but hoped it would make a difference, though she was starting to worry that it might not.

Zara stood up straight and looked across to Arkadi who sat with his legs folded, his back straight and eyes closed, wrapped all in black. Hopefully Arkadi would answer the questions they needed to know and give the group a way out of this labyrinth. Still they needed to keep a close watch until Arkadi had discovered those elven bastards' whereabouts.

Zara stole a look down the dark hallway, but she couldn't quite see Nat at the far entrance that they had all come down. Perhaps it was time to change her, the archer must be tired.

Zara quickly walked over to where Darin sat with his back to the outer wall staring blankly at Garon and Rebba as they worked and muttered to one another over Bear.

"Darin I think it's about time to change the watch."

Darin looked up and his handsome face split into a smile, "You tired already, Zara? You've not long taken over from me!"

Zara shook her head, "No, but can you take Nat's watch. You seem fresher than the rest of us."

"That's because I am by far the fittest, strongest and best of us." the knight replied grinning impishly, "oh, and the most modest!"

Zara gave Darin a flat stare. The knight gave a laugh, grabbed his pack and helm and heaved himself up. He slapped Zara on the shoulder and then headed off towards Nat in the gloom.

Zara found herself facing the stairs by which they had camped. There was a clink of metal on stone and her head snapped up to look into the darkness up the steps. She frowned. Could that be…?

She turned around and saw Arkadi was pulling himself to his feet, his staff propped against the floor to help lift him. There was a scrape from the metal butt end of his staff. Zara relaxed and let out her breath. She watched Arkadi head over towards the middle stairwell where the gnome creature, Nossi Bee sat still and quiet. Zara shook her head and walked back towards the far stairwell away from her friends. 'I'm getting jumpy,' she thought.

As she approached, the dark maw that was the stairwell opened before her. She looked up into the inky darkness and listened intently.

Nothing.

Zara turned and looked over to her friends. Once Arkadi got his spell working it wouldn't be long before they could head out again. She really needed to see the light again.

Suddenly, there was a low, deep, guttural snarl and a scrape of metal on stone. Zara froze for a second and then turned to look at the stairwell in alarm. With surprising speed, a huge armoured arm and shoulder pushed out from the utter dark of the tunnel followed by a mountain of flesh and platemail!

Zara looked up in amazement and saw a pair of huge, dark eyes peering down at her from a face shadowed by a helm that covered a head the size of a grizzly bear's.

"Enemies!" she heard herself yell as she automatically reached for her sabres. Suddenly, an equally large arm to the first thrust out from behind the bulk of the first monstrous brute and slammed into her like a battering ram. She hurtled through the air like a child's rag doll and slammed against the back wall heavily. Stars danced in front of her eyes. Instinct and years of training took over. She pulled her twin sabres from their sheaths across her back without even thinking and ducked beneath a prodigious swing from the first monstrous man-like creature. It held the largest spiked mace Zara had ever seen. She screamed an almost incoherent battle cry and leapt forward, her sabres a blurring arc as they sliced deep into exposed flesh along the sides, upper arms and thighs of the gigantic warrior. Her attack was ferocious and would have badly wounded if not killed any smaller opponent, yet the great brown skinned brute before her merely hissed from its helm and hammered again at Zara with a huge swing that forced the agile warrior to leap back to avoid being smashed like a bug!

⁓⧖⧗

Darin of Kenarth was snatched upright by Zara's cry. He dragged his great sword from its sheath, instantly turned and ran down the corridor towards his friends. Time seemed to slow down. He could see the tall, lean figure of Nat Bero ahead of him, not yet back to her blanket to take her rest after he had relieved her. The tall huntress had an arrow already knocked to her bow. Just in front and to the side of her, the little gnome sat frozen, Arkadi was by him, his shadowy cloak still swirling outwards from his hasty turn.

As Darin rushed forward, round the bend of the corridor, he could see huge figures hacking and swinging at the seemingly tiny figure of Zara as she leapt and twisted desperately to avoid blows that would have felled an ox. An arrow sprang from Nat's bow to slam into the lead beast's shoulder and it reared back in pain. Darin could see Zara leaping to the attack...

"More of them... At the other stairs!" Darin suddenly heard Garon call frantically.

Darin's view of Zara was suddenly obscured as Garon and Rebba thrust themselves to their feet facing the middle stairs. Abruptly, a third giant figure burst into the light from the stairs nearest their camp. It swung a vicious blow at Garon who was only saved from being crushed by Rebba desperately yanking him back!

Darin saw the rotund monk pull his own mace from his belt, a look of wide eyed fear on his pale face.

The gnome Nossi Bee, cried, "Ogres" even as Darin bounded past Nat to ram his blade deep into the exposed side of the roaring creature. Its roar turned to a gurgle and Darin grinned savagely at the beast. He twisted his blade and yanked it free. He lifted it quickly to finish the ten foot lumbering brute, but an arm the size of small tree trunk hammered into him and he felt himself fly backwards through the air to land with a crash back at Nat Bero's feet, all the wind knocked out of him. Darin struggled up to see the ogre he'd attacked slump back against the arch of the stairwell, mortally wounded. However, from behind it boiled forward a half a dozen of the hideous insect creatures, arms and legs flailing madly in the shadows of the corridor. Nat's arrow slammed into one and knocked its body back into its fellows, but more of them pushed heedlessly over their injured companion. Suddenly an explosion ripped into the front row of insect men and they seemed to almost blow apart, four practically disappeared completely with others losing arms and legs. There was a momentary lull as the blast flung the creatures back, but more uninjured giant insects poured from the stairs along with a couple of black skinned goblins and darkly clad elves.

'By Alba's blood!' Darin thought, 'they've all found us!' The tall knight hurriedly pushed himself to his feet not taking his eyes off the insect men. Garon and Rebba defended frenetically, but were pushed back by the press of the creatures as they skittered into the wide hallway. The tide of bodies pushed the two away from Darin and the others towards where they'd last seen Zara fighting the two other ogre creatures. The winded knight also realised that Bear was over there, helpless before those hellish creatures.

Darin lifted his blade, anger pulsing into him, and all pain left him. His mouth pulled into a snarl and he roared, shoving himself forward to meet the rush of attackers.

Suddenly, Darin found himself facing a wall of glittering, pulsing blue energy! He dragged himself to a halt, almost skidding from his feet before the wall of light. He could see insect men slamming into the wall and bouncing back with high pitched, inhuman screams.

Darin spun to face a pale Arkadi and yelled over the screams and snarls. "What are you doing?"

Arkadi looked at him like he was insane. "I'm saving us." he snapped.

The angry knight lunged at the frightened mage. He grabbed his cloak and yanked him up close. "No, you're killing them!" Darin spat, pointing back up the corridor. The knight saw the look of bewilderment on his friend's face and he practically screamed, "How are Garon, Rebba and the others going to escape? You've trapped them!"

Arkadi was shaking his head in denial. "They can flee the other way…"

"That way was blocked, you fool!" Darin shouted.

"What do you expect him to do, Darin?" Nat Bero cried desperately. "If he lets down the barrier, we won't have a chance. They're all coming, maybe forty or fifty of them. We can't face those odds. Our only chance is to flee."

Darin turned his fury on to the dark haired huntress. "You'd flee and leave your friends to die!"

Nat Bero looked at him unable to speak, torn, not knowing what to say.

Zara was in trouble. The brute before her was bleeding badly and was starting to show signs of failing, but his partner was still barely injured and hammering at her like a child at a mouse. Zara wasn't sure she could keep dodging for much longer. It was only her agility and a great deal of skill that had kept her out of reach of those huge maces and she knew even a glancing blow from one of those could slow her down enough to prove fatal. Added to which, she could see elven faces glaring at her from between the angry giants, waiting to have their own chance at her. Zara had heard Garon's cry from down the corridor. She knew there were more enemies behind her too.

"Ishara's icy tits!" she cursed. They were trapped again, and soon, unless her friends could deal with those attacking behind her, she could have enemies at her back too! Again, Zara had failed and this time it looked like it would be the last time.

Zara growled in sudden fury. She stopped dodging the swings of the snarling ogres and darted in to bury one of her blades into the lightly injured brute's exposed thigh and with her other she jabbed up under the overstretched creature's arm to slice into its armpit. Blood splattered her and she frantically dragged herself and her blades back, but one had lodged in the creature's powerful thigh! She dodged to the side, still yanking on her left hand blade, and the creature's grasping hand missed her by inches. Suddenly, she realised she had exposed herself to the other wounded creature. In came its whistling mace. Zara forgot her trapped blade and hit the ground flat. She felt the huge weapon whistle over her and then there was a huge crunch!

Zara looked up even as she sprang almost cat-like to her feet, fear powering her muscles. The badly wounded ogre had been unable to stop its mighty swing when Zara dodged and had smashed its twin's leg! Zara quickly used the confusion to dart forward and hamstring the injured ogre as it watched its companion crumple to the ground bellowing in pain from its unintentional attack. Zara smiled for a moment as she watched both giants crash to the ground in agony. However, the smile froze on her face when she saw black skinned goblins leap to the attack over the prone thrashing brutes.

Desperately, she back pedalled and took her remaining sabre in both hands. She could hear the battle behind her getting nearer, and Garon and Rebba's curses getting more despairing. Savagely, she lunged forward and the first goblin stumbled back, Zara then feinted to go left and instead went right and caught the unprepared goblin under the chin above his black breastplate. The goblin's eyes widened as it frantically grasped at its ruined throat before collapsing to its knees. Zara only just parried attacks from the other two goblins, but had to give ground. She could also see more goblins and now elves, waiting to jump across the still thrashing and bellowing ogres. It was only their blind dying rage that was keeping the others from rapidly overwhelming Zara, and that was not going to keep them off forever. Even without that threat, the danger she could sense behind her seemed to be building like a dark cloud.

There was a sudden cry from behind.

Zara risked a glance back and despair hit; there was no sign now of Rebba, Garon or anyone else, only a mass of insect creatures!

'So this is it!' Zara thought as she faced the two goblins again, 'This is where it ends.' It was not the glorious end she would have wanted. She really wished she hadn't led her friends down here. A fatal resolve gripped her and she thought savagely, 'I'll take some of these bastards with me!'

Zara attacked hard, dodging and using every trick she had learnt against the two goblin assailants, and a parry, spin, kick and thrust took one startled goblin and left the other choking out its last breath on the cold stone floor. It was then that the first ogre Zara had attacked, heaved its last great breath and three elves jumped on the unfortunate beast's still sinking chest to advance. Behind her she heard harsh commands and she knew the insect creatures were coming. Zara had no illusions; even with both her blades she could not have defeated so many.

'Damn,' she cursed silently and then shouted, "If anyone can hear me, get yourself out of here!"

The goblins and elves leapt to attack.

Darin, Knight of the Holy Order of Saint Karodra, looked at Nat Bero, then at Arkadi and the gnome. He turned to look through the barrier's blue haze and could see some of the insect creatures still throwing themselves heedlessly into the barrier in the hope of breaking through. Beyond them it was clear a fight was still underway and that their friends were still alive. Darin couldn't leave. He had to help his friends. He would rather die than live knowing he had left his friends.

"Fine," he hissed, "You go. Take that gnome and get him back to the surface how ever you can. Those authorities still need to know what's happened down here and about that elven prince and his army." He glared at the barrier. "I'll stay and fight."

No one moved.

Darin spun and lashed around with his blade in pure rage. He screamed, "Go, damn you!"

Abruptly, the sound of battle quieted. Darin spun back to peer hard through the barrier. Everyone moved towards the barrier. The insect creatures stopped hammering at the wall of energy at some barked command and stood rigid staring at Darin and the others. Beyond them the other insects, goblins and elves began to slowly move off, around the bend of the corridor.

Suddenly above the eerie quiet came a voice bellowing, "If anyone can hear me, get yourself out of here!"

Arkadi spun and rushed over to grab his pack and a torch from the fire. "Come on, you heard what she said, get your things and let's get out of here. That barrier should hold for a while, but with the speed those mayax insect things move they could get round the corridor quickly enough."

"Whose voice was that?" Nat muttered confused. "Was it Zara?"

"It doesn't matter, does it?" Arkadi interrupted, "Let's get out of here." He grabbed what he could and thrust another pack at the gnome who was looking terrified and confused all at the same time.

Nat spun round and ran to grab her pack, her puzzlement lost in the urgency of the moment.

Darin was torn. "What about Bear?" he muttered hopelessly.

Arkadi grabbed him by the shoulder. "We can't do anything for Bear now, Darin. We've got to think of ourselves." Darin continued to stare despairingly at the barrier and Arkadi grabbed him and turned him roughly to stare into his face. "Bear would want us to survive, Darin and we need you. You're the best fighter we have. Come on." he pleaded. "The others will get out another way!"

Darin could hear the doubt in Arkadi's voice as he said it. Darin closed his eyes and blinked back the tears. He looked up to the ceiling and then turned to face the barrier. He brought his great sword up, the blade pointed to the ceiling and the hilt held two handed in front of his chest, his face pressed against the cross guard. Darin thought of his oldest friend and the others and whispered, "Goodbye. Have a good long drink for me in Tynast's hall." He thought his friends would enjoy themselves in the Heroes Hall of the God of Battles, even Garon.

Darin stood still in tribute. Suddenly he swept his sword down and spun around.

The others were staring, sorrow in their eyes.

"Well, what are we waiting for? Let's go." Darin shouted harshly, his voice thick with suppressed emotion. He began jogging, stone faced towards the stairwell ahead.

Quickly, a much smaller group fell in behind Darin.

Chapter 29

DARK THOUGHTS

The Waygates were said to be one of the greatest wonders of the Elder. How they may have been constructed and the magic needed is a complete mystery. Elven myths say that they were built by Gal'Mir Greenheart, a legendary king of all the elves so far in the past that all knowledge is lost of that time save the names and a few fragments of lore. The Waygates were used as roads between the major cities of the ancient Elder kingdoms of the elves, dwarves and other lost races. If the stories are to be believed, somehow the Waygates allowed instant travel between places thousands of leagues apart. They were permanent and could transport vast numbers. However, this goes against all the known laws of magic.

From 'The nature of the Elder' by Melkor Erin, Archmage of Shandrilos, BY1303

Prince Uh'Ram Bloodfire was displeased and he so hated being displeased because then he would have to make an example of somebody. He always found that a judicious execution sated his anger.

Looking around, his eyes scanned the great column lined hall with its broken statues. Dotted around these, in the hall, were his faithful lorewarden guard and their dark brothers, along with groups of lorewise and clerics, talking in hushed tones and casting worried glances his way. They knew he was annoyed and feared him. That was good.

Senior Parinsar Nar'Dolth, his second in command, along with his Venerable Loremaster, Cleric and Lorewarden, his three senior advisors, stood mute and still at the bottom of the stair to the raised dais upon which his throne stood. To the side of them, stood a shabby group of local goblin 'guls', the name they gave to chieftains. Some of them were physically shaking with fear as they looked on his countenance. They were pathetic these goblins, such poor imitations of his dark brothers. The goblins were shackled and elven warriors in their jet black armour stood around them. These goblin 'Guls' had dared to go against Uh'Ram's will and had continued a blood feud with another group of tribes who had pledged to Uh'Ram's service. Alongside the group of goblin prisoners was a large brutish looking rock troll, a chief of some clan to the north who had made the mistake of attacking one of Uh'Ram's warparties.

Sensing his eye on them, the goblins commenced whining and beseeching Uh'Ram. He was disgusted with their behaviour. These creatures had no honour or dignity, but then they were a degenerate race and as bestial and petty as the humans. The troll at least had the dignity not to beg.

"Hironsar," Uh'Ram called lightly to the officer in charge of the guards around the goblins and lone troll, "kill them."

The wailing of the creatures grew louder and the Hironsar pulled his sword, as did his men. With that the Hironsar thrust his blade into the nearest goblin.

"Not here!" Uh'Ram snarled over the noise. "Take them outside. We are not barbarians!" He admonished pointing to the doors.

The Hironsar acknowledged his direction, but Uh'Ram ignored the fool and looked over to Parinsar Nar'Dolth who nodded briefly. Nar'Dolth would see that the officer was suitably chastised afterwards.

The officer and his men began dragging the goblins, including the now gurgling, writhing one out of the hall. There was a stain of red across the floor. A needless mess, Uh'Ram thought in exasperation. It was likely the Hironsar would be wiping much of his own blood up once his punishment was imposed. He would not die, that would be a waste of a warrior, but he might wish he had died afterward. Another would take his place as Hironsar; fools could not be tolerated to lead.

Suddenly, there was a rough snarl and the towering troll warrior smashed the guard and a couple of goblins away and shouted in very stilted elven, "Why you not kill us yourself, coward?"

Uh'Ram looked at the creature in disdain and then at his court. "Because I don't have to." He replied simply and gave a stiff, brief smile to the creature.

The seven foot brute looked confused, but then Uh'Ram did not imagine it would take very much to confuse it, trolls did not exactly have the sharpest of minds, even a true mountain troll like this one.

The creature went berserk and started hammering around at his guards who dodged it and looked to their prince. They knew he had said to kill the prisoners outside and to go against his direct command would be a death sentence.

In exasperation, Uh'Ram found his temper slipping. He stood slowly, his mood switching instantly and his face becoming a tight mask of malice.

He hissed in pure anger, "Very well, release the troll."

His guards dropped back. Uh'Ram was aware that his lorewarden guard around the room was now poised to attack and he lifted his hand to hold them and spat, "No, leave the beast." Then to the troll who suddenly glared at him he called, "Come then troll!"

The troll hefted its shackles and began to charge, bellowing like a wounded mammoth, but before it had taken more than a few strides, Uh'Ram's anger and frustration burst free and lightning leapt forth from his suddenly outstretched arm to hammer into the troll. The creature seemed to just vaporize in the blinding conflagration. Its few remains were slammed twenty feet back to strike a column.

Uh'Ram almost purred in brief pleasure before withdrawing his hand. He then straightened his cloak before calmly sitting back down, his anger vanished and his attention on the troll forgotten. Even killing seemed not to offer more than a passing diversion at the moment.

'Shame,' he thought, and leaned back in his large seat.

Looking up thoughtfully he ignored the guards who herded the now stupefied goblins out. Gnome servants, who seemed to appear from nowhere, cleaned up the bloody smears and the troll's remains. Uh'Ram's gaze was drawn upwards. He could see the vault roof of the great hall. It was arched and looked like the ribcage of some monstrous creature with mighty ribs curving to meet a huge spine that ran down the centre of the roof. The distraction calmed him more fully. He had to keep a rein on his anger; it could just simply appear from nowhere and disappear as quickly. It was galling that a man of his genius should be plagued with such an unpredictable temper. He smiled imperceptibly, 'but then it did keep his servants on edge.'

Still admiring the roof, Uh'Ram noticed that in between the great ribs there were murals and scenes from the forgotten history of this land. That thought made the prince smile, at least on the inside, it would not be proper to beam at his court like some barbaric human, especially when he wanted all to know his displeasure. Still it was pleasing to know that this had once been a hall of some prince of the lost kingdom of El'Yaris, a kingdom that was now almost totally forgotten and his to control. Even the so-called rulers of this now barbaric land, the goblin 'guls', were barely aware that it was now Uh'Ram who controlled this land not them. He controlled it through their new leaders, the 'Guldors' or High Chiefs. It was Uh'Ram and his forces that were orchestrating the rise of unity amongst the bickering goblin nations of these northern plains. They would never have managed it themselves. The goblins actually thought him to be the messenger of the Dark Gods come again to raise them to glory. Some of them had actually believed he was sent to do their bidding… a ridiculous thought and one of which he had quickly disabused them!

Still, as stupid as these goblins were it was proving difficult to unite them, so intent were they on killing each other as well as anybody and everybody else. He'd had to commit his forces, both soldiers and lorewise, to aiding certain handpicked goblin chiefs, those who had sworn their souls to him and the Demon Lords. Thus, his attention was stretched across the whole of the northlands, carefully guiding his puppet rulers to crush any who opposed their rise. His lorewise and wargroups were spread thin. Currently, his plans for unifying the goblins under nine high chiefs across the immense northlands were going well. Already he had created a successful base of power for four such Guldor's who would eventually be able to provide him with over a hundred and fifty thousand warriors, but it was gradually becoming clear that this could not be maintained unless he could keep a closer control on events and that would need better communication. However, the difficulty was that his lorewise's strength was almost completely used up in opening magical portals across the land to communicate with him and to move his forces around to where they were needed. To add to this, the greatest of his lorewise could only open the great portal through which his forces had first come, infrequently. This meant that he could only bring through small groups of men at a time to reinforce himself and so he was starved of the true forces he would need to conquer and fully control this land. It was a frustrating problem.

Prince Uh'Ram sat on his harsh throne and played the problem around in his head. His bloodmetal armour made the throne on which he sat twice as uncomfortable, but Uh'Ram ignored it. He believed hardships bourn made you stronger. He leaned forward and slowly propped his elbows on the bare arms of the mighty chair, steepling his fingers together in front of his scarred face.

The most frustrating thing was that he knew how to solve this greatest problem, but it was becoming clear that things were not going according to his extremely thorough and meticulously planned schemes!

Uh'Ram knew that if he could somehow reopen the sealed Waygates that sat beneath the greatest of the now ruined cities of the Elder, cities that were spread across the vast northlands, he could send his troops and messages across the wide expanse of the northlands with ease, freeing up his lorewise to use their powers to aid his armies in a more direct manner. He could then fully unify the goblins beneath his rule, destroy all opposition and reclaim this ancient land!

For a moment Uh'Ram allowed himself to luxuriate in the imagined glories that would come from success, but then he hastily crushed his elation and brought his mind back to the present. He was not one to celebrate until victory was firmly in his grasp. First he had to gain the key to the ancient Waygates.

Thoughts of the lost key again turned his mind to Ry'Ana the Lore Queen and the prophecy she had spoken all those centuries ago. She believed he was the one to fulfil the prophecy.

Uh'Ram had only been a child when she had first uttered her fateful decree, she had been ancient beyond any of his people; the greatest seer his race had ever known. Over the years she had guided him and aided him, using her unique vision to help him deal with dangers. However, her warnings and advice had become irksome recently. Since they had come to these lands almost twenty years ago, she had placed too much emphasis on the humans and the threat they posed.

The humans were pathetic creatures, weak and easily corrupted. It was so easy to dominate those 'ape creatures' and turn them on themselves. Already his agents among them had begun dealing with the potential threats Ry'Ana had foreseen, not that such threats were really credible... at least that was what he had thought. Now, he worried about those humans he had instructed be killed. Ry'Ana had prophesised that some amongst the humans might threaten his search for the key to the Ways and worse might threaten the prophecy itself!

Uh'Ram had not seen how this was possible, but he was always thorough. He had ordered his pet human mage to deal with them. Uh'Ram knew that none of the humans had escaped the northlands, those threats had been neutralised, but what of the two warriors? Ry'Ana had hinted that two humans in the south might prove a thorn in his side? She had said that there was something hidden in her visions, something elusive, an unknown factor and that Uh'Ram should be sure of their deaths. Recently, he had heard nothing from the humans. His pet mage refused to respond to Uh'Ram's call and Uh'Ram had suddenly found he had very few who could get near the mage to deal with him. It was irritating to find that most of his other human pawns had mysteriously been slain; it was irritating and worrying.

Ry'Ana's belief that there were threats from among the humans seemed less and less the nonsense he had believed it to be. It now seemed, from the rumours he was hearing from his few remaining sources, that the killings he had ordered might not have gone to plan. If so then this might explain why he was not holding the key to the Waygates in his hand right now!

Oh, he remembered how he had laughed silently at Ry'Ana's departing admonishment not to underestimate the humans nor ignore the portents.

Humans, how he despised them!

Uh'Ram continued to brood.

'No!' he thought suddenly, 'I am deceiving myself.' There is no threat from the humans, there could be no threat from the humans; they were too weak to present a problem. Another thought occurred to him, one far more alarming; the other princes; his kin!

Ry'Ana had said that she would deal with his fellow princes; she could exert her considerable influence to keep them subdued and unaware. However, perhaps Ry'Ana had failed. Perhaps, it was not the humans who were the cause of the delay, but his own kin. Uh'Ram suddenly saw the hand of one of the princes of the Second House stretching out to interfere.

He was no longer sure that none of them had discovered his plans. Another thought struck him. Perhaps one of them was aiding the humans, using them. That would explain things. He knew that Im'Lak or Sky'Ina would happily see him dead regardless of Ry'Ana. The princes of the Second House were fools, but ambitious fools! They would want the key to the Ways and the glories it could bring.

Again, Uh'Ram fell to brooding.

There had originally been twelve keys to the Ways, but most were destroyed millennia ago. The rest had been hastily destroyed or hidden centuries ago in an attempt to safeguard the Elder kingdoms. Recently, his hope for finding a key had faded to naught and he had almost given up. That was until only two winters ago when one of his spies had stumbled across a lost piece of script that described the desperate plans of the last elven Lore King. There were no details in it that were of any use save for one; where they had assembled and attacked from, and that a trusted guard had been left behind to protect and seal the portals. They had left from the kingdom of Dah'Ryllah!

That was the answer, Uh'Ram had been sure of it. He knew that the Lore King had meant to seal the Ways. It made sense then that a key still remained there, for he knew none had left Dah'Ryllah's undercity after the Lore King's last attack.

It had taken some effort to actually detect the unique resonance of the key, but it was there, somewhere underground in Dah'Ryllah!

The problem was that Dah'Ryllah's greatest city now lay beneath a settlement of humans, and of lorewise humans at that! Their knowledge of the ancient lore was poor and fragmented, based on tradition and rigid spellcraft with little true understanding of the mysteries, yet potent enough in their numbers to make them dangerous. Luckily, Uh'Ram was not unfamiliar with the place, it had come to his attention early as a possible source of both opposition and allies, and he had several humans there bound to him, one of whom was quite high up in their primitive culture. Uh'Ram had quickly realised that if he could make sure that no humans would stray into the ancient city beneath, he could send through a trusted group to retrieve the key.

His worries now centred on that group.

He had sent his most ambitious and driven Hironsar, Dar'Elthon Ath'Totheariss, with his warparty to find and return the key. Dar'Elthon was a talented lorewarden and a man driven to regain his family's honour. He had proved he was more his grandfather's heir than his father or brother's in the way he had successfully carried out all of Uh'Ram's orders. Uh'Ram had been sure he would be the perfect servant for this crucial task; he would never betray his prince if he knew he could regain his family's honour and position with its success. At least that was what Uh'Ram had wanted to believe; now he wasn't so sure. Perhaps Dar'Elthon had made some alliance with another and sought glory for himself.

Uh'Ram shook his head. No, a minor house lord would not presume… unless another prince had promised protection? Again, that thought plagued him: were his fellow princes involved?

It was already past time for Dar'Elthon to have retrieved the key and signaled for the portal that had transported his warparty, to be re-opened. Uh'Ram should now have been holding in his fist the key to his people's glorious future… but he was not. Instead he was sat here in his hall brooding.

Abruptly, Uh'Ram's gaze was brought back to the present by the silent movement of the huge doors at the other end of the hall. He watched as a loremaster in the deep purple, almost black robes of his caste entered. He was briefly challenged by the guards, but with a quick word was allowed through. Seeming to float across the smooth, marble floor, the loremaster approached, head down in respect. Uh'Ram did not recognise the man, but ignored him as his Venerable Loremaster, Oth'Raan went to meet him. There was a quick discussion with more emotion than was decent and then Oth'Raan turned and approached Uh'Ram's throne. He bowed and asked if he might draw near.

With a sharp nod Uh'Ram acquiesced and Oth'Raan bent low and mounted the few steps before kneeling on one knee by Uh'Ram's throne.

"My prince, the Lore Queen has returned."

Uh'Ram raised an immaculate eyebrow, a show of his intense interest. 'Ry'Ana was here, so far from the Holy City?' he thought.

"Where is the Holy Mother, Oth'Raan?" Uh'Ram asked and was a little shocked at the unseemly urgency in his tone. He made a mental note to take control of himself.

"Highness, she awaits you in your inner sanctum."

He knelt, for he was in the presence of his Queen.

The woman before him was the oldest member of his long lived race, far older than she ever should have lived to be, sustained by her magic. Ry'Ana White Eyes had outlived her children and even her grandchildren were now old by the reckoning of their long lived race, yet none of this showed in the angelic form that moved towards him, such was her knowledge of the powers of the world.

She was tall, like all who possessed the blood of the *Ata'Gon*. Hair, black as night, cascaded down to her waist; careless tresses fell over her shoulders, partially covering her chest and arms. She wore only a simple floor length robe of black silk-lined velvet, sleeveless and cut low at the chest. The skin that could be seen was shining and youthful, a metallic coppery sheen that was flawless. Her figure was slim and seemed to exude a natural poise and elegance as she stood in his inner sanctuary. There was no trace of her age in that body and so he looked to the face seeking any trace, but as always there was none. It was a face he knew well for he had known the women for centuries; his whole life, and still the sight of her face shocked him. It was not the lack of age in that elven face with its winged, sloping brows or its delicate boned features, it was the eyes that always took him aback.

Elven eyes were always wondrous, large and almond shaped, they had dazzling irises of spectacular hues that dominated the whole eye, no whites showed in elven eyes. Not so with this woman's eyes. Hers were, as always, white, milky and blind, a startling contrast to the polished copper fire of her complexion. Blind she had always been, born that way, or so he was told for none now lived who remembered her birth, and yet she had a sight that went far beyond any other mortals. Even the *Ata'Gon*, her blessed father, the most powerful of their race who had ever lived, did not possessed his first born daughter's ability to divine the future. Hers was a unique gift and a gift that she now bent to aiding his conquest of the lands their people had been forced to give up.

Centuries had passed since that terrible time when the *Ata'Gon* had been lost and Uh'Ram's beloved father had been slain. Few knew the truth of that time, few knew how they had failed, but now that failure would be remedied, now the time was right.

All this history flashed though Prince Uh'Ram's mind as he gazed at the women before him. The history of his people had been hammered into him ever since he could remember; hatred for the enemies of his people flowed through his veins like an elixir, it had pushed him on through the long years, fuelling his desires for revenge and conquest. The knowledge of his father's death and the *Ata'Gon's* defeat was an ever present part of his thoughts, it had been taught to him by the being who stood before him; a being who had lived through it all and survived.

"Will you simply stare at me, Prince Uh'Ram?" Ry'Ana asked in a voice that sang like a small stream through a brook. "Or will you invite me to sit? I have travelled far to see you."

Uh'Ram stood and bowed in a single flowing motion, "I apologise, my queen. Forgive the inadequacy of my welcome. You caught me unprepared." he replied. "Please take your ease." Uh'Ram watched as the Lore Queen of his people sat gracefully into one of the ornate chairs he had installed in his private apartments. "Travel through the great portal is taxing."

Her head tilted sharply to face him and her blind eyes seemed to search him and he knew Ry'Ana sought his thoughts. "I have not risked a journey through the great portal, Uh'Ram..."

Uh'Ram realised as she said it that indeed before him stood only the shade of the Lore Queen, an astral projection of her form. He was impressed. He knew of her skill with astral magic, but to project herself over such a distance from the Holy City was incredible.

Her eyes were still on him, searching. Her words still seemed to hang in the air. "Is your desire for revenge as strong as it once was?" She enquired quietly. "Is your desire to fulfil the prophecy as strong?"

"It is, as it has always been since you first told to me the story of our people's betrayal and loss. I was still only a child then, but ever since I have dreamed of vengeance, of retaking the ancient lands and, most of all, of fulfilling the prophecy, your prophecy, my queen." Excitement and desire filled him. "I long to see our people raised to their rightful place as rulers of all; the chosen people. All others will bow before us as they once did." He intoned thrilling with the images that caught his mind's eye.

"Beware your feelings, Uh'Ram, my dear," Ry'Ana purred, "you know that the other princes have only sanctioned your attempt at retaking the promised lands. Should the princes of the Second House discover your attempts to fulfil the prophecy without them, they will move against you. They will see your loyalty to the prophecy as an attempt to increase your power... and to diminish theirs. They have lost their faith. They have convinced themselves that the prophecy is a mistake in their selfish desire to rule; they seek to take full control of the race. The princes of the Second House have grown jealous of the power they now wield as leaders in the council and they want more." Her tone gave a clear indication of her hatred. Uh'Ram knew Ry'Ana despised the Second House... as did he!

Uh'Ram was a prince of the Third House, the descendent of the *Ata'Gon's* third wife. Of course, Ry'Ana was of the First House, the eldest house. The *Ata'Gon's* second wife had been insane it was said and so were her offspring. Still, it had been hard to believe that the princes of the Second House would completely abandon the prophecy and seek to glorify themselves. Had he not seen their selfish desires himself he would not have believed that a descendent of the Holy line could so betray their blessed destiny. Uh'Ram's eyes blazed in anger at the thought.

"Bah! The princes of the Second House are blasphemous fools. They are blind. Even at best they have only ever wasted all our resources on a futile, furtive attempt to regain our former glory. They would have us stagnate so that they can take power."

The fine eyebrows above Ry'Ana's pale eyes rose in pleasure.

Uh'Ram hurried on, "All was lost centuries ago and what have we done?" Uh'Ram asked, caught up now in the passion of what he was saying, "Nothing, save dwell on our past glories. The Princes of the Second House wish to rule themselves, to make themselves dominant... and what then? They will fight amongst themselves, such is their twisted nature, and they will destroy what remains of our people in civil war! We need the courage to forge the path laid out for us by the prophecy; we need to be bold!" In his passion he had stood and his hands clenched at the air around him in the extremity of his feelings. He found Ry'Ana staring directly at him, her face impassive yet somehow disapproving.

"Not disapproving," She responded quietly, reading his thoughts, "Sit down Uh'Ram." She commanded, "Your outburst is unseemly if perhaps justified."

Shame touched Uh'Ram; elves did not show such emotions, it was uncouth. He sat once more, the darkness of his cloak flowing around him.

Ry'Ana looked off into some distant place only she could see. "Your search is safe for the moment, your worries about the other princes moving against you is unfounded."

Uh'Ram was surprised at her knowledge of his earlier thoughts.

"Something else is occurring amongst the humans, something I had not thought to see. You know that I support you fully, though your methods are a little too... ah, how should I say... lacking in subtlety for my taste, but then I am no warrior or commander. However, your forceful nature has got you far. You are now in a position to conquer the ancient lands, and to better search, especially if you get the key to the Ways." She insisted, some passion showing in her tone for the first time.

Uh'Ram hesitated. He had rarely seen any emotion in Ry'Ana.

Ry'Ana seemed to sense his disapproval at her breach of propriety. "Calm yourself, Uh'Ram, there is no need for alarm, even I can allow myself to indulge in emotion when the occasion warrants it." She paused and regarded Uh'Ram, amusement clearly waning. "Ah..." she said almost regretfully, "I forget how little you and your generation truly know of me."

Suddenly her face changed, as quickly as it had appeared, all animation on her face seemed to vanish and the serene visage settled back into place.

"My passion should not alarm you, Prince Uh'Ram, for it heralds the answer to all our dreams."

Uh'Ram frowned, his attention caught and Ry'Ana's blind milky gaze seemed to focus on him.

"You should be wary of the Second House but..." She paused and again her unseeing gaze seemed to look off into unknowable distances. Somewhat dreamily her voice drifted to him, "...as yet there is no danger from them. They suspect nothing. I have protected you and dealt with the Second House's clumsy attempts to place spies in your ranks. However, you must still be wary, there is another danger! The secrecy of our people's involvement is imperative until we have a complete grip on these northlands, and now that secrecy is in peril because of your search for the key to the Ways." Ry'Ana White Eyes sat forward her face suddenly harsh. "Your search party has placed our plans in jeopardy!"

Uh'Ram Bloodfire was caught cold.

"However," she continued in a thoughtful tone, "it has also brought the lines of fate into focus. Events have now been set in motion that could see the fulfilment of the prophecy. The humans of those lands that are now known as the Wildlands will soon become aware that something is wrong in the north. The humans are driven by some powerful influence. They will discover your plans, not here in the northlands, but in your searches in the south, unless you act to neutralise the threat."

"They are not a worry." Uh'Ram muttered.

Ry'Ana looked harshly at Uh'Ram. She shook her head. "Your hatred of the humans blinds you. You have underestimated them and now the humans are a danger! The humans grow large in my visions."

Uh'Ram snorted.

"They are ignorant animals. What can they do against us?"

"Such arrogance Uh'Ram, perhaps you are not the one spoken of in the prophecy, you scorn my advice and risk my anger!"

Uh'Ram sat still, Ry'Ana's words struck hard, but his blood was up now and a fury formed deep in his chest, though he dared not show it. He despised humans. They were a primitive, pathetic people. He could not bring himself to believe they could ever be a real threat.'

"The humans must be dealt with, Uh'Ram or you will never succeed." Ry'Ana snapped harshly before continuing more gently. "Remember what happened in the past. Don't repeat the mistake of underestimating them."

Uh'Ram just couldn't bring himself to believe. He had watched the humans, moved amongst them, they were little more than animals with no control over their feelings, little knowledge of the mysteries, and they put such stock in petty things that they were easily corrupted.

It was almost ridiculous and yet…

No, his plans were flawless, he had covered every eventuality. Nothing those in the so-called Wildlands could do could upset his strategies.

"You are right for now," Ry'Ana agreed, reading his thoughts again, "but if you are complacent, the minor threats you ignore will turn into major ones. Figures of power can appear from nowhere. I have seen it before."

Ry'Ana paused a moment and then continued. "I can see the patterns of the future forming. The future is not set, choices and decisions will change it, yet most choices can be guessed at and the possible future made manifest to one with the eyes to see, and to one with the support of the Gods." She nodded at Uh'Ram's doubting countenance and then her tone became harsh, cold, "Your failure to deal with the threat of the humans in the south has now set events in motion whose outcome is unclear to me." She insisted, her face taut.

Suddenly, the Lore Queen, stopped, her head snapped back and she quivered. Uh'Ram was awed despite the fear and anger warring within him. He had seen the Lore Queen enter these prophetic trances before and always her words were true!

"In your future I see power, great power, the Lifestone I see..." Ry'Ana whispered in a voice heavy with power and doom.

Uh'Ram almost gasped such was his sudden elation.

"... yet insignificant seeming decisions and individuals could spell your doom, Uh'Ram." the Seeress warned. "I also see humans seeking the talisman of power."

Uh'Ram's mind was brought back from elation with alarm and his gaze fixed to the unseeing one of the powerful Lore Queen. How could humans even know of the ancient talisman?

Ry'Ana seemed to come back to herself and gave an almost imperceptible shake as if to restore herself to the here and now. "I can help you with these dangers." She asserted coolly.

Uh'Ram was stunned by her words. He knew she did not lie, he knew for sure that humans were now a real danger; Ry'Ana's prophecies had never been wrong. Even so, emotions warred within him still; fear, anger, hatred, disbelief, joy. He found it hard to prevent his emotion from reaching his face and he was glad he was alone with the ancient seeress.

Uh'Ram made the only decision he could, "What is your bidding my queen?"

Ry'Ana leaned back into the large chair in which she sat and regarded Uh'Ram placidly; content, patient, confident. Slowly the ancient Lore Queen spoke, her voice heavy with certainty, "This is what you must do..."

As Uh'Ram entered his throne room, he was met by Venerable Loremaster, Oth'Raan, who bowed briefly. "Highness, we have now received information from our spies about the secret proceedings of the human leaders' council, but not from the human mage. Our people are closely watched and cannot get to him. He still refuses to answer the call and so we cannot verify if he has dealt with the human threats the Lore Queen identified. However, it is now clear that the humans are aware that the goblin tribes around their northern frontiers are uniting. Word has escaped of Guldor Marog's rise in the Bloodlands in particular."

"And our involvement with the goblins?" Uh'Ram asked, knowing what the answer must be as he mounted the steps to his throne.

"Not as yet. Our secret is still secure." Oth'Raan replied smoothly.

Uh'Ram nodded and then carefully and calmly turned and looked out at his court for a moment before sitting. Ry'Ana had already told him that knowledge of the goblin unification had been revealed, though she was unclear how.

Knowledge of the unification of the goblins getting to the humans was inevitable, and Uh'Ram had planned for how this would happen and how his people would infiltrate the humans. However, Uh'Ram was a little perturbed at his human mage's failure to kill the threats that Ry'Ana had identified; too many of his carefully laid plans were starting to come apart and from what Ry'Ana had told him, those shabby humans could well be responsible for Dar'Elthon's tardiness!

Uh'Ram had planned for the eventual resistance and possible unity amongst the humans of the Wildlands, had arranged for their own people to undermine such an alliance, but he had underestimated the humans again it seemed.

Uh'Ram briefly wondered if there were some guiding hand at work, someone who had the vision to foresee the danger from the north, someone who knew the secret behind the goblin unity, but then that led to the question of how much did this someone know and why had they kept it to themselves.

Nevertheless, the unity of the Wildlands would only be a minor setback to his great schemes. The Wildlands, even united would only be able to provide a tiny force to oppose the army he would eventually raise. What was more worrying was that the humans knew more than he had expected and now it seemed as if his enemies suspected his other objective. If it were true, it would make acquiring the talisman twice as difficult and could lead to it falling into their hands. That could not be allowed to happen.

Uh'Ram had miscalculated recently and he hated miscalculation. He liked to think he had put things into motion that made the choices of his foes predictable and suddenly there were possible aberrations to the carefully worked sequence of events he had arranged.

He sighed, his emotions switching completely. 'Ah, but that was the joy in such an endeavour,' he allowed, 'if he was never surprised, never tested he would never be able to prove his genius.' Thus, in some ways he resented the aid Ry'Ana had given him, even though it would help him put things back on track. He shook that thought away. He needed to focus on the way forward and not let his personal feelings cloud things.

He would have to change his plans to deal with that city of magic users far sooner than he had originally planned. He would need to begin assembling his forces ready for an attack. He already had people in the city and the college. He had long ago developed his strategy for isolating the city, something made easier by it being an island, and then annihilating its populace. It would also be made much easier by the humans' complete lack of knowledge of his people's true goals.

Uh'Ram quickly summoned his faithful Senior Parinsar and gave him instructions to begin gathering the forces and informing their people in the city, ready for the attack on Shandrilos. Parinsar Nar'Dolth knew exactly what to do and immediately crossed over to begin a whispered conversation with his senior officers.

However, what Uh'Ram needed while that was happening, was more information about the college. Ry'Ana had said that information about their people was close to being revealed and that needed to be delayed until the city could be destroyed. They needed to prevent the knowledge of their race from spreading beyond the city. This also meant he would have to delay killing the human mage until he was no longer needed. Uh'Ram had need of the mage for now and he needed to speak with him.

Uh'Ram thought.

What he needed, Ry'Ana had suggested, was to send a spy to that ape infested city, a powerful spy who could be trusted totally, who would blend in perfectly, who could never reveal anything if captured. They needed a spy of sufficient power to cow that upstart of a mage and bring him into line until necessary, while reporting directly back to Uh'Ram at all times; a spy who could eradicate any threat from the humans and remain undetected. It was a difficult and subtle proposition, but one with a very obvious solution, albeit a very dangerous one. A slight smile began to form on Uh'Ram's face at the thought of the plan Ry'Ana and he had created. 'Yes, we will send a spy none will expect,' he thought viciously.

Uh'Ram forced his face blank and looked down to the unmoving bowed head of his most powerful loreman. "Oth'Raan, we will be sending a messenger to visit our servants in Shandrilos. You will assist me."

"Highness?" Venerable Loremaster Oth'Raan enquired.

"I will send a greater servant of Eleora'Ashar." He said in satisfaction at the idea of sending a servant of the netherworld.

Oth'Raan's head came up and looked at his master in surprise. "A Changeling!"

Uh'Ram frowned at his first loremaster. "You forget yourself Oth'Raan." he admonished sternly. None were to address him without title or to look up at him on the dais without his permission.

"I beg forgiveness, my prince." Oth'Raan hastily replied, dropping his head, "the… ah… use of such a powerful creature somewhat startled me. They are unpredictable and difficult to control."

Uh'Ram stood. "I am well aware of the shortcomings of using a changeling, but there are many advantages."

"Yes, my prince." his advisor agreed.

"Come, Oth'Raan," Uh'Ram ordered and headed for the summoning room, "and bring those necessary for opening a portal to Shandrilos."

Chapter 30

DANGERS IN THE DARK

The northmen or Nordic and their druid priests worship many gods. These gods are primitive representations of the forces of nature. They are limited in influence and power to their own area of nature. Thus their fire god controls fire and some key aspects of life that are linked to fire. In turn these gods show human aspects such as rage, joy or hatred. The northmen do not easily see how there could be one all powerful loving God as we do. It is too far removed from their concept of what 'god' is, just as their limited view of a god is anathema to us.

From the war journals of Emperor Kilimarius the Great, BY412

The mage smiled politely at the First Minister of Hadek as he turned to leave.

Yet another seed sown, he thought, but still he had to admit he was finding it hard to create a solid opposition to the elves joining the Grand Council among the Olmec leaders. Only the First Ministers of Torunsport and of Kalizern had agreed to oppose the elves, even Sir Arleas of Karodracia was non-committal! Still he'd had more success with the opposition amongst the magi. Many were shocked and appalled by the Archmage's insistence on leading without consent from the Conclave or from the Assembly of Masters.

The mage quickly made his way out of the apartments of the Hadek contingent and was swiftly on his way back towards his own rooms. It was getting very late now and he'd had little time to do anything other than visit members of the Grand Council, but he still had much to do. He had made a point of introducing Sardyk Andar, the skilful halfling thief and assassin, and on his recommendation the halfling had been made an investigator working on the theft of the cloaks from the enchanters and the mystery of the goings on below ground. The Watchmasters had questioned the use of an outsider at first, but had finally accepted it with the mage's support. The mage had also managed to get three of his most trusted masters as investigators. Two of them were already ostensibly looking into the disturbances underground while the third was looking into the stolen cloaks.

It had also just come to his attention through a note from one of his informants that his assassins in the south had disappeared and their targets had survived. The mage had no idea how they had failed, but couldn't spare the time to look into the matter further until he had dealt with his problems here.

Waiting for him outside his quarters was the halfling, Sardyk Andar. The lithe little man was lounging casually against the door jam and the mage brushed past him into his rooms and gestured for him to follow and close the doors. The mage moved swiftly over to his desk, slammed his staff into its holder and almost threw himself into his chair.

"Tired?" asked the child faced Andar.

The mage nodded wordlessly and clasped his hands together in front of him on his silk robes.

"Busy bending the ears of those rich lords." Andar added as he strolled cat-like towards his master's large, oaken desk.

The mage nodded again.

The halfling assassin opened his mouth, but the mage cut him off.

"Would you sit somewhere quietly, I need to think." he snapped at the diminutive killer.

Andar merely smiled slowly then wickedly bowed in elaborate sarcasm before moving off to the main room.

The mage ignored the halfling and put his mind to the problems at hand. The enchanted stave that his master used to gain his attention had been jabbing at his senses. He knew his master wanted to speak to him, but the mage had ignored it for now. It was a dangerous move, but he needed to get things disrupted here so that he would have good news for his master. He needed to distract his master from events in the catacombs. If his master learnt of his involvement underground, as well as the failed killings in the south, the mage might not survive the meeting. If he could report himself as the new leader of the College and the Grand Council he would be safer, he would be useful. However, he had to balance things finely as he had to be rid of his master's people at the college without being obviously responsible. Things were proving difficult, only two of the twelve lords on the Grand Council were open to expelling the elves and only two others were undecided. The mage could only hope that Sir Arleas of Karodracia's advisors would persuade him to oppose the elves inclusion too. The Grand Abbot Alinus' insistence that such an inclusion was not unholy would hold a lot of sway, but there were still large factions in the Karodracian Brotherhood who resented the Grand Abbot and his Sironacian order and would argue the point. Still, it was now obvious that there was little chance, as things stood, of changing the decisions of the Grand Council to accept the Elder so the mage had to be patient. He just hoped his master could be equally patient without it proving lethal!

"Hmmm," he muttered and thought to himself, 'Perhaps this particular puzzle would unknot itself if he applied pressure to his other problem. Perhaps the one could influence the other.'

His second major problem was how to manipulate the Assembly of Masters to formerly strip the Archmage of his rank for improper use of his office. He then had to manipulate himself into the position of heir to that title. The latter would prove far easier than the former. The argument that the Archmage had not consulted either the Conclave or the Assembly on his decision to ask the elves and dwarves to the Grand Council was a strong one. However, at present it was not strong enough to do more than give the Archmage a reprimand, as the Archmage well knew, but that was just at present. What the mage needed to do was to implicate the Archmage in much more damning and obviously self interested crimes. What the mage had to work with was the theft of the cloaks and the magical happenings below ground. Rumours had already been started that the Archmage and his elven allies were somehow responsible, but that wouldn't be enough. What the mage had to do was to produce convincing enough evidence of the Archmage's guilt in these matters.

Of course, he thought in sudden inspiration, Master Drollin, one of the investigators he'd had put in place, was a seer. He could walk the paths of the past and see the Archmage doing the deed. None would doubt him. Few knew his desire for power and he was generally known as an eminently trustworthy soul. But if the mage could give good Master Drollin the right incentive he had no doubt the seer would damn the Archmage, he had no love for him… nor his own Head of Seers, Allseer Corvindar. Master Drollin lusted after the title of Allseer.

'Yes… but of course, that was the incentive Master Drollin would respond to. Allseer Drollin, the mage was sure he would respond to that particular incentive. For such a rise in his fortunes he would be persuaded to name the Archmage the thief!'

The only problem with that was that the mage was not sure even that would be believed, Baden Erin had a good reputation as Archmage, people would doubt the evidence and then they might dig for the truth. No, the cloaks would have to be the first step, it would need something much more damning than that to overthrow Baden Erin quickly enough for the mage to take control in the confusion and prevent a thorough investigation.

The mage's mind was working over time now.

What if the Archmage had needed those cloaks in order to disguise his elven allies and send them through the college to do his bidding? Perhaps he would need the elves to dispose of any who stood against them. Perhaps the Archmage was in fact under the control of the elves who sought to gain control of the rulers of the Wildlands through him!

That would be difficult to convince people of, but if all these things were done quickly enough and enough confusion was generated, it could work. Many of the leaders of the provinces would be eager to believe ill of the elves… but how to create the confusion.

A sudden thought occurred to him. What if someone died? What if the Archmage were linked to it? Excellent, he thought, but who to die? He mused for a while.

Well, if he was going to make Master Drollin the Allseer then he needed to get rid of Arimenes Corvindar, the present Allseer, he thought wryly. He would be an easy enough target; the man had barely any abilities at aggressive magics. The mage frowned. How then to implicate the Archmage? No, he answered his own thoughts, not the Archmage, but the elves and then he would be discredited by default. If an elf was found in the dead Allseer's rooms, the murder weapon held in the hand of his badly disfigured body, apparently from a final desperate spell of the Allseer, the link would be obvious, especially if one of the missing cloaks was found on the elf's body!

The mage pushed himself up to his feet, his exhaustion forgotten in his new excitement. There would be difficulties later, but the initial part of his plan could be put into motion immediately. He would then have to work fast to make the best of events as they arose. First of all, what he needed to do was visit Master Drollin for a quiet discussion, and on the way there he would need to pay a visit to other key masters in order to spread the rumours that he wanted and to gain their support in the Assembly of Masters. However, the more important work this night would be done by his faithful little assassin.

"Sardyk," he called sharply.

Almost immediately and soundlessly the small child-like halfling appeared, a light smile creasing his small face. He wore nondescript dark brown clothing, with lightly padded armour underneath. The mage also knew there were various knives and throwing weapons hidden about his person along with two slim, curved shortswords strapped upside down to his back that somehow slid out from behind him when he wanted them.

"I need your particular services tonight."

The little man's cherubic face lit up. "Do I get to kill a mage, my lord?" he asked eagerly.

The mage smiled at the halfling's perverse excitement. "A mage and an elf." he replied earnestly. The halfling's smile got wider if that was possible. 'Sardyk Andar was so suited to his needs,' the mage thought. "Listen carefully my little friend; this is how I need you to do things."

Ivello the black monk sat his prodigious bulk back deep in the shadows and watched. His quarry was moving towards the back room of the inn, moving towards the hidden entrance to the catacombs beneath Shandrilos. He would not have credited Koros with the courage to return below ground, but the master had given him good incentive. However, the mercenary was not a complete fool. He had at least gathered together another group of fighters to go down with him, though they were hardly the most impressive.

Also, from the mental link that he still preserved with his quarry, he knew that the mercenary leader had no intention of going down deep into the catacombs, only to the first great hall where the main tunnels met. There he intended to ambush the woman he now needed so desperately to find – the brightly clad thief who had taken the key from him at the inn.

Ivello waited for a few minutes after he had seen the last man enter the backroom and then followed. One of the inn's hired toughs moved to stop Ivello. He then obviously thought better of it after assessing the monstrous, great ape-like monk and thinking it less than worth the risk. Ivello smiled a hideous gap toothed smile and ambled through to the back room.

Ivello knew from the minor link that he had maintained with Koros that the mercenary and his men were now navigating the long, sloping tunnel towards the college's cellars. Ivello had decided that he would follow and watch and wait. If the brightly garbed thief who took the key did not turn up soon he would break the mercenaries neck and be done with it. He could then return to the master to find out what to do next.

Ivello had to admit, grudgingly that the mercenary was sensible in his plan. Earlier he had quickly returned to the inn and picked up the trail of the thief. Ivello remembered smiling at the mercenary's fear as he discovered that the thief had actually gone back down into the catacombs from which the mercenary had only just barely escaped with his life. However, the resourceful warrior had quickly formulated a plan and a prudent one at that, but it was not one that would guarantee success. Still, Ivello would wait and see. He wasn't hungry at the moment and he had nothing else to do, but if he did become bored he would always enjoy killing the mercenary. Ivello had no doubts he could do it. The mercenary was a formidable warrior, but unsuspecting, and a simple sleeping charm could put the already weary man to sleep. Then in he could creep and…SNAP! Ivello smiled at the thought. Yes, that would cheer him up. He would have much preferred his victim to struggle, but then he also preferred his victims to be women and children, there was more pleasure. Still it would amuse him.

Shortly after, Ivello found himself watching from above as Koros and his group of poorly armed and armoured fighters settled down in the first level of the catacombs. They quickly set up a little base in the first hall and organised to go out into the tunnels in turns to watch and listen for the thief and her friends. Ivello settled down on the balcony that ran around the hall and down which Koros and his men had come from the college's cellars. The balcony ran around the perimeter of the hall to a large set of stairs on the north side that came down from either side to meet and then turned and led down to the great floor of the hall on which Koros' group had made camp. The doors on the balcony level that led up towards the cellars of the college were opposite the stairs in the south wall, while doors leading out of the hall itself, below the balcony, were in the east, south and west walls; the great stairway from the balcony taking up the middle part of the north wall.

It was a good place for an ambush so long as you knew which door your enemy would come through and kept a good watch on them all.

Ivello sat down to watch as those below him set themselves ready to catch a thief!

⌒⌒

Unknown to Ivello, not far from where he sat, in the cellars of the college, another mage waited.

In the quiet of the cellars the mage worried and twitched at every sound. He had never been down here before and certainly the dim light and dusty, silent rooms would not normally have been enough to worry the young mage, but the reason for his being here worried him. He had only recently joined the secret society to which his master and tutor had introduced him. He longed for power and his tutor had promised him just that. He had promised that if he was brave enough to make a pact with otherworldly beings he would receive great power in return. That thought almost settled him, but not quite. Sitting here in the darkness, he was having second thoughts. He was not an evil man, he just wanted real spells, not the pathetic ones that the masters taught and gave, secretly holding their best spells to themselves. They pretended that they were too dangerous to give to young adepts who they said had not yet developed enough strength to be able to use them safely. The young mage knew that this was just a lie to keep them down, to make the younger, brighter students serve those old men who did not have the courage to really seek power. That familiar bitterness made the mage angry and gave him more courage.

Suddenly, there was a rush of air and the space in front of the mage appeared to peal apart like curtains on a window. Light poured forth and the mage threw his hand across his eyes. Only moments later, the light was gone and there was an almost perceptible thud that reverberated through the air. At last, he thought, the chance to gain real power. He looked around, his eyes slowly adjusting back to the dimness. The portal, he had seen open, was gone?

Almost frantically the mage looked around, but there was no sign of anything.

Had this been a trick or a prank maybe? Was this some kind of test for new recruits?

He began to curse, but then abruptly a feeling of dread crept up his spine and he knew there was something else here in the room with him. Fear, thick and cloying, rose up to almost gag him. Slowly, so slowly, he turned his head around to look behind him.

There was a figure, indistinct in the darkness; shaped like a man, the shadow stood still and quiet, but with a menace that the mage could not explain. He had never believed in evil as a force, but the figure, unmoving, unthreatening seemed to exude evil.

He gulped hard and the figure moved. Arms suddenly reached out and grasped the mage's head and chin. The mage's eyes widened in pure terror at the figure before him; it was man-like in shape, but completely featureless like a dressmaker's dummy. It was pale white, like a dead fish with no hair and no face!

The mage sat; held, still and quiet as the thing seemed to twitch and heave. The mage watched in paralysed fascination as the thing's skin began to bubble and boil. Its skin stretched and the bones underneath the skin seemed to be thrusting and moving. Hair started to grow on the head and body, muscle definition started to appear on the legs, arms and torso, and on the blank face, the skin started to split and stretch as first a mouth, then a nose and eyes began to form.

The young mage began to pray silently to the gods he had never believed in, fervently hoping that something would happen, someone would come, yet still the transformation continued. Now the young mage felt energy begin to flow from him, draining him. He became frantic, but he was unable to break the creature's iron hold. Slowly, the mage's mouth widened in horror as he began to recognise the face before him; eyes identical to his own looked down on him, unfeeling and uncaring; a mouth the same shape and size was silently screaming back at him in cruel mimicry.

Suddenly the vice like grip tightened and with a savage wrench the mage's neck snapped and the last thing he saw as life was taken from him was his own image coldly observing the life draining from him.

A Changeling had arrived in Shandrilos.

Chapter 31

MURDER IN THE COLLEGE

There are traces here and there in this land of a once great civilisation, but what happened to it is a mystery. As I move through the land, I hear more and more rumours of how great this kingdom once was. Prisoners we have captured speak of a Great King years earlier, draining the land to take the mightiest host to fight a war in the north against some ancient evil, a war from which none returned. I find this hard to conceive. Perhaps this is some metaphor or misinterpretation of their language. I think it more likely that some disease struck down these people, leaving cities, towns and the land bereft and ripe for conquest.

From the war journals of Emperor Kilimarius the Great, BY413

Sardyk Andar the halfling assassin, made no sound as he moved down the corridor, or at least no sound that any human would have heard, yet he was not so sure he would be as silent to an elf. His quarry was up ahead he knew, a lone elven guard in his peculiar, earthen coloured armour and cloak, carrying a sabre-staff, a weapon virtually unknown to humans save for perhaps weapons experts. It was like a short staff about three feet long with a long slightly curved blade on the end. Apparently, it was wielded two handed and in the hands of a skilled elf it was said to be a devastating weapon. Some elves even carried sabre-staffs with a blade on either end, incredibly difficult to use, but incredible killing implements in the right hands. Of course, most humans would not have the agility and dexterity to use such a weapon effectively; Sardyk was not human.

'Perhaps a miniature version' he mused.

The halfling race was well known for their incredible agility and he was outstanding amongst his kind.

Still, all of Sardyk's speculation on the elf's weapon would hopefully be academic. He had no intention of actually fighting him, only of killing him.

He walked carefully and purposefully along the corridor. He did not want the elf to think he was trying to sneak up on him if its sharp ears picked up the halfling's approach. Sardyk wanted the elf to see a single, small halfling, not particularly dangerous. All the elf had to do was let Sardyk get close enough.

Sure enough there was his target. The elf was standing perfectly still in the shadows and would have been undetected until you were almost upon him unless, like Sardyk, you knew exactly where he would be. The elf made no obvious move, but Sardyk knew it had taken note of him already. The halfling made a note to never underestimate an elf's senses, particularly an alert one.

Wearing his customary smile, Sardyk ambled up the corridor pretending not to have noticed the elf. As he got within ten feet of the doors to the guest rooms in which the Archmage had secreted his new elven friends, the elf stepped out smoothly and stood resolutely in front of the halfling without a word, simply blocking the way. Sardyk hesitated and then continued to advance.

"Stand fast." the elf chimed firmly, its voice soft and high. Its beautiful eyes were intent on Sardyk.

Sardyk stopped and then quickly stepped forward again, opening his mouth to speak. He found himself almost walking onto the blade of the elf's sabre-staff. The elven guard had moved it with startling speed. He stared at the blade only inches from his chest and then up at the elf.

"I must speak with your superiors," Sardyk found himself saying.

There was no answer.

"I am charged with investigating the strange occurrences under the college in the old elven city catacombs and I have some questions of your Lords." He tried.

He was met with silence. Just as he was going to try again, the elf responded.

"My people have no knowledge of these occurrences."

"I'm sure, I'm sure," Sardyk quickly replied, "but it is their knowledge of the catacombs that once were yours that concerns me."

The elf simply looked at Sardyk.

This was not going how Sardyk had anticipated. He needed to get closer and quickly, he did not want witnesses and more delay meant more chance of discovery. He also needed time to activate the device his master had given him to transport him and his victim. It would take them the short distance to the Allseer's rooms where, Allseer Corvindar's body was already cooling!

That killing had been easy. The trusting Lord Seer had accepted Sardyk into his room easily and had even confided in the halfling that he'd had disquieting dreams and visions of evil to come, little knowing the evil had already arrived.

"Look, I am sorry, but this blade in my face is making me nervous. Would you mind…" he asked pushing the blade away with his hand.

The elf's face showed nothing and Sardyk was disconcerted by the lack of anything to read in those smooth features. He was used to victims he could read. It was part of the pleasure in playing on those feelings and seeing the final emotions that flickered across the victim's face as they died.

Abruptly, the elf snapped the sabre-staff upright, the blade pointing at the ceiling and the staff held firmly at the elf's side, at the ready.

"Thank you," Sardyk breathed in mock relief, "Now all I would like is the chance to ask a few questions of your Lords to see if they can at least clue me in on the likely layout of the catacombs and what to expect." As he was talking, Sardyk slowly stepped closer to the elf. He deliberately lowered his voice slightly, hoping the elf would lean in to hear better; all the time smiling his smile.

The elf stayed straight as an arrow and responded firmly, "My Lords know nothing of the old city of Dah'Ryllor beneath. It has been centuries since we set foot upon this island or visited the lost glory of our past."

'Damn,' Sardyk thought, and then decided to change tack.

"Perhaps your Lords would take a look at this," he said conspiratorially, taking his pouch from his belt and beginning to open it. "It was found below and had some sort of writing on it, elven we think."

Sardyk pretended to take something from his pouch making sure the elf was watching. He lifted his hand and the elf unconsciously leaned in to see. Sardyk's arm straightened and he flicked his wrist, tripping the poisoned dart thrower he had strapped to his forearm inside his sleeve. There was a small 'whoosh' as the dart exploded out and a wet thud as the dart went through the elf's left eye and into his brain. He fell instantly, dead before he even realised.

Sardyk half caught the elf's weight as he fell. He quickly lowered the weight to the ground with a grunt. The slight elf was a prodigious weight even for a strong halfling like himself. Halflings were definitely not built for strength. Sardyk, from habit, quickly and carefully reloaded his secret dart thrower with another dart he had in a thick case attached to a leather band on his other forearm. He had to be careful; the poison on the darts was lethal within a matter of a couple of dozen heartbeats. Of course, the poison hadn't mattered in this case, Sardyk had been careful to make sure the elf died instantly and without sound. It had become a habit of his to get up close and fire the dart through the eye, but it could also be used to kill from a mere scratch.

Sardyk took out a rag and quickly mopped up the small amount of blood that had spilt onto the stone floor and then took out the strange device his master had given him, a metal object with strange runes on. He grabbed the elf and then pressed the whirling pattern rune as he had been instructed. There was a flash and the two disappeared from the corridor as if they had never been. The night was going well for Sardyk Andar.

⁂

Thud, thud, thud!

The doors to Eliantha's rooms practically shook with the urgency of the blows.

The Mage Master looked round in surprise from her table where she had been going over a recent paper written on the use of glamours on high intelligence creatures.

Thud, thud, thud, went the door again. It was still only two hours past dawn and Eliantha had been up for more than an hour. She rose early by habit.

Quickly, Eliantha Shamass pushed herself from her chair and hurried to the door. Whatever it was, it must be important for them to bother her so early. Even the hasty summons of the Assembly of Masters was not to happen for another couple of hours. That would still give the masters at least three hours time to debate and then get ready for the great procession that officially started the Grand Council just after midday!

Eliantha pulled open the heavy doors and was confronted by Master Tayvon, her deputy in the school of magi and Master Rill, the Second Watchmaster of the College. Master Rill was breathing heavily. Obviously, the old, yet sturdy Watchmaster had rushed over from the main college building and had scaled the six floors of the mage's tower to talk to her.

She silently stepped back for the two to enter, but immediately the Watchmaster began shaking his grey haired head. With a gulp he gasped, "You must come Mage Master, there has been murder in the college and all is in uproar. The Conclave must be summoned."

'Murder! In the college!' A deep foreboding settled on her and she nodded and quickly went and gathered her staff of office.

As she returned, she could see the Watchmaster was already heading back to the stairs. The stocky, matronly Master Tayvor looked at Eliantha in concern.

"You must rouse our masters and inform them that I may have need of their support in events to come today. I fear that our college of magic faces the sternest test of its existence." Eliantha responded earnestly.

"I will Mage Master. The masters will rally to you or they will have to face me." She insisted.

Eliantha smiled. It would take a strong person to resist the stern Abertha Tayvor's will. "Thank you." she breathed and then hurried after the Watchmaster. Dread sat in her stomach as her imagination took her fears and sought to magnify them.

She didn't catch up to the Watchmaster until the door to the mage's tower over five flights of stairs later, such was the rush in which the old fighter mage seemed to be. Eliantha had to admit that the old soldier was still fit even if he was over eighty. The resistance to aging that magic use tended to engender would not have preserved a fighter mage in so good a condition as to tackle those spiral stairs of her tower without some fatigue. Just going down them was a task, especially at speed.

Hurrying along at Master Rill's side, she sought to question him and between breathes he gave her blunt statements of facts so much a trait of the stern Rill. What she heard gave Eliantha pause.

The Allseer had been murdered in his rooms by an elven assassin! What's more the elf had been wearing one of the missing camouflage cloaks that had been stolen two days ago! The college was in uproar. Apparently, it had been discovered by the Allseer's aide, a young adept who had panicked and run through the seer's wing screaming the news. This, the gruff Watchmaster reported with a snort, meant it was virtually impossible to contain the news and prevent further panic. Now it seemed there were masters calling for the arrest of all the elves and even the dwarves.

Eliantha tried to get her mind around this dire news as she shadowed the Watchmaster into the college's Black Hall. This would make unity with the elves virtually impossible if it was true.

As they passed through the lower hall, Eliantha noticed novices, adepts and even masters gathered in groups, talking in hushed yet urgent tones. No doubt the news was growing with each telling and making the prospects of the alliance with the Elder races less likely with each. Master Rill was right to worry over panic, it could easily cause more trouble, but Eliantha feared the murder itself had already irreparably damaged the Archmage's alliance.

Eliantha suddenly realised that they were not heading for the seer's wing, they were heading for the main stairs to the upper floors.

"Are we not to meet at the scene of the crime?" she asked.

Master Rill didn't even look around as he replied. "I have had that area sealed off and guarded and no one is allowed in at the moment. I also have the elves' rooms guarded as a precaution. We are meeting in the Chamber of the Conclave."

"On whose authority was this carried out?"

"My own, and that of First Watchmaster, Sintharinus." The still fierce old master responded harshly. "In the event of such a... crime, it is the Watchmasters who have authority for the investigation, though that busybody, Xameran Uth Altor seeks to stick his nose in."

Eliantha frowned. "Stick his nose in?"

"Yes, though his suggestions are sensible precautions in these unusual circumstances."

"What of the Archmage?"

At this the Watchmaster halted and turned to face her. "The Archmage is currently informing the elves of the matter and he is accompanied by two of my best men. He should be along shortly.

"These guards with the Archmage, are they perhaps one of Master Uth Altor's helpful suggestions?" Eliantha snapped acerbically.

The Watchmaster merely stared at her and then turned and continued his climb up the stairs.

Rill had always been surly, but today it seemed he was in no mood for unnecessary discussion. First Watchmaster Sintharinus was a different matter. He was far more congenial and also far more easily swayed. Eliantha would have much preferred Master Rill in charge despite his manner. He could be rude at times, but no one would doubt his word or his dedication to duty, nor would anyone sway him with words. Rill judged people by deeds. Xameran Uth Altor's sharp tongue would have been blunted on old Gardon Rill.

Less than half an hour later saw the whole Conclave assembled, all save the ill-fortuned Allseer. Also in attendance were the three Watchmasters of the college, and the senior administrators of the college, the Chancellor and the Chamberlain. The atmosphere was subdued and it was the First Watchmaster who called the meeting to order.

"It is clear now that during the night a lone elven assassin, using one of the enchanter's missing camouflage cloaks, entered Allseer Corvindar's rooms and slew him with a sword thrust through the heart. The elf was, in turn, killed from a fireball type spell from the Allseer, no doubt cast in self defence against his attacker." The wand slim First Watchmaster, swallowed. He was obviously uncomfortable with delivering such difficult news. "It is clear that the elven attacker was from the contingent of those elves currently here at the Archmage's request." He stopped and looked around the room uncomfortably.

A silence developed before Atholl Dorard thumped his fist on the table and declared, "We must act!"

"That is obvious, Atholl," was the dry response of the Chief Druid, Marillia Aronis, "but it is the correct course of action that we need to decide upon."

"Bah! That is the obvious thing," he snapped, "We must put the elves under house arrest and find out the reason for their attack!"

Eliantha could already see the Archmage's face darkening. It was no doubt as obvious to him as it was to her where this was heading.

As if on cue the urbane Sorceror Supreme put in smoothly. "This also calls into question the decision to include the elves in the Grand Council." He levelled a cool stare at the masters around him. There was a clear nod of agreement from the Magus General. "I, no doubt, don't have to remind the members here of the rumours that have been circulating." He then looked directly at the Archmage. "I think even our learned leader would acknowledge that the elves are clearly up to something." He paused dramatically and then continued firmly, "However, what I would like to know is how much the Archmage knows of these events?"

All eyes turned to the Archmage whose face was almost white with suppressed emotion. His eyes like dark ice.

Eliantha found herself leaping to her feet immediately, "How dare you try to imply that the Archmage is in some way responsible for the Allseer's death. I think you forget yourself, Xameran."

The infuriatingly smooth sorceror lord merely looked at her before responding, "In that case, the Archmage will no doubt authorise the elves be arrested and taken for questioning as it is clear they had something to do with the Allseer's death."

All eyes turned to the Archmage again and Eliantha slumped back to her seat now seeing the trap that Xameran had set for the Archmage. Both he and Eliantha knew the Archmage would never authorise such a thing. He had pledged on his honour that the elves would be safe under his protection.

Through clenched teeth the Archmage replied coldly, "Is it clear that the elves were involved, my Lord of Sorcerors? I have yet to see the evidence."

"What!" the savage Lord of Enchanters exclaimed, "Are you deaf or just stupid?"

The look that the Archmage turned on the diminutive Atholl Dorard gave even the irascible old mage pause, such was the ferocity held in that look.

"I am neither," he spat in barely controlled fury, "I have only heard of the findings of two bodies and a preliminary judgement based upon that. There is no evidence that either killed the other save the proximity of the bodies. I have never heard of the Allseer using a fireball spell nor have the elves any reason to kill that peaceful man. There is nothing to say they killed one another. It may be that the two were killed and placed there. There is no motive for this attack!" The Archmage finished almost shouting.

"That is what we must find out from the elves." Atholl Dorard snapped back, his dour features snarled in anger.

"Now, now gentlemen," Xameran put in smoothly, ever the diplomat, "It may well be as you have said my lord Archmage, yet we cannot ignore that the elves attacked and killed the Allseer simply because it is the most obvious thing that could have happened, neither should we allow the chief suspects in a murder to move around freely and not seek to find answers from them, so I will ask you again. Will you authorise their arrest, my Lord Archmage?"

Eliantha dreaded the Archmage's response, but she knew what it would be even as he surged to his feet and snarled, "No that I will not do, Xameran. There are other important issues at stake here and this act, no matter how heinous cannot be allowed to jeopardise them. Had this murder been committed by a human would you have me place all humans under arrest?"

Eliantha could see that few agreed with the Archmage's argument and there was shock on several of the Conclave's faces, notably on the thin, noble features of First Wizard, Zarina Agroda and the coppery skinned face of Abbess Tariadarmin. Anger showed on the dark skinned Magus General's huge face and on the less than favourable features of the Lord Enchanter whose hatred of the Archmage was now clear. None of them expected the Archmage to defend the elves safety over such a terrible crime to one of their own.

"You won't, my lord Archmage?" Xameran returned rising to his feet, "Is that perhaps because you have some knowledge of these events?" he hissed.

"What?" the Archmage gasped in surprise, "You dare to accuse me of a hand in murder…"

"Indeed I do" the sorceror lord interrupted. With that he moved from his chair and addressed the rest of the conclave. "I had thought to leave this until the Assembly of Masters as it seemed so amazing, but in light of what I have just heard, it now fully verifies what my investigators have discovered in their search into the matter of the missing cloaks." He turned, strode purposely over to the double doors to the chambers, pulled them open and called to someone outside. Everyone in the room looked around in puzzlement seeking enlightenment from anyone else.

Through the door came Master Drollin, a senior member of the school of seers, probably one of the most gifted seers after the unfortunate Allseer Corvindar.

"Perhaps, Master Drollin, you would relate to the Conclave the information you gleaned from your scrying into the matter of the stolen cloaks." Xameran Uth Altor suggested motioning for the master to step forward.

Master Drollin seemed somewhat taken aback. "What here?" He seemed somewhat reluctant.

Xameran nodded.

"Don't fear, Drollin," Atholl Dorard quickly called, "Now is the right time."

Eliantha thought it an odd comment and frowned at the old enchanter.

Master Drollin cleared his throat a little nervously, "Well, I spent considerable time in the Enchanters hall where the cloaks were held and sought to... erm," he thought for a moment, "walk the paths of the past, to see who had entered and left the room in the past few days."

Eliantha nodded. It was a known and fairly straight forward use of a seer's powers; the events of the past left energy resonances and spiritual and mental signatures that would persist for a time. A skilled seer could trace events back over several days.

"I have spent a lot of time verifying the whereabouts and actions of all those that I saw entering the safe room. All the people that I observed could provide clear reason for their being in that room and what they were doing there, all that is save one person who had gone to some length to obscure their identity through the use of shielding spells. However, I have successfully pierced those spells, unravelling their signatures from that of the individual and it is now clear that person is..." Here he seemed to catch himself and look even more nervous.

"Yes, master Drollin, have no fear of the truth." Xameran prompted.

Master Drollin nodded and stood up straighter. "That person is the Archmage, Baden Erin." he declared.

Eliantha gasped in surprise as did a number of others. She looked at the Archmage whose face was a mixture of disbelief and surprise. Eliantha realised all eyes were now on the Archmage who looked back at them shaking his head. "That is simply not true." he insisted.

"Are you now trying to tell us that not only are the elves innocent of any involvement, but that Master Drollin is also lying?" Xameran insisted.

"I knew it!" Atholl Dorard crowed. "You are a traitor to our college and our people. You are trying to manipulate us all for your own ends, for your own power!"

"That's a lie!" Eliantha almost yelled back so furious was she at the vindictive old enchanter.

"Spoken like the true lapdog." he stormed back, "You're no doubt as guilty as he is."

"Is this true?" the tall wild haired Chief Druid asked of the Archmage in the silence that Atholl's accusations brought. She was clearly very confused and finding it hard to believe that the Archmage was capable of such actions.

"No!" the Archmage answered, "this is all wrong." Baden Erin was clearly taken completely aback by the accusations that were being aimed at him.

"If we all just calm down and sit. We need time to get our heads around this. It is clear that something very wrong is happening here." Eliantha insisted seeking to pacify her colleagues and gain some time for thought. "We cannot act hastily. We should be looking for ways to verify these accusations both against the elves and the Archmage."

Eliantha could see that the Chief Druid was nodding in agreement, but before she could continue the Lord Enchanter cried, "No! That is precisely what you want us to do so that you can seek some way to save your precious Baden! Well it's not going to happen. I am not going to allow this traitor to continue to lead us any longer. I vote that we should imprison both him and the elves." He finished, spittle splattering his patchy beard in his anger.

Silence fell on the group.

Suddenly, the Archmage spoke, his voice subdued, "I would like the thoughts of all those gathered here. I know the feelings of the Lord Enchanter and the Mage Master what of you others?"

The formidable Chief Druid, Marillia Aronis responded first. "I find it hard to believe any of this. You still have my faith, Archmage though I do want these charges investigated."

The Magus-General was already shaking his head. The dark skinned Tanzabari replied in his accented speech, "I also find this hard to believe. However, I think the evidence points to duplicity and I would rather have those implicated locked away until these issues can be resolved."

The Archmage nodded wearily before turning to the sturdy built Abbess of the school of clerics, his dark brows raised in question. Eliantha found it hard to believe he was taking this so easily.

Abbess Tariadarmin looked deeply concerned by what she had heard and she spoke slowly, "I find myself in agreement with the Magus General, though I hasten to add that I fully believe that you will be vindicated, Archmage."

The Chancellor and Chamberlain regretfully agreed with the Abbess and Baden turned to the First Wizard like a man awaiting his execution.

The skeletal Zarina Agroda looked harsh. "I believe that we must follow the laws of the college as we have set them down and in such a case as this the proper procedure is to suspend the member of the Conclave until the charges have been investigated."

Xameran Uth Altor quickly put in, "I think in these circumstances, when the person in question is the Archmage, the matter should be put to the Assembly of Masters to decide whether the Archmage is guilty and I believe the Archmage should be confined to his chambers until this matter is resolved."

"Am I not then even to be allowed a hand in my own defence, allowed a chance to represent myself and those others accused before the Assembly, my Lord of Sorcery?" Baden Erin snapped at Xameran in cold, controlled rage.

Before the Sorceror could reply, Zarina replied in her aristocratic accent, "A person shall be appointed to investigate this matter."

"A person already has, Zarina." Atholl Dorard put in, "The Sorceror Supreme here." he said pointing.

Eliantha was shaking her head and called out, "No! Xameran is clearly biased in this matter."

The sorcerer lord looked surprised and she could see him mouthing the word 'biased' in surprise.

"Who would you suggest then, Mage Master? You!" sneered the ungainly Lord Enchanter.

She could see that the others would also see her as in favour of the Archmage and though they might trust her she would not be seen as a fair judge. Quickly, she turned and said firmly, "No, I would nominate Second Watchmaster Rill." The old warrior mage showed his surprise with a raised eyebrow on his stoic face, but out of the corner of her eye she could see the frown that flashed across Xameran Uth Altor's face. He wanted the authority, it was what he always desired, she knew.

The ever officious and correct Zarina Agroda quickly asked if the Second Watchmaster would take up this task and if the Archmage consented.

The Archmage then stood slowly and all turned to watch him. Eliantha could feel his pain at the distrust he could see on some faces. She made the effort to try to smile reassuringly at him and got a brief crooked smile in return.

"I would like to say that I am totally innocent of these charges and will await the results of Master Rill's investigation," the Archmage began, "I will confine myself and my guests, the elves and the dwarves to the upper levels of the College and we will deal with any questions needed there. No one will try to arrest my guests unless they can prove without doubt and after a thorough investigation that they are guilty of the Allseer's murder," As he said this he sent a fierce look at both Xameran Uth Altor and Atholl Dorard, "Any attempt to go against this will be seen as a direct attack upon myself and the Elder by people acting against the good of the college. I will also name, Eliantha Shamass as my acting Deputy until this matter is done."

Xameran and Atholl both moved to stand, but Eliantha was quick to give her formal agreement and Marillia Aronis quickly followed, as did the First Wizard, Magus General and the Abbess. Xameran looked at them in consternation and Eliantha took the chance to end the meeting and quickly ask the Watchmasters to arrange matters.

"Wait..." The sorcerer lord began, but Eliantha cut him off.

"All is in order and accordance with the laws of the college, my Lord of Sorcery. A majority of the conclave has agreed and I now need to consult with the main officers of the college to ensure the continued smooth running of the college in difficult circumstances." Xameran again sought to speak, but Eliantha continued, "You are dismissed my lords, I must see to the quelling of panic in the college and the needs of the Lords of the provinces for the upcoming procession and Grand Council."

Eliantha could see Xameran's chin twitch, but then Atholl Dorard took his arm and turned him around whispering some comment into his ear. She watched as the Archmage was escorted out and the Watchmasters went to begin settling the college populace and seeing to the investigation of the murder.

Once everyone had left she slumped down in misery. Her heart went out to Baden Erin. A gentle hand on her shoulder made her start. She had forgotten the Chancellor and Chamberlain. She really did need to take over the running of the college.

"Should we fetch the others," Chancellor Yarith suggested.

She nodded dully and the two filed out. Sitting in the empty silence of the large chamber she hung her head and almost succumbed to the tears she knew were near. Everything she had feared had come to pass. Xameran was intent on power and Atholl's hatred of Baden Erin had finally been given an avenue for attack. She had no idea what to do. Her choice of Master Rill to investigate had been a spur of the moment decision, but she felt it was the only thing that had given the Archmage a chance at being cleared.

What was worrying her though, was that the more she thought about what had happened the more she had to come to the conclusion that Atholl Dorard or Xameran Uth Altor had had a hand in the murder of the Allseer and the elven guard, or they both had! She would not believe the Archmage had; she had known him too long now to believe he was capable of cold blooded murder.

Whichever way it had happened it was clear that someone was ruthless enough and uncaring enough of human life to kill to get what they wanted and to end this alliance. Suddenly, the stakes in this matter seemed to have grown beyond what she really wanted to have to deal with, but if she was to save Baden she would have to come up with a way to deal with those two mages or Baden would be facing a murder trial.

She was sure the Archmage would not sit around idly waiting for the results of the investigation. She would go and visit him as soon as she had seen to this morning's organisation. She could serve all best by keeping the college together so that the Archmage still had a chance to create a new alliance that could possibly resist the coming goblin threat from the north.

For one black moment she wondered if she was up to the task. No, she shook her head, Atholl and Xameran were out for themselves. The danger the Archmage had seen was still far off in the northlands. They still had time and she needed to help the Archmage.

She looked up to see an adept pass the door to the chambers and look her way. She shivered for some reason. Perhaps she was feeling the chill.

Chapter 32

THE RISING THREAT

A week ago we hit a great sea that my scouts tell me may be an offshoot of the Middle Sea. We have also heard from our scouts and spies that the Great King's heir dwells across the water, North of the lands of the Mikad. We hear tales of great discord and calamity from those lands. Some whisper that the Great King was lost along with his armies and that only a boy, grandson of the Great King remains to rule. Nothing more has been discovered of the loss of the Great King, but if true this offers a great opportunity.

From the war journals of Emperor Kilimarius the Great, BY413

The changeling pulled its eyes away from the female mage that the young mage's memories told it was the Mage Master, Eliantha Shamass. If it stayed here, that one might get suspicious.

The changeling's master had been clear in its instructions; find out what was taking place here, make contact with the human mage that its master wanted to speak with and deal with any threats; anyone who knew too much about the master and his people.

So after killing the young mageling, the changeling had been slow to leave the cellars. It had known instinctively that the initial kill and entrance into an unknown place was when it was most vulnerable so it had bided its time, seeking to digest not only the mageling's physical remains, but also the knowledge it had gained from the mental communion before it had killed the human.

Later it had headed for the stairs to the surface.

The changeling had known little of the layout of the huge building, the pathetic human's mind had given up its name and main memories, but its mind had been so awash with terror that the detailed memories were hazy.

The changeling had headed upwards in a search for someone from which it could gain more detailed knowledge. As it had reached the first floor, it had noticed a pair of humans in differing coloured robes heading out of a room to its left. From the mageling's memories it had known that these two were the chancellor and chamberlain of the college. The chamberlain, in particular, would have a very detailed knowledge of this place. The mageling's memories were clear on that.

The changeling had ignored the chancellor human as it had walked past and moved after the chamberlain, but as it had passed the doorway from which the two men had emerged the changeling had noticed the human female in silvery grey robes and had stopped.

The changeling had hesitated, watching despite the threat, fascinated. This one was a talented mage, the changeling sensed its power which seemed at odds with its frail body and it longed to test that strength. The female might prove dangerous, but she was a target for another time.

The changeling quickly brought itself back to focus upon its mission and moved to follow the chamberlain mage. It moved swiftly and silently to the door the chamberlain had used and pushed it open, stepping in quickly and without sound. There was a key in the door and the changeling turned it. The chamberlain turned at the sound of the door locking and looked in puzzlement at the adept that had entered without knocking.

"You don't simply walk into a master's office, adept!" the chamberlain began scathingly. The changeling simply ignored him and headed forward. The chamberlain stood in surprise at the lack of respect.

A chill seemed to wash over the chamberlain. The changeling extended a finger and simply pointed at the chamberlain's chest. The mage began a question, "What do you thi…"

His voice was cut off as the changeling's finger suddenly shot forward changing and lengthening as it did, becoming as sharp as a knife blade. It pierced the chamberlain's chest and came out of his back to stab into the wall behind him, pinning him in place.

The chamberlain gasped in horror and shook and then, an instant later as the agony hit, his mouth opened to scream. The changeling's other hand slid into his mouth gagging him. Slowly and carefully the changeling then began to change. It would do things slower this time and fully absorb this human's mind as it died. The human's wounds would not prove immediately fatal.

Less than an hour later, as Eliantha Shamass mounted the stairs to the Archmage's room at the top of the college, she wondered at her mood. Throughout the meeting with the main officers of the college she had felt a chill and deep foreboding. Luckily, the meeting had gone well with everyone knowing exactly what had to be done. The chancellor had been clear about the necessary arrangements for the Grand Council and the procession, though the chamberlain had seemed a little distracted. Luckily, the college had done this sort of ceremony a number of times before.

The Watchmasters hadn't attended, they already knew their duties for the moment and the Chief Archivist, Scribes Master and Novice Master knew their roles and would seek to make sure the rumours and panic would stop. Still, it was only now, that she felt the chill leaving her. She felt relief, a relief that went beyond just simply getting out of a meeting.

Eliantha shook her head at the thought and moved purposely to the main doors to the Archmage's apartments. They took up most of the huge dome structure that sat atop the mammoth Black Hall of the college.

Quickly, she moved past the four guards and opened the door, entering without announcement. Inside she found more guards and walked purposely past them into the second hall where the Archmage had held his meeting last night that had seen elves, dwarves and men mixing freely. Now, the hall was empty.

She quickly went back and asked one of the guards where she might find the Archmage and was told that he was currently in the rooms assigned to the Suthantar Elves. When she looked blankly at him he pointed and informed her that was the first set of apartments out of the left exit to the hall.

Through the left set of double doors from the semi-circular hall, she went purposefully. Outside of the doors to the first set of rooms, Eliantha could see there were in fact half a dozen guards, two dwarven, two elven and two human! It took only a few moments to get past the guards though the elves and dwarves needed reassuring form the college guards that she was in fact no threat to those within.

Inside the first large chamber, Eliantha found herself the scrutiny of a dozen or more sets of eyes; human, elven and dwarven. The faces from which these peered were grim.

"Come in, Elie and take a seat, I would welcome your council." Baden Erin called lightly.

Even with this cordial invitation, the eyes of the elves and dwarves never left her as she moved over to the large table that was now serving as an impromptu council table. She sat herself carefully, fully aware of the charged atmosphere in the room.

Around the table were all seven elven lords and all five dwarven, and Eliantha couldn't help but notice that most were armed and armoured! Added to these though, Eliantha was surprised to see Elgon of Ostia and even more surprised at the presence of Grand Abbot, Alinus Quan Sirona! Eliantha would have thought the old saint would have sought to avoid the presence of the Elder races despite his pronouncement in the council yesterday. They were still considered by most of the Alban faith as kin to demons!

"What is your assessment of the situation Elie?" Baden asked her gently.

"Well... I...that is...difficult." she responded struggling with where to start.

Baden smiled and said, "Yes, difficult."

"What I mean is that it will be difficult for you to pursue your plans for the Grand Council." she insisted.

Baden just nodded and looked thoughtful before muttering, "Difficult, but not impossible."

Eliantha was amazed at the comment. "Surely you can see that you must first of all deal with the college and settle these charges of murder and deception. You will not be able to continue with the Grand Council if you do not have a seat on it and if the others vote to have the Elder races expelled or even arrested!" she insisted. She was completely surprised at the Archmage's seemingly dreamy attitude to the events that had seen him suspended.

Suddenly the Archmage's dark eyes flashed to life and she could hear a stirring amongst the elves and grumblings from the dwarves. "No one will be arresting anybody." he exclaimed, as much for his guests benefit, Eliantha thought, as for hers. "The matters relating to my suspension are being dealt with and with your appointment of Master Rill to investigate on my behalf, I expect myself to be cleared given time and fair dealings but it is those things which I want your opinion on." he said looking sharply at her. "Do you believe that we will have time and a fair investigation?"

Eliantha opened her mouth to answer but the Archmage held up his hand and continued.

"Or, like myself, do you believe that whoever is behind the cruel murder of the Allseer will allow us neither of those."

She frowned. "Yes, I agree." she answered firmly.

"Who do you think is behind this act, Elie?" he then asked quickly before she could add more.

She paused. "I believe it is likely that both Atholl Dorard and Xameran Uth Altor are involved in some way."

The Archmage was nodding and she continued with the thoughts that had plagued her for the last hour or more.

"Atholl's hatred of you has increased with the years. He still resents you for taking the leadership of the college when he felt he was the most senior. Added to this, your agreement to split the school of enchanters to allow the seers their own school he saw as an attack on himself and his demesne. He had no love for the Allseer either for the same reason. Xameran, I believe just wants power, though I did not know until now how much he desired it. It seems clear now that he will go to great lengths. I had not thought him so impatient for it before but now…"

"Yes," the Archmage agreed, "I agree with your assessment, but are they both working together? Are they both responsible for the Allseer's death and my suspension or is one merely going along with the other's lead and using events to further his own ambitions?"

"It is hard to say, though it would seem prudent to treat both as dangerous and out to be rid of you and your… guests." she finished, looking uncomfortably at the Elder lords who watched her every move like hawks about to attack.

"Yes, you are right and it is not so important now who is behind this, but what we need to do to counter them. I have been blindly looking to my own actions and not trying to predict what those against me would try to do." the Archmage said grimly.

Baden Erin then looked out at the lords around the table. "I am sorry for the accusations levelled at you. It seems you have become caught up in an attack upon me."

"Are you so sure of that, my friend." the saintly old Abbot Alinus put in quickly.

Baden frowned at him.

"It seems a large coincidence to me that this should happen just as you are pushing to include the Elder races in our council. Could it be that some enemy has perceived our designs and has acted to prevent an alliance that could strengthen our defence against it?"

This set all to whispering, while Baden asked clearly surprised. "Do you think Atholl and Xameran are in some way linked to events in the north..." He shook his head, "I find that hard to believe, Alinus."

"Perhaps," the old monk mused stroking his long white beard thoughtfully, "but we may well be being manipulated."

"It is worth considering, Archmage Erin," the ghostly elflord Val'Ant put in. "The goblins are very cunning and capable of guile as well as direct force."

"A common tactic in defeating a foe is to set it against itself." came the gravelly voice of Chief Afindor of the Ironcleaver dwarves."I just would never have credited goblins with the subtlety needed.

Others nodded at this.

"However, we do not know this is not merely a power play amongst your people, Archmage" the ghost prince added in a cautionary tone, "and we will not be kept here to be arrested by your people. If need be we will fight our way free!"

Baden closed his eyes and sighed before nodding almost to himself. "Though it may destroy all I have sought to build here, I will see this college torn apart before I will allow it to hold you, my lords. I have given my word that you would be safeguarded above all and I will stand by my word, though I am hoping that it will not come to war in the college." Baden's pale face was rigid with emotion and no one in the room doubted his sincerity. The elves nodded their understanding and the dwarves growled and slapped the desk in approval.

"We will give you whatever aid you need in the coming struggle," Lord Val'Ant added, "we each have brought a score of our best warriors, as have the dwarves and those will back you."

"Thank you, but I feel this battle will first of all be fought in the Assembly of Masters and in the hearts and minds of my colleagues." Baden drew a deep strengthening breath and then glanced at Eliantha. "There is not much time Elie, but we need to canvas as many masters as possible in the next hour to rally our support. If need be we must resort to muddying the waters if only to delay any vote of no confidence that I am sure Xameran and Atholl will call for."

Eliantha Shamass nodded earnestly and gave the Archmage the warmest smile she could muster. She would see him defeat that vile pair!

"Meanwhile, my Lord Elgon and Alinus, I would like you to do the same with the Lords of the Grand Council in case we should fail. Perhaps, then we can at least prevent the Lords of Sorcery and of Enchantment from destroying what we are trying to build."

As Eliantha turned to leave she noticed that the elves and dwarves were deep in conversation and then one elflord and one dwarven chief made a hasty exit before her. She frowned and turned to catch Baden's eyes, but he was too engaged with the ghostly, elven lord, Val'Ant. However, she did notice others of the elves nodding, the briefest of smiles touching their flawless faces.

Chapter 33

TO THE SURFACE

I had never thought to push so far into the unknown west, but the northmen fall before us. They are disorganised and strangely bereft of men and the will to fight. We met the boy-king in battle. He was foolish and sought to strike us without warning, seeking the element of surprise to break us. His army was hastily created and poorly trained, all save a small but disciplined core that fought with great fury. The boy-king Bardon the Brave, earned his name that day. He may have been little more than seventeen summers but he and his guard cut a bloody swathe through my best legion before they were cut down.

From the war journals of Emperor Kilimarius the Great, BY413

Sir Darin of Kenarth felt like he had been running for hours rather than just minutes. Around him, his friend's gasped and groaned as they forced themselves onwards and upwards. They were onto the second set of stairs now; they had passed through the middle hall that they had descended through what seemed like days rather than hours ago. Nat Bero led the way with her long, loping stride and appeared to be suffering the least from the exertions. Arkadi had his robes pulled up slightly, like a maid in her skirts, to show his hairy, white legs above his ankle high boots as he ran. Behind Arkadi, occasionally blinded by the swishing of Arkadi's cloak, was their newest companion, Nossi Bee the gnome.

Originally, Darin had led them up the stairs, but although he was fit and strong, the weight of his armour began to drag on him and so his friends had, one after another, overtaken him. His breath was now starting to burn in his throat and he feared that an army of those insect creatures could be right behind him and he wouldn't know, his wheezing and gasping was so loud in his ears.

Darin tried not to think of what he was running from. It wasn't anything to do with fear, he was not afraid of those behind him, he wasn't afraid of dying. He had always fought and though he had been afraid at times, he was used to it; trained and experienced in dealing with it. No, it was the shame of running, the shame of leaving behind friends, and of leaving behind one in particular who had lain helpless. He wanted to turn around, though he realised it was too late. Bear would have been killed almost instantly in the attack. Darin had been fooling himself earlier about how bad Bear had been, ignoring the looks from Rebba and Garon. Now all that drove him on was that he had to protect his other friends, and he had to get that gnome to the surface or else his friends' deaths would mean nothing and his own desertion would be just that, a desertion and not for the greater good.

"The stairway is clear!" Darin heard Nat call from the front, "We can go up to the entrance room."

'Hopefully, the way isn't still blocked by that great stone.' Darin thought and then wryly changed his mind.

"On second thoughts let's hope it is" he gasped to himself mockingly, "then at least I can catch my breath!"

Pushing himself heavily up the last few stairs he emerged into the rough hewn room from which they had all fallen. He held the torch he was carrying towards where he knew the entrance would be and saw more clearly. His friends were clustered around the doorway. It was blocked!

'Typical,' Darin thought in both exasperation and relief. "Can we open it?" He asked.

Nat Bero called back, "Don't panic. I can open it... just give me some time."

Arkadi was looking back and must have seen the skeptical look on Darin's face. "Don't worry if she can't I know a spell that should just about blast the way through."

Arkadi smiled stiffly at Darin and the knight knew the mage was not sure of his claim.

Darin turned back to the stairs and dropped himself to sit roughly on the top stair. They would need to keep watch for pursuit, but there was no need to do it standing. Besides if he didn't sit he was sure he wouldn't be able to move his feet even to get out of the way of one of those huge ogre creatures, his legs were so leaden.

Staring down the stairs, Darin could only see about twenty feet before the dark got too thick to see anything. He'd have time to draw his sword, stand and call the others, he was sure, before anyone could get up to him. He watched and listened as he heard Arkadi and Nat mutter at each other furiously. Occasionally, even the gnome tried to give advice! Darin focused on the stairs. Minutes passed.

Suddenly, there was a grinding noise and Darin half went for his sword before he realised it was the stone blocking their escape, moving. He stood and turned to see his friends all smiling and Nat already moving off, torch held above her head.

"Excellent, Nat, at last your starting to get things right." Darin snapped.

The archer replied quickly, "It was nothing," as she headed off.

Arkadi snorted. "Actually, it was nothing. It was Nossi here who found the mechanism that released the door." The black cloaked mage responded nodding to the diminutive figure that stood at his side.

Darin was surprised and then he called out, irritated, "Reeaaalllyyy!" after Nat Bero.

Darin then nodded his head to the child-like man and said, "Well done, little fellah. We are in your debt." The creature appeared to blush as Arkadi hustled him into the tunnel.

Darin gave one last look at the stairs for sign of the enemy and then almost regretfully turned and began trotting wearily after the others. 'A fight might have been preferable to this,' he thought.

Two hours later, Darin slumped to the ground in exhaustion. "We have got to stop now, otherwise I will collapse and you will have to carry me," he announced.

They were in a small chamber that was a widening of a long corridor. It seemed to be rising slightly upwards; the way that they so desperately wanted to go.

They had come out of the rough lower tunnel, through the hidden panel in the alcove Bear had crashed through only hours earlier. From there they had carefully navigated the corridors and rooms in the darkness. It had taken perhaps half an hour or more of hunting around before they finally found a way up to the next level. However, they were then greeted with more featureless tunnels and rooms. They had been scouring this level for what must have been another half an hour and finally Darin had had enough.

The others took one look at Darin's face and quickly acquiesced, following the tall knight's lead. They sat themselves, Nat by one entrance and Arkadi by another.

Sitting there, Darin actually found himself wondering why the elves, if they built this place, couldn't just put one big stairway for people to go up and down in one place and actually decorate their walls and rooms with more than just large swirling patterns in the rock. Arkadi had suggested that maybe a lot of their possessions and decorations had been lost over the centuries, but that still didn't explain why the elves had made this place such a pain to get in and out of.

Darin lay back and closed his eyes for a moment, his padded under jacket and trews feeling slick and hot against his skin. His armour plating and chain mail prevented air getting in to cool him. He tried to relax and slowly felt his leg muscles easing.

As he sat there, he began to worry again about what had happened to the others. When last he had seen them through Arkadi's barrier, they had all been sorely pressed, Zara against those monstrous giants and Rebba and Garon against another with some of those bug creatures thrown in. He knew at least that Zara had had enough time to yell for them to flee and Darin hoped that the others had enough time to do that too. However, Darin knew that even if they had fled, those insect creatures moved like the wind and the old stories said that elves could run faster than any human. The others would have been hard pressed to escape, but Darin clung to some hope. There was a chance that Rebba or Garon could repeat something of Arkadi's feat and create a barrier. However, Darin's mind seemed to taunt him with the knowledge that neither of those two had Arkadi's skill or knowledge of magic, and both had been sorely tired.

Of them all only Zara had the skill and savage determination to have a chance, but even she would have found it hard to run and fight. Nevertheless, Darin would not mourn them until he had seen their corpses, even if that meant coming back down; a prospect he was hoping would be possible. He would happily go to his order and beg permission to take down a company of knights to wipe those foul creatures out. He would take great pleasure in hunting every one of them down, especially if they had killed his friends. The loss was twisting Darin's gut and threatening to unman him!

All was quiet in the little room save for Arkadi and the little gnome nattering away to each other. It seemed Arkadi was not going to miss the chance to learn from the gnome all that it knew about magic that he did not. Darin listened closer. Arkadi was explaining that he had known nothing of inverted weaves, or even weaves themselves, though Darin was unsure how weaving was anything to do with magic. It seemed this was not because his master had not taught him, but because no one above in the college even knew anything about inverted magic. From the little gasp and surprised response, it seemed the gnome found this hard to believe, if not amazing. Darin was none the wiser on the subject. He quickly switched off from the conversation and decided to take a light nap.

He was snapped awake by the sound of Arkadi moving towards him.

"I don't know how you could possibly sleep when there could be enemies almost on top of us." Arkadi snapped.

"Because I need to," Darin snapped back. "How long have we been sat here?"

"Half an hour at most."

Darin cursed. He pushed himself up and was glad to feel much of the soreness in his legs had receded. He was not so out of shape after all. "We need to get going."

"We are just waiting for you." Nat Bero declared sternly.

Darin nodded and indicated that he was ready to go.

"We'll go a little slower for now," Nat whispered as they all drew close in the small, dark chamber. "I think I am beginning to recognise some of these tracks on the ground." They were down to their last torch which the rangy huntress held low to show the dusty ground. "The tracks are now heavily confused, though this looks like your tracks here, Darin." The hunter pointed. Darin could make little of the scuffs and marks he saw.

They set off at a fast walk with Nat at the front, bent low watching the floor intently. 'I just hope she doesn't walk into anything like that,' Darin thought.

Twenty minutes later, they had gone up another level and Nat seemed sure of the route now. On several occasions she had stopped to point out particular tracks.

Abruptly, Nat stopped and tilted her head, seemingly puzzled. "Does it seem to be getting lighter to you?" she asked.

Everyone looked around and Darin began to see what she meant, the whirled patterns on the walls did seem to be clearer.

"I think you're right." Arkadi replied. "What do you think it is? We cannot be near the surface."

The tall huntress shrugged and no one else had any answers so they decided to move on cautiously.

As they walked, it became clear that the light was coming from a large room up ahead.

"I can see a fire in the centre of that hall up ahead, but I see no one there, not even the movement of shadows." Nat whispered unslinging her bow.

"Could it be a trap?" Darin asked.

Nat Bero stopped and beckoned everyone closer. "I think I know what that room is," she whispered earnestly. "That is the first hall. It is on the map Zara got. We did not come down that way. We bypassed that hall, going down that steep ladder thing. I must have lost our tracks somewhere back there and picked up that other groups that Nossi mentioned." Nat looked confused for a moment then shook her head. "To the left of that door is a large staircase from what I remember of the map and that led up to a balcony that went around the room to doors that lead to the cellars of the college," she whispered. "We could be almost out. I'll go ahead and have a look at the hall."

Nat handed the torch over to Arkadi and moved off cat-like along the walls, sticking to the shadows to have a better look. Soon she was huddled by the entrance to the hall.

Nat stood and turned, beckoning quickly with her hand for them to come up. They all stood and began hurrying down the corridor, suddenly keen to put these ancient halls and corridors, and their thick darkness behind them. The thought of escape from the dangers down here spurred them all on.

Just before they got there, Nat darted out and to the left, obviously heading for the stairs she had mentioned. Darin and the others burst out into the hall and squinted at the brightness of the large fire that was burning in the centre. They all began hurrying towards the stairs. As they passed, Darin noticed there were packs around the fire and it was immediately obvious that someone had made camp here, but where they were was anyone's guess.

As if to answer, a group of men appeared in the large doorway on the opposite side of the hall and Darin heard the armoured leader muttering in anger.

"Next time make sure you've actually heard something before raising the alarm…" The leader stopped at the sight before him. He looked at Darin and his friends by the stairway to the balcony in complete astonishment.

For a moment both groups looked in surprise at each other. Darin was just about to call out a greeting when the leader snarled and pointed, "They must have been with that thieving bitch!"

Darin's greeting died in his throat.

"Kill them. I want that key!" the livid warrior cried.

Chapter 34

ESCAPE FROM THE DARK

The campaigns of Emperor Kilimarius brought into the empire more new territory than any other emperor before or since. Kilimarius is credited with reforming the armies of the Carnacian Imperium to form the modern legion system which is still the basis for the Holy Alban legions today. Kilimarius' conquest of the Nordic was swift, lasting only around five to six years. However, he then spent the next twenty years subduing the lands he had conquered. The province that is named after him became the biggest in the empire. His conquests also spread the teachings of Blessed Alba into the northern lands.

From 'The Holy Lands of Alba' by Arch Prelate Jorus Enarius Florian, BY1180

'This was getting ridiculous,' Nat Bero thought in frantic exasperation, 'couldn't they just get out of these bloody tunnels without someone else turning up to try and kill them? Maybe, that man she cheated at cards on the boat here was going to turn up too,' Nat thought sarcastically, 'or even that old man whose house she had pelted with horse muck back when she was nine!'

She turned back towards the stairs to the balcony and yelled, "Run, we can make it out!"

She grabbed the gnome by the collar and half dragged him up the first flight of stairs even as she shouted, "The door out is just up here." At least she hoped it was!

She reached the first landing, let go of the gnome, knocked an arrow and let fly. 'Let it hit that bloody warrior,' Nat thought. She realized he must have been part of the group that had been in the catacombs earlier. 'Ishara's icy heart but that man really didn't give up. You'd think evil elves, giants and insect creatures would put anyone off being down here ever again!'

Nat turned without looking what the arrow hit, and ran up some more stairs before she risked another look back. A man was down, one of her arrows sticking out of his chest, but the vengeful warrior was still leading the mad charge across the hall. Nat knocked another arrow and fired. She missed the warrior again, but was satisfied to see another man was punched from his feet. However, that still left at least ten of them. She looked back to where she was going and leapt long legged up the next set of stairs. Darin and the gnome struggled after him, Arkadi just in front of them.

'We are lucky the warrior hasn't any men with bows or spears,' Nat thought.

As if in answer, a spear ricocheted off the wall in front of her and bounced wildly almost tripping Arkadi who had almost caught her up. Nat then realised that the gnome with his short legs, and Darin in his armour, were starting to fall behind.

'Damn,' she thought, 'someone needs to think of something.'

Nat stopped again and knocked another arrow which she fired and then ran without looking where it went. She heard the screech of metal on metal and knew the arrow had hit a shield and not a man. She made it to the balcony level just behind Arkadi and glanced across to where the door out must be. As she ran, she shouted, "If we can get to the doors we might be able to make a stand there or even barricade the doors."

Again, she risked a look back and could see the more lightly armoured men were catching up with Darin and the gnome. The huntress realised that all it would take was for one to get close enough to one of her companions and then they would all have to turn and fight. No one would make it to the doors. She stopped and looked back unsure of what to do. It looked like Darin and the gnome would be caught.

Suddenly, she had an idea, though it was not one that she particularly liked. She ran back towards stairs that Darin and the gnome were still climbing, their pursuers hot on their heels. She quickly pulled out her hidden second purse. In it was her emergency stash of silver, at least thirty pieces. Her hand almost baulked at the idea, but she quickly unstrung the purse and spun and tossed the coins from within into the path of the chasing men. They clinked and bounced in a silvery shower and the chasing warriors, hesitated and then stopped to make a grab for the money. Nat laughed to see them scrabbling for the money. She turned and ran to catch up with Arkadi, just ahead of Darin and the gnome.

Over the clanking and thumping of feet on stone, Nat heard a voice yell ferociously, "Leave that you fools, the master will give us ten times that." There was a thud and a grunt and Nat peered back over her shoulder to see the chief warrior slamming at his men with the flat of his blade. "Get on with you," the warrior shouted in fury, "or I'll gut you where you stand!"

The men were already beginning to leave the coins to pursue them. Nat cursed. 'Bloody waste of money! You just couldn't get the money hungry fighters you wanted these days,' she thought, but the ploy had given Darin and the gnome enough time.

Nat stretched her long legs and accelerated past Arkadi to reach the doors first. She turned and began firing arrows at the pursuing men, but most were hitting only shields. Arkadi ran by Nat to stand at her shoulder just inside the doorway. Nat had managed to thin their pursuers with her shots. Only around eight men were still running and they had slowed to a cautious jog with shields leading the way.

A terrified Nossi Bee, hurtled between Arkadi and Nat into the corridor that led to the stairs to the college's cellars. Then Darin pulled up in front of them, spun and drew his huge great sword at the same time. The men chasing them slowed and came to a stop only a few feet away, wary of Darin's blade. Nat shouldered her bow and pulled a short sword and dagger, though she was loath to fight hand to hand.

Darin signalled to Nat and the others to begin backing up while he never took his eyes off the men in front of them.

At Nat's side, Arkadi suddenly stopped still like a statue and began looking around him. "Nossi, do you sense something," he hissed urgently.

From behind them there was no answer. "Nossi?" Arkadi called again.

"What is it?" Nat snapped sarcastically, "Have you just sensed the group of angry men that want to kill us?"

The mage looked at Nat and almost yelled, "No, you fool there is magic here, strong magic."

"We are in elven ruins beneath a college of magic," Nat snapped back.

Arkadi never got the chance to answer as the warrior yelled at his men to attack all at once and overwhelm them. There was a roar and the group of men charged. Nat threw her dagger and a man fell clutching his head. She pulled another dagger, her last. Darin yelled some battle cry and hammered into the approaching men slashing this way and that, taking down two men instantly with huge wounds. Nat knew better than to move forward when Darin was in full swing, though as men tried to dodge around Darin's lethal blade, Nat took them down with quick efficient thrusts.

At a sharp command, the men pulled back from Darin, leaping to avoid his savagely efficient blade. They left six men dead or dying at his feet. Attacking a knight in full armour was always going to be a difficult move in such a confined space. Nat could see the leader of the group was now eyeing Darin with greater respect. It took great skill to wield such a large sword with such speed and accuracy, but then Nat knew Darin had spent years honing his skills with all kinds of weapons. The knight, along with Zara and Bear had always had an unhealthy fondness for swords in Nat's opinion. Not that she was complaining now.

Darin suddenly called out to the men, "Not many of you left. I suggest you abandon this venture before there are none of you left to collect on it."

Nat thought she could hear a slight tone of pleasure in Darin's tone, but then the man was mad; always keen for a fight!

Nat could see that the two men left with the warrior were looking one to the other in silent agreement with Darin. It seemed the warrior could see this too because he moved forward and snarled, "Very well, if you cannot deal with this, I will."

The warrior carried a bastard sword, not quite as big as Darin's blade, but big enough. He was also well armoured with a shirt of chain. Plate mail was attached at chest and shoulders, and this was finished off with armoured gauntlets, helm, and greaves. He was a much tougher prospect than the fighters he had obviously hired.

"Now let's see how good you are master knight." the warrior snapped.

Darin snapped over his shoulder to Nat and the others, "Start heading out of here, I'll deal with this."

Arkadi started to back up, still looking around him, a worried frown on his face. Nat hesitated until Darin snarled at her to get the others out of there. Nat was just about to start backing up too when, on a whim she suddenly threw her last dagger at the approaching warrior, hoping to catch him by surprise. With startling speed the man swayed and flicked his blade out to knock the dagger aside in midair.

'Blood and sand,' She thought, 'that takes a bit of skill'. She was suddenly glad Darin was there. She did not fancy their chances otherwise.

"Very good," Darin acknowledged. There was no fear in his voice. "Let's see how you do against a bigger blade." With that he attacked with a sudden burst of speed, his great sword lunging for his opponent's stomach. The warrior swept his blade down and parried neatly, following through with his sword to swing viciously at Darin's leading leg.

Nat hurriedly moved back into the corridor where she could just see the two swordsmen. She heard Arkadi ask where Nossi was and turned to frown into the dark corridor that led to the last flight of stairs to the college's cellars.

"Is that him by the stairs?" Nat answered and then called out the gnome's name. He could see a huge shadow at the foot of the stairs, it looked too big to be the tiny gnome, but the dark often threw confusing shadows.

Nat saw Arkadi shake his head not listening. "Something's not right here." He began to head for the stairs and Nat backed up, not taking her eyes off the entrance to the corridor as she followed the mage. She could no longer see Darin but she could still hear the clang of swords. She was worried about leaving Darin even though she knew she would be of little help to the knight. She glanced behind her and saw the shape by the stairs move. It seemed like it was struggling. She whispered to Arkadi, "What is that?" She paused, "Is it Nossi?" but the mage was distracted, looking around him like a blind man just seeing the light.

"I just can't quite get a feel of it" Arkadi mused, "It's like those inverted weaves down below but not..."

Nat could still hear the clash of blades behind her and looked back. She wanted to keep an eye on Darin even though she'd been told to go. Nat started to retreat further and turned to see Arkadi still gazing at the walls in thought. Nat also noticed that the shape seemed to be struggling up the steps. It had to be Nossi. Maybe the gnome was just too terrified to come back down the corridor?

Suddenly Arkadi looked over to the shape and yelled urgently in fear, "Wait…" he stumbled sideways towards the stairs, his arm stretched out in a sudden desperate plea. Nat was startled by the mage's dramatic reaction.

Suddenly, there was a blinding flash and a deep rumbling and the roof of the corridor began to shake. Something like lightning seemed to flash down the corridor and Nat was slammed to the ground. Arkadi yelled something and there was another flash then everything went black.

Darin of Kenarth, Knight of Karodra attacked again, but his opponent parried and riposted and Darin had to retreat to avoid losing his head. He had to admit the man was good, but he knew he could take him. It was just those two men trapped behind the warrior by the narrow balcony. They made it difficult to change his point of attack from anything other than straight ahead in case they took a hack at him.

Darin smiled savagely, enjoying the test of his skills. He attacked again, high then low as before, forcing his opponent to retreat. He then went for the warrior's blade, predicting the man would turn his attack as before. He caught the warrior's riposte on his blade, trapping his sword against the balcony rail, and stepped forward to punch him hard in the face. Blood sprayed and the man stumbled back and sideways into the railings. Darin didn't follow, but raised his sword. A look of pure terror passed across his opponent's face as he realised he wouldn't recover himself in time and he was about to die.

Suddenly, there was a flash of intense light and a crackle of energy. Darin felt himself hammered forward into his opponent and both almost rolled over the railings.

There was an immense rumble and Darin half turned in horror to see the corridor his friends had disappeared down collapse! Dust blasted into the hall. He tried to raise himself up, but just then there was an alarming cracking noise. Abruptly, the men along the balcony cried out and Darin spun to see the men seemingly bounce as the balcony beneath them heaved and buckled. There was another crack, louder than Darin had ever heard and that section of balcony fell away and the men simply plummeted out of sight, screaming. Darin frantically looked for an escape but it seemed the whole hall was falling apart. He tried to stand on the shaking balcony and he caught a glimpse of the floor of the hall below give way and disappear as if sucked into the depths.

A third almighty crack pealed through the hall and Darin was thrown forward as the section of balcony he was on shifted. The warrior beside him gasped and looked wide eyed at the floor. Darin's eyes followed in time to see cracks spreading across the stone floor like spider webs.

"Blessed Alba," he whispered, and then "Gods of earth, sea and sky." Just to be on the safe side. "Don't let me die like this. Give me a warrior's death."

The balcony began to tilt and Darin threw his body at the wall in a desperate attempt to save himself. His opponent was a split second behind him. Darin managed to grasp at the wall as the balcony gave way beneath him and dropped into the dark crevasse in the hall floor. He felt his grip slipping and he slid down. He grabbed at an outcropping and saw the warrior at his side, slide past him to plummet screaming. Darin couldn't hold on, he knew instantly, and he cursed even as his hands slipped and he dropped.

꿰ㅇ

Ivello sprang clear just as the rocks began to fall, pulling the struggling little man with him.

"No!" He heard the little creature's muffled shout, but Ivello yanked him along, hand over the little creature's mouth, desperately trying to out-run the falling ceiling.

He had an urge to just crush the little man's skull, but resisted. The creature had been with the thief's friends and might know something of where the Waygate keystone was. Ivello made it to the first landing and was swallowed by a huge blast of dust. Slowly the rumbling ceased. Ivello coughed and put his arm over his face and eyes, still holding tight to the small man he had grabbed in the dark.

Gradually, the dust began to settle and Ivello looked back to see a mass of rocks and rubble blocking the corridor and stairs below. The small man was suddenly straining to go back down, fear and worry on his smooth, child-like face. Ivello decided he needed to act the part of friend and saviour to try to find out who the creature was and more importantly what had happened to the keystone, but... if that failed he would have to resort to more pleasurable means, pleasurable for him at least. For a moment he was tempted to skip right to the torture, but restrained himself with a grimace.

"Wait, wait!" he pleaded gently to the struggling man, "You can't go back there it would be suicide, the rest of the roof could come down at any moment."

The strange little man looked at him, his eyes wide with fear, "But my friends. You pulled me away." He stammered in confusion. "You would not let me go!"

It was clear to Ivello that his massive frame and somewhat brutal features, as well as the fact he had grabbed the little man, were scaring the tiny figure.

"You startled me in the dark, my friend." Ivello said gently. "I had been following some strangers, some thieves in the cellars and then you ran in to me. I grabbed you as much out of fear and surprise as anything else. I thought you and your companions were going to attack me!" Ivello lied as he thought back, trying to cover his actions. "Then the roof began to fall and I just ran." he finished. The last at least was true.

Ivello had just been reaching the point where he had grown so bored with the mercenary, Koros and his antics that he had been contemplating ending his miserable life. However, just then Koros and his men had all stormed out of the hall at a call from one of the men on watch and Ivello had been amazed to see the thief's friends walk warily into the hall with his companions from the opposite direction. Ivello had watched silently from above as the group entered the hall. The big monk remembered thoroughly enjoying the irony of the group stumbling into the mercenary chief's trap just as it had been sprung by some nervous hired idiot down the other hallway!

Meanwhile, the thief's companions as Koros called them, none of them was the big one from what the monk had seen in the mercenary's memories, had suddenly made a frantic dash for the stairs, straight for where Ivello hid. However, they had then paused. Apparently, Koros and his men had returned and a chase ensued. Ivello had retreated into the darkness of the corridor and when the thief's friends had made a stand at the door, the small man had hurtled past them and Ivello had taken the chance to grab the diminutive creature, not entirely sure what he was.

Ivello brought himself back to the present and realised that the child-like man was looking at Ivello in suspicion.

"Look," Ivello pressed, "I don't know what is going on here, but the mages will want to know and you are the only witness." He looked firmly at the timid creature upon whom he still had a firm hold. "What exactly were you doing down here? This is the college's property and people are not allowed down here!"

Ivello's captive was looking more and more confused, which was good.

"We were…lost. We were trying to get to the surface to speak to the mages." the large eyed little man responded hesitantly.

"Really, then we should take you straight there…" Ivello began and started to turn the small man towards the rest of the stairs up to the college's cellars.

Immediately, the man began to struggle against him. "No, my… friends."

He had struggled over how to describe the others and Ivello wondered at the creature's relationship to the thief and her group and… now that he thought about it, he wondered at the creature's race.

He had taken it for a strange kind of halfling, though now as he watched the creature pull against his strong grip, he realised that the little thing reminded him more of a dwarf, but without the beard or thick build. It was almost a mix between a halfling and a dwarf.

"Friends?" Ivello said warily, "Your friends could not have survived that collapse," he said earnestly, even as he thought that, if the group had the keystone his master would need to be told. He would want to dig out the corridor. His master would have to be here and in control soon as Ivello was sure this place would be heaving with mages and guards very soon. No one up above could have failed to have felt the collapse. "Who was that back there and why were you down there?" he asked, making his voice harsher now. "I am sorry about your friends, but you should not have been down there."

"I, that is we…" The small creature was obviously struggling.

"Come now, the truth please. I sensed magic and you clearly have talent. Did you cause this?" he pushed, knowing the creature could not have been responsible.

Ivello found this act of being the good monk irritating. It was a role he had been forced to play for years and had hated it, especially when he wanted to simply beat the information out of the creature.

The pale faced dwarf man looked horrified at the accusation. "I did not do this!" he gasped incredulous. "We were coming to tell the mages of the Great Masters in the tunnels below and their invasion."

"Invasion? Great masters?" Ivello responded, genuinely surprised.

"Those you call elves. They have been in the tunnels below looking for…" the little man hesitated.

Ivello found his hand clenching unconsciously and forced himself to ease his grip on the man as he urgently pressed, "Looking for what?"

"The key to the Ways."

"Where is it?" Ivello snapped forgetting himself and his role, "Did your friends have it?"

Ivello realised from the small creature's look that he had made a mistake and he quickly stuttered, "I mean… the elves, do they have it?

"The others had it…" the little man began.

"What those in the collapse?" Ivello interrupted.

The little man was already shaking his head, though suspicion was beginning to show on his features again. "No," he murmured, "we got separated when the Great Ma… elves attacked. I am not sure where they are, maybe dead?" He finished quietly, now very wary. "Are you going to take me to the mages?"

Ivello realised he was frowning savagely at his captive and had him held tight, his strong hand a band of iron on the little man's arm. He forced himself to relax and answered, "Yes of course. If what you say is true then the master, er… masters of the college need to be told." He turned and said, "Come we must get you up to the college."

This time the little man did not resist, though as he was pulled along he asked meekly, "What of my friends? They might be alive!"

"We will send help down to try to free them." Ivello snapped as he headed purposely for his master's quarters.

Chapter 35

REVELATIONS

Kilimarius conquered the lands that would later become the provinces of Tarsia, Zaran, Mikadia, Cumbra, Varitia, Tutonia and, of course, the province of Kilimar that was named after him. Campaigns were mounted into the lands of the Norns, Stellici and Calones, but despite victories, those highland lands were never brought within the empire. Indeed of the lands conquered, only Tarsia, Zaran and Kilimar provinces remain within the empire today. The others gained independence during the upheavals of the 9th century when the empire had to call back many of its legions from the outlying provinces.

From 'The Holy Lands of Alba' by Arch Prelate Jorus Enarius Florian, BY1180

Eliantha Shamass stumbled against the wall and the giant, Jammu Quadai Pendi, the Magus General, caught her. She had been working to help shift the rubble for several hours now, adding her telekinetic spells to those of other mage's. She would gently support the fragile corridor as others worked to carefully move the rocks and rubble beneath by means both magical and mundane. Now she was nearing exhaustion and she finally accepted the Magus General's insistence that she go and rest.

The last few hours had rushed by in a flash. She had just finished organising the procession of the Lords of the Provinces that officially began the Grand Council when the rumbling began. Tremors had caused vases and statues to topple in the lower hall. She had been there trying to canvas and persuade as many masters as possible of the innocence of the Archmage and the Elder races. There were gasps and cries of fear as objects smashed and people fell. Then it had been over. Eliantha had been at a loss, but she knew it was magic, had felt it, and with all the other events that had been happening, she had feared the worst.

She had reacted quickly, and sent for the Magus General and the Captain of the Guard. It was clear that whatever it had been, it had come from below the college and that it was big. She had ordered the two warriors to gather some guardsmen and head down carefully. She had been in the process of gathering some masters to help with the investigation when Xameran Uth Altor had come hurrying up and informed her that he had information from below and as head of the investigation into the happenings down there he would take charge.

She had come very close to swearing at the arrogant Sorceror Supreme, but had been forced to swallow her comments as she acknowledged his role, yet insisted that this was now more than an investigation, it was an emergency and any information he had, she needed. Even then he had tried to force her aside, but she had been adamant. Reluctantly, he had drawn her aside and confided that enemies beneath the college were on the loose and a small party of humans that he had sent down led by Master Arkadi Talcost, had been down there investigating and had been attacked and trapped when the first hall beneath the cellars had collapsed. He insisted that a rescue be attempted.

Eliantha was suspicious of the Lord of Sorcery, yet she could not argue. She knew Arkadi Talcost, he was an up and coming mage of her own school, gifted and ambitious and known to favour Xameran in the college's politics; that had been a bit of a disappointment to Eliantha who'd had high hopes for the young master. Nevertheless, she could hardly refuse to send help because she was suspicious of Xameran.

It had only been later as she was caught up in the rescue that she had realised that the sorceror lord had not given her any details of this enemy below or even of how he knew of it.

Eliantha brought herself back to the present and stumbled up the steps to the lower cellars and was greeted by a young adept. He handed her a large cup of water which she drank greedily.

Everything else, even the murder investigation and the procession, had been put on hold as the college rallied to help. Even now there were well armed groups of magi, fighter-magi and guards heading down the other entrances to the deep tunnels of the old elven city, intent on reaching the collapse from below and dealing with any enemy. Apparently, Xameran had briefed those groups on what to expect. What suddenly hit Eliantha was that Xameran seemed to know an awful lot about what was happening and she did not. The rest of the Conclave needed to know what he knew.

Eliantha handed her cup back to the adept and stood up straight, stretching her tired muscles. It felt almost like she had been holding the roof up down there with her own muscles rather than her magic. Looking around the cellar's wide corridor, Eliantha watched as a long line of volunteers from the college carried various buckets and containers of rubble or struggled to carry large rocks or help feed or water those who worked.

The only good thing that had come out of this was that the Assembly of Masters that Xameran had called for, had been postponed. Just as she was thinking this there was a commotion from up ahead and bustling into view came the sour faced little Atholl Dorard accompanied by the much taller Xameran Uth Altor, though it wasn't the sight of the two masters she least wanted to see that made her take an involuntary step back, but who was accompanying them. It was this company that was no doubt responsible for the angry looks on the two mages' faces.

Marching along purposefully at the two masters' side was the short, burly and powerful figure of Chief Jarlis of the Hammerhand Clan. The heavily built dwarven chief was moving towards her with a look of determination on his face that said nothing would prevent him from reaching her. Behind him marched at least a dozen of his kinsmen.

"Mage Master Shamass…" the warrior chief began, but Atholl Dorard spoke over him.

"This cannot be tolerated. These…" he pointed at the dwarves, "have been ordered to remain in their quarters!"

Chief Jarlis ignored the High Enchanter and continued, "I am here to offer my people's aid in the rescue. My people have great experience in working in these conditions."

Atholl Dorard opened his mouth to continue his tirade. Eliantha cut across him, quickly accepting the dwarf lord's offer and then turned to the spluttering Lord of Enchanters, "High Enchanter, Dorard" she almost hissed in fury, "I believe you will find it was the elves, not the dwarves who were asked to remain in their quarters."

Surprisingly, Xameran quickly agreed and Atholl looked at him in astonishment. "Mage Master," Xameran then continued, "we need to talk."

Eliantha looked hard at the pale face of the Lord of Sorcerors and replied firmly, "Yes, I believe that we do!"

Eliantha quickly snagged a passing master and informed him that Chief Jarlis and his men were going to be helping to clear the collapsed tunnels at her orders. The golden haired burly dwarf nodded firmly at her and she quickly thanked him and then motioned to the sorceror lord to lead the way. She followed the tall robed figure as he strode along in his splendid robes of office. As they mounted the stairs up out of the cellars, she suddenly became aware of how she must be looking, covered in dust and sweat after the hours down below. She squinted at the light flowing down the main corridor from the lower hall on one side and the great hall on the other.

Xameran Uth Altor hurried up the next flight of stairs and Eliantha wearily followed. She really did need to rest. The day was only half gone and already she felt exhausted from the revelations and toil of the day. She was so tired that when Xameran finally stopped and offered her a seat in the Hall of the Conclave she completely missed the presence of anyone else in the room. So, as she sat back into her seat, she was surprised to see the other heads of the schools of magic already seated; all that is save Atholl Dorard and the Magus General who were still below. She turned to ask Xameran what he was up to when the door behind her closed and she turned wearily to see the missing Dorard and Magus General behind her.

"Ah, good. We are all here then."

Xameran's smooth voice caused her to turn back. She was finding it hard to concentrate; fatigue was making her mind sluggish.

"No doubt you are all wondering why in such a time of urgency I have called you all here." Xameran began in that even and reasonable tone of his. "Well, I am afraid I have grievous news that could change everything, even the minds of those so skeptical yesterday."

"What are you about, Xameran?" Chief Druid Marillia Aronis snapped, "Must you weary us further with your attacks on the Archmage!"

A hurt look covered Xameran's face, "My lady, Marillia, I am saddened that you should think that I have attacked the Archmage. I have done nothing more than what my conscience has dictated I must. It is clear that the Archmage believes that the elves are a force for good and will greatly benefit the Wildlands and I respect him for his beliefs," Xameran looked around at the gathered masters, a look of sincerity on his urbane features, "but you must respect that I too have strongly held beliefs and that I too will defend those beliefs even if it means opposing a man who has done so much for this college and our lands." He paused and seemed to take a moment to collect himself and Eliantha noticed that both Zarina Agroda, the First Wizard and Izonda Tariadarmin, the head of the clerics, were nodding in agreement with the sentiment of following ones beliefs. "I cannot in good conscience hold back any longer this information that I have found. The conclave, yes, even the Archmage, must be made to see the truth!" Xameran continued in earnest determination.

"And what is this vital information, more accusations with little proof?" the Chief Druid asked harshly, though it was clear from the look of genuine worry on her wide, handsome face that even she was not immune to the sorceror lord's words.

Xameran looked at Marillia, clearly hurt by her disparaging comment. "This morning, as you all know, a magical explosion destroyed the first hall of the catacombs beneath us. I was perhaps the first to understand what had happened... and I know many of you were puzzled by this, but it had been part of my investigation to look into the mysterious magical emanations and disturbances that were coming from below. Master Arkadi Talcost and a group that he himself chose were already below." The Lord of Sorcery paused and swallowed. He leaned his fists on to the large table at which they all sat to support himself; he seemed to struggle with what he was about to say. "Now also, as you now know, Master Talcost and his friends were caught in the collapse and we struggle hard to find them... hopefully alive!" Xameran looked down and grimaced. "I feel somewhat responsible for those men and fervently hope they are found." He looked at the members of the Conclave a little nervously, and many of the masters gave understanding nods back. "However, not all were caught in the collapse!"

Eliantha looked sharply at the sorceror lord.

"However, the one who luckily escaped the collapse was not actually one of the people who went down with Master Talcost, but someone who actually joined their group in a desperate attempt to escape from his former slave masters!"

Xameran straightened and turned to look and nod at Atholl Dorard who in turn looked to the small doors to the hall and called out lightly, "Please come in, Nossi. Do not be afraid."

All eyes turned to look at the doors which remained still for a moment and then slowly creaked open. In the doorway was a small figure, about the size of a child and Eliantha could see many of her colleagues frowning at one another. Then into the room and the clearer light walked the small figure and Eliantha was taken aback to see a small man in non-descript clothes. The creature moved slowly to stand by the sorceror lord who motioned for the creature to mount one of the chairs in order to stand clearly above the oaken table top.

"Nossi here is of a race known as Gnomes, I believe they are akin to the dwarves. But it is not his race that is important; it is what he knows about the threat both from below us and from that which the Archmage spoke, a threat in which I now wholeheartedly believe. However, I now fear that the Archmage has been cruelly misled about the nature of that threat!" With that Xameran Uth Altor turned to the little gnome creature, Nossi and prompted gently, "Please, my little friend tell us about yourself and most importantly about your Great Masters; who they are and what they intend?"

The mage watched the faces of the other members of the Conclave as they listened to the gnome's story. The mage took great delight in watching each little detail hit home on the pathetic little Mage Master's bland face. He also loved the dawning of truth that gradually spread across the haughty Chief Druid's features as she listened to the gnome's story.

The mage had been very careful in how he had moulded the trusting little gnome creature to his will before he handed him over. He wanted the Conclave to hear Nossi Bee's story, but to hear what the mage wanted them to hear. He wanted them to hear of how it was the elves that were behind the threat from the north! He wanted them to hear of how the harsh, cruel and sadistic elves were planning to use the goblins to slay them all. The Conclave would then realise that the elves were manipulating everybody, including the poor deluded Archmage. The mage would then allow their imaginations to work while slowly maneuvering himself into the position of Archmage; they would have to choose another after this one had been so devastatingly misled!

The mage had to stop himself from smiling. Soon he would have the Conclave exactly where he wanted them and would take his rightful place at their head. The little gnome was in no position to add any details. He would definitely not mention the keystone to the Ways; that was the mage's secret. Little Nossi Bee knew now that his life depended on not mentioning that fact, and he was such a fearful creature. The mage even went so far as to allow the Conclave to ask the gnome their disbelieving questions, to begin to understand the scale of their Archmage's mistake in trusting the elves.

Questions ceased and all eyes turned to Xameran Uth Altor. "I know that this is hard to take in but…"

"How do we know what this creature says is the truth? He may believe it, but it may not be the truth?" Eliantha Shamass snapped over the Lord of Sorcery. However, no matter what she said, she was very troubled by what she had heard. Everything seemed to fit. The Archmage must be wrong!

Xameran smiled benignly, "You do not know if it is the truth, my dear Mage Master, but we can find out." He paused and then leaned forward to add intensity to his words, "We should not believe blindly, but we should treat this information seriously and question the motives of a race who have avoided our kind for centuries only to come forward now in our time of need. There is no loss in that, and we can seek hard to save Master Talcost and his fellows and question them. We can seek to discover the truth in the catacombs below." He stabbed a finger at the oaken table. "Atholl Dorard and I will lead the search below and we shall see if we can verify what little Nossi Bee here has told us."

"We should also bring these questions before the masters; matters of such import to all of us must be debated between us all." Atholl Dorard put in. "The very existence of our people is at stake and I for one do not believe Baden Erin is the man to lead us against the grave threat that hangs over us. He has already made too many poor judgements."

"Well I for one disagree with the ever predictable Lord Enchanter. We all know where your bias against the Archmage comes from!" Eliantha Shamass bit back at the hunched Atholl Dorard who went purple with rage.

"And this…" Xameran put in, referring to the hatred between Eliantha and Atholl, "is why we must take this to the Assembly of Masters. If we do not, this will end up tearing this college apart." Xameran insisted.

"The college is in uproar. We cannot call an assembly now." Eliantha gasped.

"My dear Mage Master, we must call the Assembly now in order to settle this uproar. We must, and it must be soon." Xameran replied and all heads, save the defiant Mage Master, nodded in agreement.

PART TWO
NEW HEROES AND OLD ENEMIES

Chapter 36

DREAMS AND DECISIONS

The first king of the ancient Nordic was of course, Cumb'Rai the Horselord, who was said to have led our people to leave their ancient homeland far to the East. He it was who found and wielded the Sword of Ice, the most famous weapon of the Nordic, and helped defend the Elder Kingdoms. His son Sed'Cumb succeeded him but little is known of this king. My'Sed the Mighty was the third king who finally settled the Nordic in what is thought to be the present lands of Cumbra. The fourth king was Ghan'My, My'Ced's grandson, who was in turn followed by both of his sons Anda'Ghan and then Aru'Ghan, the fifth and sixth kings who both spent their lives driving off enemies from the south and expanding the realm and power of the horse lords.

Extract from 'The Lost Druid Scrolls - Scroll 6' Author unknown. Discovered beneath the Academy of Mikadia, BY1096. Thought to date back a thousand years. These are hotly debated by Imperial scholars as faked to show Nordic civilisation as far older than that of the Olmecs!

Jon 'Bear' Madraig watched as the men thundered into the small courtyard in front of the keep. Chickens squawked and half leapt, half flew out of the way of the crashing hooves. Two dozen men, wearing leather armour with steel breastplates, and carrying swords on their hips and shields on their backs, came to a hasty halt. A tall, slim man at the front swung down. His hair was thinning, but what he had was braided in the Calonian manner and around his waist was strapped a thick swath of Calonian plaid; the tartan of the Madraig clan, held in place by a leather belt.

Jon looked down and saw his own small hand clasped by a strong, thick fingered one, a ring of precious gold with a single emerald, glittered on the middle finger. The hand was so familiar to him; it was his mother's. Her hand was not that of a soft noblewoman, only concerned with the running of her household; this was the hand of a strong and vibrant woman, a woman who was familiar with the outdoors and hard work. Jon looked up to see the face he knew so well, a broad strong face; attractive, but not with a delicate beauty, there was nothing truly delicate about Lady Orella Madraig and yet she retained her femininity. She was a tall woman with a fine white linen dress over which flowed straight, raven dark hair down to her waist. Around her neck, a silver torc shone; the symbol of her station. She was unusually broad of shoulder for a women, an inheritance of her Varitian father, who was famed for his prodigious strength. Jon's grandfather, Jarik Orendar had been a formidable warrior, compact and thick limbed, a man who had won the bare knuckle fighting at the great Mikadean games! His daughter had inherited much of his iron will and strength of character.

To his child's eyes, Jon's mother seemed so tall and strong, her presence at his side reassuring amidst the great crowd in the courtyard. It was the most people Jon had seen in his young life. There must have been almost a thousand! It seemed that all of the people of the Madraig lands had turned out in the courtyard, but then this was a time of celebration.

The tall, slim warrior strode confidently across the courtyard. He was Jon's father.

Maelor Madraig had always been a warrior; he was a Calonian with a proud tradition in battle. The highlands of Calon produced the bravest warriors in the Nordic lands it was claimed and Maelor was accounted a fine swordsmen and a charismatic leader in the area. He was well known for the hospitality of his hall; the free flowing drink and good food. It was also widely known that Lady Orella Madraig bred the finest war horses in the region and so Maelor had been a natural choice to lead the men of Redvale into battle.

The warriors who had ridden in with his father to the cheers of family and friends were part of the warband that had just battled and destroyed the Dagwart Goblins. They had been part of the great tribe that had attacked Ostia, but they had been left behind in the rout that followed and had taken shelter in the Redwoods nearby, to stay and kill any who entered. Jon's father had led the warband of local warriors to deal with the goblins.

Jon felt his mother's hand slip from his and he watched as she stepped down and moved out to meet the tall slim warrior. She was smiling, and he was too. They drew close and hugged passionately.

This moment came back to Jon from the mists of his mind. He remembered this. It was one of his earliest memories. He had been only around four years old at the time and so proud. His father was a hero.

Yes, Jon remembered this day, it was the last time he could recall that he had seen his mother and father truly happy together!

Images flashed and whirled; faces, times and places flickered and swirled and sense was lost. There was pain and sorrow, fear and anger. Jon had no idea where he was or what was happening, he only knew he was lost. Darkness fell once more and his mind fled into its comforting embrace.

Suddenly, light... sound... a voice screaming!

Jon was stood in the small chamber that he shared with his two older brothers. It was at the top of the keep that was his family's stronghold. They were on the fourth floor, just above his parent's chamber. Jon lay on his cot, curled up on his side like a babe, clutching his thick woolen blankets to his chest, chewing them and crying.

Again he heard the screaming, voices were raised in anger, but he refused to listen to them.

"Why do they have to fight?" asked his brother Mael in frustration. Mael was the eldest of his brothers, twice Jon's age and on the verge of being accounted a man at the age of twelve. He was Jon's favourite. He was patient and willing to answer his youngest brother's incessant questions. He always looked after Jon and stopped their other brother, Alrin from beating him. Alrin was only three years older than Jon and had a mercurial temper. He could switch from joy to hate, calm to agitated in a heartbeat and found it hard to even sit still, such was his energy. Jon, on the other hand, was placid and quiet. 'Like chalk and cheese, those two' he had often heard his mother say. However, both Alrin and Jon had inherited their father's bad temper and so they clashed. Mael, on the other hand, seemed to have inherited aspects of both his parents in moderation; Alrin and Jon had the extremes. Mael was by far the best of them Jon was sure, even at the age of six. Mael was Jon's hero!

There was crashing and banging down below. Things were being thrown and the anger in the voices was rising to a new level.

The fighting had grown worse over the past year. It was difficult for Jon to accept that his mother and father fought. He longed for that time when they had touched one another with quiet respect and love. When smiles had come easily to his mother's face, but those times were passed it seemed. His brother Alrin took it worst. His temper, so much like their fathers, could not handle the atmosphere that hung between his parents like a poisonous cloud. His frustration at his inability to understand or to help; drove Alrin to bouts of savage rage and destruction that brought equal rage from their father, while their mother rushed to defend her son from the battering that would be dealt out. Jon couldn't understand why his brother drove his father to such extremes. It was like Alrin craved his father's ire, like Jon craved his mother's love. Yet Alrin seemed more successful in his desires than Jon. Lady Orella was too concerned with dealing with their baby sister, Pemara and with defending Alrin from her husband to notice her quiet third son and his growing fears.

Jon heard his mother's voice, high pitched in a plea.

"That's it. I've had enough!" stormed Alrin, leaping to his feet from his own bed. "I'm not going to lie here and cry," he snarled, looking at Jon accusingly, "while he beats mother again. The drunken fool needs to be stood up to." Alrin was only nine, but quick witted. He stood up straight and resolute, anger giving him courage.

Alrin was right, Jon knew it, but to face father, especially when he had been drinking, as he so often did lately, was madness!

Father had always drunk, but since the battle with the goblins, father had become not just a local hero, but a figure of notoriety in Ostia as a whole and the rich merchants and nobles of the town had drawn him into their circle. He was taken in with their wealth and their lives of ease and luxury, their gambling and drinking. Father had taken to having grand feasts, inviting these new friends, and drinking late into the evenings. At first his mother had been compliant, but she was not a woman to hold her opinions for long and she slowly became more and more resistant to her husband. She would not have him gambling and drinking away the wealth they had… and so the fights had begun.

Jon watched from his bed as Alrin headed for the spiralling stairs in the corner where the eastern tower wound up the side of the keep. As he went he grabbed Mael's sword from its sheath that hung on the wall pegs. Jon sat up in alarm.

"Alrin, what are you going to do?" Jon cried out terrified.

At the same moment, Mael sprang towards Alrin shouting, "Oh no, you can't take that, you fool." but Alrin had already darted for the stairs. Mael leapt after him and Jon found himself leaping to follow. He was petrified at going downstairs, but also afraid of what Alrin might do.

The scene that greeted Jon as he cleared the last of the spiral steps and entered his parent's chambers was one he had spent years forgetting, yet here it was clear as if barely a day had passed. His father stood over his mother in the centre of the room, his mother half propped against the strong box. Her face was bloodied and already the area around her left eye and cheek were starting to blacken and swell. His father's face was a twisted snarl, a thin line of spittle was spattered on his chin and his eyes were like ice as they rose to fix on Alrin charging at him, sword held high and screaming incoherently at the top of his voice. Mael was close behind in pursuit of their fiery brother.

What happened next would be indelibly etched on Jon's mind.

Jon's father stepped over their mother and almost casually swept the sword from Alrin even as he swung it. Alrin didn't give up though, he screamed and launched himself bodily at his father, but again with ease, Jon's father caught his second son, turned and tossed him cruelly into his mother as she tried to rise. Both tumbled heavily to the floor. Mael stopped at the sight and stood, fists clenched facing his father's back. Mael was rigid with indecision and Jon's heart was thumping with fear.

Jon so loved his father. It would have been easier to hate Maelor Madraig if he had been a monster, but the truth was that when he was sober he was a kind and charming man, quick witted and full of fun… at least with Jon. With Alrin, their father found it difficult. Alrin was his mother's defender and would not forgive his father the beatings he gave her. Maelor saw his own guilt in Alrin's eyes, in Mael's too sometimes, though Mael was more forgiving as well as more able to hide his feelings.

Jon just didn't understand his father anymore and desperately wanted everything to be alright again.

Jon heard Mael say, "Father, please." But Maelor Madraig was in no mood to listen to any pleas. His temper was in full flow and rational thought was almost gone. Father hurled a curse at his wife and son. Before their mother could prevent him, Alrin sprang to his feet and spat his own curses back. Bellowing, Father swept back the sword he had taken from Alrin. Jon knew his father had never meant to strike anyone. It was meant as a threatening move. He did not know that behind him, Mael had sprung forward to try to put himself between his father and brother. The sword's blade slid almost easily into his chest! Jon watched in horror as the point of the sword appeared from his brother's back, cutting through his thin linen shirt.

Almost instantly, Jon's father had turned and snatched back the sword in surprise. The anger and intoxication that had clouded his eyes, immediately drained out along with the colour in his face. Maelor Madraig's mouth was a circle of horror. Jon heard a scream and saw his mother shrieking even as his father caught Mael's body as it sagged to the floor, but Mael was dead before his father's arms encircled him.

Jon had never seen his father cry, but a gasp of pure grief burst from his father as he saw the light of life leave his firstborn child and he buried his head in the shoulder of his boy. Mael's head fell back and lifeless orbs gazed into Jon's wide, disbelieving eyes.

Jon's mind fled.

He had walled away this memory, spent every day trying to forget the torment of that day. Why had it returned? Where was he? What was happening to him?

Darkness, soothing darkness came again, but not the absolution of unconsciousness this time, this time his mind would not let him flee.

He had wanted to help that day. He didn't know why he had remained by the stairs so helpless to the drama that was to unfold. He wanted to go and join his brothers, wanted to stop his father, to calm his anger. He wanted to make his father smile, to make him become the man he had once been, but Jon had been afraid and his fear had meant he stood by and watched while his beloved brother died. He knew he should have done something. To have done even something would have made that day easier to bare. Had he tried, his brother might not have died. Jon had known he had the most sway with his father; he was the one who could calm his rages when no one else could. Why hadn't he done just something… anything?

He had vowed that day he would never allow fear to rule him, never allow fear to stop him doing what he should. It had been a vow he had found so hard to uphold, the fears were always there, waiting. What had kept him going was the vision that sometimes haunted his dreams, a vision of his brother's head lolling back and the dead eyes staring at Jon accusingly.

Again images seemed to flash by him and this time Jon recognised them. They were faces he knew, places he'd been. This was his life he was seeing! Why? He couldn't seem to concentrate. Everything was awhirl, light stunned him and darkness blinded him.

He saw a sword in front of him, a shield on his arm but they weren't his… or were they. They seemed familiar… Of course, they were his, gifts from his mother when he had entered manhood. According to Nordic tradition, he was a man at thirteen, a strange idea; he hadn't really had a full grasp of the world and how it worked at that time. A thought occurred to him. He had lost these weapons when he was twenty in those caves, when they'd been attacked by…

He looked around him. Caves! Could it be…? He tried to turn, but he found he had no control over his body; it carried on walking forwards, straight towards disaster!

'Oh by the gods, I don't have to live through this again do I?' he thought desperately.

Why did it seem his mind was intent on viewing those harshest times in his life, those times that he had spent so long trying to bury?

Jon and his friends had been down in these caves on the fringe of the Darkheart Hills. They had never been this far east into goblin country before. Jon and his friends had got the insane idea that the best way to earn some serious money for themselves, as well as the chance to have young village girls swooning over them as Darin had put it, was to sign up with the Ostian mercenaries to aid the beleaguered villages that lay on the eastern border of Ostia province. These villages lay in the mouth of Darkdale. The problem was that on the other side of the Darkdale were the Darkheart Hills and goblins, trolls, kobolds and other less savoury creatures that raided and attacked constantly.

Arkadi, just back for the summer before his final year as an apprentice at Shandrilos, had said the villagers were idiots to have settled so close to such wild country and Jon had agreed with him, but High Lord Elgon was offering money to warriors willing to deal with a particularly stubborn tribe of goblins that were raiding. So Jon and his friends had agreed.

However, the job had been easier than expected with many warriors answering the call. The goblins were baited, trapped and slaughtered with relative ease. The money had been less than expected because so many had volunteered.

Nevertheless, while using some of their earnings to celebrate and to try to get some of those swooning village girls, they had heard of another threat that needed dealing with. Apparently, there was a clan of trolls in some hills a few miles up the Darkdale that had lately become very bold in raiding. Now, as far as Jon was concerned, trolls were a different kettle of fish to goblins. Goblins were little green or grey skinned freaks usually no taller than an adolescent and probably no stronger. Trolls, on the other hand, were big and mean. Most trolls stood over six feet and were as strong as an ox. What's more they lived underground and fighting in the dark was not what Jon relished at all. The others were all fairly negative about the whole idea as well, all that is save Zara and Darin. Darin admitted that he just wanted more of a challenge, stupid as that seemed to Jon, but then Darin spent his time actually looking for danger! Excitement, Darin called it. Zara, on the other hand, wanted money!

Zara could be very persuasive when she wanted to be and in those days, Zara and Jon had been close and Jon backed her despite his own misgivings. They'd fought side by side in the training arena and in battle; they knew one another well and trusted one another totally. Jon always backed her. Zara had pointed out that trolls inevitably meant metals and stones... precious metals and stones! Trolls were greedy and they were hoarders. They mined and were good at it; they had a keen eye for ores and metals. This was, in fact, their only saving grace intellectually otherwise they were about as intelligent as a rock! Zara was convinced they could sneak in to the troll tunnels, deal with those they came across and plunder their hoard while Arkadi shielded them with his magic. Eventually, Zara had them all believing it was going to be easy, a sure thing!

There had only been a dozen of them that year, but they had split into two groups to search the troll caves; with Jon and Zara were Arkadi, Garon, Darin and Gael Machay, a warrior who made Darin seem cautious; a real wild man in battle.

However, the key to this plundering was to avoid most of the trolls.

All had gone remarkably well as Jon recalled, but they should have been warned by the ordered nature of the trolls in this clan. Jon had only raided one other troll hole, but had heard of a number of others from veterans. As far as was told, trolls were savage, stupid and chaotic, sometimes even fighting one another rather than their enemies. This troll hole seemed well organised; the trolls actually carried proper weapons and some armour. It was unheard of, but the group of friends had forged on, unheeding of the signs.

Jon now found himself looking again at those slick limestone walls, the slow burning dung in the braziers on the wall giving off minimal light and maximum smell! He was leading, with Zara on one side of him and Gael Machay on the other. Jon knew that around the next bend in the corridor was a sharp turn.

It was strange. Jon could see the caves around him, smell the fetid stench of the place, hear the breathing of his companions and feel the heat, yet he could also remember this place. He was there, living the events as they happened and yet also not there, instead remembering what had happened, knowing what was to come.

With all his will he tried to turn his body from its course, but to no affect. He watched through his own eyes as he stepped around that bend, confident that they were nearing the hoard, confident that no one had even sensed their approach. They had slipped past the organised sentries covered by a skilful, but simple camouflaging spell.

As if in slow motion, Jon stepped around that corner in the corridor. Suddenly, events seemed to zoom back to full speed with horrifying abruptness. The cry, that would haunt his sleep for many months to come, roared out of the darkness, a savage snarl of bestial ferocity that shook him to his core. Too slowly, he reacted as almost a quarter of a ton of angry troll hurtled forward and slammed into him. Jon was thrown backwards through the air smashing Gael and Zara back with him. For a moment Jon was stunned, he was a large man, but this creature was twice his bulk! This was the largest troll he had ever seen. It stood well over seven feet and was impressively muscled, its heavy ridged forehead was covered by a thick, horned helm and its tusks were large and protruded from a wide slash of a mouth. What was even more impressive was that this troll was armed and armoured and its movements were not those of a lumbering beast, but of a trained warrior.

Jon pulled himself to his feet to see Darin and Garon dodging back from prodigious swings of a mighty spiked-head mace while a flash of fire streaked from Arkadi to hiss into the face of another more ordinary seeming troll who was rushing in with yet another to attack. The third troll was bearing down on Zara who was still down, but Jon saw Zara flip herself acrobatically to her feet to meet the rush. Screaming in savage joy, Gael also leapt up and bounded across to hack at the troll Arkadi had blinded.

However, after springing up himself, Jon stood still. Terror hit him at the thought of facing the brute that had smashed him aside, and the thought of all those trolls who had no doubt heard the sounds of battle. Suddenly, the armoured troll backhanded Garon who dropped like a stone, unconscious. It moved with surprising swiftness to catch Darin's great sword on the shaft of its mace before stepping in and smashing a fist into Darin's armoured chest, hurling him back to slide across the rough floor in a heap. The creature turned and saw Jon. The small dark intelligent eyes locked on his and Jon could have sworn its cruel, tusked mouth smiled. Fear, thick and heavy hit him and the monstrous troll launched itself at him, a mountain of armour and flesh. In his mind, Jon saw again the accusing eyes of a brother and with a startling scream of madness he threw himself at the approaching creature. He saw a flash of surprise on the grotesque face and a fierce smile twisted his own.

There was no finesse in his attack, his shield led the way and took the blow of the giant mace. His arm went numb as his shield crumpled under the blow, but it did the job. It cleared the way for his sword to drive straight through from behind. His weight fully behind it, the sturdy blade went straight into the throat of the snarling brute and the snarl turned to a coughing gurgle. The force of the two coming together punched Jon backwards and he went down, the troll smashing down on top of him. The crashing weight snapped Jon's blade even as it sent the shards up under the troll's chin and into its skull. A massive crunching sound reverberated through Jon's whole frame and the breath was forced out of him in a gasp as the troll came to rest on top of him. Pain lanced through his whole body.

Jon felt it all and yet he didn't. Part of him was removed from the scene, clear headed, but nevertheless caught up completely in the emotions of the moment, while the other half wandered in and out of consciousness beneath the smothering mass of the troll. Jon knew what happened next from what he was told later. The others had managed to free him, but had found his arm smashed and his left side caved in from the mace's blow and what ribs the mace hadn't smashed, the creature's weight had! The worst part was that he was losing blood and his lungs were punctured. The only good thing was that no other trolls turned up to attack and his friends were able to rig up a stretcher of sorts and carry him out.

Without a healer of any kind in the group, as Garon had not yet joined the Sironacian monks, Jon had almost died on the way back to the village. Luckily, in the village were some monks who had been treating the injured from the fight with the goblins. Once there he was patched up. His friends were generous, all the money they had earned that summer paid for the monks to save his life and speed his healing, but even with this it was to take him almost a year to heal fully, at least physically.

Mentally, for a man whose fragile courage was based on his strength and skill, that year of helplessness and weakness were devastating. Jon had become even more withdrawn and a new fear was added to his arsenal of terrors.

"And yet this experience eventually improved you."

"What?" Jon thought.

Already his vision was dimming, he could no longer see the beast that lay atop him, could no longer smell its foulness as death loosened its bladder or feel the steady drip of blood as it pulsed from his broken side. Light flashed again and images whirled afresh, yet this time he seemed more aware. He could make sense of what he was seeing.

"That is because your mind is growing in strength as is necessary for the joining."

This time Jon was sure that the voice had not come from him and yet the voice had read his mind, answered his question?

Just as he was about to phrase a question, he found himself standing in a room. It was his room, his class. It was here he had spent the last two years tutoring. The room was empty now and this did not seem to be one of his memories. Jon turned around full circle taking in the seats and benches and the large circular arena that dominated the centre of the room. The circle was about thirty feet across with wooden barriers around the edge, save for two openings. The chairs and benches spread around one half of the small arena, each row on a step going higher as it went back so that anyone at the back could see the arena above the heads of those in front. Jon's chair and table were off to the side of the arena close to the entrance to the class.

This was where he had virtually lived the last two years. Happy years they had been. It had almost seemed like he had fallen into this by accident, but it had been a fortuitous one. The trauma with the troll had led him here.

Jon had never had any intention to teach others only to learn himself. When he had returned to studying magic, after the battle with the troll, after so many years spent drinking, fighting and wasting his life, he had only one intention; to get away, to start again and to make something of himself, but it had taken a period of deep depression and misery to get him to change.

After the battle with the troll, he could no longer face the wars and skirmishes. The troll and the injuries had taken all his confidence from him. The damage from the fight with the troll, both physical and mental, had forced Jon to look at his life through new eyes. What he saw did not fill him with pride: fights, drunken stupidity and no direction or good from his life. He was a man who had been educated to a level far above that of the common folk, a man with knowledge of the mysteries, yet he could often be found drunk in the gutter, bloated and forgotten.

There were still some good times, times he would always remember with a smile, that was what made it so difficult for him to lift himself from the low he had fallen into, but for every gem of joyous remembrance there were ten regrets, ten shames.

The inactivity and depression finally forced Jon to look hard at where his life was heading. He'd not had the courage to strike out and do anything save dwell in self pity for two years, even with the realisation that his life was being wasted. Finally, it was the argument and fight with Zara that had forced him to get his life moving.

One evening, Jon had let his frustrations loose yet again after a few drinks, but this time it was aimed at the ever confident, Zara.

Jon had protected her, helped her and loved her for years; ever since the death of her uncle. From then they had been inseparable, the best of friends. However, for Jon it had slowly changed. He had grown to love her. He knew she never saw him that way and had vowed to keep it secret, yet Zara was twisted by her youth and was self destructive, hell bent on the pursuit of pleasure as if that could make her happy and fill some void within her. For Jon, every time she took a lover, it hit him hard, especially since they were such worthless scum. However, he kept his feelings in check and sought only to guide Zara.

After the frustrations and fears from the injuries in the battle with the troll, Jon had lost that control and that fateful evening he had sought to prevent Zara from taking yet another warrior to her bed. They had argued and fought and destroyed a trust that had been total.

This was the final regret to add to so many others. This fight had severed his last strong tie to Redvale and Ostia; he had no reasons to stay anymore. He had no friends; Zara was gone and Nat and Karis with her. His oldest friend, Darin had already headed off to join the Knights of Karodra; and Arkadi, Garon and Rebba were finishing their studies at Shandrilos and were about to begin new lives… Jon had nothing. He had no choice, but to pluck up what courage remained to him and leave for Shandrilos to finish the studies he had abandoned five years earlier.

It was the best decision of his life!

His time at Shandrilos had been a revelation in itself. There he had discovered a side to himself he had never thought he had. It was here he learnt the self discipline needed to study and to take a grip of his life. He had also turned out to be a bit of a notoriety amongst the apprentice Fighter Magi. He was older and by far the most accomplished warrior; arena trained and battle hardened. He was also one of the most gifted and the most driven. He suddenly had his confidence back and a direction. Also, the years missed and wasted seemed to press him to make up time, to push himself harder and faster than any other student. In only a few years, he had caught up to his peers in the mysteries and passed them. It was almost like he couldn't do anything wrong. The school asked him to help with the tutoring of weapon skills and this led into tutoring magic allied to sword skills too. What's more the teaching forced him to understand more deeply what it was he himself had learnt. He also discovered an aptitude for teaching that made him more content than he had ever been before.

All his aimless talents that seemed to never quite fit in other situations became strengths in this one. His surprisingly wide ranging knowledge, his skill with arms, but lack of love for war, and his patience, were so suited to the task of instructing students. Even his famous temper was chained and suppressed, and drink was almost completely forgotten in the seriousness of study. The only problem Jon had was his lack of social skill, yet he learnt what was needed in the classroom and this gave him the framework in which to confidently lead and communicate. Aspects of command came through from his time as a lord's son and his confidence in his own abilities surpassed what it had once been.

When they had asked him to become a tutor at the new guild school in Lauria, he had jumped at the idea.

Jon looked around the spacious hall in which he had become a complete person, in which he had forgotten the past. This was his room, he knew it from the marks in the benches and tables, to the collection of writing implements that were so neatly ordered on the side tables ready for use. Here, he had taught students as young as ten or eleven, helping them to understand the scripts of the common tongue, High Alban and even the ancient language of the mysteries. Here, they had learnt of the world in which they lived, how to act, how to fight and how to craft, and their imaginations had gained wings. His older students, those who had decided to stay on, those in whom the spark of talent was strong, had received his instruction in the basics of spellcraft and warfare. In the sand circle he had sparred with and guided those who wanted to follow his example and ally spell with sword.

Turning round to take in the full extent of his stone walled hall, Jon took a deep and contented breath. This place was a sanctuary against those other memories.

Abruptly, he stopped. There was a figure in the sand circle, a figure still and silent. Jon squinted in an effort to make out the details of that figure, but it was like a blurred image that would not resolve itself, dark and foreboding. This was definitely not one of his memories.

Chapter 37

THE LORE KING

The son of King Aru'Ghan of the Cumb'Rai was named Dari'Aru the Builder. He became king and continued the settling of his people. He moved away from the nomadic life of his ancestors. He was followed by his daughter, Tan'Dari Elf-Friend who it is said strengthened ties with the Elder and adopted much of their beliefs, beginning the order of Druids. Her grandson, Odar'Tan succeeded her and was given the name 'the Wise' for his sponsoring of the development of the mystic arts, literature and the Bardic tradition. Finally, Nam'Odar the Fisher-King, tenth ruler of the ancient Nordic, came to the throne. He was an accomplished mystic who promoted the Nordic to develop their sea and river trade. He travelled widely, even to the Elder kingdoms where he met and fell in love with the elven princess, El'Ariel.

Extract from 'The Lost Druid Scrolls - Scroll 6' Author unknown. Discovered beneath the Academy of Mikadia, BY1096. Thought to date back a thousand years. These are hotly debated by Imperial scholars as faked to show Nordic civilisation as far older than that of the Olmecs!

"No, it is not."

It was the musical voice he had heard in his mind. Did it come from the figure? But how could it? It had spoken an answer to his thoughts!

The realisation hit him that none of this was real. It could not be real; it was all part of his memories and, if none of this were real, that would explain the way the voice answered his thoughts. If this were all from his mind then the figure might just be a part of his mind and that would mean... he was talking to himself! He laughed at the thought.

Maybe he was going mad? ...And yet that seemed to make no sense! Not the fact that this was obviously some part of his own mind or that he was mad, he had enough knowledge of the mysteries to know that in the realm of the mind, dreams, fears, and thoughts were very real in their own way, but the fact that this figure was from no part of his mind... unless... could it be a part of his subconscious, a manifestation of his inner self to his conscious mind? It was possible.

Jon began to move down the steps towards the circle and the puzzle that stood frozen there; a shadow rooted in the pale sand.

Another realisation struck him and his step faltered on the last step. How had he got here? He couldn't remember entering any kind of trance or meditative state; it was not an area of magic at which he had been particularly adept. A cold feeling began in his stomach as his mind threw up another possibility. If this were some mental or astral realm and he had not entered, but been pulled here by some other magic user... a flash of a coppery elven face flashed before him, a duel, a pair of menacing dark cloaked magi... Could this figure be an enemy?

"I am not your enemy, Jon Madraig." echoed the light voice in the stillness. "Indeed, I want... and need, more than anything, for us to be friends and to understand one another."

Jon frowned. "Then you are magi?"

Jon saw the figure nod. The first movement it had made and he almost missed it, it was so slight.

"Why have you brought me here? Who are you and why would you want me to be your friend?" Jon called across the space.

"I understand your suspicions, Jon."

Jon felt that the creature before him smiled, though he had no evidence to back this.

"Your first question is the easiest to answer, while the second will take some time to explain, time that I am not sure either of us has."

There was a pause and the black shadow started to almost glide towards Jon across the sand. It was only then that Jon realised how tall the figure was. Taller than he, it must have stood almost seven feet tall and was so thin as to appear almost like a pole wrapped in a cloak, like those that some farmers used to scare away crows.

There was a dry tinkling chuckle and the voice from the figure muttered, "An interesting comparison my friend."

The figure stopped in front of Jon and though it stood no more than an arm's length from him, Jon could not make out any more details. It was like the darkness seemed to hug to it, obscuring all features and keeping its identity secret.

Again, in response to his thoughts the figure seemed to look down at itself, the vague outline of its cloaked head dipping. "Yes, that is the purpose of this form, I have worn it so long now that it has almost become my true self in this place of ghosts and memories." the creature murmured to itself in solemn contemplation.

Abruptly, the head came up and the dark hole that was its face stared at Jon.

"To answer your first question, I did not bring you here, I merely found you, you were already here, lost and oblivious save to that final imperative."

"Final imperative?" Jon asked confused.

"Death, Jon Madraig, death! That is the final imperative."

"What, you mean I came here because I am dead!" Jon gasped in horror. Such an idea seemed so impossible. Surely he would know if he was dead. Wouldn't he?

"Not dead, Jon Madraig, but dying. Your mind sought refuge in oblivion as your body failed."

Jon was growing more panicky with each word.

"Your body still lives, though even as we speak it is failing, kept alive only because of the actions of your friends and, perhaps through an innate stubbornness in yourself, or more accurately an inner belief. However, neither of these will maintain you forever. Your brain has suffered injuries and danger is all about you."

"How..." Jon began.

"How did you gain the injuries?" The figure interrupted in its soft almost sweet voice, "Do you not remember the duel, Jon... with the elf lord?"

As the tall, dark figure spoke, Jon could see in his mind a coppery skinned elf, garbed in midnight black armour, attacking. He saw his blade split the merciless figure, his sword driving through its strangely armoured chest. Then he had attacked yet more elves behind the first; elves robed ominously in black, spells forming in the air around them. One died by his blade, the second going down, though not finished. There was a dive, a sense of desperation, a blast then... nothing.

"Although I did not see what happened to you Jon, I believe from examining your memories that the blast was from a fellow magic user, most likely an Arkadi Talcost. Not aimed at you, probably aimed at those elven warriors about to attack you. However, your last conscious thoughts are of sliding off into darkness along with the elf mage and there, I believe, you must have sustained your injuries, for there are no memories after that event."

Suddenly another memory struck Jon. The musical voice of the elf he had dueled and the voice of...

"You are an elf!" Jon hissed taking a step back and looking around for weapons that weren't there.

The long dark robed shadow lifted its arm and held its hand out seeking to placate Jon. "Well, guessed Jon. You are right, but I mean you no harm. I am not of the kind that attacked you. I assure you."

Jon was wary. Elves were elves weren't they? This could be some kind of trick. This was obviously a powerful magi he faced.

"Yes I am..." replied the figure in response to his thoughts, "and I could have harmed you had that been my intent, but I have not." The figure must have seen that Jon was unconvinced for he continued. "You are unaware that there are different kinds of elves in this world. Elves who have different beliefs, cultures, colour of hair, eye, skin... much as your own people. The elf you fought is not from the elves that live in the deep forests of your lands."

Jon frowned and repeated. "There are different kinds of elf?"

"You must have noticed the black eyes and hair of the elves that attacked you, and their fiery red skin."

Jon nodded.

"My people possess silvery skin, fair hair and lightly coloured eyes."

Jon frowned, "I have never seen an elf to know, But even if I had that does not mean you are different, I know that Nordic and Olmec people have different skin, but that does not make them good or evil."

"Quite right, Jon, but it does often make them different people with different beliefs and ideals," the figure replied, "and the beliefs of those elves you fought are hideous and twisted. They are anathema to all my people, whom your forebears were allies with, and to all for which they stood. These dark kin are cruel, hateful and sadistic. They revel in death. My people have always revered life."

Jon thought about this for a long moment. "So you are a forest elf… from my land?"

"I am of their kind, though not of the forests and not from those lands that we once called Dah'Ryllah."

Jon knew this was the old name for the Wildlands amongst the Elder races, when it had once been one of the legendary nine kingdoms of the elves.

"That is correct," responded the figure to his thoughts, "I was born in the greatest of the ancient kingdoms, in El'Yaris, seat of the High Kings of those you now know as the elves of the wild forests. In fact I am of the line of the High Kings and indeed you know my name if only from story."

Jon looked confused. "El'Yaris was destroyed centuries ago. The land it once was is supposed to be far to the north, inhabited by goblins, trolls and monsters of all kinds."

"So I have learnt from your memories Jon." responded the lyrical voice mournfully and there was a depth of sadness that Jon had rarely heard. It reminded him painfully of his brother.

"And I know you?" Jon queried. "How can that be? I have never seen any elves until we came into the catacombs beneath Shandrilos, and I have spoken to none save that…"

"Dark elf" supplied the tall shadow smoothly.

"Dark elf?"

"Yes, Jon, that is how we once knew them, though they refer to themselves as the True Elves. It was they who led our enemies against us, their kin. They, in turn were led by a creature of pure malice and cruelty, a living avatar of the Lords of Darkness."

Jon gasped. "The Elder kingdoms were destroyed by these Dark Elves?"

The shadow nodded solemnly.

"But why was this knowledge hidden?" Jon asked in amazement.

The shadowed figure was silent for a moment, seemingly reluctant to speak. Eventually, the musical voice whispered forth from the darkness. "You must understand that the dark elves were a great shame for our people. We have always revered life and for an elf to kill another is a terrible thing, to kill another elf is the greatest crime known to our people. I can only think that the survivors of the Dark Elves onslaught and the fall of the Elder kingdoms refused to speak of such shameful knowledge and so that knowledge was lost."

Jon nodded at this, though he didn't really understand fully. His thoughts wandered in chaos at the repercussions of what he had heard. He wasn't sure what this had to do with him.

Suddenly, Jon remembered his earlier question. "How could I know you?"

"You know me through the tales of your people and the teachings and myths learnt from your lorewise, the druids. They may not have known the whole truth of what happened, but they passed on much, including knowledge of me. My name is Tal'Asin."

'Tal'Asin!' Jon thought, "But that's…"

"Impossible." interrupted the shadow as it stepped closer.

Jon sensed that the shadow was smiling like a benign father upon his son, though he could not see it. "Yes, Tal'Asin was the Lore King of the Elder kingdoms from long, long ago, the greatest mage of all, a legend. He died centuries ago."

"Not quite, my friend. I did not die… at least not fully, though I have remained trapped like this for centuries," sighed the shadow in a tone that conveyed deep weariness. "Not quite dead, yet not quite alive either; trapped between life and death like a fly in amber." He paused for a moment, "However, like the fly I have remained preserved, an unchanging shade while the world that I knew has passed away."

Jon's mind was flailing around, desperate to think of a question that would make sense of what he was hearing. "I don't understand. How? Why?"

The shadow glided over to Jon who stood now like a child before a parent, only coming up to the cloaked figure's chin. It looked down on Jon.

"I am not sure either of us has the time to answer your questions fully, but you must trust in me if we are to save one another."

Chapter 38

GUARDIAN OF THE ELVES

One of the most ancient and yet popular folktales tells of how Nam'Odar the Fisherking met and fell in love with an elven princess of El'Yaris. It is said that after many trials Nam'Odar proved himself worthy of the hand of the elven princess, El'Arial. However, their love was doomed to fail; man and elf are not meant to be together. El'Ariel knew this and yet she loved Nam'Odar and thus sought the aid of the Lore King, Tal'Asin the Wise. He used his magic to transform the princess. It was said that for her love of Nam'Odar she gave up her elven nature and became human. Legend tells us that from Nam'Odar and El'Ariel came the fabled line of the Druid Kings of the ancient Cumb'Rai.

From 'A collection of Folktales' by Rogarin Draghar, Bard to the King of Tutonia, BY1107

With that, the figure lifted its hands and threw back the cloak that covered its head. At the same time, the shadows that had clung to the figure, despite the light from the burning braziers around the sand circle, seemed to swirl and wash away like smoke on the breeze. From beneath, the features of an elf were revealed, but no ordinary elf. This elf's silvery skin seemed to glow from within and the eyes were large and such a colour of deep blue that they seemed purple, like an Alban emperor's robes, with swirling patterns and flecks of light gold within. These seemed like the eyes of a god with an inner light that shone with power and passion. The face was long and thin with high prominent cheekbones and the skin was smooth and without blemish like a new born babes, yet an ancient intelligence radiated from every feature of the face. The nose was fine and the brows arched up like the wings of an Alban angel above the eyes; the brow was high and the hair that framed the face was long and golden, falling lightly to the shoulders; the tips of the pointed ears, that all elves had, could be seen through the hair of straight spun gold, but Jon found his eyes always drawn back to those magnificent orbs that gazed on him with polite wisdom. The eyes were incredible!

"This is a great risk I am taking Jon, the Lords of Darkness are ever watchful" said the tall mage earnestly, laying his long, slim silvery hands upon Jon's shoulders, "but from what I have learnt from your memories and from those of your fellows, the great enemy may be moving again and the same darkness that destroyed my people has again returned and will seek all our dooms as once it did before unless a defence is made against it." The tall elven mage looked heavenward for a moment before turning its burning blue gaze upon Jon once more. "I must tell you that I require your aid, but it is aid that must be freely given."

Jon's confusion was deepening. He had a good mind and was quick, but he was being inundated with information and needed time to think. He couldn't see how this really related to him.

Reading his mind, the imposing figure before Jon stepped back and gazed calmly at him. "Forgive me, Jon, I am rushing you."

"Yes," said Jon latching onto a thought, "you have mentioned time on several occasions now. Why have we little time?"

The elven mage looked serious. "For a number of reasons, Jon, firstly, I sense danger all around you and your friends and I see the hand of the enemy stretching forth once more to swamp our peoples, yet more immediately, for you in particular, time is running out and you are the only hope I have!"

The great elven mage whispered almost fiercely. "Your hold on life is failing, Jon. Your friends have fed your body with energy and healed your superficial wounds, yet they were unable to heal the deeper ones. Soon you will die unless I aid you, and if you die, all hope I have of combating this threat dies too."

"If you can heal me then do so." Jon responded, worry making his tone harsh.

"It is not that simple I am afraid."

Jon stared at the mage lord in disbelief.

"I did not mean for that to sound like a threat or a bargaining point, Jon." replied the mage quickly in a placating tone, "but I am afraid it must at least partly be the latter."

"A bargain?" Jon muttered puzzled.

"I would have healed you already," continued the elford passionately, "if I could affect the world directly, but I am shackled; a prisoner. I am a spirit trapped without a physical body within the Ways. I cannot heal you."

"Then why say you can!" Jon growled through a jaw clenched with growing anger.

"I said I can, Jon and I was not lying. What I am saying is that I cannot as I am," insisted the angelic figure before him, "I need your help, Jon and then I can help you. However, what I am asking is not easy or even certain and it involves great risk and… great trust." the elven mage pleaded, his fine, long fingered hands reaching out almost tenderly to Jon.

"What use am I to you? How can I help so great a mage?" Jon's tone was turning bitter at the realisation that his life was ending even as he spoke and he had no control over it. He was also growing suspicious as his understanding of what he was hearing failed.

"I understand your ire and your fears, Jon, but you can aid me and in so doing, aid not only yourself, but give me a way to aid our peoples against this threat that is now coming."

Jon was shaking his head, "How?"

"A joining"

Jon looked blankly at the silvery being before him. "A joining of what?" he asked, "Do you mean join our spirits to heal…" He trailed off not knowing where to go with this line of thought.

Tal'Asin, the archmage of a lost elven people, looked at Jon in a measuring way. "A complete joining Jon, a joining of spirit, body and soul; my spirit and soul would become one with yours and reside within your physical body. This would give me the freedom and power to affect the world once more."

Jon's eye widened in surprise, "Is that possible?"

Tal'Asin put his hands behind his back and started to stroll around the sand circle as if avoiding looking at Jon. "It has never been done between one of my race and one of yours. Long ago, it was common among my people for dying elves to pass on their knowledge and wisdom to their offspring, but that was a minor sharing to what I propose." Again there was a pause as those wondrous eyes looked hard at Jon. "Jon, I do not know whether it will work or how it might turn out between us." he paused. "As I have said there is risk. There is no knowing how this will change you... us. However, I am fairly sure that without my aid our peoples will fall before the enemy."

Jon was starting to get annoyed now. This Tal'Asin, if indeed that was who he was, was starting to talk nonsense. 'Our people will fall before the enemy? There had only been a few of these so-called dark elves. It would take more than that or did this Tal'Asin think humans so weak? All that had happened was that Jon and his friends had run into trouble with some of these dark elves and their foul creatures and now he was reaping the rewards of his stupidity. The Wildlands and its people were not in jeopardy, only him, and this elven mage was trying to tell him that without his aid his lands would face ruin! It was ridiculous.

Reading his mind again, the mage responded, "It is not just you who are in trouble, Jon. Your friends sit now in those same catacombs, labouring over your body while danger approaches. From what little I can sense of them, they are torn and hurt. They refuse to leave you, but need to flee if they are to survive and if they do not survive, all knowledge of the return of the dark elves will be lost. Then, the Dark Gods who guide the minds of those foul creatures will have no opposition and soon your lands, the lands in which you grew to manhood, will be lost to a dark horde. Your family and friends will die!"

Jon frowned hard at the stunning figure of Tal'Asin, who now stood swathed in robes of verdant blue that sparkled and shone like they were made of metal not cloth. It was difficult to credit that this imposing figure was anything other than what he said, or that what he said was not the utter truth, yet it was so unbelievable. This whole situation was beyond belief. Jon shook his head, it just seemed so fantastical: a return of an evil that had wiped away the Elder races! However, one thing did seem very credible and that was that his friends were in trouble. The elves and insect creatures, not to mention those massive brutes that had attacked them, were a very real danger.

Suddenly, Jon found the long limbed Tal'Asin before him, his long, slim arms grasping Jon's shoulders. Jon looked up and the power in the tall Lore King's gaze gripped him.

"Jon, the group that attacked you were merely a search party, a scouting group. In the northlands I sense great danger. The mind of some great power is searching; it seeks to reform its power of old, I can feel its malevolence! Jon you must believe me!" Tal'Asin pleaded. "The danger to you and all you know is very real…"

Jon was stunned by the sheer force of will that was pressing upon him.

"Jon, I can help stop the dark elves. You see, I believe I know what it is that they desire and why this group was here in the ruins of Dah'Ryllah. If they get it then your lands and peoples will be wide open to them!"

Jon wasn't sure what to say. He was astounded by what he was hearing and by the passion that drove the words from this potent figure before him. Confusion raced through Jon's mind, questions formed and possibilities flared. Were such things possible? A dark horde… dark elves… some great power in the north…a joining… was he really dying and would this joining save him? It all seemed too incredible! His mind reeled.

Long moments passed. Finally, Jon managed to speak.

"There are one or two things more that I would like to know before I agree to anything?" Jon asked cautiously.

The near luminous figure nodded, calmly, yet Jon could sense impatience building.

"Why me, first of all? Why not find another to join with?"

Tal'Asin blinked his large magnificent eyes. "I cannot reach anyone else, my friend. My own people are far from here, they never returned to the city you know as Shandrilos after the last battle with the dark elves, and even if they had, they would have had to know I was here and have searched for my spirit. No, my people think me dead, as I almost am.

Even your friends who sit so close to you, I cannot reach. I am afraid that my spirit and soul have been imprisoned within the Waygate for too long. The Waygate now lies hidden at the heart of the ancient catacombs. My physical self has been destroyed and my spirit and soul are shackled in this place between realities."

Jon nodded in partial understanding and added, "That brings me to my next question, how? How were you trapped here and why?"

Tal'Asin nodded his large head and his golden hair cascaded across his shoulders. "These are very good questions, Jon yet we have little time and I am not sure I can fully answer you... but I will try. This is very important and I can see this is very overwhelming for you."

The mage took a deep breath. Abruptly the room around Jon melted away and in its place appeared a circular room, a deep fire blazed in a large fireplace and the whole room was decorated in blazing colours and swirls of pattern that beguiled the eye. Jon found himself seated in a large and comfortable high-backed chair, like those that he had seen in the great houses of the nobles of Lauria. Tal'Asin now sat before him, his long slender legs crossed in a way that looked uncomfortable to Jon though the look on Tal'Asin's shining face was relaxed. The great mage seemed to be gazing off into the distance to some place or time beyond this strange room.

Abruptly, Tal'Asin looked hard at Jon and for the first time he felt menace in that stare... anger, though it was not directed at him he knew instinctively.

"First of all, I fought long ago to destroy the ancient enemy and its dark horde. I finally succeeded, though the cost was high for my people, and cost me my mortal shell. However, I am not fully dead because I am not so easily destroyed, my knowledge in the mysteries has allowed me to preserve myself and so, though perhaps I should have died, I have persisted in the hope of aiding my people, of passing on the ancient lore. You see my apprentices were all killed in the battle against the dark elves and when I realised I would not survive, I sought to preserve my spirit. Unfortunately, my spirit became trapped within the energies of the Waygates. I waited long here for someone to find me, not knowing the terrible fate to which my people had succumbed.

Jon, I did something terrible to my people, something I should never have allowed to happen. I was too confident that I could defeat the *Ata'Gon* and in my pride I was destroyed and with me the line of knowledge of the Lore Kings was broken for the first time in thousands of years! The first tenet is to preserve the succession and in that I failed. The line of Lore Kings that goes back to Dah'Nu the Great Mother, has failed with me. I could not pass into the next world with the burden of such a failure and so I have remained, banished here waiting for my people to find me... but they have not."

Tal'Asin's head sank and a feeling of such sadness gripped Jon.

"And now the enemy has returned and my people, our peoples, are ignorant and incapable of protecting themselves. There is no one to guide them."

"You keep saying the enemy." Jon interrupted, "Do you mean the dark elves or this ancient leader you said you killed, or someone else?"

"When I speak of the great enemy I am talking of the Lords of Darkness, those whom your people call the Death Gods, but, more particularly, the enemy are the dark elves. Who now leads them I do not know, though I feel the influence of the one I destroyed and that puzzles me. He was the Chosen One of the Lords of Darkness, and indeed he did have a name, Jon, though it is a name that I will not speak lightly. It is a name that fills me with hate. To his own people he was a messiah. They called him the *Ata'Gon* or Great One and, though I thought his line extinct, I fear it must be one of his ill spawned offspring that has returned."

The anger that had been hinted at before in those magnificent alien eyes was now clearly revealed; it was deep and abiding and Jon was glad that he was not the target of that cold rage.

"How I was able to survive here, trapped, is more complicated," continued Tal'Asin, "it is bound up with who I am and what I am."

"The position of Lore King amongst my people is ancient and more than merely just the title of the most learned of the Lorewise or magi as you call them. The Lore King is responsible for the moral, cultural and spiritual well being of our people. In many respects it is a position that is more important than even that of the High King, indeed once the two were one and the same." Tal'Asin mused.

"It is my responsibility to guide and protect my people." he continued. "By tradition, the position of Lore King goes back to the earliest times, to the legendary days after the Wars of the Gods, as you Nordic people know it. That war saw the Gods, or Lords of Light, cast out the Lords of Darkness and their demon minions from our world; they could not or would not destroy their ancient enemy. However, according to legend, this Great War devastated our world. The gods healed the world as best they could, but they were weary and so they left it to the Elder races who had survived the ancient conflict. The Gods were wise and realised that their ancient enemies might seek to influence and corrupt the people of the world from afar and so they left behind Guardians, descendants of their own immortal bodies, who were half mortal, half immortal to guide the races. Also, each God gave to their Guardian a talisman to help them in their task. The Lore King is that Guardian for the elves."

Tal'Asin paused and looked at Jon and smiled. "I sense your skepticism, Jon. These are tales you have been told as legends from your druids and you are a man who believes in logic and reason. You have never felt the presence of the gods or felt there was anyone deciding your fate other than you." Again the tall, angelic creature smiled benignly at Jon, "And yet there is a core of belief in you; a belief in Tynast's hall of heroes, in Ishara's icy touch and even in good and evil, right and wrong. You live your life by the teachings of the druids and the way of the warrior, even while doubting their truth."

Tal'Asin leaned forward and Jon found himself mesmerised by the powerful stare of the Lore King. "You are a good man, Jon, despite your misgivings, and that is why I have hope that the gods still work to aid us for they have delivered a man to aid me who believes in honour and justice, believes in doing the right thing no matter how skeptical he might be about the reasons why." Tal'Asin slowly sat back and Jon felt himself released from that powerful stare. "In a way," Tal'Asin mused as he settled himself comfortably into his chair, "this makes you a better man, for you do what is right because you believe you should, not because you worry about some god watching over your shoulder, judging your every action. I have watched your memories and seen the moments that defined your being. You are a man full of fear and yet a man afraid to be afraid lest you somehow fail someone around you as you believe you did your brother."

Jon wasn't sure how to respond to this. It was uncomfortable to have someone lay bare his soul.

"Worry not, Jon for you are a good man and your weaknesses are in fact strengths. In time you will come to see the truth of this, and of the gods who have sent you to me… but where was I?" The silvery skinned being asked himself, no doubt sensing the chaos that was taking hold of Jon's feelings, "Ah, yes, the Guardians… Amongst my people, the first Guardian was named Dah'Nu and she lived long guiding our people. The talisman that she was given came from the Goddess most revered amongst the elves, Elysia, the Earth Mother, whom your people name Sarahiri, Queen of the

Gods. The talisman she gave to her Guardian was known as the Lifestone and was placed by Dah'Nu within the mighty Temple she created to honour the great goddess. It became known as the Temple of Life and within it, that most powerful of artifacts, was placed!"

Tal'Asin looked pointedly at Jon as he said this and Jon nodded. He had heard in the legends of the druids of the fabled temple and of the Lifestone of Elysia. Its powers were supposedly immense, one tale told of how it had been used to bring peace between the warring dwarven nations after the last great war with the trolls, another tale told of how an entire army had been destroyed through its power! Jon had always thought it a myth.

Jon noticed the great mage frowning at him slightly, the most facial expression he had seen on the other, save in his eyes and in the ghost of a smile that could shimmer across his metallic face. "The Lifestone was never meant as a weapon." Tal'Asin admonished. He then dismissed this with a slight wave of his hand and continued. "From Dah'Nu, the first guardian, has come the line of the High Kings and Lore Kings, and from them all the lines of the noble elves have some claim of descent. Indeed my people call themselves the Children of Dah'Nu." Tal'Asin looked at the ceiling for a moment in remembrance it seemed. "So, I was not the first Lore King as your memories suggest; however, as far as your people are concerned I am the only Lore King they have known because the power of the Lifestone and the temple, of being its Guardian, greatly extends the life of the individual even for a long lived race like my own." Tal'Asin turned his intense gaze back on Jon and finished, "I have been the chosen Guardian of my people now for around three thousand years!"

Tal'Asin smiled at Jon's stunned silence and nodded as if to confirm his own words and encourage Jon to believe. "Before me, Tel'Emnar, known as 'the Crafter' was Guardian for well over two thousand years, and so the position of Lore King goes on back through our long history to Dah'Nu, though I have not the time to go through all that history. What is important is that I am the Guardian of my people and the great temple and the Lifestone were given into my care to protect and preserve my people. It is because of this duty and through my knowledge of the Temple and Lifestone that I have preserved myself."

"You mean that, somewhere this stone still sits in this temple and the temple still remains after all this time!" Jon asked and then almost immediately looked apologetic. "Sorry, go on."

Tal'Asin shook his large yet fine head solemnly. "The Great Temple of Elysia has existed for millennia, and is the most potent place of power known to my people. It still endures. However, the Lifestone does not still reside within it. It was that talisman that the foul *Ata'Gon* sought to steal and twist to his use so long ago when his Dark Elves ravaged my people. He failed and I destroyed him and sealed off the great temple."

Tal'Asin looked at Jon and tilted his head in a way unfamiliar to Jon. Suddenly the tall, potent figure leaned forward. "The Lifestone I was forced to send elsewhere. However, I retained a tenuous link to the Great Temple, yet recently my connection has been tainted, evil draws near the Temple, and I can no longer sustain myself. Slowly, I begin to fail."

"Somehow, the dark elves have returned, led by some agent of the Lords of Darkness, some scion of the cursed *Ata'Gon*. I feel his evil in these lands again and in the ancient heart of my people, the great city of Althazar, beneath which the Great Temple lies. Somehow that evil has gained control of that most holy site and seeks to corrupt it. Already they may have managed to use its energy to force open a great portal, albeit for only short periods, and bring through their servants. How? I do not know. Yet there is hope still, for the great temple's inner sanctum is still sealed by a mighty barrier that I put in place to trap my enemy so long ago. That barrier still endures and it prevents whoever this new threat is from reaching the most holy centre of our people." Tal'Asin paused and looked around him, searching. He muttered darkly, "I feel the evil influence of the Dark Lords and I feel their will searching for a way to pierce the temple barrier. Yet they have not found it. The barrier cannot be undone save with the Lifestone and that lies elsewhere. I thrust it through the Way Gates along with all those near me in my final battle with the *Ata'Gon*. I needed the temple clear for the final death spell I had conceived to destroy my enemy."

The elven mage's eyes clouded for a moment in doubt and worry. "However, my ancient enemy struck back at me in that crucial moment when I cast and I was forced to use all the mystic energy I had, even the energy of my mortal body itself, to give full potency to my spell. I drew the very life essence from the *Ata'Gon* and cast him down, there in the inner sanctum of the great temple, in the shadow of the great Waygates. My physical self was destroyed, but my spirit and something more was spared, and now I am, for the most part, an astral creature held together by my will and power, and bound to the Waygates whose mystic energy trapped me. To the physical world I am dead. The only consolation I have is that I destroyed that foul being the *Ata'Gon*, with my last efforts and saved the Lifestone!"

"So you don't know where this Lifestone is now? Do these dark elves want it?" Jon couldn't help but ask, this was fascinating, though he was losing track of some of what the ancient elflord was saying. Jon had always been intensely interested in the Elder races and their magic. He had spent some time learning some of their language, albeit poorly as there were no elves willing to talk with humans anymore. He was totally enraptured by what he was hearing.

"I can only think that they do desire the Lifestone and yet I sense their thoughts are focused more on the Great Temple of Elysia. Perhaps they believe the Lifestone is still trapped within, I do not know. It is puzzling. I sense they want something more." Tal'Asin sat back in his chair and blinked long and slowly. It was an unusual mannerism that Jon could not decipher.

"The answers to these questions now bring me back to the danger that faces us all once more." Tal'Asin mused in his beautifully lyrical voice.

Jon's enthusiastic fascination was quickly squashed as the fact of his imminent death was painfully brought back to him.

"You have heard the tales of the Elder races from your family and from the druids who helped teach you. You know of the nine kingdoms of my people and now of the Dark Elves that destroyed them, but you did not know the truth of how and why and who was behind that foul army. You now know and your understanding of this is key. Do you now see the threat that faces your people?"

"Yes, but why did these dark elves, these followers of this *Ata'Gon* attack? Why did the *Ata'Gon* hate your people so much? I do not understand why they would want to destroy their own kin then or now!"

Jon saw Tal'Asin's face go even blanker, if that were possible, to become almost stone like. No emotion showed on the face, yet Jon could sense the tall elven archmage's anger clearly… and something else too… Fear… Shame? Jon could not identify it.

Suddenly the Lore King thrust himself to his feet and he towered over Jon who was taken aback and sat back into his chair in dismay.

"They are evil. Is that not enough? Their dark gods drive them!" Tal'Asin stormed.

Jon could sense there was something more that Tal'Asin was not telling him.

The Lore King looked hard at Jon and it was clear he knew Jon's thoughts.

In a quiet, dangerous tone Tal'Asin said, "What you ask is forbidden, Jon Madraig. It is a tale no elf has spoken in over two thousand years!" the elven archmage thundered. "You do not know what you ask and this delay helps no one!"

Jon could see that Tal'Asin had become rigid as conflicting emotions and desires rushed through his tall frame. The very air about the mage lord began to darken and the cosy room in which they stood, vanished like smoke and was replaced by a tortured wasteland of twisted trees, broken buildings and swampy lakes as far as the eye could see.

Jon gasped at the scene and looked back wide-eyed at Tal'Asin. The Lore King was struggling to retain his calm expressionless demeanor and Jon could see that a vast fury was beginning to twist his beautiful features. Jon felt suddenly very small and helpless, like a child before a raging storm. Was this all a mistake? Was this ancient spirit really an enemy?

All at once, reason seemed to flee from the blue orbs of the Loreking and he lunged at Jon!

Chapter 39

LEGENDS AND LORE

The line of the so-called 'Druid Kings of the Cumb'Rai' is traced from the legendary King Nam'Odar the Fisher-king and his 'Elder' princess. It was said that their descendants were blessed with long life and great affinity with the mysteries. There were said to have been seven Druid-Kings and the Nordic tales say that they ruled over a golden era in Nordic history that lasted a thousand years! This was said to have come to an end with the great invasion and subsequent abduction of the last king by the mysterious 'sea people'. Of course much of the tales of the Druid-Kings are myth; embellished and distorted from the truth, but it may be that the 'sea people' were in fact the ancient Etoshans whose empire has always raided across the sea for slaves to build their mighty monuments.

Except from 'A discourse on the myths of the people of the Empire and beyond' by the historian, Casinian, BY456.

Jon was snatched up like a child and found his feet dangling off the ground and his eyes bound by the powerful gaze of the Lore King. His face was still serene, but a kind of madness glinted from those deep blue orbs and Jon knew he was utterly helpless. He knew that if Tal'Asin so chose, he could destroy Jon with a thought.

Long moments passed as Tal'Asin's savage stare seemed to rip through Jon to the core, then, as suddenly as it had come, the madness seemed to pass and with a snarl of half rage, half pain, Tal'Asin slammed Jon down. Jon stumbled back and fell. His hands sank into the stinking wet mud and he found himself sitting at the feet of the incredibly tall elf lord. Tal'Asin's face was suddenly ravaged by emotion, but the Lore King was slowly getting himself back under control.

"I am sorry…I…" Jon stammered.

"Enough, Jon Madraig, do not speak. My mind is too over wrought. Instead, listen."

Jon nodded, fear coursing through him. He feared he had gone too far.

Tal'Asin's musical voice cut through his fears. It was discordant, like each word was being torn from the elf lord.

"Much of your knowledge is confused Jon Madraig, but there is much truth in the legends and stories you learnt in your youth, just as there is truth in the beliefs of your forefathers in the Gods, the Lords of Light, though you doubt their voracity."

The great elven mage's stunning eyes looked keenly at Jon, certainty now seeming to emanate from his gaze. It was impossible to doubt this figure of power before him. Tal'Asin began to speak with a passion that was hard to ignore.

"My story starts here." Tal'Asin announced sweeping his arm around him at the tortured wilderness. "This is Hy'Deeria, the last of the fabled nine kingdoms of the elves. At least this is what it became. Once, in ancient times, it was a land of verdant forests and fertile fields. It is back to that Ancient Hy'Deeria that we must go, back thousands of years." Tal'Asin paused and leaned down. He held out his hand for Jon who hastily wiped his and accepted the Lore King's grasp. Tal'Asin pulled Jon to his feet, a calm look once more settling on his features.

"What I am about to share with you, Jon is lore long forbidden to my people and long lost among them. This terrible lore has been eradicated from our history."

Suddenly, the land around them seemed to fade and Jon found himself once more in the room they had been in mere moments before. Tal'Asin seemed to slump back into his chair, resignation seeming to deflate him.

Jon wondered if he should sit. He could still feel the dampness of the foul earth he had just been sat on.

"Sit Jon, you needn't fear ruining a chair." Tal'Asin stated, knowing Jon's mind almost better than he himself did. "The dampness is not real, anymore than any of this is." Tal'Asin waved at the room around them. Jon sat and found all dampness had indeed vanished.

"Over three thousand years ago, the elves ruled much of the lands of the north; the nine kingdoms of the elves were governed in peace and plenty. However, the ninth kingdom, Hy'Deeria was the newest then and, in truth, was not truly a kingdom of one race of elves, but of two; the silvery skinned elves who are the Children of Dah'Nu and the golden skinned Children of Tal'Osir. We met them in peace and created a land in which both races could mix and share knowledge, craft and wisdom. This was Hy'Deeria, a land of two great races and of their desire for peace. Later, this kingdom was to become the home of a new race, a race that would later term themselves the 'True Elves'!

Now these so-called True Elves were a new race created unknowingly when my people mixed with the Children of Tal'Osir. Hy'Deeria was the most easterly of our lands and stood between our kingdoms and the lands of the Children of Tal'Osir. Hy'Deeria was to be a symbol of our friendship. It was the great vision of our then Guardian, Tel'Emnar the Crafter, my master. I was but a youth, yet I can remember the joy and hope we had for the glorious future. We had met more of our own kind and though slightly different they were of like mind.

Our two races began to mix, but we did not foresee that the mixture of our two races would produce a new, more powerful race; a race more talented and driven, more passionate and powerful than those from which it was derived. However, unlike the older races, this new race of elves sought knowledge and power over the world, not power in tune with it, and they loved contest and contrivance and not the ways of the wilds and the knowledge of the lands as we had. They built tremendous cities and huge machines with magics fearsome to behold. At first we took pride in their incredible achievements, were stunned by their passion and drive, so much so that we could overlook any flaws, any differences. In all ways they looked like us save that their skin was dark and coppery while its forebears had been light and silvery or golden."

"Dark elves, like the one I fought." Jon whispered.

"Yes though that was a name they earned later.

You see in those far off days, peace reined in our lands as it had for millennia, and no elf would ever have consider harming another, but the rise of these new elves was quick as we reckon time and we did not see anything untoward in their rise until too late. Of course it was the obvious flaw in the race and our arrogance that eventually led to disaster."

Jon frowned, "Obvious flaw?" he asked quietly in spite of his fear at upsetting the strangely subdued Lore King.

"Yes. You see the inter-marriage of golden and sylvan elves produced the coppery skinned elves that you know of as dark elves, a race that is blessed with great knowledge, skill and power even more so than our own, but for every dark elf born, a dark twin was born, a lesser twin, black skinned and twisted like no elf."

"The dark goblins that accompany them," Jon gasped in astonishment.

"You are perceptive. Yes, those you know of as goblins. And it is in this lesser race that we, a fair minded race, made our greatest mistake."

"You mean the elves and goblins are kin!" Jon exclaimed then quickly grimaced as the terrible anger returned to Tal'Asin's face. Thankfully, it swiftly passed, but it was replaced by a look of intense pain.

"Yes it is painful," Tal'Asin acknowledged Jon's thoughts, "For I was a child of the time and saw this evil growing within my people." He shook his beautiful head, his golden hair flowing gently side to side. "You see, we elves are also a proud race and we saw these twisted goblin offspring as an affront to our very nature, not so much in the dark skinned twins, for they retained some of our race's long life and power. However, when they themselves had offspring, they produced grey, green and yellow skinned goblins that you now know so well. Their bodies were not only a twisted parody of our own, but their nature was twisted and chaotic too; so much less than our own. They resented us and we shunned them, even though they were our relatives, our grandchildren, nieces, nephews. We called them 'geh'obla nar' or twisted ones!"

"Goblins," Jon breathed.

Shame was clear in Tal'Asin's eyes. "For a people, to whom family and descent is vital, to disown a member of our family is terrible and yet we did that and more. We could not look on them and hated them and sought to prevent more being born. We strove to isolate them and to cure our new kin of this terrible affliction of birthing this degenerate race. Yet it was too late for that, and our view of our kith and kin, no matter how twisted they seemed to us, was one doomed to lead to conflict. It was there that evil first blossomed amongst my people. There were already many dark elves and their dark skinned twins and they, as is natural, wished to marry and have children. However, we wanted an end to this 'geh'obla nar' breed. Yet how could we end one without ending the other, they were inextricably joined. Now these new elves, as I have said, were a more passionate and aggressive people than we, and their dark brethren were even more so. Thus, it was inevitable that they would see our views and actions towards them as an attack on their very race. This was our greatest shame. We could not accept the geh'obla nar and their kind for what they were and seek to love them. Perhaps if we had things would have been different, but perhaps not; there was always a seed of chaos in our coppery skinned kin and their brethren, a touch of darkness and fiery desire that we could never understand. The trouble finally came to a head when a true leader rose amongst them.

You see when the kingdom of Hy'Deeria was created as a joint kingdom, joint rulers were sent from both races. The guardian and Lore King, Tel'Emnar the Crafter came from my people and a great princess came from the golden elves, Kiri'Thalasa Nightstar, daughter of their God-Emperor. It seems fated now, though by which gods I do not know, that those two would fall in love, and from them would come a dark elven prince and his dark twin." Tal'Asin paused in pain and remembrance.

Jon realised Tal'Asin was not now telling a story, but reliving the past.

"Tel'Emnar was my uncle, I his student, and he was the Lore King of my people. At first his children grew well and it seemed they had avoided the nature of the other dark elves. They seemed as good and noble a pair as any that had been born, yet even with the best will in the world, it became clear that Tel'Emnar's first born, the dark goblin, Tah'Rokin could not be a true heir to his father. The elven people would not accept him. Tah'Rokin knew this too and became bitter. His brother..." Tal'Asin stopped here and it seemed like he was struggling with himself, "Bah'Athamin, who was perhaps the most glorious and powerful of elven kind ever born in thousands of years, was chosen as heir in his stead. Tah'Rokin left and went into exile to rule the segregated geh'obla nar offspring who had been forced away from their families to live out of sight of tender elven eyes."

Tears suddenly ran down Tal'Asin's face. "Oh what folly!" he suddenly gasped. Tears ran down his pristine cheeks, "Our pride knew no bounds."

Tal'Asin carefully stroked the tears from his face with a delicate finger and stared at them as if he could read something from them. "Bah'Athamin became everything his father had wanted in his heir; he was gifted beyond any born to our kind since Dah'Nu and he was good and honourable in all things. In those days, all loved Bah'Athamin and saw in him the hope for the future. What we could not know then was that it was also Bah'Athamin who was in fact the dark seed amongst us. In secret, it was he who had always encouraged the hatred and rebellion in his weaker brother. He wanted his brother forced into exile for his righteous views of elves living hand in hand with geh'obla nar.

Now that I look back I dare to think that perhaps such a possibility could have been were it not for Bah'Athamin the Beautiful One." Tal'Asin's mouth twisted as he uttered that name.

"It was Bah'Athamin who wanted power more than anything. It was he who wanted to rule all elves everywhere, it was he who manipulated us all, and it was he who first contacted the Lords of Darkness to aid him; perhaps his greatest crime!"

Jon could see Tal'Asin's proud and stunning face, knot at the jaw as if the Lore King was chewing and biting off every word.

"In exile, Tah'Rokin had become the unofficial ruler of the new 'goblin' race. As Bah'Athamin acted the dutiful son and learnt all his father could teach, Tah'Rokin led the resistance to the new laws that banned the mixing of the races that inevitably came, and eventually the black goblin prince led the armed rebellion, aided of course by Bah'Athamin, the beautiful one, who betrayed all from within. It had been he who had constantly and secretly blocked all efforts at peaceful conciliation on both sides! It was he who turned the dark elves against their sylvan and golden skinned kin while pretending he was the peace maker. Bah'Athamin and Tah'Rokin allied themselves to attack and kill all who were not dark elf or goblin, in Hy'Deeria. They began a vicious war." Tal'Asin hammered his fist down on the arm of the chair and fury shone in his eyes.

"And thus the kingdom of Hy'Deeria, the hope for the future, was corrupted and became savage. So quickly, it seems now, the war came upon us and elf was killing elf. The great peace that had so long prevailed was riven asunder. Peace was sought, but the goblins and dark elves, the True

Elves as they now called themselves where implacable and intent on total devastation. We did not know it, but they had turned their worship to the Lords of Darkness under Bah'Athamin's guidance and had summoned demons and monsters to wage war on our people and on the golden elves of the east. It was all guided by Bah'Athamin, all masterminded by him and his infernal masters. Eventually, he even slew his own brother to take total control. It was Bah'Athamin who the goblins and dark elves saw as their great leader, their messiah who would free them from the evil of the sylvan and golden elves, and make them the rulers of all. Eventually, they came to call him the 'Great One', the *'Ata'Gon'*.

My people were finally forced to face the truth and pursue a war against their own kind, yet we were not prepared for the ferocity and power of the dark elves. We combined our strength with the golden elves of the east against Hy'Deeria, whose lands lay between our two, but it was not enough. We were beaten back time and again and tens of thousands died at the hands of the terrible demon allies of the dark elves! We saw no end to the war save our own destruction.

It was Tel'Emnar, the Lore King, who finally realised the truth. Finally it was he, the Guardian, who in the great extremity of our certain destruction, raised the powers of the Lifestone against Hy'Deeria and its dark prince. He drew upon the power of the Temple of Elysia and the energies of our greatest Lore Wise and focused them with the power of the Lifestone. He knew even as he cast down those great energies on Hy'Deeria and changed that once beautiful land into a poisoned hell, that he was perverting the use of that great talisman. It would cost him his life, but he was so far gone in despair at the thought of what his son had done that he would have rather died than live in the knowledge that he had allowed such a monster to live.

Some goblins survived the destruction, but the lands of Hy'Deeria were laid waste and the dark elves destroyed."

"You knew this Bah'Athamin?" Jon asked quietly, humbly, knowing the answer. "You knew this *Ata'Gon*?"

Tal'Asin did not look at Jon as he replied. His eyes looked elsewhere, into a past, long distant, and memories long buried. "Yes, I knew him." The great elven mage sighed and seemed to return from his past. He looked straight at Jon. "We were cousins, Bah'Athamin and I. I helped guide him and teach him and I trusted him, loved him. I can still remember standing by our master's side, my uncle, his father, when the son rejected the father utterly and sought to slay him. Tel'Emnar could have killed Bah'Athamin then, but as a father he could not bring himself to destroy his son, he believed him mad or ill. However, had we known then that Bah'Athamin had given his soul to the Lords of Darkness, and had we known of the terrible things he would do, things might have been different. It was only on that final day of the great war so many years later, when all had been tried and the true depths of Bah'Athamin depravity had been revealed, that Tel'Emnar could bring himself to raise his hand against his beloved and cursed son. We stood in the Temple of Elysia beneath Althazar, the high city of the Lorewise, thousands of leagues from our enemy in Hy'Deeria. Tel'Emnar used the Lifestone to destroy his only remaining family and the kingdom in which he had placed such hope. That great man was broken even before the casting of that terrible spell and did not survive the destruction of an entire race and land… his land. So it was I who took up the Lifestone and the burden of guiding our people." In an odd motion, Tal'Asin passed his hand before his face, closing his eyes wearily before continuing, "and it was I who forbid knowledge of what had happened to be passed on."

"The war had seen a great slaughter amongst our people and our allies who aided us. Although our kingdoms continued, the strength of our people was seriously depleted and would never return to the glory it had once been as the troll kingdoms and surviving goblin remnants attacked us constantly, sensing our weakness. In time, and with the constant struggle, the dark elves were slowly forgotten. However, long years passed and the knowledge of our connection to the goblins was buried and forgotten until only hatred remained. Even contact with our golden elven kin was lost as the lands between us that had once been Hy'Deeria were now a barren, poisoned wasteland from the energies that had been released in Tel'Emnar's final spell. Even if that were not so it was thought best to avoid contact in case any mixing of our blood could begin again the taint of the dark elves.

I, and all others at the time, thought the dark elves were destroyed in those poisoned lands that had once been Hy'Deeria. We searched as best we could, but it was clear that no elf could have survived the great blast of that final spell and no elf could survive there for long, the land was poisoned and the poison was anathema to us. Terrifying monsters grew there and would have quickly slain any who survived the poisons. Only goblins lived there with the monstrous mutated creatures, and they became as primitive as animals. All they remembered through the centuries was their hatred of us, but not the reason why.

However, no one ever dreamt that a remnant of the dark elves, led by Bah'Athamin, had somehow transported themselves out of those lands as the final spell struck, nor that they had husbanded their strength and their hatred for centuries to again attack us, guided still by that foul and hated creature, the *Ata'Gon* who had preserved himself with the aid of the Lords of Darkness.

Around ten centuries ago, it was Bah'Athamin and the dark elves that unified the goblin tribes under Gah'Lorg the demon possessed goblin king, a distant descendent of the twisted prince Tah'Rokin. It was the dark elves who gained the alliance of the mountain trolls, and it was they who summoned a foul army of demon spawn.

From nowhere it seemed, came a dark horde, a monstrous army that was bent on our destruction and, at the same time, there came an army of dark elves through the Waygates to attack our cities from within. Both were intent on taking the Lifestone for their dark lord so that he could enact his revenge upon our people and take his place as ruler of all!"

Jon was totally wrapped up in the tale he was hearing and couldn't help but ask, "Why? Why the armies? If they were thought long gone, why not simply come after you and the Lifestone in secret?"

"Oh, it was tried, though we did not know it was the dark elves. The dark forces have sought my death, but I am not easily killed, and in those days, even if they killed me another would take my place. My people were then well aware of the importance of the Guardian, and I had many successors. Also, had the dark elves come themselves in secret amongst us, we would have sensed their chaotic and evil nature. I also believe that Bah'Athamin wanted his revenge. He wanted my people to suffer and be destroyed. The dark elves hated us fiercely and blamed all their hardships upon us, driven, I think, by their Dark Gods and their first disciple, Bah'Athamin, the *Ata'Gon*!"

"This is incredible." Jon gasped. "I had no idea!"

"No, no one does in this time, and that is the greatest danger." Tal'Asin insisted sitting forward to look straight at Jon, his large eyes burning. "It was a grave mistake to bury the knowledge of the wars against the dark elves so long ago; our pride got the better of us; we did not want to remember such shame, to have to face our own actions in that terrible time. Later, for different reasons that mistake was repeated. Our peoples have forgotten the dark elves once more and lost much of their lore. Worst of all, the Guardian of the elves is also lost to them. This is the great scheme that I see. The dark elves are raising a new dark horde knowing that our peoples are weakened and lost; ignorance will see us fall now, as surely as battle and war. Yet, if we can join together, I can free myself and heal you. We can then start to forewarn and fore arm our peoples. We can find the Lifestone and use it against the dark elves. Without it I fear we are lost, but if the dark elves find it and open the Temple of Elysia then there is no hope!" Tal'Asin hissed; such was his passion.

He slowly blinked his large, azure eyes and Jon found himself breathing heavily, fear, anxiety and excitement coursing through him. Again, Tal'Asin made that strange gesture of passing his hand before his face and closing his eyes. A sign of respect or grief it seemed it must be.

"From your memories, I have come to understand that the final battle centuries ago between our armies and those of the dark horde went badly and that none ever returned home. The greatest leaders among our people I had gathered and taken with me to attack the *Ata'Gon* and his demon allies in Althazar as they sought to open the Temple of Elysia. We destroyed them, but were in turn almost totally destroyed. The horde was split without its leaders or demon allies, but also without our greatest leaders, the remnants of the horde were no doubt able to hound and slaughter my people." The angry Lore King shook his head in what seemed like despair. "Also, it seems that the survivors of our battle in Althazar, those I thrust through the Ways, did not ever return to our peoples and were lost somewhere here in the Ways along with the key and the knowledge of what had occurred in the Temple of Elysia."

Jon Madraig sat rigid in revelation, his eyes wide as the reason for the dark elves being under Shandrilos became clear. "They are here to find the key and reopen the Ancient Ways. They want to find the Lifestone!" he exclaimed.

"Yes," Tal'Asin whispered fervently, "Here they hope to discover the key. With it they will find the Lifestone, use it to open the Temple of Elysia, and then bring forth a second dark horde that will destroy all that is good in the world!"

Jon slapped his fist into his hand in stunned realisation, "That must have been what that dark elf thought we had and why it attacked us."

Jon slumped back. If only he and his friends hadn't decided to go down into the catacombs they would have been safe. As quickly as he thought it, it struck Jon that they would not have been safe, the danger of the dark elves would have eventually reached them and destroyed them.

Silence had settled on the strange room and the crackling of the fire could be heard. Tal'Asin sat like a statue watching Jon intently, not pressing him, but allowing him to digest what he had heard.

Jon was now privy to the most vital information in the history of his world and it seemed clear to him that he was now caught up in the middle of events that made his life seem insignificant.

Turning his gaze back to look straight into the angelic features of the Lore King, Jon found his decision was strangely still not clear to him. He had the choice of joining with this near godlike creature and giving his people, his friends and family a chance to survive the dark wave that was thundering towards them, or he could ignore all he had been told and die quietly, in some lost catacombs within a forgotten city. Why couldn't he bring himself to say yes? The correct choice was obvious.

"Your fear holds you, Jon." Tal'Asin said softly. "You fear that somehow you are still being deceived, you fear the inevitability of the choice and the fact of your impotence in influencing your destiny. You are caught up in events that are far beyond you, events that make you feel small and insignificant, and your mind and emotions cannot handle such a situation. Thus, your mind stubbornly retreats into its familiar fears. It takes comfort in them, for fear and you are old friends…"

Tal'Asin took a slow breath and his deep gaze turned stern, "but you must abandon such comforts, such fears and take the warrior's path once more. You must look your brother's shade in the eyes and act as you have always striven to do!" the tall figure proclaimed. Then, softly, he reached out and his large hand took a firm hold on Jon's shoulder and his eyes linked to Jon's. "Will you join with me, Jon Madraig of Redvale? Will you take the risk of the unknown and give our peoples a chance?"

Jon 'Bear' Madraig took a deep, strengthening breath and gave a single nod of his head.

Chapter 40

DEATH AND REBIRTH

It was said that with the loss of the last Druid-King, that the people of Cum'Rai fragmented. They had long spread and settled in different lands where their cultures diverged. With the Druid-King and his family gone, many claimants arose descended from the royal line and unity was lost. Indeed those times were dark for the Cumb'Rai who warred amongst themselves for many years and much was lost. Eventually lesser separate kingdoms came into being. Prime amongst them was Cumbra, the ancient heart of the people. However, powerful leaders and lesser princes of the royal line such as Calon the Highlander, Norn Sealord, Stell Stongarm, Varic Longstrider and Tuta the Hunter carved out their own kingdoms, while Mikadia, Zaran and Tarsia became republics ruled by powerful merchants and sea traders.

From 'Legends of the Nordic Realms' by Talinar Bal'Othir of the Mikadian Academy BY654

Zara Halven readied herself as the elves moved in for the kill. All their eyes fixed on her. Suddenly, one of the two ogres spasmed in a final death throw, its huge armed flailed out to strike the rear elf who was flung forward into the elf in front of him and both went down. Zara needed no second invitation, she quickly parried an attack from the leading elf and darted forward to slash twice at the unbalanced elves, gutting one with a slash across its lower abdomen just below its belt and then following through her swing to slice across its neighbour's thigh, crippling it. A blow to her side caused Zara to leap back sideways just dodging a disembowelling thrust from the remaining elf. Her side hit the wall and she turned to see a blade thrust coming straight for her throat. She did the only thing she could, she dropped. There was a metallic clang and Zara desperately shoved herself up and off the wall, shoulder charging the elf from its feet. She stumbled and almost fell, but kept her feet and even managed to scoop up an elven blade. She then ran. She knew she had to get away from the mass of insects that would be coming. She hoped to get past the entrance in front of her before any other enemy came down.

She ran towards the downed giants in front of the black hole that was the entrance. She saw an elf in midnight black armour and matching cloak step from the darkness of the stairs, a wicked smile on his thin, black lips. Time seemed to slow. The elf's eyes met Zara's and she felt the hatred in that large, black eyed gaze. Zara knew instantly that this elf was no common soldier. He must have been the most senior officer left. This was the creature that had obviously planned this ambush and probably killed her friends.

Rage arose within Zara and her face contorted in fury. She forgot about fleeing and with a roar of pure emotion, she sprang at the grinning elf, her two blades leading the way. She had no thought for the mass of insect creatures that no doubt bore down on her. Somewhere inside herself, she had accepted that she would die, but she wanted to at least take this slanty-eyed bastard with her and get some vengeance for her friends!

So it was that her attack showed no finesse. It was almost a diving leap, sword points aimed for the elf's thin chest. The elf was clever though and quick. He had obviously guessed what Zara's reaction would be, what she would do. The elf was already moving to parry and dodge to the side of Zara's mad attack even as she began it. Desperately, Zara tried to change her attack, to slice sideways at the agile elf. It was no use, the elf had slipped around her attack and Zara struggled to catch herself on the first steps of the stairwell. She knew she had no time to turn or parry the elf's next blow. The foul creature would skewer her through the back.

In a last ditch attempt to give herself a few more seconds and fight to the very end, Zara simply threw her whole body backwards. Instead, she was slammed forward and pinned to the steps! She felt no pain, but then she had heard it was sometimes so. Suddenly, she could feel no weight on top of her. She waited for death to take her...

"Are you just going to lie there all day?"

'What!' Zara spun around and looked up. She could see a figure, a large figure. It was in shadow from a blazing glow of fiery energy that was stretched across the corridor blocking the attack of the small horde of insects and goblins beyond. Zara leapt to her feet. Out of the corner of her eye she saw the body of the elf at which she had lunged. It had been almost completely cut in half. There was a huge wound in its side that had crashed through its armour.

"Who...?" Zara began and then stopped, the words sticking in her throat as she saw her saviour's face. "Bear!" she gasped.

"I can't hold this for much longer... I didn't even know I could hold it for this long." Bear replied a wide grimace on his face, his bald shaven head gleaming in the light from the magical shield he had created.

Zara reacted quickly. She spun around, grabbed her swords from the steps and leapt up. She saw Bear still standing, holding the magical barrier. Zara couldn't believe who had saved her and didn't understand how, unless Garon and Rebba's healing was more powerful than she, or even they had thought. She turned and jumped towards the stairs to dash up when Bear's voice stopped her. "No, not that way, we must go to Garon and Rebba in the Portal Hall."

Zara stopped and turned in surprise and confusion, "We must what?" She shook her head. "They are alive? Where are they?" She asked quickly.

Bear responded by nodding back through his magical barrier to where they had set up their camp.

Zara looked at her friend like he was insane. 'Perhaps the blow to his head has driven him mad' was the thought that flicked through Zara's head. The cuts and scars had been healed through Rebba and Garon's efforts, but obviously the internal damage was untouched.

"We can't go that way, as soon as your barrier goes we will have more than a score of elves, goblins and those bug men on us in an instant!"

Bear seemed to nod in agreement, but then replied in a voice tight with exertion. "I think I can warp my barrier to surround us and can use its energy to drive through them!"

"You are mad!" Zara snapped angrily. "That blow has addled you wits and you're now having dreams of grandeur. I know enough about magic from when we were younger to know not even Arkadi could manage that. It goes against those immutable laws of spell craft or whatever."

Bear seemed to ignore Zara, so deep in concentration he seemed. Zara decided to grab the mad fool and pull him up the stairs. As she stepped out to grab the big man, the energy shield seemed to twist and bend around them. Insect men fell forward in confusion. They quickly skittered to their feet and threw themselves at the barrier that now curved around Zara and Bear, hammering at it in renewed fury. A high pitched wail issued forth from their smooth heads.

Zara looked around her in fear. She was only a hands breadth from her enemies now and she could see the fiery energy of Bear's shield reflected a thousand times in those inhuman, insect eyes.

"Walk forward with me, Zara. You must stay close to me I cannot extend the shield and I can feel my control slowly slipping so we must move quickly."

Zara shuffled up to Bear's back and hissed, "This is unbelievable. When did you learn to do this?"

Bear didn't reply. He continued to walk forward slowly, pushing the enemy back out of his way. However, Zara could see around Bear's armoured shoulder that the elves had quickly deduced their purpose and were barking orders at their jet skinned goblin allies to throw themselves against the front of the shield.

Bear grunted with strain from their efforts. "I'm afraid, Zara that you might have been right." Bear gasped. Sweat was pouring from him now. "I think that…" He stopped suddenly and tilted his head as if listening to something. He shook his head and muttered something under his breath and then nodded sharply.

Zara wondered whether she had been right after all about more than just which way they should go. Bear appeared to be talking to himself!

"Kneel down now, Zara and cover your head!" Bear hissed and crouched down to grasp a sword lying at his feet.

Zara looked at him.

Bear's hand shot back up and dragged Zara forward by her breastplate. "Kneel down, you fool!" he snapped.

There was a sudden whoosh of air and then an almighty crack. Zara felt herself pushed down painfully. Quickly she leapt back up, Bear following her up. Around them the insect creatures and goblins were lying flat out like grass knocked over in a strong wind. Bear had released his shield in a way that had somehow blasted outwards.

"How did you..."

Zara began, but Bear grabbed her and snapped, "Oh you're just full of questions today aren't you?" He dragged Zara forwards, "Run!"

With that the burly warrior jumped over the groaning goblins in front of him and dashed for the wall just opposite the stairs they had come down what seemed like days ago.

"Run where?" Zara cried desperately even as she gave chase. She made sure to step on as many goblins as she could on her way past. This all made no sense to Zara.

Suddenly, she almost stopped dead in surprise even though behind her she knew the elves, goblins and insects were already rising to pursue them. Out of the wall ahead she saw Rebba's fiery haired head and upper body poke out as if she were a ghost or spirit.

"Come on Zara." Bear yelled and Zara ran on in utter confusion.

She had no idea whether she had gone mad, was still asleep and dreaming, or had died already and the gods were playing some kind of cruel joke on her, but she ran. She saw Rebba disappear into the wall and Bear leap after her. Zara held her breath and launched herself, closing her eyes, expecting the crack of her skull on solid rock and the laughter of some cruel deity, but it never came. Instead she felt the crack of her head into Bear's armoured back and heard Garon's voice shouting, "Seal the entrance, Rebba!"

Chapter 41

A HIDDEN SANCTUARY

King Earondar Greatheart united all the lands of the Nordic. This began with his fortuitous birth as he was the heir to the Kingdom of Cumbra through his father and the Kingdom of Calonia through his mother. In his youth, he then married the heir to the Kingdom of Tutonia. With these three powerful kingdoms as his base, along with the training and guidance of the greatest druid of the time, Gilarnur the Grey, the Greatheart quickly managed to conquer the powerful Mikadian Empire, which at that time controlled Tarsia and Zaran. The Varitian Principalities then quickly fell into line after that. Eventually, even the fierce Norns and reclusive Stellici agreed to join him. In a generation, Earondar had managed to reunite the Nordic as they had not been united since the fall of the Druid-Kings centuries before.

From 'Legends of the Nordic Realms' by Talinar Bal'Othir of the Mikadian Academy BY654

Several hours later and Bear could see that Zara still struggled to understand what was going on.

"I don't believe it!" she almost yelled, "That is the most fantastical and ridiculous tale I have ever heard."

She paced back and forth in the huge hall. Zara had been pacing for some time now, listening to Bear's story.

They were in the great empty space that lay somehow hidden and blocked to the outside world, the Portal Hall as they now knew it. It was within the circle of the great corridor in which they had so recently been camped and then attacked.

The group already knew from looking through the magically hidden entrances to the Portal Hall that the surviving elves and their allies had tried in vain to enter after them. However, the enemies' efforts to get at them had meant that Darin, Nat and Arkadi had a much better chance of making it to the surface.

The hall they were in was wide and empty save for nine archways that dominated the centre of the room. Each of them pointing in different directions and each was as wide as two carts and as tall as a two storey house! Otherwise the walls and ceiling of the gigantic Portal Hall were completely white and featureless. Zara, Rebba and Garon had been there for some time as they listened to Jon's incredible tale of what had happened to him.

"It explains a lot." Rebba said thoughtfully. "A lot of what we knew of those times has come from story and it fits with every tale I have ever heard tell..." Zara moved to interrupt, but the druid continued, "and..." she stressed, "it explains the whole reason for not only those fiendish elves and their creatures being here in these tunnels after this key," she held out the ordinary seeming stone that had allowed them entrance to the hall, "but also the whole reason for the fall of the kingdoms of the Elder!"

"Horse crap!" Zara barked. "It is a fanciful tale that gives credit to other fanciful tales."

"Then how else do you explain these things, Zara?" Garon asked quietly from where he sat with his back against the wall.

Garon Vale looked weary eyed at Zara. The stress of the last few hours was clearly showing on the monk.

Garon was almost camouflaged where he sat, his holy white tabard blended with the near perfectly smooth white stone of the rounded outer wall. "You would discredit all the teachings of your childhood, all the beliefs of your people in the Elder races so quickly and so easily?"

Zara merely threw up her hands and shook her head angrily. She walked around somewhat aimlessly for a moment or two before throwing herself down to sit in a heap on the floor, disconsolately.

Abruptly, her head came up and she stared with red rimmed eyes at her three friends, "This just doesn't make sense to me, that's all. It's all too big, too grand." Her head went down again and Garon and Rebba both looked at her in surprise and then at their newly recovered friend whose tale seemed so fantastic. They had never seen Zara so affected.

Jon Madraig sat motionless, watching while Zara sat huddled on the stone floor. He knew her better than anyone and was wary about how to explain. She was always at her most violent and volatile when emotional.

However, even before Jon had a chance to respond to the silent plea he could see in Rebba Korran's eyes to do something, the angry warrior woman muttered, her head down and her voice muffled slightly, "I'll grant you that those slanty-eyed freaks were after that key and for that alone we should make sure they don't get it, but open up these damned Ways and go after some lost stone. It's madness!"

The dark haired head of Zara Halven rose wearily, "Surely we have done our part? We can't go off to the gods-only-know-where hunting this thing. We have no idea of the danger on the other side of those gates." She pointed at Jon, "Even our suddenly all-knowing friend here doesn't know where exactly this artifact might be and what might be with it!"

"There is no one else, Zara. Don't you see? We are being given a quest from the gods themselves!" Rebba said fiercely. "The merging of Bear and Tal'Asin was meant to happen, Tal'Asin is a servant of the Earth Mother herself and so is Jon now!"

"Bah, you're such a trusting fool Rebba. Bear... a servant of the gods... ha! You are so eager to believe because you want to. It is everything you ever wanted in the world, you and your bloody druids. We only have Bear's word on this," she paused, "and who's to say that whack on his head didn't drive him insane." Zara snorted derisively."He always had too much of that Elder shit in his head!"

Garon sat forward suddenly, "Zara, his healing was a miracle. There was no way he could have survived those injuries, certainly not recover from them virtually instantly and be hale and whole again, and then perform the feats of magic he did to save us! You can't deny that." the monk insisted.

Zara face dropped at this, she couldn't deny the truth in that.

"There is some divine hand involved here, whether it be the old gods or not." Garon finished firmly.

Zara Halven nodded loosely and thumped on her leg with her fist, "Okay... If that's the case then why couldn't these gods have performed this miracle a little earlier." the warrior snarled. "Then our friends wouldn't be fleeing for their lives out there and we'd all be together." Zara looked angrily at her friends. "We should be out there helping them!"

Silence fell over the room for a few moments.

"Well? What about our friends?" Zara asked. "They are out there..."

"And well on their way to the surface," Jon interrupted firmly, no room for doubt in his tone. "Those elves spent the best part of an hour trying to find a way in here and none of their creatures pursued the others." He shook his head. "The dark elves want the keystone; that was their purpose. The others are safely away and have an important mission of their own. I cannot sense them close by." Jon looked to Rebba for confirmation.

Rebba stared at Jon. "It is hard to sense far over the magical emanations of this room and I am absolutely exhausted. I can't even think straight."

"Aye," Garon nodded his agreement.

Rebba Korran said earnestly, "Our friends are away and there is no way we should be making any decisions now. We need rest." She climbed slowly to her feet to retrieve her pack and blankets.

Soon all followed suit, all save Zara who sat still and quiet, hunched over, her head down. Jon knew that she blamed himself for what she saw as the mess they had got themselves into., though she would never admit it.

It was not long before Garon was asleep and Rebba soon followed. Jon was just about to settle down too when Zara looked over bleary eyed.

"Do you think we need to have a person on watch?"

Jon could see the pain in her eyes and knew this was a tender question for Zara who had been on watch earlier when the ambush happened. Jon stared hard into Zara's blood shot eyes. "This is the safest place we could be right now, Zara. It would take a force of massive magic to locate this place let alone enter it."

Zara looked worn out both mentally and physically. "Could we have avoided this, Bear?" she asked quietly.

Jon knew what Zara needed to hear from him and answered without hesitation. "No, Zara. I believe this was meant to happen. Without this... and us, the elves would now have the keystone and all would be lost. I think maybe the gods have a purpose in this."

Zara smiled, "You really think so, Bear. Neither you nor I ever had much faith in the gods, old or new. I always saw life as just a struggle and when we die we're simply worm food. Do you really think someone is up there looking out for us?"

Jon simply nodded, though he still had his own doubts.

Zara heaved a weary sigh. "Well let's hope that Darin can run fast in that bloody armour of his then or he'll be swatting bugs off his arse soon."

Jon smiled at the image and Zara chuckled. It was good that she seemed to be returning to her old self, though Jon could clearly see the stress in her still. "Sleep, Zara. Rest." he urged.

The two old friends stared at each other for a moment, each reading in the other a reassurance that they needed. Both blinked and then Zara sighed and nodded before reaching for her pack. Jon lay back and wondered where the voice of Tal'Asin had vanished to. However, sleep took him almost as soon as he closed his eyes.

It was a sleep so deep for all of the bone weary and soul weary group that none of them even stirred with the rumbling that shook the room not long after. Far above them the catacombs reeled with the collapse of the first hall.

Chapter 42

THE MERGING

The excavation of the tomb has shown that this is part of a large complex of rooms that house a remarkable collection of relics. Of course after so long, little other than metal and stone remain. The workmanship on the relics is crude and of a style similar to that on ancient standing stones. We know that the monoliths erected by our earliest ancestors date back almost three thousand years. The similarities in script and art itself indicate this tomb could be as old. Crude translations of the runic script on the tomb itself point to this being the final resting place of one of the earliest kings of the Cumb'Rai, perhaps even that of My'Sed the Mighty, who settled our people in these lands!

Excerpt from a letter from Alenur Uldarin, Duke of Sakoom to the Council of Princes in Cumbra, BY1287.

There were faces and places he had never seen before; places of wonder and magnificence beyond what he thought possible. He saw elves, everywhere elves. They walked the twisting lanes of a city of soaring spires, a city glowing with power. Scenes switched to deep forests with the mighty trunks of trees rising as tall as any spires, and amid them almost unseen, buildings of such natural hue and architecture that they seemed to merge seamlessly with the silent glade. Then again things changed. He was riding on some mighty beast, flying at a terrifying speed, the wind whistling in his face; then he was floating gently amid the clouds, a mighty ship beneath him; again a change and he was aloft and could see the world spread out below him like a map.

Places changed to people. He saw the faces of elves, dwarves, men and other races he could not quite put name to, yet knew nonetheless. Faces started to blur and colours whirled in his mind, but amid all this he saw a stone, carved with ancient symbols and thrumming with power. It was a gem the size of his fist, a green emerald that glowed with an inner light. He knew instantly it was the Lifestone, the talisman given to the elves by Elysia, Lady of Light and Life. He knew it, though he had never seen the stone before.

'Jon, awake. We must go. Time is pressing.' whispered a voice in Jon 'Bear' Madraig's head, a voice he knew so well and yet was so alien to him; the voice of Tal'Asin, the long dead Lore King of the elves.

Jon's eyes snapped open and pain pierced him. He gasped even as he sat up. He grabbed his head in both hands, shutting his eyes. The light in the hall was too dazzling. Sharp points of pain exploded in his eyes and his head and body ached as fiercely as if he had been beaten.

'What, by the nine hells, was wrong with him?' he thought. When he had gone to sleep he had felt healthier than he had in his entire life. Now, suddenly, it was hard to think, hard to remember and pain was swelling larger. He gritted his teeth to prevent a harsh cry from escaping his lips.

Slowly, the pain began to recede, leaving only the harsh aching throughout his body. He wondered if he should try to open his eyes again and then tentatively squinted.

"Gods of Light!" he exclaimed and opened his eyes fully. 'What was he seeing?'

'You are beginning to see as an elf would.' came the silent response in his mind.

'As an elf...' he thought in wonder. He looked around the large open expanse that was the circular hall of the portal. On the walls he saw pictures and patterns that had been hidden. Before the walls had seemed white, blank and featureless, now he saw landscapes and figures. He looked around at his friends still sound asleep. This had been the first decent sleep any of them had had in the last two days. However, now when he looked at them he did not just see his friends, he also saw that they seemed to glow with a reddish-light and that reddish smoke seemed to emanate from them.

'You are seeing their body heat. Elves have vision that encompasses a greater spectrum.'

'This is incredible... but how?'

'Your body is changing Jon. It is an unexpected result of the merging.'

Jon felt a slight chill. 'Unexpected?'

'There was no way to know what would happen with our merging. I am not of your people and neither am I purely a spirit. Somehow our merging has begun changes in you that I did not foresee. I had thought that my spirit and soul would reside with yours within your physical body. My spirit and soul would be linked to you, allowing me to communicate through you and travel with you and even give you aid as I did when you saved your friends, but it seems more is happening. I believe that the legacy of my connection to the Lifestone has allowed me to maintain myself as more than a spirit and soul and this is affecting you, changing you.'

Jon was shaking his head. 'I don't understand. How am I changing?'

'I believe you are becoming something new, something that has not been before. My elven nature is fusing with your human one and it is remoulding you to fit with this new elven-human hybrid.'

'I definitely don't like the sound of that. I am me. I don't want to change. I'm happy being me... at least for the most part. What is going to happen? Am I going to get pointy ears and silver skin?'

There was silence in his mind. 'Well?' he shouted into that silence even as he realised what a ridiculous question he had asked.

'Jon, already you have changed. Your eyes have become more elven in looks as well as in vision. Your senses are increasing and your body is changing to more match my elven nature but...' Tal'Asin's voice insisted sensing the rising panic and anger in Jon, *'you are also still fundamentally the same. There is more of you than I. You will still be you'.*

Jon calmed a little at this. A thought occurred to him. 'So, are you saying that I will develop elven senses and abilities, but will also retain my own nature as a human? I will still be me?'

'I believe so...'

'Well that doesn't sound too bad so long as I don't begin to look like some kind of freak... well no more than I do already.' Jon chuckled to himself. 'I suppose I can't get much uglier.' He paused and thought hard. 'Certainly, elven senses would be handy and elven speed and agility, if that is allied to my strength... No offence, but you elves are a bit too spindly for my liking... Well then that should give me something of an edge in fighting these dark elves, shouldn't it... and with your magical knowledge and some of your magical ability then we might actually have a chance of retrieving the Lifestone.' Jon realised he was beginning to babble, but he suddenly felt more like they had a chance of achieving what still seemed near impossible.

There was no answer to Jon's thoughts.

'Well, Tal'Asin, what do you think?'

'What you say could well be true. However, there is something else...'

Jon swallowed slowly. There was an ominous feeling to Tal'Asin's thoughts. 'What is it?' he managed.

Again, there was a long silence from Tal'Asin and then, just as Jon was about to ask again, the ancient Lore King responded.

'I believe that not only is your physical self merging with what was preserved of mine, but also your spirit... your mind.'

Jon frowned. "But hasn't that happened already? Isn't that why we can share thoughts and talk in my mind?'

'No. I simply reside with you. However, already I can feel my spirit and mind becoming entangled with yours. Already you are starting to see into my memories. Before long our memories will merge and then our thoughts.'

Jon was confused. 'I don't know why you're worried about that. It sounds like we will be able to work together better if I share what you know and we think as one.'

'Jon, you don't understand what will happen. We will in essence both cease to be!'

"What, die!" Jon said out loud in surprise. 'But I thought this merging would save my life and allow you to help us defeat the Dark Elves.'

'Yes, yes, as did I, and it has Jon, but this is new to me and too unpredictable. This has never been done before and I had no way of knowing exactly what would happen, yet it was the best option for both of us.'

'But you just said we will die! How is this better with us both dying. Did it simply allow us a little more time?' Jon thought desperately.

'It was you who said die. Die is not the correct word. We will cease to be as we have been. I believe you will become a new being, a spiritual hybrid with the thoughts and memories of us both though essentially still yourself.' Tal'Asin seemed to muse.

'What?'

'We will cease to be as we were before. I will merge with you fully and will cease to be as I was. You on the other hand will retain more of who you were but may well... suffer' Tal'Asin finished quietly, hesitantly.

'Suffer?' Jon cried in the silence of his mind. 'How will I suffer?'

'You may well be driven insane by the merging.'

Jon's mind reeled and he blinked in mute surprise and dismay. It took him a moment to regain his thoughts. 'Dying, now insanity, at least that's a slight improvement for me.' Jon snapped bitterly, his mental tone dripping sarcasm.

'Don't be foolish, boy!' Tal'Asin's voice admonished in Jon's skull. *'There is too much at stake for you to be flippant. The fate of both our peoples depends on us retrieving the Lifestone and we are their only hope. Fate has placed you at the heart of great events. Do not joke!'*

Jon quailed inwardly at the thunderous rebuke, but then his familiar response to his fear arose and anger boiled up. 'I did not ask for this nor want this! You may be on familiar ground with saving the world, battling dark elves and mighty magic but I am just a man, AN ORDINARY MAN AND I DON'T WANT TO GO MAD.' Jon calmed at the enormity of the situation and finished, subdued. '... or die!'

There was a pause and then Tal'Asin's response was both gentle and understanding, *'Forgive me. Things have not gone the way either of us would want. You and I were both chosen by fate and we cannot avoid our destiny.* Tal'Asin insisted. *'I do not know why the gods have placed us in this position, your mind was never meant to hold the knowledge I have or to contain the memories of millennia. Your mind could easily be torn apart by the inundation of knowledge and experiences so much greater than the human mind was meant to cope with. A human of talent in the mysteries might live a century or more of your years. I have already existed for thirty times that. Thirty lifetimes into one human mind; I cannot foresee that you will survive the process with your mind intact. However, if fate is kind to us, the process will be slow enough that we can recover the Lifestone and find a new Guardian to take my place...'*

'Before I go insane,' Jon finished the thought.

'Yes.' was the soft reply.

Jon's head dropped and he stared at the floor which he now saw in more intense detail than ever in his life. 'And are you so sure of this? Could you be wrong?'

Silence again answered his question. Jon waited, determined to gain a reply.

'It is possible your mind may survive the merging...but unlikely. However, if a new Guardian is chosen, they may well be able to take my spirit within them so that I might pass on what I know and leave you unharmed.'

Jon heart rose at this.

'However, even if this is possible, we need to strive to remain separate so I think it is better if I communicate with you as little as possible and try to keep my spirit free of yours. Perhaps then we can delay what is to come.'

Jon nodded slowly, staring disconsolately at nothing.

Tal'Asin sensed his feelings. *'You must not doubt yourself, Jon. We can do this. Fate has chosen you and you are worthy, Jon Madraig. You are a strong man with a hero's heart. Believe me. I have known many such men and they all had their doubts and fears. Even Earondar, your king of legend, had his doubts. It was how they overcame them that proved their worth and you will do as they.* Tal'Asin paused for a moment to let his words sink in and Jon could not help but be affected by them. This was a man who had known the greatest heroes in his people's history. He would know.

Tal'Asin's voice returned urgently. *'You must convince your friends to help us find the Lifestone. We need all the help we can to find it and we have little time to do so, I fear. Already our enemies are searching. We have little time. Your rest was necessary, but now we must move or lose any initiative we have gained. I will seek more information of our enemies and set a shield about you to prevent any scrying by others while you search for the Lifestone.'*

Jon suddenly knew that Tal'Asin was no longer there. It was like a hole had appeared in his mind. 'Damn,' he thought bitterly, 'saved from death only to face a descent into madness.'

He rose slowly allowing his aching body to stretch and found it took a moment for him to gain his balance, his senses were all over the place and the light was giving him a headache already. His eyes might have changed, but his mind was struggling to keep up!

Jon moved over to wake his friends. He gave them a quick shake and said it was time to be up and then headed off to have a better look at the Waygates themselves; the gates they would have to open and pass. The passage itself was not a worry; it would be over in an instant. It was what would be on the other side to greet them that worried Jon. He knew Tal'Asin's thoughts.

401

The Waygates here in what had been the Elder kingdom of Dah'Ryllah joined to a number of others, including the holy city of Althazar where the final battle had been fought centuries before. There was a brief flash of memory in his mind of elves, dwarves and men, heroes all, waiting to enter that Waygate to face the might of the *Ata'Gon*.

Of course, Jon and his friends would not pass that gate. Tal'Asin had already said that the enemy held the holy city. It would be certain death and pointless too as Tal'Asin had sent the Lifestone away from there. No, the talisman would lie elsewhere. Where, was the great question and one Tal'Asin had been unable to answer. He could sense the stone, but not locate it. It had been a desperate last spell that he had used so long ago and he could not say where he had sent the Lifestone in that final cataclysmic moment.

Tal'Asin had told Jon that the Waygates connected like a spider web with Althazar at the centre of a web of connections so that it connected with five other ancient kingdoms. Two of those could be reached from where they now stood; Shah'Namir, the great forest kingdom; and the ruined kingdom of ancient Hy'Deeria, the former homeland of the dark elves that had been destroyed two millennia ago. Tal'Asin had not even speculated on what they might have to face if they had to go to Hy'Deeria. Jon had decided not to inform his friends of that possibility. It was his hope that the talisman would lie in Shah'Namir or one of the other kingdoms that could be reached from there. His friends would be wary enough of going through the Waygates without the possibility of entering a hellish place like the dead swamps of Hy'Deeria.

Focusing outwards on the Waygates, Jon found that even without the presence of Tal'Asin in his mind, his own perceptions had greatly increased. He could now see the weaves of magic that made up the myriad of spells and enchantments that were laid across them. Just a day ago he'd had no knowledge that such weaves existed. His knowledge of spell craft related to pre-constructed spells that he had learnt from his masters or from research. He had only just begun trying to manipulate spells to adapt their results, something only masters were capable of. Now it seemed he had gone far beyond his masters, at least in perceptions, though he was sure his magical talent was growing too.

The Waygates were made of the same kind of unidentifiable black rock that the college of magic was made from. Jon was suddenly surprised to realise that he knew where the rock had come from and how it had been made. It was steelstone from the mountains of Cor'Tuvor, the lost Elder kingdom in the far north. The steelstone rock had been magically altered to make it more durable and resistant to magic using something he could only term as 'antimagic', a negative energy that opposed ordinary magic – if that wasn't a contradiction in terms!

Jon shook his head. Such concepts were beyond him and he was finding it hard to concentrate. He was being inundated with information. In his mind he could see the process of enhancing the steel stone being carried out, and could see the weaves and hear the magical intonations and see enchantments and feel energies and...

"Ahh." Jon gasped and rubbed his hand across his brow. He clenched his teeth and tried to shut out the information. What he could see were magics that he was not equipped to deal with or understand. He stumbled forward and leaned on the smooth surface of the nearest Waygate, trying to get his mind back under control. It was like he had accessed something, had opened a door in his mind and a flood had burst through it. Slowly, he gained control and stood, slamming the door in his mind.

"You alright, Bear?" he heard Rebba call out.

"Yeah, fine." he replied and turned...

He was unprepared for his friend's reactions. Zara swore and Rebba just stared at him open mouthed, while Garon reflexively made the circle sign of Alba and muttered some kind of blessing. Jon stared at them in turn.

He stepped forward, "What is it?" he asked perplexed.

His friends moved forward warily. "What happened to you, Bear?" Zara asked staring intently at his face and then moving her gaze across him with a look like she had just seen a dog speak and didn't believe it.

"What do you mean, what happened to me? Nothing..." he responded puzzled.

Zara moved forward, a deep frown marring her smooth forehead. "But your eyes... and skin?"

Jon suddenly remembered the changes that had begun in him were both mental and physical. He saw Zara shake her head in near disbelief.

"Your skin has some kind of silver sheen to it and your eyes... your eyes are blue and they seem to shine!" the warrior finished, somewhere between aghast and amazed. "Is this some kind of elven magic, Bear?"

Jon looked to Rebba and Garon. They both nodded at his unspoken question. Rebba moved to stand before him, a look of genuine intrigue on her open face.

"I think you have also got thinner, Bear."

Jon looked at the druid and frowned. He looked down at himself then raised a hand to his face as if to touch his eyes. He saw his hand. He stopped and stared. His hand was silvery. Not quite like an elf, but certainly not human either. "The merging…" he managed to mutter. His friends looked at him blankly. Even though he knew what was happening, it was still a surprise to see. "I am changing as my human nature mixes with that of Tal'Asin. Some of what he was, is affecting me, altering me."

"What are you going to change into an elf?" Zara gasped.

Jon shook his head, "No," he grimaced, "I am still human, though I am also becoming partly elven too. It is a consequence of Tal'Asin's spirit merging with mine."

Rebba was nodding. "The physical shell will always mirror the spirit and soul and yours are now changed so the body seeks to mirror that change." Rebba looked to Garon and Zara. "It is not unheard of amongst the druids. Those among my order who seek to become more at one with the wilds will sometimes link themselves with a powerful animal spirit and in so doing seek to become like the animal. It is an integral part of shape shifting."

"Shape shifting is evil." Garon put in firmly. "The teachings of Alba forbid it. A man must retain his pure spirit if he is to enter heaven. Merging with beasts is an abomination in the eyes of God."

"Maybe to your god, Garon," Rebba snapped, before quickly calming and adding, "However, shape shifting is dangerous and frowned upon as many lose themselves to the animal side and go insane!"

Jon started involuntarily and Zara looked at him sharply, a question on her lips, but Rebba continued.

"Still this is not a merging with an animal. Jon has merged with a great and holy being, the beloved of Sarahiri, the Earth Goddess herself!" Rebba added. She had a gleam of joy in her green eyes.

Zara responded to this by snorting and going over to sit by her pack and blankets and begin packing things away. Rebba looked at Garon and then Jon as if to say, 'What?'

Chapter 43

PROPHECY AND DECISION

*Of the seven lords of colours, many stories are told,
Unsleeping and unfailing, they guarded the king.
Dragon wrought legacy of elder lore and craft,
Each an armour with weapon given; duty bound.*

*Blood red the killing axe, bourn by Aelfin of Uth Dar,
Silver the heralding spear, taken forth with Garin the Bold,
Golden the hammer, in the just hand of Haru'My,
Black the blade, bane of evil, swung by Fin the Seeker
White the shield of healing on the arm of Maru'Dor
Green the avenging arrow from the bow of Loth'Arn
Grey the mystic staff wielded by Maidhlin the Wise*

*To the sword of ice, greatest weapon of Cumb'Rai,
They were sworn to serve till the end of their days
That mightiest of blades holds still the minds of all.
Defenders of the realm from darkness' lords.*

Translation from an inscription found in a collapsed tomb complex discovered beneath the city of Sakoom in Cumbra, BY1287 (translated from ancient Nordic by Alenur Uldarin, Duke of Sakoom)

Garon Vale grimaced slightly and then said out loud. "So what is the plan then? Do we go after the stone or not?"

Zara stopped packing and looked over at the others with a harsh look. Rebba and Jon took the opportunity to sit down.

Zara looked at them both, "I still think its madness to even consider it." She looked each of her friends in the eyes seeking signs of agreement. "We are four people, four! We are not heroes." Zara spat. "Where are our magic swords, our armies?" she asked savagely, looking at her friends in turn. "We are not equipped to fight something that not even the Elder races could defeat," she insisted.

"We don't have to defeat anything, Zara, we just have to find the stone." Rebba replied, her tone soft and persuasive. "We go through the Waygate and on the other side are lost cities and ruins, not dark elves or goblins. No one has lived in those ruins for centuries. There's no need for magic weapons or armies. It will be quickly in and done before they even know what is going on. Isn't that right Jon?"

Jon shifted slightly and he couldn't help the slightly pained expression that crossed his face. "Yes we pass through the Waygate and..."

"Hold on a minute," Zara butted in, "I saw that look, Bear; things aren't that simple, are they? After all, we all know what can be found in ruins and lost cities, remember." Zara exclaimed, gesturing around them at the ancient city. "We are in one now and look what happened to us." she said bitterly. "Quickly in and out, yeah I remember saying just that not more than a day ago, Rebba. Things just don't always work out that way."

Rebba sat forward and put in quickly, but gently, "You should not feel responsible for what's happened."

Zara growled angrily and glared at Rebba. The druid pressed on nevertheless.

"We all chose to come. We are all responsible for where we are; we all knew what we were doing. We were just unlucky to be in the wrong place at the wrong time."

"Or the right place at the right time." Garon Vale softly added.

Zara immediately scowled at the white clad monk's piety.

"What God has ordained..." Garon began.

"Don't you dare bring your bloody religion into this, Garon." Zara stormed, leaping up. She pointed at the pained looking monk, who seemed to have half expected his friend's response. "You and your new found belief in the 'oh so pure' Alba... Bah! Only a few years ago you were a washed up drunkard who was having trouble speaking and keeping the contents of his gut down. You've gone from a fat loser spewing out vomit to a fat loser spewing out crap!" Zara snarled. She had always mistrusted religion of any kind.

Rebba leapt to her feet and grabbed Zara as she moved threateningly towards the large monk. Garon merely stood meekly accepting the abuse.

"You go too far, Zara. Garon has done something with his life. He has something to believe in, something to live for. You, of all people should be careful of what you say." Rebba added anger now clear on her face too. "You have nothing in your life. You believe in nothing and have spent your own share of time in the gutter and worse from all the stories we have heard!"

Garon said quietly, "Please Rebba, let her speak, it is nothing that I have not said of myself. I have come to terms with my past and am secure in my faith. Her words are merely that... words."

Rebba looked at Garon in surprise. Eventually, she nodded, sensing the depth of her friend's belief. Zara too seemed somewhat taken aback by the monk's response.

Garon looked understandingly at Zara, "You are right about what I was, but you cannot understand what I am now. I have faced my demons and am better for it. I do believe in the teachings of Alba, but not in dogma and strict church law that you think of as the beliefs of the Alban faith. I believe in the true teachings of the great Prophet, teachings that the Grand Abbot Alinus was forced from the holy lands for discovering and seeking to spread. The true followers of Alba do not believe in the strict laws of the church. The Albanite church has become corrupt and intolerant, unbending and occupied with irrelevancies. Alba believed in good and evil, in God as the personification of goodness, order and life and the devil and his minions as the personification of evil. Do good to those around you and evil diminishes; do evil and it flourishes. For many this seems too simplistic a view of life, yet if a person sticks to their beliefs, it really is that simple. That message has been lost by the church. The church has interfered in people's lives and forgotten what it is really there to do."

Garon nodded at Zara seeking her understanding, but the angry warrior merely snapped. "Albans believe that you should not fight evil because in doing so you become evil yourself. What kind of a belief is that?" Zara asked spreading her arms and looking to the ceiling in mock dismay. "If we all followed your beliefs we would be lying back saying come and do what you wish and all of us would be dead."

Garon was shaking his large head, his eyes closed. He stopped and looked hard at Zara. "If everyone did follow that teaching there would be no one to do anything evil to you, but that is not the point, Zara, Albans do not believe in leaving evil unopposed. They do understand the danger in doing so. There is the danger that someone who fights evil may well become as evil themselves. That is why we constantly seek guidance from God and strive to defend the weak while not succumbing to the temptations to punish our enemies." the portly monk insisted. "We forgive our enemies even as we fight them. To hate them is to succumb to evil."

Zara seemed practically stunned. "Forgive your enemies as you fight them. You are mad!"

"No, Zara, he is not," put in Rebba quickly. "The druids too believe that hate is the first step towards darkness."

"Oh, marvellous!" Zara called out in exasperation and sat down heavily. "Now we must love our enemies! Well, we had best get going then, so that I might kiss the backside of every black hearted elf I come across and maybe then I can invite them to share my home!"

"Now you're being ridiculous, Zara." Jon said quietly. He had deliberately kept out of the conversation letting his friends sort out their feelings. Despite Tal'Asin's urgency, he would not force any of his friends to accompany him.

"I'm being ridiculous!" Zara snapped, her eyes wide. "You're turning into some kind of freak and have a thousand year dead elven spirit in your head, these two religious fools…" she hissed, pointing at Rebba and Garon, "are asking me to love those bastards who damn near killed us, and you call me ridiculous!"

Zara was in full flow now and Jon let her get rid of the anger she had pent up.

"You say I believe in nothing." She asked of Rebba, not wanting a reply. "I believe in what I can touch and taste and feel. I believe in what my eyes can see and my mind perceive. You have no proof that any gods exist or that they guide us in some way, have you?" She asked harshly. "Prove to me that some god or gods have placed us here to do their bidding. Prove to me that we are meant to be here and meant to find this Lifestone and save the bloody Wildlands, and not meant to get ourselves out of here by the quickest exit!" she thundered.

Rebba looked helplessly at Zara and then at Jon. It seemed the sleep had reinforced Zara Halven's feelings. However, it was Garon who quietly answered.

"I can prove that we are meant to be here, that we are meant to get the Lifestone."

Zara stared at him. Silence fell.

"Go on!" Zara prompted still angry, though a touch of uncertainty had entered her voice. It was clear to Jon that Zara was finding Garon's quiet dignity and belief hard to understand. An out and out shouting match would have been what Zara would have preferred.

The monk seemed to compose himself. "This is hard for me for I swore not to reveal this as it was told to me in trust, as a friend."

Jon frowned, while Zara looked like she was thinking Garon was just stalling. She gave an impatient disbelieving snort.

"Just before I met up with the rest of you in the tavern, before we came down here, I met up with Nat first." the Alban monk said reluctantly, swallowing slowly and licking his lips. "Nat was in a bad way. She was obviously being eaten up inside by something and when she told me things were bad I knew she wanted to talk, to confide in someone." Garon paused for a moment again, clearly uncomfortable. Garon began to speak.

Jon listened as Garon related what Nat Bero had told him and as the story unfolded he began to feel more and more alarmed. 'Nat a bounty hunter... Killing for money? She must have been desperate, but to kill in cold blood? At least she was hunting killers and murderers...'

All these thoughts ran through Jon's head and then Garon spoke of two so-called murderers that Nat and her two companions were to kill. One was a warrior mage and very dangerous, and the other was masquerading as a Knight of Saint Karodra! Jon found Garon's eyes boring into his as the earnest monk related how Nat and the others had been told where the men would be several weeks in advance; how the details of who they were only came later from their shadowy employer.

Jon frowned. How could they know exactly where the men would be, but not who, until later? That generally wasn't how bounty hunting worked as far as he knew. People did generally follow patterns, but to know so far in advance and be so exact in where they would be had to be supernatural. Magic must have been involved, nothing else made sense! Criminals especially were not likely to be forthcoming about what they would do, they were generally unpredictable in their movements and travel, and they would not have advertised such things.

Jon listened carefully as Garon told them how Nat had waited in ambush, the plan set... and slowly realisation began to dawn on him. He had been travelling that road... on that day...?

Like a thunderbolt it hit him. "That was me! Nat was hunting me!" he exclaimed.

Garon nodded slowly, deliberately.

Jon heard Zara and Rebba's puzzled queries, but he ignored them and focused on the round faced Garon. "I am no murderer. Why were they going to ambush me?" Another thought occurred to him. "That bloody thief... on the road who attacked... almost took my head off." He was confused and rambling and he knew it. "What the hell is going on Garon?" he finished.

"Someone used Nat to hunt down their enemies. It almost tore her apart when she realised she had not been hunting murderers, but innocent people like you and Darin..."

"Darin?" Jon interrupted surprised even as the answer came to him, "Of course the Karodracian knight, the so-called impostor."

Garon nodded and continued. "The most obvious questions that spring to mind from this are who was manipulating Nat and why."

Zara and Rebba nodded in agreement.

"It seemed clear to me that whoever it was must have incredible knowledge of the people they wanted dead. To know where your enemies would be in advance you must know them or have lured them, but that solution didn't fit because I knew that both you, Bear" the monk said nodding at Jon, "and Darin were not lured by anyone. In fact what really puzzled me was that Nat had been told where you would be even before we had finalised when we would meet, let alone when we would travel. There was no way Nat's employer could know where you would be… unless…" He left his statement hanging and Rebba picked up the strand.

"Unless they knew magic and had a talent with prophecy." the druid muttered. She then sat forward, a frown on her face, "But even then their talent at prophecy would have to be incredible."

"You're right Rebba." Garon agreed.

"Right about what?" Zara asked, clearly confused by the talk of magic.

"Prophecy is more an art than anything else. It is the most unpredictable and least understood area of magic. A seer would have to be incredibly powerful to be able to see such events in the future with such accuracy." Rebba explained.

"And insightful." Jon added. "The future has a multitude of possibilities, to see one so distinctly would need incredible vision."

"Indeed," Garon concurred, a serious look on his usually cheerful features. "So we know that whoever Nat's mysterious employer was, they were very powerful and wanted to kill Bear and Darin!"

Zara was shaking her head, a bewildered look on her tanned face. "This is, I'll grant you, very worrying for both Jon and Darin, as well as for Nat, but I am struggling to see what this has to do with us in the here and now. This does not mean we are meant to be here, in fact it probably means we need to find out who Nat's employer was and do a little bounty hunting on him!"

"No, no, Zara, you are missing the point." Garon responded shaking his head in return.

"Oh, am I?" Zara bit back acidly. "What is the point?"

"The point is why were they hunting Darin and Bear." Garon stated firmly, staring hard at Zara.

The warrior merely looked back at him blankly and then looked at both Jon and Rebba, clearly annoyed. "Shouldn't that be what we need to find out?"

There was a moment of silence as Garon simply closed his eyes and sighed. Then it occurred to Jon what Garon meant and he slapped his shaven head as the revelation came to him. Zara and Rebba looked at him blankly.

"I think what Garon means is that we already know why they were hunting Darin and I…" he paused, "Nat's employer was obviously powerful and used prophecy, and if they could use prophecy to see where Darin and I would be, perhaps they could have looked ahead and seen more," Jon could see Garon nodding excitedly now, "that would be why they were so intent on killing us in the first place." Jon took a deep breath at the enormity of what he was saying and noticed Zara still struggling with what she was hearing. Jon said to her, "Perhaps this enemy who sent people to kill Darin and I is the enemy we now face, the dark elves and their infernal allies. They looked into the future to see who would be a threat to them and then moved to kill them before they could ever become a threat!"

"They knew you would be a danger and that we would go after the Lifestone!" Rebba cried in excitement. She turned to Zara and grabbed the warrior's strong arm. "Don't you see we must have been destined to be here or the enemy would not have tried to get rid of Bear and Darin!"

Zara growled and snatched her arm away, still confused. "Is this true Bear?"

"True! I don't know Zara, but it makes a kind of sense." Jon replied. "One thing I do know from Tal'Asin is that prophecy is a difficult gift for even the most powerful and very few who have ever lived could have done the kind of scrying of the future that Garon is hinting at, certainly no human. The difficulties are immense, only one with divine aid could do such, if you believe in the gods. If the dark elves have that kind of support, it is possible and so in a way it makes sense that we are supposed to be here."

"That seems a bit of a stretch, Bear." Zara put in dubiously. "They looked ahead to see who might be a problem and then figured out where they would be at a given time and organised to have them killed!" Zara shook her head, "it's a bit farfetched."

"Yes, but so is the idea of dark elves from the ancient past trying to kill us." Bear replied.

Zara frowned, but had to acknowledge the point. She then sat bolt upright as something obviously occurred to her. "But doesn't that mean that the enemy knows we are coming and will be waiting for us?"

"Possibly, but not necessarily; as we have said prophecy is unpredictable, it is an art that is difficult to control. Much of it is often divinely inspired so the seer might not have seen all that was to happen. Also, even when they saw possible futures, they still failed to kill both Darin and I. Jon suddenly smiled, nodded and looked to Garon. "I see now what you meant, Garon." He then turned back to Zara and asked, "Now why weren't we killed, Zara?"

Zara's frown deepened. "Well, I suppose because Nat recognised you and couldn't kill her friend."

"And who or what placed Nat in that position instead of someone else?" Jon prodded.

"Who? I don't know who? What do you mean?" Zara said in exasperation.

"I mean, was it simply a fluke of fate that placed Nat Bero, our friend in the position to be one of the attackers?" Jon's gaze held Zara's blue eyes with a fixed stare. "Now that seems a huge coincidence doesn't it? Even a skeptic must admit that perhaps there is a divine hand out there guiding events and seeking to aid us in defeating our enemies, either that or we have been hugely lucky."

"It seems obvious to me that the gods are guiding us," Rebba said quietly and Garon nodded in clear agreement.

Zara blinked and looked at each of her friends in turn, finishing by looking hard into Jon's eyes. She seemed to take a deep breath and then smiled wryly. "I prefer the idea of luck myself, but alright, this does seem…" She searched for the right word, "strange, yet I find it hard to believe that the gods would pin their hopes on a druid who hates fighting, an overweight, ex-drunk monk, a failed mercenary and a warrior-mage with a dead elf in his head! Surely they could have done better."

Jon and the others smiled at this, for it had all been said with a sudden merry twinkle in Zara's eyes, and it was clear that the warrior, although not fully convinced, had acknowledged their point, albeit grudgingly. She would go after the Lifestone, though more perhaps, because she was convinced at least that her friends were convinced it was the right thing to do.

"Well stop grinning at me like fools and let's get ourselves organised." Zara muttered gruffly. "If we are going to do this we'd better get on with it. The sooner started; the sooner finished." she recited.

Everyone began to move, but then Rebba stopped them with a question.

"Nat was employed by a mage, probably from Shandrilos. Doesn't that then mean that the enemy has humans working for him here?"

All frowned and nodded slowly. They all knew their friends were heading towards the surface and Shandrilos.

"Nat believes she can find her ex-employer." Garon murmured softly, "I just hope she doesn't do anything foolish. She was almost inconsolable about the killings. She has a lot of anger and hate to deal with."

413

Jon looked at Rebba who had a sympathetic look on her pale, youthful face, and then looked to Zara whose features seemed to be saying 'Damn right!'

"She and the others need to get the information they have and the gnome to the Archmage first. If she is wise she will mention about the other mage and get some aid." Jon said firmly. "Let's get ourselves moving."

The group quickly gathered their few supplies together. They had a little water and dried food, and a few bundles of kindling for torches left, along with their bedrolls. The food and water was worrying Zara until Rebba quickly assured her that she knew a spell to summon up fresh water from the earth and to produce some nourishing food the same way. Zara was a little taken aback by this. Jon knew her opinion of Rebba had never been high, the battle with the giant ogre creatures had somewhat changed this, but of course Zara had never put much stock in either druids or priests and her opinions were often hard to change.

Jon quickly explained to his friends that they would search the ancient kingdoms around the elves' holy city of Althazar, as that was where the Lifestone was going to be, and that they would begin with the Waygate to Shah'Namir, the fabled land of endless forests and hidden cities in the glades. If the stone were not there, they would go on from there to the northern highland kingdom of Cor'Tuvor and so on around the five Elder kingdoms that had Waygates that joined directly to Althazar. Eventually they would find the stone.

"Are you sure there will be no one waiting for us?" Zara asked a little warily.

"Sure? I am not sure, Zara, nothing is certain, but these Waygates connect to halls like this, halls that were sealed when the Waygates were closed. It would take tremendous force to break into these halls, and all of the Waygate halls are deep below the ground." Jon answered. "So it is unlikely anything will be waiting for us."

Zara seemed to take heart from this and got on with organising herself.

Only a few minutes later, the four friends stood facing the Waygate to ancient Shah'Namir. They all looked at one another. Each seemed to gather themselves with a deep breath.

Zara was right in a way, Jon thought, they were not heroes, not used to such battles or such high stakes, but Jon knew he couldn't have chosen a better group with which to face the unknown, save to perhaps have their other friends here too.

Zara and Jon drew their swords almost in time with one another, while Rebba and Garon grasped their staff and mace respectively. Jon then bade Rebba place the keystone in the Waygate to the ancient forest kingdom. Rebba moved forward, taking the keystone from a hidden pocket and placing it in the rounded hole in the Waygate arch, Bear had indicated. There was an audible click as the stone linked to the mighty carved frame of the portal. Then the stone popped out again.

Nothing seemed to happen!

"Well, that was less exciting than I expected." Zara laughed lightly, "I thought there would be some great spell or a peal of thunder or some..." Zara's voice was cut off as there was a mighty hiss and crackle. There was a palpable rise in energy around them. Abruptly, a searing blue sheet of energy leapt into being in the empty space in the arch of the Waygate. The energy swirled and boiled and then pulsed and spun out ferociously at the four stunned friends before sucking backwards like a tornado pulling them with it. They didn't even have time to scream before they disappeared into the vortex of blue power!

Chapter 44

VISITORS

Of the legends of the Green Man of the Forest, there are many. It was said that he would hunt the forests of Cumbra and would kill any he caught. Only the truly pure of heart were said to be safe from the Green Man.

From 'Legends of the Wild Northmen' by Alrin Ul'Dar, BY686

Nat Bero seemed to drift. She remembered pain and movement, though now both seemed to have faded in intensity and time. She felt strange, yet warm and comfortable. Slowly, she began to become aware of herself; her arms, her legs, her eyelids. All felt heavy and her mind seemed to swirl at the thought of moving any of them. It was an effort merely to think.

She seemed to hear a voice. Did she know that voice? It seemed so, yet she couldn't place it. The voice faded and her mind drifted.

Someone was touching her. She didn't know how long had passed, and the voice had returned, more insistent this time. She concentrated on her eyelids. She would open her eyes. However, even with such determination it seemed all she could do merely to make them twitch. With a groan, that she realised only afterwards was her own, her eyes opened.

Whiteness! That was all she could see. Was she blind? No… details in the white began to emerge. Some grays and darker whites seemed to give the impression of... a roof? Abruptly, a face came blearily into view. It was a happy face, it seemed. She could make out few details, but the smile was wide in the tanned face and the dark eyes glinted with pleasure. Words came to her ears as if from far away.

"Nat, you're awake."

She thought she managed a smile before she drifted off again.

Sometime later, perhaps, a minute or perhaps an hour, she had no idea, she found herself staring at the roof she had glimpsed earlier. She wasn't sure when she had come awake again, though she could now see the roof quite clearly and without effort. It was high, curved and arched. It was made of stone and yet the stone was crafted in such a way as to appear like a canopy of leaves as if she lay in a forest beneath mighty trees, all white. As her eyes followed the curve of the roof they came to a mighty stone column. Here was the trunk of one of the trees of that stone forest. With effort she moved her head and followed the column down. Off behind it, she saw other columns just like it, and then a wall with what seemed like large double doors set in it every twenty feet or so. This was a white hall of columns and doors! She had no idea where she was.

"So you are awake this time", a voice called.

She tried to move her head, to lift it from its pillow, but she could not. A man came into view. It was Arkadi, though he wasn't wearing the dark cloak he had worn below ground. He appeared to be wearing some kind of thin, long gown that left his arms bare. Nat tried to answer and only a croak came out.

Arkadi leaned over her and smiled. "Don't worry. Your voice and energy will return; the healing has taken a lot out of you."

Nat frowned. Arkadi didn't seem to notice.

"We have been very lucky, my friend. We have been given the finest healing. The Grand Abbot himself has attended us."

Nat listened as Arkadi spoke and slowly things began to come back to her.

It seemed it had been almost two days since they had been fleeing the tunnels beneath the college and the last thing Nat remembered was a massive blast. Apparently, it had been some sort of spell and it had collapsed the tunnels down onto them. They had been buried under tons of rubble for hours until mages from the college had dug them out. Arkadi had been conscious throughout, he said, though it was obvious from the dark look that he didn't want to talk about it. Arkadi only briefly sketched out how he had been pinned down, his legs both broken. All that had saved both himself and Nat from death was a spell of some sort, a contingency spell he called it. It had formed a shield around them. This hadn't saved them fully, though it had caused a small gap to form around them as the rock fell.

Nat had sustained more injuries: broken limbs and damage to her body. However, once saved from the rubble, teams of clerics had worked on them, including the Grand Abbot himself, and in only a day their bones had been rejoined, their muscles and flesh stitched together, their injuries healed! This was the kind of healing that only kings could afford. Soon, Arkadi assured her, she would be up and as good as new.

Nat managed to croak, "What of the others?"

Arkadi looked grave and Nat's concern grew.

"What of Darin and the gnome?" Nat asked hoarsely. Her voice was starting to function more as she wanted it to.

Arkadi stared fixedly at Nat for a moment and then almost glassy eyed as if looking elsewhere he replied, "Nossi Bee was unhurt and is with the Conclave, I believe, being questioned. Darin is gone!"

"Gone?" Nat coughed.

"Gone," Arkadi repeated staring blankly, not seeming to believe what he was saying. His voice was distant and matter-of-fact as though he feared to think about what he was saying too closely. "The whole of that hall we fought in collapsed through the next two levels. There's tonnes of rubble that has plummeted sixty feet or more. They have not found any bodies yet, though the dwarves have said that in such a fall the bodies are often pulverized."

Nat squeezed her eyes shut, tying not to picture anything in her mind. The thought was too horrible to conceive. After a few moments she opened her eyes and saw Arkadi looking thoroughly miserable.

The mage muttered quietly, "It may only be you and I that have escaped those tunnels, Nat."

The thought was too much for her. She shook her head and whispered. "There is no word of Zara, Rebba and the others?"

Arkadi merely slumped down onto Nat's bed.

Nat closed her eyes and let the fatigue she had been fighting wash over her. Sleep took her.

It was some hours later that Nat was snapped awake by nightmares. In them, she could see the faces of her children; they cried out to her, begged her to help them, but rocks were falling and she could not reach them. Quickly, they were smashed from view, and then the rocks had struck her and she felt blood flow down her brow. It was then she had awoken, heart pumping, hand going to her head automatically.

She realized, as her heart slowed to a normal cadence, that she did actually feel stronger and clearer, though it took awhile to push away the dark images from her nightmare. Slowly, she managed to push herself up into a sitting position and she took in the full view of the hall in which she had slept. It was large, very large, and spacious, airy and clean. Beds were spread around the room and a few men in white and grey robes moved around slowly; some bending to help people in the beds, others carrying food or merely cleaning. The men were monks, mostly of the Sironacian order, the same order to which Garon had belonged. She quickly pushed away an image of the large monk that came unbidden. She didn't want to think about her friends.

This place seemed like some kind of place for the sick, an infirmary or something. It was not full, most beds lay empty, but the place looked like it could comfortably hold a hundred people. She recalled someone mentioning that the Clerics Dome of the college had an infirmary in it and the town's folk would sometimes go for care. It was even said that it was becoming a place of pilgrimage. It was one of the benefits of having a college of magic in your town. Certainly, nowhere else Nat could think of had such a place. Elsewhere in the wilds and beyond, death was a much more common outcome to most illnesses and injuries.

The thought reminded her of her friends and family and images from her dreams appeared again. She thrust them aside, thrusting the covers of her bed back at the same time. She swung herself round to sit on the edge of the bed and noticed scars on her legs. She had no recollection, thankfully, of the injuries she had suffered, and from the looks of the scars they had been numerous.

A bout of dizziness hit her, but it quickly passed and she looked around. Her bed was against what she had taken to be a door. It was in fact a panelled section of wall. However some of the panels were doors she noticed looking around the hall. The wooden panels, both door and wall sections, did not seem to be part of the original design of the place and Nat guessed that this hall was originally open to the outside. It seemed odd to have so many doorways, but then it had been elves who had built the place. An image of coppery skinned elves; demonic, black skinned goblins; and giant insects came crashing back upon her and she looked around anxiously. The moment passed and she frowned ruefully. Those bastard creatures couldn't get her here. The mages would know of them now and would have sent warriors and magi down to deal with them. Perhaps there was news of her friends!

She turned to look behind for Arkadi, but the bed next to her was empty. In between the beds, Nat noticed a small cabinet of some kind. It was half open and inside she could see her clothes and armour stored neatly away. Surely they had been badly damaged?

She stood slowly and the dizziness struck her again. She held on, determined to not let it get the better of her. Slowly, the dizziness receded and she was pleasantly surprised that she felt no further weakness. Her strength was returning. She walked around the bed and opened the cabinet fully. She took out her clothes and spread them out on the bed. Yes, she realized, they had been repaired in a number of places and some of her clothes had been replaced with similar. They were generous these monks. A thought then occurred to her and she turned and opened a tall thin cabinet by the side of the one her clothes had been in. Inside, as she had suspected, she found her bow, short sword and a dagger. The dagger was not hers, though it was in one of her sheaths. She had lost the others below ground, fighting that lunatic mercenary.

Just then she heard soft footsteps and turned to see a monk approaching. He was an older man, balding and rake-thin, though he had a smile that softened the hard lines of his gaunt face.

"It is good to see you awake, Mistress Nat."

She had not been called 'mistress' since Karis had died. She smiled and thanked the monk.

"You must be careful not to over exert yourself too much. The healing costs the body much energy. You should eat and get your strength. In a day you should be back to your old self."

"I am feeling much stronger already, thank you," Nat replied, "but food sounds wonderful." She had realised as the monk mentioned food that she was starving. She was going to take advantage of the hospitality of these monks. She was not one to look a gift horse in the mouth.

Later, as she finished off her meal, she saw Arkadi returning. He looked weary and Nat guessed that he too had not yet fully recovered. Arkadi was back in the grey master's robes of the School of the Magi. He smiled when he saw Nat up and alert.

"It's good to see you fully with us, Nat. How are you feeling?"

"Better," she replied gruffly, "but you look like crap!"

"Thanks, Nat. I see you are feeling more your old self." Arkadi muttered a small grin on his lips. He sat himself down heavily, using his staff almost like a walking stick. "The teams that have been scouring the tunnels have found nothing it seems, not even bodies!"

Nat raised her eyebrows at this and Arkadi nodded. He too had been taken aback by the news. Arkadi suddenly leaned in close and whispered. "Nat, there are elves here, in the college!

Nat gasped out loud. Arkadi nodded at her surprise.

"It seems they are seeking an alliance, if you can credit it!" Arkadi continued, "The Archmage is protecting them, refusing to believe what we have said. If what I have heard is true, he believes the elves are here to help us defend against a goblin army from the northland. Our story of the elves working with the goblins has half of the Conclave ready to attack any elf on sight and the other half believing we are liars trying to stop an alliance!" He shook his head wearily and then threw up his hands, "Though why they would want an alliance with those swine is a mystery to me." Arkadi snapped. "No one wants to really tell me anything. All this is being kept quiet, but there are some who even think we made it all up! One of the Conclave even tried to hint that maybe I had caused the damage below ground!" Arkadi snapped bitterly. "No one seems to know where Nossi has vanished to and the college is a hot bed of intrigue and politics. There are all kinds of rumours."

"Rumours? What rumours are those, Master Talcost?" a voice asked from behind them.

Nat looked around and saw a dark haired man in bright blue robes marching purposely towards them. Arkadi rose to his feet and smiled, "Sorceror Supreme, Uth Altor."

"Let's forget the titles, Arkadi. We need to talk."

"Of course, Xameran." Arkadi replied, "This is my friend Nat Bero." Arkadi continued, pointing, but the mage was already turning away.

The blue robed sorceror then pointedly ignored Nat and looked at Arkadi. "We need to talk… in private, Arkadi."

Arkadi nodded and headed away with the newcomer.

Nat hated secrets. In her recent work, information had become a currency and old habits died hard. Slowly, she stood and began to casually circle around Arkadi and the other mage until she was out of sight behind one of the tree like columns. She then slipped closer and listened.

"What is going on, Xameran? The college is in uproar. I mean I understand about the explosion, but why does no one want to listen to what I have to say."

"Hold on, a moment, Arkadi." Xameran said calmly. "There are other things going on in the college, things of which you are unaware. However, what concerns me first of all is why you were down in the ancient catacombs, Arkadi? You and your friends have gone where it is forbidden."

Arkadi frowned. "It was hardly a major breach of college law, Xameran…" He began, but the Lord of Sorcery cut him off.

"I'll ask again," Xameran said firmly, "Why were you and your friends down there?"

Arkadi stared at the Lord of Sorcery for a moment, taken aback by his tone. "There was no real reason. My friends and I had arranged to meet up after years and then there were rumours of treasure below in the old elven catacombs and we thought it would be fun to explore as we used to when we were younger." Arkadi explained. "It was just a bit of foolishness. No one actually thought we would find anything. Mages have scoured those tunnels for the past century."

Xameran Uth Altor frowned at Arkadi for a moment and muttered, "I see, and this Nat Bero is one of your friends?"

Arkadi nodded, confused. "It's not like we caused the explosion or anything else! People have been down there before and no one has really bothered." Arkadi insisted.

"That might have been the case had we not had theft in the college and then murder!" Xameran Uth Altor insisted firmly.

"Murder! In the college?" Arkadi looked at the blue robed master in confusion. "Who has been murdered and by whom?"

"The Allseer has been murdered!" Xameran said harshly, "And it was done by elves, elves that the Archmage is protecting, elves that it now seems are causing mischief and murder below ground and according to you, are amassing a huge army in the north!"

"I can understand the elves, but the Archmage wouldn't be a party to murdering a mage, surely!"

"I wouldn't have thought so either, yet the evidence is that it was he who stole the camouflaging cloaks from the enchanters and then gave them to the elves who used it to aid their attack and murder of the Allseer."

Arkadi stared at the stern master in dismay. His mouth opened and closed, but no words would come.

"Questions are being asked, Arkadi. People believe you might be responsible for the destruction below ground, that you are part of the Archmage's plotting." Xameran stated, looking hard at Arkadi.

Arkadi shook his head, his eyes wide in disbelief. "How can... I mean we..." He stumbled to a halt, not knowing what to say.

Xameran's face softened and he raised his hand to stop Arkadi's ramblings. "Peace my friend. I can help you, but you must tell me all. Everything. Leave nothing out."

Arkadi nodded and began to tell his tale. Suddenly, the tidings he had about the elves beneath the college and the threat from the goblins in the north seemed twice as urgent. The college Arkadi loved was falling apart with its leader apparently, orchestrating that fall.

As Arkadi spoke, Xameran asked him searching questions and he strove to explain clearly. He wanted the danger to the college to be seen and be believed. The college needed to unite and quickly, to get rid of these elves or the threat from the north would engulf them all! He tried to emphasise this as he recounted his story of the last three days.

After almost an hour, he was finished and he found Xameran staring at him intently. "I hear what you are saying, Arkadi, and you are right; we do need to deal with these elves in the college quickly. We need to face this terrible threat you have uncovered."

"So you believe me?" Arkadi asked, almost pleading.

Xameran smiled warmly, "Of course my friend. What's more, I can help you, Arkadi. I just needed to be sure of you, that you would tell the truth. The stakes are too high for me not to be sure. You see the threat from the north has been discovered, ironically by the Archmage's own spies! However, what you have uncovered about the elves being behind it is too important to be obscured by any allegations against you. We must push the debate in the Assembly. Too long already has the Mage Master delayed us so I have already suggested that you and your friends were investigating for me. It was my responsibility to look into the strange goings on under the college and you have done my job for me, my young friend." He smiled. "It was not exactly a lie to claim you were investigating, was it?" He nodded at Arkadi, "Hmmm?"

Arkadi took a deep breath and closed his eyes. He smiled slowly, relief evident in his voice. "No it was not, master." He opened his eyes and looked gratefully at Xameran.

The lord of sorcery nodded, "And with that matter not an issue, the Assembly can then start to deal with the allegations against the Archmage so that we can unite the college and deal with this elven threat." He glanced around and then leaned in to Arkadi, "This last is also why I have come to visit you." He looked deeply into Arkadi's brown eyes and said, "It is unbelievable that the Archmage and his supporters still protect the elves after all we now know and this must be the focus of the Assembly. However, this could get obscured and complicated by the matter of this key the elves were after. Nossi did not mention it to the Conclave so we should keep this to ourselves until later."

Arkadi frowned, "But surely this key is important?"

"I agree fully, Arkadi, but if the Archmage is our enemy, knowing or otherwise, then we must deal with that first... and maybe even hide what we know."

The sorcerer lord raised his eyebrows at Arkadi, seeking agreement.

"This key is obviously vital though..."

Xameran cut Arkadi off. "You don't need to worry about the key, Arkadi, I have teams searching below for your other friends already and they know of the key! Atholl is adding his men to the search too. We have this under control," the blue robed mage placated, "but the Archmage and the elves here have to be dealt with first!" Xameran insisted. "Don't you agree?"

Arkadi looked worried. Xameran leaned in close and put a reassuring hand on his shoulder.

"You must trust me," he whispered. "Arkadi, do you trust me?"

Arkadi paused a moment then leaned in and answered earnestly, "Of course, Xameran."

"The Archmage is suspect, Arkadi. No one knows what part he has played in this, but it is clear that he is supporting the elves even with what we now know."

Arkadi shook his head and frowned, "This is incredible, Xameran. I mean, the Archmage was always the most determined protector of the college and the Wildlands. I would never credit he would support the elves against his own, or have a hand in murdering someone."

Xameran nodded and chewed his lip. "Yes, it is perplexing. There is more that you do not know about the Archmage." He paused. "It seems from Master Drollin, the Allseer's second that there may have been a motive for the Allseer's death." Xameran licked his lips and looked around again, checking no one was close. "It seems the Allseer had a vision. It was a vision of the elves leading foul armies from the northlands. The poor Allseer had no idea he would be killed because of his vision."

"It is surprising. The goblins were always believed to have been the greatest enemy of the elves." Arkadi mused. "Had I not seen it with my own eyes, I would not believe the elves and goblins could unite. They have always hated and hunted one another with a passion."

"Yes, some of this just does not make sense, but then our knowledge of that time is sketchy at best." Xameran stressed. "The Allseer was said to have seen visions of elves meeting with goblins and other races of the northlands and making bargains and swearing to dark powers."

Arkadi grimaced. "Really, the Allseer saw this?"

"Master Drollin was quite certain. He had sat in with the Allseer in his scrying sessions." Xameran looked around briefly before continuing. Now, Master Drollin is more an ally of High Enchanter, Dorard, but Drollin is well thought of and he has no reason to lie." the blue robed sorceror lord pondered. He looked intently at Arkadi's face. He could see the young master was still a little confused. "The elves must have murdered the Allseer to prevent this coming out... or at least delay things," the sorceror lord continued. "The elves are the enemy, that is clear, and the Archmage should be the one leading the attack on them... and yet, instead he protects the elves."

"I cannot believe he is defending them!" Arkadi repeated dumbfounded.

Xameran Uth Altor simply nodded. He let Arkadi think for several moments and then added, "The Archmage's leadership must end. Eliantha Shamass seeks to delay any discussion or decision. I had thought she would see reason after she heard what Nossi had to say, but she is too much the Archmage's puppet in this. This division could destroy us. We need to be whole and focused more than ever." Xameran insisted urgently, "What we need is new leadership and quickly. Eliantha plays on politics to delay things. She calls on those who cannot make a decision without thinking on it for days. We cannot leave this in the hands of the slow moving Moderates, Arkadi. They refuse to see the danger!" Xameran placed a hand on Arkadi's shoulder. "You and I are Progressives. We have been saying for years that the college be more active and forceful." The now fierce Lord of Sorcery added, "Support my lead in the Assembly, Arkadi. Tell the Assembly what you saw with your own eyes and we can end things quickly, unite the college and deal with these elves before their forces in the north can move against us. Otherwise, I fear we will not survive this!"

Arkadi stared at Xameran Uth Altor admiringly. This was the man to lead us, he thought. Those elves were arrogant to come here, to the heart of our lands and try to deceive us. In his mind he could hear his friend, Zara saying, 'Elves are elves... no knowing what those slanty eyed freaks are thinking, but you can bet you can't trust them!' Blunt speaking Zara. She could be vicious but she had always supported her friends. She had deserved a better end!

Xameran's quiet voice cut across his thoughts, "As Archmage, I would need a Mage Master I could trust, Arkadi. Eliantha Shamass is too loyal to Baden Erin and radical times call for radical measures. Are you ready for the responsibility?"

Arkadi looked at him in surprise, "Me!" he exclaimed. "But no one so young has ever sat on the Conclave of the college!"

"Come, come, Arkadi. You are the most talented young mage this college has seen in a generation. Do you really think it beyond you?"

Arkadi gazed at the Lord of Sorcery who looked back earnestly. Slowly Arkadi shook his head.

"Then let us go and prepare, my friend. We have much to do if we are to save our college and our land." With that the Lord of Sorcery led Arkadi towards the nearest of the many doors in the Cleric's Dome.

Nat stood still and quiet as she watched her friend leave with the blue robed mage whose name she now knew was Xameran Uth Altor. She had never heard of the man before, though already she found she was wary him. The man was a mage and Nat wasn't that comfortable around them, even after growing up around so many, but more especially because one had deceived her and made her into a murderer. Also, this mage was very smooth and self assured, and Nat was irritated by his confidence. You didn't smuggle without being able to spot a charmer and usually they were trying to set you up. Still, Arkadi seemed to trust him and that said much.

Nat shrugged and moved back to her bed. She was feeling better, but the floor was cold and the bed seemed inviting. One should always take the chance to rest and relax, she thought, after all you never knew when it could all be taken away.

She climbed into bed, pausing only to look over at where Arkadi had disappeared. She still had vague misgivings. Nat sighed and sank into her bed. Let Arkadi deal with things, she thought wearily. She could join in later.

Nat was just drifting off to sleep when something woke her. She was not sure what it was, a noise, a change in the air, she couldn't say, but she opened her eyes just a fraction and looked around furtively. It was always best to let others think you more vulnerable than you were. Not that she felt in danger, but after what she had just heard about elves in the college, she was not going to let her guard down fully.

Sure enough she saw two men walking purposely towards her. She studied them.

They stood at odds with one another. Both were tall, though one was robed in white, his ancient face and long white beard clear to see, while the other was robed in black, his hood up and his face in shadows. The two men looked first at Arkadi's empty bed before focusing in on Nat. She closed her eyes quickly.

"Come along Mistress Bero, please do us the credit of opening your eyes," said a voice.

Nat carefully opened one eye and saw the old man in white smile with genuine amusement at her. Nat smiled ruefully, opened her other eye and propped herself up on her pillows.

"Can I help you, gentlemen?" She'd known it was only a matter of time before people began to question her.

The tall bearded old man in white looked to his companion. The man in black moved forward and sat on Nat's bed, uncomfortably close.

"Would you ensure our privacy, my friend?" came a deep voice from within the voluminous cowl of the dark robes. The question was not directed to Nat and the man in white nodded, a serious look on his face. "The Dome is strongly warded and I will make sure none of my order come near," he said firmly. "However, I can give you no more than an hour before suspicions will rise as there are other people here needing treatment, Baden. Others will surely want to talk to this young woman."

The man in black seemed to nod, the movement hardly visible in the deep hood. Nat was a little worried by the man. It was off-putting to talk to a dark hole in a cloak instead of a face.

The tall old monk in white turned slowly and moved away, gesturing to those other few monks who were around in the hall. They gathered around the old man who led them from the hall after a few words. Someone important it seemed. No one questioned his commands.

Nat had kept her attention away from the man in black to watch the old monk leave, partly out of interest and partly to avoid looking at the dark shadow that sat on her bed. When she looked back the figure had not stirred at all. Nat grinned nervously and nodded, she hoped in a friendly way. She was just about to speak when the man spoke.

"You are Nat Bero, a former innkeeper and huntress out of Ostia, though Lord Elgon believes there is more to you recently. You are a childhood friend of Master Arkadi Talcost. There were others with you below ground, also childhood friends, all educated at the college's guild school and in the court in Ostia." The man in black stopped and a small sigh came forth. "I know something of you and your friends and what has befallen you over the past few days… you on the other hand know nothing of me."

Nat nodded slowly, not sure what to say.

Pale hands rose to the hood and swiftly tossed it back to reveal a pale faced man with dark hair and even darker eyes. There was a touch of silver at his temples. The face was a strong one. It seemed to radiate both firm resolve and sadness at the same time.

"My name is Baden Erin, I am the Archmage of this College, and I am in need of your help, Nat Bero."

Nat could feel her brows rise in alarm. 'The Archmage of the flaming College of bloody Magic!' she thought. 'Crap!'

She knew from the conversation she had 'overheard' between Arkadi and the sorcerer, Xameran that this Archmage was in league with the elves, and though Nat hadn't fully trusted the overly smooth sorcerer, she trusted Arkadi.

The Archmage was watching her intently, reading her response. Nat tried to make her face blank as she responded, "I am not sure I can help you, my lord Archmage. Events have just taken me along. I don't pretend to understand the big picture here."

"You seem a little cautious of me, Mistress Bero. Can I take it that the absence of your friend, Master Talcost is due to a visit from either Xameran Uth Altor or Atholl Dorard?"

Nat stayed silent, unsure how to avoid the political situation she sensed was coming her way.

The silence grew. Nat suddenly said, "I have been unwell, my lord. I am beginning to feel a little…"

"Please, Mistress Bero, hear me out," the Archmage cut in, "There is much that has happened to you that I need to understand and there is also much of which you are unaware, and much truth that has been twisted." He leaned forward and his powerful gaze locked on to Nat's. "All I ask is that you listen first before you make any judgements." The Archmage's dark eyes flashed with passion for a moment before he lowered them and finished quietly, "Please, Mistress Bero, this is of the utmost import."

There was little Nat could say to this so she simply nodded and muttered, "O…okay."

The Archmage began to speak. At first it seemed that he was talking about things long past and irrelevant to what had happened over the last few days, but slowly Nat began to get caught up in the Archmage's tale. She listened as the powerful mage laid bare his soul about his dreams and plans for the College and for the Wildlands. How he had come to know first the dwarves and then through them, the elves of the wilds, and how he first learnt of the terrible threat brewing in the north. Nat was engrossed.

As she listened on, the Archmage outlined the recent events in the college, events hinted at by the sorcerer, Xameran Uth Altor to Arkadi earlier. However, the Archmage's version of events was subtly different. The elves were not to blame for the murder of the Allseer, they had been framed, as had the Archmage himself. It was a plot by someone within the college to prevent an alliance that could give them a real advantage against the enemy.

The Archmage paused at this point and looked directly into Nat's eyes. "I cannot be certain, but it is my belief that either Xameran Uth Altor or Atholl Dorard is an agent of the enemy!"

Nat kept her face blank. The Archmage's story was compelling as he told it. She had the feeling that this powerful man before her was honest and had told her what he truly believed. However, Nat had seen what the elves could do. Her friends had died because of them. She would not trust them. This man was either being deluded or deluding himself. Arkadi had trusted this Xameran Uth Altor, and although Nat couldn't quite go that far, it was clear that this Archmage was utterly wrong!

The Archmage's seemed to read her doubt. He held up a placatory hand and said quietly, "I can understand you suspicions, Mistress Bero, especially after what you have been through, but all I am asking is for you to have an open mind... and also I would like to hear your story of what happened below the college... if you can trust me that far?"

Nat frowned. It couldn't really hurt; in fact it might convince this Archmage of the truth, but... "Haven't you already heard this from little Nossi Bee?" Nat asked.

"The gnome Nossi Bee has vanished! I cannot find him anywhere. He was allowed to speak to the Conclave briefly, but since then he cannot be found." the Archmage said with a frown. "I was not present when Nossi Bee spoke and no one has been able to question him fully about the details... save perhaps Xameran and Atholl. It was they who brought the gnome before the Conclave and then..."

The disbelief and anger must have shown on Nat's face.

"I know you will think this another ploy to blacken the name of my opponents, but it is the truth."

Nat snapped angrily, "Has no one searched for him? I lost friends trying to get that gnome back to the surface. Surely, somebody has organised a search? If you are so innocent why haven't you organised one?"

"Peace, Mistress Bero," said the Archmage softly. "I am constrained. I have tried my best to find Nossi, but I am under suspicion and supposed to be locked away in my rooms. I can do little..." Nat was about to argue, but the Archmage held up a finger to stall him, "Little that is save talk to you and try to puzzle out what is going on here." He looked hard at Nat again. "Will you tell me your story, Mistress Bero?"

Nat was angry. She had to take a deep breath to calm herself and to stop thinking about what had happened to Nossi Bee. Then she nodded. She still did not believe this Archmage, but there was little harm in telling him what had happened. However, she would not mention the key the elves had been after, Arkadi had agreed not to so Nat would not, but she would have to have a long talk to Arkadi once he got back. Nat was out of her depth here. She knew little of what was going on and she needed to find out what had happened to Nossi. She was damned if she would let anyone harm that gnome after her friends had given so much to get him to this college in the first place!

She spoke quickly, keen to get this over with, but the Archmage made her stop and go through things in detail at certain points. Nat was annoyed, but she held her temper. It was difficult; there were a lot of painful memories. She hadn't been that interested in anything other than surviving for a lot of the time. Still most of Nossi Bee's story came back, which she was surprised at, though the names of the people the gnome had talked about were gone. At one point, the Archmage appeared confused. Nat had described the elves and their allies and she expected it was the giant insect creatures or even the gigantic ogre creatures, but it was the elves that caused him to frown!

"They had coppery skin?"

"Yes, a kind of coppery or fiery bronze, why?" Nat had answered.

The Archmage looked slightly perplexed, but after a few moments he had waved for her to continue.

It took a while to finish the story and by the end she felt bone weary. The Archmage stood and lifted his deep hood back into place. "I thank you for your trust, Mistress Bero. I know that you still do not believe me and, in your position, I would find it hard too. However, I do ask again that you keep an open mind, and that you warn your friend Arkadi to be careful. I believe he is being manipulated."

Nat said nothing. She was confused by the earnest nature of the Archmage. She wanted to believe him, but his view of the elves was so obviously wrong. Nat wiped a hand across her brow. Her mind seemed to be working so slowly at the moment. She knew she was terribly tired!

"The healing has wearied you and you must rest. I shall continue to search for your little friend, Nossi Bee, though it is difficult as I am supposed to be staying in my rooms." He leaned towards Nat and asked carefully, "Would you keep my visit here a secret… at least from any of the mages… at least for now?"

Nat nodded. She wouldn't tell any mages, none save Arkadi, but then he was a friend.

The Archmage hesitated then seemed to sigh before turning and walking silently back towards the doors on the far side of the hall.

Nat felt her eyes closing and thought, Arkadi better be back soon. As she drifted off, she was again tormented by images of her lost friends.

Chapter 45

RELICS OF THE DEAD

One of the most chilling legends surrounds the creature known as the Dark Destroyer. This legend has grown over time from a number of traditional stories. These originate from almost all the kingdoms of the Nordic. The great King Earondar is also linked to the legend in some stories, but stories seem to go back much farther than this mythical king.

From 'Tales from beyond the Empire' by Boria of Var, BY615

Zara Halven stepped through more carefully this time. She was actually starting to get used to this travelling through magical portals or waygates or whatever they were called. This was her third time through and it was easier each time. If truth be told, only the first time had been difficult... well, if she was honest... bloody scary... the other times had only been a step, like moving from one room to another. The power that radiated from those giant stone arches was enough that even a non-adept such as she could feel it and magic still made her uneasy. She was used to her friends' magic, but magic on this scale was frightening, though she would admit that to no one.

She quickly scanned around the Waygate hall. Her swords were out and she was conscious of the sudden appearance of Bear, Garon and Rebba. They had weapons ready as they appeared from the sheet of blue energy that filled the Waygate's ancient black stone arch. Each of the halls they had entered had been identical; empty and forgotten. They had visited two since leaving the one beneath Shandrilos. However, this one was very different!

Zara looked around aghast. Bodies littered the floor of the hall; bodies armoured and armed, and from more than one race. Zara looked to Bear and saw a look of horror on his familiar and yet strange face. Rebba gasped audibly.

"Wha…?" Garon began, but Bear's hand on his arm stopped the big monk.

Zara looked at Bear carefully, puzzled. There was no danger. It was clear these people had died long ago; their bodies decayed away to leave only skeletons in armour of all kinds, and yet Bear was clearly hit hard by the place. Bear seemed to notice her questioning look and he blinked those alien, elven eyes slowly, deliberately. He forced a smile, but it was clear to Zara that all was not well with him. Zara frowned and turned away. She began to carefully step over the bodies while studying them. She noticed out of the corner of her eye that both Rebba and Garon began doing the same. Bear just stood staring.

The bodies were spread liberally about the large hall. There must have been almost two hundred bodies in here. The huge hall could easily contain them, but it was alarming. The bodies were crowded around two places in particular. One was the Waygate arches, the second was what Zara now knew was the main exit from the hall.

It was strange. Some of the bodies seemed to have merely sat themselves down and died, there was no sign of violence; others had quite clearly gone down fighting. Here and there, there were severed skeletal limbs.

Zara heard Rebba call out and turned to look her way. Rebba was over in a corner bending over what appeared to be a pile of bodies.

"Goblins and trolls," she said. "They seem to have been piled over here. Some of them must have been pushed here through the Waygate too."

Zara nodded. She knew that the elven Lore King Tal'Asin had pushed people through the Waygates at the height of his battle with this *Ata'Gon* creature, trying to save them.

Zara shook her head ruefully. She would never have thought it, but she had now become something of an expert on the war against the Dark Elves. They all had. Oh, those old bookworm masters who had taught her would have been astounded to know that possibly one of their worst and most reluctant students knew far more than they. She chuckled to herself. She had always been bored silly in those lessons on history and languages and herb lore and so on. She had been interested only in learning how to fight and kill. They had always said she would amount to little. Now she could go back and teach them a thing or two.

"Look here," Garon called. He had gone to the other side of the Waygate arches and was kneeling in his white armour, his shield on his arm. "These bodies have been laid out neatly in rows. There's about a score of them; elves, dwarves and men by the look of them."

Zara looked around the hall. What had happened here... a battle?

"I think these must be the losers then," Rebba said gravely, pointing at the rough pile of what looked like about thirty or forty goblins and trolls. "The elves, dwarves and men killed them though they must have lost people..."

"And they laid those out here." Garon finished for her nodding towards the neat rows of bodies by which he stood.

"Yes," Rebba acknowledged, "but that doesn't explain these others." She said pointing at the bodies in front of the archways and the main exit. "Who did they fight?" The brown robed druid asked, leaning on her gnarled staff and studying the room.

Garon Vale walked back around the archways in the centre of the room, rubbing one of his large ears in thought. "Maybe they were defending the hall. Maybe someone was trying to get through the archway and the hall entrance and they fought them off, a kind of heroic last stand." the monk mused.

Zara shook her head, "No," she called, "that doesn't seem right. These people have fallen in all directions. If they were fighting some trolls and goblins their bodies would be here amongst them." She pointed with one of her swords as she moved through the fallen warriors.

"But they moved those bodies over here, Zara." Rebba replied, nodding to the pile of trolls and goblins.

"What, they took the trouble of moving the enemy dead and left their own where they fell?"

Rebba frowned at that and Garon put in again, "Then they must have been fighting to keep someone out after defeating the trolls and goblins that were in here."

435

"No, they were not fighting to keep someone out."

Zara, Rebba and Garon all looked at Bear who had spoken in a voice filled with sadness. They all looked at him, confused.

"Then what…" Zara asked.

"They were fighting to get out!" Bear whispered.

Zara looked again at the bodies.

"They would have tried to force their way out after defeating the trolls and goblins." Bear continued dolefully. "Eventually, after their attempt to escape their magical prison failed, they would have grown desperate; angry and afraid. They then would have started to starve. They would have fought each other for what food there was left. Those are the bodies you see, hacked up and left. The survivors would have been too few and too starved to move anymore bodies." Bear slowly walked over to the bodies slumped against the walls by the main doors, the bodies Zara had noted earlier. "These are the survivors. Eventually, starving, they slumped here in despair to fall into unconsciousness before finally death took them."

Bear fell silent and Zara, Rebba and Garon looked to one another. It was a truly horrible way to die. Zara saw Bear slump down by a body that lay in its jet black armour. Shudders wracked his body and then an agonized gasp as he began to cry! Zara was stunned. She couldn't remember ever seeing Bear cry.

Rebba and Garon hurried over to their fallen friend and Zara followed, not sure what to think. It was a bad way for someone to die, but such grief? Zara watched as Rebba put her hand on Bear's back. Slowly Bear sat up and his face was a ruin of tears.

"Good gods, Bear. Don't fall apart on us" Zara snapped. Both Garon and Rebba gave her disapproving looks and Zara felt guilty, "Bear, this happened centuries ago. It's nothing to do with us." She finished helplessly. She just wasn't equipped to deal with this kind of thing.

Bear looked up at her, his glorious blue elven eyes, pale with moisture and tears. "You don't understand, Zara. I sent them here." he cried and her mouth fell open. "I sent them away. I tried to save them and instead I condemned them to this… a slow death. They'd have been better off if I had just slaughtered them myself."

Zara was shaking her head. What was Bear on about? Had he lost his mind? He was about to speak, but Rebba's look stopped her.

"Don't you understand, Zara?" The druid said harshly, "It was Tal'Asin who sent them here all those years ago. Bear's mind is inextricable linked with his. What one feels affects the other."

Garon was nodding and Zara realised what she meant. "But I thought this elf lord was gone. Off searching... erm, astrally... or whatever."

"Yes," Rebba responded impatiently, "the spirit is elsewhere but the soul is bound up with Bear's, the memories are there with Bear's."

"Well, how was I supposed to know?" Zara snapped back. She was getting a little irritated with the druid's superior attitude.

"Perhaps, you weren't, Zara," Garon put in, trying to calm things, "but you could have shown a bit more understanding."

Zara looked from Garon to Rebba. She knew she was in the wrong, but it irritated her just the same. It wasn't her idea to come here. She cursed at them both angrily, turned and stomped off. Let them pamper Bear.

He heard Rebba snap, "Leave her, Garon. Let her cool off."

This just annoyed her more. She moved over to the wall, took off her pack and sat down. 'Bloody do gooders!' she thought. She sat and glowered at the floor in front of her. She wasn't an expert on magic.

Slowly, after a few minutes of cursing to herself, her anger began to recede and she glanced back over to her friends sullenly. She wasn't going to apologise. She couldn't have known Bear was going to react like that. This was just another thing that wasn't right. The last three days had been full of such things.

It was worrying really. Over the last two days as they had searched, Zara had watched her old friend change, just a little, just here and there, and it wasn't just physical changes to his eyes, skin and hair. His mannerisms seemed odd at times, the way he spoke and what he said. Zara had heard Bear speaking to himself in languages she had never heard. Sometimes Bear had just stood there, still as a statue, his eyes unseeing; at other times he seemed lost, not knowing where he was or what was going on. The big man even seemed almost in pain at times. Zara wanted to understand, to help even, but she didn't know how to even approach him anymore. The years made things difficult. She and Bear still had the hangover from their fight years ago and they had seen nothing of each other in the intervening years. Once they had been as close as family, now Bear was changing before her eyes and Zara wasn't sure it was for the better.

She found herself staring at the gaping eyes of a skeletal head. It was the head of what must have been a large man. He lay as if he had laid his head down to sleep with his helm by him. He was wearing curious grey armour. At least it looked like that beneath the layers of dust. It was dull, but as Zara looked more closely, the grey colour seemed to move like smoke, like storm clouds in an angry sky! The armour was made of interlocking plates of scale, like Zara imagined dragon skin would be. There were no gaps in the armour, no clasps or bindings, and it covered the warrior completely. By the warrior's hand lay a strange staff, longer than she was tall. It seemed to be made from the same material as the armour and it was clearer to make out. The material had the look of wood and yet it had no grain to it. It couldn't be wood, when she thought about it, no staff so thin would be made from wood, it would be too fragile, and yet this was a man from the Elder times. Was there some wood that could be made so tough it could resist steel? It was said there were many wonders in those ancient times. Perhaps the armour truly was some kind of dragon skin!

Whatever it was, it was well made, though a staff was an unusual weapon for a warrior to have. A quarterstaff was effective to use against multiple enemies, but it would not easily deliver a killing blow to a man in armour. Zara suddenly noticed that the two men either side were armed and armoured exactly the same way, though their armour didn't seem to beguile the eye in the same way! Interesting!

She heard footsteps and looked up to see Rebba, her open face tight with worry.

"We're going to set up here for the night, over where the hall is empty." She pointed and Zara saw Bear and Garon heading over, unslinging their packs.

"In here?" she asked surprised.

Rebba nodded then looked around. "It isn't ideal, but we need to rest before we go through the Waygate again."

"Are we not going to search the surrounding tunnels?" she asked. She was tired and needed a rest, but she wanted to get this bloody Lifestone as soon as she could and then get the hell out of here.

"There's no point. Bear says this hall was sealed just as these people arrived, that's why they were trapped. If the stone were sent here, it would have been trapped here too and Bear cannot sense it."

Zara nodded in relief, she hadn't really wanted to traipse about any more dark halls. She gestured for Rebba to head over to the others as she pushed herself up. Rebba seemed about to say something, but then just shook her head and turned away.

"Is he alright?" Zara muttered gruffly.

Rebba stopped and without turning, answered, "I think the memories swamp him, Zara. I'm not sure how long he can hold things together. Try to be more understanding."

Rebba moved off.

"Yeah, understanding," Zara scoffed. Very little here made any sense. Understanding was something she was starting to feel she had little of, but she'd try. She rose and trudged wearily after the druid.

Rebba Korran sat down, crossed her legs and put her staff across her knees. Garon had opened up one of the packs and was eating some dried beef. He offered some and she took it and began chewing it without enthusiasm. They had started to run low on rations yesterday. Rebba had used her magic to call up water from the earth and they had refilled their water skins. She had then impressed both Garon and Zara by causing several kinds of berry bushes and a small apple tree to grow in front of their eyes out of a patch of earth in one of the tunnels. They had saved their rations and feasted on the fruits. It was a tricky spell and taxing. It had taken her long hours to master. It always seemed that the destructive spells were so much easier than the creative ones; another sad fact of the world.

Zara had dented Rebba's pride in her spell by asking if she could produce a roasted pig for them to feast on and then she had roared with laughter. Zara Halven was a pain, though Rebba knew her well enough to know that her 'humorous' comments were often to stop things becoming too serious. Zara seemed to have spent her life in search of pleasures and fleeting happiness while avoiding actually feeling anything too deeply. She had always found emotions other than superficial pleasure and humour hard to deal with. Something she had proved yet again with Bear.

Rebba looked over at the big warrior. It was interesting how his features were changing. The lines of his face seemed softer and he seemed thinner. His brows were now more arched, and his eyes seemed larger as well as completely blue; no whites now showed in his eyes. It was very distracting looking into those incredible eyes. Bear also seemed to be growing hair back; stubbly golden hair was starting to show all over his once bald head and the scars he had carried for years seemed to be fading, even his broken nose seemed straighter and more noble. There were times when Bear's expressions were clearly not his own and Rebba wondered if she were getting a glimpse of the ancient Lore King in Bear's face.

It wasn't just interesting though, it was also worrying. Rebba had studied shape shifting. It was an incredibly difficult area of magic and one few indulged and even fewer mastered. Those who could shift their shape would often take on characteristics and features of the creature they became and some said those who were weak would lose their mind if they stayed in that form too long. Rebba didn't want Bear to lose his mind. Perhaps when Tal'Asin's spirit returned it would help, but until then... well Bear was strong willed.

Bear caught her looking his way and he smiled sadly. "I can see them you know."

"See who?" said Rebba carefully.

"See them." He waved at the bodies lying around the room. "I can see them as they were hundreds of years ago. I can see their faces. I can remember them as we... as they prepared for the battle. Tal'Asin's memories are broken, but... well many of those here were great warriors and leaders. They followed Tal'Asin to attack the *Ata'Gon*."

Rebba frowned and asked, "What were they like?"

"Ah, Rebba. It's so hard to put into words. It is confusing. To me they seem like heroes, with fabulous armour and powerful weapons and magic, yet to Tal'Asin they were comrades or followers." He paused for a moment in thought. "In here there are people from three races, people who are now part of our legends. There are elven Dragon Lords, princes amongst their people, chosen to wear armour made from the skin of the great wyrm, Cormithiniar. They could command dragons, their armour was proof against most magic, and their swords could cut through even a demon's hide with ease. Amongst the dwarves were the Invincibles, the berserker lords whose enchanted weapons and armour made them a match for even the monstrous troll kings. Lastly, there were men, warriors of the fabled Rainbow Guard. They wore many-coloured armour and carried fearsome weapons. They were led by the

Lord Champions, the personal guard of the greatest of the Nordic Kings, Earondar Greatheart." Bear was almost ecstatic; he was so caught up in what his mind's eye could see.

Rebba was worried he would lose himself to his memories and yet at the same time, she too was enchanted by what Bear was saying. To her and all others in these times, the people he spoke of where legends. Much was lost and much had been added so that the truth was hard to find, but Bear was now a treasure trove of knowledge and Rebba knew he spoke the truth. You only had to look around this room to know. The room itself glowed with power and Rebba, beginning to use the senses that Nossi had shown her, could now see the glow of this power if not the strands of power she knew were there. Rebba could see the glow of magic emanating from almost everybody, they all wore enchanted armour and had enchanted weapons. It was incredible!

Arkadi would have been beside himself. He would have been like a child on his birthday, not knowing what treat to start with first. Rebba was not Arkadi though; to her all this power was frightening. As her masters had taught her, ancient magics could be dangerous. People today just didn't have the knowledge or power to use them.

As students they had all been told the stories of people that had come to nasty ends with ancient artifacts. However, it had not worried Arkadi in the least, but then he would probably have the luck not to get hurt. No, someone else would end up getting hurt. Rebba had no intention of it being her. She was here to search for the Lifestone and that was enough. Zara thought her madly enthusiastic for any kind of adventure that involved elves or the Gods, and she was; it was something of which she had always dreamt. However, the reality had tested her beliefs. She was not in love with danger and it had taken all her courage to say they should go hunting for the Lifestone.

"So there are members of the Rainbow Guard here, with their magic armour and weapons?" Rebba heard Zara ask, suddenly interested.

Rebba knew that most of the history and myths they had studied years ago had bored the warrior, but any stories about the Rainbow Guard and Earondar Greatheart had always fascinated her.

"Yes, I have seen the bodies of a number of the members of the Order of the Healers and the Order of the Slayers, as well as Aelran Sa Vern, the Lord Champion of the Order of the Mystics himself." Bear answered. "His

441

body lies over there with two of his Lord Captains." He was pointing over to where Zara had been sat.

"What, the men in the grey armour with the staffs?" Zara asked, excited.

Bear nodded and Zara looked as if she might go over for another look.

"So, maybe I was asleep when we studied this, but what was so special about them?" Garon Vale asked.

Zara looked at Garon like he was an idiot. "The Rainbow Guard were the greatest warriors amongst the Nordic. They were founded by Earondar Greatheart perhaps the greatest of the Nordic Kings." Zara took an exasperated breath. "You're not going to tell me you haven't heard of him are you?"

Garon gave Zara a disparaging look; everyone had heard of Earondar, there were more legends about him than any other king of the Nordic people.

Bear interrupted. "The Rainbow Guard weren't founded by Earondar. Their history goes back much further, though there are none who now know it."

Zara looked at Bear in wonder, "Really." She gestured for Bear to continue.

"The Rainbow Guard is the name that King Earondar gave to them because of their coloured armour, but in fact the order goes back over a thousand years before that to the beginning of the Nordic people's time in these western lands… and their story is linked to Tal'Asin's."

Bear paused and looked around at his friends and smiled at their rapt expressions. Even Zara was caught.

"Okay, to start with, I will need to take you back even further to before even Tal'Asin was born. Over seven thousand years ago, when the sylvan elven civilisation was nearing the zenith of its power, Gal'Mir Greenheart was the Guardian. He was perhaps, the wisest and gentlest of all the elven guardians. It was he who created the Waygates, using magic and knowledge now beyond the comprehension of even Tal'Asin. However, a great evil came upon the elves in this time. It was the great wyrm, Cormithiniar the Black. Now a wyrm is not like the mighty dragons we have heard tell of that have destroyed whole towns. A wyrm is to a dragon as a lion is to a kitten! Cormithiniar was huge and ancient and clever. It was said he was one of those creatures who had fought against the gods in the time before even the Elder days. Cormithiniar attacked the elves and, when Gal'Mir sought peace with that ancient being to prevent the wyrm's destruction of his people, it slew him. However, Gal'Mir's son, a mighty warrior named Gwin'Dor took up the Lifestone and pursued the great wyrm. In a battle that is still sung of by the elves today, Gwin'Dor the Avenger slew the great wyrm."

"It's a wonderful tale Bear for elves, but what has this to do with our people and the Rainbow Guard?" Zara asked.

"The elves preserved the skin and bones of the wyrm as a reminder of their great loss and great victory. Centuries later, when Tel'Emnar the Crafter became the Guardian, and the Kinslayer Wars, as they became known, had begun against the dark elves, Tel'Emnar took the skin and bones of the great wyrm and from them he crafted the armour and weapons of the hundred Dragon Lords. They were perhaps Tel'Emnar's greatest achievements. The armour was for the elven High King and his greatest warriors."

"Could they really command dragons?" Rebba had to ask. The idea seemed incredible.

"Indeed, the High King and his guard each commanded a silver dragon and were the scourge of the enemy."

"I still don't see what this has got to do with the Rainbow Guard. The dragon bit sounds good, but I'm not that interested in elves." Zara put in impatiently.

"I am coming to that Zara." Bear responded.

"Now after the Kinslayer war when it was thought the dark elves had been destroyed, the King of the Nordic, My'Sed the Mighty asked Tal'Asin, the new elven Guardian, for aid in protecting his people. They had been severely weakened in their fight to aid the elves. It came to Tal'Asin that he would do as his master had done before him, he would create armour and weapons for the Nordic king and his bodyguard. He took what was left from the great wyrm's hide and bones and created a suit of armour for the King and seven suits of armour for his guard. Now in his pride, Tal'Asin sought to surpass his master and he decided to give each armour a distinct spirit and purpose and so he created a will for each armour and gave each a distinct colour and weapon."

"Only seven? But there were over a thousand men in the Rainbow Guard." Zara said.

"Yes, but only seven Lord Champions. The others had lesser armour and weapons made in imitation at King Earondar's behest. The original bodyguard consisted of seven and it guarded the Nordic Kings for over a thousand years before the line of Kings failed and the armours were… lost."

"Lost?" Rebba asked, sensing Bear's hesitation.

"Yes…" Bear replied slowly, "at least in a sense." Bear licked his lips and his almost luminous blue eyes looked down into his lap. "You see the armours were Tal'Asin's greatest success and his greatest failure at the same time."

"I'm not sure I understand." Rebba said and Garon and Zara both nodded agreement. "By all accounts the armours were amazing; they granted long life, great physical strength, speed, healing, resistance to magic and…"

"Yes, yes, it did, but there was a price."

Everyone looked at Bear in surprise. The manner in which he had snapped at them had been odd. Rebba suspected that this was perhaps how Tal'Asin might react, not Bear.

"Let me explain," Bear went on more normally. "There were seven armours with a weapon chosen and forged for them. For example, the grey armour was paired with a staff. It was made for a mage to enhance their abilities and to provide mystical guidance and protection for the king. The spirit… the will of the armour was focused on magic and on protecting the king, following his will. All the armours followed the will of the king and were linked to the rightful king of the Nordic through the great icy sword of Cumb'Rai, their first king. The king would choose who was to wear the armour and carry the staff. The person chosen would don the armour and their will would merge with that of the armour. This was done to give certain advantages. The armour's will would enhance the desire to protect and to be loyal. It would also increase the wearer's will to resist magic and, in the case of the grey armour, to enhance their ability and desire to wield magic. They would become a tireless, loyal defender." Bear looked at them all in turn, "It all sounds good doesn't it?" He asked not wanting an answer. "Save there was one flaw, one thing overlooked. What would happen if there were no king? All of the armours and their spirits were geared to the true King of the Nordic people through the Kings great sword. When the line of kings failed and the heirs were lost and divided, the sword disappeared and the spirit and will of the armour lost its controlling influence. It grew and fought for dominance so that it eventually took control of the person in the armour and took its nature to the extreme. The will of the grey armour became obsessed with finding and protecting the king at all costs and became obsessed with magic."

"Well I can see that might be a bit of a problem but…" Zara began, but Bear cut him off.

"You still don't understand. With the grey armour and staff it created little problem, the armour would seek to do magic. This was also true of the white armour and shield of the healer. However, the red armour and axe of the executioner drove the wearer to kill, the black armour and blade of the slayer became an engine of death!"

Bear stopped and looked at Zara directly. "I know Zara that you have heard of the legend of the Dark Destroyer."

Zara looked at Bear incredulously and Bear nodded.

"The dreaded Dark Destroyer is a terrifying legend from the time after the line of kings failed, but the Dark Destroyer was the Lord Champion of the Ebon Order; one of the seven Lord Champions of the Rainbow Guard. It was Earondar Greatheart who reclaimed the kingship of the Nordic, rediscovered the sword of Cumb'Rai and managed to slay the Dark Destroyer. Eventually, Earondar was able to kill or summon to him all the seven armours and from them he formed the Rainbow Guard with the seven at its heart."

Rebba sat back. She too had heard the tale of the Dark Destroyer. It was a tale to scare little children. She had never thought it was real.

"Hold on," Zara said suddenly, "what about the story of the Green Man, the great hunter who would hunt men in the depth of the forests? You're not saying…"

Bear nodded, "The green armour and bow of the hunter."

"Tynast's fiery breath!" Zara exclaimed. "That story gave me nightmares for months when I was a child!"

"But couldn't they just take off the armour?" Garon asked.

It was Zara who quoted in response, "The armour of a Lord Champion can only be taken off when death has taken its wearer."

Bear agreed, "Though the wearer can will the armour to vanish away, it is still there only a thought away. No man can escape the armour once it is taken up. Even sleep is denied them."

"So you mean that armour over there is that of a Lord Champion."

Bear nodded. "He would have been one of the last to die. The armour would have preserved him for a long time before starvation finally took him. Also, with King Earondar dead and no will to guide him, the torture must have been horrific!"

They ate in silence after this.

It was always light in the hall, but Rebba could feel her eyes getting heavy and she rolled out her blankets and lay down. Soon the others did the same and sleep came quickly.

⌇⌇

Rebba snapped awake with a cry as she felt the touch on her shoulder. Garon sat back in surprise and Zara laughed from where she was packing her bedroll away.

"Sorry." Rebba said a little embarrassed.

She had been dreaming of someone calling to her, someone she could not see, and then elves with demonic, screaming faces had leapt at her and a giant snarling brute had slammed a cruel club down on her.

She took a soothing breath and sat up. Bad dreams were inevitable now it seemed. They had plagued her these last two days.

She saw Bear was now talking urgently with Zara about something. Zara seemed worried at first, but then whatever Bear had said seemed to convince her, even excite her. Rebba packed her things away. She wasn't sure she wanted to know what they were discussing. It would have to do with the search.

At the start of the search, Bear had driven them on and Rebba had been just as enthusiastic, but two long days searching ruined tunnels, halls and buildings had dampened her enthusiasm. Now she was just weary and the nightmares were getting worse.

She thought back. The first journey through the Waygate had been scary. None of them had been prepared for the explosion of energy that had rippled out and sucked them through. This only happened when a Waygate was first opened they had found out. If the gate was left open as they had with the one that had brought them here there was no problem, you just stepped through, and when you closed it the energy simply died. Bear couldn't explain why, it was just the way it worked, though Zara was a bit peeved that he had not remembered this until after they had opened one and nearly scared themselves half to death.

The first place they had visited was ancient Shah'Namir and it had once been the heart of a great forest kingdom. The hall they had found was identical to the one they left, save that it had been breached, though not by the enemy. It had collapsed in places because huge roots had broken through the walls. They were the roots of ironwood trees, Bear called them. They were trees that could grow to over three hundred feet tall and had a trunk inside which you could build an entire house. Apparently, the elves of Shah'Namir had been renowned for their cities in the trees, cities built into the trunks and branches of the trees, cities with buildings wrought so cunningly that they resembled the trees themselves and few could tell them from the surrounding forests. It would have been marvellous to see them, but the few tunnels they could reach were choked with roots and they found that the tunnels and passages had collapsed long before they got anywhere near the surface. That had been an exhausting day. Bear had provided the light while Rebba had used her magic to cause the roots to move aside. Without that they would have got nowhere. The day had exhausted Rebba's strength. Then, as now, they had slept in the Waygate hall and then, as now, dreams had left her feeling like she hadn't rested at all.

The following day they had moved onto ancient Cor'Tuvor, the kingdom of stone. It was far to the north of Shah'Namir. The kingdom was one of highlands and mountains according to Bear. Its hall was once again identical, however, they had found it sealed and intact. They used the key to get out and had spent a day searching the tunnels and halls. The lower halls provided nothing save bones. The elves that had dwelt there had died there, though it was hard to tell how as they had been disturbed and they didn't need Nat's hunting skills to tell them by whom. As they moved up towards the surface the tracks of trolls became heavier and heavier. Then they had reached the walls in the passages. Apparently, the trolls had blocked up the passageways. They had walled them closed. Bear had then used something he had picked up from Tal'Asin's memories to go into a trance and send out his senses in search of the Lifestone. It was not there, and had never been, Bear had reported and Rebba did not doubt him. It was clear to both Garon and Rebba's mystical senses that Bear's talent was growing. Already his talent surpassed Arkadi's, and with Tal'Asin's memories, Bear's knowledge and mastery of the mysteries was increasing. Soon Rebba believed he would be one of the most powerful human magi ever, if he could still be called human!

They had then packed up and left Cor'Tuvor to come here, to ancient Dal'Thanda, the fiery volcanic kingdom where, Bear told them, the elves had delved for metals and forged their closest links with the dwarves of old. Here too there was no sign of the Lifestone, only the bodies of heroes long dead.

Rebba sighed. This quest, for want of a better word, was everything Rebba had dreamt of as a girl; lost cities, magic and danger, and yet, the reality was fear, confusion, futility and fatigue. They never mentioned those in the epic legends.

Rebba moved over and quickly used the keystone to close the Waygate back to Cor'Tuvor. They would be moving on, but where next? Which of the nine ancient kingdoms next? They had already visited four. Bear would tell them soon, no doubt. He had shared his knowledge of each before they had arrived, seeking to give them some warning of what to expect.

Rebba saw Zara and Bear wandering round, pointing here and there at different bodies, talking excitedly. Rebba looked to Garon, silently asking what was going on. The big monk shrugged. She and Garon put away the rest of their things into their small packs and waited for Zara and Bear. They didn't have to wait long.

Zara approached them with a big smile on her face. "Bear's had a great idea."

"Yes, I thought about it and though Tal'Asin's memories suggest this is a violation of the dead, Zara and I feel this is a necessary evil."

Rebba didn't like the sound of that and neither did Garon.

"Violation of the dead?" the monk asked warily.

"Don't worry Garon, we are only talking about arming ourselves from the artifacts left here." Bear said trying to be reassuring.

"Yeah, don't try and get all moralistic on us. We are talking about the same thing we have done before. We originally went down into the tunnels beneath Shandrilos hunting treasure, treasure that would have been left by the dead, long ago." Zara lectured, "And Bear tells me that the ancient armour and weapons here are priceless. I mean I thought most of it was going to be useless by now, but much of the magic still works even after hundreds of years!" she added in near awe.

"Well isn't that a reason not to take it Bear?" Rebba said slowly, "Weren't we to stay away from magical items as they are often set with safeguards?"

Garon nodded and added, "And Arkadi has told us before that the Elder races often geared their enchantments to individuals so that their magic could not be used against them."

Zara frowned at this, her face screwing up in disgust as she saw her idea of priceless ancient weapons disappearing into mist.

"All of that is true." Bear replied and Zara's face almost went purple, but Bear quickly went on, "However, with my new knowledge and skill I can make the enchantments safe for us, change the enchantments to link with our life force."

Zara let out her pent up breath in a huge guffaw. Bear smiled with the now gleeful looking Zara.

"Oh, yes! My own magical weapons like some hero of old." Zara laughed and then she slapped Garon on the shoulder. "You know I think you might just be right Gar. Maybe the gods are on our side."

Garon wasn't so convinced of the merit of this line of thought, but Rebba could see he couldn't deny the fortuity of such weapons.

"Are you sure you can do this, Bear?" Rebba asked.

The big man nodded and then said, "I would suggest some dwarven armour for you Zara, it is lighter than it looks, at least for your upper body, then some elven blades." Zara beamed and then turned to have a hunt around. "A dwarven warhammer or mace would be good for you Garon, along with a dwarven shield, or maybe the armour and shield from one of those Lord Captain's of the White Order of Healers. It seems appropriate somehow." Garon nodded a little dubiously. Bear looked to Rebba, "and maybe the grey armour of the mystics for you Rebba, if you don't mind too much, it will enhance your talent."

Rebba looked over. She was tired and couldn't think of any objections. Indeed her mind seemed to have turned to treacle pudding this morning... if indeed it was morning. She had lost track of time down here.

Zara called out to Bear to come over and help her with some armour and Bear headed off.

Rebba walked over and began to carefully strip one of the skeletons of its armour. It was not easy as the armour was unlike any she had seen, it was all connected and more like taking off clothing rather than armour. It was not a pleasant job either as she had to be careful with the bones which she knew could give off dangerous dust. As she worked, she was vaguely aware of Bear working some magic and of Zara crying out with pleasure. By the time Rebba had all the armour off she could see that Zara was leaping about practising with two new blades; magical auras gleamed strongly off both. Bear was now helping Garon into some white armour. It seemed a bit tight the way they were struggling. Rebba smiled as she watched Bear heave at the straps trying to pull the portly monk into the armour. Without thinking, Rebba placed the helmet from the armour on her head to try the fit.

Suddenly, a blinding white pain exploded in her head and she cried out.

Zara heard Rebba's scream and looked sharply at the druid. She was sat rigid with a grey full helm on her head. All the muscles in the druid's body seemed to be twitching and writhing as she shook and spasmed.

"Blood and sand!" she spat and sprang towards the thrashing druid, even as she called out for Bear and Garon.

Somehow, Bear got to the druid before her. He knelt urgently and grasped Rebba's head in both her hands and the hairs on the back on Zara's neck stood up. Bear was doing something with magic. Zara and Garon stood helplessly for what seemed like forever, and then abruptly, Rebba's body relaxed and Bear pulled the helm from the druid's head. All of them seemed to let out a sigh of relief at the same time, all save Rebba who moaned weakly and then collapsed back. Garon quickly knelt and sat her up. He pulled out a water skin and the druid grabbed it and drank deeply.

"Gods of earth and sky," Rebba gasped after a moment, "I don't want to do that again."

"No, that I don't doubt," Bear replied, deadly serious. "You should be careful which armour you choose, Rebba. I do not think you are ready to don the armour of a Lord Champion. Without a high king the will of the armour would quickly overwhelm you, enslave you and drive you insane."

Rebba nodded in fervent agreement.

"What happened?" Garon asked quietly.

"Well, when I put on the helm… I suddenly found myself in some lifeless plain and a warrior dressed in the grey armour was facing me, not twenty feet away. The warrior suddenly called forth a fireball and hurled it at me and it was all I could do to leap out of the way. I could never have defended myself against such a spell. I fled. Thankfully, Bear then appeared and pulled me away somehow." Rebba gasped and then gave an involuntary shudder. "There was something truly terrifying about that figure. I don't think I have ever been so scared."

Bear nodded. "You were lucky. Had you not dodged and then run you would have been in essence excepting the armour's challenge. The landscape and the battle are a metaphor for the greater contest of wills." Bear smiled gently at Rebba. "Your weakness against such a strong opponent actually saved you, though had I been any slower you all would have been looking at the new Lord Champion of the Order of the Mystics, willing or not!" Bear said dramatically and then finished in a softer tone. "Thankfully, we still have Rebba Korran with us."

Garon smiled and added, "And glad I am or otherwise I'd be left with these two lunatics." he said gesturing at Bear and Zara, "And then there would be only me to try to give a voice to reason."

"Well said, Garon the Mighty, wielder of the Hammer of Azerlin Trollslayer" Bear laughed, nodding at the rune carved hammer the monk now carried.

"You see what I mean!" Garon insisted.

Rebba managed a weak smile. She wouldn't wish that experience on anyone.

Chapter 46

BETWEEN A ROCK AND A HARD PLACE

Sometimes called the ebon knight, other times the shadowed death, the legends of the Dark Destroyer are truly gruesome in their relentless tales of slaughter and death. In some stories this creature is almost human while in others he is a winged monster, but in all he is death to those he encounters! However, it is interesting to note that in the earliest legends the creature is known as a hunter of evil, a terrible warrior against dark magic and demons.

From 'Tales from beyond the Empire' by Boria of Var, BY615

Sir Darin of Kenarth awoke in pain and darkness… and not for the first time! He had lost count of the number of times he had blacked out. He knew he had been trapped here for hours, his legs crushed, his arm broken and useless, his chest pinned. How many hours, he wasn't sure and yet it seemed a lifetime. It seemed that it was all he could do to remember a time when he hadn't been here, when he had been in the light.

He set his teeth once more against the waves of pain that coursed through him. They came with less regularity now and he supposed that was probably a sign he was dying.

He could remember endless hours earlier crying and screaming with the fresh agony of his injuries and the almost greater agony of knowing he was helpless and alone. He had pleaded and begged with all the gods he knew, with friends, with family, and finally with death itself. But none heard. He had wished for death to take him quickly so that the pain would end, but even that would not come. He could barely move his head and the only limb that worked could scarce be moved more than a few inches. The rock pressed in on all sides. He couldn't even end his own suffering.

Thinking back now, he was ashamed at how quickly the pain had reduced him to a whimpering wreck. He had always thought of himself as strong and brave, yet when it came to it he fell apart as quickly as any other. It seemed he was not brave enough to die slowly, in pain.

Now, the pain was fading and his strength along with it. He was light headed with blood loss and lack of water. His lips were cracked and split, but the pain from them paled into nothing beside that he had suffered since waking here, slammed down like a bug beneath a giant's boot, crushed and writhing.

There was no hope for him now, he knew, and with that acceptance came some measure of sanity strangely enough. He gained a measure of clarity with an acceptance of death. He smiled and laughed weakly. It turned into a coughing, rasping choke that stirred up the dust and sent new waves of pain through him.

'Good gods' he thought. 'Let it end soon.'

Once more the pain subsided and his mind began to drift. He thought he could see his mother and called out to her, but she was washed away by the pain his call prompted. He cried silently, there were no tears anymore, they had dried up long ago, but locked inside his head, he wailed like a babe in arms at the cruelty of his end. He would not even die with his sword in his hand like a warrior. He would die a mewling retch.

Time passed and Darin drifted through memory. He could remember his father giving him his first sword. It was a wooden practice sword and he was little more than four years old. "You'll be a warrior, my son," he heard his father's gruff voice say, and that's what Darin had set out to be. He would be a warrior and not just that, but a great warrior, a warrior men would look on in awe, women would swoon at, and about which bards would sing. Yes, that was how it was meant to be.

His father had begun his training. He was a harsh taskmaster, a self-made lord who had cut, slashed, killed and bribed his way to becoming a respected baron. He had taught his son to show no fear, to bury it deep and to take any advantage. He had taught his son how to fight dirty, and though Darin learnt later the more subtle forms of sword play, in a battle his father's rough teaching served him well.

Later, he had benefited from the teaching of warrior magi at the Guild school in Ostia who had studied the art of sword fighting from various cultures; the hacking, swinging styles of the Nordic warriors; the blocking and stabbing techniques of the Carnacian Legions; the dancing, whirling methods of even the far off Etoshan dervishes; they had all added to Darin's growing knowledge and skill with the blade. These skills he had honed in mock fights with friends such as Zara Halven, Gael Machay and his best friend, Bear. All three had developed different techniques. Zara Halven was a dancing warrior who fought with twin sabres and fast cutting and slicing attacks. She was a dodging, weaving opponent with uncanny speed and agility. Gael Machay was a savage, fearless, reckless warrior, all nastiness; an attacking opponent with little thought to defence. Jon 'Bear' Madraig was strong and fought with calm and caution, at least to begin with. Once his fear passed, he became a ruthless, powerhouse. Darin had practised with them, taking something from all of them. He became a thinking, cunning warrior with unorthodox moves, though it wasn't until later he learnt how unorthodox. After all, you have to learn how to fight the orthodox way before you could go beyond it. It was with the knights of Karodra that he went beyond the ordinary.

When he first joined the knights, most of his friends and family saw it as an odd move. He didn't even believe in the Alban god or the teachings of the prophet Alba. However, he did believe in the strong protecting the weak, at least a little. He seemed to have picked that up from his friends. It certainly hadn't come from his mercenary father! Even more though, he valued the respect and admiration the knights gained and he definitely respected superior sword play and the knights had the best sword master in the Wildlands. Later, he came to appreciate the discipline and training of the order, and the other perks were a bonus too. He had seen senior knights of the order with women gazing at them with rapt expressions, they wore expensive armour and men looked at them with envy. He wanted to be like them.

He had loved the order. He had quickly risen to prominence as a swordsman, though he had found it harder to master the mace, morning star and lance. The lance came with a horse involved and Darin had always hated horses. Nevertheless, he had continued to learn and improve. He learnt the ancient art of swordplay from the master; Anton Di Sandor, an Alban noble in exile. The eastern techniques were full of intricate forms and moves with beguiling names; the 'Rising Hawk' and the 'Dance on the Waves' and so on. Darin had taken little interest in the fancy names and pretentious posturing, but he had mastered the forms such that only two other men in the order were his equal, Master Di Sandor, and the champion of the order, Barristes Salivardu, another Alban, though he was no nobleman. After several years in the order, Darin was sure he could have defeated even them. He was good, everybody said so. He had combined all the divergent techniques he had been taught and had been forging them into a new style, all his own, of course he rarely got to practise it, most robbers and thieves he fought against were easily overwhelmed simply by a man with a big sword.

Something disturbed his thoughts. He realized his good hand had wandered. It was touching something, something hard and smooth, though it took a while to register in his water starved brain. He couldn't have opened his eyes, they were caked shut, but there was little need, no light shone deep beneath the rubble he was trapped under. He was puzzled though. What was it?

Suddenly, a thought occurred to him and he forced his hand further, prompting fresh pains. He didn't care. This might be his sword and if so he could at least die with his father's great sword in hand. That was important, though in his confused state, he was starting to forget why.

It was not a sword, but it was metal. It felt more like a shield. He felt around. It was smooth and could have been anything to his stiff fingers. Pain coursed through him again as he stretched slightly to reach an edge. His fingers hooked around and pulled the thing closer. His questing fingers slid inside. Was it full of sticks? He could feel smooth sticks and bits of twigs. No, sticks weren't this smooth. What were they?

The effort of reaching had exhausted him and though he desperately fought for consciousness, his failing body could not maintain him. Once more his mind drifted and he lost this battle, his head slumping.

Suddenly, he found himself in the field outside his father's keep. He was lying down for some reason. His father stood before him, a harsh frown on his thick features. 'Get up boy' he heard him say and Darin struggled to obey, but how ever he tried he couldn't get up. He was confused and when he looked down he saw his legs twisted and broken and the horror returned.

Darkness again.

He couldn't tell if his eyes had opened or whether he was staring at the back of his own eyelids. He was struggling to remember how he had got here. His hand felt warm for some reason, though he didn't know why. Colours began to swirl in from of his eyes... or in his mind. He couldn't tell which anymore. He smiled inside. The colours were pretty.

Slowly, the colours began to fade and Darin could see a dark, grey landscape. He couldn't remember how he had got here or even where here was. He was sure he had never been here before. In fact, wherever here was didn't seem right. The landscape was barren. There were dead trees here and there, but nothing else as far as the eye could see. The land itself was flat, cracked and lifeless. The sky was the colour of storm clouds without any difference; a dome of dreary grey. He seemed to be standing on a road of some kind. At least he thought it was a road, though it was little different from the surrounding land save it was a little flatter and had a small, shallow ditch running along each side of it. He turned and looked down the road. It seemed to go straight as an arrow off to the horizon. He turned again and looked the other way. The only difference this way was that there seemed to be a bridge a short way off before the road continued on. He couldn't make out any of the details.

In sudden realization, he looked down and saw he was wearing his armour and had his great sword in hand. This seemed odd to him at first. He couldn't say why, but it seemed wrong somehow. He shook his head. Why wouldn't he have his arms and armour? He was a knight.

A sound made him turn to look back along the featureless road. A warrior all in black stood twenty paces from him. Darin frowned. How had he got there? He hadn't been there before and there was nowhere he could have hidden.

The warrior stood still and silent. Darin was at a loss. He took a step forward to speak, but something made him swallow his words. Something about this mysterious warrior was wrong.

Darin studied him carefully. The armour he wore covered him completely, even his face was covered by a smooth featureless and faceless helm. There didn't even appear to be gaps for his eyes, nose and mouth. Could the man even see? Or breathe? The majority of the armour seemed to be made up of almost hexagonal plates of different sizes. The pieces were large to cover his chest, stomach, legs and shoulders and then became smaller and smaller as they moved towards joint areas. They made up a seamless suit of plate mail. Even the gauntlets and boots were part of the armour. There were no gaps between the large plates and the finer ones that made up a kind of chain mail, they merged as one. There were no straps or bindings either. The suit was like a bulky second skin with small spikes and jagged edges around knees, elbows and shoulders. Along the lower arms and legs there were serrated edges like those on the giant insects he had fought.

The armour reminded him a little of those grotesques creatures, though this armour was far sleeker and, in some ways, more elegant. In fact, now that he thought about it, the armour reminded Darin more of... dragon skin. Yes, though he had never seen a real dragon, he had heard enough descriptions and seen some pictures in some of Arkadi's books.

The armour's colour seemed odd as well. It wasn't just black, it almost seemed to absorb the light around it. It was mat black and no light reflected from its surface. The warrior also carried a sword. It was large and the handle and blade were jet. The warrior stood there, black against the grey around him. He seemed to draw in the light.

The warrior stood in what seemed like a relaxed pose, the sword held one handed by his side, its point inches from the ground.

Darin just stood and stared and the warrior stared facelessly back. There was no wind or noise of any kind to disturb them and Darin was starting to get a little irritated. Was the man just going to stand there? Where were they anyway?

'I'm getting bored of this', Darin thought.

"What's going on here?" he said, harshly, as he took a step forward, "Who are..."

Before he could finish, the warriors sword came up and a feeling of intense cold struck Darin. Suddenly, the warrior was attacking. Darin backed up frantically. The man in black lunged for him with startling speed. Darin brought up his blade and blocked the whistling arc of the black blade. The force of the two swords coming together sent Darin reeling back. 'Gods above!' he thought. 'The man was as strong as an ox...

and quick too!' He blocked another whistling attack and was forced back again, and then again.

The warrior was hammering at him from all sides it seemed. Darin was backing up and parrying desperately. 'Tynast's arse!" he cursed silently, 'Enough of this.'

Darin leapt backwards as fast as he could, opening up a gap between them. The warrior in black stopped his blade held ready. He said nothing.

"Right," Darin snarled, "Let's try that again." With that Darin launched himself at his mute attacker.

Attack after attack, Darin launched. He battered at his assailant from first one side then the other. Minutes passed and only the ringing of steel could be heard. The warrior in black blocked, parried and dodged every attack, but Darin pushed on. Few men could match his stamina in a battle and it must be almost impossible to breath in that armour. Darin could already hear his own breath and feel the beat of his heart. The other man must be sweating and struggling for breath like a fish out of water. He was incredibly strong Darin knew, but he would weaken. Darin had fought men stronger than he before. However, what was becoming obvious to Darin was that this man was good. His defence was impeccable and he used an economy of movement that spoke of a true master, a man in control of himself and his blade. Darin smiled. 'At last a real test!'

Darin stepped back, eyes on his opponent, looking for any unsteadiness or slowing. There was none. This man was more than good, whoever, he was.

"You are well trained," he called. "Will you not tell me your name so that I might at least know my enemy?"

The only answer was silence as the warrior advanced.

Darin knew what was happening, the pattern to a duel between masters was often similar. Both of them had tested the other and both now had a measure of their opponent and knew they had a fight on their hands. However, what did concern Darin was that the opening part of this duel had obviously gone to the man in black. Darin had been beaten back by the silent swordsman's initial assault, where as he had made no ground in his! Still, the man would be tiring.

Darin caught the warrior's next attack, intending to turn it and riposte, but the force of the blow meant he had to retreat. Again and again, the dark attacker came at him and Darin parried skilfully, and yet was forced to step back. The man in black did not seem to be tiring at all. Perhaps Darin had underestimated his stamina, perhaps that strange armour allowed him to breath more freely than he had expected. It certainly didn't seem to slow him at all. It was only Darin's own prodigious speed that kept his guard intact against the warrior's lightning attacks.

It seemed that though Darin was outmatched in strength, they were matched in speed and stamina so far. It would come down to skill and nerve. Darin quickly dodged the warrior's next blow and switched to attack. He used the forms he had been taught. The warrior matched him form for form. There was no way through.

Darin realized he was getting nowhere. He was using the styles he had been taught and his opponent knew them all, matched them all. Darin was being driven back relentlessly. Even when he attacked, his opponent's parries and blocks were of such strength and power he was forced back. This was the best he had ever faced! For a moment the strangeness of this whole situation struck Darin, then the man in black attacked.

Backwards, Darin fought the battle of his life; the warrior's sword was not getting close… not yet. However, Darin was not sure how long he could keep this up. Soon he would begin to slow and this bastard in black didn't seem even close to tiring! He fought on, his mind working furiously. He would never defeat this warrior using the techniques he had been taught. He had varied his attacks from wild Nordic assaults, to darting Carnacian lunges, even whirling Etoshan slashes, they were all blocked. The forms of the eastern Alban masters had brought some gaps, but the warrior was so strong and quick, Darin could not exploit them. He gnashed his teeth in frustration. A seed of doubt was creeping in to Darin's mind, a seed that had never taken hold before. Could he actually lose?

"No!" Darin called out loud, "You miserable whoreson!"

Darin launched a furious, reckless attack. The warrior was ready, he blocked, sliding Darin's sword to the right and whipped in a blow that smashed across Darin's midriff.

"Oooof!" An explosion of air burst from Darin's lungs as he was hurled back like a child slapped by an adult. He landed hard, rolled and fell into the ditch by the side of the road. 'Fool!' he thought, even as he reacted.

Instantly, he continued to roll, trying to put as much distance as he could between himself and his enemy. Then he desperately scrambled to his feet, expecting a black blade to fall at any moment.

Darin brought up his sword and looked around for his dark clad enemy. The man stood at the top of the ditch, on the road, looking down on Darin. There was no sign of tension in his stance and he stared down silently.

'Arrogant bastard' Darin thought, 'he didn't even come after me! Does he think he can afford to give me advantages? Is he that confident?' Darin moved back along the ditch, backing to where he could get back up onto the road. He never took his eyes off the man in black.

None of this made any sense, but Darin didn't care. He had trained all his life to make himself the best swordsman and here was the test he had always dreamed of; a warrior of consummate skill who could test him to the full.

Darin moved carefully up the slope and back onto the road. He had let himself lose control; that was a mistake he wouldn't repeat. He was not done yet. This warrior had given him a chance, he thought Darin finished, thought he was the superior. The mistake Darin had made was to think so too. A duel was also a battle of wills and Darin refused to be so easily defeated. His will was strong. He would not simply give up, he would fight.

Darin noticed that the bridge he had glimpsed earlier, was now barely a hundred yards away. It was a thin, stone bridge with a low rail along both edges and it appeared to cross a sheer sided ravine of some sort. He had been forced back further than he had thought.

Darin took a deep calming breath and rolled his shoulders before grasping his sword firmly in one hand, his other went to the pain in his stomach. He felt around. His armour was the finest money could buy. It should have prevented any real damage. However, the plate covering his stomach and the chain beneath it had been cut through and he suddenly felt blood running down into his groin. No sword should have been able to pierce his armour so easily. It was made of dwarven fired steel!

Darin wiped the blood off his gauntlet and took his great sword in two hands. The warrior seemed to take this as a sign to continue and he began walking casually forward. There was no doubt now in Darin's mind that he would have to try something different if he was to win this battle. He had been practising his own fighting style for some time. It merged several disparate techniques together. He had not yet perfected it, but he had nothing else. This was no longer a duel for Darin. The damage he had taken and the skill and relentless nature of this enemy meant it was now a fight for his life. Darin sensed that this was the last break he would be allowed. From now on there would be no quarter.

The warrior attacked and Darin used an eastern form to parry and ride with the blow. He let it spin him and as he did he hammered his elbow into the man's eyeless face plate and swept his lead leg as his father had taught him to do long ago. It was like elbowing a tree and kicking a wall, but the warrior swayed and stumbled and Darin slammed his sword down two handed. With incredible speed, the warrior recovered his balance and managed to partly deflect his attack, but still the blow forced the warrior to stumble back.

Darin grinned. "Not so bloody cocksure now are you, freak?"

The battle was joined and Darin used every new combination he had managed to link together. A variety of forms and attacks merged as he forced his opponent to defend. Still the dark swordsman managed to hold off most of Darin's attacks. However, some were getting through and though they failed to pierce his enemy's incredible armour, it was starting to have an effect. For the first time Darin could hear some sounds that showed his enemy was mortal after all. And Darin had the feeling that his opponent was unused to his skill falling short. Darin's confidence grew and with it his strength. Darin suddenly found he was enjoying himself more than he had ever done before. This was his finest hour, the pinnacle of his endeavour, the culmination of all his effort with the sword over the years.

As the minutes passed, Darin pressed his attack. Repeatedly, he breached his opponent's defence, but always his sword rebounded from the jet black armour! The man in the armour however, was feeling each attack. Very slowly though, the warrior began to anticipate some of Darin's attacks and he seemed to be forming new defences so that Darin broke through lest frequently.

Darin found himself in awe of the man's skill; whoever he was, he was forming, in minutes, new defences to attacks Darin had spent years creating! Darin was also starting to feel the fatigue in his arms. His muscles were beginning to burn with each attack or parry.

Abruptly, Darin realised he was again being pushed back towards the bridge. It was a slower retreat and still Darin managed to get in hits on his opponent, but now the dark swordsmen was starting to get through Darin's defence. Darin could still ride the blows, but he was slowing and his armour was taking a beating. The ebon armour of his opponent showed not even a scratch, while Darin's was now bashed, bent and broken in places. Also, the man in black was not slowing at all.

It was so unfair. Darin should have won by now. No ordinary man could fight for so long without tiring at all! No ordinary man could take that kind of beating and then come back as strong as before! And no ordinary man could have armour so strong it prevented the strongest steel from even scratching it! Darin cursed. He was going to be beaten not by a better swordsman, though the man was obviously the best Darin had ever met, but by some magical armour that sustained its wearer and was proof against any ordinary blade.

Slowly, Darin could feel the bridge approaching and with it whatever ran beneath. He couldn't see it behind him, yet he could feel it there. Could he use that?

He broke off and took quick steps back. He felt the slope of the bridge as it rose to arch over whatever depth was beneath it. He continued to retreat. He risked a look around and saw over the low rail on the bridge, a dark chasm. He couldn't see the bottom.

Swiftly, he raised his blade and managed to partially parry the warrior's overhand swing. The man had nearly cut him in two! As it was the blow slipped to the side, clipping Darin on the shoulder and adding another dent to his already battered armour. He felt the blow reverberate through his body, but forced himself to attack. He must force the man over the edge. It was his only chance now.

Desperation gave Darin added strength and speed, and he threw every attacking combination he had contrived at the unspeaking swordsman. It was working. The warrior was driven back. The man's heel was back against the foot of the rail. However, the exertion was too much and Darin's weary body could not maintain it. Suddenly clumsy, Darin overextended his lunge and the dark warrior spun out of his way to come at Darin from behind. Darin twisted savagely to face the warrior, but he had lost the advantage and now it was he with his foot to the rail and his back to the open chasm. Darin tried everything he could to get away from the fall. His every effort was countered. He was too tired, too slow, too weak.

In his mind the truth dawned. He was defeated. He had nothing left to give.

In that instant he saw the face plate of his opponent seem to melt away and the face of a pale blue eyed man appeared. The eyes were wide, wild and mad; the mouth cruel, twisted into a silent scream. In that face, Darin saw horror he had never thought existed. Then the face flickered and he saw a dark-eyed, bearded man, then a swarthy, narrow faced man with a long drooping moustache. Face after face flickered past, but for all, the eyes and mouth remained the same, the same expression of silent horror etched into them.

Suddenly, Darin heard a voice in the depths of his mind, though no word was spoken.

"You have lost. You have surrendered to the armour. You are mine now!"

Instantly, he rebelled. He didn't know what he was rebelling against, but his every instinct cried out against the horror he had seen. He dropped his sword and grabbed the warrior in black as he leaned towards him. With every last ounce of strength in his body, he threw himself backwards, heaving the black armoured creature with him.

"No! What are you doing?" Darin heard the voice scream in his mind, but he laughed and screamed back in denial, 'I never surrendered, you bastard! AND NOW WE BOTH LOSE!!!'

With that, Darin and the black armour tumbled from the bridge, clasped together like lovers.

Chapter 47

CAPTIVITY

What are demons? To the followers of Alba they are fallen angels who serve the great Deceiver. It is they who tempt the wicked and inflict tortures in the seven hells. Albanites see them as beings who inhabit the spirit realms, they are not corporeal beings of the physical world. Indeed, many of the more scholarly clerics believe they are merely manifestations of the evil within humanity. However, they are wrong! Demons or 'deavas' as we Etoshans call them, are very real and very dangerous. If they are drawn into our world they are the enemies of all life and are unrelenting in their desire for death and destruction. I have seen what a true demon can do and only a joining of many Viziers was able to banish the creature, and not before a number were lost to its foul strength!

Excerpt from the musings of Abdari Sulim Dan Duafa, Grand Vizier to the Satrap of Dur Bandar BY501

Tal'Asin's astral form sat wrapped deep in shadow and even deeper in his magic, shielding himself from all who might have the talent to look. There were many below who had strong talent, particularly the princely dark elf on his throne, but none approached Tal'Asin's knowledge and skill with the mysteries.

Tal'Asin looked down on the former great hall of the holy elven city of Althazar, a city over nine millennia old, founded by the Guardian Dah'Nu over the site of the Great Temple of Elysia, Lady of Light and Life. Once this had been Tal'Asin's home; now it was the home of the enemy.

The journey here had been terrible enough for the Lore King. The lands and people he was sworn to protect lay ruined and desolate. The only inhabitants were the very enemies he had fought so hard to defeat. It cut deep into his soul that he had managed to defeat the cursed *Ata'Gon* only to lose his lands to those evil creatures that had followed that foul being. Logically, he knew he could not have done anything more to save his people and yet his heart would not allow him to truly believe this. Surely, he could have done more, his mind taunted him. Surely he could have been quicker or cleverer.

So it was that he found himself gazing despairingly down on a hall he had once presided over, with rage and confusion in his heart, for in that place that had once been his home sat a dark elven prince and his following, and Tal'Asin could not help but think it was partly his fault.

Tal'Asin had learnt much in the past hour as he floated, cloaked and hidden above the fiend whose name he had learned was Uh'Ram. It was a name which in the ancient Elorien tongue meant 'dancing flame'; a beautiful name for a disgusting creature. It was clear to Tal'Asin that this being was steeped in evil, well versed in the cruelties and savageries of serving the Lords of Darkness; a demon lord! This was the source of evil he had felt, a source so akin to the *Ata'Gon*. This Uh'Ram was a creature who thirsted after power and to whom life, other than his own, meant nothing.

Yes, he was a fitting heir to the *Ata'Gon*. He had not that vile creature's talent nor yet his power, but he was rising in his knowledge. Already his power surpassed any that Tal'Asin knew of in this shattered world where humans held sway and the Elder races were a shadow of their former selves. If this prince were to gain the Lifestone, he would be a power that could not be stopped, not even by the combined forces of these lands in this new age. Luckily, the key to the Ways and the location of the Lifestone were still mysteries to this cruel being.

However, it was clear that this Prince Uh'Ram was already well on his way to dominating the northlands as his ancestor once had. Tal'Asin had learnt of Uh'Ram's plans as he had watched and listened. Uh'Ram had begun uniting the vast numbers of goblins that dominated the former lands of the elves. Uh'Ram also had thousands of his own people and their allies spread throughout the lands, setting up leaders loyal to him and the Lords of Darkness amongst the goblins and trolls. However, what was even more alarming, was that he knew everything that was going on in the only potential centre of resistance of which Tal'Asin knew; Shandrilos!

Tal'Asin had quickly realised, as he opened his mind and absorbed the thoughts and feelings of this new world, that Shandrilos was the one glimmer of hope in a sea of ignorance. Only in that place were there now people who knew of the threat rising in the northlands.

Tal'Asin had known through Jon Madraig that Jon's friends were heading to the surface with the gnome, Nossi Bee. They would spread the word about the dark elves and their plans. As Tal'Asin had risen up through Shandrilos, he had realised that knowledge of the goblin threat was clear to many already, and that the leaders of the remnants of the Elder races were in Shandrilos too, seeking unity in defence against the ancient enemy. His hopes had risen. However, Tal'Asin also confirmed that even his own people had forgotten or denied even to themselves the true nature of the enemy so the gnome and Jon's friends were key to making people aware of the true nature of the threat. Yet, as Tal'Asin had listened to the comings and goings of this dark prince's hall, a sickening realisation had dawned on the Lore King; the gnome knew no difference between elves and dark elves, and also Prince Uh'Ram had already known how key Shandrilos would be and was using evil humans to twist the truth and oppose the elves. The threat from the north was being blamed on all elves! The enemy had been ready. Prince Uh'Ram was already on the way to dividing his enemies. Somehow, like his vile ancestor, this dark prince seemed to possess an uncanny ability to read the future, to predict the will of the Lords of Light and move to frustrate that will.

Tal'Asin was deeply troubled. He needed to know more, especially about Shandrilos. The truth was being obscured through ignorance. The elves would be alienated from the humans. Something had to be done.

Tal'Asin began to draw in his perceptions and withdraw from the dark prince's court.

The only bright side Tal'Asin could see was that this enemy knew nothing about Jon and his friends and their search for the Lifestone. Tal'Asin needed to seek more knowledge in Shandrilos and then to find Jon; the human warrior would need Tal'Asin's aid.

Tal'Asin mentally eased his astral form up towards the roof, concentrating on not disturbing the hidden magical alarms and traps set about the hall. They had been well set, but it seemed no one in this time yet knew of the higher mysteries, even the powerful prince below had not the knowledge or power yet, and so the forces of light still had some advantages. Tal'Asin smiled, perhaps something may be done to turn the tide yet, he thought. It was only as he slid seamlessly and smoothly through the roof of the great hall that he realised his error.

Astral fire crackled around him as he rose into the open air and he screamed in pain. Someone had cunningly interwoven a nasty astral trap using the higher mysteries. An attack he could not evade. Swiftly, Tal'Asin's reactions drove forth a negating spell and the fire hissed away, yet even as it did, Tal'Asin realised that the fire was just a ruse, the true intent of that weaving was the astral trap that hammered Tal'Asin's mind and caged him like an animal! Tal'Asin threw his best astral storm against that prison, but the force holding him was immense and without the resources of his true body or the Lifestone he had little chance of breaking free. The astral cage formed around him, binding his mental self tightly.

Quickly, he ceased all struggling, his mind working furiously, seeking an escape. The trap was well conceived and the thought that dominated his ancient thoughts was… 'Who had such power?'

Archmage Baden Erin sat quietly at his desk, trapped. He was confined to his quarters and while his quarters where spacious; they took up the whole upper domed section of the main college building; he still felt his captivity keenly. True he could wander in secret, but he could do little. Events were happening that he had no control over, and worse, had little chance to affect!

The revelations of the gnome creature, Nossi Bee had been relayed to him by Eliantha and he had confirmed it with this Nat Bero: elves beneath the college, killing; elves behind the rise of the goblin tribes; and elves ready to betray us all! This was on top of the huge explosion and collapse in the catacombs. Even loyal Eliantha had confided that she was now less than sure about the elves and the only thing preventing an emergency assembly of the Masters was the collapse itself and that would not delay things much longer.

Despair rose up in Baden's chest and sought to choke him, but he forced it back. He needed to think, needed to come up with a course of action, yet it seemed like everything that he had built was being pulled down around him. Even now his leadership was being stripped bit by bit from him. Baden Erin had no pretences about that, no matter how cheerful a face Eliantha put on it, the revelations from Master Drollin combined with those of the gnome Nossi Bee would sway things enough for him to be suspended and would give the seemingly heroic and decisive Xameran Uth Altor or Atholl Dorard the leadership of the college. Of course, this would only be temporary, until the matters could be fully investigated, Baden thought wryly. Baden could almost see the smooth sorcerer uttering the words, though Baden was sure no investigation would ever reveal the truth. But then what was the truth?

Baden was sure of little at the moment, little other than his own innocence in the matter of the murders. Of the elves it was less clear.

No, he thought suddenly and shook his head, I cannot doubt now.

He had spoken to the elves as soon as he had heard the gnome's words and their surprise and shock had been genuine. The gnome's revelations took them back and they quickly had retreated to discuss things. However, they had stressed instantly was that they knew of none of their people below. Baden was at a loss. He could do little but wait now. It seemed he was powerless to affect either his own fate or that of the plans he had begun.

As soon as Baden realised this, he rejected it violently. He would not sit back and allow all he had built to be decided and dictated by others. He needed to do something. The enemy, whoever or whatever it was, was clearly working against him to a degree he could never have predicted in his own college. The Grand Abbot Alinus was correct, he was now beginning to see; Xameran and Atholl were just pawns, either willing and knowing or not, and Baden needed to take back the initiative and defeat them… but how and who were the puppet masters?

It seemed in all this that the gnome and Master Drollin were central to his problems. Drollin had an impeccable reputation and none would question his word on what he had seen, none that is save Baden who was in the unique position of knowing for sure that Drollin was lying. It was clear to Baden that Drollin had been bought, no doubt with the offer of heading the school of Seers, but Baden could not convince others of that, they would believe Baden was simply trying to save his own reputation. The gnome was a different problem, less clear to Baden, but perhaps more tractable.

It was clear from Eliantha that this creature's race was definitely unknown to her or anyone else, unless it was some kind of deformed dwarf. Also, that the gnome had spoken what it, at least, believed to be the truth. Eliantha had been certain and Baden trusted her senses. However, the Conclave had not been given a lot of time to question the creature and he had conveniently been protected by Xameran and Atholl as the gnome was very 'sensitive' and 'fearful' as the sorcerer lord put it. This led Baden to the obvious thought that the gnome might have told the truth, but what else was there, what were Atholl and Xameran protecting? Their sudden concern for others was unconvincing. Perhaps the gnome creature had not told the whole truth just as Nat Bero had not?

Baden had been intrigued by the tall huntress' story, but it was clear that she could not remember all the details and that she was hiding something. However, the Archmage could not press her without her becoming resistant. It was clear that Mistress Bero did not trust him, and why would she?

Baden's thoughts turned to Atholl and Xameran for a moment and he cursed silently. He had been so wrong about them. He had always known about their opposition and antagonism, but he had badly underestimated the depths they would go to get what they wanted.

Baden needed to find the gnome that was clear. Eliantha had said the gnome was a timid creature. Baden was sure Atholl or Xameran was intimidating the creature. If Baden could find the gnome, he could find out what was being hidden and why. He also needed to talk to the elves again. Some of what Nat Bero had told him seemed odd.

With a clear purpose and a determined look in his dark eyes, Baden Erin stood and moved to prepare his magical disguise.

⁂

"So it seems you were not destroyed all those centuries ago?" a musical voice chimed, hatred clear in its beautiful tones.

Tal'Asin remained silent, waiting. He could do little else except wait and try to discover more about his captor.

Slowly, the scenes of the ebon roof and dome of the great hall of Althazar began to haze and swirl and in its place a cavernous, flame-lit room came gradually into focus. Tal'Asin sensed that the vast hall he found himself in was far removed from the normal astral plane. This was some constructed annex of that realm, a place apart, controlled and maintained by an enchantment of true complexity and power. Only a mage of great power could have created such a place. Tal'Asin had created such a place for himself as a refuge in his enforced centuries in the astral realm. He had taken Jon Madraig there. This was the kind of place in which a seer could dwell in safety to perform their scrying. Tal'Asin's scrying had been limited by his link to the Waygate. However, his captor's obviously had not. This one had been watching and waiting.

Tal'Asin once again mentally tested the astral bonds that confined him, but the instantaneous move through the astral realm had made no discernible difference.

"The shadows enchantment that surrounds you is quite impressive." The musical voice chimed again. "But is it still necessary? There are few who would still recognise you, few who have your image indelibly etched upon their memories. There are few who would scour the planes for signs of your remains?"

Tal'Asin looked to the centre of the flickering hall and by a large pool in the centre of the cavern stood a single figure, tall, slim and female. A chill ran through him as he realised that before him stood a dark elf! Her coppery skin shone in the fiery chamber and her jet black hair and her… pale, blind eyes… a second chill shook him as memory took hold of him. He knew of only one elf of any race that had such eyes.

"Ry'Ana?" he whispered in horror. "You're…"

"Dead." Ry'Ana of the White Eyes finished for him. "No, I'm afraid when your people attempted to destroy all of my kind all those centuries ago, I was one of those who escaped your annihilation. Hundreds of thousands of others were not so lucky!" She spat, rage clear in every inch of her posture. "Your time has finally come."

The dark elven woman turned away and looked into her scrying pool.

Tal'Asin quickly examined his surroundings and the prison that held him.

"Oh, you will not be escaping dear Tal'Asin. My prison is well beyond you in that weakened form," came her voice, even as Ry'Ana turned back to view him with her pale stare. "Just how did you manage to survive? I am not displeased to see you so weak, but I am intrigued. I had thought you long dead and beyond my reach or I would have hunted you down centuries ago."

Tal'Asin merely stared at the dark elf mutely.

"Oh come now, you did so love the sound of your own voice, have you no desire to speak with an old friend?"

Tal'Asin blinked slowly and then closed his eyes. He needed to think.

"Rest all you want Lore King, you will be here a long time, I promise you that. However, your presence does change things somewhat. So before I can indulge in slowly and painfully..." She almost purred as she spoke, drawing out the words, "...tearing your spirit and soul apart, I must speak with Uh'Ram."

Tal'Asin opened his eyes and found that Ry'Ana was smiling as no seemly elf should. Slowly she began to fade from view.

Despair and sadness hit Tal'Asin like a blow; Ry'Ana was still alive and he was helpless!

⁓⁂⁓

The changeling knew its master's will and opened its thoughts to him. Quickly it communicated all it knew. The information was not welcome. The Archmage, the so-called leader of the college was behind the alliance with the Elder races. This information brought interest from his master.

The expedition to retrieve the key to the Waygates had failed and a party of humans had brought a gnome survivor to the surface who was now in the college being questioned. This information prompted deep rage and while the changeling feared nothing, its master's rage was to be avoided. The changeling quickly communicated that the gnome was held by their agents here in the college and the information it knew had been twisted; knowledge of the dark elves and their true purpose beneath the college had been hidden and the master's pet mage was using the information to drive a wedge between the college and the Elder races here.

This was received better, but prompted a question 'What of the mage?' was the silent thought. The changeling had tried to contact the mage and yet he always seemed to be elsewhere or surrounded by others. It communicated this. Annoyance came through the mental link and along with it instructions, clear and concise. 'Kill the gnome and those who had brought it up from below. Kill this Archmage who sought to create an alliance with the Elder races. Find the mage and make him contact the master.

The changeling closed the link with its master and stood up from its desk. So far it had worked hard to allay any suspicion of itself. It had done the duties of the chamberlain perfectly. The changeling smiled using human lips. It did enjoy deception, but now its orders were more clearly defined, now deception could move onto murder. Murder was far more to its tastes, but where to start?

The survivors of the humans who had brought the gnome were healing in the cleric's dome, a sanctified place. The clerics were the magic users of which the changeling was most wary. Their magic dealt with the spirit and the soul and their knowledge of his kind and of evil was the most defined. Walking into their stronghold was not possible without setting off magical wards they had worked hard to create. The wards could not hold against one such as itself, they were wards against lesser spirits and undead, but they would alert all to its presence. That was a task to be done later. The gnome presented a different problem. Its whereabouts were unknown, save to the master's pet mage it seemed. So in order to kill the gnome it must first talk to the mage.

Its path decided the changeling, in its guise as the chamberlain, left its office. It would find the mage and impress on the human the importance of communicating with the master.

⁂

"My prince!" The Venerable Loremaster, Oth'Raan called urgently yet quietly, not letting unseemly emotion disturb his finely aged features.

Prince Uh'Ram Bloodfire tilted his head slightly, a question on his thin black lips and the slightest of lines marring his near flawless forehead, only the savage scar that ripped diagonally across his whole face spoilt the perfection.

Uh'Ram was distracted, still digesting the information his changeling had given him and did not want to be disturbed. His midnight eyes clearly warned his servant that this interruption had better be justified.

"The blessed Lore Queen is here and wishes to see you." Oth'Raan insisted fear and awe in his countenance at the presence of the legendary head of his order.

Ry'Ana had returned. Uh'Ram was pleased, and it was a good indication of her mood that she had not just appeared in front of him. She was not one to follow etiquette if she was irritated. His throne room should have been impossible to penetrate in such a way, it was a place warded with the strongest enchantments against such intrusion, but Ry'Ana's knowledge of magic, and her talent, far exceeded any living elf's. Millennia of knowledge and the favour of the Lords of Darkness gave her an advantage that more than made up for her blindness.

In her earlier visits, she had given him the knowledge of where and when to strike, and who to deal with before they became a threat, but her last visit had brought questions and irritation. She knew that he had employed assassins to deal with the human threats she had perceived, and she also knew they had failed. To him, it had always seemed she gave the humans more respect than they deserved, but he could not deny that these humans were starting to be a thorn in his side, not a large thorn, but a thorn nonetheless. The news from his changeling about the events at the human city of Shandrilos had confirmed that. Perhaps that was why she had returned, perhaps she had learnt more about the humans and about the key to the Ways. Uh'Ram still worried and exalted over the Lore Queen's last foretelling; he would gain the Lifestone, but that humans were searching for the talisman!

Uh'Ram knew Ry'Ana had been scoring the northlands from the astral realm. She could not bring her physical self all the way from the Holy City through the Great Portal. She could not leave her place of power, not with the princes of the Second House becoming so great a threat and so jealous for power. Uh'Ram had no doubt that they watched her constantly. The princes of the Second House would not face her openly, not yet, but such an opportunity as the Lore Queen travelling alone into the wilds would be too good to miss.

Uh'Ram quickly nodded to his Loremaster who turned to go and present the Lore Queen, but even as he did so her astral form shimmered into being at the foot of the dais and began to climb. Oth'Raan was taken aback for a second and then bowed. He opened his mouth to address her, but she merely waved him away.

Uh'Ram raised a puzzled eyebrow and waited. As she came towards him, he stood and bowed deeply. Strangely, she smiled slightly as he stood, a show of emotion for which he was unprepared. He had expected annoyance at the worst, placidity at best.

"I trust you are well, my queen." he enquired softly as he gestured for his court to leave. Only his bodyguard would remain.

A throne appeared behind her, a manifestation: an astral throne for an astral queen. "I am well, surprisingly so, considering you have yet to deal with Shandrilos."

He sat himself carefully as the last of his court filed silently from the hall. "I am dealing with the threat we discussed earlier. Matters are in hand, my queen." he replied carefully. "I have learned who is behind the alliance of the Elder with the humans and have placed a servant of Eleora'Ashar to deal with him. This 'Archmage'" he emphasised the word mockingly, "will not be a problem for long."

She shook her head slightly and Uh'Ram frowned. He had allied himself closely to her, but he would not be treated like a child to be dismissed by her. He opened his mouth to continue and Ry'Ana held up her hand to silence him.

"I do not think you a child, Prince Uh'Ram." She stressed his title. "I merely am disappointed that you did not pay closer attention to my advice sooner."

Uh'Ram merely stared. She had again read his thoughts. He was wary.

"This Archmage is not one of the threats I counseled you about. The Lords of Light are subtle. This Archmage is important certainly, however, other individuals are now on the rise of which we must be more careful. You let your personal feelings about the humans blind you and now they are waxing to greater potential as we speak."

He was puzzled. Only two of the targets she had identified had not been dealt with and he could see nothing of how they were important. She had said this Shandrilos was the key and yet his agents had found no sign of them there. Frustrated, he asked carefully, "What threats are these, my queen?"

"The two humans you are thinking about have vanished from my visions. I can no longer see them or find them on the astral plane." Ry'Ana was clearly irritated. She suddenly shook her head, "I believe now I know what has happened." she paused. "They are being shielded from me."

"Surely, there is no one with the…" he began.

Ry'Ana leaned forward and fixed her milky gaze on his. "Tal'Asin has returned." she hissed.

Uh'Ram's eyes widened as what she had said began to register, yet before he could respond, Ry'Ana continued.

"And I have his spirit trapped on the astral plane!"

Uh'Ram didn't think his shock could heighten and yet… Tal'Asin, the Lore King of the sylvan elves, was not only alive, but his spirit was captive to Ry'Ana. He didn't think it possible. Then another thought occurred to him. "The Lifestone?" he asked urgently.

"Don't be foolish, had he the stone, I could not have contained him." Ry'Ana thought for a moment, "No, as I saw long ago, the Lifestone was sent away at the peak of the Great One's battle with Tal'Asin, yet somehow that hated creature has avoided death… though it has weakened him it seems." She seemed to drift off, musing.

Uh'Ram couldn't contain himself, "If Tal'Asin is alive, it is surely he who has been working against us and with him captive we can push forward more confidently." Uh'Ram could almost have sung with glee. He looked to the youthful, yet ancient Lore Queen. There was no sign of pleasure. In fact there was a hint of displeasure.

"Perhaps…" Ry'Ana almost whispered, looking off to some unknown place with her milky white gaze. "And yet, something is not right here. I am missing something." She looked firmly at Uh'Ram fixing his dark eyes with her white. "There is more that you do not know. The Waygate beneath Shandrilos has been opened!"

"What!" Uh'Ram exclaimed. "By whom?"

"That is the question, isn't it, my prince. It was not by Tal'Asin. As I said, other threats have arisen."

Uh'Ram suddenly felt a rush of shame and fury. 'Foul ape animals!' Uh'Ram cursed silently.

"Yes, Uh'Ram, the humans." Ry'Ana snapped reading his thoughts again. She gracefully rose from her throne and it wafted away as if it were smoke and a breeze had taken it. "Events move on and we can no longer afford for you to neglect the humans. You must deal with this, Shandrilos. The time for subtleties is over. I believe you have already a plan to deal with the place." It was a statement, not a question. "Gather your forces, Prince Uh'Ram. I shall seek more answers on the astral plane from Tal'Asin and about the Waygates."

With that she simply vanished.

Uh'Ram continued to sit. It seemed events were getting out of his control and he so hated that, especially when humans were involved. Yes, he had a plan for Shandrilos, a plan of annihilation and it was already in motion, but it would still take time. He needed time to summon enough forces to deal with the place and then gather the Lorewise needed to move that many warriors through gateways. It was not a small undertaking and would still need several days to organise. He would get it done in one if at all possible. Yet he still did not summon his advisors. He found he did not like the feeling of failure. He found he was tapping rhythmically on the arm of his throne. He was irritated. He needed more information and he would not simply rely on Ry'Ana. His changeling would find the mage in Shandrilos soon and this time he would know all. The mage would hide nothing from him. There would be no more games!

Chapter 48

A DISCOVERY BENEATH THE GROUND

According to Druidic Lore, the Elder believe that there is one spirit of all, the mother spirit known as Ea. She in turn gave birth to the twin spirits, Eru and Mor. The great mother Ea represents time, fate and the eternal balance. Her children are opposites; Eru is the spirit of goodness, creation and order. Mor, on the other hand, is the spirit of evil, destruction and chaos. Both are seen as necessary, but that Eru seeks to maintain the balance and protect his mother, while Mor desires to destroy the balance and devour her instead.

Knowledge passed down through Bardic tradition. Recorded by Prince Afdar SaTell of Stellicia BY78 - thought to be directly quoted from the legendary 'Lorebooks of the Druid Kings' said to have been begun by King Nam'Odar the Fisherking a thousand years earlier.

Nat Bero sat up suddenly in bed. She hadn't meant to slip off to sleep, it had just crept up on her. She had meant to watch for Arkadi's return. She looked quickly round, but Arkadi's bed was still empty. However, something had woken her.

Over by the far doors, which seemed to be the main ones, there was some sort of commotion. Brothers in white robes milled around and the doors were open. Someone in the black traveling robe of the magi was talking quietly, yet urgently with one of the brothers, and pointing back out of the Clerics Dome, the way he had apparently come. It seemed to be light outside from what Nat could see. Then into view came a small group of men in black robes with four men in the armour and tabard of Shandrilos. They were walking awkwardly and it wasn't until they entered and the brothers moved back to let them in that she realised why. They were carrying some sort of stretcher between them!

Had they found someone from below? Could it be Zara or Rebba or one of the others? She had given up hope. It had been so long. Yet them bringing someone here meant they were alive! Surely it was one of her friends.

Nat hastily pushed back the sheets of her bed and leapt up. She was pleased there was no dizziness this time. She realised at the same time that she was still wearing the white, loose gown that she had first woken in. Ordinarily, this would not have bothered her, but they did not segregate in the Clerics Dome. She had been attended by female monks when she had asked for anything but there were males in the dome too. Since Karis' death, she hated anyone seeing her less than as the tall huntress, yet she had been gravely injured, and she would then rectify her lapse once she knew who was on that stretcher.

The brothers led the way across the large hall towards where Nat stood barefoot. They moved to a bed down from Arkadi's and began pulling covers back. Behind them the Shandrilosi men-at-arms, along with the small gaggle of black robed magi flanking them, followed along. It was then that Nat noticed Arkadi hurrying in through the main doors, a look of concern on his face.

By the time Arkadi had caught up to the other magi, the soldiers and brothers had crowded around and lifted the mysterious person off the stretcher and onto the bed. The soldiers quickly departed, but it wasn't until one of the more senior monks began shooing some of the other brothers away that Nat got her first look at the man on the bed.

He seemed to be clad all in black; some kind of black suit. He was lying rigid on the bed with a huge jet black sword clasped in his hands in front of his chest, like a knight formally laid to rest.

Nat moved forward and peeked over the shoulder of one of the magi. It wasn't a suit the man was wearing, it was armour of some kind! She couldn't see the face; some kind of hood was over the man's face. No, it wasn't a hood, it was a helm... and yet it had no eyeholes or air holes to breathe through. What a ridiculous piece of armour! Nat knew these knight types were stupid; all that armour had an effect on the brain, but this was downright suicidal. Fancy having a blind man fighting and gasping for air in that, she thought disparagingly.

She saw Arkadi push through to take a good look. "Is this one of you companions, Master Talcost?" one of the magi asked.

Arkadi frowned and shook his head, "No... at least I don't think so. Not unless they changed armour..." he drifted off. The thought was implausible even to Nat.

"Where did you find him..? If it is a him." asked Arkadi quietly.

The oldest of the magi Nat could see, replied, "We found him in the third level down, below all the rubble from the collapsed first level hall. We discovered a way into that area by chance, through what must have been a concealed entrance before the collapse. However, the force of the falling rock must have blasted the door partially open." The elderly mage paused thoughtfully. "It must have been a powerful door to have even partly withstood that kind of force. Inside, the walls were intact too, split into small... cells is the best I can describe them. The walls and doors must have been made of incredibly strong stone to be still standing. Indeed, it was only because of these walls that there were some voids in which this man must have been shielded."

"In the rubble..." Arkadi mused, "that would mean he was one of that swordsmen's men, though I don't remember seeing anyone like this, and I think I would have remembered this armour. Did you see this warrior, Nat?"

Nat simply shrugged her shoulders, eager to get attention off her. She didn't want to get involved in this and she certainly didn't want a group of magi staring at her in only a flimsy gown. Nat couldn't go and dress even though she wanted to either, she needed to speak to Arkadi urgently about Nossi so she stayed where she was. Hopefully, the other magi would leave quickly.

"Has anyone tried to take off his helm?" Arkadi inquired, looking around at the other magi. There was no answer forthcoming. "Do we even know if he is alive?"

"He's alive," said another of the mages, "that's the puzzle. From what my senses can tell, he is in perfect health. My senses also say this armour is... odd. I think magical, though none of the others sense anything."

The elderly mage put in to the younger one, "You are a seer and I would not argue with your senses, Master Foran, but the armour has no aura."

Arkadi's head snapped up to look at the old mage at this, then to Nat. He suddenly remembered what the gnome had said about the key to the Ways, about it being 'invented' or 'inverted' or something. It was something that stopped it being sensed easily, whatever it was called. Arkadi's eyes seemed to be saying 'don't say anything'. Nat kept her thoughts to herself.

"Well", Arkadi said taking a breath, "we can at least have a go at this helm then." He stepped past the others and though Nat noticed the eldest mage frown a little, he said nothing to stop the grey clad, Arkadi.

Arkadi leaned over the bed, but as he did so, the helm's featureless face panel seemed to simply melt away and a face was revealed, placid and peacefully unaware of anything. Arkadi's eyes widened and he fell back a touch. The mages around the bed gave a collective gasp. For a moment Nat's mind wouldn't process what she was seeing but then she realized...

"Darin!"

All eyes then turned to look at Nat, who was so dumbfounded by the sight of her friend in this strange armour that she didn't notice. Arkadi seemed equally stunned, but was quick to recover.

He leaned forward swiftly and put his fingers to his friend's throat. After a moment he nodded and smiled over towards Nat. "He's alive, his pulse is strong."

Nat sighed, relieved. However, she saw the look of bafflement that passed across Arkadi's face and then frowned herself. How had Darin escaped the collapse seemingly unharmed, and from where had he got this bizarre armour? It was obviously magical, no matter what the elderly mage said, even he must see that now.

The elderly mage moved forward and tapped Arkadi on the shoulder. "Is this a member of your party, Master Talcost?"

Arkadi ignored the question and began to gently shake Darin. There was no response. The mage repeated his question, but Arkadi cut across him and asked, "Has anyone tried any healing?"

Before anyone could answer the elderly mage snapped, "Answer the question, young man?"

Arkadi spun and looked hard at the old mage. "Yes it is," he hissed, "and at the moment I am concerned for his well being more than I am for your questions. Now has anyone tried any healing on him?"

The old man looked like someone had slapped him and Nat chortled quietly to herself behind a hastily raised hand.

"How dare…" the mage began, but before he could finish the seer who had spoken earlier answered. "We tried below ground. The magic simply was absorbed… it had no effect."

The old mage cut in fiercely, "Silence, we will speak of this later." He glared at the young seer who stammered to silence. "Now, Master Talcost, you will answer my questions!" he thundered at Arkadi.

"Grandmaster Percale," Arkadi began slowly. He was struggling to contain his anger. Nat had rarely seen Arkadi angry, "If there is some information that will aid my friend's healing I would hear it now!" Arkadi punctuated his last word with a snarl.

"You go too far, *Master* Talcost." the mage replied just as fiercely. "This is a matter of magic. Your friend's health is not at stake. However, discipline towards a senior mage is!"

Arkadi's eyes flashed, but he held his temper. Through clenched teeth he replied, "You do not know whether my friend's life is at risk, you didn't even know there was magic involved here. I suggest that any information you have could help." Arkadi took a hold of his temper and in an almost normal tone he finished, "Would you please, share your information, Grandmaster?"

The old mage was still fuming and was about to deny Arkadi's request when a voice called from behind the group, "Yes, would you please share your information, Grandmaster!" It was not phrased as a question.

Nat looked over and saw the tall, stork-like old monk with the flowing white beard who had come with the Archmage earlier. He was looking sternly at the old mage who now seemed so much younger compared to the ancient man in white.

"Grand Abbot…" Grandmaster Percale began in protest, "these are matters for the senior officers of the college to hear, the Conclave…"

The Grand Abbot stepped forward and Nat suddenly realized how tall he was. He must have been several inches over six feet and he was wide shouldered. He would have been a prodigious man in his youth. Of course Nat now knew enough to know that was a very long time ago. Everyone had heard of the 'Grand Abbot'. He was Alinus Quan Sirona, head of the Sironacian Monks and ruler of the town of Sironac that he had founded before even Nat's father had been born.

"Enough, this man may well have some kind of ailment of which we are not aware. It certainly seems he is possessed of some ancient magic that is beyond our ken and until he wakes…" The tall saintly man raised a finger, "or if he wakes, we must strive to ascertain what magic this suit of armour possesses."

Grandmaster Percale still seemed to hesitate and the saint's face turned stern. "The Conclave will understand, Grandmaster, I can assure you of that!" he warned firmly.

Suddenly, all the air seemed to come out of the old mage and he waved to the young seer who took this as a gesture to carry on.

"We cast magic on the… er, man here." he began quietly, gesturing at Darin on the bed. "However, all of our spells seemed to have no effect. Indeed, they simply vanished as if they had never been, like the armour absorbed them." A couple of the other magi began nodding. "It was Master Evram who found the book, though."

"Book!" both Arkadi and the Grand Abbot said at the same time.

"Yes, your grace," Grandmaster Percale cut in, "It was old and frail, made of some material we couldn't identify and whatever ink they had used to write with had faded in places. We could make out little, but Master Evram found it in a small side room that was only half collapsed. It must have contained more because similar tomes could be seen beneath the rubble, though they were almost completely pulverized." The Grandmaster smiled wanly, "I had hoped to take another party to investigate later."

"I am sure," the Grand Abbot replied disapprovingly. "Where is this book? What did it say? Anything pertaining to this young man."

"We do not know, your grace, it is written in some elven script and none of us are sufficiently proficient to read it," the young seer responded eagerly.

"Though, it is unlikely an ancient tome of the elves would have any information about a young warrior." Grandmaster Percale put in quickly.

"Let me see." the regal seeming Grand Abbot replied.

"You can read elven script?" said Percale, clearly surprised.

"Well, I am familiar with some of the ancient tongues," Alinus Quan Sirona snapped.

Nat saw one of the other magi bring a small book out of a sack he'd had hidden in his voluminous robes. He came forward smartly and handed the book to the Grand Abbot, who took it and opened it gently. It looked like the small books that Nat had seen Arkadi carry for notes and ideas. The Grand Abbot moved forward through the magi, who parted easily for him. It was clear they were respectful of the old monk. The tall man seemed to fold as he sat himself by Darin on the bed. He took the book carefully and opened it up. For a number of minutes there was silence, save for a slight shuffling of feet or swishing of robes.

"It seems..." the old, white robed monk began, "that this is some kind of journal. It was written by a young elf and he was responsible for what I can only translate as a prison of some kind, though it seems different to our view of a dungeon or gaol." He slowly turned over a fragile page, read for a while and then turned another. "Much of it is hard to see and a number of the words I am unfamiliar with, but from what I can piece together, this prison had only one guest at the time when this was written, a human man by the name of Riga Sa Dor. He was well known to the elves as a warrior of the king, though it does not say which king. It does say that 'he returned where no other did' and that 'after using the key to close the hall, he seemed of clear mind', but then shortly after he 'became like a savage animal, at once grieving and killing'. The elf who wrote this reports him saying over and over, 'the king is dead, the king is dead'!" Grand Abbot Alinus looked up at those around him and saw them all staring back at him spellbound by what they were hearing. "The last part is unclear, but it says quite clearly that this Riga Sa Dor wore jet black armour and was a champion of the king. The journal then ends suddenly and is not continued."

Everyone seemed lost in thought. Nat had started slightly and looked nervously towards Arkadi at mention of the key, but Arkadi had acted as if he had never heard of a key. The silence stretched. It was Arkadi who voiced the obvious question.

"Why did Darin put on this ancient armour?"

The Grand Abbot spoke, "For an answer to that we shall have to wait until your friend awakes or we can awake him. However, I believe from my knowledge of the history of this land that this man in black, Riga was here when the elves yet dwelt here centuries ago. Obviously his armour lay undiscovered down in the ancient elven catacombs. If so this armour will have strong enchantments on it. This would explain the affect on your spells." He nodded at the seer and the other magi.

"The king he mentioned must be the legendary high king of the Nordic, Earondar Greatheart." Arkadi added.

"That is speculation, Master Talcost." Grandmaster Percale argued. "We know little of verifiable fact from those times."

Arkadi looked as if he was about to argue back, but the Grand Abbot stood suddenly and all eyes turned to him. Nat was surprised he could still move so swiftly since he was allegedly well over a hundred years old!

"There is no answer in this journal to help your comrade, Master Talcost. I am afraid we must investigate further." the old saint said sadly.

"Very well... perhaps then you could give me some privacy with my friends." Arkadi said firmly.

Nat saw the elderly Grandmaster Percellen's eyes harden, but it was Alinus Quan Sirona who nodded and said simply, "Come" to the group of magi and began walking away.

The magi fell in line behind the Grand Abbot, though the old man, Percale looked almost menacingly at Arkadi, and Nat guessed that he would be trying to cause trouble for Arkadi later.

Nat waited a moment and then moved quickly over to Arkadi. She could see the dark eyed mage was lost in thought. He was muttering to himself, but he looked at Nat as she approached and saw her gaze at the departing magi.

"That bloody old fool, Percale," he snapped, "the man couldn't even light a candle with the talent he has. I am surprised he ever made grandmaster."

"Arkadi, we need to talk." Nat said urgently.

"Darin seems fine, Nat. He seems to be just sleeping." Arkadi replied misunderstanding her comment. Arkadi went on, "It was always difficult waking him. Do you remember that time..."

"No, Arkadi. It's about Nossi Bee and that Archmage person, not Darin."

"Nossi... Archmage?" Arkadi frowned at Nat. "What are you talking about?"

She quickly told Arkadi about her visit from the Archmage and what he said.

"Do you think he might be right?" Nat asked.

"About what?" Arkadi mumbled not really paying attention. He was deep in thought. Obviously some of what Nat had told him was troubling.

"About Nossi having disappeared, about your friend, Xameran, or the other guy, whatever his name is, having been the ones who made him disappear!" Nat snapped exasperated.

Arkadi turned and looked at him, his brown eyes wide with indignation. "No! The Archmage is trying to discredit, Xameran. He doesn't want to lose his position, Nat. It's politics!"

"Then where is Nossi? Do you know?"

Arkadi's stare wavered, "I don't know. The Archmage was right about that," Arkadi saw Nat's face darken, "but Nossi was with the High Enchanter, Atholl Dorard, not Xameran." he said quickly.

"How do you know? From this Xameran?"

Arkadi nodded warily.

"Can you really trust him? I mean you know these people better than I do, but this Archmage couldn't have taken Nossi, he was apparently locked up."

"The Archmage is powerful, Nat. He came to see you when he was supposed to be locked up. He stole cloaks and aided the elves in killing another member of the Conclave!" Arkadi insisted.

"You only know this from this Xameran" Nat muttered, "and he seemed a bit too smooth for my liking. Anyway, that is beside the point." She moved up close to Arkadi and stuck her finger under the mage's nose. "We lost friends getting that little gnome back to the surface. You said he was important and now you seem more interested in politics. What about this great threat that is coming? Have you forgotten that?" Arkadi opened his mouth to answer, but Nat spoke over him, "We need to find Nossi. I've lost too many friends to let him and what he has to say get squashed in some political struggle between you idiots in robes!"

"You don't understand."

Nat ignored him and turned away. She was determined she would find Nossi, even if she had to search himself.

Suddenly, Arkadi's hand fastened on her arm and spun her around. "Don't ignore me!" He snapped. "You listen. I am trying to make sure we can get things back under control here in the college. If we don't do that we won't be able to get the Wildlands united and without that we have no chance against the elves anyway."

"And what if the Archmage is right, what if one of your magi is an agent of evil…"

"He could be the agent of evil, you fool." Arkadi hissed.

Nat ignored him and continued, "…then that means Nossi could be in trouble. Now, I know he may not be a friend as such, but he shouldn't be left at the mercy of these magi, whichever it may be. He came to us for help, remember."

"Of course I remember. I don't want any harm to come to him either, but I must help Xameran first."

"And while you play politics with this Xameran, Nossi is 'Olwyn-knows' where." Nat replied harshly.

"I have already tried to find, Nossi. No one seems to know where he is, but I don't have time to look for him, I have to go and help Xameran with the up-coming Assembly of Masters." Arkadi pleaded.

"Fine, I'll look for him."

"You can't wander around the college…" Arkadi began.

"I am not going to," Nat growled, "I am going to talk to the servants and then, I figure, if no one can find him in the college then he isn't in the college. I'll go into Shandrilos and see if he is there. I can at least move around a town and find things others can't!"

Arkadi stared at Nat helplessly for a moment and then threw up his hands, "You do that… and try not to gamble too much while you're doing it, Nat." He turned and stormed across the hall.

Nat ignored him. 'Go and kiss up to your little sorcerer lord, Arkadi' she thought, 'but I don't trust these magi.' She grabbed her clothes and began to dress.

Chapter 49

SEARCHES

From the two eternal spirits, Eru and Mor were born the 7 Lords of Light and the 7 Lords of Darkness. These are those to whom the Elder pay homage. Each of the races seems to favour one of the Lords as their patron while acknowledging the others in a lesser way. Even the Lords of Darkness are given their due, despite their evil natures. The Elder acknowledge the role of the Lords of Darkness in the great balance while supporting the Lords of Light. However, there are groups and even some races who have been seduced by the Lords of Darkness and pay homage solely to them.

Knowledge passed down through Bardic tradition. Recorded by Prince Afdar SaTell of Stellicia BY78 - thought to be directly quoted from the legendary 'Lorebooks of the Druid Kings' said to have been begun by King Nam'Odar the Fisherking a thousand years earlier.

Baden Erin stepped through the small magical portal back into his quarters. His search had produced nothing. No one knew where this gnome creature had gone and all the hiding places Baden could think of, he had either checked himself or had allies check. The gnome was not in the college.

He stepped quickly over to his desk and sat himself down heavily. Nothing seemed to be going his way. The enemy had planned well. It was now likely that he was going to lose his leadership of the college and if that happened, it was only a matter of time before the elves and dwarves were asked to leave. All the years of work would be for nothing.

For long moments he sat, thinking of nothing, allowing despair to rule him, but such was his nature that he couldn't dwell on it too long before he began to look for something that he had missed. He knew now that Xameran and Atholl were well on their way to gaining the Assembly of Masters they wanted. Eliantha had been masterful in keeping those two off balance and delaying any decision to even have a full debate in the Assembly, and while doing this she had kept the Grand Council going, had kept the High Lords of the provinces pushing on with constructing some kind of agreement on how the elves and dwarves would fit into the Grand Council, what votes they would have, what boundaries and borders would be accepted, what trade concessions would be allowed. Indeed, Baden Erin knew he couldn't have done better himself. He was surprised and elated with Eliantha's boldness and skill, even he hadn't expected it from her and he had known her since they were novices together. However, it was clear that the burden was draining her.

Also, Xameran and Atholl weren't likely to give up their advantage; an Assembly of Masters would take place today and once that happened, it was inevitable now that Baden would lose the leadership of the college, and more than likely Xameran or Atholl would be the next Archmage. Once that happened, Eliantha would be made to step aside and all that both Baden and Eliantha had managed to do would be undone. Baden did have the small hope that his long time allies Grand Abbot Alinus and High Lord Elgon of Ostia would seek to keep the Elder races at the Council. However, that tiny glimmer of hope was just that, tiny. The revelations about the elves being involved below ground and potentially leading the enemy would finish any chance of an alliance... and perhaps it should. Perhaps he was being deceived.

Baden Erin sighed again, leaned his elbows on the desk and put his head in his hands. He did now know more of the nature of the enemy at least. The hunter's tale had yielded more information than had all his long years of sending spies to the far north... if it was true. It all really came down to that; who to believe.

It was clear that the gnome and Mistress Bero believed what they said. However, the idea that the elves were behind the new threat in the north was unbelievable: that elves had allied with the goblins and trolls and taken control of them, their sworn enemies. Could it be true, could the elves be in league with the enemies of mankind or had the gnome and the huntress been deceived?

Certainly he knew what Xameran wanted people to believe and it was so easy to play on people's fears of the unknown, of the elves who hid away in their forests and killed any who entered. Yet Baden couldn't shake the nagging doubts.

'No!' he thought, 'I know the dwarves and they are not easily deceived. They trust no one easily. It had taken him twenty years to get the dwarves trust and support. The elves would never deceive them. He would stake his life on it! In fact, he realised, he had.

So if that were so, what was really going on?

Something the huntress Nat Bero had said had been bothering him for a while. It had surprised him at the time. Nat Bero had said the elves that had attacked her and her friends had coppery skin, dark hair and dark eyes! It could have been a trick of the light, but the woman had been adamant. Yet, Baden knew of no elves with such hair and skin colour; dark hair and eyes were unknown amongst them, he had checked and the dwarves confirmed this. They all had light silvery skin.

Could these new elves be false? Could they be some agents of the enemy in disguise?

It was a straw he was grasping at, he knew, but he could think of nothing else that would help solve the mystery, save that he had been deceived and he refused to allow himself to think such.

Baden Erin gathered his resolve as he gathered his robes and climbed slowly to his feet. He would speak with the elves again, he had no other choice now.

Baden quickly moved over to his wardrobes and switched his long, dark travelling robes and cloak for his robes of office. He might not be the Archmage for long, but while he was, he would let no one forget it.

⁂

Nat had no luck with the servants. Most of them simply brushed off her questions or asked her who she was and what she was doing in the college. None of them seemed to want to chat or gossip and Nat didn't have any money to lubricate their tongues. After an hour, she gave up with the servants and headed out of the college into Shandrilos… and the Changeling watched her go.

The Changeling had heard that someone from the group who had gone below ground was asking questions and had hurried down to find them. It knew if it was quick it could deal with them before meeting with the mage. It had taken longer than expected to find the human and by the time it had, she was already passing through the gates, going into the human town. The Changeling watched the dark cloaked woman keenly, memorizing her face, tasting her scent. It couldn't follow her, not yet. It had finally managed to get an excuse to get close to its master's pet mage. Since the death of this Allseer, as well as the disappearance of a number of novices that the Changeling couldn't refrain from killing, security had increased.

It had to go visit the mage now, its master wanted to speak to him. The woman could wait. Now it had her scent it would be able to find her even in the busy human town.

Baden Erin knocked on the door and waited. Elven guards flanked him without seeming to acknowledge his presence, but had he not been known, he would not have got within a dozen feet of the door without being challenged.

The door was opened by another elven warrior, his luminous blue eyes shadowed slightly by the elf's slight frown of inquiry that was replaced with a placid, seeming featureless acknowledgement of who stood waiting. Most would see that face as wooden and expressionless, but Baden took the serene look as one of acceptance and welcome.

"May I speak with Gonhir Val'Ant and the other Gonhiri? I have an important question."

The elf blinked in agreement, cloaking those wonderful eyes for a second. "You will find the Gonhiri in conference in the hall beyond, my lord Archmage." the elven warrior responded with all the grace of a lord.

Baden Erin thanked him and strode past. He moved across the stone floors into the next room through an open door. Baden had been here often in the past few days. Six of the elven lords were sat, as before, around a large oval oak table. They stood with sinewy grace and blinked slowly in greeting.

"My Lord Archmage," the grey haired Val'Ant, the most powerful of the elven lords, acknowledged. "Please take a seat, we would welcome your council."

Baden smiled his thanks and sat down. The dwarves were not here today and Baden frowned. Also, the elflord who had left during the conference when Eliantha had brought her worries about Atholl and Xameran was still absent. He had been gone for three days and Baden had been given no reason as to why. He acknowledged again that he knew little of these elvenlords and was basing his trust upon his dwarven friend...

"We were just discussing the agreements so far in the Grand Council…" the ghostly Val'Ant began.

Baden cut him off, "I am sorry, my lord, but I have another more pressing matter I would discuss with you." He looked around. "Some of you are missing?"

"Gonhir El'Caron has other important concerns that he must take care of, my friend." was the quiet response.

"Might I inquire as to these concerns?" Baden asked politely. He had never pushed the elves before, but he needed reassuring.

It was the forbidding, one eyed elflord, Dag'Nir who replied, "These concerns are… private, they will not harm anyone. You need not worry, my lord Archmage."

Val'Ant must have seen the dubious look that Baden quickly tried to conceal.

"You have our word that it is nothing that will threaten you or your people, indeed if we are correct, it will be a great help."

Baden frowned again and almost chewed his lip; a habit he had thought long gone.

"Now, how can we help you, my friend? You seem perturbed. Is it with the matters of the Grand Council or with the allegations against us all?" the ghostly prince of the Suthantar elves' voice sang and managed to convey both reassurance and interest at the same time.

Baden swallowed and forced a smile. He needed to push on, he was not sure he wanted the elves planning things behind his back, but he couldn't blame them the way things were going and the fact that he had lost control of events. "I have received some worrying information from those who went beneath the college."

"Is it to do with the idea that we elves are somehow responsible for the explosion below ground and have been attacking people." the fiery haired, female, An'Tiara snapped, "Or the preposterous idea that we somehow were responsible for our own people's downfall or that we are somehow responsible for the goblins uniting?" The look on her face was unseemly for an elf as disgust was written large on her smooth face.

"It is…" Was all Baden got out before the curt Dag'Nir cut him off.

"We have answered those charges honestly, Archmage. Do you presume to call us liars?" he asked anger touching only his eyes. He was in better control of his features than An'Tiara.

"No, my lord," he said firmly, "but I have received new information that I need to discuss with you!"

"Go on, my friend." Val'Ant cut in smoothly, his voice again reassuring. The stern Dag'Nir's eyes were hard.

Thankfully, the others would still take their lead from Val'Ant. He had seemed very honest and fair-minded so far.

"It seems that the gnome left out the fact that the elves that attacked the group below ground and caused the explosion were different to your people. The woman Nat Bero, gave me a clear description."

"In what way were they different?" Val'Ant said, his head tilting in clear puzzlement.

"They had coppery red skin and jet black hair and eyes." Baden said clearly.

If he had been hoping for some kind of dramatic intake of breath or jaw dropping surprise, he was disappointed. The elven lords looked unblinkingly at Baden and then at each other.

"Coppery skin?" Val'Ant asked, "No elves have such. Are you sure this woman was reliable?"

"I believe so." Baden responded, "I would have sensed had she been lying. She believed what she was saying. Could it have been some kind of disguise?" he asked, grasping at straws.

The elves clicked their small pointed teeth, a clear sign of strong agitation. "We know of no one who would do such and the magic is beyond the goblins or trolls that we know." The surly Dag'Nir said, still irritated.

Baden pushed on, "He told me that the gnome spoke of an ancient story that these coppery skinned elves had once lived in the northlands long ago, and that they have come to take those lands back. They apparently may have tried unsuccessfully centuries ago and have now returned. This is partly why the Conclave believes you are here, that you are in league with these other elves to take your ancient lands back from us!" As he was speaking he could see them all shaking their heads, all that was except, Stor'Gan, the eldest of the lords. His wrinkled face was looking decided odd. Baden had never seen such a look on an elf's face and he couldn't help staring. Baden's gaze must have been obvious because others of the Gonhiri began to look at Stor'Gan and once they looked at him they too began to stare.

When Baden finished it was Val'Ant who asked what was wrong. At first the old elf simply continued to stare at some fixed spot. His face bore a kind of slightly pained expression, like he was suffering from some kind of ailment. The elves waited patiently, but Baden had the urge to call out or go over and shake the elf out of his stupor.

Finally, Stor'Gan spoke. His voice was quiet and croaked as if he found it hard to speak. "I have lived a long time. I have seen out over six hundred years according to human reckoning and I can still remember when the humans first settled the town they now call Lauria. It was on the edge of the lands that I hunted with my father. In those days we could wander freely throughout the land and had only goblins to worry about.

Listening to this, Baden began to get a cold feeling down his spine, but he kept his thoughts to himself.

"We were not confined to the deep forests as now and humans were new to me then. Of course my father knew them. He remembered them from tales from his mother and grandfather. His father had been killed in the battles that saw Dah'Ryllor destroyed, but his grandfather had been a great Loremaster and had survived the fall of our ancient kingdom. He was privy to much lost lore.

Back in those times, Lauria was just a collection of mud huts and the humans were simple folk. Nevertheless, I was worried. I was not yet fully grown and these strange people were different. We camped out and watched the humans. We even went among them in the night and listened to their rough voices and course behaviour. It was then that I had the first great shock of my life. I saw two humans, intoxicated with some foul smelling brew, fight one another. They swayed around, grunting and snarling then one pulled an iron knife and stabbed the other in the stomach! I was so shocked I gasped aloud and the man looked my way and saw me. My father and I fled. We disappeared into the night. It turned out that the human blamed the murder of his 'friend' on the wild creatures he had seen in the night. Demons he called us."

Stor'Gan looked around at the other elves, his eyes sad. Baden was now completely unsure about what this elf was saying. He feared the worst as it seemed it was about how evil and untrustworthy humans were, but the old elf's face was one of such sadness that he didn't know what to think.

The old elf continued, "I was distraught by the time we reached our camp and my father sought to console me. It was not that we had been blamed; the people were obviously ill-educated and superstitious. It wasn't even the sight of killing; I had killed goblins. It was the fact that one human could so easily murder another! To me this was the behaviour of animals, of goblins and lesser creatures. No elf would ever harm another." Others of the elven lords began nodding, "I became self righteous. Were these the ancient allies of our people who had helped us in our fight against destruction? I condemned humans as below us."

An'Tiara growled her agreement and Stor'Gan looked at her with shame in his eyes and shook his head. "You know so little, young one. My pride and arrogance were such that my father became ashamed of me. He spoke harshly to me and for the first time I argued with my father!" Stor'Gan insisted.

Baden Erin knew this was almost unheard of; an elf did not argue with a senior. Baden was surprised. This was certainly not something an elf would easily admit to in public. The others too were taken aback by this admission. Baden knew this kind of public display was distasteful for them. Something important was occurring here, though Baden was still none the wiser what it was.

In a voice heavy with sorrow, Stor'Gan continued, "My father became angry with me and he forced me to sit and he sent all away. I was prepared for his reprimand, such was the righteous anger I felt, but he did not reprimand me. Instead he told me a story. It was a story that had been whispered to him long ago by his grandfather, a story that was forbidden among our people so that by the time of my youth it was unknown, and by the times of your births was long forgotten." Stor'Gan finished, looking at the elves around him.

Baden was listening intently, and so too were the other elven lords. Stor'Gan spoke of how his father told him the story of a terrible war amongst the elves. He told of a race of mad elves that, in their pride and arrogance, turned on their kin and sought dominion over them, who brought savage war. He told of how these elves had finally been destroyed using a great spell. It was the lowest point of elven history and it was forbidden to be taught by the Lore King himself, and so it was only whispered of amongst the lorewise as a warning against a surfeit of pride and arrogance. It was told to me as I would one day lead and as a warning against my pride; elves are not a race above others as they would believe."

Silence followed this. Finally, Stor'Gan added, "This story was one that scoured my soul as a youth and later I believed it was simply a tale told to teach me a lesson. I have not thought of it since. I eventually convinced myself of its falsehood that my memory of it was lost, and yet I never looked again on humans with the same pride as many of our people." He looked at An'Tiara with a stern eye then he sighed deeply and passed his hand before his face and the others copied, even An'Tiara whose face still showed shock at his admission and his implied reprimand.

An'Tiara stiffly responded, "Why do you relate this tale now? Do you now believe there was truth to it because some humans cast doubt on our race?"

Stor'Gan replied softly, "No, An'Tiara, it is because in the tale my father told me, the mad elves were said to have fiery coloured skin and dark soulless eyes!"

The mage walked swiftly to his chair and sat. He was ecstatic. Soon the Archmage would be finished and soon he would see that arrogant swine cast down.

There was a knock at the door and he remembered his meeting. He was over an hour late and the Chamberlain would no doubt be annoyed, not that he cared. He was a little confused at the need for this meeting though, he had other things to attend to and so, presumably, did the Chamberlain.

The door swung open and the Chamberlain marched in, swinging the door firmly shut behind him. The mage frowned, the Chamberlain may have had to wait, but who did he think he was striding in here. The mage was a member of the Conclave and head of a school, even the officers of the college needed to show respect. He rose from his chair to say just that when the Chamberlain's face seemed to melt and a hideous visage appeared, part humanoid, part wolf. The rest of his body changed and before the mage could even gasp the now huge lupine creature was leaping across the room at him. He quickly snapped off a cantrip even as he leapt sideways towards the stand where his staff stood.

Whatever this creature was, it brushed through the cloud of gases he had thrown up to hide his leap and smashed into his chair, snapping it into kindling with six inch long claws. It looked to the side at the mage with cold clear malevolence even as the mage grabbed his staff.

What was this thing?

With a low growl, it again hurled itself at the mage. He stood and jabbed his staff at the creature and yelled a killing spell. The spell hissed out and crackling energy slammed into the creature, blasting it back, but before the mage could even take a breath, the creature twisted in mid air and landed cat-like against the wall like some giant spider. It bent its legs and leapt back at him. His spell had hardly even slowed the creature! The energy just seemed to roll off it. He needed time to think and threw up a multi-shielding spell, one of his best. He smiled as the creature slammed into it and was hurled back. His smile curdled though as the creature hit the ground for only a split second and then was back up, slashing with those wicked claws. The mage could feel each blow draining his shield. The blows were incredible in their power!

"What are you?" he cried, half in fear, half in anger.

The creature reared back and slammed its hand like a blade at his shield. The mage cried out as pain erupted in his head and his shield collapsed. A steel hard hand grabbed him by the throat and his next spell died, unspoken. The mage's eyes widened in terror as huge jaws with needle like teeth opened in front of his face… but then the mouth continued to open, impossibly wide and from within the mouth flesh bubbled out and a new human face pushed though as the jaws folded back on themselves and moulded into the now human head. Hair sprouted. It was the chamberlain's head though it sat upon a monster's body.

"Do I have your attention now?" a sibilant voice hissed.

The mage nodded and he felt the grip at his throat loosen enough that he could croak, "What are you?"

"What I am is of no concern to you." The hand dragged him close. "The master has sent me. He wishes for you to commune with him... and he wishes you to do so now!"

"The master... wha... what master? I..."

The impossibly strong hand shook the mage like a rag doll. "Cease these games human, Prince Uh'Ram calls." the creature spat.

It shoved him down and the mage fell to his knees.

"Open your mind!" commanded the beast.

The mage looked up and a hideous finger with a wicked claw appeared in front of his face. He nodded hastily and cleared his mind. He cast the spell he had cast so often, but had avoided for the last few days.

A grey slash appeared in front of them and it widened to reveal a scene in which a throne stood large, and upon it sat his master.

Prince Uh'Ram Bloodfire looked down at the mage and the mage looked up and saw anger. Suddenly, all the mage's fears came boiling forth and he gabbled like a child. He confessed that he had put off communing with his master. He tried to hold back from saying anything about the key to the Ways. For that he was punished.

Pain blossomed in his brain and he writhed helplessly, dangling from the rigid creature's hand, almost throttling himself. His master's voice boomed in his mind. He found that his master knew all about the key, the gnome and the men who had gone below ground, though it seemed he did not know of the mage's own attempts to get the key. His master wanted to know about Master Talcost's group and if they had brought anything to the surface. The mage confessed that they had found the key and his master's thoughts bombarded him. He cried out loud and answered silently that it was lost below ground when some of his master's servants had attacked the group. They did not have it with them. He found himself pleading. He told of how he had managed to hide any knowledge of his master and the key, of how he had organised a search for the lost key to make sure it was given to the master. Silence answered this and the mage dared to hope this would not be the moment of his death. Abruptly, his master's commands came through, clear and concise; the gnome and those who had been with him had to die, so too this Archmage, the mage would see to it and the master's Changeling servant would help. However, the key was to be left, the master would deal with that himself.

Suddenly the communion was over and the mage found himself sagging over, his hands still clinging to the terrible hand that held his throat.

A voice said at his ear, "Where is the gnome? I will deal with him first."

The mage looked at the creature beside him. A Changeling! The mage had heard of them, servants of the Demon Queen, Mayvar, but he had never heard of one that could change so swiftly between forms. This must be a greater demon, a powerful enemy and a powerful ally. With this creature to aid him he could face the Archmage with confidence.

The creature seemed to sense his thoughts, "I do my master's bidding, human. If you seek to do my master's bidding I will aid you. If you seek to thwart him, I will kill you… slowly."

The mage nodded and the hand released its grip. Pain coursed through him and for a moment stars seemed to flash in front of his eyes. He coughed and rubbed at his throat until the pain began to fade. Slowly, he stood and before him stood the chamberlain once more. Any signs of the Changeling had vanished completely save for the evil look that twisted his old features.

"The gnome is not important, we need to…"

Suddenly, the chamberlain's hand flashed up and changed. The mage found himself staring at the thick, gnarled finger with the wicked claw again. "Do not seek to divert me. That would be…foolish."

The mage nodded. He did not want to face the Changeling again, not without proper preparation beforehand. He would also look up everything he could on the nature of such creatures. He would be a more difficult challenge next time… if there was a next time.

Quickly, he told the creature of the house he kept just outside the college walls. The gnome was there guarded by a servant of his, a monk by the name of Ivello.

The Changeling turned and walked to the door, once more completely the old chamberlain. The mage rubbed his sore throat again. He had survived and what's more his plans were still intact. The Assembly would be called soon. Eliantha Shamass could not delay any longer. Yes, there were still things that he could salvage.

Nat had not been slow to track down her old contacts. She had returned to get her things from the inn first of all. She needed money and a change of clothes. It had been a shock to see Zara's bags. They were still on the bed across from her own, in the room they had been supposed to share. That stopped her for a while, but she wouldn't give herself time to grieve. Rebba, Bear, Zara and Garon had given their lives so that she and the others could get away and get Nossi to the surface, and she would find the little gnome if only for her own piece of mind.

She had left the inn more determined than ever to find the gnome.

Nat had quickly purchased some more knives and put them in the sheaths she had secreted about her person. She didn't have a lot of money, but she had some favours she was owed, favours from those with whom she had traded back before Karis had died. Back when life made sense.

She paused for a moment and thought of her children. When things had gone badly underground, she had tried not to think of them too much, to keep herself focused on staying alive, but she had thought about them often since the collapse. She was glad they were safe with her parents. Her mother had always been wonderful with them, but she missed them bitterly. She came very close at that moment to simply heading home.

Focusing back on her old contacts, she quickly made her way around and after no luck with her first two contacts, she found out about some interesting goings on at a house over by the college. There was knowledge of a small man over there, but it turned out to be a halfling thief by the name of Andar or something. Nat had been disappointed, but one of them then mentioned a group of mercenaries who had visited the place several times and who had now disappeared. This had really upset his contact as they had owed him. He had been searching for them himself and had discovered that they had been seen in the very inn that Nat and his friends had met. This got her to thinking. What if those men were the same men that Zara had 'bumped' into in the inn, the ones from whom Zara had stolen the key to the Ways, and what if they were part of the group she, Darin, and Arkadi had 'bumped' into underground? They seemed to know her and had been after the key. Could they be involved with the mages?

A sudden thought occurred to her; the mage who had hired her to hunt people had relied on mercenaries. She hadn't thought about that in awhile with everything else going on. It seemed a terrible coincidence, but Nat knew the mage who had manipulated her so badly was a powerful mage at the college. Could all this be linked?

This house she had heard about might well be where the mage had met their hired help. It might also be where they had Nossi. It would be the perfect place from what she had been told; out of the way and out of the college, secret and safe.

Nat got directions. She was going to get that gnome back... and maybe even find out who had used her as an assassin!

Chapter 50

DEADLY PLANS

To the Elves, the Altai Eru or Lords of Light, are seen not so much as gods but seemingly as powerful ancestors or predecessors from whom their most influential claim descent and power. For example, the ruler of El'Yaris, the Lore King Tal'Asin the Wise is said to be the most direct descendant of Elysia, Lady of Life and Healing, whom we call Sarahiri, Queen of the Gods. The elves also see the Altai Mor, the Lords of Darkness as fallen ancestors and to be respected but shunned. Thus the Elves see Eleora'Ashar, Lady of Death and Disease as a necessary balance to Elysia while avoiding even mention of her if at all possible. She it is whom we would know as Mayvan the Enchantress, Queen of the Underworld.

Knowledge passed down through Bardic tradition. Recorded by Prince Afdar SaTell of Stellicia BY78 - thought to be directly quoted from the legendary 'Lorebooks of the Druid Kings' said to have been begun by King Nam'Odar the Fisherking a thousand years earlier.

Ry'Ana White Eyes sat on her astral throne and stared into her scrying bowl. It was ten feet across, filled with what looked like liquid silver, and it did not exist save on the astral plane. She had created it to help focus her thoughts and help her to scan the astral and physical planes. It also occasionally provided her with clues, guidance and visions from the Lords of Darkness.

She had found those who carried the key to the Ways and knew where they must go!

For a moment she allowed herself to smile. Oh, the Dark Gods favoured her now. She had captured Tal'Asin and soon the Lifestone would be found!

Within the scrying bowl she could see a hall of one of the Waygates. It was the Waygate hidden deep under the ancient city of Dal'Thanda and it was strewn with the bodies of elves, dwarves and men, long dead. However, within the hall stood four who were very much alive; four humans! Their auras were sketchy and their faces blurred. Someone had cast a powerful camouflaging spell on them. It would hide them from all but the strongest of scryings and it was a spell that only a master of the higher mysteries could cast, a master such as Tal'Asin.

As if prompted from her thoughts, Tal'Asin said calmly, "You cannot reach them Ry'Ana, they are sealed up in the hall of a Waygate. Your spell might be able to penetrate it from the astral plane, but you cannot reach it on the physical."

Ry'Ana moved her milky gaze from the image of the four humans to the astral form of Tal'Asin, last Lore King of the Sylvan Elves. He stood passively within the astral prison she had crafted for him. The prison shone fiercely, the weave of energies surrounding him writhed with power so quickly the eye could not follow them and left a bewildering image etched on the mind. It was perhaps her finest and most complicated astral spell save the one that maintained this sanctuary for her. In here she was safe from astral intrusions and could observe, hidden from all others. It would take a huge amount of psychic energy to intrude upon her here, as it would to break free of her prison.

Tal'Asin seemed quiescent in his incandescent cage. Ry'Ana was not fooled.

"Oh, even the strongest of spells may be broken, even that which protects the Waygate Halls." she hissed back.

"Oh, yes, Ry'Ana you are quite correct about that, even the most powerful of spells can be broken" He smiled and gazed at the blazing astral energies that surrounded him.

Ry'Ana seethed inside, though nothing showed on her fiery visage. She longed to make him suffer, his confidence irked her. She longer to make him cry out as he had when she had first closed her trap on him, but since then he had proved that he was still the great master of the mysteries he had once been. The probing spells she had cast had been turned, deflected or even absorbed; a prodigious show of mastery. There was also the issue that his presence had begun a chain reaction of memories. Sudden flashes of images long lost were returning to her, the visions were disturbing. She had thought the cunning Lore King was casting spells on her somehow, yet that was impossible. It was puzzling.

Tal'Asin was an enigma to her. She had waited for him to weaken, with his spirit trapped, held back from his body, it was inevitable; the body could not survive long without a will to guide it, move it, maintain it. When the body weakened the spirit would too, until eventually both body and spirit would perish. Of course, Ry'Ana had no intention of allowing Tal'Asin to escape her so easily; she would ensure he suffered a torture sufficient to the suffering her people had. However, Tal'Asin endured! His spirit had not weakened and she could not find where his body resided! It was most frustrating. It was not possible that even such a powerful mage could be sustained for so long. The only explanation she could think of was that someone was preserving his body, giving it energy. She had looked exhaustively for signs of such magic and found none. It was most galling, and what was more, Tal'Asin seemed to know her frustration and be enjoying it. Bitterness had filled her, but now she would have her revenge, with the aid of the Lords of Darkness. She would strike against Tal'Asin's pawns; these humans and Uh'Ram would find the Lifestone. She had foreseen it! It was ironic that it was Uh'Ram's very mistakes that had led to this opportunity.

She smiled inside. "You are right," she acknowledged quietly, "but now I know where they are and where they will go. Once they leave those halls my people will be waiting for them."

A shadow of doubt appeared and then vanished from his silvery skinned brow. "You cannot." he replied.

"Can't I?" She smiled slowly and menacingly. "The Lords of Darkness have shown me their favour as they did my father before me. We will have that key, Tal'Asin, my sweet." she said coldly. "I know where they must go and Uh'Ram Bloodfire will go there too." This time she laughed out loud, enjoying the worry that reappeared on Tal'Asin's arrogant face. "Soon we will have the Lifestone. The Lords of Darkness have shown me this. Uh'Ram is destined to hold the Lifestone and with it, open the Great Temple."

She stood and walked confidently around her scrying bowl and stood in front of Tal'Asin's prison. She might be blind on the physical plane, but here she saw clearer than all. The ancient Lore King stared at her, his face carefully blank. She checked her wards and enchantments that held his astral prison in place. All was still well.

"You will break, Tal'Asin. I will break you. I will bring before you every one of those whose lives you have touched, every one of those who carry out your will. These four humans will die in agony, and then I will discover where your body lies and you will die!" With that she willed herself to vanish, she needed to pay another visit to Prince Uh'Ram. He needed to visit the cursed swamps and ruins of Hy'Deeria; the kingdom in which she had been born, the kingdom in which her people had almost been destroyed.

Prince Uh'Ram Bloodfire sat his throne and listened to his advisors. His senior Parinsar, Nar'Dolth stood foremost, a group of other Parinsars clustered behind him in their dark witchwood armour, their jet and silver cloaks of office flowing from their shoulders. Beside them stood his Loremasters and Clerics, though they would have little to do with these discussions; their roles would be to transport the army and to minister to its wounded.

"We have managed to muster the nearby goblin tribes. We have armed and armoured them and assigned some of our Hironsars to take command of them." Parinsar Nar'Dolth, his chief commander reported.

Uh'Ram nodded. They had begun to train the goblins and try to impose some discipline on them, putting some of their own young officers and their warriors in charge, but it was difficult; the goblins still saw them as enemies. They had been raised with tales that instilled hate for all elves. They had forgotten any distinction. Still they hadn't had to kill too many before they began to remember and fall in line. These grey and green skinned goblins were easily cowed. They made for poor soldiers, but they would make excellent shock troops and battle fodder for wearing down an enemy.

"As of today we have in excess of six thousand goblin braves, my prince." Nar'Dolth added.

It was few compared to the numbers of goblins he knew were in this part of the northlands. He knew they could muster upwards of twenty thousand, but that many could not be transported; the magic portals his people had spent long years perfecting, could not take such numbers. This was also why they couldn't bring more from other parts of the vast northlands.

"And what of our troll allies?" Uh'Ram asked quietly.

"We have almost a thousand, my prince, well armoured and organised, though they are more stubborn than the goblins."

Yes, trolls would be a strong part of their army, if they could get them to do as they were told. Goblins suffered from too much cunning and not enough courage, while the trolls lacked nothing in courage, but were not the quickest thinkers and could get it into their heads to do whatever they decided was important! Still a firm hand with the whip or magical lash brought them into line.

"That is a good number of trolls, Parinsar" Uh'Ram acknowledged, "And with two of our own Warbands that gives us almost ten thousand." His commander nodded and bowed. "How many warriors do we think the humans have at Shandrilos?" he then asked though he knew the numbers. He and his Parinsar were simply going over things carefully.

"The town of Shandrilos will be able to field around six to seven hundred men, though the majority will be ill armed volunteers. The contingents from the other towns will add perhaps another three hundred."

Ten to one odds would be enough even if all the human forces were formidable, but his intelligence told him that only around two to three hundred would be well trained soldiers. The only other concern was the magi of the college. Around two hundred of them would be of sufficient ability to cause a concern, but the mage and his disruption of the college should cause enough distraction that any magical resistance would be split and muted and, even if it wasn't, the odds were in his favour and his strategy would mean time was on his side. The longer the humans held out the more time his lorewise would have to recover from the effort of teleporting his army to the island of Shandrilos. He could then bring them into the battle. The humans would not be able to stand against a bombardment from two hundred elven lorewise!

He allowed himself a small smile before he again addressed, Nar'Dolth. "Have we chosen the Gonhironsari to command the five sections?" The army would split into five to attack the town. Two sections would attack the dock area on the western side of the town, from north and south. They would quickly move in and sink all vessels in the harbour. No one would be allowed to escape. The next two sections would attack the main part of the town from north and south, preventing any from fleeing into the hills. However, they would push in more slowly, allowing the people to flee from the dock area, east through the town. Uh'Ram wanted the people to flee into the college and swamp them. It would also then be easier to surround them and move in and massacre them. The final section of the army would move in from the east, cutting off any escape to the other side of the island. None would escape Shandrilos and later when people came to the island they would find a place only for the dead. His army would leave the way they had come and none would know the fate of the town and college. With one swift attack he would then destroy the vast majority of magic users in the Wildlands as well as the leaders of the provinces.

He sat back. It was a good plan. There was even the chance that he would be able to kill all the leaders of the Elder races too, though he expected them to use their own arts to flee. However, even if they did, it suited him perfectly; his spies had instructions to start rumours that it was the Elder races that massacred the humans at Shandrilos. No one would believe the elves or dwarves if they claimed it was goblins and trolls that had wiped out the town!

Suddenly, his magical senses detected something. His Loremasters sensed it too and began forming defensive spells. His bodyguard of Lorewardens was already leaping forward to place themselves between their prince and any danger. Uh'Ram sat calmly, he knew what was happening. His own magical senses told him that Ry'Ana had returned.

In the air before his throne, in front of his startled advisors, the astral form of Ry'Ana White Eyes formed. She looked around at Uh'Ram's advisors and bodyguard and a small crease on her perfect coppery brow marked her irritation. Uh'Ram let the confrontation stand for a moment and he sensed Ry'Ana's irritation increase. 'Let it' he thought, 'if she was going to intrude in such an unseemly manner on his court. Besides it was good to keep his bodyguard alert.

"I suggest you tell your guard to stand down, Uh'Ram." Ry'Ana said curtly.

Uh'Ram smiled inwardly. He respected Ry'Ana's power, but he was a prince of the holy blood, he would not allow anyone, even her to take him lightly.

Still it did not pay to irritate her too much. He nodded and gestured for his guard to return to their posts. To his advisors he said, "Go and make the final preparations for the attack on Shandrilos. We will leave when the sun begins to set."

They nodded and withdrew and Ry'Ana drifted closer. Uh'Ram noticed that this time she had not fully manifested her astral form. It was still completely ephemeral. She must have noticed his scrutiny.

"I need to preserve my strength. Tal'Asin is proving more resilient than expected."

He raised an eyebrow. He would have liked to have seen the most hated enemy of their people. "Perhaps, I can be of help?" he mused.

"I can deal with Tal'Asin. He will break, that I promise."

She stopped and looked hard at Uh'Ram then and he felt a touch of unease. A strange, faraway look crossed her face and then vanished.

"The Lords of Darkness have spoken to me." She announced. "They have shown me what we must do." Her blind eyes opened wider, orbs of ivory in her fiery complexion. "I know who has opened the Ways, I know where the key is!"

Elation filled Uh'Ram, but he kept control of himself. Fighting for calm, he asked "Who? Who has the key? Where are they?"

"Four humans have the key. They opened the gate beneath Shandrilos and have since been searching the ancient cities of the Sylvan ones." Ry'Ana intoned.

Uh'Ram was aware she was watching his reactions carefully. "Searching!" His mind worked furiously, "They are seeking the Lifestone!" He found himself on his feet, advancing on the shade of Ry'Ana. "Do they have it?" he asked harshly.

"Calm yourself, Uh'Ram. They have not yet discovered the location of the Lifestone."

Uh'Ram relaxed slightly and began to think, "Four humans... they must be those of the group who went below Shandrilos. They should not be difficult to deal with."

"There is one problem. They sit within an intact Waygate Hall, protected by its ancient spell wards and..."

Uh'Ram cut in, "and they could go to any number of other Waygate halls with the key."

Ry'Ana nodded.

"I do not have the resources to have guards around all the Waygates. It would take time to find them and great effort to then make a portal to transport my men there." Uh'Ram turned and walked back to his throne and sat. "Still, if you have found them once with your scrying, you could do so again." Uh'Ram said, voicing his thoughts as they came to him. He needed to plan carefully and so he didn't see the look of clear anger that touched Ry'Ana's face for a second.

"Tal'Asin has cast a spell to obscure their images and aura. It would be very difficult to locate them again." Ry'Ana said stiffly.

Uh'Ram's head snapped up and he looked at her incredulously. She had found that bit of information difficult to admit, yet before he could speak Ry'Ana continued.

"However there is no need to. I know where they will go, my dear Uh'Ram," Ry'Ana went on, a look of pleasure returning. "The Lords of Darkness have shown me where the stone lies and you must go there!"

"You know where the Lifestone lies!" Uh'Ram gasped, losing all control of his emotions for a second.

Ry'Ana's blind gaze was implacable, though Uh'Ram sensed her emotions. She too was struggling to control her elation.

"You must send your men to assault Shandrilos as planned, Uh'Ram, but you must take a Warband and go to Hy'Deeria. The Lifestone lies there." Her voice dropped off at the last and the impact of what she had said hit Uh'Ram like a physical blow.

"Hy'Deeria?" He slumped back on his throne, his bloodmetal armour creaking in protest and pushing into his back. "Our ancient homeland is anathema to us now. When last our people tried to go there, the twisted beasts rose up against us and even the very air was poisonous to us." He closed his dark eyes. "The ruin of Tel'Emnar's great spell laid waste to all."

"Yes," Ry'Ana uttered quietly, "It seems almost just that the stone should lie there."

Uh'Ram looked at her and saw the wariness in her.

"You are certain of this vision?" Uh'Ram asked, though he knew the answer. Ry'Ana would not have brought this information if she was in doubt, and he had no reason to doubt her. Her visions had all proven true so far, even the one about the humans. He was surprised at her forbearance. She had not mentioned that the humans who had the key were most likely the ones he had failed to have killed.

She ignored his question, "You must go quickly. The humans will soon enter the Ways once more. They will soon be searching in Hy'Deeria. You must get to the Lifestone first or remove it from their lifeless hands." She drifted closer to Uh'Ram. "I have seen you holding the Lifestone and it shining as it opened the Great Temple beneath Althazar." She moved close and leaned forward. "You will bring the Great One back to us, Uh'Ram, my dear, and you will be his Gonkaldesar, his Grand Warlord when he conquers all!"

With that she vanished.

Ry'Ana White Eyes shifted herself carefully back into her hidden annex of the astral plane and quickly checked the wards and spells on Tal'Asin's astral prison. The weaves were still in place, still strong, unfortunately so was Tal'Asin it seemed!

He stood there, unmoving. He seemed serene and content and Ry'Ana knew he was resting himself. How was he resisting? How was Tal'Asin still strong when everything Ry'Ana knew said he should be withering away both in body and in spirit; neither could be without the other for long? How could he endure? Ry'Ana's flawless brow crinkled slightly at this. She had seen his body destroyed, she had been sure. In every vision of the past she had watched that climactic moment at the height of the Great One's battle to open the Great Temple, to bring through his demon allies. Tal'Asin and his forces had interrupted them, had hammered into the Great One's bodyguard. Tal'Asin had waited, letting others carry the attack. He had waited until he could bring the power of the Lifestone to bear against the Great One. The visions of that battle were painful to behold, such power had flown between the two, Tal'Asin's magic augmented by the Lifestone and the Great One's by his link to the

Lords of Darkness. Neither would have prevailed but for… She paused and her frown deepened. Of course, Tal'Asin couldn't have survived that battle, it was only his sacrifice that had given him the power needed to defeat the Great One, to strip his life force from him and thrust it into the void. He had not used the Lifestone; it would have been a violation of its purpose as Tel'Emnar's had been when he destroyed Hy'Deeria. Tal'Asin had drawn his power from his own life force. As a consequence his body had been consumed.

Of course, it all seemed to fit now. Tal'Asin had not been seen in these lands since that time. Had he been alive, he would not have sat back in secret while his lands and people were hounded and harried to near extinction, he would have fought back, Tal'Asin would have found the Lifestone and led his people. What a fool she had been! She had thought him alive. A smile appeared on her face for a moment with the revelation, then… the frown returned, but that made no sense either. If he was dead and this was merely his shade, it would not have had such power, such strength. It would have been a ghost, a lost spirit, its soul gone, with little influence over the astral realm and even less over the physical.

Ry'Ana moved over to her throne, an exact copy of the one in which she sat in the physical realm, in the Holy City, half a world away. Luckily, she had returned to her body not long before capturing Tal'Asin and renewed her strength otherwise she too would have begun to fade. She needed to unravel the mystery of Tal'Asin before she again needed to return to her physical self. The prison she had constructed would endure without her, but she did not trust to leave Tal'Asin for long, he seemed to know far more of the mysteries than she had thought possible. She had thought she had learnt all the mysteries, attained all the levels of mastery, but perhaps not. She was still unsure how Tal'Asin had been able to seemingly absorb the higher magical attacks; it was possible to absorb the spells born of the lesser magic, but not of the higher, at least not that she had thought. It was another conundrum and it made her feel like a student again, a feeling she liked not at all!

Her thoughts were interrupted as Tal'Asin's deep blue, almost violet eyes opened and locked gaze with her. She snarled inwardly, but kept her features blank.

"Soon your human pawns will be dead, Tal'Asin, soon Prince Uh'Ram will have the Lifestone and soon the Great One will return."

No emotion marred the tall Lore King's silvery face. "Your father is dead, Ry'Ana, he cannot return."

"So sure are you, oh wise Tal'Asin?" Ry'Ana purred. "The Lifestone can heal and the Great Temple preserve."

A frown appeared on the Lore King's high brow and uncertainty appeared in his eyes. "Your father is dead," he asserted, "you cannot bring him back!" he finished firmly. His features became serene once more.

"You are wrong, Tal'Asin, as you have been wrong about everything. You constantly seek to deceive and have instead deceived yourself."

"Are you so sure, Ry'Ana?" Tal'Asin whispered, "Perhaps it is you who have been deceived?"

"The Lords of Darkness have shown me the truth." she replied, smiling sweetly.

"Like they showed you centuries ago?" he asked quietly. "I am presuming that it was your vision that guided your father's attacks, that it was your insight and guidance that allowed him to destroy my people." he asserted, seeming like he didn't want to believe his own words.

"Your people were weak; it was that which allowed us to destroy them. They were not worthy. The Lords of Darkness guided us…"

"Through you, Ry'Ana, through you!" he insisted. "Your father had their power driving him, he understood their will, but it was you who interpreted the future for him, wasn't it?"

Ry'Ana stared silently at Tal'Asin, a slight smile on her lips. 'Of course it was me', she thought, but she would not say it, Ry'Ana was not sure what Tal'Asin's purpose was.

"All those times that I wondered how he could know just where to strike and when, and it was you." He seemed to drift off at the end and a deep look of sadness seemed to wither him. He hunched over slightly, the strength ebbing from him.

"Of course it was me!" she snapped, "My father has always been guided by me. It was I who told him where…" Tal'Asin seemed to slump a little more, "and when…" It was like each word was a blow, "and who!" Tal'Asin seemed as if he were going to collapse.

Ry'Ana pushed herself up and hurried over to his prison. Her eyes were wide and her face flushed. Could she break him so easily? How curious, that he should be so affected by this knowledge.

"Does the power of the Lords of Darkness cause you pain? Does my gift bring you despair?" She asked in mock worry. Her anger cut in then and her tone turned harsh. "Are you sorry your great spell did not kill me along with all my kith and kin?" she finished viciously.

He was shaking his golden maned head and as she stepped closer to the prison, Ry'Ana saw him look up and she took an involuntary step backwards. His face was a ruin of sadness and tears streamed down his face. She frowned, was it so easy to break this man that she had feared for as long as she could remember?

"No," he replied, his voice barely audible, "I am so sorry you have been twisted so. You were such a wonderful child…" He looked at her, his gaze piercing, yet tinged with the sheen of tears. "Your mother's soul must be writhing in torment."

It was like a physical blow. Ry'Ana reeled back. Her face must have shown the horror of her response. The horror was quickly replaced with anger, fury. She had never been so livid. How dare he of all people speak of her mother, and in such a way, he who had slain her!

She couldn't contain herself, couldn't control herself, she called forth her astral might with wild rage and hurled it at Tal'Asin. "How dare you!" she screamed as the conflagration leapt from her outstretched arms and rigid fingers.

Tal'Asin seemed genuinely taken aback at the suddenness of her reaction, but he was the consummate master and too wily to have no defence in place. Nevertheless, the raw blast of Ry'Ana's attack slammed him back against the far war of the astral prison. For a brief moment strain appeared on his startled face, then the energy began to simply vanish as it reached him!

Ry'Ana realized what was happening and immediately ceased her attack. Again he had shown he could absorb her attacks. Frustration made her clench her fists and her face contorted with the need she felt to destroy this being. Her hate burned like a furnace inside her.

With deadly passion she howled, "You, who killed my mother, dare to speak of her! I would draw out your death over a thousand years!"

Tal'Asin's hated sylvan features looked aghast. "I… I… did not kill…" He seemed to choke on his words, "I did not kill your mother!" he gasped.

"Liar!" Ry'Ana screamed, "You killed her, you. You sought to seduce her from my father and when she chose him over you, you killed her!"

He was shaking his head fervently. "That's not true… surely you remember… your father…"

"Silence!" Ry'Ana cried interrupting, "you will not spread your lies!"

"I do not lie!" he called back angrily. His brows were drawn down like a stern father. "I did not seek to seduce you mother, she was my sister…"

Tal'Asin continued speaking, but Ry'Ana was not listening. The words 'sister' reverberated through her mind. 'Madness', she thought and yet all her senses told her he was telling the truth.

"…she was a princess of the Sylvan elves, she found out about your father's betrayals and his allegiance with the Lords of Darkness, she was horrified and sought to leave him."

Ry'Ana was shaking her head. Such vile lies, her father had told her the truth. Somehow, Tal'Asin had managed to affect her senses. Yes, that was it. He was trying to deceive her as he had her mother. Her father was right, he was clever.

"Enough!" she spat and threw up a wall of silence between them that would prevent his words from reaching her while he could hear her. "You will not seduce me with your lies, as you tried with my mother," she called, "and soon Prince Uh'Ram will slay your humans and my father shall return and we will see an end to you. My people and my mother shall be avenged. We shall take our rightful place as the rulers of all!"

With that she turned and moved back to her throne, but in her mind his words still echoed and, for some reason, from the depths of her mind came images of her mother unbidden and in them her skin was not the lovely copper of the True elves, but the silvery skin of Tal'Asin and his kin. 'No', she shook her head. Tal'Asin had cast some strange and subtle spell on her. His power was great. She must steel herself if she was to break him.

Sitting on her throne she looked into her great scrying bowl and summoned up the image of the humans in the Waygate hall of Dal'Thanda. She saw them preparing to step through a Waygate arch, presumably to Hy'Deeria. She would not be able to observe in the country of her childhood, it was a virtual dead zone to magic and no scrying would show her what happened there. She had to trust in Uh'Ram, he had arranged to create a portal to that wild and dangerous land straight away with a Warband of his elite guard; the humans didn't stand a chance.

Chapter 51

THE FATE OF NOSSI BEE

The dwarven peoples see themselves as the blessed of Estarn, Lord of Earth and Stone, who to us is Tynast, God of Battle. While Thalos, Lord of Famine whom we know as Yarvik the Destroyer, is spoken of only in whispers. Meanwhile the trolls are seen as having forsaken Uroth, Lord of Forging and Dreams long ago. It is said they now revere the strength of Xarloth the Dark Lord of Flames and Nightmares whom our people call Taythan the great Fire Giant!

Knowledge passed down through Bardic tradition. Recorded by Prince Afdar SaTell of Stellicia BY78 - thought to be directly quoted from the legendary 'Lorebooks of the Druid Kings' said to have been begun by King Nam'Odar the Fisherking a thousand years earlier.

Nossi sat, curled up tight in a ball, deep in the shadows of the dark room. He had got as far as he could from the giant, fearsome man in the dirty grey robes. His eyes were dry now; he would not shed any more tears, and the pain had dimmed to a throbbing throughout his body. He had done nothing to prompt the beating; the man seemed to enjoy hitting him. Nossi now realised that he would die here, it was just a question of when. Despair filled him. He had come so far and avoided so much only to end up here in some unknown house, in an unknown city.

He had thought that his luck had started to change after he had fallen in with the humans. Things hadn't gone well at first, he had been afraid of their strange ways and these were backed by the stories he had heard of humans. He had fled, but with nowhere to go he had returned to them, he wasn't entirely sure why. He had sensed something about them, though it wasn't until later that he had realised what it was. He had slowly begun to understand that the humans he had fallen in with were friends in a way he had not known could exist. They argued and seemed to delight in baiting one another, yet Nossi came to see that this was just another way of showing they cared for each other; they laughed at each other in small ways as if to hide their regard. Yet, it showed when they had been attacked, how they would lay down their lives for one another without thought. None of them had wanted to leave their companions behind, none of them had thought to flee and save themselves at the expense of their friends even though it could mean death to stay. This kind of regard for each other was alien to the culture in which he had grown. In House Tothearis it was everyone for themselves. You turned a blind eye to the problems of others. Even with the Great Masters, who need not fear closeness like their subject races, they only would do what their duty demanded of them. The kind of regard that these humans showed one another was utterly alien. Even with his father, with whom his relationship was close to the point where many considered it strange, he had always been careful to keep a distance, to not care too much in case caring brought suffering. Of course all that had changed when he had found his love, though his biggest mistake had been in not hiding his feelings.

He pictured her face once more and though the pain still remained it was not so sharp now as to pierce him through the way it had. The man in white had somehow changed something in him. There was a wonder in the kind of magic that human had possessed and he had helped Nossi without thought to recompense. Now Nossi could at last look back on the good times he shared with his love. It was those times that Nossi had retreated to in his mind when the brutish human had beaten him. Soon he hoped he would be meeting her. His time would come soon. Nossi just hoped it would be over quickly.

He looked across at the horrible creature that held him captive. In some ways he was more disgusting even than the ogres and the skriegan that Nossi had grown up with. The human was not physically as imposing or ugly as those two races, yet he was more repulsive for that. He at once reminded Nossi of those foul creatures, but also of the humans who had taken him in; of the kind man in white who had given Nossi a way back to his love. It was that comparison that made this man in dirty white robes all the more grotesque. He was a parody. So too that other human who had questioned him and tortured him and made him say just what he wanted him to say. He reminded Nossi of the Great Masters and of the man, Arkadi at the same time.

At first Nossi had been wary of Arkadi too, yet as they had made their way towards the surface, Arkadi had shown a true admiration of Nossi's knowledge; rather than a need to rip it all from him, Nossi had felt that Arkadi saw him as a fellow 'mage' as he called it, an equal almost. He had chatted to Nossi in a relaxed and friendly way and had even talked Nossi through the translation spell he had cast so he could cast it himself. Not so the 'mage' he was now a captive of; this gaudily robed loreman had scared Nossi through to his very core. He was only interested in what he could get.

Nossi wished Arkadi or the man in white was here now, or the others with their bright swords. They would have dealt with these horrible creatures; these poor reflections. All of the humans he had met below the ground had been kind, even when it was plain they were all afraid both for themselves and for their friends. No Great Master would ever have treated Nossi like that, even in the best of times.

It had crushed Nossi yet again when the friends were separated and he had been completely devastated when the others had been caught in the rock fall. He felt responsible too. He had not been present at the time, but he had known about the trap the Great Masters had set. He should have warned them. Now they too were dead. They would not come to help him. He was helpless just as he had been when they had taken his love away. It seemed that whenever he raised his hopes they would be dashed. Grief rose up and caused him to gasp and cry once more.

"What's the matter little friend?" came the strangely smooth voice of his captor out of nowhere. "Are you in pain, crying like that?"

Nossi looked up in terror to see the toothless smile on the face of the ponderous human as he marched towards Nossi. He shook his head silently, knowing nothing would stop the attack that was coming, yet hoping the man would take pity.

Nossi saw the brutal fist as it rushed towards his face and he dodged his head sideways. It was a mistake. The miss only made the man angrier and Nossi felt a boot hammer into his side. He cried out as he was lifted and hurled sideways by the blow. Then the fists started to fall and Nossi saw lights flashing and felt the floor rush up to meet his face. Thankfully, his brain took pity on him and he faded into oblivion.

※

Nat crouched by the door silently with her eye was pressed to the slight gap that ran along the hinged side. Hardly breathing she watched as the ape like man in the dirty robes of a monk of the Karodran order stomped angrily over to a large wooden chair and slumped his brutish bulk into its embrace almost sullenly. He was obviously disappointed the gnome had not lasted longer before unconsciousness took him.

Nat was struggling to control her breathing. She was furious! This troll-like excuse for a man seemed to like inflicting pain. Nat had met people like him before. They were always big in her experience, big men with little intelligence. However, Nat had heard this one talk and although the lack of many of his teeth made his voice lisp, it was clear from his cultured tone and range of vocabulary that he was no simpleton as she had first took him to be. He had the cruel face and small piggish eyes, but there was more to this one than met the eye. Another issue was the fact that this man was almost twice as wide as most normal men and muscle clearly stretched his woolen robes at chest, shoulder and arms. Even Bear would have struggled with this man!

So although Nat was angry, she was not stupid. She wanted to help Nossi, but she would not face that behemoth unless she had to. No, there were always other ways.

Nat had found this house with a little searching and had scouted around it; a large town house with two floors. She had counted from the windows at least eight rooms on the ground floor alone. No lights showed in the house, and no movement. All had been quiet and still. The huntress was experienced with traps and locks and had quickly managed to get the simple lock open on the small side door, one of three entrances to the building. She had then carefully scouted through the house. One room, in the centre of the house, had four doors, one in each of the walls of the room. Nat had been especially cautious here. Through one door she had found a large room with what looked like blood stains on the floor. In a few weeks, no one would have noticed, but at the moment the room stank like an abattoir. Through a second door she had found a small room and a door, but something had stopped her from going through it. She felt something. It had taken her a moment to put her finger on it. Others might not have recognised the strange feeling, but Nat had spent a long time around magic users, both in Ostia in her youth, and with her friends. She knew magic when she felt it. Something magical was behind that door. She had, very carefully, examined the door and its handle. As far as she could tell the magic had nothing to do with the door, but she did not want to stake her life on it. If it was powerful enough for her to sense, poor as her magical senses were, it was powerful enough to kill her.

It was through one of the other doors that she had found a way down. The steps had been hidden in a storeroom under a trap door. The steep ladder-like steps led down into a narrow corridor with a number of doors leading off. Nat had discovered that these rooms were small and used as storerooms. However, the room at the far end of the corridor had been large and it was against the door to this room that she now had her eye pressed.

She needed to get that brute out of there so that she could steal away the gnome, but how?

What would bring the man out? What would force the man out of the room?

'Wait a minute' Nat thought, 'wasn't that a grate to the surface she had seen?'

Nat gingerly edged herself around until she could see the left upper corner of the room.

'Yes!' She could see a wooden and metal grating through which some light could be seen faintly. She could go up there and cause some sort of disturbance that would bring the hulking monk out. She could then slip in and free Nossi.

Nat frowned. As plans went that seemed pretty poor; she needed a better one. Turning, silently, she crept back along the corridor and up the steps. She quickly made her way out of the side door through which she had entered. She needed some distraction that would bring the monk up, but would occupy him long enough for her to get in and out with the gnome. What would be important enough to bring the man up quickly and to take a little time to deal with?

Nat glanced around the small muddy yard at the side of the large house. The grating must be near here, yet she hadn't noticed it on the way in so it wouldn't be obvious. She crept about the yard. There were bits of old wood and weeds strewn about the whole surrounding walled garden of the house. Nat carefully knelt by the wall of the house and then began to move slowly around the wall, looking for a grating. She moved around the side of the building, round one corner and then another. With all the turns inside the house, she couldn't say which side of the house the cellar grating would be beneath.

Suddenly, she saw it, half covered by mud and weeds. Quickly, she stepped back. She didn't want her shadow alerting the man too soon. However, she needed to get the big monk up here and keep him here.

She turned and looked around.

'Of course!' she thought bitterly, thinking of poor Karis, 'what do all people in towns fear – well apart from plague… war…robbery…!' Nat stopped herself. 'Get on with it!' she thought angrily.

She quickly assembled what she needed from back the way she had come, making sure to keep low and out of sight. Thankfully, the sun was starting to go down and no other houses overlooked this one – probably why it had been chosen. Out of the small pouch attached to her belt, Nat pulled out her flint and tinder.

Fire!

That would bring the monk up sharpish, no doubt, and by that time Nat would already be in the house waiting. Then, while the monk tried to put out the fire, she could get Nossi out.

'An excellent idea', she thought smiling to herself.

Ten minutes later, Nat was crouched in the gloom behind the ladder-like stairs that led up from the cellar. She was starting to worry now. She had not even heard a sound from the room at the end of the corridor and by now that fire should have taken hold. The crackle of the flames and the smoke and light from the flames should have been clear to that bloody oaf in there.

'Damn' Nat cursed silently, 'Was she going to have to bloody well shout 'fire' herself to get this 'walking mountain's' attention! If the damned monk didn't do something soon, the house would burn down with them all in it!'

Nat was just about to move forward when the door at the far end of the corridor was almost wrenched off its hinges by the ugly brutish monk. The look on the man's face almost made Nat chuckle out loud. His piggy eyes were wide with alarm and his almost toothless mouth was agape. The monk hurtled down the corridor and his feet stomped urgently up the stairs inches from her eyes. She could hear the man cursing something under his breath about his master.

Nat waited a good count of twenty before cautiously moving out from her hiding place. She looked up the stair to check the man had gone and then hurried down the corridor and stepped slowly into the room beyond. She had a dagger in one hand, a short sword in the other, and was crouched, her muscles taut. She was sure there was no one else in the room save Nossi, but it paid to be careful.

She scanned around. The room was empty save for the little gnome who lay slumped in the corner, bruised, battered and bleeding. He was so small he reminded Nat of her children.

She sped across to him, knelt, and whispered his name as she rolled the prone little man over.

Nossi's eyes opened slightly. They were swollen almost shut from the beatings. There was no flash of recognition. The gnome just stared up at Nat silently. She gently slid her arms under the gnome's head and shoulders and lifted him slightly.

"Nossi" she whispered urgently and gave him a slight shake, "Nossi, come on!" There was still no response. The gnome was obviously conscious, but was completely out of it. "Come on, snap out of it!" Nat hissed a little impatiently. She didn't really have time for this. She'd expected the gnome to get up and for them to get out. It seemed like she might have to carry the little fellow.

Abruptly, a noise came to her. Her eyes widened and she looked around the room quickly. There was only one way in or out of the room. The noise she had heard and recognised instantly became louder. It was the big monk. He was coming back. Nat could now hear him muttering that he had to get the gnome out of the house. Nat lowered the gnome down and swiftly turned just as the brute walked into the room. It seemed she had set the fire too well. The monk had returned quickly because the fire couldn't be put out. 'Damn and damn again!' Nat thought. 'Weren't heroes supposed to be able to rescue people? Wasn't it supposed to be easier than this?' She crouched.

The monk pulled up short and his buttress like forehead lowered as his mouth became cruel. "Well, well, what have we hear? If it isn't the thief's friend," said the monk, pulling a wicked looking spiked mace from his wide, stained belt. "You know you're supposed to be dead under that rock fall. I hear the mage survived too." He moved forward menacingly, "We'll have to rectify that mistake."

With a growl the monk leapt forward his mace whistling towards Nat's head.

Nossi watched as if from a distance. It all seemed like a dream. He heard the green clothed woman's voice, recognised it, but he would not believe it. He had given up and no tricks his mind could play could touch him. He would not give in to false hope again. He had been disappointed too many times. Soon he hoped he would be with his love, in a place where no one could hurt him anymore.

It was curious how his mind worked though, of all the people he could have conjured up to save him, this woman was not one of them. He only vaguely remembered her really. She had been the one who had accidentally tripped the stairs that they all had fallen down. 'Nat' that was her name, 'Nat'.

Never would Nossi have thought his mind would produce her. She had died in the trap the Great Masters had set in the catacombs.

Nossi frowned. The fantasy was very real.

Nossi heard his captor's voice and shivered 'Not dead in the rock fall?' Was that what he had said? The words only came to him slowly. Nossi watched as the monk attacked and frowned. Had the man said the mage too? Was that possible?

For a moment his hopes rose, but then despair quickly followed. Even if they had survived the rock fall, they would not come to help him, they owed him nothing. His mind was playing tricks. He watched the fight through swollen disbelieving eyes.

Nat threw herself sideways and rolled to her feet. The big monk was strong, but he was not so quick. Already, the monk's dirty robes were stained red where her knife and short sword had slashed him.

Again, the prodigious man snarled, spun and attacked. She feinted one way, waiting for the swing of the mace then darted the other, slipping under the swing and slashing her knife quickly along the monks exposed ribs. The monk grunted, but did not cry out. He turned, slowly this time, and his thick brows came down as he regarded Nat balefully.

She grinned impishly, giving the appearance of confidence, while secretly swallowing hard. The big bastard was hardly even concerned by the wounds she had inflicted. Nat was quick and quite agile, but she was not sure it would matter against this brute; he was possibly as strong as Bear and she was pretty certain she would slow before the brute did.

The man advanced again, this time slowly, more cautious. Nat decided she needed to risk a more straightforward approach. As the brute lifted his mace, this time obviously going for a downward swing, she leapt forward. The grotesque monk's piggy eyes widened and he hurriedly twisted, but it was too late. Nat's knife and short sword were already burying themselves into the monk's ribs, one from either side. The monk gasped and Nat grinned fiercely.

'Have that!' she thought.

She stared into the big, vile man's face, enjoying the look of pain that stretched his near toothless mouth wide. The monk threw his head back and roared loud enough to shake the wooden beams of the room and the spiked mace fell with a thump to the floor.

"Yeah," Nat snarled, "Don't like the pain yourself do you, you ugly whoreson!"

Abruptly, the monk's head snapped forward and eyes filled with fury bored into Nat's. The power of that gaze chilled her and she started to pull away, but vice like hands clamped down onto her wrists and held her. Nat felt the pain as the monk's monstrous hands squeezed mercilessly. She struggled and pulled. The mammoth's hands didn't even budge. She looked down quickly from the huge monk's face to her hands and then back. A cruel grin twisted the brute's thin mouth as he leaned towards her. The tall huntress felt the pain intensify and she desperately tried to twist the knife in the brute's side. She looked up to see if it had any effect and was shocked to see the beast's big ugly face scant inches from her own, leering like a lunatic.

Nat felt her hands being pulled back. Her weapons slowly pulled free of the brute's body with a sickening, sucking noise. Blood pumped free, but it didn't seem to have any effect on the crazed monk whose face was heading towards hers, his near toothless maw wide.

'Tynast! He's going to bloody well eat my face!' Nat thought. She increased her struggle, but it made no difference. The man might as well have been made of rock. Nat could feel her wrists being crushed in the unforgiving grip.

"Somebody bloody help me!" she cried.

Nat looked around desperately for help, none was in evidence. She was here alone save for the gnome, but Nossi was still as a statue.

"Nossi!" Nat almost screamed, "Nossi, help me or we are both going to die!"

Nat thought the gnome heard her. His head moved slightly and he was looking straight at her, but then nothing.

"Damn you, you little fool. I came here to save you." Nat thundered in fury, "My friends died to get you out and you lie there making their sacrifice, nothing! Nothing! Do you hear me?!"

Nat didn't wait for an answer. The gnome was a lost cause. With a suddenness that surprised even the monk, Nat Bero slammed herself forward, butting the monk and pushing her weapons back at the brute. In the instant the monk reacted and pushed Nat's hands back, she leaned back, brought her knees up, planted her feet against the big monk's stomach and heaved back with all her might. For a moment it seemed even this would not be enough and then her hands pulled free and Nat hurtled backwards through the air. She tried to flip herself in midair so that she would land on her feet and she might have managed it too had the wall not been just a little too close. Instead she crashed into the wall chest first. Air burst from her and she slumped down cracking her head on the floor. Stars flashed in front of her eyes and she felt her weapons slip from her hands and go skittering across the floor.

She tried to twist herself over so that she could rise, but she couldn't seem to see clearly and the room was spinning. She got half way round and then felt a hand grab her by the neck and yank her up. Her vision cleared a bit to show the insane face of the monk. A second hand slammed down and Nat saw stars again. She was pulled forward and she knew the monk was about to smash her head against the wall and reacted instinctively, sweeping her foot around. There was a growl of pain and Nat saw she had kicked the brute in the ribs where blood streamed liberally from his wounds. Nat quickly took advantage of the monk's distraction to slam another kick into his ribs. However, this time the reaction was different. The burly monk grabbed her leg with one hand and then spun and heaved with the vice-like hand he had on her neck.

For an instant, Nat felt weightless as she flew through the air. She tried to twist in midair to ease her landing, but she still slammed hard into the wall. Thankfully her twisting meant it was her back that hit not her head, and she slid down to land on her knees.

Nat looked across to the monk. He was standing, glaring at her. One of his hands was pressed to his side and his face was knotted with pain. It seemed the wounds were at last starting to have an effect. All Nat had to do was survive long enough for the brute to collapse. Those wounds were serious. However, Nat could already feel her own face swelling from the monk's fist and her whole body ached from the collisions with walls and floor. She sat up and reached to grab another dagger from her hidden sheath behind her lower back, but as she did so pain shot through her hands and up her arms like fire. The monk's crushing grip had damaged her more than she had thought. Still, she pushed on. She needed her knife.

Suddenly, Nat felt the hair on her neck rise. Magic! Desperately she threw herself sideways towards the corner next to where Nossi lay. A blinding light flashed where she had been and the smell of sulphur filled the room. Nat turned. The monk was mouthing a second spell.

'Damn! Life just isn't fair,' she thought even as she sat up and drew her hand back to throw her knife. If she could distract the monk, the spell would be disrupted.

Nat got as far as drawing her arm back when the spell struck. She felt her whole body go cold and her muscles cramped. She went rigid and even the cry of pain stuck in her throat as her vocal cords froze. She couldn't move, not even blink!

The monk grunted painfully in satisfaction. He walked slowly forward. "I am going to suck your eyeballs out of your filthy little head." the monk growled, hatred clear in each slowly spoken word. "I am going to slit you open and pull out your innards then stuff them down your throat, you miserable bitch!"

Nat's fear rocketed out of control as she realised there was nothing she could do. She was helpless.

※

Nossi Bee watched the monk advance menacingly towards the human. Something was gnawing at him. Something wasn't right here. This was too real. What was it the human had said? She had come to save Nossi! Friends had sacrificed themselves for him! Was that true? He had never considered it. Arkadi had said that it was imperative Nossi speak to the other human magic users in the 'college' he called it. The others had all agreed. They had fled to the surface and left their other friends below, trapped by the Great Masters and their mayax and ogres. They had gone to escape, but they had also said they must get Nossi to the surface. Yes, Nossi was to tell those above of the Great Masters and their plans. He had done so, but not as he wanted. The mage had told him what to say and what not to, had terrified him into submission. Somehow, Nossi didn't think this was what Arkadi and the others had intended.

So could this woman have survived and then come to save Nossi, come to give Nossi the chance to do what he had been supposed to do. It seemed unbelievable to Nossi that anyone would care enough, but it was possible and what's more it was something Nossi did not think he could have thought up himself. There was no way his mind could have conceived of that!

Nossi struggled to make his body move and realised that the near paralysis that had gripped him was one of his own making. He had given up, he had been ready to die and so he had lain helpless, wishing for it to all end. However, if this was real and Nat was here and fighting for him... He paused. 'Fighting for him!' The idea seemed so ridiculous. No one would fight for him, and yet if she was... she was about to die. Despair hit Nossi afresh; there was nothing Nossi could do; nothing. He was no one, small and useless. These humans were big and strong. Nossi was weak.

He watched unable to move as the gigantic seeming man in dirty, blood soaked robes loomed over Nat. Why was Nat just sitting there? Nossi frowned. Of course, the monk has used some kind of paralysis spell. Nat was helpless, just like Nossi.

Something small sprang to life inside Nossi at that moment. It burned dimly at first and then grew in strength. Nat was helpless. This grotesque man was going to do to his new friend what he had done to Nossi, only worse. His friend! Yes, this woman was his friend. She had come to save Nossi. She cared what happened to Nossi and was willing to risk her life for him.

The flame that had ignited in him, burst inside his mind like a conflagration.

Nossi Bee was angry!

Fuelled by years of repression, months of anguish and days of fear, his anger blazed inside him. Nossi sat up. Nat was helpless against the spell, but Nossi wasn't. He could dispel such a simple spell with ease. Pain sliced into him as he sat up though, and his resolve began to disintegrate. He had been beaten hard and his body was a mass of agony.

The monstrous man had taken a hold of Nat's head in his large, powerful hands. He was leaning in close. Nossi could see the sheer panic in the huntress' eyes.

"No!" Nossi coughed. He sat up with every muscle in his body seeming to protest and the dispel cantrip flew from him.

Things happened suddenly. The monk looked up and over at Nossi, startled by the little man's surprised outburst... and Nat's knife lunged forward and buried itself into the monk's throat just above the collarbone. The thrust of the blade didn't even seem to register with the monk at first. The blow didn't seem to even nudge him. He just stood there bent over, looking first at Nossi and then down at Nat who dragged herself back, frantically jerking her head from between the monk's cruel hands. Then the apish human stumbled back a step, his hand went almost gently to his throat. Blood seemed to gush from around the knife quivering below his chin, and from his half open mouth, simultaneously.

Nat wasted no time watching. She pushed herself painfully to her feet, stumbled over to Nossi, swept up his arm and half dragged the gnome out of the room, only pausing to grab one of her knives as she left.

Minutes later, the changeling entered the now smoke filled cellar room. It was in the guise of the young mage it had first killed, wearing a dark cloak and deep hood. It took in the scene in the room in an instant using both its human eyes and its other senses. The blood drenched man against the wall was still breathing and partially aware, but with his blood and life draining slowly from the wound in his throat, he was not of interest to the Changeling. The scents in the room told it a gnome had been here, but so too had the woman it had seen earlier, the one in the green clothes from the Cleric's Dome.

Quickly the Changeling turned, its body lengthened and twisted, it became something sleek and feral. It took up the scent and began to hunt. The gnome and the human were not far ahead. It could deal with two of its prey at once.

Chapter 52

THE NINTH KINGDOM

Legends tell us that there were many lands that the Elder races inhabited, but the greatest were seen as the nine kingdoms of Elvenkind. They were: Dal'Thanda, Kingdom of the fire mountains; Dah'Ryllor, Kingdom of the river lands; Pry'Dein, Kingdom of the western isles; Ald'Orea, Kingdom of the lakes; Eld'Erin; the hidden Kingdom; Cor'Tuvor, Kingdom of stone; Shah'Namir the forest Kingdom; El'Yaris, the first Kingdom; and Hy'Deeria, the lost Kingdom. This last, ninth kingdom of the elves was the most mysterious, it was said to have been lost to some calamity so great and terrible that no elf would speak of it lest grief overcome them!

From 'The nature of the Elder' by Melkor Erin, Archmage of Shandrilos, BY1303

Jon 'Bear' Madraig stood anxiously by the Waygate arch to lost Hy'Deeria. "Are we ready for this?" He asked quietly, looking to each of his friends.

Zara Halven, Rebba Korran and Garon Vale all nodded.

Jon took a deep breath and turned to face the archway. With the new vision he had inherited from Tal'Asin he could see the intricate patterns on the arch, worked in the most ancient of elven script, Altaic script; a form of writing that even predated the High Elorien that was the common language of the elves when these archways were formed well over ten thousand years ago. Altaic was said to have been a language derived from the gods themselves and all languages of magic were born of it.

From Tal'Asin's memories, Jon had also gained a knowledge of their destination. Hy'Deeria, the ninth kingdom of the elves had once been the newest kingdom of the elves, a land of hope for uniting two elven peoples, the sylvan and the golden. Now, thousands of years later, thousands of years after the Kinslayer Wars and thousands of years after the great spell Tel'Emnar had cast perverting the Lifestone's purpose, the place was far different. Gone were the rolling plains, the fields of golden crops and green pastures; the bread basket of the elven people. In its place was a land drowned by floods, sunk into stinking swamps and festering marshlands. It was poisoned by magic that affected every living thing. It was a place of nightmare that had given rise to twisted monsters of every kind. Evil lurked there, it hung in the air, dripped off every leaf and stem, seeped through every bit of rock and soil. Even magic there was twisted and malevolent. No spell could be trusted save those of enchantment that had been cast elsewhere. Any magic cast in that place would go awry. It was a place where the forces of life and death contended endlessly and in its centre was the ancient city from which the land got its name, Hy'Deeria. Once it had housed thousands, now it was shattered; a tomb for any who entered.

Jon had shared all this with his friends. It had all come from Tal'Asin's memories of a time he had visited the place, through the Waygates, before the final fall of the Elder kingdoms. Then the elven Guardian had harboured dreams of healing the land. Instead, he had barely escaped. Only the fact that he had a Waygate to flee through had saved him. His own magic had rebelled on him and even the magic of the Lifestone had been muted.

His friends had not received this information well, but Jon had assured them that from Tal'Asin's experience, if they used no magic, none of the creatures that dwelt in that foul place need know they were even there. The creatures there seemed inexplicably drawn to magic and to elves. They just needed to be careful and stay out of sight. Jon would quickly be able to tell if the Lifestone was there even with magic being unreliable.

They had seemed mollified a little with this and Jon had gone further. He had explained about the powerful enchantments on the weapons and armour they had acquired. If they were discovered those enchantments would help them slay almost any opponent. This was a bit of an exaggeration, but his friends needed the boost. The staff Rebba now carried would enhance her magical prowess and the shield Garon carried could aid his healing spells so that he would be better than any of his clerical brotherhood. Also, the armour Rebba and Garon now wore was made by the elves in imitation of the armour of the original grey and white armour of the Rainbow Guard. They were incredibly light and yet tougher than steel and resistant to most minor magics.

Zara's armour was similar though it had been made by the dwarves, while her two swords were elven and very powerful. From High Elorien their names translated as 'Spellcutter' and 'Darksbane', one would protect the wielder from almost all spells, cutting through the weaves of any attacking spell, the other was designed to enhance the wielders physical abilities and increase their ability to slice and pierce armour and magical defences.

If truth be told the little group was now one of the most powerful ever seen since Elder times. It even made Zara comment that perhaps the Gods were with them.

Jon was also astounded at how he and his friends had changed so rapidly. It did make you believe that there was a divine hand involved.

Jon signaled to Rebba and said, "Open the Waygate."

Rebba stepped forward, but Zara called out, "Hold on a minute, I just have one more thing to ask."

Jon turned around and frowned at the now magnificent looking warrior in her shining, dwarven silver chain and platemail. "Can this wait, Zara? We really need to be moving."

Zara shrugged, "I only wanted to know if we could use this stone thing. You know, what we are looking for." Zara looked at Rebba and then at Garon on either side of her, "If we find it, can we use it? I mean if it is such a powerful... magic... erm, item... thing?" She drifted off helplessly.

"It's an interesting point, Bear, what if we come up against those twisted creatures you mentioned or such. If this stone is powerful we could defend ourselves at least." Garon put in.

Jon looked at him. He hated to quash their hopes. He knew they just wanted something to give them a little more chance against what they still saw as worrying odds against them.

He slowly shook his head and closed his eyes. "I am sorry, but the Lifestone can only be used by one of the holy line, one of the royal blood of the elves. It would strike down any other who sought to use its power, even if their intentions were good. Once, it is said, the Lifestone was wrenched from the hands of Gwin'Dor the Avenger by a mighty Troll King. He sought to use the stone against the elves, but instead it destroyed him. It is said it sent a blast of power through his skull that was so powerful it destroyed even those close by!"

Jon could see Garon mouthing the word 'oh' and Rebba simply stared at Jon in dismay.

Zara murmured, "A blast of power through his skull!" and shook her head.

Jon looked at his three friends seriously, looking into their eyes, weighing them. "Are we ready for this?" he asked again.

Again they all nodded. They were not certain, they were all afraid, but they would all step forward and give it their best. Jon could not ask for more than that.

Rebba moved forward and quickly slipped the keystone into the arch. She then stepped back hurriedly, moving a good distance from the archway. After a brief moment the now familiar blue energy burst out and then sucked back to leave a sheet of blazing force where before there had been simply an empty archway. They moved closer and stopped.

They all took a deep breath and then stepped through the Waygate.

Zara stepped out. Immediately she stumbled to her knees and began coughing. The air seemed acrid and had a smell like rotten eggs. It seemed almost like a thin fog tinged the atmosphere making it as though you were looking through a thin film, a little bit like when you had just woken up from a deep sleep and your eyes refused to clear. All of her friends were down and coughing harshly.

Bear was the first to recover, then surprisingly Rebba, but then Zara reasoned her druidic magic must give her a better tolerance of such things. Zara was still opening and closing her eyes carefully against the stinging that plagued them. She was slowly finding her breathing easing and the stench seemed to be lessening, either that or she was getting used to it.

Rebba was already closing the Waygate they had come through as Zara managed to stand up and look around, wiping the tears from her eyes. What she saw gave her pause. This was nothing like any of the other

Waygate halls, indeed there was no Waygate hall! Zara stood at the bottom of what appeared to be some kind of enormous hole. On all sides rubble and rocks and earth spread away from them at a slope. It reminded Zara of the arena in Ostia where she had fought, but instead of applauding people, bits of broken masonry, columns, archways and boulders looked down on her silently.

She heard Rebba ask, "What happened here, Bear?"

"The great spell was sent through the Waygate and what you see here is the results of the enormous explosion that started here. It blew this hole straight through the city and leveled this whole area, destroying almost everything in the city save some of the more outlying larger buildings whose enchanted walls and foundations resisted the blast. However, that was not the end of the spells affects, it was merely the beginning. The blast threw out a magical cloud that engulfed the land around and killed everything. Beyond that it was worse..."

"Worse!" Garon gasped, "What could be worse than such an attack?"

Bear turned and looked at the white armoured monk, "Slow death, Garon!" he answered gravely. Beyond the explosion and the killer cloud, the people, animals, plants and trees were all poisoned and died slowly or, even worse, they were twisted and changed into something vile, a parody of their former selves."

Even Zara found this idea repelling. She was quite untouched by the idea of elves killing elves thousands of years ago, but to die slowly or even change into something awful was an idea that touched even her. She could still remember the disease that had killed her parents and the monstrous scarring and swelling it had caused. Fear of such a fate had haunted her since her childhood.

Zara noticed that Bear was slowly turning on the spot and he seemed distracted, "Bear are you..."

A swiftly raised hand from Bear stopped her and Zara looked to Rebba and Garon who were both watching Bear too.

"It is here," Bear whispered, "It is here!" he repeated more firmly.

Zara looked at the others.

"You are sure?" Rebba asked, "This place confuses my senses completely."

Bear nodded and then added, "But I cannot get a firm sense of where or what direction. We must get out of this hole."

Zara nodded, checked the light pack on her back and cast around for where best to start the climb. It would not be a hard one, but it would be long and draining.

Rebba spotted what looked the easiest path and they quickly set off.

Perhaps a half hour later they reached the lip of the gigantic crater. The sight that greeted them was ghastly. They stood on the lip of a mound looking out over the long forgotten remains of a once great city.

A pall hung over the landscape like a damp blanket, but what lay within it was forbidding in the extreme. Immediately around the large crater that had been the centre of the ancient city was a wasteland of overgrown ruins, mounds and broken buildings. Zara noticed that the ruined buildings and what must have been streets, had now turned into small almost natural looking canyons with many of the collapsed buildings having been completely over grown and covered.

Beyond this, in the distance, was a seething mass of low lying, twisted groves and trees, interspersed with wetlands; swamp and marshy ground stretched as far as the eyes could see. There were small lakes of still water between moist grassy rolling mounds and copses of dark, dank trees.

As they looked around the panorama that was laid out before them, Zara could hear some far off strange noise, but she couldn't place it.

"Over there," Bear called excitedly, "the Lifestone is that way."

The rest of the group looked where Bear was pointing. Not far off, Zara could see a large building that was almost completely intact, though it was covered in vegetation. It stood up from a deep valley that must have once been a wide thoroughfare sided by large buildings. The buildings had now been swallowed up beneath rubble, soil and plant life.

As they looked, they noticed movement for the first time. Creatures that couldn't quite be made out at this distance could be seen on the high points of the valley and they were disappearing in large numbers over the edge. Zara frowned. It was also from there that the strange noise was emanating.

Bear suddenly snapped, "Quickly, we must get down off here. We will be seen." He sprang towards the more steeply descending slope on the outside of the crater and signalled for the others to follow.

Zara quickly hunched down even as she too sprang to follow. Garon and Rebba came after her.

As Zara caught up to Bear, with Garon and Rebba close behind, Bear added, "We must get to the Lifestone. From what I can hear and sense others are here too, seeking the stone," Bear smiled at Zara suddenly, "though it seems they have caught the attention of the denizens of this foul place."

Zara shook her head at Bear's enthusiasm and wondered about these denizens, who they were after and how Bear could sense what was going on down there. The answer came to her almost straight away when she looked at the black armoured Bear. He was wearing the magically adjusted armour of an elven Dragonlord, but the helm was slung on his belt and Zara could clearly see the upswept, pointed ears of an elf. Of course, those ears weren't just for show, nor the magical senses he had gained either.

Bear was looking more and more strange to Zara. His once bald head was now covered by short, spiky golden hair and his skin was looking more and more silvery. He was thinner too. Bear had always been impressively thick limbed and still seemed to retain his large build, but his limbs seemed to be longer and his waist slimmer. Bear was no longer clearly human, more elven features showed with each passing hour.

Bear moved off and Zara followed, ill at ease with the continued changes in her oldest friend.

It took them maybe five minutes to get down the steep incline and on to leveller ground. Another five minutes saw them crouched at the edge of a steep sided valley with columns and what must have been statues sticking up in odd places from the grassy, lightly tree spattered slopes. However, it was not the odd valley and scenery that held their attention, but what was taking place within it. Zara heard both Rebba and Garon gasp involuntarily at what they saw and look fearfully around for a moment before looking back down.

Along the centre of the valley's uneven floor, a phalanx of now familiar, dark elven warriors and their black goblin, ogre and insect-like allies stood tightly packed in disciplined lines fighting off a rabble of disgusting and misshapen creatures.

It was odd to think of the dark elves and their allies as familiar, but those who attacked them with wild abandon were truly strange. They were twisted versions of animals, beasts and even the races of the northlands; goblins, kobolds, dwarves, trolls and yeti. Some of them were grossly disfigured with lumps and limbs where there should never have been any, and some were enormous, massively swollen and enlarged beasts.

Zara watched as what looked vaguely like a mountain lion, but twice the size and with horribly oversized jaws and teeth, dragged one of the large ogres from the defensive line by its leg. Around five or six smaller goblin-like creatures then leapt on it and it went down smashing around with it huge hammer. It killed most of them before the huge lion creature lunged forward and ripped its head from its shoulders.

Zara found herself actually impressed with the dark elves, though she felt no sympathy for them. They had obviously drawn every beast for several miles around and maybe a thousand of them assaulted the dark elven lines, but the outnumbered dark elves were maintaining a disciplined defence against terrifying creatures and still managing to not only hold their own, but forge ahead and move at a slow march along the valley floor. Dark elves and black goblins calmly shot down monsters with swift efficiency, while mayax systematically hacked down anything that came close, silently replacing any of their number who fell. Ogres were spread through the lines holding back unless some larger beast broke through and then slamming forward with their own great bulk and weapons to seal the breach. It was an impressive sight. The dark elven forces would eventually defeat their enemies, but unfortunately their enemies were maddened beasts with no desire other than to kill. They showed no regard for themselves and would not retreat. They would take a heavy toll. Zara could not see even one of the twisted creatures looking to flee instead they almost queued up to throw themselves at the dark armoured elves and their allies.

Rebba grimaced. "How did they get here and how did they know the Lifestone was here?"

"Maybe they don't", Garon answered quietly. "They may be here for a completely different reason."

Zara snorted, "They are heading straight for where Bear says the stone is. I doubt they are here for the delightful local wildlife."

Rebba gave Zara a withering look and then looked back to the spectacle below.

"At least we don't have those beasts all over us." Garon added earnestly.

It was clear that the creatures below scared him, and Zara had to admit they scared her too.

"It is lucky the dark elves have attracted such local attention," Bear whispered, acknowledging Garon's point, "It has slowed them down and drawn the danger away from us, but we must stay focused, we must make haste to that building." He nodded down the valley where about a mile away stood what must have once been a mighty stone mansion. Now its white, carved stone was almost completely hidden by choking vegetation.

Rebba and Garon nodded and all said nothing as they pulled back from the edge. No one wanted the kind of attention the dark elves were getting. Bear broke into a hunched trot along the ridge-like top of the valley. Zara saw that they would be able to move easily along here for the next few hundred yards and get ahead of the dark elves, but then they would have to descend into the valley to get to their destination. She didn't relish that idea.

They quickly got to the point near where they all knew they must go over the edge and down into the valley. Bear kept peering over the rim as they trotted to a halt. He nodded to them. They would go down here. They all hunkered down and crept to the edge until they could see over. They were now well ahead of the battle that was still raging along the valley floor, maybe two hundred metres ahead. Bear looked at them and nodded. It was now or never.

Zara could feel her heart pulsing faster. It had already been beating strongly, but now it stepped up a gear.

"Let's do this," she muttered and as one they all stood and went over the edge running.

It was a steep drop and soon all of them were finding it difficult keeping their feet as the gradient forced them down faster and faster. They slipped, slid and leapt down. Zara kept glancing nervously up towards the slowly advancing riot of monsters and dark elves, but so far no one... or no thing had noticed them.

"We're going to make it," Garon half laughed, half gasped.

The slope began to level out as they got nearer the valley floor and their pace increased. It was then that they noticed two things at once. One was the call of an elven voice behind them; they had been seen. Two was the group of beasts hopping up and down and generally enjoying the show of their brethren killing the dark elves and their allies. The first was not as important as the second, as the group of beasts was standing on the broken and pitted steps of the building they wanted to enter... and what's more they had noticed the humans too!

"Ishara's icy ti..." Zara began.

Rebba growled over her, "Would you stop cursing the gods, we need all the divine help we can just now!"

The beasts snarled, whooped, coughed, growled and hissed as one and bounded forward at the group. Everyone already had their weapons out. No one had sheathed them since arriving in this cursed place. Zara found herself screaming a wordless call back. Rebba, Bear and Garon joined her and the four of them went charging at the hellish creatures like mad devils themselves.

The lead creature; a mix between some kind of troll and giant wolf, pulled ahead and went for Bear. Bear didn't even pause, he slammed his shield into the creatures open maw and side stepped neatly, hammering his sword down with an over hand cut of stunning power that almost beheaded the beast. Meanwhile, Rebba had her grey staff held out like a spear. It glowed with greenish power and it plowed into a goblin-like creature with four arms and a bulbous, deformed head. The momentum of the two coming together caused both to stall, but Rebba's staff knocked it down hard and it started to writhe around in obvious agony. The druid quickly recovered her pace, looking wide-eyed in shock. She was on the edge of panic, but swiftly recovered and slammed her staff in a huge roundhouse at a creature that Garon was already smashing with his warhammer. The monk was also fending off another wolf like creature with his shield. His shield shone white and the beast was suddenly repelled like it had been hit by a giant fist!

Zara didn't even slow as she opened up a wolf-like beast from hip to shoulder with one blade while sidestepping the charging leap of another and slicing her second blade across its throat. She spared no glance back and charged on hacking left and right. Her blades were magnificent, they cut through, hide, flesh and bone with ease, and both weapons and armour seemed to weigh nothing as her adrenaline and fear fuelled her limbs.

"Yes," she shouted. "Come on you freakish bastards, come to Zara!"

Things were going just as well for the others who were wading through the beasts.

As suddenly as it had started, it finished. The four of them stood there panting and looking about for more enemies, but all half a dozen or so of the beasts lay dead around and behind them. It was incredible and both Garon and Rebba whooped with exultation. Zara smiled at them fiercely.

Just then there was a call from a high pitched elven voice behind them and Zara turned to see that the elven advance had gathered pace. There were fewer of the dark elves and their allies, but there were far fewer of the beasts too and a tall elf in blood red armour and black cape was gesturing savagely for his men to push on with what Zara now recognised as a particularly long sabre staff, a peculiarly elven weapon.

"Quickly into the building, we must find the stone!" Bear cried out and they fled.

Up the stairs they went, two at a time, and then into the shadowy cavern of the building's huge entrance. Their feet echoed on the still shining floor. Zara's eyes adjusted to the twilight and she looked around to see they were in a huge hall with light beaming in through cracks in the walls. Vines and creepers climbed the walls and hung down from the broken ceiling, the place had a stillness to it and a musky, damp smell like decay. They ran through a large doorway with doors that had long since disappeared. They burst into a smaller hall. Zara could hear the gasping breath of her friends as they all galloped along.

"There!" Bear called out and Zara looked ahead as she ran. Bear was pointing at a raised dais with a throne on it. Was there a figure there, on the throne, in the gloom?

It had taken Ry'Ana several hours to get her thoughts back in order. Her hatred for Tal'Asin had now risen to a point she had not thought possible before. However, she would not let him disrupt her plans. She was now scanning each of the possible Waygate halls that anyone could flee through. She was sure that Uh'Ram would be able to take care of the humans, but it paid to be careful. She couldn't see within each Waygate, to do so would take a vast amount of energy since they were all powerfully warded, but she could watch for anyone moving in or out of them. The only Waygate hall she had penetrated was the one at Althazar where the inner sanctum of the Great Temple stood surrounded by the other Waygates. If Uh'Ram succeeded, he would take the portal keystone from the humans and open the Waygate to Althazar. He would then open the Great Temple and retrieve the body of the Great One!

"You know that if you succeed in opening the Great Temple you will only find your father's dead body!"

Ry'Ana's head snapped up and she stared at Tal'Asin in horror. Had he read her thoughts? How had he broken through her barrier of silence?

"Your father is gone, Ry'Ana and it is better for all that he is!"

Ry'Ana recast her wall of silence spell, but it had no affect!

Tal'Asin was still talking, anger clear in his melodic voice. "Your father was twisted by jealousy, hate and the Lords of Darkness, Ry'Ana. I don't know how he has managed to brainwash you so that you do not remember the truth, but you knew it once! As a child you dwelt with your mother during your father's exile. You must remember, Ry'Ana. You must know the truth! You cannot allow the Great Temple to be opened; it will bring only death and destruction. The gentle child I knew would not allow such."

"You did not know me as a child, vile liar! You will not spout your filthy lies!" Ry'Ana screamed in complete fury.

Ry'Ana cast again desperately. What was preventing her spell?

Tal'Asin continued relentlessly. "I think it all began when your father knew that his own father, Tel'Emnar would not pass on the Lifestone. He was jealous and became enraged. I believe that was where it all began. He refused to understand that Tel'Emnar could not pass on the Lifestone to any other than a pure blood Sylvan elf. It was not fair, but the sylvan elven people would not have stood for anything other than a pureblood Guardian, their prejudices would not allow it."

Tal'Asin looked saddened by what he was saying, "However, we all thought he had accepted this, but he had only hidden his rage and frustration... Initially, when he and your mother fell in love we saw the greatness in him. She was as rapt with him as he was with her. I knew both and loved them both..."

"Liar! You hated my father, you were jealous of him, and you wanted my mother for yourself!" Ry'Ana cried even as she sought to find what was wrong with her spell. The astral prison that held Tal'Asin was still strong.

"Your father was my fellow student," Tal'Asin asserted firmly, "we both studied with Tel'Emnar and though I was the senior, he was the more brilliant, but I was never jealous of him, I was proud of him. It killed me to discover he was using his brilliance only to twist people and cause discontent and discord, to try to raise the other elves like him to rebel. When Tel'Emnar discovered this, he cast your father out into exile in the wilds.

He meant it as punishment to give your father the chance to meditate and see the error of his ways. Instead he saw it as another deadly snub from his father. In the wilderness he did not seek for enlightenment, but for ways to get revenge. You and your mother dwelt with us. I helped raise you. I took you with me to all the ancient kingdoms and allowed you to see through my eyes!"

Ry'Ana shook her head. How could he know about the visits to the other kingdoms? He was getting inside her mind somehow? She cast around with her senses desperately. The spells were working! Now three walls of silence were in place against Tal'Asin so why could she still hear his voice?

"He found the damned of elven society out there in the wilds. He found those who had been exiled and forgotten about. He found the goblins, and he found their leader, Tah'Rokin, his lost other half, his dark brother! The two fed each other's hatred of their father and of the other elves, the Sylvan and Golden elves who had exiled them. The people who treated elves like you and your father with fear and distrust. It still remains the greatest crime in the history of our people that we treated our own offspring with such callous disregard.

Ah, but that was the curse of my people; their pride. They could only see themselves as perfect. Those who were different were obviously inferior. Your people inherited our flaws too."

"So you admit your crimes, foul creature. The only truth you have uttered deceiver is your mistreatment of my kind!" Suddenly, it came to her what he was doing. He was simply casting a spell on himself. He could not affect anything outside of the prison she had constructed for him. She should have realised this at first, but the retched Sylvan trickster was getting to her. She was not thinking. Her hatred for him was causing her to lose her reason. She must be stronger otherwise he could escape her.

"Your father eventually returned, but at the head of an army. He caused all those of your kind to rise up and attack us and he called on the Lords of Darkness to support them. He came to your mother then and he asked her to follow him. She might have too had she not learnt of his alliance with the Demon Lords. It was too much. She sought to flee and to take you with her. He wouldn't allow it. He killed her!"

It was too much for Ry'Ana, her control slipped, his lies were the foulest insults of which she could ever have conceived. All her rage boiled up and she hammered at the hated Lore King. Her power leapt from her, almost of its own accord. However, he was ready for her and the power she hurled was deflected. It slammed into the astral prison she had spent long hours creating and shattered it apart in an instant. What had she done?

"I am truly sorry to bring you such pain, but I cannot allow you to open the Great Temple, Ry'Ana. Your father is no more, the great man he could have been began to die when he allowed his rage and avarice to lead him to the Lords of Darkness."

Ry'Ana hurled yet another astral storm at him. He threw up a wall of force to break it.

"The man I loved as a brother died when he betrayed us all and killed your mother." Tal'Asin almost snarled such was his passion.

Ry'Ana White Eyes ignored him and began forming a more powerful spell.

Tal'Asin continued, "Even if you somehow succeeded in your diabolical plan and return life to that foul creature I sent to the abyss centuries ago, it would be a hollow shell."

Ry'Ana hurled her spell at him. He reeled back as his wall of force disintegrated and he was smashed backwards. With impressive control, he cast several spells at once and brought himself to a stop, another defensive spell already in place, but Ry'Ana already had her defences ready and her next astral attack almost got through.

Tal'Asin seemed to nod at some internal decision. "If you will not see reason, Ry'Ana, if you will not remember the truth about your past, then I must defeat you."

Tal'Asin was good she had to admit, he might even be better than her, but her last spell had two functions; one to test his defences and two to assess his strength. It gave her valuable knowledge. Tal'Asin's strength had all been stolen from her. He had been absorbing her magical attacks because he had no choice. How ever he had survived the long centuries he had not the strength of his true body. Tal'Asin would not hold out long!

※

Zara raced along. The figure on the throne began to resolve itself. It was an elf! And it was holding something! As they got closer it became clear that the elf had been dead a long time. His skeletal remains were all that now sat upon the throne, encased in undimmed shimmering golden armour and cloak.

The four of them raced forward.

Suddenly, Bear called out sharply, "Stop!"

They all skidded to a halt and looked at the tall form of Bear, silently asking the same question.

"There is a magical barrier here." Bear responded to the unspoken question. "It is very faint and inverted, but it is there."

"What does it do?" Rebba asked, puzzled. It was clear that she and Garon sensed nothing.

"I am not sure." Bear replied hesitantly, "I need a moment to study it."

Zara grimaced. "Sorry to hurry you, Bear, but we have several hundred evil bastards not far behind us. We don't really have time for study." Zara stepped forward and before Bear could stop her, she lunged forward calling, "Let's see if this 'Spellcutter' sword is all you said it is!"

Zara heard Bear yelling something about higher magic and her being a bloody fool, but it was already too late. Blinding light dazzled her. She heard the buzz of some kind of energy and smelt something burning. The next thing she knew she was on the ground and smoke was rising from her armour.

Rebba reached her first and knelt anxiously scanning her for injuries. Then Bear was standing over her.

"You idiot!" he snapped, "You don't just lunge in at unknown magics, even with that blade. This spell was cast using the higher mysteries, probably even with the stone itself." He shook his head like one of Zara's old weapons tutors when she had managed to stab herself "You're lucky your armour is powerful or we would have been putting out your burning carcass."

"Er... Bear?" Garon called nervously, "What's happening?"

They all looked up to see that the elf on the throne was watching them and he no longer looked dead!

Zara scrambled to her feet in astonishment and the four of them stood ready.

"He was dead wasn't he?" Zara whispered to Bear who nodded not taking his eyes off the now rejuvenated elflord.

Zara heard Bear mutter something and said, "What?"

"I said he wears the arms of the royal house of El'Yaris." Bear's scrutiny was intense. "That crest on his armour is the arms of the High Prince Ara'Niss!"

"Who?" Garon hissed.

"He was the nephew of the high king of the elves. He was at the last battle against the *Ata'Gon*."

"Over a thousand years ago?" Garon asked, grabbing Bear's arm in fear.

Bear turned to look at him sharply, "Yes, Garon. Now stop asking me questions and let me concentrate."

"It is a shade," Rebba said hesitantly. "This spell was left here before the creature died."

Bear looked at the druid and then at the elflord. "Yes, I believe you are right, Rebba... but why?"

Zara looked at the figure. It was now an extremely tall elf with flowing golden hair and blazing blue eyes. It reminded Zara of Bear a little, but it was completely elven with long thin limbs and body.

A noise behind her distracted Zara and she turned around to glance back the way they had come. The noise of battle was still in the distance, but now some of the cries and clashes of weapons were echoing. The dark elves had reached the first hall. They were inside the building!

"Now, I don't mean to hurry you or anything," Zara called out, turning back, "but we need to find out quickly. I don't think those elves are going to sit down for a lunch break or anything."

"Let's find out then." Bear said with a half smile that was pure Bear and more or less said 'what the hell' without words.

He stepped forward and the elflord's voice suddenly cried out something in the musical language of the elves.

Zara kept her mouth shut. She had no knowledge of elven tongues, no experience with talking to the dead and no intention of developing either.

"It is I, Tal'Asin." Bear replied in High Elorien.

The figure of High Prince Ara'Niss stood as he must have looked all those years ago. Bear's eyes could now pick up the complex weaves of magic that made up the shade. Using the senses he had from the ancient Lore King, Bear could still see the skeletal remains of the elven prince through the image before him.

"Tal'Asin?" The image of the prince said softly. "Is it really you, come at last?" The image seemed to lean forward and looked down on Bear who now stood at the foot of the dais on which the throne stood. "You do not seem to be as I remember you."

"You must look deeper, highness, past the mortal shell you see." Bear needed the elven prince to recognise him quickly and had no time to explain fully what had really happened to Tal'Asin. He just hoped the prince would recognise Tal'Asin's essence within him for it was now clear to Bear that this final spell, cast with the aid of the Lifestone was meant to protect the talisman. It would form a protective shell around the stone and destroy any who sought to reach it. If the elven prince did not give them the Lifestone freely, they would not be able to unravel the spell in this place where magic was so unpredictable!

For long moments nothing happened and Bear could almost feel the dark elven presence at his back getting nearer. He could certainly sense the fear rising from his friends.

Abruptly, the shade of Ara'Niss replied, "Long did I hold the beloved talisman of our people, long did I suffer in this hellish place and long did I seek to free myself from this land, but the Waygates were closed and nobody came. There were many of us to begin with, elves, dwarves and men. Many times did we seek to flee this place; I used the Lifestone to help us fight our way free of this cursed city, but the swamp and its monsters resisted us and we were forced to return. Time and again we tried, yet each time we were pushed back and each time we became fewer; people were taken by the foul spawn here or by the swamp. Some simply vanished in the night. Soon I was the only one left. In despair, I determined that I would protect this most precious of artifacts the only way I could. My life was bleeding from me, but I would not let those spawn of the Dark Lords take it."

"That was well done, my prince." Bear replied a little abruptly, "But time is pressing and the enemy draws near."

"Enemy?" the shade questioned sharply, "Here after so long?"

"Yes, my prince," Bear snapped impatiently. He could feel the danger at his back, like a palpable force now and he could here, Zara muttering 'come on' repeatedly. "We must take the Lifestone and flee or they will take the talisman of Elysia for themselves!"

Again, long moments passed and Bear had to fight the urge to lunge forward and snatch the Lifestone from the dead prince's hand. He could see the rune covered stone clearly; the mighty emerald was clasped in the dead high prince's fist!

As if he had willed it, the Lifestone was suddenly thrust upon him with such force that he almost fell over. He grappled with his shield arm to grasp it. "Go then, Lore King, take it and flee this tainted land. I will welcome our ancient enemy in the best manner I can with what puissance still remains of me." With that the shade shot forward and Bear felt its presence go through him like a blast of icy cold air. He spun and watched as it screamed off down the hall like a hurricane.

Zara thought at first that the shade had attacked Bear and she was half leaping forward, her sword swinging when she realised Bear had the emerald talisman and the shade was halfway down the hall!

She didn't wait to see what would happen when the shade reached the dark elves. She grabbed the startled looking Bear and dragged the big man sideways. She had already seen a large rent in one corner of the hall where light flooded in. It looked big enough for them to fit through. Bear resisted for a moment as he juggled the huge green stone and his shield, but Garon and Rebba needed no urging. They had seen Zara pulling Bear and exploded into a run.

Zara risked a look back and could see the now ephemeral shade at the doorway to the second hall. "Can that ghost thing actually do anything?" she asked Bear.

Bear had got the Lifestone in hand now and was stretching his long legs. He said something, but Zara could hardly hear him over her own breathing, the thud of running steps and the clanking of armour. "What?"

"I said, not much more than surprise them." Bear barked, "So stop bloody asking me things and run!"

Zara let go of Bear's arm and set herself to running for all she was worth. Behind her she heard, a shrill scream and some choking gasps, but then an imperious elven voice roared a command and there was a sudden clatter of armoured feet. The thrum of bows followed along with the whistling hiss of arrows. Zara ducked and sidestepped instinctively. Arrows screeched and bounced off the hard floors around them. Zara saw Rebba stumble slightly as an arrow struck her in the back, but it bounced off the grey armour beneath her brown robe. The dark elven arrows were no match for their enchanted armour, at least not at this range. However, the speed those elves and their insect creatures could run, that might not remain true.

Rebba was in the lead and she simply dived bodily at the hole in the wall. She disappeared from view and Garon, slightly more hesitantly began to slow until Bear, who was hot on his heels, bellowed at him to get a move on.

Zara was at the rear and her back suddenly felt ten feet wide as she thought about those elves behind her. She could now hear hard, insect feet tap tapping furiously on the stone floor.

Bear was through the hole in a single diving leap. Zara hoped there was nothing painful on the other side as she hurled herself after the big warrior.

There was a sudden burst of light and a flash of green and Zara slammed into thick, damp grass and slid in cold wet earth. She came up virtually instantly, spluttering mud. She pulled a bit of grass from her mouth and looked around urgently, left then right. She was in a narrow, natural pathway formed by the vine covered wall of the huge building and a steep sided, grassy mound almost as tall. Down one way the path ran along the building back to the valley along which they had just come, and more importantly, along which the dark elves had come. The other way was almost identical save it had the hurrying backs of Bear, Garon and Rebba!

Zara bolted after them.

At the rear of the building, the pathway turned at almost a right angle and opened out slightly. It then split between mounds of grassy rubble into almost half a dozen smaller pathways. They ran blindly down one of them, paying little heed to anything other than running. They were all panting by now, but so far Zara had heard nothing from behind her and if they were lucky none of their pursuers had seen which pathway they had taken.

It would only slow them for a moment or two at most, but it could be the difference between life and death.

Five minutes later and they were all slowing down and gasping like broken bellows. It was not easy running for long in armour, even in armour as light as they wore. They were now in a pathway narrow enough to force them to run almost sideways. They had passed several forks in the path and had continually taken the right path. However, those paths had not always gone in a straight line and they were now hopelessly turned about.

When they reached the next fork, Zara called for them to stop. "We're lost..." she began breathlessly.

"Good..." Rebba interrupted, leaning over and holding herself up with her hands on her knees, "it means those foul creatures won't find us."

"Not necessarily," Zara snapped over her. "And as I was about to say, we need to get to somewhere high where we can see where we are. We need to get back to the Waygate!"

"Agreed!" Bear nodded.

Garon nodded too, but was too busy trying to catch his breath to put it into words.

Zara walked forward and pushed past the others to get into the right hand path. She looked up and studied the almost vertical muddy sides. Bits of rock and building stuck out in places, but it was mostly soil and earth held loosely together with the roots from plants that grew further up where the slope lessened. "What do you think Bear? If you gave me a boost up, could I reach that rock?"

Bear glanced up, "Yes, definitely, and then you could grab that other piece off to the left and from there you could use the roots to pull yourself up to where it levels out a bit."

Quickly, Zara was boosted up with little difficulty by Bear. She had to use her small knife to stab into the soil to balance her, but she was then able to pull herself up. When she reached the top, she stayed low on her belly until she could get a good look around. It was like they had been in a maze of kinds, made between collapsed lesser houses that must have made up the city. Zara could see the pathways through which they had come as little canyons between grass and bush topped cliffs that must have once been the tops of houses.

She felt Bear slide up alongside her. "Any sign of the dark elves?"

Zara shook her head. "They must still be down in the pathways we came along."

Zara looked back down and could see Rebba's head just coming over the lip of the steepest part of the climb. Garon was still at the bottom, just rolling a fair sized rock into place because he had no one to boost him up. Zara was impressed, Rebba and Garon had managed to boost Bear who weighed enough for two people.

Just as Rebba scrambled up the last part of the climb on hands and knees, Bear's hand grabbed Zara's shoulder and turned her around to look back along the narrow path, the way they had come. There were about half a dozen of those vicious insect creatures accompanied by a dark elf and a black goblin. They were moving warily along the path. They were following their tracks! Zara's blood froze. She twisted back and looked down to see that Garon had seen them too and was now pressed against the side of the path just out of their sight.

"Quick," Rebba whispered as loud as she dared. "Garon, you've got to climb, they haven't seen you yet."

Zara knew as soon as Rebba said it that Garon would never make it high enough before the enemy saw him. They would find him an easy target. What's more he would give them all away. From the agonized look on Garon's face he knew it too. Garon looked up at them and his eyes met each of them in turn. Terror showed clearly in his eyes. He was on his own down there.

"Damn it!" Zara swore and sat up a little. She began pulling her swords.

Bear's hand clamped firmly down on his. "We cannot." he whispered harshly and he nodded again to the way they had come.

Further down the path, almost out of sight, at least another score of dark elves and their allies walked along warily. The first group was just the scouting party, the trailblazers. Zara knew they might have dealt with the lead group, but not before the others fell on them.

Rebba looked at Bear's hand on Zara, holding her sword in place. The druid's eyes rose to meet Bear's gaze. She began shaking her head. Bear looked at Rebba with a look of pure wretchedness and shook his head. They could not go back down, it meant suicide, and the dark elves would get the Lifestone. Rebba knew the truth, but it was clear she couldn't; she wouldn't accept it.

Zara hated it and she could see that Bear did too. All three of them knew the necessity of the situation, but were still loath to even think about leaving their friend. They could not make that kind of decision. It went against everything that made them who they were. Even Zara, though she had done many things in her life of which she was not proud, would not leave a friend.

As it was Garon made the decision for them. "Go," he called up softly.

They all looked down. Rebba was already shaking her head, tears forming in her eyes.

"Go," he said more firmly, swiftly peeping round the bend to see he hadn't alerted the elves. "They are following our tracks and not going too quickly. I will lead them on and look for somewhere else easier to climb."

Rebba looked like she was about to argue, but Garon snarled as loud as he dared. "Don't you dare argue with me, Rebba Korran. The stone is too important to lose over some fat monk." He chanced another quick look round the bend before looking back up. "Besides I can lose them. I have learnt a few things about woodcraft from Nat."

They could all see Garon was scared, but they all smiled when he did. Even Garon knew his chances of evading the elves were now slim.

Garon took a deep steadying breath. "Now go. Don't make this a waste. You understand! I'll meet you back at the Waygate, okay." he said firmly, taking hold of his fear.

With that Garon turned and ran down the path. Zara watched him go with an admiration she had never thought she would have. That bloody fat monk was braver than she. She'd have cursed them all and tried for the climb and probably got them all killed.

Bear caught Zara's eye and they both nodded. They needed to go. Bear grabbed Rebba and half dragged her up the last little slope. Rebba was deeply upset by Garon's departure.

"Come on, Rebba," Bear said gently, "He'll make it, his god is with him. We will see him at the Waygate."

Rebba looked at Bear with tears now streaming down her cheeks. She swallowed hard and nodded.

All three of them knew Garon's chances; he could not stay ahead of those elves for long, but Zara knew that Garon would give them time to escape. She also knew he would give a good account of himself if they caught him. He was not the Garon she had known years ago.

The three of them set off back in the direction of the Waygate. They used the huge building they had recently fled as a guide.

It took them maybe two hours to get back to the lip of the huge crater in which the Waygates stood. They had moved slowly and carefully and had dodged a number of dark elf patrols. None of them spoke. All of them were thinking of Garon.

In the end they had to go almost all the way to the opposite side of the crater before approaching. As they looked over the edge, their hearts sank. Down below them, perhaps as many as a hundred dark elves, mayax, goblins and ogres were camped!

How were they going to get through them to escape?

However, almost immediately they came to realise that things were even worse than they had thought. In the midst of that camp, upright, spread eagled and tied to one of the Waygate arches was a man! His once white armour and tabard were split open and drenched red, his stomach and chest had been sliced open numerous times, a gag had been pushed into his mouth and his face was swollen and battered.

As the three friends watched, the man sagged in his bonds, his blood dripped down to the mud covered floor and his head lolled back drunkenly to reveal the battered face of Garon Vale!

Chapter 53

TRIALS AND TRAGEDIES

The eternal races or Elori Mai are believed to be the lesser kin or servants to the great Lords of Light and Lords of Darkness. We would know them as elementals or demons. Each Lord has servants whose nature matches their own and whose powers are linked to their Lord's. There are also different seeming ranks within the Elori Mai; greater and lesser kin. For example, the lesser servants of Eleora'Ashar, she who perverts life, are the were-beasts who appear as half beast, half man. However, far more dangerous are the greater servants, the changelings who can take on any form!

Knowledge passed down through Bardic tradition. Recorded by Prince Afdar SaTell of Stellicia BY78 - thought to be directly quoted from the legendary 'Lorebooks of the Druid Kings' said to have been begun by King Nam'Odar the Fisherking a thousand years earlier.

Arkadi Talcost walked into the vast bowl-like space that was the Hall of the Assembly. It had a slightly curved circular floor in the middle and was surrounded by steps, about a dozen of them, going around the hall in concentric loops, each one getting higher. All of the hall was made from the same black stone as the main building and was incredibly tough and resistant to magic. It was here that the college's students were tested and given their trials to achieve a new level of mastery at the college. The hall had a magical seal on it too. This had been added later to keep students both in and out. However, tonight the hall would be used for its other function. Here all the laws of the College were debated; here the great disputes came to be settled. Tonight would be no different, tonight they would settle the dispute that had riven the Conclave and had pitted the Archmage and his supporters against Xameran Uth Altor and his.

Arkadi was there to support Xameran.

Soon this hall would fill with those members who had attained a sufficient degree of control over magic as to allow them to be called masters; some were even grandmasters; all were long time servants of the college. Of course, not all the masters could be present, some were away, but those who weren't would need a strong reason to miss this session. It was likely to be the most important in the recent history of the college!

Archmage Baden Erin was on trial. He had pursued courses of action that were radical to say the least, but ones that had endangered the college and had done so in a way that was against the laws of the college. It was also alleged that he had stolen valuable articles from the School of Enchanters and that he was involved in the murder of the poor Allseer; far graver allegations. Many of the masters had already condemned the Archmage, but many still could not believe such of a man who had served the college for over half a century and who had led it for two decades.

Arkadi was thinking about what Nat had said to him. The Archmage alleged that Xameran or Atholl Dorard were agents of evil. Arkadi simply could not believe it. Maybe Atholl Dorard would betray them all, but not Xameran, and anyway it was the Archmage who was defending the elves, their clear enemy, not Dorard.

Still, Arkadi had to be sure. He went through scenario after scenario. He tried to examine the information from all angles, yet it always came down to the fact that Xameran was against the elves and the Archmage supported them. The other things he knew about events in the college were based upon what he had been told by Xameran and what he had heard from the Archmage by way of Nat. Arkadi simply had to go with who he trusted. He trusted Xameran. He didn't distrust the Archmage… didn't know him.

Was it really that simple? Again he went over what he knew in his head. As he was doing so he found himself fingering the small shackles and chain that had once restrained Nossi Bee. Arkadi took them out and looked down at them. They still looked like ordinary shackles, though with concentration he could now perceive the weaves that prevented magic being used without any aid, and he was beginning to discern the individual strands of the weaves and their colours. Where could Nossi have gone? Had he been taken, and if so, by whom?

He shook his head. His thinking was just going round in circles. He thrust the shackles back inside the deep pocket in his robes as masters began filing in to the hall. Arkadi sat in the area that had now become the place where Xameran Uth Altor and his Progressives sat. The Traditionalists, Independents and Moderates each had their own little areas of the hall, though the leaders of each group would always occupy the lower circle of the round hall.

When the hall sat in debate the great double doors to the hall would be locked and a magical force field would be put in place by a triumvirate of senior magi. At the moment they stood open and masters were now beginning to stream in in greater numbers. The doors led under a section of the hall's banked seats and into the central circle of the hall which was large enough to house at least half of the two hundred or so masters of the college.

The hall filled up quickly and the leaders of the college took their seats in the lowest circle. Arkadi sat on the second circle and waited as the opening rituals took place. Soon he would be called to speak in support of Xameran and to give his story about the elves and their attack on him and his friends below the college, attacks that had taken the lives of four of those friends!

Nat Bero ran as fast as her long legs would carry her. She struggled with her own pain and with the weight of the half conscious gnome on her shoulder; the little man was surprisingly heavy for his size.

Back along the main street she ran. It went parallel to the college walls, under the silent, implacable view of its fortifications and by the mighty keep that Nat knew was the home of the School of Warrior Magi. By the time she reached the gates, she was beginning to tire and had to slow to a fast walk. She had no difficulty entering the gates; the guards recognised her from earlier and knew something of her story. They greeted her pleasantly but with frowns at the bloodied state she and the little man on her shoulder were in. She smiled a little painfully and waved them back and she hurried on wanting to answer no questions. They knew from Nat's own questions of them earlier that she had been looking for her little companion.

Nat headed straight for the Clerics Dome. She hoped both that Arkadi had returned and that some of the clerics would be able to offer some healing for Nossi Bee and herself. She was so intent on reaching the college that she did not see the dark shadow that slipped warily past the guards at the gate, she did not sense its frustration as it watched her enter the Clerics Dome.

Nat burst through the main doors and into the large hall. Two monks saw her enter and rushed over as she crossed to the bed she had once occupied.

Nat's face was a knot of pain and she grimaced and wanted to ask for healing herself, but she was too concerned for Nossi. She laid the gnome down on the bed. Nossi was still conscious, but obviously weak. His injuries were not severe individually, and not yet life threatening as a whole, it was the mental trauma that was clearly still laying the gnome low.

Nat waved the two monks forward and gestured for them to look after Nossi. She then crossed over to look at Darin who was still completely unmoving. Nat then slumped on her own bed, her own pains throbbing as she heard the monks chanting and healing the gnome's wounds.

Nossi Bee, in the next bed, sat upright so suddenly that one of the monks stumbled backwards in surprise.

Nossi cried out, "She came to rescue me, she saved my life…" and then slumped back down wearily. It was obvious that the gnome was not fully aware of what was going on. "She battled a huge brute that had tortured and beaten me. She was a hero!" Nat heard the gnome mutter. She could see a look of pure joy on his battered little cherubic face.

Minutes passed and the clerics spent a little time treating her injuries before returning to Nossi Bee.

As she waited, Nat realised she was genuinely touched by the little man's emotions. It made the huntress feel good about herself for the first time in a long while.

Suddenly a light voice interrupted her thoughts. "Such a touching scene." the voice said happily, yet the voice's tone was laced heavily with sarcasm.

Nat swung around, as did the two white robed monks. Even Nossi struggled to sit up. They all stared at the surprising figure that stood in the centre of the hall looking over at them.

It was a halfling. Nat recognized the creature instantly. She had known a number of the little people. They made exceptionally good pick pockets and burglars with their impressive natural dexterity and agility. This one was of average size for a Halfling. He was about four feet tall and slim built. Like all Halflings, he possessed the large eyes and pointed ears that were so similar to those of the elves and he looked like nothing more than a child standing there. He was completely relaxed with a grin on his lips and his hands were inside the small waist length cloak he wore. The cloak was a nondescript colour, as were the clothes he wore beneath it.

"So you fought the mouldy monk all by yourself did you?" the halfling asked in a nonchalant manner, "And freed your little friend." He walked leisurely forward. "You must be a great hero." he said mockingly to Nat.

Without warning the halfling skipped sideways and Nat started in surprise. She swore at herself, but there was something worrying about this cocky little man. The halfling looked hard at Nat for a second.

"And aren't you the great huntress? The woman my master was so upset to find had disappeared after failing to deal with her last two targets."

The halfling's words hit Nat almost like a physical blow. Her mouth opened and closed. A fury she couldn't seem to find words to express rose in her chest. She began to pull herself up.

"Oh, don't get up, great huntress," The halfling said in mock concern and then he giggled.

He threw back his head and laughed with such pure joy that even in the midst of her mounting anger, Nat was astonished.

"Why you, cheeky, little…" Nat began.

The monk nearest the halfling suddenly stepped forward and interrupted.

"I do not know what your business is here, but it is at an end!" the stern monk said firmly, marching forward.

"I think not," was all the halfling said, smiling.

The halfling's cloak swished back and almost casually his hand came out and then whipped forward with startling speed. There was a glint of steel and then the monk keeled over and hit the floor dead, a small, slim dagger sticking out of his left eye!

Nat jerked and gasped, "By Ishara!"

"No, by Sardyk Andar," the halfling laughed and gave an ostentatious bow.

The other, younger monk was staring wide eyed at his fellow on the floor. Blood was now pumping from around the dagger which seemed to be pulsing with the man's failing heartbeat. He then looked at the little halfling like he was a devil come to take his soul and he fled.

The halfling reacted instantly. The same hand that had cast the dagger rose languidly and gave a slight twitch of the hand and something zipped from out of his sleeve. The now galloping monk didn't even notice the small dart that struck him in the back. He ran on. The little man watched him with a look like a child with a new toy, eager to see what it did. The monk almost reached the door before he stumbled and fell to his knees. He arched his back once and made a strangled cry before collapsing.

The halfling laughed and did a small gleeful little dance. Nat stared at him fixedly. Her brain didn't seem to be able to process what was happening. The halfling stopped its little jig and looked excitedly at Nat, a small grin on his lips.

"Now, I regret I cannot allow any of you to live."

He said it in such a way as to make it sound like he regretted nothing. In fact it seemed he looked forward to it.

The halfling's other hand came out and whipped forward, Nat was almost too stunned and bewildered to move, but at the last second she sprang back and the dagger whistled past her. The surprise, and the fact that she had come a hairs breadth from dying, galvanized Nat. With all the speed and agility she could muster she rolled, spun, drew her shortsword and dagger and found her feet all in one go. She looked around, crouched ready, expecting the halfling to be coming at her or to have to dodge another throwing blade. Instead she saw the little man standing, looking down at Darin who had not even twitched.

"How fascinating," the halfling muttered.

He knelt then and stroked the black armour as if petting a dog. Nat froze. She could do nothing if the halfling sought to kill Darin.

"I will kill you in just a moment great huntress," the halfling said gently as if he were soothing a child. He turned and looked Nat straight in the face. "For your betrayal of the master, you can watch me kill your friends first." He said it all gently and danced away laughing as Nat growled and launched herself at the little fiend, desperate to get him away from Darin.

The halfling turned his gaze upon Nossi. That playful little half grin returned to his face. Nossi was rigid and wide eyed looking at the halfling in abject terror. Nat too was afraid of this creature. In some ways, this little child-like man was far more frightening than even the ape-like monk had been, but she was damned if she was going to let that stop her killing the bastard. This halfling worked for the mage who had deceived her. It seemed that whoever had abducted Nossi was also responsible for turning Nat into an assassin. All this was indeed linked and made her twice as determined.

Nat half grabbed Nossi with her knife hand as the halfling stood back, watching. The little man began ambling forward and Nat pulled Nossi off the bed and onto his feet. Nat then moved out to face the seemingly unarmed halfling. She was going to get Nossi to run while she attacked, get the gnome to get help. Nat instinctively knew she was not skilled enough to defeat her opponent on her own.

With a practised speed that had Nat jerking into a fighting crouch, two short swords appeared in the little killer's hands almost as if by magic. Nat sprang forward a step, at the same time calling for Nossi to run. The halfling reacted instantly. Leaping forward like an acrobat, he did a series of forward flips, parried Nat's attack and then cart wheeled past her. Nat slashed despairingly at the little man, knowing she would not reach him. Nossi had only just started to run and the halfling caught him without effort and sliced its dagger across the back of the gnome's pumping leg while at the same time blocking Nat's angry attack at him from behind almost without looking. Nossi went down with a shriek, rolling into an agonized ball and grabbing his left leg.

The halfling whirled away from Nat as she tried to skewer the little fiend. Nat looked down at Nossi and then moved to stand over him protectively. The little killer walked around her slowly, casually, smiling.

Nat would have much preferred running and then shooting the halfling from a distance, but she couldn't. She wasn't even sure she'd be able to hit the halfling who seemed to move like lightning.

She glared at the little bastard, breathing hard through her nose. "I'm going to gut you, you arrogant little swine!" Her words were more optimistic than she was.

"Show me," the child-like man replied impishly.

Nat promised all the gods that if they got her out of this alive she would never try to be a hero again. She took a steadying breath; she knew she was hopelessly out classed with the blade, but she moved forward nevertheless.

Arkadi Talcost sat and looked on, watching the closing arguments. He had said his piece almost twenty minutes ago and that had been after almost an hour of debating. All the time he had listened as the evidence was presented.

The Archmage and his supporters had spoken eloquently about the lack of evidence and the reliance on the word of individuals about the theft and the link between the elves and the murder of the Allseer. However, Xameran and his allies had talked these points down, pointing to the fact that an elf had been found with the Allseer, with one of the stolen cloaks. It was obvious the elves were the culprits.

The Archmage argued that it had been staged to look like the Allseer had been killed by an elf, that there was no evidence that the elf found had done it. This was widely greeted with derision.

Should the assembly doubt the word of its own members and put that of the unknown elves before them? After all why would they lie?

Xameran argued that the Archmage was just trying to shift the focus of the argument. People like Master Drollin were not on trial!

When Arkadi had told his tale about the elves and the story he had been told by Nossi Bee, much of it was still treated with disbelief, it was too incredible for the magi. However, Xameran emphasised how we knew little about the elves and much was possible. Xameran also argued that although much they had heard was farfetched, there was no doubt that the elves had attacked Arkadi's group and that the elves were connected to the goblins and the goblins' unification in the north. The elves were creating a huge army, Xameran insisted, of that there was no longer any doubt, and the elves would be aiming that army at them. Why else would they be scouting around beneath the college?

There was uproar at this and Xameran hammered the point home by pointing out that this was the very people the Archmage would have them ally with!

The Archmage rose amid hoots of derision, but he still held some sway over the masters and soon silence descended. The Archmage then stunned the whole assembly by agreeing with Xameran that elves were behind the goblin unification in the north! Even the Archmage's own supporters were agog at this. Into the stunned silence that followed, the Archmage hit the assembly with another revelation; there were two races of elves! The Archmage spoke of the different races, of one with red coppery skin that worshipped evil and sought to dominate all; and one with light silvery skin that dwelt in the Wildlands. The two races were enemies and had been millennia ago. It had been the coppery skinned elves who had led the dark forces centuries ago and had destroyed the Elder civilisations.

This was too much for Xameran and his supporters. It was too convenient. Why was this story coming out now? Why hadn't this incredible story been known before? Xameran had asked the Archmage how he could expect the Assembly to believe such an obvious attempt to save himself and his alliance with the elves. It was outrageous!

The masters had almost all stormed to their feet, shouting back and forth. The Archmage was clearly furious. He tried to insist over the raging debates that his story was the truth, that the elves had long ago buried this knowledge of their hated kin, thinking them long gone. They had no wish for everyone to know of the shame of the mad elves who led the destruction of their ancient kingdoms. It had only been the encounter below ground and Arkadi's story that had brought the truth to light.

Slowly, the Assembly came to order, but the majority could not accept such a tale from the Archmage. Atholl Dorard had even laughed out loud at the Archmage's story. Xameran then took the initiative and called for a vote of no confidence in the Archmage, for the Archmage to be removed and another elected in his place.

Minutes later the vote was taken and the Archmage was surprisingly, only just ousted from his place. He still commanded loyalty from many it seemed, even with such a wild tale. Arkadi felt sorry for Baden Erin as he took off his cloak of office and gave his staff to the Mage Master to hold. Eliantha Shamass seemed on the verge of tears, but then Arkadi knew she was the Archmnage's staunchest supporter.

It did not take long for the assembly to vote in the new Archmage. Xameran was the only choice, though one or two other of the Grandmasters put their names forward. Xameran Uth Altor smiled kindly to Baden

Erin as the Mage Master draped him in the cloak of the Archmage and passed him the great staff of the college. Eliantha Shamass looked like she might physically attack Xameran, but a touch on her arm from Baden Erin seemed to calm her.

Xameran quickly thanked the Assembly and promised to get to work on putting things in order in the college as soon as possible. He did have one last thing to do before the assembly dissolved and that was to announce that both the School of Seers and School of Sorcerors had chosen new leaders; Master Drollin was to be the new Allseer and Grandmaster Gregan the new Sorceror Supreme. Both were Progressives and both were staunch allies of Xameran.

It was obvious to Arkadi that Xameran was bringing in advocates of a more forward thinking attitude.

It was only as the masters were leaving that it also occurred to Arkadi that it was Master Drollin who had been the person who had used his mystical vision to see Baden Erin's theft of the enchanted cloaks; a master the former Archmage had cast doubt upon.

Arkadi mulled this over for a moment and then disregarded it. Drollin was a well respected master. What did seem a little odd was that he was only a master! Why had the seers chosen a master, no matter how talented to be head of their school? Grandmaster Rejis was the most senior surely... but hadn't Xameran hinted that Arkadi could soon become Mage Master!

And why not? Arkadi reasoned. He was one of the most talented mages the college had seen. Drollin was talented too so why shouldn't the school of seers make him their head?

Arkadi stood up then and noticed that all of the masters had now left the hall. Only the members of the Conclave still remained. They were stood in the centre of the hall talking quietly. Arkadi waited, he wanted to talk to Xameran about what was to happen next.

As he waited, he toyed with the idea of becoming the next Mage Master. The idea thrilled him, though he did feel a little guilty. In the back of his mind a voice was muttering about him not being ready, about how he had not served enough time and earned the position. He pushed the thought away.

Nat parried frantically and used all her speed and agility to avoid the flashing, whirling blades of her diminutive attacker. The little halfling seemed to just bound and leap around all over the place. It was all Nat could do to keep his swords from her. Once or twice she did not and it was only the light shirt of fine chain beneath her clothes that kept her from being injured. As it was her clothes, that had recently been repaired, now had several new cuts. She really would have to visit a tailor soon.

Nat was being pushed around from one place to another, Nossi had dragged himself under a bed for shelter. Nat hoped he would find some weapon or come up with some magic to help.

Abruptly, the onslaught stopped and the little fiend skipped backwards. "You really aren't much fun," he snorted derisively, the grin not leaving his face. "I am starting to get bored with this."

Nat backed away towards the bed she had originally woken up in less than a day earlier. She held her short sword ready, her dagger in her other hand. It really was galling that such a little creature could be so good. If only Darin would wake up. The halfling wouldn't be smiling then. Darin would cut the little swine in half. However, Darin hadn't so much as twitched.

Suddenly, there was a clatter from over where Nossi was lying on the ground. What was he up to? The halfling looked over that way and raised a short sword and waggled a finger at the gnome.

"Now, now, who said you could get out that bow, cripple." The little man exploded into action, even as Nat heard a feeble twang. Nossi was too small to fire it properly and the arrow hissed haphazardly through where the halfling had been and shattered on a stone column behind. The halfling moved with such speed that it was almost on top of Nossi by the time Nat reacted.

She leapt up on the bed in time to see Nossi swing desperately with the cumbersome bow. The little man dodged easily, but Nossi had distracted him enough that he did not see the dagger that Nat hurled. For the briefest time, she thought she had done it, she'd got the little bastard, but with incredible agility, the halfling twisted and the dagger sliced along its neck rather than burying itself in his chest. Nat stared agog for a moment, but Nossi did not. The gnome had developed some real backbone. He swung again with the large bow, putting all his hatred behind the blow. Somehow the off balance killer managed to step inside the swing; the bow connected solidly, but the little man had managed to go with the blow, riding out the impact. His instinctive return parry, narrowly missed taking Nossi's hands off and the flat of the blade thwacked the bow from the gnome's grasp, but with a crack, the halfling's blade snapped. Nat leapt forward, down from the bed, determined to press the advantage. Her overhand swing should have split the halfling's skull, instead the swift little man parried his attack with a lightning block and punched upwards hitting Nat in the face. The halfling wasn't strong, but with Nat coming downwards, the punch upwards, the blow stunned her and she fell back onto the bed she had just leapt over.

"Though it's been fun, I think we should end this charade." the evil little man snapped, showing some annoyance for the first time.

Nat almost cried out at the unfairness of it all as she realised that the halfling was darting forward and his sword was heading unerringly for her stomach. She knew it would gut her before she could get her own sword down to parry. Her thin armour would not turn the sword.

Abruptly, the halfling's lunge halted and a pained look appeared on his evil child-like face.

"Get him, Nat!" Nossi called from down on the floor. Both his arms were desperately wrapped around the halfling's leg and it appeared he had bitten the little killer.

The halfling's blade quickly, changed direction, heading down towards the gnome's exposed body, but Nat yanked herself up and thrust her blade at the halfling's chest with all the speed and strength she could muster. The little monster tried to dodge, but with his leg held tight and his sword down, even he could not avoid the blow.

"Dodge this!" Nat screamed as her blade slammed into the halfling's chest.

The little man looked down at the sword in his chest and began to giggle. The giggle quickly turned into a gurgle and the now frail seeming little body collapsed on top of Nossi, sliding off Nat's blade.

Chapter 54

BEFORE THE STORM

The forces of the Elder were great indeed, but the greatest were the Dragon Lords! It was said they possessed armour and weapons far beyond any other and the skill to wield them, but by far the greatest power they had lay within their bond with a dragon! They would ride these mighty beasts as a knight rides a horse. They would fly through the skies and bring justice. Few they were in number, but even fewer there were who could stand against them. Only the greater demons ever opposed them with any success.

From 'A collection of Folktales' by Rogarin Draghar, Bard to the King of Tutonia, BY1107

Senior Parinsar Nar'Dolth strode out of the portal his Loremasters had created. He quickly looked around to assess his surroundings. He had already seen them in the scrying pools of the Lorewise, but it was good to see things with one's own eyes.

His force of almost three thousand stood arrayed in battle lines in the slight valley that hid them. They were just to the south of the human town of Shandrilos. The sun was starting to go down and soon twilight would be upon them. By the time morning came, Nar'Dolth intended to have the town emptied and this 'college of magic' surrounded, ready for the slaughter.

Nar'Dolth gave the order to commence moving towards the town. He knew already that the two forces to the north and south of the town docks would have begun their attacks. They would scupper the river boats in the harbour and kill anyone they found. This would force the humans to flee towards the college. Nar'Dolth would then bring up his own forces to flank the college from the south. Later he would move his own Warband to opposite the college gates from where he would direct the assault.

He looked around, scanning for the Venerable Loremaster and Cleric. He would need their advice with these 'mages' as the humans called their lorewise. Quickly, he spotted them. They were over with their brethren who were wearily forming a camp around the now closed portal point. The Lorewise would take little part in the battle, most would stay here; it would take them at least a day or more to recover their strength from creating the portals. The Venerable Loremaster had assured him that the human 'mages' would be unable to launch any kind of co-ordinated attack against his troops, and what they did send, he and his few fresh Loremasters would be able to deal with.

Nar'Dolth was unconvinced of this, but these northland goblins would be taking the brunt of the initial attacks and he would see how these humans fared.

It did not take long to get his forces moving, the goblins were barely more than a rabble in his opinion, but they listened well to their elven leaders… and their whips. The trolls; however, marched in a solid regiment almost as well as his own Warband. Yes, these mountain trolls took to discipline well and would be a force to be reckoned with.

By the time they reached the top of the hill that separated them from the town, his forces were moving smoothly and silently. Looking down the long slow incline, he could see the lights of the town spread out in front of him. These humans were peculiar creatures. They had built an entire town with no walls, save around the college, and they lived completely above ground, their dwellings easy to find! It was madness, but this was a soft land, not like the unforgiving lands he had been raised in. He supposed they had trusted the river as a barrier to attack – fools!

Already, as his elven eyes adjusted to the distance and coming twilight, he could see the warriors from two of his other divisions attacking the town's docks from the south and north. Some screams and noises were just audible to his acute hearing. The docks were in clear view from up here and he could see humans scurrying like ants to flee his warriors. Some were heading for their ships and boats, but most were fleeing into the warren of low houses that was the town proper.

He watched with a stern eye as his men pursued those who sought to reach their boats and sail out. Few were able even to weigh anchor before they were shot or hacked down. The larger river boats were being swarmed over by goblins and soon they began to wallow. Nar'Dolth knew his sappers had holed the boats' hulls. No one would be allowed to flee the island.

Nat watched in a detached way as monks milled like headless chickens. The sight of two of their own, dead in their sanctuary, was a shock with which they were finding it hard to come to terms. It had taken Nat almost half an hour to explain what had happened, but eventually the monks seemed satisfied, at least for the moment. While they had been explaining, the monks had moved the dead bodies away, including that of the halfling killer, though before they had arrived Nat had taken the halfling's knives and short swords, the fancy scabbard the little bastard had for them and the vicious dart thrower he had on his wrist. The monks were now clearing up and a few of them were tending to Nossi.

Nat just stood and leaned against the tree-like column and wondered what the hell was the matter with her. She had just faced not one, but two vicious killers and she felt nothing. She could put down her lack of a reaction to the events underground as partly due to her unconscious convalescence after the collapse. Yet here she had no such excuse, she had almost been killed and all she felt was numb. Oh, she had been afraid at the time, no terrified, yet now – nothing!

Somebody must be looking down on her with favour for there was no way she should be standing here, almost totally unhurt with the blood of two madmen on her clothing – that was a point, she really did need to get her clothes cleaned and patched. She looked down at the torn, bloody and cut clothing and smiled wryly. Who was she kidding, she didn't need them cleaned she needed them burned; even a beggar wouldn't be seen dead in them now. What she really needed was new clothes, a set of the finest!

She was still looking down at herself, imagining her next visit to the tailor when she noticed her hands had begun to shake. She frowned.

Then, suddenly, she was shaking all over, her hands, arms and legs all seemed to have turned to jelly. Her cheek began to twitch uncontrollably. Then... oh god, she thought and began to look around urgently. Oh god! She saw something that might do. It wasn't the best choice. The feeling came again. No, it would have to do. She stumbled across the room, brushing monks out of her path and grabbed desperately. She could feel the rhythmic spasm, and could hold on no longer. She heaved her guts up.

One of the monks called out indignantly, "That's my bucket!"

Nat had to ignore him as she spewed the rest of the contents of her stomach.

As soon as she was able, Nat looked over at the monk and said weakly, "Sorry." She sat back onto the bed next to Darin's. She managed a weak smile and then added to the monk, "Look on the bright side, I think I might have improved the smell a little."

A snort was all the reply she got as she passed the bucket back. The monk moved off shaking his head and grimacing at the contents of his bucket.

Nat waited for the sick, weak feeling to pass. Already the shakes were subsiding. Thankfully, the gods were smiling on her as one of the monks took pity on her and brought a cup of water and some dry bread and tended to her wounds.

Not long after, the monks finished cleaning the floors. No one would have thought anything had happened save for the frightened looks on some of the monks' faces. Nat then noticed a change from earlier; at each door stood two burly looking monks with weapons held ready, and armour under their robes. They reminded Nat of Garon for a moment and her mood darkened as she remembered her friends.

This made her think of all that had happened. Going over it all appalled Nat. It was clear that the mage who had hired her all those months ago was also the one working against them and, presumably, for the elves. The mage wanted them dead and had wanted some of them dead long before they had even gone into the catacombs. Nat could make little sense of that, but it all must be linked in some horrible way.

Nat looked around to find Nossi now being left to recover on the bed that had once been Arkadi's. Nossi was looking a little less pale and beaten. In fact, he seemed eager all of a sudden. Nat had been impressed with the change in him. He was rapidly developing some backbone. In the fight he had risked his life and saved hers!

It occurred to Nat that Nossi might be the one who could unravel some of the mysteries here.

"Nossi, how did you end up in that cellar and did you see the halfling and monk's master at all?" Nat asked.

"The little man and the monk were both with a mage from the college." Nossi Bee replied.

He seemed suddenly eager to talk to her where he had been wary before. He must want to help and to get back at whoever had locked him away she thought. Nat was pleased to see that Nossi was still confident. It struck Nat that it was a strange reaction considering the little gnome had been tossed from one bad situation to another.

"He was the one who made me talk to the leaders of the college and tell them what he wanted." Nossi Bee finished firmly.

"He must be the one who was paying for the killings and ordered the attack on Bear and Darin." Nat added, hate in every word. "What was his name?"

Nossi shook his little head sadly. His brown eyes were morose and he seemed to deflate. "No one ever said his name. They just called him master."

"Well what did he look like, Nossi?" she asked trying to reignite the gnome and get some clues.

Nossi's eye sparked a little and he sat back up. He spoke quickly, but it was clear he hadn't seen the man clearly and that most humans were generally alike to him save for big distinctions. In the end the description Nat got could have been one of a number of the senior magi.

Nat sighed heavily and then stood up. Nossi looked at her. "It looks like there is nothing for it," she said firmly and the gnome looked at her in confusion. "I will have to take you into the college, to this Assembly of Masters thing that Arkadi is at."

Nossi frowned at her, his eyes worried.

"If this man is a powerful mage, he will be a master and will be at this assembly… and Arkadi will be there…" she finished not knowing what should happen if they did find the mage, "…he'll know what to do." Nat paused for a moment and then looked down at her newest friend. "I'll find this mage for you, Nossi, and for me. We'll get him!"

Five minutes later, Nat was back to grumbling again. She was again going to have to carry the gnome and the little man hadn't got any lighter in the last hour. It wasn't that the gnome couldn't at least hobble now after the cleric's healing, but they needed to move quickly. They couldn't trust that no one else would try to kill them. Cautiously, Nat, with Nossi on her back, stepped out of the light of the Clerics Dome and into the twilight. Here we go again, she thought.

The changeling was on the other side of the Dome when the tall dark haired human bolted out and across the lawns. It immediately sensed her and gave pursuit. However, the changeling was still a good distance away when the woman, carrying the gnome, entered the main building. The creature hissed in frustration. Enough was enough. They would both die tonight, even if it had to track them for the whole night and fight its way through all of these pathetic humans!

With that furious thought it transformed itself into the chamberlain once more and hurried into the Black Hall, following the dark haired woman's stench of fear and desperation.

Arkadi Talcost waited patiently as the conclave talked. The former Archmage, Baden Erin was haranguing Xameran about the Grand Council and warning him that he could not dismiss the elves and dwarves from the council without the consent of the other town leaders. Arkadi didn't bother listening to the debate, he moved around the group and over to near the doors. He would wait until they had finished and catch Xameran on his way out.

The Conclave was clearly split, even with the way they were stood. Baden Erin was flanked by Eliantha Shamass and the Chief Druid, Marillia Aronis while Xameran was flanked by Atholl Dorard and the new Allseer and Sorceror Supreme. The First Wizard, Zarina Agroda, along with Abbess Tariadarmin and the huge, armoured Magus General were clearly unsure who to support and stood slightly off to the side of the two factions.

Xameran had said this would unite the college, but it seemed the Conclave was still split. Also, Arkadi wasn't entirely happy with his new allies. He now realised he had the nasty old High Enchanter Dorard as an ally and the oily new Sorceror Supreme. Still he was sure Xameran was the right man to lead them. The Archmage was still holding to his delusion of the elves as allies!

Abruptly, he heard someone huffing and puffing as they ran along the passageway that led to the hall. He frowned and moved down into the shadowed entrance to see who it was. There were braziers burning at intervals along the way and they created patches of light and darkness. Into one of the patches of light came a familiar figure stumbling like she was about to collapse and panting like a bellows.

What the hell was Nat up to now?

Arkadi wasn't going to allow the fool to embarrass him in front of the Conclave. He marched forward. It was only then he noticed the bulky lump Nat had on her back. Was she giving someone a ride?

"Nat what are you…" he stopped in surprise. "Is that Nossi you've got there?"

The lanky hunter stumbled to a halt, breathing heavily. She nodded and slipped the gnome from her back. "Little fellah weighs a ton!" the huntress gasped.

"Where did you find him? What happened?" Arkadi asked, grasping Nat and holding her up while she tried to catch her breath.

"We don't have time for that, Arkadi," Nat replied, "We have already almost been killed twice." Nat took another gulp of air. "Listen, Nossi here was being held by a mage who used him to twist what he told. He was told to hide the fact that the elves were after the Waygate key and that the elves that attacked us were different to those in the college."

Arkadi's eyes widened. That was exactly the point the Archmage had tried to stress! Why was that important?

Nat grabbed Arkadi by the arms and looked him in the eye. Arkadi was unused to such a fierce look from the usually flippant huntress. "A mage has manipulated us all!" she snarled.

Nat told Arkadi all that had happened to her over the last year, about the assassinations and the mage who hired her and that it was the same mage who had captured Nossi and almost killed both she and Nossi.

Arkadi was completely taken aback. For once he was lost for words!

"Arkadi," Nat almost shouted, "Nossi knows who this mage is. He has seen him!"

Arkadi looked at the little gnome who was looking at him with a look of such hope and determination. He nodded at Arkadi confirming the huntress' claim.

"We have got to stop this mage. He is obviously powerful and important here and he is a ruthless killer!" Nat said with total sincerity. "He has tried to kill me, Darin, Nossi and Bear, and would no doubt have killed us all eventually!"

Arkadi nodded. He trusted his friend and knew from the extremis he saw in Nat Bero's eyes that this was no joke. He took a deep breath. Suddenly, he felt nervous. It was the Archmage who had supported the elves. Could the Archmage have duped everyone so thoroughly? But why then seek to hide the fact of the elves differences if he was going to reveal it himself anyway?

"Okay, okay... we will go into the hall and let Nossi have a look at the members of the Conclave, but stay quiet. We don't want to draw attention to ourselves."

Nat was frowning at him, but she went forward with Arkadi who had a hand on Nossi's shoulder. They got to the last shadowy area before entering the hall and Arkadi and Nat both knelt by the gnome.

"Look carefully, Nossi. We cannot afford to make a mistake here." Arkadi warned.

Arkadi held his breath while the gnome looked over. It was only a second before the gnome was pointing. Arkadi looked at where he was pointing. He frowned. It was difficult to tell who he meant.

"Do you mean the man in the dark robes, the old Archmage?" Arkadi whispered.

The gnome shook his head and pointed, "The man with the tall staff next to him!" Nossi Bee insisted, no doubt in his tone.

Arkadi felt like he had been kicked in the stomach. The gnome was pointing at Xameran Uth Altor, the new Archmage!

<hr />

First Watchmaster Sintharinus stared at the sergeant in dismay.

"Are you sure of this, soldier?" he asked.

"As sure as I can see you sitting there, First Watchmaster." the soldier replied gruffly.

The sergeant was a veteran of the guard and not one easily scared or prone to exaggeration.

"An army of goblins and trolls is attacking the docks!" Sintharinus gaped, "It's unbelievable!"

"Nevertheless, it's the truth, sir." the sergeant replied immediately.

"What do we do?" came a voice from behind him.

Second Watchmaster Rill stood at his shoulder.

First Watchmaster Sintharinus sat, not knowing what to do. He had never been faced with such a thing before, had never thought he ever would. It was utterly incredible!

"We should tell the Archmage and call the guard to arms." Second Watchmaster Rill announced, "We will also need to alert the Fighter Magi."

Sintharinus turned to face his second. "And what if this is nonsense?" he asked. "We could look like fools."

"Then we will have tested our men's readiness for combat." was the immediate reply, "but if we do nothing, we stand the chance of being overrun."

Sintharinus nodded. It was a good point. "Very well, Master Rill, see to it."

"We should also see to sending a company into the town to offer some defence and allow the town's folk to get away. They will be heading this way, seeking protection if the docks have been attacked. We must leave the gates open, but guarded to get as many people as we can safe behind our walls."

He frowned at the old fighter magi. "Should we not move out into the town in force?"

The old veteran magi shook his head. "Only once we know what we face. It is getting dark out there now. For the moment we should hold our position. It could be a hundred or so goblins and trolls who thought this was an easy target and boated across here, or it could be a thousand. Until we know, it would be foolish to risk our men in the town where we could not form a coherent defence."

First Watchmaster Sintharinus nodded. He was no fool; his expertise was in administration and organisation. He had no experience of battle. He was from the school of enchanters not fighter magi. This was a peacetime position. In a situation such as this he would bow to Master Rill's experience.

"See to it then, Rill. I will inform the Archmage."

Rill turned to go, the sergeant too, but Sintharinus thought he heard Rill mutter, 'Which one,' as he left.

Which one indeed; whoever was now Archmage, it would be an interesting discussion.

⁂

Nat was saying something, but Arkadi wasn't listening. He was shaking his head.

The tall huntress was suddenly shaking his arm and whispering urgently. "Snap out of it, Arkadi. It's your friend, isn't it? He's the one!"

Arkadi looked at Nat, but there was nothing he could say.

"We need to do something." The huntress said firmly, standing up and moving forward.

Arkadi lunged after her and grabbed her. "What are you doing, you fool! We can't just walk out there and declare the Archmage of the College as a villain and a killer!" Arkadi was keenly aware that they were now out in the hall, in the light.

Nat turned to him in a fury, "Why not?" she hissed. "That bastard turned me into an assassin and murderer of innocents and had Nossi beaten and…" Nat's voice rose as she went on, "…his bloody henchmen almost killed me twice!" By the end she was yelling.

Arkadi looked over at the members of the Conclave in the hall. They had all stopped and were looking at Arkadi, Nat and Nossi. Arkadi looked to Xameran who was staring at the gnome like he was a ghost come to haunt him. However, the look did not last and the urbane mage quickly hid his emotions. It was Baden Erin who spoke first.

"So you have found your little friend, Nat Bero." the former Archmage said. "That is good to see. Is there something you wish to say to us?"

"Yes!" Nat practically bellowed. "That man," she snarled, pointing at Xameran, "tried to kill my friends, had Nossi kidnapped, and his men tried to kill me!" Nat declared. She had taken a step closer with each accusation and Nossi had followed. Arkadi stared at them in dismay.

The Conclave was all looking at Xameran; Baden Erin and Eliantha Shamass had looks of vindication while the rest looked confused. The Conclave seemed to step apart, the magi moving away from Xameran almost without thinking.

Xameran Uth Altor smiled and said. "Come, come Baden, could you not have come up with a more plausible way of discrediting me?" Xameran looked around, a look of incredulity on his face. "Surely you don't believe this nonsense!"

He gestured at Arkadi, "Tell them Master Talcost, tell them your friends are mistaken."

Nat turned and looked at Arkadi. Her face was neutral, carefully so, but her eyes gave a look that silently asked, 'Are you with us or with him?'

Arkadi looked back at Xameran. Why did Nat have to yell things out like this? She had no idea of the bear trap she was putting her head into. This could have been handled far better.

Seconds ticked by and Arkadi thought furiously. What if Baden Erin hadn't lied? Was it possible? What if Nossi wasn't mistaken? He definitely seemed certain, and Arkadi had never seen Nat so angry. By the gods, could Xameran have just been using him? Yet Xameran had always been his friend and mentor, a man of principle...

Arkadi was paralysed by indecision. He looked again at Nat and Nossi. The gnome's eyes were trusting and open while the hunter's were stern and seemed to be asking what the problem was; she expected her friend to support her. Damn it all to the Seven Hells! Arkadi cursed silently.

"They are not mistaken," Arkadi snapped, making his mind up. He had to stand by his friends. "I stand with Nat and Nossi."

Xameran stared hard at Arkadi. His eyes seemed to bore into Arkadi's. "So be it," he muttered, looking away from Arkadi. "You have declared your loyalties."

"These charges are serious." the Abbess said.

"These charges are ridiculous!" Atholl Dorard snapped gruffly.

The stately, old Zarina Agroda shook her head. "We must investigate these charges as any other, High Enchanter Dorard. We must follow the laws of the college."

"Laws of the college," the new Archmage snapped. "No, this is nonsense. They have no proof." Xameran barked, ruffled. "Are we to take seriously every fool who comes in with an accusation?"

Eliantha Shamass smiled cruelly at his discomfort, "I think that this Nossi Bee is central to matters and he is backed by a master of the college. You were keen to abide by the laws of the college when they suited you, Xameran."

Xameran seemed about to argue again when something caught his eye. He stopped dead for a moment and then smiled.

Arkadi turned and looked where Xameran was staring. In through the doors of the hall walked the chamberlain.

Why would Xameran react so to him?

Xameran's next words brought Arkadi's head back round sharply.

"Oh, why bother, any more," the suddenly smiling new Archmage said. "Yes, I did all those things and much more, but I did it all for the good of the college and of this land!"

The reaction of the Conclave was immediate. Everyone stared at Xameran in shock and stepped away from him, everyone except those who had supported him. They were obviously a little surprised and uncertain, but they also obviously either had been aware of his dealings or believed that this was a ploy to discredit Xameran. The new Archmage looked around and then back to each side at his erstwhile allies and smiled.

"It seems we will have to deal with things now, rather than later, my friends." Xameran gestured and all of the other magi reacted, ready to call up spells, but it was not they who were the target of his casting, it was the hall. The great doors slammed shut and Arkadi knew that Xameran had called into being the spell barrier around the hall.

"What is your purpose here, Xameran?" Baden Erin asked angrily.

"My purpose is to destroy all those who oppose me. We cannot let the college be divided. You either stand with me or you die!"

"You cannot hope to defeat us all, Xameran." Baden Erin said warily, "This is foolish."

Arkadi firmly agreed with Baden Erin; the more powerful magi stood against Xameran. Nevertheless, he realised what was to come and grabbed Nat and Nossi and began dragging them back towards the rings of stepped seats around the hall. He needed to get some distance between them and the Conclave.

"Oh, I don't think so, my dear Baden." Xameran laughed and then looked over at the chamberlain standing silent and still by the doors. "Now is the time, chamberlain. We have them all here; all the enemies that our master wants removed."

Arkadi, along with every other magi in the hall was looking at Xameran and then at the elderly chamberlain in confusion. Xameran looked at the others in the hall and a deep, wild laugh burst from him.

He stopped almost instantly and said to the chamberlain. "Kill them!"

Arkadi was looking at the chamberlain as Xameran spoke and felt his jaw literally drop open as he watched what he had thought was an old man flow and change smoothly into some massively muscled and scaled, feline monster! It was no beast of which Arkadi had ever heard tell.

There were gasps all around the hall. It was Baden Erin who realised the truth. "Demon!" he exclaimed.

Chapter 55

THE COMING STORM

There are thought to be three states of being, though more have been hypothesised. The first is that of the body, the physical or corporeal state of being. The physical form inhabits the normal world as we know it. The second is that of the spirit. The spirit is often equated with the mind or consciousness of the individual. Those with a knowledge of the mysteries know it is this state of being that inhabits the astral realm which exists alongside that of the physical, and interaction between the two happens continuously, though direct conscious interaction is rare. The third is that of the soul. It is here that least is known. The soul is thought to be eternal, a spark of the divine that gives life and consciousness meaning and free will. The soul is thought to inhabit the eternal realm where the gods dwell. It is believed that the soul returns there when a person dies.

Excerpt from the musings of Abdari Sulim Dan Duafa, Grand Vizier to the Satrap of Dur Bandar, BY501

'DEMON!' The word echoed deep though Darin's mind. Where was he?

'*We lie on a bed in the ancient elven dome that was once part of the great palace complex of the kings of Dah'Rhyllor.*' A voice said in his mind. Was it one voice or more than one?

'Dah'Rhyllor?' He thought to himself. 'That name sounds familiar.'

'*Your memories tell us that it is now known as Shandrilos and the elves are long gone*'

A thought occurred to him. 'Who are you? What are you doing in my thoughts?'

'*We are you and you are we.*' The voices replied and a cacophony of laughter echoed through his skull.

It went on and on until he could bare it no longer. 'Stop it!' he screamed silently into the darkness of his mind.

'*We must be away*' one voice suddenly called above the others, '*a demon is loose.*'

'*Yes, we must go*' said another voice, '*it is our purpose.*'

Darin felt the voices becoming insistent, trying to get him to move. Darin held firm to his resolve.

'We do nothing...What am I saying! I do nothing unless I decide to!' he shouted silently.

'*It is true. He resists us. We must have his consent.*'

There was a burst of angry calls, furious screams and almost animal growls.

Darin screamed at them again to stop. Everything went instantly quiet.

'Very well,' an imperious voice said, '*your friends are here. Their lives may be in danger. We must act.*'

Again, stubbornly, Darin resisted, 'I do nothing until you explain.'

'*You know who we are. You are conscious of everything around you if you wish to be, but you have barricaded yourself deep in your mind...We are the voices of those who have worn the armour, who took up the black blade. We are the armour, now, its spirit, its knowledge, its experiences. You became one with us when you took up the challenge.*'

Suddenly, Darin remembered the man in the strange black armour he had fought.

'Yes,' the voices prompted, '*you are now the wearer of the armour, you are the new Lord Champion of the Ebon Armour and you must act.*'

Darin was bombarded with images and knowledge flooded him.

'Yes, I am the wearer of the Ebon armour and I must act.'

The monk was busily strapping wooden slats to the broken legs of the man who had sought their healing. He was wrapping the bandaging tightly around when out of the corner of his eye, he saw the black armoured man in the bed opposite sit up.

The monk stopped in surprise.

The man sat there rigidly for a moment and then he swung himself around and stood.

The monk saw the man's face. He was incredibly pale and his eyes seemed somewhat dull, as if they were out of focus and he was not seeing what was around him.

The monk smiled over at him and called out, "Are you okay?"

The black armoured warrior said nothing. His eyes didn't even twitch the monk's way and then, to his astonishment, the armoured helm on the warrior's head seemed to flow down his face like some kind of horrible black treacle and a moment later a featureless face plate covered the man's face. A huge black sword swung up at the ready and the jet armoured warrior stood, turned and headed towards the main doors. He was accelerating all the time and by the time he reached the doors he was running at a speed the monk would have found hard to emulate even without armour. The warrior vanished through the hastily opened doors into the night, leaving two warrior monks holding the doors and staring after with looks of astonishment.

Roslyn Shanford was closing up the apothecary as usual when she heard the scream.

'What on earth was going on?' she thought. 'Was someone being attacked?' This wasn't the usual place for such and usually the mages and their guards kept a lid on things in the seedier parts of town.

She listened. It had been faint and far off.

Nothing. She waited.

Oh well, maybe someone had been scared by something, she thought. It had better be something serious, she thought frowning, or she would have to go out there and give them something to scream about, frightening people like that.

She caught a look at herself in the expensive looking glass that her grandfather had bought long before she was born. She rubbed at her forehead. Whenever she frowned the lines on her forehead would form into a kind of triangle and she had been told that her frown would send even an angry troll fleeing for the hills. She knew she had a reputation as a formidable women; not someone with whom to argue.

She casually straightened he long mousy blond hair, brushing it back from her heart shaped face. She did not look her age, she thought. Indeed she still looked quite young. She was now past thirty, but she had always been small, barely reaching five feet, and that had always added to her youthful appearance. People naturally thought she was younger because she was smaller. It was a puzzle. Still she had heard many say that for such a small women she had a big character. She was out going and knew her own mind and was well respected in the town as a gifted apothecary and healer. She had carried on her grandfather's business and it had blossomed under her stern hand. She now had two journeyman and six apprentices working for her, though they had left early tonight. With the Grand Council on, the town was holding celebrations and hosting its many visitors. Her apprentices had wanted to go off to some dance that a prominent river trader had organised.

She looked around at her shelves stacked with neatly labelled bottles that held everything from wolfsbane to deadly nightshade and every kind of powder, tincture and cream in between. She had done well. She was now a wealthy woman with investments and a large house full of her treasured possessions. Many men had courted her over the years, but she had never found any that she could live with for long and she would not marry and let some man take what she had earned.

In truth, the big house had been left to her by her grandfather as had the business, but she had kept them going and had taken the business to new heights. It was now well known that Roslyn Shanford was the best apothecary in the Shandri valley.

She moved around the shop, carefully going through her routines, cleaning the work benches, sealing the bottles and putting them back in the correct places. She filled her large leather bag with small vials, pouches and the other paraphernalia of her profession; everything from forceps to knives. She took the bag and put it next to the cloak rack where her long, hooded cloak hung. On the inside her cloak had numerous pockets, just like a mage's, and, just like a mage's, it was filled with herbs and powders. Roslyn prided herself on being as fine a healer as the monks and druids of the college.

Was that another cry? She frowned. She wasn't sure. It was starting to get noisy outside, it always did this time of evening when people were heading for the large inn at the end of the lane. Most of the shops and workshops along the row would be closing and the journeyman and apprentices would be in a boisterous mood. It was partly why she had let her lads go early. At least she knew then that they would get home first and grab something to eat. It was better to have something in your belly before you filled the rest of it with ale.

She picked up the broom and began to sweep the floors. She had not done these jobs in a long time. Her apprentices now did the routine things about the shop. She had trained them well. Once she had performed these duties often when her grandfather ran the shop. She had always helped out and tried to learn all she could from him. She felt she owed it to him.

Her grandfather had been a student of magic long ago when Melkor Erin had first formed the college. For some reason he had never taken his trials to become a mage. Roslyn had heard rumours about a falling out or something, but her grandfather would never talk about it. He had started an apothecary shop, using the knowledge he had gained as a student. Years later, he had paid for Roslyn to attend the new Magic Guild's School. He hoped that Roslyn would go on from there to the college and become a mage as he had not.

Those were not happy years for Roslyn. She had worked her hardest, but just couldn't seem to get a grip of the writing. She could read well and understood things, but whenever she sought to write things down it would all go wrong. She would miss words, misspell words and get so frustrated she could have screamed. He tutors didn't understand her difficulties; they just kept hammering away at her. Eventually she began to turn off; frustrated, and began to think that she was just stupid. Her tutors thought she was lazy.

She left the school at sixteen, but was not allowed to go on to the college. Her talent was clear to her tutors, but her writing was not good enough. Oh, she was far more literate than most people, but she would not be able to study without the ability to write and record her spells accurately.

In depression, Roslyn had returned to work in the shop with her grandfather. She knew he was disappointed, though he never said anything to give her that impression.

Over the next few years she had thrown herself into helping her grandfather. She still had the same problem with writing, but she had a fine mind and a determination and tenacity that made up for her lack of literary skills. She could learn how to make the potions and tinctures her grandfather needed if she did it often enough, and he had the patience and grace to allow her to make mistakes.

What changed everything for Roslyn was when her grandfather fell ill. He was everything to her and she worked hard to nurse him and also to keep the business going. She was an accomplished apothecary by then and could tend to most ailments and problems in the town. Also, she had secretly learned to use her talent. She had enough knowledge of how spell craft worked to experiment and soon came to realise that her ability to heal others needed no writing. Once she learned how to do a thing physically it stuck in her memory.

She worked long and hard on her grandfather and used her talent to heal him. No one had expected him to live, he was already past seventy, but she had succeeded. She had also proved to him that she could work magic. He wanted her to go back to study at the college, but by then her dislike of the mages was set and she refused. Her grandfather knew he could not argue with her so he let things pass. They had worked together then and her talents became known throughout Shandrilos. Some people would even come to her rather than go to the monks or druids, certainly most brought their minor ailments to her. Things had gone wonderfully for several years, but then her grandfather had been killed. He was knocked down by a runaway cart in the main street. She had been devastated. Six years on she still missed him.

The noises outside were getting louder and nearer. Roslyn frowned again. What on earth were they up to out there? It sounded like a riot was going on. She walked over to the shop's small window and looked out. The narrow street outside was dark, save for one or two dim lights inside the shops opposite.

Suddenly, a man ran past the window. He was in a hurry.

As she turned away she saw others flash past the window. What was the hurry and what was all the noise and shouting about?

She went over to the corner where she kept the broom. She was going to find out what was going on. As she put the broom down she heard the door open. She turned around.

"What is going on out..." she stopped; her question unfinished.

Standing not ten feet from her was the most ghastly looking creature she had ever seen! It was a little taller than her and wiry thin, though it had a muscular look to it that said it was stronger than it looked. Its skin was a sickly grey like old stone, and it had huge dark eyes, a bulbous warty nose and ears like a bat's wings! It was wearing crude armour and carrying a wickedly curved and serrated sword. Worst of all, its foul little eyes were looking at her and an evil grin split its overly large mouth to reveal pointed teeth.

She froze. She knew what it was even though she had never seen one. They were in most evil tales she had ever been told. They were always the ones who carried off little children or tortured the innocent.

'What was a goblin doing here in her shop?'

It hissed and sprang forward a step and Roslyn screamed and stumbled backwards into her workbench, knocking over jars that she had left neat and ready for tomorrow. It laughed then, a cold heartless sound. It enjoyed her fear.

Roslyn's heart was beating like a hammer in her chest and her eyes were wide. What was she going to do? The goblin moved forward menacingly, still laughing to itself.

'Bloody, foul creature' Roslyn thought her fear giving way a little to her anger. She scrabbled around with her hand and grasped a handful of powder she had spilt on the workbench. Her eyes searched around looking for anything else she could use as a weapon.

Without warning the goblin sprang forward again, sword raised, screaming at her. Roslyn screamed herself and flung the contents of her fist into the creature's face. Its scream turned into a screech and it wiped frantically at its eyes. Roslyn leapt out of the goblin's way. It slammed into the workbench and both went over. She quickly sprang past the thrashing, howling goblin and grabbed at one of the pans she used to heat and melt materials. The goblin was still wiping at its eyes and trying to get up. Roslyn screamed out all her fear and hatred and brought the pan down on the creature's scraggly haired skull with all the force she could muster. The goblin was slammed back by the blow and lay still. Roslyn looked at the beastly thing in horror. What by the seven gods was going on?

She quickly yanked the sword from the creature's hand and spun towards the door. She ran across and grabbed her cloak and swung it on, switching hands with the vicious looking sword. Her eyes kept darting back to the goblin on the floor to check it had not moved. Roslyn then grabbed her bag and headed for the door. She was almost there when she saw the shadow on the window. It was of someone's head, but as it turned Roslyn could make out the now unmistakable outline of a goblin's head. There were more of them!

Without a second thought she bolted for the room to the workshop at the rear. She shot through there and frantically began unlatching the back door to the little alley. She almost moaned out loud with fear as she heard the front door swing open. Then she was flinging the door open and fleeing into the dark.

Senior Parinsar Nar'Dolth watched from on high as his first two divisions poured into the town. The docks were now taken. No one moved down there save some of his own troops left to watch for any humans hiding. Now the battle was moving through the town towards the college, though it could hardly be described as a battle, more like a rout. Nar'Dolth could see the occasional skirmish in some of the wider streets, but for the most part his vision was blocked by the buildings. However, he could see the wide street that separated the front walls of the college from the rest of the town. There he could see that human soldiers had set up a wall of shields and were funnelling the fleeing humans from the town through the gates into the college grounds.

Things were going exactly to plan. Fear was rife throughout the town and the mages in the college would have little idea yet of what they faced. By the time they realised they were hopelessly outnumbered they would be surrounded and burdened with thousands of pathetic humans from the town! Their walls were more for show that anything else, Nar'Dolth knew, they were barely twenty feet high and not more than a foot thick. They were also long; the humans did not have enough warriors to man the whole length of them, unless they put their untrained boys and old men on the walls, so the wall could either be breached or scaled easily and then the humans would provide little resistance.

He allowed himself the briefest of smiles before giving the order to advance. This division would flank the college from the south while his own warband would move to join the two divisions now moving through the town to lead the frontal assault on the college.

Nar'Dolth had no illusions here; unless the humans simply fled wildly in all directions, he would have them bottled up and ready for the slaughter by morning!

Roslyn Shanford bumped and pushed her way through the crowd of terrified townspeople and into the college grounds.

It had only been ten minutes earlier that she had bolted down the alley from her shop and out on to the main street that ran the length of the town from the docks to the college gates. It had been madness out there. People were screaming and running headlong towards the college. The wide street had been choked with desperate people; men, women and children running for their lives. Down towards the docks, Roslyn had seen a mass of seething goblin warriors marching forward, hacking down anyone who came within reach. Some men had tried to fight with whatever they could, but they had been quickly overwhelmed.

Luckily, a company of Shandrilosi guards had burst from a side street where the main street narrowed. They had formed a shield wall. They had been hopelessly outnumbered, but the width of the street meant the goblins could not overwhelm them. The guards had not been stupid either; they retreated steadily. Their orders had obviously been to slow the advance not face it.

Roslyn had pushed her way into the river of people and had been swept along to the college and through the gates.

Now as she slowed and looked around her, the occasional person bumping her as they came past, she realised there was little less than chaos here too! People stood on the front lawns and pathways of the college and milled aimlessly. Some people were forming together into little clumps as families found one another. Others moved about frenetically searching for those they had lost. There seemed to be no one organising things, only the Shandrilosi guard seemed to be doing anything. They were lining the walls and had formed a cordon at the gates, but once inside there were only a few soldiers and they appeared to be guarding the stairs to the walls, the stables and the main doors to the imposing Black Hall that was the main section of the college. Roslyn could see no magi. Where were the Archmage and his Conclave? What was happening here? The town was being invaded, people killed and there was not a magi to be seen!

Making a swift decision, Roslyn marched over to the nearest guardsmen and asked to see his superior. She was passed from person to person until finally she saw several men in the arms of the guards with cloaks of office that marked them as Watchmasters. Now she would find out what was going on.

First Watchmaster Sintharinus was at a loss. He had been trying to get to see the Archmage, the new Archmage. Alba! He would have seen the old Archmage, anyone from the Conclave, but they were all locked in the Hall of the Assembly, apparently debating. So for the moment it was going to be all down to him.

He had made his way outside, through the main doors and had been greeted with a scene of utter chaos. Master Rill had obviously been organising the guard, but things had been clearly worse than anything Sintharinus had believed possible. Several thousand people crowded around the gates and were dotted here and there on the front lawns; at least half the townspeople were there!

It had taken him only a short time to find Second Watchmaster Rill and Third Watchmaster Feris, along with a guard captain and his sergeants. Rill had brought him up to speed on what was happening.

Rill had mustered all four hundred of the guard and the one hundred of the reserve militia. He had also spoken to Magus Commander Bargus who had summoned all eighty of his fighter magi that made up the college's most feared defenders.

Rill had the fighter magi guarding the main gates with a heavy infantry company held in reserve. Another heavy infantry company was spread out along the walls, patrolling and keeping watch. Rill had then sent their two light Cavalry companies out of the rear gates to scout the college's perimeter. He wanted no surprises. Sintharinus couldn't fault that sentiment. Also, he had placed the two archer companies and the two reserve companies on the walls over the main gate and wall facing the town. They were ready to provide cover to the retreating townspeople. The last two heavy infantry companies, Rill had sent into town to try to help the townspeople and to slow down the goblin army's progress. It was clear now that it was an army... of at least two thousand!

It was unbelievable, Sintharinus thought, where had two thousand goblins come from? There hadn't been more than a few hundred seen in Shandri vale in the last decade!

Sintharinus couldn't fault Rill's preparations. He did think it was dangerous to send two of their precious heavy infantry companies into town, but he could see that they could not sit behind their walls while these goblins hacked apart their families and friends!

"Master Rill, you have done well." Sintharinus looked out at the dazed, confused and terrified townspeople, "What we now need to do is sort this lot out."

Sintharinus took a deep breath. Master Rill was an old warrior whereas he was an administrator; he might not have a gift for warfare and strategy, but he was an experienced organiser. This sort of mess he could cope with.

"Sergeant," he said to the nearest officer, "I want you to take a couple of your most experienced units and move through the crowd. Find every able bodied man you can and begin forming them into companies of fifty. You will assign two of your men to lead them and organise them and then bring them to the keep's hall." He turned to a second sergeant. "You will take a unit and go to the keep. Break open the armoury and begin bringing all the spare weapons and armour we have to the keep's hall and begin arming our new companies." He looked at both of the sergeants. "By morning I want at least ten companies up on the walls ready to fight. Do you understand me? This is vital." The sergeants thumped their fists to their chest in salute and without a word, spun and ran off, shouting for their men. Sintharinus could see Master Rill and Master Feris nodding in agreement. Good they were happy with his orders so far; however, the next bit was the hard part; Sintharinus knew soldiers would not like it.

He turned to the Captain. "Captain, you must use your remaining three units to begin organising these people." The captain's face dropped immediately, he did not want to have to start nannying the town's folk. "Captain!" Sintharinus said harshly. "I know this is not what you want to do. I know you want to be out there facing those bastard goblins, but we must organise our people, otherwise some of them will not last the night." The captain nodded somewhat reluctantly. "Now, I need you to send one of your units on a mission of some danger." The Captain perked up a bit at this. "Over the next few hours I need a unit to go out to the houses, shops and inns nearest the college and raid them for any kind of supplies we might need; food, blankets, firewood, water, ale, anything. Do you understand?" The captain nodded. "They must do this as often as they can right up until the enemy is upon us. Is that clear?" Again the captain nodded. "If you can, find some sturdy women or young boys who can help and some carts to load things onto." Sintharinus looked around again and could see some of the townspeople now settling down in fearful groups. Some were now heading his way, seeing him as the only person in charge. "Your other two units and you yourself must begin organising these people and offering support…"

A voice suddenly interrupted him, "We can help with that."

Sintharinus glanced around to see a young woman in a voluminous cloak holding a goblin scimitar. She was accompanied by several other townspeople.

"I am Roslyn Shanford and these are some of the city councillors."

Sintharinus acknowledged the group, but before he could say anything, the young woman continued.

"We need somewhere for the injured, the sick and the old." Without waiting for a response she carried on, "I suggest we use the Cleric's infirmary. It has beds already and is big enough to hold maybe as many as five hundred if we put down palettes and blankets. I know they have those in there. Also, Crandor here," she hurried on, pointing at the man who stood next to her, "lives just outside the walls and runs a warehouse, the only one this far into town. It holds all the kind of things we need. He also has several carts."

Sintharinus was just about to express his thanks when she stepped past him and spoke to the captain. "Now Crandor can go with you captain and help you organise the supplies. You could then lend me a unit to start rounding up the injured and spread the word that anyone in need of immediate medical need should go to the Cleric's Dome."

The captain looked over at Sintharinus, a question on his lips. Sintharinus simply nodded. Meanwhile the young woman had turned back to him and was right under his nose, looking up at him.

"What we should do is get as many of these people inside as possible," she insisted sternly. "We should start taking groups of families and friends into the Black Hall and putting them up in any spare rooms or even in the corridors. They would be better off in there for the night than out here. We could even use the stables since you have sent out your cavalry."

Sintharinus began to try to stop the woman, but she continued to give her ideas, though they sounded more like commands. She continued for a moment before she finally noticed Sintharinus' increasing irritation.

"Madame, we have not got the Archmage's permission to allow people into the Black Hall, nor the Abbess' for the use of the Clerics Dome." he managed to say.

"Well where is the Archmage and why isn't he doing something?" the feisty young woman snapped.

"Madame, that is none of your concern," Sintharinus could see this was not doing anything to improve the woman's temper, which he realised probably had a short fuse. "However, I agree that the people should be moved. I would be obliged if you would lead the efforts to organise the Clerics Dome," He was sure the monks would not protest, it was the sort of work they did every day. "Also, captain, send you sergeant and his unit with this man, Crandor to get us those supplies."

Sintharinus was pleased to see that the young woman was satisfied with her task and had already turned away to begin organising the councillors to help her. She was a little firebrand that one. Still her idea for getting the townspeople inside was a good one. The problem was getting permission. He needed the Archmage! Where was he?

"Master Feris," he called and the Third Watchmaster stepped over. "Find out why all the magi are hiding and get a group together and take them to the hall of the assembly. Have them smash down the doors and the force field if need be, but get me the Archmage." The young master saluted, an excited look in his eyes as he headed off.

"The magi are probably still debating, that or talking with the lords and officials from the provinces." Master Rill said from behind him, "The Chancellor organised a banquet for them in the upper hall. I think he was trying to promote trade. Many of the magi were going to go."

"Well, at least it's stopped them from coming out here and panicking or adding to the chaos." Sintharinus muttered. "However, that's not going to last, the news will spread like wildfire."

Master Rill nodded.

"I need to know what kind of provisions we have here in the college and the different schools, Rill." Sintharinus said thinking hard. "If we end up facing a siege, I need to know what we have."

"The chamberlain would know best." Master Rill answered.

Sintharinus nodded. "But where is the chamberlain?"

Chapter 56

DEMON AND MAGE

It is possible to invest great power into an item, either to perform a specific purpose or to be a repository for energy that can be called upon by the magic wielder. Different materials are more conducive than others for the creation of such items. The dwarven folk of old were said to have known much of this form of magic, but research and experiment have allowed us to develop anew, a clear body of knowledge upon these matters. In simple terms, some materials hold more mystical energies more efficiently, and some even enhance energies applied to them. We have forged many simple items that could one day improve the lives of all, but our best creations are the staffs and staves of the magi here at the college.

From an introduction to a treatise entitled, 'The Development of Enchantment; crafting items of power.' by High Enchanter Atholl Dorard of Shandrilos. BY1336

For a split second everyone in the circle of the hall stopped. Then spells began to form. Arkadi didn't waste an instant. He pulled a stunned Nossi and Nat up the banked, stepped seats of the hall away from the conflict he knew was coming. He barely even stopped to glance when he heard Baden Erin snapping out orders.

"Zarina, Marillia you deal with Drollin and Gregan. Izonda, you and Jammu take the demon." He was about to say more Arkadi saw, but the hidden shield he had cast was suddenly, hammered by a fiery burst from Xameran. Old and new Archmage faced off against each other.

"And I suppose you will deal with me, will you Baden?" Xameran gave a short, harsh laugh. "You have no idea what you are dealing with."

"Why don't you show me then, traitor?" Baden Erin growled back.

Arkadi suddenly found it was he who was being dragged back as Nat, now realising the danger, was trying to get them all as far up and away from the fighting as possible. Arkadi slapped at the huntress' hands and barked, "Wait!"

The hunter stopped and Arkadi looked down on the battle below.

Fiery bursts leapt towards Baden, but already his hands and mouth were moving and a wall of coruscating light sent the energy careening off towards the ceiling.

Beyond them Arkadi could see that Eliantha Shamass, the dainty little Mage Master, a woman he had thought as timid as a mouse, was hammering spells at the twisted, savage old High Enchanter like a wildwoman!

Nat jerked him and pointed to the new Allseer, Master Drollin. Arkadi was just in time to see the aristrocratic, old First Wizard, Zarina Agroda blast a lightning bolt at him. Drollin's shield of force was shattered instantly and he was smashed down with a smoking hole the size of a child's head blasted through his chest. He was dead before he knew it.

"By all the gods!" Arkadi exclaimed. He had heard that the withered stick that was the First Wizard was a powerful warmage, but he had never believed it until now. Drollin hadn't stood a chance.

Neither too did the new Sorceror Supreme, Grandmaster Gregan. Arkadi could see that he was losing the fight against the spell wrought Death Roots that the tall Chief Druid had conjured. He was burning them as they appeared, but more were growing all the time. Abruptly, his flames sputtered to an end and Arkadi saw his eyes widen as he desperately began another spell. However, the determination on the furious face of Marillia Aronis never wavered and roots spread around Grandmaster Gregan like webs. Before he could finish his casting they bound his arms and then pushed on to ram themselves into his mouth and down his throat.

Arkadi grimaced and turned away as he heard the poor sorceror's bones begin to break in the Chief Druid's unforgiving grip.

Arkadi found himself instead looking at the Abbess and the huge Magus General as they faced the demon. The magus general had his huge sword in hand and was darting in to hack at the monster, distracting it while the Abbess began a long and complex banishing spell.

He heard Nat mutter behind him, "Tynast! These magi don't mess around."

Nat was right. This was the most incredible spell battle of which Arkadi had ever heard. He found a small part of him that wasn't terrified, was excited at the chance to watch these true masters of the art do battle.

Arkadi had known straight away that Drollin had stood little chance against Zarina, a seer against a wizard was no contest in battle, but the First Wizard had dealt with Drollin with brutal efficiency. Also, the ferocious tawny haired druid, Marillia was renowned as a formidable opponent; she had fought in the wilds against all manner of beasts. However, the contest between the demon and the Abbess and Magus General was less clear. The Abbess' strengths were in spiritual and healing magic, while the giant that was Jammu Quadai Pendi was a fighter mage of great reputation. He would augment his own fighting skills with his magic.

It seemed he needed to. The demon moved like lightning, dodging and weaving away from the Magus General's attacks and slicing back at the big man's enchanted armour. Claws like knives screeched across his chest plate sending sparks flying, but the Magus General could hardly land a blade on the whirling, writhing demon.

Nat nudged Arkadi again and pointed. Zarina and Marillia had finished their opponents and were turning their attention to the demon. The infernal creature must have realised this too. It suddenly, bounded forward, slid past the Magus General's swift, but despairing thrust and leapt past him. It swept his legs from under him as it passed. The poor Abbess was caught unprepared as the demon sprang for her, but she reacted with a speed that surprised Arkadi. Her banishment fell apart as the demon came straight for her, yet the wide eyed Abbess caught the demon's raking blow on her staff and then whipped the butt end into the creature's ribs. She then called out a word and a shimmering barrier appeared between her and the hell spawn. The demon had already launched itself, jaws wide at the Abbess and couldn't stop. It crashed into the barrier and howled in pain as sparks ran painfully up and down its scaled hide.

Arkadi was impressed. He had thought the Abbess was finished. Arkadi saw the Magus General regain his feet and the First Wizard and Chief Druid closed on the shuddering demon.

"Yes!" Arkadi found himself saying out loud in triumph.

Without warning, a long, wickedly sharp tail seemed to flow out of the demon's lower back and in a lightning fast lash, swung around the mystical shield and sliced across the Abbess' throat!

Suddenly, the shimmering barrier vanished and bright red blood gushed down the Abbess' white robes. Her mouth was open in a silent scream and horror contorted her coppery skinned face. Zarina and Marillia stopped in their tracks, shock writ large on their aged faces.

The demon wrenched itself around and slapped the roaring Magus General's lunge aside. It contorted and lengthened as it soared a prodigious way across the hall in one bound. It turned and its face twisted back into the face of the chamberlain. It laughed then; a laugh that stretched the chamberlain's mouth impossibly wide. Jammu Quadai Pendi roared again like an angry bear and threw himself wildly across the hall, sword held high.

Arkadi was snapped away from the Magus General's attack by an explosion not five feet away. It threw Nat sideways into Arkadi and the two stumbled. Poor Nossi was lifted and thrown several feet.

"Blood and sand!" Nat exclaimed, busily extricating her limbs from Arkadi's. "What was that?"

Arkadi didn't answer. He was looking at where the spell had come from. Tiny Eliantha Shamass was now almost toe to toe with the irascible old High Enchanter. Atholl Dorard's face was filled with strain, while a seemingly insane Eliantha bombarded him with bolt after bolt of energy from close range that was pummelling his multilayered spell barrier. Eliantha seemed to have no concern for her own safety as her energy bolts went ricocheting all over the place. However, Arkadi could not deny the effectiveness of her assault. It may have been reckless, but it was blasting away layer after layer of the now appalled looking lord enchanter's barrier.

Suddenly, he seemed to make some decision and he pulled a wand from his robes. Arkadi saw his lips move and then there was a dramatic flash. The High Enchanter vanished and an inrush of air to where he had been, dragged Eliantha from her feet and almost over balanced those nearby.

"I never knew Eliantha had it in her." Arkadi murmured as he picked himself up. "She beat the High Enchanter!" Nat was already pulling Nossi Bee back up and over to them.

Baden Erin used the distraction from the High Enchanter's exit to blast the floor beneath Xameran's feet that lifted him up, over and onto his back, but the wily sorcerer did not lose his concentration for a second, and in a moment of incredible skill, released several spells at once; one to catch him on a cushion of air and right him, one to reinforce his suddenly wavering shield and one to blast back at Baden Erin who had been about to cast another attacking spell.

Arkadi looked back to the other side of the circular floor of the hall and saw that the Abbess had fallen and was choking out her last breath, with Zarina and Marillia looking on helplessly. It was too late to save her; Arkadi had known it the moment the demon struck. The wound was too severe, the blood loss now too great. Marillia knew this too. She knelt and gently closed the Abbess' eyes and whispered something to the old woman. Arkadi suddenly realised that all three of those women were no longer young. Each was past sixty, their magic kept them seemingly young, but of the three, the Abbess had been youngest.

Abruptly, the Magus General reeled back across Arkadi's line of sight, down near the steps below Arkadi, Nat and Nossi. The demon had changed again and it now resembled some gigantic mantis. Its arms were like swords and it hacked at the Magus General in wild abandon. The burly Jammu was skilfully blocking its attacks with his sword. He barked something and his sword suddenly blazed with blue energy and the demon's next attack was sliced through by the Magus General's sword. It hissed like an enormous snake as its limb fell to the floor, smoked, sizzled and vanished! Jammu Quadai Pendi bellowed triumphantly and swung again, but the swift demon, changed again, produced another arm and slid under his blow. It pinned his sword arm. The mighty Magus General called another cantrip and he heaved a massive blow with his free arm. His armoured, spell powered fist slammed into the beasts head and its neck snapped with a loud crack! The demon's head lolled back hideously.

Arkadi heard Nossi gag, while Nat practically crowed with delight.

However, the demon seemed unphased by its broken neck and with its other arm, pinned the big fighter mage's free arm. Zarina and Marillia hurried over ready to cast, but they could not now attack without hitting the Magus General. He, meanwhile, was snarling like a wounded lion and had wrapped his arms around the demon too. The two seemed matched in strength and reeled around like drunken prize fighters. They fell, and rolled, each one battering at the other in a fury.

A laugh caught Arkadi's attention. It was Xameran. He was now throwing out strange lashing strands of energy that were whipping at both Eliantha and Baden Erin. The now weary looking Mage Master had gone to aid Baden. Arkadi could see the strain on both of their faces and wondered where Xameran was getting the energy to batter down such powerful magi. He knew Xameran was one of the most talented magi, but Eliantha was talented if tired and Baden Erin had been fresh and was one of the most powerful magi in the college's history! It just didn't make sense.

Arkadi looked hard, straining his magical senses to the limit. He frowned and without taking his eyes off Xameran he said to Nossi, "Do you see the weaves that Xameran is using, Nossi?"

The gnome climbed onto the step behind Arkadi and stood so that his head was at the same height as Arkadi's.

"He weaves his spells with precision and can cast multiple spells at once." Nossi said quietly.

"Yes, yes," Arkadi said impatiently, "but can you actually see all of his weaves?"

There was a pause and then the gnome said, "No, he is obviously inverting some of his weaves to give himself an advantage in his battle… and he is drawing power from that staff he is holding." The gnome added almost as an afterthought.

"Of course!" Arkadi exclaimed, seeing the truth now. It was a mystery how Xameran had learnt how to invert his spells when no one else could, but more importantly he had the Archmage's staff, the Staff of Melkor. The school of Enchanters had worked long and hard on that. Xameran was using it to fuel his spells. Thinking about it, Baden Erin had done well to last as long as he had. If he could not see all of the spells that Xameran was constructing he would have to react almost intuitively, casting with incredible speed to counter spells that were already manifesting. No wonder the strain was showing. Arkadi wouldn't have lasted more than a minute; he was in awe of Baden Erin's skill!

The former Archmage was still resisting Xameran and was even managing to send his own attacks now and again. It was a breathtaking display. Unfortunately, it wasn't going to be enough. Already, Eliantha was showing she could not match Baden in dealing with Xameran's assault. She was simply trying to defend herself and take some of the pressure off Baden.

"Look at that!" Nat suddenly cried.

Arkadi looked across and saw what Nat was talking about. The Magus General, with a burst of magical strength, though still pinned himself, had lifted the demon. It was changing almost constantly, but the Magus General was crushing it in a massive bear hug. The big warrior's face had gone purple with the strain. The demon was changing and twisting more and more rapidly, obviously in pain. Then the big man's strength spell failed and he was forced to collapse. He managed to fall on top of the demon, but now the creature was no longer writhing in pain. It was leering at the Magus General with a face that was partly human. Its arms lengthened and twisted around the huge warrior's body and yanked him close in an even tighter bear hug, preventing him from moving at all.

Nat gasped then and Arkadi found himself fascinated. The humanoid head swelled and massive jaws grew out from the face. Soon the demon's head resembled something like a drake or crocodile. Its sawtoothed jaws split wide in front of the snarling Magus General's face. Nat swore and looked away. They all knew what was coming, even the Magus General who spat curses at the creature in defiance. Zarina and Marillia called out and summoned their magic, but it was too late. The jaws lunged forward and clamped down. With a cracking, gurgling crunch, the demon ripped the Magus General's head from his body!

Arkadi wanted to look away, but he couldn't. Some kind of morbid fascination held him fixed, watching the blood spurt out like a jet and the body twitch. Thankfully, the impact of the two female magi's simultaneous magical blasts at the demon blinded Arkadi and forced him to close his eyes for a moment. The noise of the ferocious attack was immense and when Arkadi opened his watering eyes he could make out flames and smoke rising up from the place where the demon and its victim had been. His eyes slowly cleared and he could just make out Zarina and Marillia, arms still held out, fingers rigid, ready to cast. Their eyes were fixed on where the demon had been. Slowly, the smoke drifted away.

The demon was gone!

A small crater was left in the magical black rock of the floor, a rock that was almost impervious to magic, and in it were the burnt and melted remains of the Magus General and his armour. There was no trace of the demon. Could they had disintegrated it or sent it back to whatever abyss it had been summoned from?

"Where did it go? Did they destroy it?" Nat asked from beside him.

Arkadi ignored him. His eyes scanned around. They had done it. It was gone.

Suddenly, from nowhere, the demon was behind the two magi. Arkadi went to call out. Two long blades appeared to spring from Zarina and Marillia's chests! Their mouths opened, but only blood came forth.

Nat was swearing uncontrollably at the side of him. She began grabbing at Arkadi's arm asking what they were going to do. It was clear even to her that the battle was definitely going against their side.

Arkadi shrugged her off and snarled, "Let me think!" However, Arkadi could think of nothing. He could not break the magical barrier that held the doors closed, nor blast his way out. He had known that at the start. Could he even slow the demon? He had just seen it kill four of the most powerful magi in the college. What could he do?

The demon let the two magi slip from its arms and slump to the floor. Behind it, on the other side of the hall, Eliantha Shamass was now slumped, either dead or unconscious and Baden Erin was not looking good. Sweat poured from him and his eyes were wide, his skin pallid. His entire body showed desperation in his every move and gesture.

The demon looked over at the battle. Xameran was now showing some strain and it was clear that Baden Erin had lasted longer than he had expected, but Xameran was still smiling, still confident. The demon looked away. It was not needed there.

It looked up, straight at Arkadi, Nat and Nossi!

"Tynast's teeth, it's looking at us!" Nat cried out.

Nossi was suddenly clinging to Arkadi. The gnome had been on the edge of panic during the battle, but with the demon's eyes on him, he was petrified. Arkadi didn't blame him.

"Think, Arkadi, think!" he said to himself, but his mind had gone blank. He had his spells and he would go down fighting, but he knew he had nothing that could stop the creature before him.

The demon changed. Wings grew from its back and it began to look something like a picture Arkadi had once seen of a dragon, save the demon stood on two legs like a man. Its head changed again and slowly, the chamberlain's familiar face appeared. The demon stepped towards them.

"At last, the gnome and its friends!" the demon rasped in the old man's slightly scratchy voice. "Too long have I hunted you."

It would have been comical had it not been so frightening; an old man's face on the body of a demon!

All of a sudden there was a dull thump. The demon stopped in its advance and looked around.

'Was Baden Erin rallying somehow?' was all Arkadi could think. He looked over optimistically at the former Archmage. Baden was almost on his knees! His face was haggard and he seemed to have aged. Xameran, however, was still standing tall, though sweat now rolled down his forehead.

The large, dull thump came again, louder this time. It was clearly not Baden Erin, he could barely defend himself. A third thump sounded and the doors to the hall clearly vibrated. The demon turned and took a few steps towards them.

With startling suddenness, the doors cracked, dust bellowed out and a piece of one door flew violently across the room. The demon stepped back in surprise and raised its arms to cover its face. As if launched from a catapult, a shadowy figure flew into the room and a huge sword hacked down and cut off one of the demon's upraised arms. The demon howled as its severed arm hissed and melted away on the floor. Swiftly, it swung its other arm, smashing at its new enemy and hurling him across the room to crash with stunning force into the stone steps.

"It's Darin!" Nat hollered like she had seen salvation. Arkadi supposed she was right though the man was covered head to foot in that strange armour. Arkadi was not as hopeful for their salvation as Nat. Darin was a superb swordsman and Arkadi was glad to see him, but this thing was a servant of the dark gods who was more than a match for the most powerful magi in the college. One lucky swipe might be all Darin would get.

"We need to go and help him." Arkadi called quickly.

Nat looked at him like he was mad. "You want me to fight that!" she almost wheezed.

"He cannot last against that thing, Nat. If we can hold it off, we can get by it and go and get help."

Nat suddenly looked towards the hole in the door and her eyes lit up. She began to bound forward, down the steps. Arkadi moved to follow her, but out of the corner of his eye he saw that Baden Erin had made use of the unexpected explosion and had leapt on Xameran. The two men were wrestling for the Staff of Melkor. Arkadi was suddenly torn. He should go and help Baden.

Ahead of him, Nat swore and Arkadi looked at her. The demon had moved itself in front of the doorway and was leering at the frozen hunter.

"Look," Nossi said, distracting Arkadi further. He was stood at Arkadi's hip, pointing.

Arkadi looked over and saw Darin in the enchanted black armour, up and marching forward, sword in hand. Incredibly, he seemed unhurt and he was moving confidently. Well, that was Darin, confident no matter what the danger.

The demon leapt forward towards Nat who back pedalled frantically. Darin ran in from behind and attacked with blistering speed. The demon sensed his attack and dodged, but too slowly. Darin's sword sliced down its body and it screamed and fell back. Darin pursued it with relentless efficiency. The demon produced two arms again and its wings disappeared as it dodged and weaved. Its arms turned into the long blades it had used to cut down Zarina and Marillia, but every time it used them to block Darin's ebon blade the sword bit into them and the demon howled in agony.

"Whatever that armour and sword are, they are bloody impressive." Nat called.

Arkadi had to agree with the archer's crude assessment. However, as they watched the two combatants, Arkadi noticed that the demon's wounds were healing almost instantly and it was not tiring at all. Suddenly, it stopped its retreat and lunged forward, screeching fearfully. Its bladed limb sliced through the jet armour and Darin cried out loud, his voice muffled by the jet helm that covered his head.

Nat grabbed Arkadi's arm in concern and Arkadi thought, 'Oh gods!'

However, Darin was not overly concerned it seemed. He leapt back, retreating from the hellish creature and placed his hand over the gapping split in his armour. A second later when he removed it the split appeared to have vanished! Even the demon was taken aback by this.

Nat laughed almost hysterically and shouted, "Not so sure now are you, you freakish...thing!" she finished a bit lamely not really knowing what to call the creature.

Arkadi was suddenly more confident. It was obvious as Darin leapt back to the attack, that the armour he now wore was powerful indeed. However, things still weren't certain. Darin could still be killed and if Baden Erin fell too, Darin would not be able to face both the demon and Xameran. Arkadi was suddenly determined that would not happen. Xameran had used Arkadi and he hated being used. What's more it was obvious now that he was a servant of these dark elves who had killed his best friends. Arkadi would repay Xameran in full!

"Nat," he called and the huntress looked at him. "I want you to get yourself over near the door." Arkadi instructed. "When you get the chance I want you to get out of here and get help, okay?"

Nat nodded, a look of relief on her face at the thought of escaping this hall. She turned to go and then stopped and looked back.

"What about you and Nossi... and Darin?"

Arkadi looked down at the gnome still clinging to his robe like a child at its mother skirts.

"Darin can take care of himself. Nossi and I have a mage to take care of." Arkadi said fiercely.

Nat looked hard at Arkadi. "You've got that nasty look on your face again, Arkadi. I take it you have some clever plan."

"Never mind, Nat, I don't have time to explain. Just go!"

The huntress nodded and skipped across the steps, heading for the door, but going around the circle of the hall to avoid the demon and Darin who were leaping, slicing and whirling like dervishes.

Arkadi knelt and took Nossi by the shoulders. "Do you want to get back at that man who had you tortured and beaten?" he asked urgently yet softly of the gnome.

Nossi looked at him fearfully. Arkadi held his breath. The gnome suddenly nodded vigorously. He had obviously come to some inner decision.

"It will mean some danger. You could get hurt." Arkadi warned.

The gnome looked at him earnestly. He was clearly frightened, but something in his demeanour had changed. "Nossi Bee will help you. He is through being beaten and used. He will fight."

The gnome had such a fierce look on his innocent little face that Arkadi would have laughed out loud had things not been so serious. Quickly, Arkadi whispered his plan to the little gnome. By the end, Nossi was smiling. He clearly liked Arkadi's plan. Arkadi just hoped he could carry it through. It was a gamble, but the gnome had a look of steadfast resolve in his eyes now, and Arkadi was convinced the gnome would not fail for lack of trying.

Over on the far side of the hall, the two archmages had thrown each other down in their hand to hand struggle. The Staff of Melkor had fallen to the side of them. Spells were again flying between them from only a couple of feet apart. However, Baden Erin was still on his knees, unable to get to his feet again, while, Xameran had regained his feet and was slowly edging towards the fallen staff, hurling quick cantrips to keep his opponent off balance. Arkadi sent the gnome off around the steps, waited a few moments willing Baden Erin to hold on, and then headed down to the circular floor of the hall.

Arkadi mentally went through his repertoire of spells. His best chance was to simply defend. As he marched across the stone floor, he conjured up several spell barriers. He was about to summon more, in fact all the defensive spells he knew, but Baden Erin suddenly groaned and collapsed. Xameran stopped his assault, smiled and picked up the fallen staff of Melkor.

"At last we come to it, then Baden." Xameran Uth Altor said suddenly pleasant. "You put up a brave fight, my friend, but now it is over."

Arkadi sensed Xameran summoning a spell. He realised he could wait no longer. As quickly as he could he summoned and cast a fireball spell at his former mentor's back. He put all his anger and bitterness at being deceived into that spell.

Xameran sensed the spell the moment it formed and with a skill that came from years of practise, he spun and wove an energy barrier. Arkadi's spell slammed into it and both barrier and fireball exploded apart. Arkadi began a second spell, an ice storm spell. His concentration was shattered as a bolt of blazing blue energy pounded his first spell barrier apart.

"So, Arkadi, I see you have finally allowed your ego to take you too far." Xameran sneered and fired off another bolt of energy. "Do you really think you can face me?"

Arkadi gave up on any thought of attacking the former sorcerer lord and concentrated on creating more layers to his spell barriers. Already, he had lost two of his three. Had he not pre-cast them he would be a smoking ruin on the floor by now. He could not match Xameran's speed at spell casting nor his stamina. Arkadi focused on keeping more barriers in place than Xameran could pummel away. This wasn't a strategy for victory. Arkadi just hoped he could survive long enough. His defences were being stripped away too fast. Where was Nossi?

"You are trying to give Baden a rest, Arkadi?" Xameran smiled. He was as aware as Arkadi that it was only a matter of time. "Because we both know you cannot beat me," he chuckled.

Arkadi ground his teeth in frustration, but didn't allow Xameran to disrupt his focus on forming his defensive shields. He did glance over to the prone Baden Erin, but there seemed little chance the former archmage would get up again.

Arkadi was now barely getting his barriers in place before Xameran would hammer them down. Where was Nossi?

"It is a shame you have chosen to fight against me." Xameran said magnanimously, "In a few more years you would have been a formidable mage." He paused as if in thought. "Mind you, I would have had to kill you then, wouldn't I? Couldn't have you challenging me!" he laughed again.

Arkadi stared daggers. 'You just keep on talking, scum' he thought savagely. It would slow his casting down enough for Arkadi to stay alive, but then Xameran always had liked the sound of his own voice.

Abruptly, Nossi Bee appeared by Xameran's hip. Arkadi's eyes widened. The gnome sprang forward, grabbing at the mage's arms, disrupting his spells. Arkadi swiftly stopped forming his shield and began his most powerful attacking spell, a lightning burst. Xameran was still wrestling with Nossi. However, he quickly slapped the little gnome, knocking him back. The gnome held onto Xameran's arms for a moment, but a second blow sent him spinning away. Xameran's eyes met Arkadi's. He smiled his glib smile and the look in his malicious dark eyes seemed to say, 'bet I can get you before you can get me'. Arkadi knew it was true. He had foolishly started a longer more powerful spell. Xameran lifted his arms to cast. It would be short and deadly, Arkadi knew.

Xameran suddenly writhed in agony and fell to his knees, dropping the staff. His hands went to his wrists; a small metal bracelet encircled them with a chain hanging down. Nossi had done it. Xameran now wore the magic inhibiting chains that Nossi had once been forced to wear!

Again, Xameran's dark eyes met Arkadi's. This time it was Arkadi's turn to smile.

"Bet you can't get me before I get you." Arkadi spat as he released his spell.

Lighting speared out and Xameran began to spring back trying to avoid the deadly energy, but too slowly; the lightning lanced into his chest. Xameran Uth Altor was lifted and tossed backwards like a rag doll, daggers of energy jolting his body. He landed limply. Sparks played briefly across him and his back arched. Then, as swiftly as it had stuck, it ended, his last breath rasped from his smoking corpse.

Arkadi stared for a moment and then he was hit by a small body. Nossi was hugging him and shouting, 'you did it' over and over. Arkadi hugged him back for a moment in disbelief and then he saw Baden Erin move. Arkadi gently pushed Nossi away and then hurried over, pausing to grab the staff of Melkor on the way. He knelt and thrust the staff into Baden Erin's hand. He then quickly cast a simple healing relief spell.

Baden Erin groaned and opened his eyes. He didn't seem to know where he was for a moment and then he jerked up. Arkadi put a hand on his chest and said soothingly. "Xameran is dead. Lie still. Try to use the staff to regain some of your energy." Arkadi knew that the spell battle with Xameran had taken almost all the energy Baden had. In some battles it was said magi had simply dropped dead because their spells used up all the energy in their bodies and it could no longer even keep their heart pumping.

Baden seemed to relax a little and then he hugged the staff to him like a lost lover.

Arkadi stood and looked around. There was no trace of Nat and Arkadi hoped she had gone for help. Darin was still engaged in a furious cut and thrust with the demon. However, it seemed to Arkadi that somehow the demon looked smaller. Arkadi watched Darin slice yet another arm from the demon and suddenly knew why. The arm was quickly replaced, but Arkadi realised that, with every bit cut off that sizzled away to nothing, the demon got smaller and weaker. Darin was literally cutting the thing down to size.

Arkadi could have cheered.

Behind him there was a scraping sound and Arkadi spun, arms out, ready... it was Baden Erin, he had pulled himself to his feet. Arkadi could sense the energy flowing from the staff to the mage. Its reserves must be huge. It must have taken years to build up such a reservoir. Baden Erin, still a little shaky, stared at the battle between Darin and the demon.

It was an incredibly display, Arkadi thought, turning back to the fight. Arkadi was amazed to see that neither was tiring and both were healing themselves. Arkadi had no idea what the armour was, but it must be old magic. Nothing like that was even remotely possible today.

With dazzling swordsmanship, Darin suddenly, loped off another arm, but this time guessed which direction the demon would dodge and spun and cut its head from its shoulders in one lighting fast blow. He didn't leave it there either, with a titanic overhead swing, he sliced the demon's body in half! There was a huge unearthly scream and a breeze blew up from nowhere pushing Darin back. The scream turned to a deafening howl and then the parts of the demon's body simply exploded into nothingness, knocking everyone from their feet.

Arkadi's ears were still ringing when he struggled back to his feet. Baden Erin used the staff to help him up and then spotted Eliantha lying still. He cried out and ran over to her. After a moment, he called out that she was alive.

Arkadi began hurrying over to the door. He passed Darin in the faceless black armour and called for him to follow. Darin never even twitched he simply stood still like a statue. Arkadi stopped and frowned at him, but then turned and headed for the door, shouting for help as he got near. He could already hear feet pounding down the long passage that led to the hall. Arkadi stopped and looked back. Only then did it hit him; in the still aftermath of the battle, the assembly hall looked more like a charnel house now than a meeting place.

"Sarahiri preserve me," he sighed, invoking the Queen of the Gods. Suddenly, it was like a weight had been lifted from him. He had survived.

A thought struck him. He remembered something he had said to Rebba and he cursed sadly to himself, thinking of his lost friend. 'Life is definitely no longer dull at the college!'

Chapter 57

AT THE WAYGATE

It is believed that each of the Lords of Light had a favoured people and that they gave to each race a powerful talisman to guard that race. A guardian was selected from amongst the most powerful of the race to wield the talisman. To the Elves, Elysia, Lady of Life gave a mighty gem which contained much of her power. Thus, the elves were ever the healers, in tune with nature, bringing life to even the most barren of lands. It is from this example that our own people were inspired to form the druidic order to continue to heal and aid all life.

Knowledge passed down through Bardic tradition. Recorded by Prince Afdar SaTell of Stellicia BY78 - thought to be directly quoted from the legendary 'Lorebooks of the Druid Kings' said to have been begun by King Nam'Odar the Fisherking a thousand years earlier.

Rebba Korran looked down at the Waygate arches that would take them to safety and was appalled. Strapped cruelly to one of them, Garon Vale hung helpless and tortured. Rebba wanted to run down there and free her friend, but she could not. To do so would be suicide for them all, Garon included. It was obvious that the only reason the dark elves had kept him alive was because they did not have the Lifestone. They knew who did and would use Garon to try to lure them down.

Rebba looked around. She, Zara and Bear had the stone; it was there, in Bear's tight grip.

It was so easy to say that this trap the dark elves had set would not work, would not lure them in, but when it was your friend down there, it was not so easy. When it was a man you had known almost your whole life, a man you trusted completely and who had not long since saved you from the fate he now suffered, it was not easy at all!

Rebba seethed with worry and frustration. What were they going to do?

Rebba again looked at the Lifestone. All that had happened was for that stone. Rebba looked up and found Bear's now alien eyes on her. He blinked those large luminous orbs at Rebba silently, his face a mask. She looked away. It felt as though Bear was looking into her soul. Rebba had no doubt that Bear knew her thoughts. Had it been she alone, she would have already been trying to go down to aid her friend.

"Well, what do we do?" Zara whispered, looking back and forth between Rebba and Bear.

Rebba looked away. She could not say what she would do. Instead she looked over the rim of the gigantic crater that had once been the centre of the ancient elven city of Hy'Deeria. Once the Waygates that now stood open to the sky, had been hidden beneath the earth, but the ancient spell that the sylvan elves had sent had burst up from the ground and annihilated the city, poisoning all for miles around. Looking down the slope of the crater, Rebba could see ruined bits of statues, buildings and masonry amongst the mud, grass and bushes that now grew. On the far side of the crater, she could see where the dark elves and their allies had descended. They had cleared a muddy, rugged path that wound down to the still polished floor of what had been the Waygate Hall. They had set up camp in there, a hundred or more of them. Added to this, Rebba could see there were sentries posted on the lip of the crater. More elves, black goblins and mayax were moving back and forth over the rim; obviously search parties still going out and coming back.

"We cannot give them the Lifestone. We would inevitably be killing all the Wildlands and letting loose those monsters in the world once more." Bear insisted quietly. "They would see our whole world plunged into chaos and subjugate all to create a world where demon kind ran free at their bidding. It would mean the end of all the free peoples, the dark elves would not tolerate them to live save as abject slaves."

Rebba nodded, but she could not get over the feeling that they should go down and save Garon, or at least try.

"You're right Bear we can't let them have the Lifestone, but what do we do with it?" Zara asked and then pushed on not waiting for an answer. "Soon the dark elves will find us if we don't move and from what I can tell those arches down there are our only way out… unless we can go through the swamps?" The lithe warrior asked without any enthusiasm.

"Even with an army we could not go that way." Bear muttered darkly.

"So what do we do? Do we spend the rest of our days dodging dark elves and monsters in this gods forsaken place?" She looked up at the sky and held up her hands, "Or can we expect more divine intervention?"

It was said with deep sarcasm and Rebba snorted.

Zara looked at her and snorted back. "I thought not!"

"Aren't we forgetting something here?" Rebba asked acerbically. "Garon is down there," she said, both she and her voice rising in indignation. "He is still alive and suffering!"

Zara grabbed her to pull her down, hushing at her, but Rebba resisted, slapping Zara's hands away.

"He risked his life to lead those dark elves away from us. We cannot leave him like that." Rebba cried, "They are torturing him!"

Zara roughly grabbed Rebba by the front of her robe and hauled her down to her knees. "You fool, you'll give us away."

Rebba opened her mouth to argue, but Zara yanked her forward so that their faces were scant inches apart.

"We know he is down there, Rebba, we haven't forgotten," Zara hissed, "but Garon is a grown man. He made his own decision." Zara shook her. "And I respect that decision. I won't make it count for nothing because you can't get a grip of yourself. Do you hear me?"

Zara glared angrily into Rebba's eyes for a moment, shook her one more time before pushing her down.

Rebba rocked back on her haunches. She looked bitterly at the silver armoured warrior woman.

Bear leaned over and put a placatory hand on Rebba's shoulder. "None of us like the idea that he is down there, but we need to keep our heads, there are more important things at stake here."

Bear looked at Rebba for understanding, but she just couldn't shake the feeling that they should be doing something and looked away.

"Look, we need to get through one of those Waygates." Bear said more severely. "If we can do that, maybe we can take Garon with us when we go."

Rebba looked back at Bear and found the big man's elven eyes staring right at her.

"However, if we sit here arguing we will never get anywhere and Garon is as good as dead!"

Again, Rebba found she could not hold that potent gaze. She looked away. Bear was right. They needed to think.

Silence settled on the group and Rebba found herself staring around again. The dark elves were still making their camp, they did not look to be in any hurry to leave, after all they had dealt with most of the larger creatures in the area so they could sit in relative security for now. Casting her eyes down the slope, Rebba again noticed the rocky, uneven terrain. It would be possible to get almost to the dark elves without being seen. That was good. A thought occurred to her.

"Bear," she called softly, "How did the dark elves get here?"

Bear shrugged, "They would have made a portal..." he stopped, "Ah I see where you are going, but I have only some sketchy knowledge of making portals from Tal'Asin's memories, but what I do know is you need either a lot of mages working together or a person or enchanted object of some sort on the other side to act as a beacon and aid to the casting. Both would be preferable unless you are a very experienced master. Added to which the suppressing and warping of magic in this place makes things virtually impossible."

"Just what can you do with this Tal'Asin's memories?" Zara asked puzzled. "You seemed to be fine with magic when you were altering this armour and stuff, and you saved my hide back beneath Shandrilos."

"Altering the weaves of enchantments is far easier than creating them and back in the catacombs I had Tal'Asin's spirit with me to guide me." Bear answered solemnly.

"So where is this Tal'Asin when you need him?" Zara snapped exasperated.

Bear shook his head, a look of deep worry on his face. "I do not know, but he should have returned long ago. I fear something has happened to him."

Zara frowned. "How do you harm a spirit? It's not like you can cut it or anything."

"There are things on the astral plane that can kill as surely as a sword through the heart." Bear warned and then went on. "But I cannot risk trying to take us out using a portal, not unless it is the last resort. Even if I could control the magic enough to cast the spell, you really need to know where in relation you are to where you want to go and I don't even know exactly where we are!" Bear exclaimed, "It's not like anyone has been in these lands for around three thousand years!"

They all went back to thinking again.

As Rebba was thinking, her hand went to the keystone she still carried in the inner pocket of her cloak. She rubbed it and held it in her hand as she thought. This little pebble had caused people's deaths, she thought. So much had happened because of this little rock. Her life had been changed for the worse because of it.

She thought hard for a few moments and realised that wasn't entirely true. While she had been chased, attacked and scared half to death, she had seen some truly incredible things, things she would never have got to see otherwise. Was it worth it? Not when weighed against Garon's life and yet she had seen elves, ancient magic, learnt things no other knew, not even the finest scholars. She had even seen two of the ancient wonders; the Lifestone of Elysia and the Waygates! Not only that either, she had travelled through the Ways and visited some of the long lost cities of the Elder. How many people could claim that?

'Travelled through the Ways...' that gave her an idea.

Quickly, she sat up and looked down at the dark elven camp again. The camp was set up around the edge of the clear smooth rock that had been the floor of the Waygate Hall. The dark elves had formed a wall of warriors facing out and were now building fires with branches and dry grass as kindling just back from the outer ring of warriors. Only the dark elven leader and his senior men or body guard were actually near the Waygate arches. Occasionally, they would look at the barely conscious Garon and then return to talking.

Rebba frowned. It might just work... if they could time things right.

She thought it through again. They would have to wrap the Lifestone up, hide it, maybe under a cloak or something. If the dark elven leader saw they had it on them, he would simply attack them straight away.

Rebba licked her lips. It would be risky. They could all be killed, but if it worked it could get them all free, including Garon. It could also maybe even up the odds a little.

With a feeling of trepidation that the others would think her a fool, she turned to them and began telling them her idea. A minute or two later Bear and Zara were looking at Rebba with unreadable looks on their faces.

"What do you think, Bear?" Zara asked looking at the big warrior. "It's better than any idea I can come up with."

Bear nodded a fraction, "Yes, but it is risky, very risky. If it doesn't work we have lost everything," he warned, "Not only our lives, but possibly those of everyone we know. The dark elves would have the Lifestone!"

"Yes, but we would have to take it with us. We'd have to risk it or it would get left behind." Rebba insisted, "We didn't come all this way to leave it behind."

Zara looked at Bear for a moment and then looked at Rebba. A smile spread across her tanned face and her brown eyes twinkled. "All or nothing!" she said, thumping her thigh. "I like it. Those are my kind of odds!"

Rebba looked at the warrior in bemusement, while Bear shook his head sadly.

"Come on Bear," Zara said, thumping Bear on the shoulder. "You know it's the best idea we're going to come up with." Zara looked over at Rebba and winked. "After all, do you want to live forever?"

Rebba suddenly felt, shaky. Actually, she very much wanted to live forever!

<hr>

Prince Uh'Ram Bloodfire was getting increasingly irritated. Had he known that the beasts of this place would be waiting for him, drawn by the portal, he would have brought more men. Nevertheless, they had dealt with them, though he had lost too many. Still if it gained him the Lifestone it would be worth it. However, that goal still seemed to be out of his reach at the moment.

Humans, they were the flaw in his plans. He cursed the humans. How could they have got here so quickly and got past that Sylvan elf shade? It was obviously a guarding spirit and it should never have been so easily convinced to give up its charge.

Deliberately, he left that puzzle. It had been done and nothing could change that now. The immediate problem was that those humans were still out there. Uh'Ram had been pleased when they brought in the round one. It did not have the stone, but Uh'Ram was sure it could be persuaded to tell where its friends were hiding and to enlighten him on how they had got the key and how they had convinced that damned Sylvan shade. Humans were inherently weak and had no real sense of loyalty; they could always be bought whether with the metal coins they so treasured or with the chance of life. There was always something they would do to save their own piggish hides.

However, this human had frustrated him. He had repeatedly called on his god and someone or something called Alba to be with him, or save him or some such. No divine aid came and Uh'Ram had taunted him, but the human had persisted in his primitive beliefs. Uh'Ram had come across these priestly types before and had managed to break them. Thankfully, here the human could not call on any primitive spiritual magic to end his own miserable existence, yet neither could Uh'Ram use any magic to torture him or, even worse, heal him. He had to use the simple methods of the flesh. Irritatingly, the human had continued to resist his questioning, and to call incessantly for his pathetic god!

Uh'Ram had to take a deep breath to calm himself.

The air here was foul, but he could now tolerate it. He looked around at the ruins of what had been his ancestral home. It was not a place he would care to return to. The Sylvan elves had seen to that and for their crime he would take all their ancient lands and see them all die painfully. That thought cheered him slightly.

Looking at the Waygate arches, Uh'Ram was amazed that they still stood, seeming as untouched as the day they were crafted, but apparently they had been created with magic that none now understood. Uh'Ram had hurried here as soon as he realised the humans might allude his men. The one place they would have to go was the Waygates and they would not escape him. Now with their escape route safely cut off, Uh'Ram just had to wait. They couldn't elude him forever. However, he did have a tiny nagging worry that they might take the Lifestone and simply cast it into the swamps, but he could not see that they would throw away their greatest and most potent weapon. In the hands of a sylvan elf of sufficient royal blood, the stone could prove a formidable force. No, they would not throw it away. Suddenly, another thought struck him, humans were stupid creatures, perhaps they didn't realise what they had!

Uh'Ram smiled. If they threw it into the swamps he would summon an even greater host when his Lorewise reopened the portal. He would have an entire Warhost searching this cursed place if need be. If it took a century he would find that stone.

Abruptly, his thoughts were disturbed. Someone had called out. He quickly scanned the slopes around him. It hadn't sounded like one of his warriors. He was right. There on the southern lip of the crater-like hole, not far from where he now stood, were three humans!

Already his mayax were skittering across the rubble strewn slopes to reach them.

The voice called out again, this time in Elorien! "Keep your creatures back or you will never see the Lifestone."

Intriguing, Uh'Ram thought, a human who spoke the common elven tongue!

"I mean it. The stone will never be yours." the taller human stated firmly, his voice showing no sign of fear.

Very curious, Uh'Ram thought. He casually signed an order to his Gonhironsar and his order was quickly signalled. A shrill blast stopped the mayax dead in their tracks. The telepathic link his commanders shared with their mayax was disrupted here.

Uh'Ram saw the humans relax, though the one who had spoken changed little. This one could hide his body language and his feelings.

In the glare of the sun on the slopes, Uh'Ram found making out the individual features of the humans difficult. However, they were all armed and armoured, though the smallest one was covered with a long robe that disguised his shape somewhat. One of the humans did not hide anything. This one carried two curved blades and wore plate and chain armour that shone brightly in the sunlight. However, it was the taller one that intrigued Uh'Ram. Something about the way he moved and held himself seemed odd to Uh'Ram. He had a long cloak on and the hood raised. His face was in shadow.

"We have a proposition for you." The hooded human called again. "We will tell you where the Lifestone lies in exchange for our friend and free passage out of here."

Uh'Ram stared at the humans and let the silence build. If he took them now, he might be able to torture the location of the stone out of them. They would not have brought it with them; even humans were not that foolish. However, these humans had already proven unusual, Uh'Ram wasn't sure he could rely on torture to locate the talisman. There was also the chance that if he sent his men now, the humans might escape back into the city. He needed to draw them in, if he was to take them safely.

It occurred to him that they may well keep their word; certainly, the human he had tortured had shown remarkable loyalty. Perhaps they were kin or something. Uh'Ram knew that could sometimes make a slight difference with humans, not much, but some. Perhaps these humans would give up the stone they could not use for a kinsman.

It was a conundrum. Uh'Ram was undecided.

Suddenly, he realised that either way, they would have to come down. Uh'Ram decided he would wait and see what whim took him when the humans came down. Let it be a surprise even to him. He needed the surprise. Life was just starting to get interesting again. It had been so tedious for so long with his plans going so perfectly. A little 'unpredictability' had kept his blood hot recently.

"Agreed," Uh'Ram called. "You may come down and collect your friend."

Bear heard the dark elven leader agree and looked around. Warriors all around the crater had their eyes fixed on them.

"What do we do?" Bear heard Zara mutter out of the side of her mouth.

Bear looked down the slope towards the dark elven forces. Already their leader was gesturing for them to make a gap. The way through was not so difficult, yet it was the hardest thing in the world to get himself to move forward. It was like putting your hand into the fire. You knew what would happen and you knew you shouldn't. Bear steeled himself. They had to go down. They had committed themselves now, there was no choice anymore.

Bear glanced over at Zara and said far more calmly than he felt, "We go down and get Garon."

With that, Bear forced himself to sheath his sword and to take a step... and then another. He felt more than heard his friends follow.

He could hardly breath as he walked. The unreadable, insect faces of the mayax, the ebon, uncouth faces of the black goblins and the handsome, if cruel faces of the dark elves all followed him and his friends. Everything seemed to have stopped; stillness and silence reigned in the devastated bowl of what had been the heart of ancient Hy'Deeria.

Soon they were walking warily between the ranks of warriors. Bear was biting his lip and he had not let go of the handle of his sword. His grip on it was tight! Against his stomach, under the cloak, the Lifestone felt suddenly heavy. He had a sudden feeling that the enemy could see the stone, but pushed it aside. He had to hold his nerve and he couldn't give any indication that he was hiding anything. The dark elves would fall on them instantly if they suspected they had the Lifestone.

They passed the warriors and began the short walk to the arches of the Waygates and the leader of the dark elves. He was an impressive sight. He was clad all in dull red armour worked with elaborate patterns. It was moulded to his body with a combination of superbly made interlocking plate and chain mail, a little like the dwarven-made armour Zara wore. The dark elf carried a short staff at his hip and Bear recognised an elven sabre staff from Tal'Asin's memories. When released a long blade would spring from the shaft of the staff.

Bear switched to examine the creature's face. This elf was no doubt a descendent of the *Ata'Gon*. From Tal'Asin's memories, Bear knew that foul creature's face. It was, surprisingly, a face of extreme beauty. Bear had expected a man so evil to have it show somehow.

The face of this elf before him was also very handsome, but a large, jagged scar across his face marred his looks. Bear could see a slight resemblance to the *Ata'Gon* in this elf's face. As he approached, Bear realised the leader was tall too, just as the *Ata'Gon* and all the elves of the holy line had been. He was as tall as Bear, though slightly built. He reminded Bear of Nat Bero, tall, lean and long limbed. The thought brought the tall huntress' face to mind and Bear wondered what his other friends were doing. They should have warned the college by now.

Bear was brought back to the present as he noticed the leader call forward two of his men. Bear tensed, but the two moved over to Garon and began cutting him down.

Would this work?

Rebba's idea had seemed so ludicrous, but ten minutes after the druid had given it, Bear was still wracking his brains for a better one. He had finally realised that it was their only reasonable chance, if reasonable was the word for such a plan that could go wrong in so many ways.

Their armoured boots clinked as Bear, Zara and Rebba crossed the stone floor. Bear's now acute hearing also began to pick up Zara's voice. She was swearing under her breath, over and over. Bear just hoped that the explosive warrior would be able to contain herself. They needed to time this perfectly. Rebba needed to get to the arch.

All of a sudden, Bear found the dark elven leader in front of him, head tilted, looking completely at ease and apparently puzzled. He was looking at Bear trying to make out his face under the hood.

"Now, be so good as to tell me where the Lifestone is, human." The dark elven lord said, his musical voice even and sedate.

"We will take our friend first." Bear said firmly and gestured to Rebba and Zara.

Out of the corner of his eye, he saw Rebba walk a wide path around the dark elven leader with Zara following her, trying to shield Rebba from the dark elves with her body. Bear hoped the dark elven lord would just take it as fearful humans huddling together, avoiding getting too close.

Rebba suddenly stumbled a little and put her hand out to right herself against the arch Garon had been tied to. Bear twitched! He couldn't help himself. He snapped his eyes back to the elf before him. Thankfully, the foul creature had noticed nothing. Instead he was staring at Bear as if he would look straight through him. Something seemed to be still puzzling the bloody creature! 'Well, at least it will keep him focused on me.' So far no one had noticed that Rebba had activated the arch she had fallen against!

Time seemed to slow. Bear tensed himself, waiting for what he knew would come. However, this time the dark elf lord did spot his reaction. His eyes widened and with snake-like speed, he began pulling his sabre-staff. His mouth opened to call out and Bear did the only thing he could think of; he stepped forward with a speed he didn't know he had and snapped a vicious head butt into the elf's face and felt a satisfying thud as he connected solidly. Rebba, Zara, the elf lord's bodyguards and every warrior around, saw this at the same time.

Bear screamed a warning and Rebba looked back at Bear her eyes wide and horror on her face. It was too soon!

Zara wasted no time and pulled her sabres. The body guards let go of Garon, who dropped like a stone and began pulling their swords. They stood little chance as Zara's blades flicked out and opened their throats.

The elflord reeled back for a second from Bear's surprise attack, then sprang sideways with incredible speed as Bear pulled his sword. Zara turned and Bear noticed her eyes widen. He twisted around, a horde of warriors were hurtling towards them!

"You dare to attack me!" The dark elven lord practically shrieked. "You will regret…"

A burst of crackling energy sprang into being in the archway, cutting short the elf's words. Then a sheet of blue energy boiled out and everything was washed away in a moment of blazing light.

⁓⁂⁓

Rebba reacted instantly. She had been through this enough times now to know what to expect. She let her sense of balance return and then she lunged at the archway. She didn't pay any attention to her new surroundings, she just concentrated on closing the Waygate. She had to stop anyone else coming through. She had a vision of that horde of ferocious dark elves and their allies pouring through the open gateway at any moment.

She scrabbled to get the keystone into the correct niche on the archway. It clicked in place, warmed a little and then dropped back into her hand. As she caught the stone, the blue sheet of energy held for a moment that stretched uncomfortably long and then flickered and… several bodies plunged through. There was a flash, the gateway closed and something crashed to the floor; heavy and flopping. Rebba almost gagged. Two black goblins had been caught as the gate closed and it had sliced them clean in half! One twitched and then both lay still.

Abruptly, Zara whirled across Rebba's line of sight. Two elves had made it through and Zara was on them like a predator. Before they could even catch their balance, Zara sliced the head from one and spitted the other one through.

Where was Bear… and that elflord?

Rebba turned around and noticed Garon lying deathly still on the floor. Beyond that Bear stood. He had his sword out ready for battle. His hood had been blown back and his large eyes were fixed on the dark elven lord not ten paces from him.

The dark elf must have darted away from the Waygate before he even knew where he was. He had his sabre-staff in hand, the blade out and ready. He was still backing away. Rebba thought he must be trying to get a bearing on where he was. A trip through the Waygate was disorientating.

Rebba looked around too. This hall was not one they had been to before. It was very different to any of those. It was far larger. They stood in an immense space and echoes reverberated around the vast hall. The Waygate arches were not the same either, at least not in position. In all the halls they had been in, the arches had been arranged in a large circle in the middle of the hall. Here the arches were spaced out and set in the walls. In the middle, stood two huge monoliths; the Waygate arches were big, but these dwarfed them. They were around fifty feet tall, circular and easily ten feet thick. They were decorated, carved and in relief. They were as far apart as they were tall. Rebba wondered what they could be for.

Apparently, the dark elf did not. He seemed to recognise them and after a momentary start, barked a harsh laugh. "You brought me here, you fools, you…"

The dark elf stopped whatever he was about to say as his eyes settled on Bear. His eyes widened. "You have the Lifestone!" he cried in wonder, obviously now sensing the powerful talisman.

"Yeah and we are keeping it." Zara snarled marching forward, all swagger and confidence. It was just the three of them alone with the dark elf now.

The dark elf pulled his longing eyes from Bear and frowned at Zara. It was clear to Rebba that the creature had understood Zara. It reached up and touched a small jewel on a chain, tight about its neck.

'It's enchanted,' Rebba thought, 'that must be how he understands.'

"Oh are you so very sure of that, human." the dark elf smiled. "Do you even know where you have brought us?"

Zara glanced around the huge hall as she came up alongside Bear. "Makes no difference."

"Oh, but it does, ignorant animal." the dark elf laughed. "You see magic works well here." He paused, lowered his blade and stood completely at ease. "Unlike in Hy'Deeria, where magic is either completely suppressed or else wild and unpredictable, here it is stronger than anywhere else."

He glared at Zara. "You know nothing, human. This is…"

"…Althazar, seat of the Lore Kings of the Sylvan Elves, where you will die!" Bear voice rang out, finishing the elf's sentence.

Immediately, the dark elf roared with rage and with a speed that Rebba thought impossible, he summoned and cast a spell more powerful than any Rebba had ever seen before. Lightning appeared to leap from the dark elf's suddenly outstretched hand. It was a spell Rebba had seen before, but never so potent. It dazzled her senses. With a massive boom of thunder it hammered into Bear and Zara.

Rebba was knocked down by the blast and the bodies of the dead were shoved several feet. Rebba quickly sat up and stared at where her two friends had been. Dust and smoke whirled around for a moment and then cleared. Rebba wasn't sure what she expected to see; charred bodies, smoking fragments, instead she saw Zara and Bear standing unharmed, though Zara had a look that spoke volumes. She was as stunned as Rebba that she was still alive. Surprisingly so was Bear! The look on his face was amazed relief.

For the first time the dark elven lord looked properly at Bear. His coppery brow knit in confusion.

"Who are you?" the bewildered elflord asked, and then, as he looked more intently at Bear's partly elven features, "What are you?"

It was Zara who answered. "We're the ones who are going to kill you, you slanty-eyed freak!" she shouted, even as she dashed forward to attack.

Chapter 58

THE CALM BEFORE THE STORM

Amongst the elves, magic users are known as the Lorewise. However, these Lorewise are not all the same or have the same depth of knowledge and power. The Lorewise are split into 3 distinct groups that do mirror our own to a degree. The first group are the clerics who dedicate themselves to the gods, the second are the Loremasters who dedicate themselves to the understanding of the mysteries, and the third are the Lorewardens who dedicate themselves to using the mysteries in defence of their people.

Extract from 'The Lost Druid Scrolls - Scroll 11' Author unknown. Discovered beneath the Academy of Mikadia, BY1096. Thought to date back a thousand years, these are hotly debated by Imperial scholars as faked to show Nordic civilisation as far older than that of the Olmecs!

High Lord Elgon of Ostia answered the summons quickly and eagerly. It was late, but he would be glad to have some official word on what the hell was going on. He marched down to the great hall thinking furiously. After the council had voted to include the Elder races in their council, rather than ending debate it began it. How many votes would they have? Would they be allowed to vote on all matters or merely matters pertaining to them? What trade would they bring or receive? What forces they had? What about border disputes? Where would the borders be drawn?

It had been day after day of debates. They had debated each minute detail laboriously, mainly due to the Olmec lords and ministers who still did not trust the Elder races. At last, today they had finally come to an agreement and were on the verge of making an historic treaty.

However, adding to the debates had been the events outside the council. They had caused all kinds of consternation. First it had been the murder of the Allseer and the subsequent confinement of the Archmage; Mage Master Shamass had taken over smoothly, but it was worrying. Next, there had been the collapse beneath the college and rumours of evil goings on below ground. The magi had clammed up tighter than an Olmec's purse, but Elgon still had friends at the college and he was disturbed by the rumours of elves killing below the college. These rumours had almost derailed the talks in the council, though Eliantha Shamass had quickly acted to squash such rumours and had pushed on with their talks. As she had pointed out, until firm evidence was forth coming it would be business as usual.

However, Elgon was deeply troubled. He had thrown his support wholeheartedly behind the Archmage and his belief that unity was the way to deal with the goblin threat in the north, but these whispers about elves were alarming, especially if Xameran Uth Altor was to be believed and the elves were in league with the goblins to kill them all. On the other hand, elves and goblins uniting was ridiculous and also Elgon had never really trusted the man, though it seemed that many did for he had called an assembly of masters to discuss it and to decide the fate of the Archmage. It had taken place tonight and Elgon assumed that the summons he had received to meet in the main hall was to discuss what had gone on there. Elgon was keen to find out who was now Archmage; Baden Erin or Xameran Uth Altor! If it was the latter, Elgon feared that all the progress they had made in the council would be undone.

As Elgon hurried down the steps from his personal chamber, he passed through the chambers that were occupied first by his servants and advisors and then through those of his personal guard. Each of the lords was always granted permission to bring along fifty retainers and no more. It had been a condition of the first council in order to stop any lord bringing an army with them to intimidate the other lords of the provinces.

Fifty men would allow the lords to bring sufficient men to guard them on their way to Shandrilos. Elgon had brought thirty of his best men at arms along with half a dozen on his personal gladiatorial guard; his elite. He saw with satisfaction that they were armed and ready. He saw a number of others look at him blearily; it was almost midnight and most had been asleep. Most looked at him in confusion; he could see them wondering what was happening that the High Lord needed all of his guard. Elgon was not sure he did, but he was a careful man. Just an hour ago, Elgon's chief advisor, Surran Kantar had awoken him with the news that something was wrong in the town. Kantar could not say what exactly, but he had heard ridiculous rumours of a goblin army attacking! Elgon was realistic about the chances of that happening, but it was clear something was going on, a riot maybe, that had arisen from the celebrations in town. It had been known to happen in Ostia.

He signalled for his personal bodyguards to flank him and opened the door from the lowest chamber out into the vast great hall of the college.

It was pandemonium!

Already out there were most, if not all, of the lords of the provinces, along with a sizable number of their men at arms. Spattered amongst them were frightened looking magi, college staff and even some townsfolk. It seemed this summons was for all in the college.

Elgon's guards pushed forward opening a path for their lord. Elgon headed for the steps from the central section of the college where he could see a number of the other lords already waiting. As he passed, he heard magi and servants whispering of a horde of people in the college grounds and of some kind of battle going on. Some had it that it was a battle within the college between different factions that had got the townspeople rioting, others had it that the battle was in the town itself and was against goblins, trolls and monsters of all kinds. Elgon shook his head. To think that even these educated men would give credence to such.

He was almost to where the other lords stood clustered around talking, when Elgon saw Baden Erin enter wearing the cloak of the Archmage and carrying the Staff of Melkor. Well, that answered one question. A hush settled on the hall almost immediately. Elgon looked more closely at Baden Erin and realised the man looked somewhat wan and sickly. He was noticeably leaning on his staff. Unusually, only Eliantha Shamass of the Conclave was with him and she looked worse than he did. Bruises showed on her face and she looked to have aged over night. The rest of the people were a small group of fighter magi guard.

A feeling of disquiet stole over Elgon. He signalled for his men to push forward more urgently. He reached the front and moved over to stand by the other lords who were all looking at the pale Archmage with a mixture of surprise and worry. Elgon noticed other figures standing back from the Archmage in the shadows. He wondered if these were some of the other members of the Conclave.

"My fellow lords, magi and servants of the college, I have called you all here to give you terrible news and perhaps to confirm your worst nightmares."

The Archmage's words were greeted with gasps. Elgon heard someone mutter sarcastically about great opening lines.

"I have been advised to not overly alarm you, but I am not sure I can tell you what you need to know without doing just that." the Archmage continued. "All I would ask is that you remain calm and hear me out."

Elgon listened as the Archmage then spoke. He outlined what had happened in the town. Elgon was stunned. It was incredible. An army of at least two thousand goblins and trolls had attacked the town, sinking all the boats in the dock and then driving through the town slaughtering all they caught! If that wasn't bad enough, the college's seers had located three other armies, each of about two thousand or more warriors, advancing on the college from north, south and east. The college was surrounded on all sides by an army of around eight thousand!

The silence in the hall was deathly for several moments and then... calls for 'why' and 'where had they come from' rang out from all corners. The Archmage explained that these goblins and trolls had come through portals created by the powerful elven magi who accompanied them!

There was an instant uproar. It took the Archmage a minute or more to calm the crowd. Elgon kept silent. He was at a loss for words. Had Xameran been right?

The Archmage then explained that the elves that accompanied the armies attacking them were the ancient evil behind the destruction of the Elder kingdoms centuries ago, that they were a race of elves who hated the Sylvan elves of the Wilds and all free peoples. They hated the humans and dwarves for helping the Sylvan elves to defeat them long ago. That was why they had come; to eradicate any chance their enemies might unite against them as they had of old.

Confusion reigned again in the hall. People yelled things, turned to neighbours and argued! Elgon was dismayed. An army was on their doorsteps and the people were arguing! Many of the lords, particularly the warriors amongst them, had looks on their faces similar to the one Elgon knew he had on his.

The Archmage seemed to sense this too. He called for silence and slowly the hall settled.

"Now we have a little time before the enemy is at our walls and we must use that time to organise our defence."

Boras Del Aro of Torunsport called out. "Can we not escape?"

"No, my lord," the Archmage said gravely, "Our cavalry is out, scouting and harrying the enemy, but their noose is complete and tightening."

"Then let us set up talks with them." the obese lord of Torunsport responded.

Elgon snorted out loud, though few heard him. Always the Lord of Torunsport sought a diplomatic way out even when there wasn't one; he believed Borus Del Aro would seek a deal with the Dark Gods themselves if it saved his ample hide.

"My lord of Torunsport, you are welcome to enter into talks with our enemy when they are present at our walls, but for now we must plan a defence in case such talks are impossible or fail." the Archmage replied smoothly.

Elgon silently applauded the Archmage. That would keep the cowardly lord quiet at least for the moment.

"Servants of the college are to report to the chancellor to be assigned tasks." The Archmage then instructed. "I would also ask that my fellow master magi who are here, seek the First Watchmaster and his men in the Lesser Hall. They will assess your strengths and assign you to commanders, tasks or walls to aid in the defence. Also, any adept level magi should report to their given masters to support them in their tasks. The novices will remain in their halls." The Archmage looked across the hall with a commanding stare. "Now!" he called out sternly, "Time is pressing."

There was a burst of chatter and then the servants and magi began pushing through and hurriedly mounting the steps. They filed past the

Archmage and headed through the doors towards the lesser hall at the rear of the main building.

The Archmage waited patiently, seeming to take a moment to close his eyes and rest or think, Elgon couldn't tell which. Finally, all that was left in the hall were the lords of the provinces and their men.

"My lords, I have a request of you all." the Archmage began sadly. He took a deep breath before continuing. "Due to the machinations of Xameran Uth Altor we are ill prepared for an attack and somewhat split. Those divisions must end if we are to defend ourselves. We are just lucky that our Watchmasters have been vigilant." The Archmage paused a moment, his face grave. "We are all in serious danger and we need to defend ourselves together if we are to survive. Unfortunately, this college is not the easiest place to defend. We have walls and a keep, but our walls are too long. We have mobilised all our forces and got volunteers from amongst the townspeople. Shandrilos can field five hundred soldiers plus about an equal amount of armed volunteers. There are also people who have volunteered to be water carriers and stretcher bearers." The Archmage paused again. "I need you and your men." he said earnestly. "Each of you brought a contingent of warriors and if we can combine them we can increase our chance for holding the walls."

"Well it goes without saying that we will aid in the defence, Archmage." Sir Arleas of Karodracia called out. "All of our heads are in the noose. The enemy wants us all dead."

The lords all called out their agreement, Elgon included.

"What do you suggest, Archmage?" Sir Arleas asked.

The Archmage nodded in gratitude to the unanimous response. "I suggest that my warriors take the front wall and gates where the attack will be fiercest. The Nordic towns of Dunegan, Dunard, Arondar, Sironac and Ostia would then unite their warriors to man the north wall under the command of Elgon of Ostia, with Raban Ironhand of Dunegan as his second. This, I estimate would produce a force of around two hundred and fifty. I would add around two hundred armed volunteers and sixty magi to give you a force of around five hundred." The Archmage looked at the lords of the provinces he had named and saw there was no dissent at his proposal so he went on. "I would do the same with the forces of the Olmec towns of Torunsport, Lauria, Karodracia, Katurem and Hadek. Along with the volunteers and magi that would give you around the same number to defend the south wall. I would ask Sir Arleas to take command, seconded by Korlin Di Vorseck of Lauria."

Again this was met with quiet agreement; all knew who the most experienced commanders were. Suddenly a question leapt into Elgon's mind. It must have been echoed in a number of the lords' minds too, though it was Sir Arleas who asked it first.

"Archmage, if you are to defend the western front wall, the Nordic lords, the north wall, we the south, who will defend the eastern wall and the lesser gate at the rear of the college?"

"Yes, we cannot leave it undefended. If one wall falls, all will." The powerfully built Raban Ironhand called out.

From the shadows of the doorway, a musical voice, impossible to mistake replied firmly. "We will hold that wall, my lords."

There were instant frowns of disapproval on the faces of the Olmec lords as the lords of the elves and dwarves stepped into the light of the hall.

Val'Ant the grey maned elflord continued. "As you, Sir Arleas, have pointed out, all our heads are in the noose, we all must defend the walls."

Mutters followed this from the Olmec men, but it was the Nordic lord, Raban Ironhand who replied. "Much as I am impressed with the fighting prowess of both your peoples, my lord, you do not have the numbers to hold that wall. I have counted perhaps fifty of your warriors here in the college."

The grey cloaked Val'Ant looked to the Archmage, and soon all eyes were looking at him.

"Ah, luckily for us all, my lords," the Archmage began a little uncomfortably, "I allowed the lords of the Elder the same rights that you yourselves have. Each lord was allowed to bring up to fifty in their contingent."

Gasps and looks of horror washed across the Olmec lords' faces and Elgon heard Borus Del Aro of Torunsport yell out that the Archmage had let an army of these creatures into the college!

The Archmage shouted over the voices. "It was fair, my lords and, as I have said, fortuitous, for we now have five hundred armed and armoured warriors of the Elder along with almost fifty of their lorewise to aid our defence!"

This brought a little quiet to the lords as the numbers sank in. It would certainly be a huge help. Then Elgon couldn't help himself, he had to ask.

"But where have these elves and dwarves been?"

The Archmage looked at Eliantha Shamass who shrugged and replied. "They are camped in the small woods behind the Mages' tower, by the eastern wall. The elves have long since learnt how to shield their encampments and I have made sure no one goes near them."

The Archmage looked around for a moment, judging the reactions of them all. Most of the lords were not happy, but at least they had a chance now to hold the walls, and they had a purpose. The Archmage seemed satisfied that there were no more immediate questions and then asked for the lords to assemble their warriors and go to their allotted walls. He asked for the chosen second-in-commands to organise the warriors on the wall, while the commanders came with him for a moment or two.

Elgon nodded and quickly told Surran Kantar to assemble his men and take them to the north wall. The other lords moved to their advisors and captains and gave their orders. Elgon then followed the Archmage who was wearily walking to one of the small doors that led to a council room. Sir Arleas and the elflord, Val'Ant also followed. Inside was a long table with a dozen chairs, the Archmage slumped into the nearest, quickly followed by Mage Master Shamass who took the second chair.

Elgon, Sir Arleas and Val'Ant took their seats. It was only then that Elgon noticed the four strangers in the room. They moved forward and sat at the other end of the long table and said nothing. One was tiny, maybe a child, while one was obviously a mage, the third was a dark haired woman who seemed vaguely familiar to Elgon, and the last was the strangest of all. He was completely encased in peculiar black armour, not even a hint of his face could be seen!

The Archmage's voice disturbed his quick study and he looked to the exhausted Baden Erin.

"I have been grievously distracted by the enemy. I was misled and deceived by those I thought were trustworthy and it has cost us dearly."

Elgon wasn't sure he knew what the Archmage was talking about.

"Earlier tonight, we had an assembly of masters. I was stripped of my title of Archmage."

Elgon was caught unprepared and simply stared at Baden Erin, while Sir Arleas gasped in surprise.

"Xameran Uth Altor was elected Archmage. However, we were horribly deceived by him. Xameran has been working for the enemy for some time. He was no doubt charged with disrupting our defence and our alliance with the Elder races. He almost succeeded."

Elgon didn't know what to say; a traitor in their midst!

"It seems the enemy planned long and well. I have no doubt that the dark elven leader outside knows our strengths and weaknesses. What he hopefully doesn't know just yet is that his spies have failed."

"Spies!" Sir Arleas exclaimed. "There was more than one."

"Yes, Xameran persuaded many to his side, though I doubt they knew the full extent of his alliances. After the assembly though, his perfidy was brought to light and a battle ensued."

"You killed the villains," Sir Arleas stated more than asked. The answer seemed obvious, the Archmage was here.

"No, in fact they would have slain me if it were not for our friends over here." He pointed at the four strangers at the other end of the table. "It was they who slew Xameran and the demon that was aiding him!"

"Demon!" Sir Arleas exclaimed again.

The knight was practically reeling. Elgon was struggling too; spies and now a real servant of darkness, here, in the college.

"Yes, that demon brutally killed the rest of the conclave who were trapped in there with it. They fought it, but alas the Magus General, First Wizard, Chief Druid and Abbess were all slain."

"Good god," Sir Arleas whispered in horror.

"What of the High Enchanter?" Elgon asked, though he felt he knew the answer. Atholl Dorard had been a staunch ally of Xameran.

"Another traitor," the Archmage confirmed bitterly. "He was defeated by Eliantha, but then fled. We know not where."

Elgon looked over at the four strangers. These people had defeated a demon and mage who had almost slain the entire conclave; the most powerful practitioners of the unseen arts in the college! It didn't seem credible.

The Archmage must have noticed Elgon's scrutiny.

"May I present the gnome, Nossi Bee, Master Arkadi Talcost, Nat Bero and Sir Darin of Kenarth."

A gnome! Elgon had heard strange rumours of such a creature. The master mage Elgon now recognised from when he had been a youth at court, so too the tall huntress, Nat Bero. Indeed the Archmage had asked him about her yesterday, but the last one gave Elgon a feeling of disquiet.

He just sat there. Elgon recognised the name, he too had been taught as a youth in Ostia and Kenarth was one of his liege lords. His son was acknowledged as a master swordsman.

The others all acknowledged the Archmage's introduction, but the last one had no way to even see in that armour.

Sir Arleas interrupted his thoughts, "Sir Darin of Kenarth?" he said puzzled. "I know that name. Sir Darin is one of my finest swordsmen." He looked to the man in the black armour. "Is that you, Sir Darin?"

Abruptly, the featureless helm seemed to bleed away and a handsome man's face was revealed.

"It is Grandmaster." he said in a flat voice.

Elgon and Sir Arleas gasped simultaneously. The armour was obviously powerfully enchanted. Sir Arleas was about to ask something more, but the Archmage touched him on the arm and then spoke.

"We have no time to really talk, my lord. We must discuss the defence."

Sir Arleas frowned. He was obviously as intrigued as Elgon at this magical armour and how this strange quartet had saved the Archmage and Mage Master, but the old, wand thin knight reluctantly nodded his agreement.

"Go on, Archmage, I will hold my questions, though the number of them is rapidly mounting."

The Archmage gave a brief smile. "My friends, I have not gone into detail about all that has gone on, but I must add more about the enemy we face. Both you, Sir Arleas and you, Elgon were at the Battle of Ostia, thirty years ago, and though you were young, you have experience of fighting goblins. However, this army of goblins is not like any we have faced in the Wildlands before. These goblins have been armed and armoured by their dark elven masters, they are commanded and bound to stricter discipline by their commanders. They will not break easily…"

"Then we target their commanders and break their hold, then the goblins discipline will fail." Sir Arleas growled.

"Yes, indeed, my lord," the Archmage agreed, "but there is more. This army has almost a thousand trolls at its heart, split between the four armies. They are not the common trolls of the hills and forests of the Wildlands that we are used to, they are bigger, stronger and well armed and armoured."

"Rock trolls," Val'Ant said quietly, "they are from the far north and are formidable enemies. They are more cunning than their southern kin."

All looked at the ghostly elflord.

"We must not allow them to gain the wall. They are poor climbers and we should concentrate our attacks on them, more even than the dark elves." the elflord insisted.

Elgon looked to Sir Arleas and the Archmage. They looked grim. Any optimism they had gained from uniting their forces was evaporating. It had seemed to Elgon, and no doubt to Sir Arleas too, that with almost two thousand men along with over two hundred magi that they had a good chance of holding the goblins out, even against odds of four or five to one. Now it was looking less certain.

"Also, I am afraid, the dark elves have brought around a thousand or their own creatures and warriors, amongst them are several hundred insect creatures that Master Talcost tells me move with incredible speed and show no fear at all, and, even worse, there are creatures known as ogres. These creatures are even bigger than the rock trolls and highly disciplined."

"Bigger than the rock trolls!" Elgon exclaimed.

"So we must plan for the possibility that we cannot hold the walls." the Archmage warned.

Elgon was finding he had an almost limitless ability to be stunned tonight.

"I will have seers assigned to all of you with a magical horn that will give a blast that can be heard for miles. If any of you are forced to give up your wall, you must have the horn blown and the seer communicate with the rest of us. We will all withdraw at once to the Black Hall of the college. Its walls are made of a magically resistant rock that is harder than steel. Once inside we can seal the doors and hold there. They will find it costly trying to take us in there." the Archmage said fiercely.

"Yes and we will find it costly abandoning the walls. A retreat to the Black Hall will be hazardous and chaotic. We will lose a lot of men." Sir Arleas cautioned.

The Archmage nodded.

"Then we must not lose a wall, my lords." Val'Ant of the Suthantar elves said resolutely.

The Archmage closed his eyes as if in prayer and then asked them all to see to the organisation and defence.

Elgon left less confused than he had been earlier, but far more alarmed. His worst nightmares had been realised, and to think he had scoffed at those people who had talked of a goblin army!

⌒〟⌒

Arkadi Talcost sat quietly for a moment after the lords had left. The Archmage then stood and looked at all of them in turn.

"I must thank you all again for your aid and for saving our lives. I would enquire more of you, Sir Darin and that armour, but for the moment other things are pressing and I must see to the defence." He looked terribly tired. "I would suggest you get some rest. Tomorrow is going to be a... difficult day." he finished with a sad look.

Eliantha followed the Archmage as he left. Arkadi and his friends sat in mute exhaustion.

"It is a good idea," Darin said, "You should all sleep."

"And what of you, Darin?" Arkadi asked, "Will you not rest?"

"It seems I have little need of rest now." he replied without emotion.

Arkadi had noticed that Darin showed almost no emotion now. He had been almost mute this last hour or so since the battle against the demon.

"Darin what has happened to you?" Nat asked, "You are about as animated and bright as that armour you're wearing."

Darin ignored her, but it was true. Perhaps the strain of controlling the armour was telling on Darin, Arkadi thought worriedly.

Darin had related to them about his ordeal, trapped underground and dying, and then of the strange battle he'd had with the armour. Darin had realised it had been in his mind, but he had awoken in the armour in the Cleric's Dome. He had told them that in his head the voices of the armour and its previous occupants had told him that it was the armour of a Lord Champion of the legendary Rainbow Guard. Arkadi was inclined to believe this and not put it down to some delusion on Darin's part. He knew a little of the legends of the Rainbow Guard and knew it had powerful magic that must have been induced by Darin touching the armour in the darkness. Somehow the armour possessed some sentience and had sensed Darin's need. It was powerful magic, unknown in the world today. However, it was still unclear to Arkadi whether the armour was a blessing or a curse. Darin had become a truly awesome warrior, something they needed right now, but Darin had told them how the armour kept trying to take over and how it desired to fight and kill constantly. Darin had said his mind was now filled with images of violence. Every time he looked at someone, the armour wanted him to kill them, it whispered incessantly that they were evil and needed to be killed. It was worrying. Darin had only been able to act when the armour had sensed the demon in the college. Such a powerful evil that both the armour and Darin could agree on, had allowed them to act. Currently, it seemed that Darin had control of the amour, but for how long was what worried Arkadi. If Darin lost control he could turn on anyone!

Darin had decided that because he had not lost his battle with the armour that it had not gained control over him. However, because he hadn't exactly defeated the armour he could not control it either. However, he was sure that he would not become a danger because if they both did not agree the armour would freeze and neither would be able to act as had been the case at first in the Clerics Dome.

Arkadi was not convinced. Darin had managed to keep control of the armour for the moment with the promise of battle against the evil army that was about to attack the college. Apparently, the promise of shedding the blood of trolls, goblins and dark elves had sated it thirst for violence… at least for the moment.

"Perhaps we should go to the Clerics Dome and rest up there and maybe get some more healing for Nossi and me." Nat suggested.

"Yes, it will be a difficult defence tomorrow!" Arkadi muttered. He was not looking forward to the battle, but he would stand on the wall and defend his home.

"Not for me, it won't." Nat replied. "I plan to keep my head down and out of this battle unless I can't avoid it."

Arkadi looked at the tall huntress in shock. "You won't fight!"

"I'm no hero Arkadi. I am not even a soldier, neither is Nossi. I want us to get out of this alive and I've been through enough fighting in the last few days to last me a lifetime." Nat asserted firmly.

"But we are all in danger." Arkadi shouted indignantly, "You can fight better than most on that wall! There are men and boys up there who have never even handled a weapon and you are a master archer. You could make a major difference in holding the wall!"

Nat's eyes flashed. "I am not a soldier; I am not made for wars and battles, Arkadi. I have barely survived up until now. That wall is a death trap for me. I have no magic to protect me, no real skills with a sword. Yes, there will be those with less skill than me and they will be the first ones to fall." Nat continued. "I know enough about battles to know that. Once the trolls reach the wall, my arrows will mean nothing and I don't have the sword skills to fight against creatures like that." She shook her head vehemently. "No! I will stay here and do what I can, but when the time comes, I'll head to the Black Hall or out any way I can!"

"You coward!" Arkadi spat.

Before Nat could interrupt, Nossi leapt in front of her and yelled, "No, she's not. She came for me and saved me when no one else would. She fought the big vile man and the little assassin." The earnest gnome's face was taut with passion. "She is brave and good!" the gnome asserted fiercely.

A hand fell on Arkadi's shoulder. Darin stood looking down at him, his face pale. "Don't be too quick to judge. You have not fought in a major battle, Arkadi. It is not something you should force on another."

As the dark clad knight spoke, Arkadi got the impression that Darin's words were at odds with his true feelings. He got the distinct feeling that Darin was eager to fight. He had the look of a coiled spring.

There was silence.

Nat looked sadly at Darin and the gnome and then at Arkadi. "Look, Arkadi, maybe I am a coward. The thought of going up on that wall terrifies me and if there is any way I can avoid it, I will. It is just not what I am suited to. Give me a forest and an enemy to hunt and I'll be there, but this... I'm sorry. I need to survive, to get home." Nat's dark eyes looked pleadingly at Arkadi for understanding. "I need to see my children. I have been away for weeks and.."

Suddenly all the air seemed to come out of the huntress and she collapsed to a chair, put her head in her hands and began to sob, her body shuddering. Arkadi felt shame rise up in him. He had not thought what it must be like for her. None of the rest of them had children.

Nat looked up, her eyes red rimmed, her face wet. "This is probably pointless anyway; the battle is likely to find us all eventually, but I miss them." She paused, "Over the last few days I have nearly died more times than I can recall. I can't take anymore. I want to see my children, to hug them, to tell them I love them. I haven't seen them in weeks. I've tried not to think too much of them, but I... my parents look after them well, but I should be with them, not here pretending I'm something I'm not!"

Arkadi felt deeply ashamed. He did not have children, did not know what it was like, but he knew it must be terrible being away for so long. He nodded and laid a reassuring hand on Nat's arm.

"Look I am tired and hurting... and confused. I need rest."Arkadi grimaced. He too was afraid but he didn't say it. He knew Nat was no coward and regretted his words. "I am sorry, Nat. I don't want to fight either, but this is my home. I have friends here..." he trailed off. He wanted Nat to stand with him, but he couldn't really force his friend to face death on that wall, just to help bolster his courage.

Nat nodded solemnly. "I understand. This is your home." The tall huntress wiped her eyes, stood and moved over to the door. She smiled wanly, "Let's go to the Clerics Dome. I am stiff as a board and parts of me are starting to throb that really shouldn't throb!"

Chapter 59

THE STORM STRIKES

> *When Earondar Greatheart recovered the lost Sword of Ice, he set about forming his famed Rainbow Guard. The Guard was formed of the greatest warriors of the age and was split into seven orders, each led by a Lord Champion and each with its own colour and purpose. The Golden Order was charged with bringing justice to all, while the White Order was charged with protecting the weak. However, the most feared was the Black Order. This order was charged with hunting down evil and those who practised the black arts.*
>
> From 'A collection of Folktales' by Rogarin Draghar, Bard to the King of Tutonia, BY1107

Arkadi awoke in his own bed in the tower of the Magi. The sky outside his small window was starting to lighten. There was something important about that fact, though he couldn't remember what it was. He was groggy and not sure how he had got there. He sat up, pulled his robes on over his heard and walked barefoot on the cold stone floor into his new main room. It was only when he saw Darin in his jet black armour, standing rigid and still by the wall that it all came flooding back to him.

They had all gone to the Clerics Dome and had found it chaos. There were townspeople on the lawns, some setting up fires, blankets and tents while others were filing into the Black Hall itself, looking forlorn, lost or horrified. It was frightening to see the scale of the danger in its starkness. Thousands had fled the town. Inside the Dome, the place was packed with the injured and infirm, and monks hurried to and fro. Arkadi had seen Grand Abbot Alinus directing his monks and some warrior monks, but it was a little woman in the robes of an apothecary who had seemed to be in charge. She had been busily ordering people around, organising and tending to the hurt. Nat and Nossi had quickly found monks to see to them and were offered a place to rest. Nat had recovered her quiver and bow and Arkadi had said again that her bow would be welcomed on the walls for the defence, even if just for a while. Nat had just stared hard at Arkadi and then shook her head. She was obviously adamant about avoiding the battle and Arkadi really couldn't blame her.

As for getting a bed and some rest, the little woman who seemed in charge had quickly made it clear that Arkadi and Darin were well enough that they didn't need beds and could sleep elsewhere or help. They had made a quick getaway, leaving Nat and Nossi to rest. It was then that Arkadi remembered his new rooms in the Mages' tower and he had taken the silent Darin there. Arkadi had collapsed soon after in exhaustion.

It had been difficult to get to sleep at first, too much was rushing through his thoughts, but eventually he had fallen into a deep sleep. His body had obviously needed it.

Arkadi now stood in his new rooms with the sunlight streaming in through his small glass window. The events and confusion of last night, and the lethargy of deep sleep were passing. He realised with shock that the goblin army would be in place by now!

Arkadi rushed around gathering his clothes; some light armour and his grey master's cloak, along with his staff. He then rushed off with Darin a black shadow at his back.

⁓⁓⁓

When they finally reached the walls, they were choked with men wearing the circle and hand tabard of Shandrilos. All were hard eyed and staring out over the walls. The gloom was starting to retreat as the sun rose above the hills and slowly the enemy was becoming clearer.

Arkadi led Darin along the wall and up the winding stairs then out on to the roof battlements of the keep. The keep was where the Shandrilosi guard and fighter magi were quartered in normal times. These were anything but normal.

Arkadi quickly headed over to where the Archmage and his personal guard stood. Eliantha Shamass was there at the Archmage's shoulder as usual and the Watchmasters were all there too, along with some of the senior grandmasters who were no doubt filling in for the decimated Conclave. The grandmasters were just moving off as Arkadi and Darin arrived.

The Archmage saw them and nodded companionably. He noticed Arkadi's eyes on the grandmasters and said conspiratorially, "I think even the former supporters of Xameran now believe I did not arrange things in the hall of the assembly. I find that rumours will start regardless of what I do, but the idea that people think I would murder my friends and colleagues is very alarming." He shrugged a little bitterly and turned to look out over the walls. "I see that you took my advice and got some rest. That is good. Eliantha and I have split the night, resting as one leads and vice versa. I must say I don't think I could have got through tonight if it wasn't for her." He smiled at the Mage Master who looked very embarrassed and hastily made some excuse to leave. "She is still so shy," he whispered gently, watching her go.

Arkadi nodded, "Yes, but a formidable woman. I would not want to face her anger. I saw how she almost blasted Atholl Dorard apart!"

The Archmage frowned, and his dark eyes flashed beneath his lowered brow at the mention of the High Enchanter. "Yes, we will have to keep an eye out for Atholl."

The sun had fully crested the hills behind them now and the town in front was starting to become clear. Arkadi watched as the light moved across the town, washing over house after house as the sun rose higher. There was not a cloud in the sky, the day would be fine. Arkadi prepared himself for the view below and leaned further out to see down to the streets below.

When the street became clear, Arkadi could see a seething mass of hideous looking goblins opposite the walls, just out of bowshot. Behind them, Arkadi could see the dark elven leader surrounded by his own people; black goblins, ogres and mayax. Once there had been houses where the enemy now stood, but they had obviously been ripped down in the night to provide space and building materials. The enemy had been active. The timbers from the houses had been used to construct ladders and towers, along with a battering ram.

"So we come to it, then, Master Talcost, we face the agents of evil and I am damned if I will give them my college!" the Archmage spat angrily. "I have spent twenty years building this college up, my father spent his life! I will not see any goblins, troll or even elves destroy what we have built here!"

Arkadi found himself looking at the Archmage in a new light today. This was not just some academic suited to study and administration; this was a man who would fight, a man of passion. It might not always burn so obviously, but burn it did.

"I have no desire to fight in this battle, my lord Archmage, but these foul creatures are responsible for the deaths of my friends and I will do my part to make them pay." He thought of Nat, down in the Clerics Dome as he said this. The archer would not fight in this battle, but she was not a coward. Arkadi wondered whether in her place, he would not already have tried to get out and off the island, back to be with his family. He could also see that the huntress was not made to fight battles. He was not sure any of them were, save perhaps Darin. It struck him then that Bear and Zara would have thrived here too, but this did nothing to ease his own fears.

"You friends will be remembered, Master Talcost, "the Archmage said seeming to read his last thought. "Their sacrifice allowed you to escape the catacombs and eventually alert us all of the true danger. We would not be here now if it weren't for you, and for them. Already the deeds of you and your friends are being spoken of; people take heart at what you have done against incredible odds."

Arkadi shook his head, "The others deserve the credit, but I do not. I was completely taken in by Xameran. I made a fool of myself and of the memory of the others."

"You are too hard on yourself, Master Talcost. You were not the only one taken in by that man."

The Archmage seemed to see that Arkadi was not convinced. He changed the topic.

"We should celebrate the lives of those you have lost, Master Talcost. Tell me about them."

Arkadi nodded and began to talk of Bear, Rebba, Zara and Garon… he felt strange talking about his friends. He caught himself talking in the present as if they were still alive and he found it painful correcting himself. It brought home how mortal they all were.

"Your friends sound like good people, Master Talcost. What do you say we…" the Archmage began. He didn't finish as something caught his eye. "What is the fool doing?" the Archmage stormed. He turned and shouted to a guard captain nearby. "Get some magi over there quickly, give him some cover."

Arkadi looked where the Archmage had and saw, about fifty yards away, a hugely fat man on the tower above the main gates. He thought he heard someone mutter something about the man making a 'really' bit target.

Suddenly the large man's voice boomed out.

"I wish to speak to your leader. I wish to discuss peace between our peoples."

Arkadi heard the Archmage curse. "I thought he had forgotten this stupid desire to talk to them!"

"Who? Arkadi asked.

"Boras Del Aro, First Minister of Torunsport."

Magi were now hurrying across the roof of the keep and down the steps to get onto the walls. Someone yelled and pointed to the enemy forces below. Arkadi looked over. Someone was coming forward; a dark elf in deep black armour along with two in dark robes.

"It is one of their leaders and he is accompanied by two of their magi," Arkadi muttered.

The Archmage looked over too. "Are you sure Master Talcost?"

"Yes, they are just like the ones we battled underground."

The Archmage turned and yelled for the magi who had just emerged on the wall heading for the gate tower, to hurry.

A voice boomed forth, enhanced by magic. "I am Nar'Dolth, Senior Parinsar to His Highness, Prince Uh'Ram Ath Arengvar Dar Uldara."

"That's a mouthful." Arkadi couldn't help muttering.

"Prince Uh'Ram has charged me with destroying you all."

Everyone jerked back as bolts of blue-white lighting crackled forth from the black robbed dark elves and slammed into the gate tower which vanished in an explosive blast of masonry and rubble. Dust swirled.

When it cleared the gate tower battlements were smashed and laid open to clear vision. Charred remains of maybe a dozen people smoldered there.

Sudden screams of challenge burst from thousands of throats as the goblins gave vent to their primal battle lusts. They charged forward in wild abandon. Shandrilosi officers on the wall called for archers to fire and arrows whistled down like rain. Arkadi saw goblins fall by the score, but the dark elven mages had a shield in place and none touched them or their commander. More fire blasted from their outstretched hands and raked the walls. However, the college magi were ready this time and blazing blue shields quickly flashed into place along the wall deflecting the fire. The leader seemed satisfied and turned to return to his former position. Goblins hurtled past him, intent on carrying their ladder to the wall and killing humans!

"I guess that means they don't want to talk," Arkadi called over the din.

Arkadi stuck close to the Archmage within his shield of warriors. He had never been in a major battle before, only skirmishes, and found it sheer madness. They were on the main walls now. The Archmage had insisted on meeting the goblins head on. The goblins themselves had taken heavy losses getting to the wall and even more trying to scale their ladders, but there were so many of them that they were still reaching the battlements with a worrying regularity.

Warriors hacked and slashed at them, there were screams and shouts and piteous cries for help and mercy. There was movement everywhere; fighting, falling, fleeing. Arkadi was glad he was relatively safe within a ring of fighter magi and guards. He had spells ready, and would send one off to blast a goblin now and again, but he was loath to enter the fray alone. The wall was a scene of utter madness. No one would relish being there; no one save Darin, Arkadi corrected.

The tall knight's face had again been submerged into the jet armour as soon as the enemy had reached the wall. He had then leapt ahead of the Archmage and his guards and ploughed into the goblins like a scythe. He cut through them as if they weren't there. He was like the angel of death the Albans believed in, come to earth to smite evil doers!

Arkadi was not even sure now where the black clad knight had gone. He had forged on ahead.

"The trolls have reached the gate, sir!" A guard captain called from ahead. "They are ramming the gates."

The Archmage nodded and signed to one of his seers nearby. "Send a message to Grandmaster Tyon to take his druids and reinforce the gates." To the other seer he asked, "Have the other walls been assaulted?"

The seer nodded, "All walls are under attack and so far hold well, my lord."

The battle raged on and Arkadi became inured to it. Soon the bloody scenes he was seeing became normal to him and he found himself more detached from what was going on and able to think more clearly. Arkadi was not sure if it was good to become like this or not, but he did begin to worry about those trolls and the gate.

"My lord," he shouted to the Archmage, "if the gates fall before we have had time to retreat from the walls we will be trapped on them. We won't be able to reach the Black Hall."

The Archmage sent a bolt of fiery energy to blast a goblin from the wall and then turned and nodded to Arkadi. Somewhat breathlessly, he said, "Yes, it is vital we know when that will happen so that we can abandon the wall, but don't worry just yet Master Talcost, the druids will hold a while and we must take as heavy a toll on these filthy beasts before that happens."

Arkadi nodded, but the idea still worried him. Perhaps this was the way a commander felt in battle. He decided command and responsibility were perhaps not so easy; perhaps such was not for him.

"My lord!" one of the seers cried out urgently. "Master Machlin reports that the attack on the north wall is fierce, but that they hold well. However, Master Opin reports that the south wall is under grave pressure. The volunteers are fleeing the wall and the rock trolls are coming up the walls. They call for aid!"

Suddenly, near the gates there was a cheer and Arkadi moved over to the wall to see what was going on. The magi attacking the trolls and the battering rams had broken through the dark elven magi's spell screen. Arkadi watched as men then came forward and released boulders, boiling water and burning oil down on the trolls below.

"Sir, if we send the magi on the gate tower to help repulse the trolls on the south wall and then return it will make little difference to our defence.

They are no longer needed against the battering ram. The dark elven magi have given up." Arkadi shouted to the Archmage.

"That is because their magi are mainly exhausted from the effort of teleporting their army here." the Archmage replied. He stopped, leaned on his staff for a moment and then nodded. "You are right though." He turned and issued the order through his seer to the seer on the gate tower.

Arkadi watched and quickly he saw, in small groups and ones and twos, the magi disappear from the gate tower.

Elgon of Ostia led another charge along the north wall. He and his men fought savagely. Goblins were cut down, smashed, bashed or thrown over the walls to plummet to their deaths. The defence was going well so far. The goblins were being cut down at a ratio of over ten to every one man he lost. However, things had not all gone smoothly, Elgon had nearly lost his volunteers when the trolls attacked, but he had seen their advance early and had been able to bombard them with arrows as they came. He had sent his volunteers to every ladder the trolls began to climb. It had nearly stopped the trolls making the walls. However, Raban Ironhand had then led a vicious assault against those that made the wall backing up the volunteers and giving them a point to which to rally. The big brutes had crushed men with their huge hammers, maces and warclubs, but they had been dealt with. Volunteers had been killed in their droves, but those who had survived were all the more determined for their victory. Nevertheless, the concentration on the trolls had almost allowed the goblins to swamp them. It was only the heroics of the young giant High Lord Wolfstan of Arondar who had led his men on a mad charge along the wall that had saved them. High Lord Tarik had been killed trying to emulate him, but by then Elgon had been able to rally a company of men and lead a charge.

The battle swept back from him and he found himself close to Raban Ironhand who was smiling as blood, mostly not his own, dripped down his head. He looked every inch the Nordic barbarian from his metal studded conical helm to his tall, bearskin boots, reinforced with steel bands.

"The gods smile on us, Elgon. The fight goes well," roared the burly warrior lord.

"Yes, but can it keep going so well." Elgon asked in reply.

"Ah, the gods love us, Elgon. Why else would they give us the chance of such glory? If I die here I shall go to Stoba Kor and sit within the Hall of Heroes at the right hand of Tynast himself!"

Elgon had always believed in the gods, but looking at Raban Ironhand and his joy at the thought of a potentially painful death only made him think how strange his people were. Still he would rather have a man like Raban Ironhand with him in the midst of a battle than any Olmec any day.

Sir Arleas felt the goblin's scimitar bang off his thick plate mail. He slammed his shield into its face as he deftly sliced its partner's throat and then turned, parried and thrust his blade through the goblin's gut. It shrieked shrilly, but Sir Arleas calmly shouldered it back and pulled his blade out. It fell back, gurgling now, and collapsed. Sir Arleas did not spare it another glance. Instead he looked along the wall anxiously.

Up ahead, a group of trolls had made it to the wall and were holding men off while others climbed up behind them.

"Di Vorseck!" he shouted, "Get more men up here, quickly!"

He then turned to his own knights and shouted, "Kill the trolls!"

His men roared in reply.

"Ready men... With me... CHARGE!"

He ran forward, his knights at his back and leapt at the nearest troll. His sword bit deep and the troll roared and swung its huge mace at his head. He ducked and let his sword meet the trolls arm at the wrist on its back swing. Its hand flew off with the mace and Sir Arleas then cut down the enraged behemoth with savage, lightning fast slashes. He turned to find another foe and found his men all around him, hacking into the trolls with lethal affect. However, they were only just beginning to turn the trolls back. They needed more men. Di Vorseck had sent two of his captains to rally the volunteers who had fled, but without support Sir Arleas' knights would not be able to push the trolls from the wall.

Suddenly, magi began popping out of thin air along the wall. They quickly sighted on the trolls and began their spell casting.

Sir Arleas bellowed for his men to disengage and with practised discipline they sprang back as one from the trolls. Within a second, the first blasts of energy, lightning bolts and fireballs began flying at the trolls.

Sir Arleas retreated and found Di Vorseck. It seemed most of the volunteers had begun to return to the fight and Di Vorseck was congratulating his captains.

"We were lucky. Another attack like that and we won't have the men to hold." Sir Arleas said honestly. "We lost a lot of men trying to hold without the volunteers and against the trolls." Sir Arleas looked at the volunteers nearest with clear disapproval.

"You must keep such feelings to yourself, Sir Arleas, we need these men and you are not inspiring them." Korlin Di Vorseck cautioned.

"I wasn't trying to!" he snarled. He expected men to show some courage and duty.

"You are too used to living the life of a knight, my lord. You have forgotten what it is to be an ordinary person. Just as you are not used to facing a field that needs weeding or goods that need selling, they are not used to standing on a wall fighting creatures from their worst nightmares!" Di Vorseck said harshly. "Don't be so quick to judge them ill."

Sir Arleas had no time to answer. He had seen another breach forming. As he ran with his men to plug the gap, he conceded the forthright First Minister might have a point. However, he certainly would know where to start with a field full of weeds. You cut them down one at a time if need be, just like the good prophet Alba taught. Looking ahead at the goblins battling the men from Hadek, Sir Arleas went to cut down some weeds!

Arkadi Talcost was filled with renewed vigour as the men of Shandrilos again threw back the trolls from the walls. By Arkadi's estimation they had almost killed all the trolls in the dark elven attack. The battering ram still lay where it had fallen. No one was getting through that gate and Arkadi dared to think they might even win this battle.

Suddenly, there was a mighty roar from below that turned his head that way. More goblins and trolls poured from between the houses and ran to the walls. Arkadi stared in utter dismay. Ishara! How many of these creatures were there? Arkadi's eyes were suddenly drawn to the dark elven leader. He was gesturing at his own troops. Damnation, Arkadi thought, even if they defeated the goblins and trolls, there was still the dark elves and their fell creatures to deal with! Despair settled on him like a cloak.

From the dark elven forces, Arkadi saw the ogres break ranks and move forward to form into a solid, massive phalanx of around fifty. The ogres then began a steady march to the wall. Dark elven magi moved up to flank them. What were they up to?

The answer soon became clear as they headed for the gate. The ogres, suddenly covered by a blazing energy barrier, quickly took up the battering ram and easily ran forward with it. They hammered with incredible force into the gates. The noise was loud enough to hear even over the war cries and screams. Arkadi panicked for a moment. The ogres would break down the gates! He turned searching for the Archmage who stood not far away directing men and magi.

"Archmage, we must retreat now. The ogres will break down the gates!"

"Calm yourself, Master Talcost, the gates will hold. We must see to holding off this new wave of attackers. We cannot give up the walls yet." the Archmage said firmly.

"But if the gate falls…"

"I know very well what will happen, Master Talcost, but I cannot send men down from the wall until this attack is repulsed. I need all the men I have to do that." He looked at Arkadi fiercely. "The gates will hold!"

Looking into the Archmage's dark eyes, Arkadi knew he would not convince him, but perhaps he was right. They could not spare men with these fresh trolls and goblins coming at them. However, Arkadi knew enough to realise it was a gamble, one that couldn't be avoided, but one that could prove very costly indeed if it didn't work.

"Are there no other men, Archmage?" Arkadi asked.

The Archmage just shook his head and returned to directing his troops.

For a moment Arkadi considered going down and finding Nossi and Nat. They had been right to stay away from the wall. Nossi in particular would be completely out of place in the battle. Thinking about the gnome and how unsuited and naïve he would be, turned Arkadi's mind to his own students he had been teaching less than a week ago. The Archmage had been right to protect them from this… and yet… A thought occurred to Arkadi. He cast it aside. It was not fair and yet… if the wall fell and the enemy reached the Black Hall…

Abruptly, he turned and headed for the steps down to the lawns.

Minutes later Arkadi was pushing through the throngs of people who were still going into the Black Hall. Arkadi could not believe that people had stayed out on the lawns so long. The Archmage had ordered the entire town's people to move into the Black Hall hours ago. They had to get in. If the warriors on any of the walls failed, they would not be able to stop to defend these people, they would get slaughtered. Still Arkadi couldn't think about that. He roughly pushed his way through the mass of people in the main hall. None of the town's people were to stop there. They were to leave it free for the retreating warriors to hold. This was the same for the lesser hall at the rear of the Black Hall. He got nasty looks as he pushed through, but people generally moved aside once they saw he was a mage.

In the hall ways, stairwells and corridors, people had camped out and Arkadi ground his teeth in frustration as he was forced to hop and dodge through them. He hoped the gates would hold.

Roslyn Shanford looked out of the Clerics Dome through the main door. She could see that the town's people had still not all got into the huge Black Hall. She growled angrily then turned and headed back into the teeming dome.

"We can wait no longer, Miss Bero." She said to the tall huntress who was now acting as her aide. "We must start moving the sick into the Black Hall or they will be trapped here.

The tall, dark haired woman looked solemnly down at her and nodded. She was over a foot taller than Roslyn. The woman had obviously been through some troubles, but she had happily agreed to help this morning. She was one of the only young and able bodied people who was not committed to the defence. Roslyn needed someone who could get the heavier tasks done and restrain the injured that were overcome with pain. The woman was strong and capable, and had obviously been a hunter or some such. She had helped, though it was obvious that she was distracted; she had confided that she was worried about her friends and her family. Nevertheless, she had been invaluable to Roslyn. Also, a surprising bonus had been the strange little man, Nossi Bee. It seemed he knew some healing magic and was also willing to help with all the menial tasks.

"I will let the Grand Abbot know," the tall huntress acknowledged her orders. "His monks will take the people across and his warrior monks will remain here to the end."

Roslyn nodded, though she was not really listening. Already she was thinking about organising the people into groups depending on their mobility and where she would get stretchers or what she could make them from for those who could not walk. It was several seconds before she realised Miss Bero had gone. She looked over and saw her talking to the thin, old Grand Abbot. Roslyn smiled looking at the head of the Sironacian order, he reminded her of her grandfather; the same quiet wisdom and dignity. However, the Grand Abbot had a steely strength to him that her grandfather had not. Roslyn had no doubt the Grand Abbot was a formidable man and her senses told her he was a prodigious magic user.

Roslyn busied herself with getting her assistants to help organise the groups of injured the way she wanted them, but it was slow and difficult. She saw a stretcher bearer bring in another wounded soldier and marched over to them. "You have been told, any injured men are to be taken straight to the upper hall of the Black Hall… you know that big, black thing over there!" she pointed angrily.

The men looked at her in surprise. "Sorry," they mumbled.

Roslyn instantly regretted her outburst and said, "No, I am sorry. I didn't mean to snap your heads off, but could you make sure you tell whoever is in charge. We are starting to move everyone to the Black Hall in case the defence of the wall fails."

The two men nodded and then turned and wearily began carrying the stretcher out again. Roslyn swore silently and called them back. She got two of her own volunteers to take the stretcher and got Nossi Bee to get the men a drink. They drank gratefully and she moved away to get on with organising people.

Arkadi walked into the huge room that was the hall of the novices. There was row upon row of beds and cupboards. For several years it had been Arkadi's home, as it was to all novices who trained at the College.

Arkadi quickly located the senior novices and called them over. They came eagerly. They wanted to know how the defence of the walls was going.

He quietened them quickly, he needed them to listen. Quickly he outlined his plan. The senior novices looked a little worried and Arkadi assured them that they could do it. They all were capable of casting at least simple spells several times over. They were magic users and could help him.

They were young and eager to prove themselves and quickly they went to spread the word and ask for volunteers. It hadn't taken much to convince them, but Arkadi's own conscience was proving more difficult to overcome.

He kept thinking to himself, 'Are you actually going to ask these youths to fight? They will be easily killed out there.' He knew that most of them didn't know more than the basics of hand to hand fighting and were liable to freeze simply at the sight of the enemy.

'No,' he shook his head angrily. 'It is dangerous, but my idea will work,' he thought. 'It has to!'

Arkadi shook his head. His argument sounded hollow even to himself and the faint voice of his conscience still whispered, 'You are going to get them all killed!'

Arkadi turned away and found himself facing all of the novices. They had gathered behind him, not one had refused his call. Guilt warred with pride within him.

One of the senior novices stepped forward, seeming to have read his thoughts. "Don't worry Master Talcost, we know it's dangerous, but we know how crafty you are, how clever your plans are and we are ready to fight, aren't we?" The last was said to his fellow novices in a loud voice. They responded with a fierce yell of agreement.

Arkadi quickly held up his hands and waited for them to quieten, along with the still nagging voice of his conscience. "Now I need your full attention, because as it happens I do have a plan, but you will need to listen carefully and well. We don't have much time and none to practise. You will have to learn quickly and hold your nerves."

The novices nodded and Arkadi began to speak.

Chapter 60

LAST DEFENSE

Under the rule of Elgon the Wise and Elgon the Golden, the city and province of Ostia has grown and developed faster than any other province save Shandrilos. Elgon the Wise, a Nordic High Lord, saw the value of knowledge and education. He it was who began to bring in the finest minds, mystics and warriors he could entice from the other provinces, the Nordic Kingdoms and even the Empire. His own son benefitted from this becoming an accomplished soldier, philosopher and mystic. Thus Elgon the Golden continued his father's policies and over time, the defence, population, trade and wealth of the province grew dramatically.

Excerpt from 'A strange land; the Wildlands of Darylor' by Grand Abbot Alinus Quan Sirona, BY1320

Parinsar Nar'Dolth was pulled from his scrutiny of the assault on the wall by the call of his senior Gonhironsar. The officer was marching over with a tight knot of his men in their dark armour surrounding something.

Nar'Dolth frowned just a touch at the officer as he approached to tell him that this had better be good to distract him from the battle at such a crucial time. The officer quietly acknowledged his look with a deep slow blink of his eyes. Nar'Dolth tilted his head in query. What was so important?

The officer gave him a bow of just the correct depth and then said respectfully, "My lord Parinsar, I have a human here who may interest you." He turned and gestured for his men to step apart. Within the centre of the elven and dark brother guard was a short, ugly little human in the red robes of a mage of some kind. He was carrying a tall staff surmounted by a red gem stone. "He was caught by our Lorewise as he sought to pass through our lines unseen. He was well armed with enchanted items, but was eventually subdued. However, he now claims he is an ally and asks to speak to you, my lord. He claims he has served us within the college."

Nar'Dolth stepped forward and gestured for the guards to retreat to let him get a better look at this human. It certainly was an ugly specimen of what was an ugly race. It was quite clearly gifted in the mysteries, but was just as obviously terrified. "You are our... ally?" Nar'Dolth asked carefully. "I am aware of my master's human servants and you are not one."

"I... that is I am an ally of... Xameran Uth Altor," the human muttered in a voice torturous to Nar'Dolth's ears, "he was your ally and I have come to... offer my aid."

"Your aid?" Nar'Dolth asked, carefully suppressing the anger he felt at such a ridiculous idea. "What aid can you provide human?"

"My name is Atholl Dorard, not human!" the human responded gruffly.

Did this petty ape think he cared? "I care not what your name is human," Nar'Dolth said in a tone that had his men standing up straighter, "Your life is in the balance, speak quickly."

The little dwarfish human stepped back in fear.

"I can tell you where the hidden entrances to the college are, the ones that run under the wall to the Black Hall. I can also tell you what is happening inside the college."

Nar'Dolth continued to stare at the human who seemed to squirm slightly under the intense black gaze. Was this human going to somehow bargain this information? Did he need to ask? "You will share this information." Nar'Dolth stated.

The human looked at him in confusion for a moment and then replied, "Yes, but I would like to be allowed to leave this island unharmed... so that I can serve you better... yes?" the human mumbled nervously.

"You will share the information," Nar'Dolth stated in a tone that his men knew was a hairsbreadth from a fatal response.

"Er... yes... er, the mages in the college are now aware of Xameran and have killed him along with a demon that was with him. There was a battle and the Archmage has regained control of the college."

Nar'Dolth stared unblinkingly at the human in disgust. The human looked back in growing discomfort.

"Er, the passageway under the wall and into the Black Hall runs from beneath that building."

The human pointed over at a partly dismantled building that had been one of the taller ones close to the college, an inn he believed the humans had called it. It was some kind of mixture of a meeting hall and a drugs den where the humans would intoxicate themselves on various kinds of liquid.

Nar'Dolth stared where the human had pointed and then looked to his Gonhironsar. The officer nodded in acknowledgement, he would look into the human's claims. Nar'Dolth then looked back to the shabby looking human. "Your knowledge is of use, human."

"So you will let me go?" the human asked eagerly.

"We will let you serve us," Nar'Dolth acknowledged. To the Gonhironsar he said in Elorien, "Take the human and sacrifice him to the Lords of Darkness." To the nearby Lorewise he said, "Shield the human and remove any enchanted items."

Instantly, the Gonhironsar signalled his men and as one they sprang forward with practised skill, pinning the pathetic human's arms and taking his staff.

"What are you doing?" the human managed before he realised his fate, "No," he cried, "I am the High Enchanter, you don't know what you are doing!"

Nar'Dolth looked at the human and said calmly, "You are an animal and to be treated as such. You should feel blessed that your heart shall be given to the Dark Lords." With that he returned his scrutiny to the assault on the wall. He heard the human's feeble attempts to cast a spell cut off as the nearby Lorewise negated his efforts and he was dragged away.

The Archmage's body guard viciously fought to hold off the trolls and goblins. They had obviously targeted Baden as a leader and were trying to kill him. The Archmage threw flaming bolts and fireballs at them, taking down several goblins and a couple of trolls, but he had to be careful; the night's rest and the energy from the Staff of Melkor had regained him some of his strength, but not all!

Baden Erin took a brief moment to look along the wall. His men were hard pressed everywhere he looked. Even with the return of the magi he had sent to aid Sir Arleas on the south wall, they were barely holding. The magi could no longer throw spells at the giant creatures on the battering ram, they had to look to their own protection and many were tiring from the constant spell casting. Most of them would have stored much energy in their staffs, but there was only so much a person could do; magic was as taxing as fighting with a sword. The Archmage's men were tired now and fighting by instinct, many of the weaker, or simply the less lucky, had perished at the hands of goblins or trolls. The Archmage couldn't help being proud though; these warriors and magi of Shandrilos had slain twice their own number at least. Nevertheless, pride or no, it might still not be enough. The Archmage summoned his will and began another spell. He would not let them down.

He fought on and lost track of time.

When next he stopped to take stock, half of his personal guard was gone and the young master seer who had conveyed his messages and orders was also gone, crushed by a troll's hammer throw. Suddenly, the walls began to clear! The goblins were fleeing back over the walls. His men had fought off another attack. Soldiers and magi began a ragged cheer. However, over the top of their celebrations, the Archmage heard their doom; a huge splintering noise. The gates were failing!

Quickly, he risked a look over the wall and saw that the goblins and the few trolls that were left were fleeing back beyond bowshot, but already their dark elven commanders were waiting for them, ready to rally, bully and whip them back into order for another attack. The Archmage estimated that around half of the goblins were gone and more than that of the trolls, who his forces had targeted mercilessly. However, the Archmage could not see the ogres at the gate, but he could hear them. He heard again the splintering sound. The battering ram was tearing the gates open. It would only be a minute or so at most before the way was open to the enemy!

The Archmage began desperately calling his captains and magi as he hurried along the wall towards the nearest stairs, "Signal the retreat to all wall commanders, we need to abandon the walls. The gate is collapsing." He knew even as he said it that his men would probably not be able to get to the gates and form up before the enemy breached them. At most they would be able to try to form up and push through to reach the Great Hall.

As he reached the head of the stairs and looked down on the now muddy lawns and paths of the college grounds, the first thing he noticed was that the injured and wounded were still hurrying to get to the Black Hall; the Clerics Dome had not been fully evacuated! He squeezed his eyes shut and wished fervently for the gods to smile on them and let them make it before the enemy broke through. He opened his eyes again to find that he was looking at the place in front of the gates where his warriors should have been to hold off the enemy. However, instead of seeing an empty area, he saw four lines of men in bright multicoloured robes about fifty metres from the gates. It was the novices!

"What in the name of all the gods are they doing there? They'll be massacred!" he shouted.

All at once he heard the great horn that would signal the retreat from the wall and the final agonised snapping of the great timbers that made up the main gates. It was too late. His men would never get there in time.

Arkadi Talcost stood nervously alongside the first rank of novices. He knew they were nervous too, and wanted to run for the safety of the Black Hall. Arkadi did too, but he knew he could not. He was committed now. He would stand or fall with these young men. He couldn't do anything else. He was responsible for them now. The thought almost crippled him. He felt the need to relieve himself. By Sarahiri and all her children, Arkadi muttered calling on the gods for strength, this was the worst feeling he had ever known. It was far worse than the ordeal of his 'master trials', worse than fighting trolls years ago, worse even than fighting the dark elves in the tunnels, and that had been as bad as he thought it could get. However, there he'd had all his friends around him, here he felt alone.

He almost bolted when he heard the huge groaning protests that signalled the forthcoming surrender of the college's gates.

Hold yourself together, he thought to himself furiously. To the novices, he shouted. "Hold steady boys, this is just like practise in the study rooms. Meditation is the first step," he prompted, "Prepare yourself. Begin summoning." he ordered. "Evoke the energy from around you and invoke the energy from within you. Start the incantation and prepare the final postulations," he lectured and watched them all as best he could. All of them knew the spell he had chosen to cast. It was a simple cantrip for a master and one of the few aggressive spells novices were taught. All of them knew it, even the first year students.

He had organised the novices into four rows for each year group of the novices. He had put the fourth years in the front line, then the first years to watch their more experienced fellows, then the second years and finally the third years. He hoped this would work. Out of the corner of his eye he could see the druids who had been trying to hold the gates. One by one, they were keeling over and passing out from exertion. He could do nothing for them. Most of their brethren had fled and the last few had given all they had to hold the gates. Seeing their sacrifice gave Arkadi fresh fire for his anger. He would not let their deaths be for nothing.

Suddenly, Arkadi heard the horn to signal the retreat from the walls, but he knew it was too late. A few seconds later, with an almighty crunch, the battering ram smashed the gates apart sending splinters flying as its ugly, blackened and hardened head burst through.

Nat Bero rushed to the doors to the Clerics Dome. She had heard the horn and realised it must mean something bad. She heard someone nearby call out that the warriors were abandoning the wall. That meant they had to get out of here and quickly. She began ordering people to make ready. Nat heard someone gasp and they called out that the gates were failing. She glanced outside and heard the groaning protests of the college gates. She was about to turn to help the evacuation when she saw something that stopped her dead; Arkadi was stood out there, right in front of the gates with a group of young lads in multicoloured robes! What on earth was he doing?

It was then that Nat heard the snapping and crunching of the gates as they collapsed. The fool was going to try and face the enemy with only a bunch of scared novices as support. He was mad!

Before she realised what she was doing, Nat found herself grabbing her bow and weapons. She turned and headed quickly out of the Dome towards her friend. She had to get the bloody idiot out of there! Just for a second the absurdity of what she was doing struck Nat, but just as quickly she brushed the thought aside. She had been able to ignore the twangs of guilt at not standing with Arkadi on the wall, but the reality, right there in front of her, of her friend's need forced Nat to act, even if only to pull her friend out of the insane situation into which he had got himself.

Behind the frantic huntress, Nossi Bee came running, his little legs pumping furiously. The huntress and the mage were all the friends that the gnome had in the whole world and he would not be left behind.

"Stand firm, boys. Maintain your concentration," Arkadi called.

The gates were shoved slowly back and then massive ogres shouldered their way through.

"Wait for my order!" Arkadi stormed. "Let them come through into range."

More and more of the brutes pushed through, then waited for their brethren to join them. Some goblins could be seen trying to get through, but it was the ogres that dominated the view. They were easily ten feet tall and as wide as two men. Their faces were covered by helms carved with the faces of beast on the front and they carried swords, axes, hammers and clubs; all manner of weapons, each twice the size of an ordinary man's!

A dark elf appeared in his jet black armour and began screaming commands in some guttural language. The ogres stepped forward and formed up with slow, deliberate discipline. At least it seemed slow to Arkadi, but time seemed to have become sluggish for him. Three lines were forming of about twenty of the mammoth creatures, but the front row was now definitely in range.

"Let's give these bastards what they deserve!" he cried.

Fifty flaming bolts sprang from the outstretched arms of the front row of novices. No one failed to cast. Arkadi could have yelled such was his pride at that moment. Ogres were struck and reeled, one fell. The dark elf yelled angrily and a grumbling roar started from the line of ogres. They began to ponderously march forward, a wall of flesh and steel.

Quickly, Arkadi yelled, "Front row kneel and prepare, second row cast."

This time some of the inexperienced novice's spells went awry, but Arkadi could not worry about that now and he spared only the briefest glances to see the flaming bolts hiss into their targets. Some ogres fell.

"Second row kneel and prepare, third row cast!"

The flaming bolts tore into the ogres again. They stumbled and howled in pain with more falling, but still the rest came on, disciplined and relentless.

"Third row kneel, fourth row cast!"

Flaming bolts hissed, whizzed and zipped past; a blazing hail. Arkadi had the first row stand and cast again, and repeated this with each line and each second the mass of ogres got closer. They had covered half the distance by the time Arkadi had gone through the lines twice. Arkadi would be lucky if these youths could cast two or three times more. Any more than that and they would surely fail, that's if the ogres didn't reach them first.

There were Shandrilosi warriors starting to stream down from the walls, down the stairs and onto the lawns, but they would never make it in time to help the novices. Their commanders must have realised this for they were forming the men into tight units as soon as they reached the lawns rather than sending them to help.

As he started with the front row again, Arkadi cast another quick look at the advancing wall of ogres. It was definitely more ragged now and maybe a third of them were down. It was incredible really to think these novices could do such damage. More and more flaming bolts slammed into the advancing giants as the novices lost themselves in the routine of casting. Could they do it or had Arkadi waited too long to begin his attack?

The ogres just seemed to get bigger and bigger, as they came closer and closer. The front row of novices fired for the fourth time. Arkadi, with a flash of an idea, changed his orders.

"Front row fall back ten metres and reform!" He yelled over the thundering of massive feet. "Second row fire and fall back ten metres and reform."

He watched as those nearest followed his orders instantly. Others hesitated and then saw their companions fleeing and turned to run. Damn, Arkadi thought bitterly, would they reform or had he sparked a rout? He repeated his commands for the third and fourth rows. And fell back with them. He hitched his robes up and ran as fast as he could. Perhaps it would be better if they all fled; at least some of them might

655

make the Black Hall. He looked ahead to the doors. They were choked with the last of the town's people trying desperately to get in. No, they would not get in, they would all be slaughtered and now it looked as if there was no way the novices could reform in time. Arkadi had been wrong to tell them to fall back. They should have stood and took more of the big bloody swines with them!

Abruptly, from nowhere he noticed Nat. The huntress had her bow and was firing arrow after arrow at the advancing horde and was yelling furiously at Arkadi to run. Arkadi could feel the ogres practically on top of him. Bitter bile rose in his throat. He was going to die; cut down by some foul creature from behind. His clever idea of an ordered attack had failed. Nat's arrows whizzed past him. The huntress was trying to cover him, give him a chance, but Arkadi could see his own fear reflected in the huntress' taut features. He was not going to make it!

"No!" he stormed, in sudden fury at himself and his stupidity. He turned and with a speed his novices could never match he summoned forth one of his most powerful spells; his earth tremor! It ripped itself from him and he almost gasped at the loss of energy. He had poured all his hate, fear and bitterness into it. The earth in front of him rippled and then exploded upwards as if some huge hand had blasted up from the ground. The front line of ogres nearest him were lifted and tossed backwards like dolls into the lines behind. The huge beasts bellowed in fear and crashed to the ground, while those behind couldn't stop themselves and slammed into their fellows in front.

This spell was no use against a mage, it was too obviously avoided, but in a moment of realisation that made his seethe at his own stupidity, he saw that this was the perfect spell to slow the ogres' advance. However, already the ones at the back were picking themselves up. The spell had shaken them up, but little more. Arkadi did not wait to see them rise. He whirled around and bellowed at the milling novices. Many of them were on the steps in front of the doors to the Great Hall. They were being screamed at by Nat who seemed to have read Arkadi's mind. Miraculously, the novices heard him and began reforming. Nat shoved them into line and shouted encouragement. The tall huntress must have realised it was their only chance. Even little Nossi Bee was there, trying his best to avoid being crushed as he tried to help Nat. Arkadi was more grateful than he had ever been in his life.

As soon as the first row was ready Arkadi shouted for the novices to cast. Arkadi looked over and heard the ogres howling again. They seemed less inclined to charge, but the dark elven commander appeared at their side once more and screamed them on.

The next row cast and the next. Flaming bolts were starting to take their toll on the ogre's bodies, but more importantly on their morale. Arkadi made a decision and paused with the fourth row. Instead of the order he stepped forward, summoned and cast, and a fireball the size of a dinner plate screeched from his outstretched arms. It leapt across the distance and engulfed the dark elf's head in flames. The elf didn't even have time to scream. His body stood for a moment, then collapsed. Nat then cried for the fourth row to cast and flaming bolts again lashed into the ogres, but they had too much discipline to give up, though a few turned and ran.

More than half of the brutes were down now and injured and burnt, but still they came on and now Arkadi realised they could not stop them all. Around twenty five ogres rumbled forward. Arkadi called for all novices, who still had the strength, to cast at will, but few managed and after a moment no more flaming bolts flew. Arkadi began to cast another earth tremor spell, but he knew before he even fully began that it would take too much energy. Instead he began summoning fireballs and hurling them. He managed perhaps half a dozen before he ran out of strength. Ogres fell, bellowing, under the fiery barrage, but too few and the rest came on, relentlessly. Luck was just not with them it seemed; they had not quite been able to do enough. Defeat began to settle on Arkadi's shoulders as he watched the last of the ogres bare down on him with a morbid fascination. So this is how it ends, he thought, too tired to even defend himself. The lead ogre ran straight at him, its huge mace held high. Arkadi fought to raise his staff, his arms felt leaden.

Suddenly, Nat was in front of him, pushing him back. "You are a bloody fool, Arkadi Talcost. You just had to try and be a hero didn't you!" the tall huntress yelled.

The huge mace came down and Nat desperately leapt aside and slashed at the huge creature with her short sword.

Then, out of nowhere, magi began to appear and throw fireballs, lightning bolts and ice storms into the ranks of ogres who faltered under the new attack. However, Nat was thrown off balance by the magical blasts and stumbled. Arkadi screamed out to his friend, but he could do nothing as the ogre's mace hurtled in from the side. It smashed the huntress' legs from beneath her and she screamed in agony.

Before the ogre could do anything more a lightning bolt tore into it, blasting it from its feet. In that instant, things changed. The ogres lost their momentum, turned and began to flee. They were met by goblins, but they crushed them in their hurry to get away. Then solid units of Shandrilosi guards slammed into the goblins and ogres from both sides.

Arkadi rushed forward, a wailing Nossi alongside him. They reached Nat together. The huntress was writhing in pain. Her legs were badly broken. For a moment Arkadi panicked and then he realised they needed to get Nat to safety.

Arkadi suddenly felt a hand on his shoulder. "Let my men take her, Master Talcost." It was the Archmage. He called to his men and ordered them to take Nat to safety. Two guards immediately ran forward and lifted Nat. The archer cried out in pain but she held on desperately to the guardsmen. A distraught Nossi Bee tried to cling to the huntress, but Arkadi darted forward and pulled him back.

"Stay back, Nossi let the guardsmen take her."

The gnome looked confused, but then Arkadi's words must have registered and the gnome sagged back against Arkadi. A huge feeling of guilt struck Arkadi and he just hoped Nat would be okay.

Arkadi lost sight of his friend as the Archmage's bodyguard formed up around them and forced them to retreat.

Arkadi found himself grasping on to Nossi Bee and stumbling back from the battle in front of the gates. The Archmage turned Arkadi with a hand on his shoulder.

"Incredible, truly incredible, Master Talcost!" the Archmage said with wonder shining in his eyes. He turned to the ragged line of novices that had retreated behind them. "You were all incredible. I am so proud of you all. You have given us a fighting chance." Then his faced turned serious again. "We will talk more of this wonder later," he said to the novices and to Arkadi. "Now you must get inside the Black Hall."

Arkadi nodded wearily and called for the novices to get inside. He headed back with Nossi clinging to his robes. The gnome was clearly not used to battle and was utterly lost without Nat.

At the doors to the Black Hall, the number of people pressing to get inside had turned into a dribble. Most had now made it inside. Once on the steps, Arkadi turned to look out over the battle.

The walls had been abandoned and the Shandrilosi guards were forming a rough wall of shields. Goblins and trolls threw themselves against the shield wall, hacking and slashing. Arkadi slowly backed towards the doors to the Black Hall with Nossi beside him. The last few novices trudged in wearily. Arkadi looked over to the smooth white curved face of the Clerics Dome. He realised that the goblins and trolls were pushing forward there, threatening to cut off the Dome from the Black Hall!

His eyes widened as he realised that the guardsmen had taken Nat that way.

"Oh Gods! Everyone needs to get out of there!" he gasped.

Quickly, he turned to find the Archmage. They needed to send more men to reinforce the shield wall over there. He was just about to call out to the dark robbed, Baden Erin when he heard a fierce roar. He looked back to see a small battle group of trolls hammer through the shield wall! Arkadi watched in horror as the guardsmen were forced apart. He could hear Nossi calling out that they needed to go and help Nat, but Arkadi just shook his head in disbelief. There was no way through to the Clerics Dome now. He clung onto the little gnome as he sought to pull away. Slowly the guardsmen who had been cut off by the trolls were cut down and the last few near the doors to the Dome hurriedly pushed inside and then slammed the door behind them. Men were left outside and Arkadi could not watch them being cut down. He bowed his head and looked down at the now still Nossi Bee. Nossi looked back in despair.

When Arkadi looked back up the Clerics Dome was now completely cut off from the main shield wall which had retreated back. The Dome's doors were being hammering on by howling goblins. "I hope they can hold out in there." Arkadi whispered.

Before the reality of the situation could fully settle in his mind, he was distracted by a call from the Archmage.

"Is that your companion, Master Talcost?"

Arkadi scanned the shield wall of warriors, but did not see Nat.

Nossi pointed and yelled and Arkadi looked at the little man and then at where he was pointing.

"There," the gnome said, "on the stairs by the main gate. There are human soldiers and friend, Darin is with them!"

Arkadi's eyes opened wide in realisation. He had forgotten Darin! He looked over to where Nossi was pointing. Darin's distinctive black armour and sword were clear among the ordinary arms and armour of the Shandrilosi guards who were with him. However, it was then he realised that the group Darin was with had been cut off!

"Oh gods, no!" Arkadi cried out.

The group of about thirty men threw themselves down the stairs and hit the ground running. Enemies were closing in on all sides and the men slowed a little and closed up. They began hacking down goblins as they came near. Occasionally, a guard would fall, wounded or dead, but no one stopped. To stop was to die.

Men behind the shield wall had caught sight of their fellows, cut off and desperately running towards them. They began to shout encouragement and a captain ordered the shield wall to push forward where they were heading. However, more and more goblins and trolls were swarming in through the gates and the number of goblins, pressing against the shield wall was increasing with each moment. The small wedge of men ran forward into a wall of goblins between them and the safety of the shield wall.

Arkadi couldn't take his eyes of Darin. The ebon armoured warrior was at the head of what was now about a score of warriors as they hit the goblins. Their forward momentum was slowed, but Darin's great sword was cutting through, flesh, bones and armour with ease. He kept the wedge going forward. The men behind flanked him, shields out, cutting down goblins that Darin missed. It was awe inspiring the way Darin hammered at the goblins relentlessly. His arms rose and fell again and again and no shield was proof against his blade. His blows moved with such savage strength that they hurled goblins back almost cut in two; they were of such speed that they parried almost all attacks and those that got through bounced off his magnificent armour with hardly a scratch left behind! However, the sheer mass of bodies was slowing them and even Darin was finding it difficult to move forward. Also, at the back of the wedge the men were finding it hard to defend the attacks from behind and were being swarmed over by goblins that had come through the gates. Slowly the wedge was being cut down. With twenty feet to go, there were only ten men and still a mass of tightly packed goblin warriors were between them and the shield wall.

"They're not going to make it," someone muttered.

Arkadi's eyes were fixed on the drama that was unfolding and he found himself clenching and unclenching his hands. In his mind he was calling out encouragement.

"Eight... seven... six..." Men around him counted, watching the beleaguered warriors fall to the goblins.

"Can't the magi do something?" Nossi yelled.

Arkadi wondered the same, but when he looked he could see many of them were either helping defend the shield wall, holding unseen barriers against arrows or utterly exhausted. Arkadi swore and looked back to see only two men still stood with Darin.

'Even he can't fight them from all sides.' Arkadi thought. 'If they get a hold of him, pin his arms, he's as good as dead, no matter how good that armour is.'

Arkadi began to move forward. He wasn't sure what he could do to help, but he wouldn't let Darin die without doing something. However, he knew he was near complete exhaustion.

Arkadi could just see over the shield wall. Darin was little more than ten feet from safety. Arkadi saw the two men at his back get dragged down almost simultaneously. He ran forward and summoned as much energy as he could into a blazing fireball.

"Darin!" he called as he tossed the fireball over the heads of the men in the shield wall and onto the heads of the goblins in between. There were howls of terror as the fireball exploded at Arkadi's command and a tiny gap appeared for Darin.

He saw it and leapt forward with inhuman power, slamming goblins aside, not even bothering to use his blade. Suddenly a huge ogre stepped into his path. Arkadi cried out in dismay. The ogre brought its immense warhammer down in a tremendous overhand blow. Darin didn't even break stride. He thrust up his sword, deflecting the massive blow slightly and twisted his body with impressive agility to let the warhammer whistle within an inch of his torso to smash into the earth. Before the ogre could even begin to pull back on its weapon, Darin sprang, put a foot on its leading knee for purchase, leapt upwards, planted his other foot firmly on its lowered shoulder and then, almost effortlessly, pushed off and soared forward, high through the air like he was diving into a river. Arkadi saw Darin wasn't going to make it and had the words on his lips to call for the shield wall to drive forward when black wings seemed to fold out from the back of his armour and Darin glided serenely over the shield wall and over the now open mouthed Arkadi.

"What…" Arkadi couldn't even frame a question or exclamation.

Darin landed, the wings folded in and he turned. His helm bled back to reveal his familiar face, though now something was different; he was smiling fiercely! It was the first time Arkadi had seen him smile since putting on the armour.

Nossi came up behind the midnight armoured figure, a look of awe on his face.

Arkadi exclaimed, "When did you learn to do that?"

"Damned if I know!" Darin laughed, "This armour is incredible. I have never felt so alive!" He yelled in sheer ecstasy.

Arkadi frowned. Darin's delight was a little odd, but he was glad the knight had made it.

"I thought you were dead for sure," Arkadi mumbled, overwrought.

"Me too," Darin laughed, "but that fireball of yours gave me the chance Arkadi. Thanks!"

Arkadi looked at his cheerful friend and thought perhaps it is not so odd to be so happy in the middle of a battle, after all he was alive!

"Still more enemies to kill," Darin responded, again a little too happily.

Suddenly, through the gates came a tide of the giant insect mayax followed by a black swathe of armoured elves and black goblins. They marched through the gates with rigid discipline. They halted in the shadow of the shattered gates and Arkadi saw the tall commander frown around at the scenes of chaos inside the college grounds. Quickly, he saw the commander gesture to one of his senior mages in the black robes. The mage headed off for the Clerics Dome with a bodyguard of elves and black goblins.

⌒⌒⌒

Roslyn Shanford could hear the pounding on the doors. They shook with each blow. It wouldn't be long before the doors would start to give.

Inside around a dozen injured and terrified townspeople wailed and cried to themselves in complete panic. An equal number of severely injured soldiers looked scared, but also, to some degree, resigned to what they knew was to come. The only people who seemed at all calm were the Grand Abbot and his monks. The Grand Abbot, like Roslyn had refused to leave until all the injured had been moved to the Black Hall, and like Roslyn, he had been trapped here.

The pounding stopped for a moment and over the panicked voices of the injured she heard a musical voice call out what seemed like commands.

"The elves have come," Nat muttered darkly at her shoulder.

The tall huntress had been dragged in scant seconds before the shield wall had collapsed and they had been cut off. The huntress had rarely been far from her shoulder earlier. She had made it her job to be there for Roslyn, to help with whatever she could and Roslyn needed to return the favour despite her fear at being trapped. She had quickly eased the huntress' pain with an herbal infusion and some magic. The monks had then begun strapping her legs. Now the huntress lay on a nearby pallet, her legs bandaged and strapped with wooden braces by the monks to support her legs.

Earlier Roslyn had thought Nat would be of little use in the Dome, but the woman knew a wide range of herbs and how to treat small wounds. Learnt in the woods she had confided, and she had thrown herself wholehearted into whatever job needed doing no matter how menial like she was trying to make amends for something. Roslyn had developed a high regard for the woman and now felt for her.

"I recognise their voices from below ground when they attacked us." Nat Bero continued over Roslyn's thoughts.

The huntress had told Roslyn of her time below ground and she would have found the tale of monstrous enemies and cruel elves highly improbable save that she had been sitting in the Clerics Dome precisely because an army of those same monsters had attacked her town.

Suddenly, the commanding voice of the Grand Abbot rang out across the round hall. "Beware, a great evil comes," he cried out, "I can feel the presence of one who is high in the hierarchy of the devil's minions!"

Some of the women began to wail and a few of Roslyn's helpers who had also got trapped here rushed across to comfort them, but also partly to comfort themselves. Roslyn turned to see the huntress struggling to get up. The monks were trying to restrain her, but the huntress was determined.

"What are you doing?" she asked.

"Pass me those crutches," Nat muttered fiercely, "I am not going to die on my back." She looked at Roslyn and smiled. "I am a hero, you know." There was an almost hysterical glint in her dark eyes.

Roslyn realised that the woman was on the verge of tears too. She gestured for the monks to leave the huntress. She then grabbed the crutches, passed them across and helped the tall woman upright. She thanked Roslyn and then quickly grabbed her bow and slung it on her shoulder before leaning fully on the crutches.

All through this the Grand Abbot had been calling out instructions. He finally called for the few ordinary monks who still remained to come to him. "I want you to join your minds with mine and together we will form a forbidding to prevent the evil ones from entering this holy place." he said to them. My faithful holy guardians," he then said to the dozen or so warrior monks who stood, holy maces and shields at the ready, "You must form a strong barrier around to protect us all should the evil one force entry." The Grand Abbot then looked at Roslyn. "My lady Roslyn, to you I would ask that you organise the injured into a tight circle within the centre of the room and my holy guardians will form up around us?"

Roslyn's mind was blank for a moment and then she nodded sharply. The next few minutes were a blur as Roslyn busied herself moving the injured to the centre of the room near to the Grand Abbot and his monks who had already entered some kind of trance. Nat suggested that they upturn the beds and palettes to form a barricade. She nodded. It was not much, but it would slow an attack down at the least. The huntress had then gone awkwardly around on her crutches scouring the place for weapons and arming any injured who could hold a weapon, whether they could stand or not. Those who could stand were placed alongside the warrior monks to give them some kind of support. The pounding on the doors had begun again almost as soon as Roslyn had started organising people, but her senses had detected a barrier of some kind holding the doors in place. However, as she now set herself with the goblin blade she had taken earlier, she could sense that whoever it was outside had begun a magical assault on the barrier the Grand Abbot and his monks had formed. Already it seemed the barrier was weakening. Roslyn just prayed help would come before it failed, though in truth, with the gate fallen she was unsure if there was anyone in any position to come to their aid.

Elgon of Ostia was lost. He had to admit it.

His troops had withdrawn from the wall safely enough; luck had been with them and the goblins and trolls had been regrouping when the horn had sounded the retreat. He had led his men through the gardens in his hurry to get to the Black Hall. However, he had forgotten one thing, the college maze! He had found himself and his men hopelessly lost in the high hedges. They had tried to hack through, but the hedges were impressively resistant. Elgon could hear the sounds of challenge as the trolls and goblins came down from the wall behind them. Soon they would catch up with his men, worse they could easily encircle and cut them off from reaching the Black Hall by going around the gardens. Something he now realised he should have done.

Abruptly, he burst out into the large gardened area at the centre of the maze. The place was large enough to hold a couple of hundred men and only had four entrances. He came to a decision quickly. It was not what he wanted, but it would be better than trying to lead his men through the other side of the maze. By the time he did that he would have been surrounded and his men would be strung out throughout the maze.

"We will form up here," he shouted, "I want shield walls at each entrance with spear men behind and reserves ready to plug any breaches." He looked around at the garden area. It was a lovely place with a nice little pond and a fountain. The ten foot hedges that walled the place were almost as good as walls, but the enemy would eventually force its way through. He looked back the way he had come and saw that he had almost two hundred men with him. He would need to keep at least half that amount in the centre of the garden ready to rush to any spot where the enemy forced their way through.

Quickly he gave the orders. A few minutes later the unmistakable high pitched cries of goblins and the guttural roars of trolls showed that the enemy had located them.

"Brace yourselves men. We stand and we fall here!" he thundered. "The more of these bastards we take with us, the better chance our friends have of beating these swine; the more of these we kill here, the less there are when the attack comes against our towns and our homes; and the more we kill now, the more the gods will smile upon us as we enter the Hall of Heroes!" he bellowed and raised his sword in the air.

To a man, his warriors raised their swords and bellowed their agreement. Elgon just hoped the others had fared better.

Sir Arleas, Grandmaster of the knights of Saint Karodra cursed his luck. He realised that any pretence at an organised retreat was lost. The wall had been as good as taken even before the horn had sounded the retreat. Now his forces were fleeing in chaos through the sparse trees that made up the southern side of the college grounds. Goblins and trolls were in close pursuit. Many of the weary and injured men were being overtaken by the fleet footed goblins and cut down without mercy.

Sir Arleas broke through with his men on to the open lawns and saw the Black Hall ahead. Off to the left, he could see that the Archmage had successfully formed up a shield wall around the front doors to the Black Hall and was steadily withdrawing his men inside. However, it seemed that some people had been trapped in the Clerics Dome as the enemy swarmed about it. Sir Arleas' spirits rose as he saw that some of the Nordic men from the north wall had obviously made it to the rear doors to the Black Hall, but then he realised that they were simply streaming into the Hall in complete disarray, there was no one organising them.

Sir Arleas ran on with his loyal knights. It would not be long before the enemy caught them too. Off to his right he suddenly saw Korlin Di Vorseck and his men burst forth from the trees. He could see the Lord of Lauria coolly surveying the situation. For a moment his eyes seemed to meet those of Sir Arleas then Di Vorseck saluted. Sir Arleas frowned as he saw the lord call a halt to his men and form his personal guard into a rectangular shield wall formation. It was a classic defensive tactic of the Imperial legions, but it was also one designed for a controlled retreat. Ordinarily, this would have been a good idea, but it was a slow moving formation and one that really needed a lot more men to hold it. Di Vorseck only had his own guard and a few others from the other town guards; little over fifty men. Sir Arleas realised that the wily old politician had realised no one was forming a shield wall by the rear doors to the Black Hall and had decided he would take as many of the enemy with him rather than be cut down piecemeal fleeing.

Despair hit Sir Arleas as he too realised it was unlikely that if he made it to the Black Hall they would be able to do so before the enemy and hold the doors.

He heard again the screams as men were cut down behind him. Suddenly, he remembered the elves and the dwarves who were to hold the rear wall. He had heard nothing of them during the fight for the wall and now they were nowhere to be seen. Silently, he cursed them, 'Foul, double dealing creatures.' He didn't care what anybody else thought, you could not trust those god forsaken animals! 'Those treacherous bastards had probably made a deal with the enemy!' he thought savagely.

He glanced back and could see wiry goblins leaping out onto the lawns, pulling down more and more men from behind. Some of the men had spotted Korlin Di Vorseck's retreat and were desperately trying to reach the safety of his shield wall, though already some goblins had reached the Lord of Lauria's men and were hammering at them.

Sir Arleas had a choice. He could flee and hope to make the Black Hall before the enemy, using Di Vorseck's retreat to cover him, or he could join the Lord of Lauria's doomed retreat.

It was no decision at all. His conscience and honour would only allow one choice.

As he ran he raised his sword and shouted his orders. Not one of his men uttered a single protest and pride almost tore Sir Arleas' heart.

"For the glory of the Blessed Prophet…!" Sir Arleas cried and led his men charging off towards Korlin Di Vorseck and his men.

⁂

Roslyn could barely stand it. The holy forbidding that the Grand Abbot and his monks were holding seemed like it would fail at any moment, but it continued to hold. The dreadful suspense was terrible. Roslyn realised she was breathing heavily and could feel the panic rising within her. A hand touched her on the shoulder and Roslyn could almost feel reassurance flowing into her from Nat Bero at her side. The tall archer seemed totally at ease. Roslyn presumed she had been in battles before.

She looked up and smiled. The huntress' dark eyes were kind and her face was almost serene. Roslyn realised that it wasn't familiarity with the fear of battle that kept the woman calm, but rather an acknowledgement that death was coming. It wasn't that the woman had given up and simply wanted an end to her life, but that she had come to terms with the idea of dying and was determined to face it.

There was a creak and then a crash and suddenly the doors were failing. Roslyn's senses detected the holy forbidding simply vanish and she heard the monks near her groan and collapse. She saw that most were barely consciousness. The Grand Abbot stumbled a little and was caught by one of his faithful guard, but he quickly stood up straight. Alinus Quan Sirona was not finished it seemed and Roslyn was glad of that.

With a final crunch, the doors were blasted from their hinges and a screaming crowd of goblins, trolls and hideous giant insects exploded into the room. Roslyn jerked back in stunned horror at the sight. She bumped into the firm presence of Nat who leaned down.

"This is it, little lady," she breathed, "Time to face death!"

Chapter 61

THE GREAT TEMPLE

Only I now live of our kin who remember how we came to these lands. We were broken, terrified and sickened. My father had saved us from certain doom, but now we were lost and afraid in a strange land, and strange it was, with creatures and people we had never seen before. We were attacked relentlessly and our numbers dwindled as we sought refuge. Long years it was before we found a new home, a sanctuary, a stronghold in which we might nurse our strength and rise again. Long years again it was before we were ready to begin to take back what we had lost, we the chosen people. None of this would have been possible without my father's power and knowledge, and that of the Altai Mor, the Lords of Darkness, who gave us their strength. This time in our history we now call, the Suffering...

Translated from 'The Book of the Suffering' by Ry'Ana White Eyes, Lore Queen of the True Elves

Tal'Asin saw Ry'Ana's distraction. Something had happened. Tal'Asin quickly withdrew his attack and fled from her. He needed to rebuild his defences. His thoughts of defeating her were starting to look arrogant at best. Ry'Ana White Eyes was a master of the Astral Plane and only Tal'Asin's long sojourn here had given him the expertise to match her.

Tal'Asin saw that the dark elven queen had not pursued him. Her hatred of him was absolute! What could have distracted her so that she would lose the chance to press her advantage against him?

Mentally, he slowed his flight and sent his perceptions darting back towards his adversary. She had encased herself in a cocoon of defensive spells and was intent on her scrying pool. Tal'Asin risked a look closer and saw what had so enraptured the blind seeress. It was the dark elven prince, Uh'Ram and he was within the Waygate Hall of Althazar! He was facing Jon Madraig and his friends, and in Jon's hand was the Lifestone of Elysia!

Tal'Asin saw the prince hurl a mighty spell at Jon and his friend Zara. Ry'Ana purred with pleasure, but this quickly turned to a growl of anger as the smoke cleared and Jon and Zara appeared unharmed.

"How?" Ry'Ana whispered furiously.

Suddenly her scrutiny snapped back to Tal'Asin who hastily retreated as he saw the woman Zara Halven leap to attack.

"Somehow this is your doing!" Ry'Ana hissed. "Who are these humans that they can stand against a prince of the True Elves?" She glared at Tal'Asin with her milky white gaze. "I will not tolerate any interference. Your human pets will die!"

Tal'Asin realised that Ry'Ana was leaving the Astral Plane. She was seeking to manifest herself in the Waygate Hall!

"No!" Tal'Asin cried out. He knew he must prevent her, even though he had little energy left, she would prove too much for Bear and his friends. However, he knew he couldn't afford to draw any energy from Jon as the burly warrior would need all he had to fight the dark prince. Tal'Asin needed to stop Ry'Ana for as long as he was able and hope that Jon and his friends could defeat the dark prince.

His astral bolt was hastily conjured, but it was enough to disrupt Ry'Ana's concentration.

"I am afraid I can't allow you to leave just yet, Ry'Ana," Tal'Asin called with more confidence than he felt, "You and I still have some unfinished business."

Zara Halven launched a blistering series of attacks with her two enchanted blades, but the dark elven prince moved with incredible speed and blocked each strike with his sabre-staff. The weapon was impressive; it had looked like a short staff, but when the elf had drawn it, an eighteen inch blade had sprung from the short staff as if by magic, though Rebba detected none. The dark prince was now using it with devastating skill. Rebba had never seen Zara move so swiftly or attack so skilfully, but the dark prince made her seem slow and ponderous. The elf danced and spun, leapt and twisted. Zara was barely holding her own!

Just then Bear ploughed forward, a silent bundle of rage and magic. The big man had managed to somehow deflect or negate the spell that the dark prince had thrown at them, though it had obviously taken some effort and now he was moving to attack. Bear had managed to secure the Lifestone somewhere and attacked with his sword and shield leading. He virtually glowed to Rebba's mystical senses, he had obviously cast spells to protect and enhance himself. The big man moved in with a grace and speed that Rebba could hardly believe. He came at the prince from his blind side with such speed that Rebba thought it was all over; the prince could never stop the big man's potent strike and defend against Zara's enchanted blades.

Rebba held her breath.

A second blade flashed out of the bottom of the elven prince's sabre staff. The lithe creature twisted his grip on the staff, now in the middle, and deflected Zara's attack with one end while thrusting back and blocking Bear's blade behind him with the other! The elven prince then leapt back agile as a cat, all the while twirling and blocking Bear and Zara's frenzied attacks, using his now double bladed weapon like a quarterstaff!

Rebba gasped out loud in sheer astonishment at such skill. This elf was almost miraculous in his fighting ability. It was even more stunning due to the fact that it was clear to Rebba that the dark prince was also still casting spell after spell as he fought. Bear was clearly emulating the dark elf prince and casting counter spells while Zara's enchanted blades were preventing spells from hitting home. Rebba could see the wide eyes of Zara and knew that she was fighting on the edge of desperation; she would have been dead ten times over had it not been for her swords and armour and she knew it. The awesome battle between the three held Rebba back; she had never seen such speed and power in the mystic arts. It was incredible! Rebba would barely be able to protect herself against such potent energies.

Nevertheless, Rebba gathered herself up and gathered her resolve. Her new staff and armour would give her greater strength. She cast her strongest shielding spell and began to move cautiously forward.

As Rebba neared the battle, she could feel the charged atmosphere around her increase. She pushed forward, resolute. If she was careful she could strike when the elf prince was fully engaged. Rebba waited for her moment. The dark elf suddenly changed tack! He clothed himself in a defensive shield and triggering more powerful enchantments on his blade and armour. He switched from defensive to aggressive and smashed Zara and Bear back for a fraction of a second. It was only a second, but it was enough. The elf spun and Rebba knew that the powerful creature had sensed her approach. Rebba found herself staring into the midnight pools of the elf prince's eyes. She did not see the spell that hit her and only her own defences saved her life but still Rebba Korran was hammered back. She slammed across the stone floor to crash in a heap by the Waygate arch she had closed only a few minutes before. She levered herself painfully up onto her elbow, even as the battle raged on with Zara and Bear hurling themselves forward once more.

Impotent anger hit the druid like a blow; even with her new staff and armour, her spells would be little more than an irritation to this dark elven prince. She glared at the foul creature, her face a taut knot of hate as she focused her frustration on the elf's face… Rebba sat forward in sudden revelation. Was that strain starting to show on the elf's coppery face? Rebba knelt up and looked hard at the leaping, twirling creature. It's midnight black eyes were now wide with exertion and sweat shone on its smooth fiery brow.

'Yes,' Rebba thought, 'the evil swine was tiring.' New resolve stiffened the druid. 'I may not be able to do much, but it may just be enough!' She thought savagely.

Abruptly, a ragged and damp cough distracted the druid. She looked around and saw that Garon was moving!

"Oh, by the gods!" she exclaimed. All thought of the battle disappearing. She had forgotten about Garon! Rebba pulled herself to her feet and stumbled across to the prone and bloody body of the monk. Rebba had to stop herself from crying out loud at the sight of her friend. Garon had been torn open in various places; cut, slashed and battered. Blood stood stark against his holy white tabard and the stain almost completely obscured the white of his leggings. Garon's blood was now pooling by his body. Rebba was aghast and had to cover her mouth. She had to turn away for a moment! Quickly getting a grip of herself, she turned back and knelt down by her friend. She gently lifted Garon's head and carefully laid it on her lap. The monk's brown eyes were open and tears squeezed from their corners to roll down his pain ravaged face. He coughed again and a thick wad of blood and spittle frothed from between his lips.

"Ah, Rebba, it is good to see you," Garon rasped, "I had thought I was surely done for, but you have rescued me."

Rebba nodded, unable to speak. Tears welled in her eyes. It was clear to her trained eye that Garon was dying, nothing could prevent that now.

"Did we..." Garon coughed again and his body spasmed and then slowly relaxed. "Did we escape, Rebba? Did we get away?"

Rebba looked up at the battle still raging away between Zara, Bear and the dark prince. She looked back into her friend's eyes. She couldn't lie, though she dearly wanted to. "We are not safe yet, Gar."

Garon went to speak again, but Rebba had come to a decision. "Don't talk, Garon. Let me help you, let me ease the pain."

Garon tried to shake his head. Even in his pain wracked state he knew the truth, but Rebba had made up her mind; if she could not save her friend, she could at least ease his last moments.

She cast and watched the agony loosen its grip on Garon's body. She didn't stop there, though she knew it was useless, she moved her magic to Garon's stomach wounds. She pulled the flaps of flesh together and sealed the wounds up and then thrust what vitality she could back into her friend. Garon eyes became a little clearer and he smiled in relief.

"Thank you, my friend, but you should not..." Garon began.

"Please, Gar, don't..." Rebba interrupted, but she did not have the words to continue.

Garon seemed to understand and nodded. He turned his head to the battle. The two friends sat in silence for a moment as the battle surged across the stone floor of the huge Waygate hall. Rebba found it almost surreal, but she gently lowered her friend's head as she stood and grasped her staff. "I must help Gar." There was more she wanted to say but she couldn't find the words. She turned and fully faced the battle.

'That evil swine must die!' Rebba thought viciously as she began to summon her spell shield again. She fixed her eyes on the elf prince, but even so her mind could not track what happened next. A trained duelist might have noticed, but such was the speed of the sword play, even that was not certain.

One second Zara and Bear were pressing the attack, the elven prince retreating before them, the next, one of Zara's blades was slapped from her hand and a kick made Bear stumble. Out shot the dark prince's hand, rigid, and a blast of force lifted Zara from her feet and sent her flying through the air. The agile warrior yelled in terror as she sailed across the hall. She hit the floor with a tremendous crash, rolled and lay still.

Rebba froze.

Bear sought to press forward, but now the elf prince had the advantage and his blade seemed to slide in at Bear from all sides. His shield was battered repeatedly and he weaved his sword in a bewildering arc trying to stop the lethal darting blade from reaching him, all the time defending against spells cast only inches from him. Had it not been against such a foe, Bear's defence would have been awe inspiring and beyond any human's ability.

Rebba snapped free of her paralysis and began to hurry forward, yet before she could cover half the distance, the dark prince slammed his staff into Bear's face. It was enough to disrupt Bear's desperate concentration and the prince then released a hand from his weapon and grasped the big man's burly shoulder. Lightning slammed through Bear who jerked like a puppet on a string. Energy zig-zagged through Bear and his head snapped back violently, his features stretched with agony. A rough scream echoed through the vast hall and then Bear slumped to the ground as the dark elven prince released him.

"Oh gods!" Rebba whispered in terror as she rushed forward.

The prince did not even look her way. He was intent on Bear. Swiftly he knelt and he reached for something on the big man's belt. He stood erect and held up what he had taken. In his elegant hand the mighty emerald that was the Lifestone of Elysia, shone forth. Rebba hadn't had time to summon a spell. She hit the triumphant elf with all her might. She might as well have struck a wall. Her staff slammed back from an unseen shield and a sudden burst of energy knocked her from her feet.

The dark elf barely gave her a glance. The ecstatic creature called out something in its musical language and a look of complete joy suffused its inhuman features. The elf had the Lifestone!

A screech of metal distracted the druid. Rebba looked over and saw Zara had dragged herself to her feet. The stubborn warrior was battered and looked like she was barely on her feet, but the look on her face said she was not finished yet.

"You can bloody well put that down you black hearted swine!" Zara snarled, pulling herself fully upright with difficulty and swinging her sword up.

The dark elven prince looked across at Zara as if irritated, but then amusement quickly took precedence.

"Your resistance was admirable, human," the prince responded, "Perhaps Ry'Ana was right that I should not underestimate your kind. Never have I been so tested, yet now it is finished."

He looked away from Zara and back to the huge gem he held in his hand. "At last I have the talisman of the Guardians, my people's divine birthright."

"Yeah, not for long!" Zara growled as she began to advance painfully. "We've got allies who will…"

"Do not be foolish, human. Accept your defeat," the dark prince interrupted.

Zara was opening her mouth to utter a denial when an unseen force clamped onto her throat and lifted her effortlessly. She gagged and grabbed desperately at the unseen force, dropping her sword. She was drawn over to face the elf and at the same time Bear seemed to rise up limply, lifted by his neck.

Rebba's eyes popped wide as she too felt the iron grip around her own neck and was dragged forward.

"Do you truly believe that there is anyone who can come to your aid human?" The dark prince asked. He was stood now, only an arm's length away, with his sabre staff away and hung on his hip. His head tilted in puzzlement.

Rebba, knew looking into the pools of ebon that were the creature's eyes, that their deaths were only a few moments away and dread washed through her. She tried to pray to her gods, but nothing would come into her mind save abject terror.

"Let me show you the power that I now have at my disposal." The dark elven prince smiled. He nodded then to himself as if in response to his own thoughts. "Yes, you shall be my witnesses to what shall now occur.

You shall witness the rebirth of a god... and then you shall be his first sacrifices. He shall sup first upon your life essence!" the cruel elf laughed lightly. He turned away then and spread his arms wide. "You probably don't even know what this place truly is, what power and knowledge there is hidden here."

The elf walked over to the huge pair of monoliths that stood in the centre of the huge Waygate hall, all the while talking, "These are the pillars of Dah'Nu the Earthmother, and this is the inner sanctum of the great temple she built to honour the bitch goddess, Elysia... and yet it is not!" the elf exclaimed spinning back to face his helpless audience for a moment. "That is the secret to this holy place. It exists here and yet is not here. In some way it co-exists with this place but in another reality, only reached when the Lifestone is used to align these two mighty stones." he explained brushing his hands delicately across the surface of the gigantic pillars. "It is in some unknown way related to the same magic that Dah'Nu's successor, Gal'Mir used to create the Waygates."

The elf stepped between the two pillars and suddenly raised the emerald Lifestone. Rebba could feel the power building and her mind was practically swamped by pain, fear and awe. Verdant green power leapt from the now blazing Lifestone and connected with the pillars of rune carved stone. They seemed to absorb the power for a moment and then cracks of green power began to glow up and down their lengths. The power then began to grow even more intense.

Something changed. Rebba could feel it, though she was in no fit state to understand it. Around them the dark air seemed to ripple and became like mist. The ripple and mist washed across her vision and she found himself looking at the same space, but it was utterly different. Gone were the Waygate arches around the edge of the vast hall and in their places stood huge pedestals with gigantic exquisitely carved statues of elves. Walls appeared and divided the space along with huge arching vaults and columns. The room they were in grew a little smaller as the walls appeared and within that space appeared wonderful delicately carved stone tables and chairs. Things appeared that Rebba could not put a name or function to, but all was lost in a blur as before her materialised a huge ball of glowing swirling energy. It reminded Rebba of the energy she had seen when a Waygate was opened, but far more intense. It floated there in the air, writhing and swirling, but untouched by anything. It defied true description.

Rebba blinked repeatedly, her mind was almost overcome by what she was seeing. Everything had changed around them and yet it was the same space; the only constants that gave truth to this, were the monumental twin pillars and the polished floor.

"Behold the inner sanctum of the Great Temple of Elysia!" the tall regal dark prince called out. He turned a full circle with his arms outstretched, the Lifestone, a tiny star in his fist. Then his eyes lowered and his dark eyes scanned the expanse of the shining floor.

Rebba's eyes followed the elf's and she noticed for the first time there were things scattered haphazardly across the floor; weapons, armour and even some bodies, skeletal and brittle. The dark prince suddenly leapt forward in excitement. Rebba heard the creature gasp what she took to be an exclamation. The elf quickly crossed the room to a body that lay almost beneath the mighty orb of energy. Rebba could not see it fully, but the body was large and clad in the same blood red armour as the prince.

Reverently, the elf knelt by the body and his hands brushed gently across the armoured chest, hardly touching it. He breathed some words, but Rebba could not make them out. Carefully, the prince gestured and softly the skeletal body began to rise from the floor. The elf stood and the long-dead body rose further, seeming to lie on an invisible bed of air. The elf's attention was fixed upon the floating body, his dark eyes wide. Rebba's fear was starting to ebb, at least a little, and she had the presence of mind to test the bonds that clenched about her throat. They remained as unbreakable as before and Rebba found Zara looking at her intensely. Her face was red and sweat ran down her brow. Rebba guessed that Zara had already spent time trying to escape the invisible fist that held her. She would never give up.

Faintly, Rebba now could see the strands of power that wound around them all, but she had no idea how to counter the spell, and certainly did not have the energy to even begin such an attempt. What they really needed was Bear, but it was clear that he was still unconscious. He looked pallid. Rebba's thoughts were interrupted as the dark prince's voice echoed through the tall, vaulted chamber.

"You shall now witness a miracle beyond your apish understanding. You shall witness the greatest of all elven kind reborn." He turned and gestured behind him. "Look upon the mortal shell of the Great One, the *Ata'Gon*!" the dark elf intoned, his blood red armour echoing that of the armoured figure suspended between him and the great spinning ball of might. "None shall be able to stand against his majestic power, none shall…"

Zara's strained voice broke through the dark elf's monologue. "Yeah that's what you think, freak!"

The dark elf spun in a fury and Zara was suddenly snatched up and forward to hang an arm's reach from the livid elf. Rebba fervently wished that Zara would keep her mouth shut, but a part of her knew the fierce woman never would and silently cheered her on.

"You think that you have it all under control here, don't you? You have no idea. Our friends will have warned all and they will be…"

The elf cut in, suddenly smiling viciously, "…raising an army; gathering their forces…" The elf barked, amusement clear in his eyes. "You have no idea what you are dealing with do you, human? But then you have no talent and are no doubt merely some ignorant chosen for your fighting prowess not your intellect."

"I know enough," Zara barked back, "I know that our people will unite and bring their armies against you. The magi will come in their hundreds and…"

"You really are very entertaining, human," the dark prince put in, his ebon eyes dancing with barely hidden glee, "I should keep you alive as a jester."

Zara went to bark an angry retort, but the armour clad elf gestured and the invisible band around Zara's throat tightened and yanked her across the chamber to face a blank stone wall near to where Garon's body lay deathly still. Rebba gasped in panic as the band at her throat dragged her and Bear across to follow.

The dark prince languidly ambled across and then jerked in to snarl hatefully into Zara's ear.

"Shall I show you your precious people and your powerful magi?" Without waiting for a reply which he knew could not come, he stood, turned and swept his arm out towards the blank wall, his fist clasped around the glowing green Lifestone. "Behold," he intoned and the wall was transformed into a crystal clear view.

It took Rebba a moment to focus properly and make sense of what she was seeing. It was the college, but it was seen as if they hung high in the sky looking down. Rebba could see the whole college and part of the town laid out before her, and what she could see did not seem right. Abruptly, they seemed to rush down and the college became bigger and clearer. Rebba gasped in dismay, as did Zara. What had seemed wrong to Rebba was now clearly wrong; a huge swarm of goblins and trolls were attacking the college, the wall had been breached and the foul creatures were now all over the college grounds. The only humans she could see were around the main entrance to the Black Hall. They had formed what looked like a desperate and fragile wall of shields around the main doors, but they were hopelessly outnumbered. As her eyes adjusted fully, she began to pick out more details. She could see that the Clerics Dome had been invaded and that there were other humans strung about the sides of the Black Hall, some in the gardens defending frantically and some being hacked down in small groups on the southern lawns. It was horrifying!

"Do you see your army, human? Do you see powerful magi?" the elf tilted his head and moved his face in close to Zara's. "Nothing to say? I thought not." The elf stood and turned to face the scene below. "A fitting first view for the Great One's eyes, I think," the elf paused a moment. "In fact, it would be fitting if all should see the rebirth of the Great One in all his glory." The elf nodded in self congratulation at his new thought, "Yes, all shall bear witness, and we shall witness the destruction of these pathetic humans." With that, he held aloft the Lifestone once more and…

Down below, the battle seemed to pause… people began to look up and as more and more people looked aloft, they began to point and gasp in clear amazement.

Rebba couldn't help her exclamation, "They can see us!"

"Of course, human." The dark prince answered, "And they shall see me resurrect our great lord…" the prince paused, "just before they die!" he finished viciously.

"And I thought I was vain," Rebba heard Zara manage to mutter.

Tal'Asin had quickly realised that he could not defeat Ry'Ana without drawing energy from Bear, and even then he was not certain he could win. He had changed his tactics from a direct assault and reverted to evasion. Ry'Ana had pursued him relentlessly and it took all his skill to keep eluding her.

Below them, the battle between Bear, the humans and Prince Uh'Ram unfolded.

Things had changed when Uh'Ram had suddenly turned the tide of the battle and smashed Zara Halven away and then sent energy coursing through Bear. Tal'Asin had felt the shock, numbly and had sensed as Bear slid into unconsciousness, his body ravaged by the dark prince's spell.

Ry'Ana had ceased her pursuit and looked down in delight. Tal'Asin had despaired. He knew that the dark elven prince had the blood heritage to use the Lifestone. He watched in mute horror as the Prince took the Lifestone. He had to do something. He began to cast, he would have to manifest his spirit and try to keep the dark elf from using the stone. Suddenly, his spell fell apart and he found himself facing Ry'Ana a look of triumph on her beautiful face.

"You shall not interfere, foul one!"

She cast and Tal'Asin countered her. Again and again she attacked and Tal'Asin was forced to hold her at bay, but he knew he was weakening. Below them Prince Uh'Ram awakened the Lifestone and opened the Great Temple.

"Do you feel the power, Tal'Asin? Soon the Great One will be reborn, the life you stole from his body will be restored through the power of the Lifestone." Ry'Ana thrilled as she cast.

Tal'Asin defended with all the skill he could. He began drawing on Bear's strength.

"You are mad, Ry'Ana. Returning his mortal shell to life will accomplish nothing, his spirit and soul are still gone."

"You think me a fool!" Ry'Ana spat, "Do you think we desired the Lifestone simply to return life to an empty husk? We wanted the Lifestone to open the Great Temple. We did not simply want my father's mortal remains."

She grimaced as Tal'Asin sought to open her defences. She caught his attack and forced Tal'Asin to desperately guard himself.

"Have you not already guessed the truth, oh wise Lore King? We needed the Great Temple because within it lies the Orb." Ry'Ana said, gloating.

Tal'Asin frowned and thrust himself violently away from the white eyed seeress. The Orb! What had that to do with bringing back her father?

Ry'Ana drifted towards him a look of arrogant confidence on her face. "This is exquisite," she laughed, "it seems the great Guardian has forgotten the true nature of the Orb? Have you forgotten why it was created in the first place by Dah'Nu, mother of your race?"

Tal'Asin thought furiously. Below them he could see the dark elven prince raising the body of his cursed relative. The Orb was created as a source of energy, it was believed, to maintain the Great Temple and to allow Dah'Nu to...

Suddenly, it hit him, almost like a physical blow! Ry'Ana laughed gleefully in response to the look of complete horror that he could not prevent washing over his face.

"Yes," Ry'Ana purred, "the Orb was a conduit to Dah'Nu's divine mother, the Goddess Elysia. The Orb was a way between worlds, a way between the very planes of existence. It could connect the Guardian to the realm of the gods themselves, the Eternal realm, and it could also connect to other places..."

"You would open a portal to the void, to the infernal realm?" Tal'Asin gasped in utter dread, "but that would be madness..."

"Only to you, great Tal'Asin," Ry'Ana mocked, "but to us it will be salvation. Our great lord's spirit awaits in the void, ready to return.

Tal'Asin was shaking his head violently and denying what he was hearing over and over. "Don't you realise what you will do, Ry'Ana? Don't you understand the true consequences of what you are trying to do? If you open a portal to the void all you will summon from that place of the damned is an undead puppet of the Lords of Darkness. All the mortal vestiges of the father you knew will have been consumed by the Demon Lords."

"Lies! You yet again seek to deceive, foul one." Ry'Ana whispered passionately. "I see through you now."

"No, Ry'Ana you must listen. Your father was once simply an evil man, but he would return from the void as nothing more than an avatar of the Lords of Darkness, his only desire to free his masters, and with such a being in this world that is precisely what he would seek to do. He would release the demon hordes to devour all life!"

"And still you persist with your shallow attempts to sway me. You understand nothing, 'mighty' Tal'Asin. You are a weak and twisted creature, one who should have long ago perished. You are a creature of lies, you are the servant of those who once sought our complete annihilation." she hissed. "The Great One shall return and he shall lead us to the birthright you and your kind sought to deny us. We shall take our place as rightful rulers of all!" Ry'Ana cried.

Tal'Asin began to argue once more, but he had allowed Ry'Ana to distract him and he realised too late as an astral web began to encase him. As the spell came to fruition, Tal'Asin began to scream.

Chapter 62

DEFEAT

Amongst our people, the descendants of the Ata'Gon rule as is their right as the greatest of our race. The Ruling Princes of those Houses govern the seven provinces. The holy line is split into three distinct Houses, each descending from the Ata'Gon and one of his three wives and each vying for power and prestige. The First House predates our time in this land and is led by Ry'Ana the great seeress, daughter of the Ata'Gon's first wife who was lost before the exile. It is Ry'Ana who is Lore Queen of the Holy City. It is she who is second only in age and power to the Ata'Gon himself!

Translated from 'A History of the True Elves' by Prince Al'Odan Mindlord

Sir Arleas stepped back from the breach in the shield wall and let one of his knights take his place. There was no retreat now. He and his knights had managed to fight their way to the shield square that Korlin Di Vorseck and his men had formed, but it had quickly been surrounded in a gathering sea of goblins and trolls. All they could do now was fight; the weight of their attackers prevented any movement. So as one man fell another stepped into the breach. However, the number of men ready to step in was dwindling and soon the shield square would simply close in as each man fell until none of them remained!

Sir Arleas took off his helm for a moment and wiped the sweat from his brow. What he wouldn't give to see his holy knights on horseback charge to their aid, lances lowered. Their heavy horses would cut through this low-life scum around them. Sir Arleas would have been happy to see any kind of aid, but he knew it was not coming. Despair settled on him and he began to make a final peace with his god. He gave up a prayer to Blessed Alba and placed his helm back on his head. As he lowered his arm he saw something he would never have thought to see in his entire life! He stared in utter disbelief. Could it be? Sir Arleas shook his head. No, his eyes must be playing tricks.

Nossi yanked at Arkadi.

"What are you doing?" he asked in annoyance. He had been watching the Clerics Dome.

"Look!" the little gnome gasped, his head back and his eyes fixed on something above them.

Arkadi was about to shrug him off so he could turn back to look at the Clerics Dome when he noticed others looking up and pointing. Slowly, the entire battle seemed to falter as even those in the thick of the fighting began to look up in shock and wonder. Arkadi looked up and his mouth literally fell open... again!

Roslyn was aghast. The bloodshed and violence were terrifying and yet the enemy had been held back. The cost was terrible and the savagery immense, but only so many could come at them at once, and the two score or so of defenders had held. The screaming goblins and bellowing trolls had been met firstly by the cold calm determination of the holy monks and then the desperate terror of the injured warriors. The warrior monks were quiet as they fought. They glowed with magic to her eyes and their serenity seemed even more insane than the desperate fury of the wounded. At first Roslyn had thought she would fall screaming, such was the madness around her; goblins were cut down and men smashed by huge trolls. Roslyn was on the verge of hysteria and every time a person was cut down or dragged from the defensive lines she felt she would fall apart; she was completely unprepared for the reality of battle.

The Grand Abbot stood like a commander amidst the frenzy and Roslyn took some strength from that. She was not sure what he was doing, but she could sense the magic he was wielding. It was subtle and took a moment for her to grasp; the Grand Abbot was bolstering the defenders, adding vitality, courage and strength to them and steadily drawing the same from the attacking mass. Roslyn was impressed... as she also was with the huntress at her shoulder.

By her side, Nat Bero was coolly firing arrow after arrow into the advancing mass. She could hardly miss, but the huntress managed to pick out gaps and chinks in armour. Her skill with the bow was undiminished by her injury as her legs were strapped and she was braced to fire her long bow. She was calmly targeting the trolls in the attack, taking the time to kill or at least badly wound all of the hulking brutes as they waded through their smaller allies. It was a clever tactic as the monks and soldiers seemed to be able to hold their own against the goblins.

Still, Roslyn knew that even all this extraordinary bravery and skill would not be enough. The monks and the injured soldiers were holding the enemy, but they were slowly being pulled down one by one. It was just a matter of time. All it would take was one bit of bad luck, one key person to fall.

A voice cried out over the battle. It was a chiming, tinkling sort of voice, one she had never heard before.

At the back, over the heads of the attacking enemy, Roslyn could see a tall, dark cloaked figure. It seemed to exude evil and a chill went down her spine as she saw a wave of utter darkness spread out from the creature. The darkness appeared to coalesce and then leap forward. Roslyn threw her arms up and screamed in fear, but the spell was not aimed at her. It careened across to envelope the Grand Abbot. Roslyn stared in shock. Her hand went to her mouth. She could hear the Grand Abbot's voice shrill with desperation.

"You shall fall to the Lords of Darkness, priest. Feel the deathly breath of the Dark Lords!" the musical voice sounded over the tumult of battle.

The black cloud around the Grand Abbot continued to seethe as dark energy ran down a single strand from the outstretched arms of the black cloaked creature. Roslyn couldn't stand the thought of the Grand Abbot suffering; he was so like her beloved grandfather. She used her talent and sent out a wave of healing energy towards him as she had taught herself to do.

At first it seemed she made no impact and then she noticed a lightening of the darkness and then... a single beam of intense light shot out from within the dark cloud. Roslyn's heart leapt with joy at the sight. She felt the pull on her as the energy she was sending to the Grand Abbot was drawn from her in greater and greater amounts. She had never given so much of herself at once and began to panic. With a suddenness that made her catch her breath, the beam of light pierced the dark cloud fully and scorched down the line of darkness. It lit up the dark cloaked elf like a lightning bolt and exploded the foul creature into flames. The creature fell screaming and the dark cloud immediately shattered. The Grand Abbot emerged from the cloud, unharmed, physically at least, but Roslyn could see he was almost totally shattered spiritually by the diabolical attack.

Suddenly, a bolt of blazing bright energy slammed into the Grand Abbot's chest and he cried out in agony and fell. The monks around him, who had still not fully recovered from holding the forbidding earlier, were slammed down. The blast reverberated around the room and all were forced to cover their ears. The goblins cowered back and the battle seemed to come to a halt. At the back of the room, by the door, another dark cloaked figure stood.

The creature shouted a command in its melodic voice and the trolls and goblins began to withdraw.

Roslyn saw the creature gesture and it was immediately bathed in mystic energy. The creature threw back its hood to reveal the features of an elf. She had listened to Nat Bero's story, but had not really taken everything in. The beautiful, coppery features of this foul creature brought the details home to her.

The elf began hurling bolts of energy at the warrior monks. The monks were well protected from ordinary weapons, but the magical assault was too much. Some of them managed to maintain their feet, but most were hammered back, their armour and weapons smoking. Roslyn found herself kneeling alongside one monk. She couldn't bear to see the damage anymore. She was a healer. This was against everything for which her life stood. It was a vision of hell. The life of the monk before her trickled away;

she could do little, even with her energy returning she could not have done more than ease his passing.

The barrage of spells went on around her and the cries of agony and fear deafened her. She put her hands to her ears and began to scream. She couldn't stand it. She sought refuge in her mind, meditating as she had long ago been taught. She drew her magic around her and instinctively channelled it to heal and preserve her mind. She looked up and saw Nat had moved ahead of her as if to protect her. She was stood, legs awkward sheltering her from the attack. She held her bow in hand and had an arrow knocked, but it hung down. She sensed that the huntress knew she could do nothing against the powerful elf. Nat glanced down at her and the look on the huntress' face was one of futility. She sensed that Nat so wanted to strike at the heart of these elves. Killing the trolls and goblins had been satisfying for her she sensed; they had been giving the huntress back some of her self respect. Earlier she had sensed that something had deeply hurt the tall archer. Her pride and courage had become fragile. Now, she realised that Nat Bero stilled ached to srike a blow against this enemy, that to kill such a creature as this elf would bring a kind of peace to her.

Around them, fewer and fewer of the monks could still resist the onslaught. The few injured soldiers and people who had survived, huddled behind anything they could; petrified and praying to whatever gods they held dear. Roslyn found her eyes drawn back to the vile elven creature who was flinging bolts of energy with deadly calm. All her hatred and fear focused on that creature and she found a strange thing happening; within her the energy she had always used for healing, began to harden and change. It became infused with her hatred and enhanced by her fear. Her eyes fixed on the dark elf and the hate fuelled energy built within her. Finally, it became too much for her and uttering a primordial scream, Roslyn unleashed her energy and sent it hurtling at the foul elf in a torrent. Everything she had poured out of her at the evil creature. The scintillating energy engulfed the elf and Roslyn's heart soared... then her eyes widened. As the energy began to subside, she could see the hated elf standing safe within a powerful globe of magic, her fading energies being deflected away. The dark elf wore a slight smile on its face and its eyes were fixed on hers. The creature had sensed her attack and reformed its defences to block her magic.

"No," she managed to gasp out loud.

Above her there was a 'twang' and she almost lost her concentration. Across her vision, something flashed. The elf staggered and looked down in bemusement. Its hand rose to touch a feathered shaft sticking out of its chest. The dark elf had neglected its barrier against an ordinary attack to prevent her magical one!

Roslyn's outpouring of energy ceased at the same moment that the elven mage sagged to the floor. She was completely exhausted, but struggled to look up. Nat looked down at her. An understanding passed between them. Roslyn knew that the tall crippled huntress was satisfied. She had struck a serious blow against the enemy.

At that moment, a huge cry of anger burst from the ranks of trolls and goblins that had retreated. A brutish troll hefted a spear big enough to skewer a bull, and threw. It struck Nat with such force that she was slammed down on top of Roslyn. She was almost smothered and she could see the massive spear shaft sticking out of Nat's chest. The huntress' face was not far from hers and their eyes met.

"Tell my children that I was a hero. Tell my friends, I am… s… sorry…" she whispered and died.

Roslyn couldn't see the charge of the goblins and trolls, but she could hear it. Nat's weight almost crushed her and the complete fatigue meant she was totally helpless.

When the screams of those still alive began, Roslyn was already slipping into oblivion and after a few seconds she felt nothing, not even the sword's blow that hammered down on her.

※

Arkadi could not believe his eyes. Hanging in the sky was a huge vision of a stone chamber of some kind with a blazing sphere of energy suspended in its midst. If that wasn't incredible enough, within that chamber stood an elf in blood red armour holding something which shone even more brightly to his senses than the ball of energy. Yet none of that held his attention. His eyes were firmly fixed on the three humans in that improbable scene. Alongside the tall elf, awkwardly hung from some spell wrought bonds, were Bear, Rebba and Zara!

"By all the Gods!" Arkadi found himself mumbling.

At his side, Nossi was shouting out in joy, "They're alive, they're alive!"

It was true. The friends they had thought lost were still alive... or at least some of them. Arkadi scanned around the gigantic apparition, seeking any signs of their other friend. He found his eyes drawn to a vague lump in the shadows just behind the powerful elf. He squinted and slowly he realised what it was. It was a body, and from the tabard, though it was stained with blood and hard to make out, it must be Garon, lying still and inert.

Arkadi grasped Nossi's arm and stopped the ebullient gnome. "Zara, Bear and Rebba are still alive, Nossi, but for how long?" he responded. He then pointed in horror to the prone form on the floor. "Look that body... it's Garon!"

Nossi stopped still and looked, then his eyes went back to their other friends and the elf that stood by them. He cried out loud as the reality of the situation sank in.

The Archmage must have overheard them. He moved over to them, hardly taking his eyes of the scene above. "Are those your friends, Master Talcost?" he asked and without waiting for an answer pushed on, "Do you know what is happening here? Who is that elf, where is he and what is that power he holds?"

Arkadi shook his head, "I cannot say, my lord. I..." he noticed that Nossi had an odd look on his face. Arkadi frowned at him and asked, "Do you know what's going on, Nossi?"

The gnome looked at Arkadi and replied, "I do not know where they are or what that power is, but I know that elf is the High Prince Uh'Ram."

"The one the elven commander mentioned earlier?" the Archmage asked.

Nossi just nodded.

"And you have no idea what he is doing or what that thing is he is holding?" the Archmage demanded.

Nossi just shook his head.

"Whatever it is, its power is immense." Arkadi muttered, looking back to the scene above.

"We must get everyone in..." The Archmage's voice was drowned out as a huge elven voice boomed out from the sky above.

"Here me my brethren," the voice thundered, looking to the elven commander and those about him. "Today you shall witness the return of our divine leader. The *Ata'Gon* will rise again..." The eyes of the elven prince then moved across to look upon the wall of humanity that stood before the Black Hall. Many cried out and covered their heads such was the look of hatred in that gaze. "And you, my enemies," the dark prince sneered, "pathetic humans. Watch and despair for your end is nigh!"

All around them people cried out in terror.

"We must get everyone inside," the Archmage cried out to those around him. There was an air of panic even to his voice. He began calling to the officers who still remained.

The beautiful and yet terrifying voice boomed forth again. "As I open the way to the void and return the Great One, let his first sight be the total destruction of these humans!"

A massive roar of agreement reverberated around as every troll, goblin and elf thundered their agreement. Weapons were raised and shaken in the air and then, all at once, the enemy threw themselves forward in wild abandon at the demoralised humans. The shield wall began to falter. The elven commander called his guard around him and marched forward into the thick of the battle, thrusting the trolls and goblins aside in his desire to get at the humans.

"I think we had better get inside," Arkadi yelled over the renewed din of battle. He was pulling Nossi along with him; the little gnome was hardly resisting.

Arkadi suddenly remembered Darin. He had lost sight of him when the black armoured knight had thrown himself back into the thick of battle. It had been barely a minute after his narrow escape. Arkadi didn't want to leave the knight, but he knew that Darin was more capable of looking after himself than he and Nossi were.

Around them, people were urgently heading for the huge doors to the Black Hall and Arkadi could see more and more soldiers abandoning the shield wall and fleeing for the doors. Soon the way in would be choked.

All of a sudden, there were screams from within the hall and people began moving back from the doors! A call went up and soon all were shouting. Arkadi could barely make sense of what he was hearing. He saw Watchmaster Sintharinus run over to the Archmage. He shouted.

"There's panic inside, Archmage. The enemy is in there! They are coming up from the passages below. What do we do?" the desperate Sintharinus asked.

From the look on the Archmage's face, Arkadi knew that he had no idea. All seemed lost. Arkadi looked from the seething mass of people at the doorway to the collapsing shield wall outside, not knowing what to do. Nossi pressed up against him fearfully. Up above, the elven prince had begun chanting in some arcane language. Arkadi could sense the power building, power he had never thought possible. There was no escape for any of them.

'This is it, thought Arkadi, this is the end!'

Chapter 63

SACRIFICE

The Etoshans and their foul priests and viziers could not stand against the power that Alba wielded for it was at once more ephemeral and more puissant than any magic, coming as it did from the one true God. None could gainsay him and so he left the cursed city of Etos, with the slavers broken behind him and the power of God within him. Blessed Alba and his loyal followers travelled far from Etosha and for many years lived in the wilderness, never visiting cities or towns but seeking a place where they might start anew and spread the word of God. At last, the prophet came upon an island set in a lake, and on that island a mighty black stone stood. 'Here is where I will begin my work' he said.

From the Book of Carnacus, fourth book of the Divine Alban Scriptures, circa BY79

Rebba was terrified. The power around them was rising and rising. She felt like she was trapped on the edge of a thunder storm. The magical energy in this place was already immense, but the power was now rising to a level that was truly awesome. Energy poured from the Lifestone in the dark prince's hand, and pumped into the coruscating ball of energy that hung in the air. A raging torrent of raw might thrummed across the ancient temple. The strain of controlling it showed even on the powerful prince's face.

Time passed and still the energy continued to rage. Rebba thought that her senses would be burnt from her. She was forced to look away and found her eyes on the body of Garon Vale lying still on the floor.

Rebba was unprepared for the wave of emotion that assaulted her upon looking at her fallen friend. Tears began to pour down her cheeks. Suddenly, all the terrors, worries and losses of these last few days seemed to come crashing down on her. It was not just for Garon that she cried, but for them all. She cried because of the terror at what her imagination told her was coming; she cried at the thought of all those she loved being killed; she cried for all those she had lost; she cried for the college and the people of Shandrilos; and she cried for herself, helpless and restrained.

Her body began to shake and the constriction on her throat grew tighter. Soon her eyes felt like they were bulging. Then, just as she thought she could bear no more, she was distracted by a faint noise, barely audible. She looked over painfully to find Zara looking at her. Had the warrior said something? She realised she was crying like a child and tried to get control of herself. Zara must think her such a coward.

"Rebba," came a faint croak. "Rebba, can you wake Bear? He could free us."

Zara's voice sounded raw and Rebba was surprised that she could speak at all, but then it seemed the woman never gave up. The band around Rebba's own neck was only just letting her breath and she could not muster a reply. Instead she looked at their unconscious friend and tried to use her senses to get an idea of how badly the big man was injured. To her surprise, she found that there was little wrong with him. Obviously, the burst of energy that had slammed through him had caused him intense pain and disrupted his mind, but it had not permanently harmed him. Indeed, the vitality coursing through the man was impressive and he should have quickly recovered. The strength and energy within him were far more than any normal person's, but Rebba put that down to the merging of Bear and Tal'Asin. Yet still the puzzle remained; Bear should have awoken, but he had not! Why?

Rebba's attention was snapped away by a primal scream that tore itself from the evil prince who had defeated them all. The powerful elf was utterly focused on the ball of energy in the centre of the room. It was changing colour; from blue it was darkening at the centre. It was like something was growing inside the sphere, at its very heart, something corrupt and evil.

Another raw cry sounded and Rebba looked again to the dark elf prince. The foul creature was taut with intense strain and his face was twisted with the extremity of drawing so much energy from the Lifestone. Yet somehow, while maintaining the vast energy he was pouring into the potent sphere, the dark prince managed to send out what looked like a shower of verdant energy to bathe the lifeless skeleton. Rebba had almost forgotten the tall, armoured skeleton; it still hung silently in the air near to the other side of the gigantic globe. The healing light of the Lifestone began to wash over it.

Rebba's eyes widened in disbelief as she watched the wasted form begin to twitch; the grey, dusted surface of the skull began to moisten and then an explosion of red and white tendon and sinew began to spread across the surface like a cloth being drawn across a table. Rebba saw vital organs blossom and grow from nothing. The body was being regenerated and at a phenomenal rate!

If she hadn't been held up by the invisible bond on her neck, Rebba would have fallen to her knees in utter amazement. This was wondrous; to be able to give life back to a form, to be able to heal and rebuild a body to such a degree! Only the gods could have such power. Rebba at last realised why the Lifestone had such significance; it held the power to restore living things. Perhaps there were other artifacts that could open the portal, but Rebba was sure there was no other that could restore living flesh. She focused back on the miracle happening before her.

Skin was starting to cover the body now, and hair could be seen sprouting from the head; the skin was coppery like the dark prince's, but the hair was not the jet black that Rebba expected, it was golden! Rebba's attention was caught then by the eyes... they formed before the druid's own. Large eyes of a wondrous deep violet coalesced in a fiery skinned face of complete perfection. The serene visage shone with an inner power and beauty that almost took the breath away. Surely this angelic creature could not be the agent of evil that Bear had told them about. This blessed form could not be that of one responsible for bringing foul demon spawn into the world, for wiping out millions of lives.

Abruptly, a line of utter darkness, a jet of something so opposed to all that Rebba knew, it scoured her senses, leapt out from the growing darkness at the centre of the ball of energy. It pierced and sullied the Lifestone that shone like an emerald star in the dark prince's hand. For a moment the darkness fought with the emerald radiance within and then it shot out to lance into the now fleshed out body. The darkness was abhorrent and Rebba felt her stomach knot in revulsion. Something was coming, something very wrong, the druid knew it instinctively.

"Come forth my lord and reclaim your earthly shell so that you might lead us." the dark prince intoned solemnly.

The astral web pressed back tighter and tighter about Tal'Asin as Ry'Ana drove the spell harder and harder. Where the web touched him, his astral form jerked as energy wracked him. The damage was not physical, but that made little difference, the pain was just as real. Tal'Asin writhed in agony for a moment and then forced the astral strands away. Desperation drove him, but centuries of hatred drove Ry'Ana; he would not have lasted even a second against her, had it not been for Jon. At the limit of his strength, Tal'Asin had instinctively reached out and drawn strength from his human host. However, Jon could not regain consciousness below while Tal'Asin drew so strongly from him, yet Tal'Asin could not break free without doing so! It was a deadly conundrum, yet in the end Tal'Asin had no choice, without him the enemy had won. That realisation had forced Tal'Asin to draw on Jon and yet even that now seemed futile, for the dark one was coming!

Below him, he could sense the opening of the portal through to the void. If he didn't break free soon the mad elf prince would succeed in bringing through his so-called *Ata'Gon*, or at least some creature that might once have been him, but it would also leave a way open to the void and that could spell utter disaster for all life. An open portal to the void could bring through a horde of demons. The *Ata'Gon* had brought a huge flood of demons through before somehow, when the dark elves had destroyed his people. The cost of destroying and banishing the hell spawn centuries ago had, in the end, broken his people more than any army of trolls or goblins. There was no force of which he knew in this new world that could stand against such a force again. This portal to the void would spell the end for all good in the world; the Lords of Darkness would take control.

Tal'Asin could not allow that to happen. He had to break free, and yet the energy from Jon would not be sufficient. He had to think of another way!

"Why won't you die, foul monster?" Ry'Ana hissed. "How do you continue to resist me?"

As if from the gods, it struck Tal'Asin; Ry'Ana had no idea how he had maintained himself so long. To her eyes he had defied all the known laws of the astral realm. She did not know of his connection to Jon; that Tal'Asin's spirit and soul in another's body allowed him to sustain himself. To her he was still a mystery. She was afraid of him, of what he might yet do. She was as desperate as he. All he needed to do was to play on her uncertainties, shake her control.

"You cannot beat me, Ry'Ana. There are levels to the mysteries to which you have not even opened yourself." Tal'Asin said lightly, fighting to keep all strain and worry hidden. "Did your cursed father withhold the knowledge from you," he asked.

Ry'Ana immediately bit back, "You are a deceiver. My father has withheld nothing from me."

"If that is so then why did he hide this knowledge from you? Why did he prevent you from reaching the highest of the mysteries? If he had you would have crushed me already." Tal'Asin challenged. He could see from her face that Ry'Ana was being affected; the seed of doubt had been planted. He pushed on. "Your father has held you back just as he has warped your memory, Ry'Ana. He has been manipulating you since you were a child. He has wanted a servant not a daughter; that is all you have been to him. He has not let you get too powerful in case you might threaten him."

"No, you lie. My father loves me. He knows I would never threaten him." Ry'Ana cried out in denial.

Tal'Asin remembered her response to her past and changed tack. "He would if he thought you had remembered the truth, Ry'Ana." Tal'Asin insisted. "You do not remember your mother, or your childhood, you do not remember how your father turned on everyone, even your mother!" Tal'Asin hissed, "Your father sacrificed everyone rather than give up his dark gods and his dream of domination!"

Ry'Ana's coppery face twitched as the anger bubbled within her, desperate for release.

"You know it is true. Deep down you know I do not lie," Tal'Asin prompted, driving the point home like a knife.

"Ahhhh!" Ry'Ana screamed; all pretence at control, forgotten. "You will die!"

Tal'Asin could feel Ry'Ana's control on her power slipping as she became more irrational.

"Ry'Ana, your father killed your mother and twisted your mind."

Ry'Ana went wild. The power pouring from her increased, but her control on it slipped and more and more flew violently around. Tal'Asin took the opportunity and hammered at the astral web, tearing it apart. He then cast every camouflaging and deceiving spell he could as he fled. Ry'Ana was so incandescent with rage that her attempts to hit him were wild and careered around him.

"No!" she screamed, "You shall not escape me!"

Tal'Asin sped away. He needed to get far enough from her that he could leave the astral plane without leaving himself open to attack. He would have to time things perfectly.

Arkadi held his staff at the ready. He could feel Nossi at his hip. They were now pressed into a defensive line about three rows back from the fighting. On both sides of them, soldiers and magi stood with looks that ranged from abject terror to passive fatalism. Slowly, the fight drew closer to them as men fell.

The shield wall was being pushed ever tighter as the enemy threw itself against them. Men were being pulled screaming from the wall by huge trolls or hacked to pieces mercilessly by insect men. Nowhere did the shield wall hold save where Sir Darin of Kenarth stood. Against him the merciless tide broke. He was tireless and moved with a speed and liquid grace that was the equal of the elves; he struck with a power that only a troll could match. If only they'd had more like him.

Arkadi had deliberately positioned himself and Nossi behind the black armoured knight. If they were to die, they would die together; Arkadi could not see the killing machine that Darin had become, being cut down before the line reached them. Soon though, the warriors between Arkadi and the enemy would be gone. Once that happened he would not last long, he had no illusions.

It had been a bolster to Arkadi's confidence that little Nossi Bee had unflinchingly stood by him. When Arkadi had said the gnome could seek to hide somewhere that the enemy might not find him Nossi had replied that he was a friend now. Very earnestly, the gnome had said he had not known what it meant to be a friend before he had met all of them down below, but he knew what one was now and he would stand with Arkadi to the end. He did not want to hide while everyone else was cut down until he was left alone. Arkadi could not blame him; he would not want that either. He could not even contemplate the idea of watching his novices, who had so valiantly defended their college, cut down by vicious evil scum like these. They deserved better, they all did. Arkadi would rather fight and die out here than hide inside waiting for the enemy to come.

Arkadi Talcost looked up and saw the scene in the sky had now changed, the darkness in the globe of power had swelled and the black stream emanating from it no longer needed to pass through the elf prince and his gem, it went straight to the figure suspended nearby. Soon these cursed elves would have their leader returned to them.

Just then a horn sounded, a clear clarion call across the morning. Heads turned and people that weren't engaged in battle stared around in bewilderment. The horn blast echoed again around the college, clearly sustained by magic. Arkadi could see the enemy looking around too. This was something they had not expected.

Gasps of surprise and calls of consternation started to reach Arkadi's ears from first one side of the Black Hall doors and then the other. What was going on? Arkadi could see the enemy forming up beyond the shield wall and running around towards the sides of the college.

"What's happening, Arkadi?" Nossi asked desperately. "What's going on?"

Arkadi didn't look at his friend; he simply shook his head as he stood up on tip toes and craned his neck. They were stood on the raised steps leading up to the college doors and could just see over the heads of those men in front of them, but the enemy was all they could see beyond that.

From behind them, Arkadi heard a clatter of feet and turned to see the Archmage along with a mass of soldiers, jogging forward. Arkadi pulled himself from the line and pushed towards the Archmage. He felt Nossi follow. As he got closer, Arkadi realised that the men with the Archmage were not soldiers of Shandrilos. Arkadi had thought at first that the Archmage must have scoured the college for every last warrior they could get to make a last stand here at the doors, but these soldiers were not men he recognised. However, marching along resolutely at the Archmage's side were two very familiar men; one was the knight lord, Sir Arleas, whom the Archmage had put in charge of the southern wall; and the other was Lord Korlin Di Vorseck! How had they got here? Had they managed to get to the rear doors and clear them? The last Arkadi had heard the rear doors hadn't been held and the enemy was forcing its way in there too.

He pushed closer.

"It is unbelievable, my lord Archmage." Sir Arleas of Karodracia was saying, "We thought we were dead for sure and then they came out of the woods at the back of the college!"

Korlin Di Vorseck interrupted eagerly. "I had never seen so many! They cut through the enemy around us and quickly put them to rout."

"I must say that I had been cursing them for traitors, may God forgive me," Sir Arleas continued, "but I have to say that I have never been so pleased to see an elf in my life... and I never thought I would ever say such at thing!"

'Elf!' The word reverberated through Arkadi's head.

"You must use your men to reinforce the shield wall, my lords, now that the rear doors are secure with Raban Ironhand." the Archmage instructed. "When the Elder folk push around the college, we will form a spear head and push forward too. Perhaps we can then break these demon worshipping fiends."

Arkadi was still not clear what exactly was going on.

"We will need our best warriors at the head of the spear, my lord." Sir Arleas put in, "It is there that the fighting will go hardest."

The Archmage nodded.

"I volunteer myself and my knights to take the lead. We will push on and with Gods favour we shall reach their cursed leader and spit him on the point of our spearhead!"

Arkadi saw the Archmage nod and Sir Arleas led his men forward.

Arkadi took the opportunity and pushed over to the Archmage's side. He called out, "What is happening, my lord?"

"Something wondrous, Master Talcost, something not seen in centuries," the Archmage replied. "Watch."

Arkadi turned and looked out over the battle. More reinforcements pushed past Arkadi and Nossi, but it was still clear that the numbers would not be enough!

Suddenly, there was a noise that Arkadi couldn't identify. It was a kind of metallic 'twang' with a dull thump and immediately his eyes were snapped to the enemy by their left. They had toppled as if knocked down by a giant hand. Screams and death cries wailed forth. Soldiers nearby in the shield wall began cheering and calling something, but Arkadi couldn't make out what. However, what was clear was the enemy was falling back. There were more of the metallic 'twangs' and more of the enemy fell. Nossi caught his attention and pointed to the other side of the college. It was happening there too.

"They are crossbow bolts," someone nearby cried in realisation.

Of course, Arkadi thought and then... but from whose crossbows?

The answer suddenly was obvious as, marching into view, came a tight phalanx of heavily armoured dwarves. There must have been several hundred of them on both sides of the college. They were steadily advancing in rows, firing crossbows as they came. The short, bulky warriors were firing what seemed to be several shots from each crossbow and then exchanging it for a second crossbow slung on their backs. The unleashed barrage of bolts was devastating on the lightly armoured goblins and was even putting down the huge bulky trolls.

Abruptly, the barrage stopped. The crossbows were empty. The goblins and trolls roared and charged. Arkadi panicked, the dwarves would not be able to defend themselves! The little warriors calmly slung their crossbows on their backs and pulled out what looked like short poles with a leaf shaped blade on the end. How where they going to defend themselves with those?

The enemy thundered down on them.

The dwarves seemed to do something as one and suddenly, the short poles seemed to grow in their hands! They now held long spears! However, they would never get them set in time to face the enemy's charge.

Suddenly, a flight of arrows seemed to drop out of the sky from behind the dwarves, massacring the leading wave of fast moving goblins. Another followed, whistling over head, and yet more of the enemy fell. Meanwhile, the dwarves had pulled what looked like collapsed metal fans from their belts. They had two handles along their length and the dwarves slid these onto their arms. They then gave what looked like a flick of their strong arms and the fan swung open, flipping round as it did so. Another flick followed and the thing locked in place, producing a round shield the length of their arms so that as the ragged remains of the enemy's charge came down on the dwarves it found itself facing a solid shield wall with spears bristling like some gigantic hedgehog.

The goblins slowed as they approached, with yet more arrows falling on them. The dwarves roared something and then began to advance once more, the phalanx changing and flowing out into a wall. The dwarves then began to charge, roaring in their rough language. The goblins turned and fled. However behind them came some of the slower trolls and behind them the elven officers who lashed at any retreating goblins, turning them around. It made little difference, the dwarves, with a lethal rain of arrows proceeding them, ploughed into the mass of the confused enemy.

The soldiers, watching from the front steps of the Black Hall around Arkadi, cheered as one at the sight. Arkadi found himself cheering along with them. Orders were called and the human shield wall began to advance and change shape. Arkadi looked back over at the dwarves and saw for the first time, the elves behind them. They were wearing dark earthy coloured cloaks, and the armour that could be glimpsed beneath was of a similar hue. In their hands, mighty longbows thrummed as they were fired with a speed and skill that was beyond anything Arkadi had seen even from Nat! Their faces were clear in the sunlight and Arkadi now wondered why he had not realised before the difference between these elves and the enemy. These elves had silver pale skin and fair hair and eyes and they seemed so much nobler, a clear contrast to the darker, fiery look of the enemy elves. That these were enemies now seemed blatantly obvious, but then hindsight was a wonderful thing; Arkadi just hoped that next time, if there were a next time, he would see things more clearly.

Arkadi looked over at the enemy leader to see how he was reacting to this unexpected turn of events. The dark armoured elflord was surrounded by his guard and his men were solidly formed around them. He was still issuing orders calmly, but now it seemed he was moving to retreat. Was he fleeing now that the odds were more even?

Arkadi looked over to the shattered gates of the college. They were clear and the enemy leader was going to escape, no one in the college grounds could prevent that, they were all locked in combat. The grounds were a seething mass of warriors. Arkadi calculated that there must have been around three or four hundred men in their shield wall and that there were around twice that number of elves and dwarves to either side of them. Arkadi had no idea how, as that was twice what the Elder races were said to have for the defence of the rear wall.

Suddenly, something else caught Arkadi's attention; there was somebody in the shadow of the gates!

A cloaked figure walked forward into the light. Were these the enemy's reinforcements? The figure stood alone for a moment and then threw back its hood. Arkadi swallowed nervously. Was that what he thought it was? He squinted to make certain. It was a lone elf... a silver skinned elf with what looked like shining white or grey hair! The figure turned and gestured behind it. The shadowed gateway was suddenly filled with running figures. Into the light burst more and more armour clad, silver skinned elves. They glowed with power and carried swords and sabre staffs. More and more poured through, and with preternatural speed launched themselves into the rear guard of the enemy. The enemy was unprepared for this new attack and the new elves seemed to carve through them.

Arkadi grabbed Nossi in excitement. He couldn't help calling out and Nossi quickly joined in as he saw what Arkadi had been looking at.

The enemy leader had seen the attack to the rear and stopped his retreat. Arkadi saw him quickly look around, assessing his chances. From nowhere, his force was surrounded and he no longer had the advantage of numbers. The defence on the walls had taken its toll; the enemy had lost several thousand getting over the walls. It had been a heroic effort by the defenders. Now, with what must have been at least two thousand elven and dwarven forces appearing and more and more humans from all over the college coming to join the attack at the front doors of the Black Hall, the forces were more evenly matched.

"Noooooo!" a huge voice stormed with such violence that all had to cover their ears in pain

Everyone looked up in terror. Arkadi, like everyone else in the heat of the moment, had forgotten the elf prince.

Above them the tall, blood-red armoured prince looked down with a face knotted with rage. Behind him, a web of complete darkness washed out from the ball of energy to envelope the floating figure; by his side Bear, Rebba and Zara dangled helplessly; and in the dark prince's hand the Lifestone blazed incandescent. With clear malice and eyes fixed on those below, the prince raised the stone before his face and took it in both hands. The power began to swell.

⌒⌒

"Get up you useless, fat wastrel," his mother yelled, "You are as bad as your father."

"Please mum, I didn't mean it," the boy wailed.

"If it wasn't for you, I could have found someone by now," his mother went on in fury, swinging at him again with the switch stick. "You are nothing but bad luck to me, boy. It was all your fault your father died, and it's your fault now!" As she was talking and hitting him, her voice got weaker and more timorous. The boy knew she was heading for tears. He continued to try to shield himself as he huddled on all fours, but the switch still managed to catch him hard stinging blows. His own tears flowed liberally and a small pool of them had grown beneath him.

Why did his mother have to hit him? It wasn't his fault was it? He hadn't meant to run out in front of the carriage, he hadn't known it was coming. His father had just reacted. Neither had he meant to spill the drink over the man, it had just happened. Not that he understood why his mother needed to have men come to call on her. They were alright on their own.

"Your father is gone, dead. That fat wastrel left me with nothing, boy, nothing except you and you're as bad as he was," his mother said weakly as she stopped the switching and sat herself heavily on the stool. Her body began to shake as the tears started to flow. The switch stick dropped to the floor, his mother's hands slumped to her lap and she cried.

The boy stayed still, afraid to move. He wanted to help, but he knew that he would just make things worse. After a minute or two, his mother's head went back and she looked to the rafters of the small kitchen.

"Why?" she cried out, "Why have the gods forsaken us? Why do they turn their eyes away in this time of need?" She looked over at the boy, "Is it you boy? Are you cursed? Did you bring evil into our home?"

The boy looked at his mother through teary eyes and shook his head in silent denial. Her face hardened again as she looked at him. She bent and picked up the switch stick.

"You are going to learn boy," she said firmly.

In his head he was saying over and over, 'I am not cursed, I am not a fat wastrel; it's not my fault.' It was a chant for him, a chant of denial. The problem was that he couldn't quite believe it.

☙

Garon's mind wandered in and out of consciousness. The visions of his past taunted him. He was not a fat wastrel he screamed into the silence of his mind.

'Then why have you left your friends to die,' his mind taunted him. 'You are a useless, fat wastrel, a good-for-nothing.' The words came tinged with his mother's voice.

'No,' he screamed, 'that's not true!'

'Fat wastrel…fat wastrel… fat wastrel…' the chant echoed through his brain. 'You have failed your friends and your family, and where is your God? He will not come because you are not worthy. No god would ever want a pathetic excuse for a man like you.'

'No,' he whispered desperately, but his voice held little conviction.

'Then why has he not come to your aid? Why does he leave you to suffer in pain and torment?'

He screamed in denial, 'My God is with me!'

'No!' the voice cried, 'you are not worthy; you are a coward, too scared to face the world.'

'That's not true!' Garon screamed.

'Then why do you hide here, coward, when your friends suffer?' the voice screamed back.

Garon fell silent. The familiar chant returned, 'I am not cursed, I am not a fat wastrel, it's not my fault… I am not cursed, I am not a fat wastrel, it's no…'

'You are a fat wastrel. Your friends suffer and you do nothing,' the voice insisted.

'But I am done, I am dying. Back there is pain. Haven't I done enough?'

'Done enough?' the voice spat, 'What have you done, you fat fool? You couldn't even lead those dark elves away. They caught you without even trying.'

'No, no, that's not true...'

'Isn't it? Then why are your friends held prisoners? Why is the Lifestone in the enemy's hands?'

'But I told them nothing,' Garon pleaded, 'even though the pain made me want to.'

'You told them nothing... you did nothing,' the voice responded acidly. 'It is your fault and now you stay here hoping for your God to take you while your friends' suffer.'

'No, no, no, nooooooo...' Garon shrieked.

Sweet darkness enveloped him. Death reached out and he moved towards its comforting embrace.

Tal'Asin raced through the astral plane, throwing up every illusion, deception and chimera he could conceive. The astral plane was a fluid dimension and he could travel at a phenomenal speed in whatever direction he wanted and not stray far from a defined spot on the prime plane. The problem in avoiding, or at least getting far enough away from Ry'Ana to escape the astral plane, was that she knew this too. What he needed was some kind of real distraction that would throw off her raging pursuit if only for a few moments. However, he had driven her so far into a fury that she was completely fixed on killing him and nothing else.

A shout sounded. It was on the prime plane, but of such magnitude and charged with such power that it echoed through the astral plane. Tal'Asin paused, as did Ry'Ana.

He willed himself to view the Great Temple and instantly it appeared.

The room was bathed in dark energies. The portal to the void was almost fully open and the vision of the still form of Tal'Asin's most hated foe was suspended in the chamber. In the midst of this, Prince Uh'Ram stood rigid, looking at a view of the battle at the College of Magic. At first Tal'Asin could not see the reason for the prince's rage, but then it became clear. There were Sylvan elves and dwarves attacking the dark elves and their forces!

Tal'Asin's heart rose, but then he noticed that so too had the Lifestone in the dark prince's hand. Prince Uh'Ram clasped the huge gem in both hands before his face. He was going to use it to aid his people.

"No!" Tal'Asin gasped.

In desperation, he began to will himself from the astral plane. Ry'Ana was distracted, it had to be now. However, even as he started, Tal'Asin knew he would be too late.

⌒⌒

Rebba reeled at the power of the cry. Her head throbbed, but it could not deny her the joy she felt at the scene below. Elves and dwarves from the Wildlands had come to the aid of the college! It was amazing. She found she was smiling as the pain and the cry subsided in the subterranean chamber.

It was the first time since the dark prince had taken the Lifestone that Rebba had dared to hope that any of them would escape this alive. She had given up hope that she or any of her friends would leave this room alive, but perhaps those below might escape the prince's vengeance.

Rebba sought to clear her mind, but the dark, foul power within this place had become so pervasive and cloying that she thought she would suffocate. The evil was palpable. The yawning darkness in the great globe of power had nearly devoured the blue energy and the form suspended in the air was now whole. It could only be a matter of moments before the dark portal to the void opened and the evil that lay within returned. It did not even need the dark prince or the power of the Lifestone anymore; the portal's opening was now inevitable.

Rebba felt the power in the room rise again and forced herself to look back to the dark prince. He had raised the Lifestone before him and was calling on its power. The target of that power was all too obvious as his beetle black eyes were fixed on the battle below. Like a splash of cold water in the face, panic and fear for those below hit Rebba afresh; it was all too much for this one ray of hope to be dashed and Rebba cried out raggedly.

She found her cry echoed by Zara, who was struggling mightily against her bonds. Rebba began to struggle too, knowing it was useless and yet unable to stop herself.

'No, no, no…' she repeated in her head, but she knew there was nothing anyone could do. It was hopeless.

As if in a dream, Rebba suddenly saw Garon stumble forward from the gloom. Rebba blinked a few times until her mind told her that her eyes were actually seeing reality.

It was Garon, the friend they had thought dead! The tortured monk looked like a nightmare, dried blood and gore staining his ragged, slashed clothing and armour. He was deathly pale and the wounds that Rebba had sealed were splitting open again. It was horrific. Garon's eyes were open, but they were glazed and unseeing. His mouth too was open and it seemed he was mumbling something over and over.

Rebba and Zara stopped their struggles simultaneously.

Garon half stepped, half fell forwards, straight towards the dark elven prince. The prince was so intent on the Lifestone and the scene before him that he did not notice the dying monk advancing behind him. Garon's arms reached up and out encircling the dark prince's shoulders as if he would give the evil creature a kindly hug.

The elf prince reacted incredibly swiftly and started to dodge forward, but it was too late, the elf could not avoid the monk's arms. Yet Garon could not hope to hold on for more than a moment, or to withstand the awesome power the cruel creature held. Rebba's breathe caught, waiting for the inevitable. Yet, it seemed Garon was driven by some unknown force. He held the prince for the moment it took for his hands to find the Lifestone in the prince's grasp. Garon Vale's hands touched the gem that was already alive with power.

"What are you doing?" the dark elven prince yelled.

Garon's reply was clear to all.

"My God is with me, He will grant me this power!"

"This power is mine, you fool," the prince snarled already starting to twist free, "You cannot use it."

Garon's last words were faint, but Rebba heard them and would never forget them.

"I know... and its power will strike me down!"

Suddenly, the Lifestone flared. It would not bare anyone not of the holy line of the elves to touch it. A blast of pure force exploded from the mighty stone straight into Garon... but he was behind the prince, wrapped so tightly to him that when the power struck, destroying Garon totally, it also tore into the elf. So much raw power could not be contained. It ripped through the prince. He didn't even have time to scream!

Chapter 64

THE LIFESTONE

One day we will return. One day we shall take back what is ours. One day we shall cast aside the so-called Lords of Light and bring the worship of the true Lords of our people to all. One day, the Altai Mor will once again join with us, enlighten us and raise us up to our rightful place as lords of this earth. We will return to visit divine retribution on our hated kin who took our birthright from us and I shall lead you to visit wrath and ruin upon them, I, the Ata'Gon of our people shall be your eternal champion, your guardian. Not even death will prevent me!

Translated from 'The Words of the Beautiful One' by Ry'Ana White Eyes, Lore Queen of the True Elves

A thunderous cheer went up as the explosion tore through the elf prince and the mirage in the sky vanished. The goblins and trolls howled in fear at the loss of their leader and instantly sought to escape. Many bolted towards the north and south walls, but quickly the elves and dwarves completed a circle around them. The now trapped goblins and trolls were so wild with the desire to flee that they turned on their own in panic and frustration. Only the elven commander and his guard of dark armoured elves and black skinned goblins retained their order and discipline. The elven commander had clearly decided that the easiest enemy to fight his way through were the humans. He called for an advance and the impressive dark-clad elves and black goblins pressed forward with the remaining insect men leading the way. They quickly forced their way through and met the human line head on. Sir Arleas and his knights awaited them. The holy warriors, made short work of the few remaining insect men, but then the line of black goblins and coppery faced elves met them and the true battle began.

Arkadi found it hard to see clearly. Tears coursed down his face. He had never seen anything so wondrous or so terrible as the sight of Garon, battered and on the edge of death, sacrificing himself to kill that diabolical prince. It was the bravest thing he had ever seen and he could not find words to express the emotions he now felt. He looked to his new friend. Nossi was huddled over, clearly shattered by what had happened. Arkadi knew that Garon's affect on the little gnome had been deep. Arkadi stood over him; his face ravaged by confusion as emotions he wasn't sure how to express washed across his face.

Arkadi wiped at his face and looked back to the battle. It was clear now that the day was theirs, the goblins and the few trolls that remained alive had lost the heart to fight and fear of death crippled them. Some were begging for mercy. The elves and dwarves showed none and cut them down relentlessly. Only the enemy commander and his personal warriors fought on. They had managed to kill most of the knights of Karodra, but for the loss of an equal number of their own. Arkadi could still see the prominent helm of Sir Arleas, but he and the few knights still with him had been pushed to the side. He was busily trying to reform who ever he could to take the attack back at the enemy, but they were pushed steadily away. The enemy was heading straight for Arkadi and the people on the steps. It seemed that their dark armoured leader had decided that the best place to escape to was the Black Hall. He could barricade himself in there and defend or even escape into the catacombs below. This was clear to everyone now, but no one could do anything to stop it. The knights had failed to hold the enemy advance and there were now no significant groups of warriors who could match the dark elves amongst the college's forces. The fighter-magi were the college's best and their strength had been used up in the battle on the walls. Those who had survived were now spread all over.

Unexpectedly, Arkadi caught sight of Darin in his jet armour. He was galloping up the steps towards them, but he didn't look at Arkadi, his eyes were fixed on the Archmage. For a moment, Arkadi thought Darin had gone mad. His face could be seen and his eyes were wild. Arkadi sprang forward and reached Darin as he stopped in front of the Archmage and his officers.

"I need someone who can cast one of those gate things, those ports." The black clad knight shouted.

The Archmage looked at him and frowned and Arkadi took the opportunity to interrupt.

"Darin are you okay?"

"Do you mean have I lost control, Arkadi?" Darin snapped. "I can see that's what worries you. How about trusting me a little?"

Arkadi stared at him a moment and Darin stared back. Arkadi nodded and lowered his eyes, acknowledging his friend's point.

"Now I need a…"

"Portal," Arkadi put in.

Darin nodded.

"What for, Darin?"

"To get me next to that foul elven commander coming straight at us," Darin said harshly, "Do that and I can kill the evil swine."

The Archmage leaned forward and said urgently. "You could do that?"

"But that is suicide, Darin," Arkadi interrupted. "Even if you did kill him, his guard would cut you down before we could get you out or reach…"

"Could you do it," the Archmage cut in over the top of Arkadi.

Darin looked hard at the Archmage, "You get me next to him and I can kill him!"

One of the Archmage's officers leaned forward and said quickly, "That would disrupt them, my lord. We cut off the head and the body should fail. It seems our best chance, otherwise they are going to be in the Black Hall in minutes," he finished, looking over at the oncoming enemy. The coppery skinned elves and their allies grew ever closer.

"The enemy will destroy the portal swiftly and they will be ready for you coming through, Darin. It's madness!" Arkadi insisted, trying one more time to dissuade his friend. "You don't have to give away your life. We are going to beat them even if they get into the Black Hall."

Darin looked at him with steely determination, "They will escape if they get inside, Arkadi. Their magi will be able to get their leader away at the least and I will not let that happen, not after what Garon has done. I'll not let any of them escape if I can help it!"

The Archmage turned and beckoned forward some magi from behind him. He spoke fervently with them and soon they were nodding. Arkadi was shaking his head. He began pleading with Darin to think again, but the tall dark clad knight brushed him away. Some sorcerors began casting a portal to the enemy leader, and the Archmage instructed Darin to leap through as soon as the portal formed and that he would send a few of his best fighter-magi with him. Three armoured fighter-magi from the Archmage's bodyguard had stepped forward. The sorcerors immediately began their spell casting. Within seconds a portal spun into life, Darin's face was immediately enveloped by the liquid armour of his helm and he leapt through with the fighter-magi at his heels. The portal flashed away and the sorcerors staggered. The enemy had cut off their spell.

Arkadi's eyes snapped to the elven leader across the heads of the struggling warriors. Power flashed and Arkadi saw the warriors around the elven leader hacking at something Arkadi could not see. He didn't need to. He knew it was his friend.

༺༻

Darin rolled as he landed, but before he could get up he was hit by several bodies and felt blades hammering down on him. He heard the fighter-magi behind him scream out in pain and knew the same had happened to them. These dark elves would not even allow a potential enemy to get to their feet let alone get near to their lord. Darin writhed around in a frenzy, trying to get his feet beneath him. Only his armour kept him alive, though it did not protect him from the pain. These elves had powerfully enchanted weapons that cut through even his armour. It repaired him and itself, but it could not cope with this for long. With an agonised cry, as another blade sought his vitals, he got his feet beneath him. With all the strength the armour could give him, he heaved up. Bodies flew from him and without even looking, he swept his blade around wildly. He had the luxury of not having to worry about who he hit, he was on his own. He knew that the fighter-magi that had come with him were dead or dying, they could not have withstood the dark elven assault, but they had at least split the enemy enough to allow him to make his feet.

Darin roared and hacked apart anything near him. His blade sliced through armour, sinew and bone, but as soon as he cleared a space before him, more of the enemy fearlessly leapt in to fill the void.

Blades started to hit and pierce him from behind and he tried to dodge around as he swept forward, trying to make himself a difficult target. He could see that many of the enemy were poised to leap on him again and simply bare him to the ground. In a lightning move, he sprang forward and simply battered into the ranks of warriors ahead of him, avoiding the dives of those behind. He then spun viciously and stepped onto the backs of those on the floor, using them as leverage for a leap that took him over the heads of those around him in the direction of their leader.

Darin soared for a moment, and in a move that completely belied the armour he wore, he flipped over the heads of those in front of him and landed right beside the startled elven commander. Darin lunged forward with a speed even the elves could not match and rammed his enchanted ebon blade straight through the elf's dark armour and on through his chest and heart.

"This is for my friend, bastard!" Darin roared.

The look on the elf's face was one of complete amazement, then his body collapsed. Blades hammered down on Darin remorselessly and he fell, pierced a dozen times.

Rebba dropped to the floor as soon as the elf died, the invisible bonds gone.

The dark power still permeated the room and the ball of energy had barely any blue left. Rebba looked over and saw Zara already springing up and looking around for her swords. Rebba knelt up, rubbed at her throat and looked for any remains of Garon, but there were none; the Lifestone had completely destroyed him.

Bear groaned and began to push himself up. Zara spotted one of her swords and dashed over and picked it up. Rebba moved over and helped Bear up, but the big man quickly pushed her away and stood, scanning around the chamber frantically.

"Bear, are you okay?" Rebba asked hurriedly.

Bear glanced at her briefly and then went back to scanning around. Zara had grabbed her second sword and looked over to see Bear.

"You took your bloody time waking up!" yelled the warrior.

Bear ignored her.

"What the hell is that?" Zara suddenly called out.

Rebba looked over and then followed where Zara was pointing with her sword. In the air something was forming. It looked like a person.

Bear dived towards it, even as it began to coalesce into the form of an exquisite elf woman. She moved to kneel and Bear slid over and grabbed at something on the floor. It was the Lifestone! The woman screamed as Bear grasped it and a spell slammed down at him. Somehow he spun to the side, out of its way. Zara had begun to charge forward, but Bear yelled for her to keep back.

The elf woman, who Rebba could now see had milky white eyes as if she were blind, suddenly smiled as Bear slid back from her and climbed to his feet.

"Human, you can save yourself a lot of pain and hand that over now" the elf woman said slowly. "You cannot use the Lifestone."

"Human, Ry'Ana, do your blind eyes not see clearly even in your astral form?" Bear replied. "Have you not guessed yet?"

The woman frowned. "How do you know me?" she asked warily.

"It is I, Tal'Asin, and I think you will find I can use this." Tal'Asin replied through Bear. He held up the Lifestone.

The elf woman, Ry'Ana began to shake her head and her musical voice whispered the word no.

Tal'Asin nodded in response and he said grimly, "You cannot stand against me in astral form, Ry'Ana and now I must send you back to wherever your physical body lies."

Power swelled in the Lifestone. The truth of the elf woman's position twisted her face into a snarl of rage and frustration, then, abruptly, the elf woman's attention switched to the globe. She smiled, "I think it no longer matters, Tal'Asin. My father comes."

Tal'Asin spun, just in time to see the globe of energy turn completely black. The darkness emanating from the mighty sphere suddenly seemed to shrink back and gather. Above the sphere it formed into a gigantic shadowy form!

"I have come." a thunderous voice rumbled. "Bah'Athamin has returned."

"Yes, my blessed father," the elf woman called out ecstatically.

Through Bear, Tal'Asin called forth the power of the Lifestone and sent a blast of energy that enveloped the astral form of Ry'Ana. Her look of ecstasy turned to one of agony as the power coursed through her, jolting her savagely.

She cried out as her form began to fragment, "Father, you must retake your earthly body and destroy your enemy." She pointed fiercely as she twisted and struggled amidst the emerald storm. "Your hated foe stands before you, clad in the body of a cursed human. Destroy him!"

With that she gave a final tortured scream and her astral form simply shattered. The explosion caused everyone to stumble back. Above them, the monstrous shape reeled back and then looked down at the human form of Bear.

"My enemy?" it queried and then it muttered, "Could it be?" The dark cloud swelled and drifted closer. "Tal'Asin!" it exclaimed with sudden savage delight, "...never did I dream that the Lords of Darkness would deliver you to me."

The cloud of darkness and evil spun and leapt towards the regenerated body that had been lying forgotten on the floor, but before it even got half way, a blast of verdant green power slammed into it. The darkness reeled back, swooped around and reformed above the dark sphere to which it was still connected.

The giant body swelled and fiery red eyes suddenly blazed forth. "You dare!" it snarled. "You will not prevent me, Tal'Asin."

Immediately, giant dark arms lanced out and swamped the big man, engulfing him. An agonised cry reverberated around the chamber. The power in that darkness was immense and made Rebba gag with the pure wrongness of it. Zara dashed forward swinging her swords, but as soon as they struck the darkness, Zara simply collapsed as if struck dead. The darkness had snuffed her like a candle in a strong wind!

"Zara!" Rebba called in horror. 'Oh gods!'

"None can withstand the power of the Lords of Darkness." the dark form bellowed ecstatically.

Rebba did the only thing she could; she began praying to the gods. She was helpless against such power so she called upon Sarahiri, Queen of the Gods, knowing it was pointless, but doing it nonetheless.

She looked at the writhing mass of darkness, a cloud of death made manifest. It surrounded the place where Bear had stood. Rebba prayed for a miracle, but nothing happened. Terrible laughter began to echo around the stone chamber. The immense being was enjoying its return to the world.

"Damn you, foul spawn of the underworld!" Rebba suddenly called out, surprising himself, but the laugh went on louder and louder. Despair settled on Rebba like a cloak of defeat. The power before her was unstoppable!

Suddenly, a strange feeling came over her; an image of Garon, wracked with pain, but still standing, appeared in Rebba's mind. A profound sense of wonder washed over her. She was suddenly suffused with joy and pride at what her friend had accomplished. She found the feeling of joy within her blossom at the thought of Garon. Then it occurred to her that all of them had struck blows against this evil. It did not matter that they had failed; they had done more than could ever have been asked of them. It was the struggle that mattered. While one person still refused to give in to evil, it had not conquered.

Rebba looked deep within herself. She stood here doing nothing while evil grew strong. So, her power was tiny, it didn't matter. This was where the gods were watching. This was where they would see what she, Rebba Korran would do in the face of evil.

Rebba saw what she must do. She must do just as her friends had done before her. She could not let them down. She looked up at the evil dark figure.

"If we are all to die, devoured by your evil, you will have to choke on me first!" Rebba snarled. She grasped her fallen grey staff and poured all the love, joy and pride she felt for her fallen friends into it. With a huge bellow, she hurled the staff like a spear at the evil being. The staff lit up the dark as it flew and seemed to fly straight to the creature's foul heart. The force in Rebba's staff was miniscule and yet it seemed the touch of that power, so at odds with the deathly force, caused it pain. It reeled for the briefest moment and its power stuttered.

In that instant, so suddenly that Rebba could hardly follow it, emerald light burst from the darkness and Bear was revealed, encased in the power of the Lifestone, the power of life itself. With a roar of savage exertion, Bear, or Tal'Asin, twisted and shaped the energy around him. With the speed of thought, he hammered the power, not at the shadowy evil itself, but at the sphere beneath it, the portal to the void.

A cry of agony burst from the long dead evil creature and it lunged at the resolute figure of Bear. He was so concentrated on the portal that he could do nothing to prevent the blow falling. He could not withstand the monstrous attack. It slammed down and struck.

Rebba was forced to look away as raw energy exploded forth and sent her reeling. She looked back expecting to see Bear's shattered body, her hand half to her mouth in horror. Instead, another form stood protectively over Bear, a ghostly figure. Rebba's eyes widened. It was the golden haired figure of a Sylvan elf. Rebba knew instinctively that it was the spirit of Tal'Asin, the long dead Lore King. It had pulled itself out of Bear and taken the blow unflinchingly. Dark energy flowed around it, but a core of light held firm against the dark, shielding Bear from the evil. The evil shadow that was the *Ata'Gon* bellowed in fury and pressed harder. Tal'Asin's spirit began to shudder as pain tore into it. Rebba suddenly knew the ancient Lore King was in terrible trouble. Tal'Asin's face slowly changed from agonised exertion to terrified desperation. Dark cracks began to appear in the astral Lore King, like the spirit was breaking apart. The cracks spread, seeking the spirit's heart and the Lore King began to scream. The force of the dark demi-god above it pressed on relentlessly. Slowly the dark evil force grew. The spirit held out for a moment more as veins of dark energy riddled it like a canker, then the astral form of the Lore King shattered!

Rebba was aghast; Tal'Asin, the most powerful mage, the guardian of light and life, had just been destroyed! How could anyone hope to stand against such power?

However, the shadow of evil that was Bah'Athamin, the Beautiful One, the *Ata'Gon*, did not revel in Tal'Asin's destruction, it reeled back in surprise. Bear still stood with the power of the Lifestone alive in his hands. Desperately, the foul creature pulled back to strike again, but Tal'Asin's sacrifice had given Bear the time to muster the power of the Lifestone and in that instant he sent an enormous blast of energy into the portal. The energy crashed into the sphere and the darkness seemed to lighten instantly. There was a massive explosion that lifted Bear and slammed him back across the chamber. Rebba too was sent sliding back, but she kept her eyes glued to the titanic struggle.

The black shadow cried out and plunged its hands back into the great sphere. For a moment the darkness stopped retreating and Rebba held her breath. Could the creature reopen the portal? Blue light suddenly shone at the centre of the sphere, burning through the shadowy hands, and rapidly spread. As it did the shadow began to shrink, screaming all the time. It roared again and huge hands grasped the huge ball, but there was nothing even it could do. A last despairing cry sounded from the dark shadow and then blue energy exploded outwards shattering the evil spectre. The massive explosion tore through the chamber and Rebba was sent spinning into oblivion.

Chapter 65

AFTERMATH

The vision in the sky changed us all. To see one so powerful, so evil, destroyed by one simple man's sacrifice is to witness a miracle. All was at an end, we all knew it, we could all sense the futility of resisting such might. Death was upon us, yet such despair was transformed to wonder in an instant. We all shed tears of joy and of sorrow for the one who saved us. We know now his name and give thanks to Garon the Brave!

Except from the writings of Sir Arleas of Karodracia, Grandmaster of the Knights of Saint Karodra, BY1346

Arkadi and Nossi picked through the bodies. They had been one of the first out to look for survivors, but one body in particular they wanted to find.

The battle was finally over. The enemy had fallen apart when its leader had fallen. It had been another hour of fighting before they had finally managed to crush the enemy, but it was now clear that although the town had lost well over thousand people and soldiers, and the college had lost almost two hundred of its magi, that the enemy had fallen in their thousands. Some were still loose on the island, but already the Sylvan elves and the dwarves were hunting them.

"We should check in the Clerics Dome too for Nat." Nossi said once more.

The gnome had been told that no one had survived in there, but he wouldn't believe it. Mind you, this search was hopeless too, Arkadi thought miserably. Darin had been brutally cut down.

"We will find Nat's..." Arkadi stopped and blinked back tears. He couldn't bring himself to say 'body'. It seemed too final, too much an admittance that his friend was dead. "We will find Nat after we have found Darin." Arkadi finished, his voice breaking with emotion.

Nossi nodded, his lower lip shaking and his big honest eyes glassy. The two of them went back to searching. It was hard to say where the elven commander had been slain. With the ebb and flow of the battle there were bodies strewn everywhere, some piled atop others. Added to which, the terrible smell of death hung thick like an invisible pall over everything. Arkadi did not want to think about the reality of death too much, though evidence of it assaulted his eyes wherever he looked. He dulled his mind and continued to scan the ground, pretending that he was not seeing the butchered remains of people.

"Here!" Nossi suddenly called kneeling by a mound of dark armoured elves.

Arkadi ran over, jumping heedlessly over bodies and weapons. Nossi was trying to roll bodies out of the way urgently, straining hard. Arkadi reached him and looked down to see the now familiar black armour.

"Don't touch it!" Arkadi cried as Nossi went to do just that.

The gnome frowned up at him. "What?"

"If he is dead the armour will look for another to wear it. Remember what Darin told us about it." Arkadi explained.

"But we have to find out if he is alive or not?" the gnome said earnestly.

"I don't think even he could have survived that?" Arkadi said sadly.

A tiny groan and twitch startled Arkadi and Nossi and they jerked back, but only for a moment. Quickly, the two of them lunged in to help free their friend from the bodies pinning him. Sir Darin of Kenarth, Lord Champion of the Ebon Order, had proved he was an incredibly hard man to kill.

"Rebba!" the voice cried urgently.

Her eyes opened and she blinked until she could see clearly. When she did she frowned and then rubbed at her eyes. What was going on?

"Rebba, come on get up!"

Rebba sat up and reached out to grab the person in front of her. "Zara!" She gasped, "You're alive!"

"Yeah," she replied vaguely, "I'm not sure what happened, I thought I was dead there for a minute." She looked around them. "I guess from the look of that big blue ball of stuff that we won."

Rebba looked around. She was still in the chamber and it looked almost as if nothing had happened. The sphere of energy shone blue and the stone around them had withstood the battle with implacable permanence. Only the fact that all the debris in the room was now plastered around the edges attested to the power that had been unleashed.

"Where is Bear?" he asked in sudden realisation.

"He is here and still alive," Zara replied quickly as she headed off behind Rebba. "Come and give me a hand."

Rebba turned and saw that Zara was struggling to lift Bear. The big man sagged in her arms. Rebba rushed over, a little wobbly at first. She lifted Bear's arm over her head and helped Zara hoist him up. Suddenly, Bear's head rose weakly and his blue eyes opened.

"Tal'Asin is gone!" he cried faintly, "his spirit was crushed protecting me and yet his soul remains. I feel his essence and yet there is a yawning chasm within me where he should be. His memories swamp me... his feelings... I cannot think... cannot make sense..."

With a groan, Bear's head sagged again as he slumped back into unconsciousness.

"Look he's got the Lifestone in his hand." Zara said.

Rebba looked down and grabbed Bear's arm. She lifted it and saw that Bear's fist was tightly wrapped around the now quiescent stone. She gingerly tried to pry his fingers apart but they would not move. It was like a death grip he had on the thing.

"Are you insane?" Zara snapped, knocking her hand away. "It's safe where it is; he isn't letting go of the thing and we don't want to touch it. Let's just get out of here!"

Rebba nodded. She was still dazed and was finding it hard to think about anything. She struggled to lift Bear, but between them they managed to drag Bear's limp body and headed slowly for the twin pillars. As they passed between them, the Lifestone flared once in Bear's hand and the familiar blue energy pulsing between the pillars vanished. The friends blinked and looked around. The hall had reverted back to what it had been when they had first entered. They were in the Waygate hall in which they had first fought the dark elven prince. Rebba stopped and pushed her arm back towards the pillars. Nothing happened. The Temple of Elysia had sealed.

"Come on, Rebba." Zara badgered. "There is no way I want to be still here if any of those bastard elves are still around. Bear mentioned before that this was where they had set up their base. Get out that keystone and get us back to Shandrilos," she insisted. "I just hope there are no more of those swine back there either. We have to get back through all those tunnels."

Rebba looked at the ever pragmatic warrior and their eyes met. A silent acknowledgement of all they had been through passed between them, then Rebba nodded. It was only as she stepped through the Waygate to Shandrilos that she realised that she had seen no elven body in the Temple. Where had the body gone?

⌒⌒

Sir Arleas and the only two of his knights still alive and not severely injured, wandered into the Clerics Dome. This had once been the centre for their holy order within the college. Now it looked like a slaughter house. The enemy had come through this place like the devil himself, bodies were strewn everywhere and the smell was almost overwhelming.

Sir Arleas wrinkled his lips in distaste and was about to turn away when he noticed movement. He moved quickly forward, calling for his men, and knelt urgently. A single tiny hand poked up from beneath a tall woman's body and twitched spasmodically. The woman on top had been pierced through by a spear and was difficult to roll out of the way. Underneath, a small woman in a long dark robe lay partly conscious. She had been stabbed and the wound was serious, but she was not beyond hope.

As the three men carefully lifted the small woman, a rattle sounded and Sir Arleas let go of his hold on the fragile woman to grab his sword and look round; many of the bodies in here where that of the enemy.

Sir Arleas turned in time to see the white haired form of Alinus Quan Sirona struggle and then sit up from beneath the body of one of his monks! The old man looked around in dismay and confusion. The man's great age was suddenly apparent in his frailty. Sir Arleas ran over to him and began pulling bodies back to free the saintly old Grand Abbot. It was clear that as his monks had died they had flung themselves on top of their leader to protect him whatever way they could. They had shielded him from the hacking blades that had executed all save the lucky young woman!

The Archmage looked around the Great Hall in stunned silence. The place was packed full of the injured. There were many. About him they stood, waiting for some kind of order. The Archmage almost didn't have the strength to hold himself up and the task of organising the aftermath to this catastrophe was overwhelming. The Archmage still didn't understand all of what had happened himself.

He had been pleased to see that Lord Elgon had survived in the college maze. Korlin Di Vorseck, Raban Ironhand, young Serales Kalizern, and the Lord of Katurem's son had survived too, but so many others had not.

He looked up to see Master Talcost and his little gnome friend come stumbling in, carrying the dark armoured knight, Darin. They had looks of joy on their faces and were calling for healers. The Archmage shook his head in amazement at the armour's power. He was glad too that the man had survived; the battle had turned decisively when he had killed the enemy leader!

Before this day, the Archmage had seen few things that could match such ancient power as that armour and it needed investigating, and yet today he had witnessed magics that had far surpassed even that of the armour. What he and so many others had witnessed in the skies earlier was a wonder; the powers involved truly awesome!

It struck the Archmage that he had no idea what had really taken place above them, but that it had been the most important thing in all their lives and that somehow they had won. What's more, their victory was down in large part to a group of friends he knew very little about; they had just been in the right place at the right time.

He looked across at Arkadi's haggard and grief ravaged face; perhaps the young mage would not agree with such an assessment.

The Archmage smiled suddenly as he remembered how Master Talcost had described his friends: 'Just an ordinary group of people, much like everyone else,' the young mage had said. The Archmage shook his head and just thanked the gods that there were such 'ordinary' people in the world.

Just then a murmur rippled around the great hall and the Archmage looked over in time to see the ghost-like elflord Val'Ant, walk in, accompanied by several other lords of the Elder. People were pushing themselves up to stare at the elves and dwarves. Men nudged neighbours and even those too injured to rise tried to see. The Archmage held his breath; he knew his people still distrusted elves and dwarves.

Suddenly, a call went up from a lone voice and then, like an avalanche starting from a single drop of snow, a cheer began. Thanks and blessings rang out and the Elder nodded their heads in acknowledgement before advancing towards the Archmage. Amidst the cacophony of cheering, the Archmage found himself with tears in his eyes. Here, from adversity, might have begun the trust and understanding between the races that he had worked towards for half a century. Just then the Archmage noticed that amongst the Elder was his old friend, Storlin, chief of the Swiftaxe dwarves!

Baden Erin, Archmage of the College of Magic, smiled through the tears that now flowed freely. He was not given to such public displays, but he could not seem to help it. Storlin pushed forward and met him. The burly dwarf grabbed him and slapped him sternly yet happily on the back. Baden, fully absorbed in the moment, threw his arms around the dwarf and hugged him fiercely to which a huge roar of approval echoed around the hall.

A few minutes later within one of the council rooms, the Archmage stood and listened as the grey elf lord Val'Ant outlined the miracle that had brought the Elder to their aid.

"Like your own seers, our Lorewise had foreseen great danger in the north. However, what we also perceived as crucial was this place," the tall, graceful elf said, gesturing at the walls around them. "In all our visions, the place you know as Shandrilos was prominent. We did not know what its importance was, but that it was important. As time moved on and your own efforts to draw us into an alliance were revealed, we were sure that we must come here and seek answers. However, we still did not know whether this place would be a place of danger or of salvation, the signs were too vague to decipher. So it was that I sought to convince my fellow leaders amongst the elves to come to your great council, but we would bring as much force as we could muster in case the dangers we had foreseen were here! We hid our forces within the lands of the Nightarrow elves, where they could be summoned quickly if necessary. We worked hard to hide our forces, and our knowledge of this ancient place allowed us to locate hidden tunnels that go beneath the great river. Thus our forces were only two days march away. It was only when we arrived that our Lorewise began to see more clearly. It became clear that this place was the focal point for some momentous events and that a battle would be fought here, though between who we were not clear, there was evidence that agents of evil were within the college. We couldn't risk speaking to you, though many of us wished to, as we had suspicions of treachery both in our own paranoia and in our visions. When we were certain of the approaching danger, we sent out Lord Storlin and Lord El'Caron to summon our forces. They arrived barely in time."

The Archmage sat in stunned silence. He found he was a little irritated that the Elder had known so much and withheld it from him, but he could not blame them. They could not possibly have known who to trust; only Storlin truly knew and trusted him. That was perhaps why Storlin had been sent away to muster the Elder's secret forces so that he could not betray anything. However, with so many lives at stake, Baden might well have done the same.

Lord Val'Ant's musical voice interrupted his thoughts, "I am sorry that we could not tell you, my friend… and I do consider you a friend, Baden Erin… but we now have a chance to make a better future, to change things. The goblin threat is still an issue and we need to discover more of the machinations of this dark elven prince."

The Archmage nodded. He then smiled at the ghostly elflord, "I have fought my whole life to achieve greater unity in this land of ours, my lord… my friend. With us all working together we can surely protect our lands."

Lord Val'Ant blinked in acknowledgement and gratitude. "With that understanding foremost, we must seek information about the miracle that happened in the sky today. Whatever it was, whatever took place, we must understand it."

"The enemy elves should be questioned..." the Archmage began.

"Those we have managed to capture alive, accept death rather than speak," the tall, one-eyed elf, Lord Dag'Nir said bitterly.

There was silence for a moment.

"We know something of what took place and that the humans in the vision were friends of Master Talcost who went below with him, but we know nothing of the place we saw nor of the emerald gem that wielded such power. We must question Master Talcost and the gnome, Nossi Bee, but I fear they know little more than we."

The Elder lords nodded and Lord Val'Ant replied, "Yet whatever clues we can find, we must. This unknown elven prince is dead, the gods be praised, but the threat from his people may not be."

The Archmage nodded. "I will summon the Grand Council, or what remains of it," he added somberly, "once we have things here more under control."

The Elder lord nodded and the Archmage stood to leave. There was much to do, but already his mind was working; tired as he was, his mood was high and the future looked much brighter than it had when he had awoken this morning.

Epilogue

A FAREWELL

Rebba Korran walked out into the bright sunlight. She moved purposely down the steps of the Black Hall, heading for the newly repaired gates. The lawns and pathways at the front of the college still showed the marks of the battle that had taken place here only four weeks ago, but thankfully the bodies were all long gone, transported to a mass grave to the north of the town. However, the once well kept lawns were torn and riven and the paths showed stains that were only now starting to fade.

Rebba walked on and quickly reached the shadow of the gates. She looked out at the city of Shandrilos. Here the scars of battle were more obvious. The shattered remains of the houses that the enemy had torn down were only just being cleared away. Many of the town's most important buildings were now gone; the large guild hall and the city hall were no more. Rebba had heard that this area would be left clear and that the two municipal halls would be relocated. It was said that instead, a town square and memorial to those who had fallen would be built here in front of the college.

As she passed out of the shadow of the gates and once more felt the warmth of the sun upon her, Rebba caught sight of her friends. They stood waiting for her.

'So few of them, now,' she thought sadly.

Arkadi was already there, released from the council earlier, and Zara stood with her pack on the ground. She was dressed for the road. Lastly, Nossi Bee, the gnome who had joined the little group of survivors as a new friend, stood hunched over, sadness clear in his posture.

Rebba waved lightly to them as she approached.

"Thought you weren't coming for a while there," Zara Halven called over. The lithe warrior wore a dark woolen cloak, but it failed to cover the magnificent armour she had beneath, nor the ornate hilts of her sabres that stuck up over each shoulder. "That collection of lords still got you going over things."

Rebba gave a grimace and nodded as she stopped by her friends. "I have been over everything three times now, but still they question me."

"Thankfully, those 'important' people," she said sarcastically, "didn't seem to think that some common warrior like me would know enough to help anymore. Not that I am complaining," she put in quickly, "At least I can get myself out of here."

Common warrior, Rebba thought, Zara was hardly that. With the armour and swords she now carried she was one of the most powerful warriors alive. She had become a celebrity around town in the weeks since the battle. She was no longer the Whore of Ostia, but the 'Silver Slayer'. She was one of the heroes of the battle and a companion to the blessed Saint Garon. It was a little uncomfortable to think of her lost friend in such an elevated way, but both the Order of Saint Karodra and the Order of Sironacian Monks had named him as both a Saint and a Martyr.

All of the friends were becoming heroes.

It was a little embarrassing to Rebba how people now viewed her. The ordinary people all knew her and the wealthy and powerful all wanted to meet her and talk to her. The stories around them were already growing, especially around Garon. However, the Grand Council's interest was also in rigorously questioning them about what they knew, and Zara was right about them; the elves, dwarves and magi on the Grand Council had placed more importance on Rebba and her magical insights than Zara's warrior's view and questioned her far more. Nevertheless, the warrior had come out of the council room claiming she would rather be back fighting the dark elves than face the lords' questions again.

"Do you still intend to go after Darin?" Arkadi asked quietly, his brown eyed gaze intense as he looked at Zara.

Zara scuffed the floor with her armoured boot.

"Darin was obviously troubled by something, maybe that armour, and he may need help. I am doing nothing else of use here." Zara said, her voice tinged with emotion. "I believe I can find him. That armour of his would leave a clear picture in anyone's mind from what I have heard of it. Besides I am more use to him than I am to Bear." The warrior paused and grimaced. "I can't sit here doing nothing!"

Arkadi nodded. "I still don't know what happened or why Dain would just disappear like that. He seemed fine after the battle, he healed at an incredible rate and was his old self again, laughing and joking. Then, just the morning you returned, he vanished. The only clue we've had that nothing terrible happened to him was that the guards at the dock saw him getting on a boat heading for Port Shandri."

"Perhaps that armour is not so under his control as he believes," Rebba muttered darkly. "If what Bear told us about the armour of the Rainbow Guard is true, Darin will face a constant struggle for control. Wherever he went he will need help."

Everyone agreed and an uncomfortable silence grew as the friends realised the time for parting was nearing.

"Any news on Bear?" Zara asked, seeking to delay the inevitable.

It was clear to Rebba, even as she shook her head in response to the question, that the warrior knew what the answer would be. Bear had remained unconscious since the battle in the Great Temple of Elysia over a month ago, the Lifestone still clasped in his fist. He had been the study of many magi, as well as Loremasters from the Elder. They had tried to remove the Lifestone from him, but some unknown force had arisen each time they tried. None could withstand it. Rebba believed that Bear's unconscious mind was somehow protecting the great gemstone. However, she couldn't prove it; no one could rouse the big man. Many had tried, including herself and Arkadi, but Bear's mind was locked away and clearly in turmoil.

"There is still hope," Nossi Bee said. "There is always hope. Garon showed us that."

All looked at the earnest little man and smiled sadly. Surprisingly, Zara reached out and ruffled the little creature's hair like a mother would a child.

"You got it right there, little guy," the warrior laughed lightly.

Rebba silently agreed. Garon Vale's sacrifice would always be an inspiration to her. It made her believe that maybe the gods were up there looking out for them... or god, she thought wryly thinking of Garon.

"Well," Zara said abruptly, hoisting her pack. "It's time I got on my way, I've got a long day ahead."

Nossi Bee abruptly sprang forward and Zara cried out in surprise as he hugged her fiercely, his little arms tight about the warrior's waist. Suddenly, they were all hugging and slapping each other on the back. None of them were comfortable with goodbyes and soon Zara was heading off towards the docks and Nossi, Arkadi and Rebba were heading back for the college. As they walked back into the college grounds, they were met by two women walking arm in arm, one old, one young.

"Did we miss Zara?" Alea Bero asked.

They nodded silently.

Arkadi and Rebba were finding it difficult talking to Alea. Nat's mother still showed the ravages of grief. They had known her for years and both felt somehow guilty that they were still here while Nat was not. The older woman had left Nat's children at their family home in Ostia with her daughter, Nat's younger sister. Nat's family had been helping to care for them while the huntress had been out seeking work and money over the past few months. The two children had taken the loss of their mother hard, but were being well looked after with the huntress' family.

Beside Alea Bero, Roslyn Shanford put her arm fully around the older woman. The two had become firm friends over the last two weeks since Alea had come south to arrange for Nat's funeral. Roslyn had taken on the role of supporting and comforting the distraught woman after she had shared her memories of the tall huntress' death. It was clear from her story and from what Garon had related to Rebba, Zara and Bear down in the catacombs that Nat had been tortured by the way she had been turned unknowingly into an assassin by the enemy. She had covered it well, but the knowledge had crippled her inside, had made her doubt herself. Nat Bero had been deeply ashamed. It was clear that she had sought at the end to prove that she wasn't a killer.

Ironically, Nat's last words had proven true, as she, like the other friends, had all been acknowledged as heroes as people began to discover what had really gone on both in and under the college. Everyone had seen Garon's sacrifice and once Rebba and Zara returned with Bear, all had hailed them as heroes. Once their story became known Nat, Darin and Arkadi had also become widely celebrated. They had already been hailed for their exploits in saving the Archmage and for their part in the defence of the College. The seven friends who had gone into the catacombs were rapidly becoming famed throughout the Wildlands.

Little Roslyn Shanford in particular had been adamant that no one forget Nat's part and few could gainsay the determined woman once she gave her opinion. Roslyn herself had become well known for her exploits in the battle and in the Clerics Dome. The Grand Abbot had spoken highly of the young apothecary and her abilities. The old holy man had insisted that she be acknowledged by the college and given a place as a mage, though the woman herself seemed reluctant to join.

"We must return to the council," Arkadi said awkwardly to the two women as the silence grew.

Roslyn flashed a frown their way, but Alea nodded. Rebba gave Alea's arm a reassuring squeeze as she and Arkadi moved off towards the Black Hall.

They walked in silence until they got to the top step then Arkadi stopped and turned to look back towards the gates and the town. Rebba stopped and turned with him.

"Everything seems so different now, Rebba," the grey robed mage muttered. "I look around me and see things afresh. Suddenly, my life before seems to have been so petty, so lacking in meaning." He looked Rebba in the eye. "Do you know what I mean?"

Rebba held his look for a minute and then looked out to the town. Over the weeks, Rebba had noticed that Arkadi seemed to be getting more and more depressed, taking the deaths of their friends hard. She knew he blamed himself for Nat in particular.

She took a deep breath. "Yes, I think I do," she replied. "Before, it seemed like we were just playing at life, like nothing really mattered. Now I feel like I have awoken into the real world and found that life is not a game. I feel that what I choose to do in my life is important and that the choices I make in my life can affect everything. When we were fighting against the dark prince and then that foul spirit, several times I felt that I was of no importance, that nothing I could do could change anything." Rebba shook her head, "Yet, I realised that even I could make a difference, even if it was a little difference it might be enough to tip the balance."

Arkadi looked at her hard for a moment, thinking hard. A grin appeared on his face for the first time in weeks.

"You are an amazing person, Rebba. You have looked into the very heart of evil and come out with your soul unscathed." Arkadi grasped Rebba's arm and turned her towards the Black Hall once more.

"You know, Arkadi," Rebba insisted, seeking to further lift her friend. "I feel we should take joy in every moment and not dwell on the unfairness of things, but celebrate the lives of those we have known and of the life we have."

Arkadi nodded thoughtfully. They walked on in silence for a few moments and then Arkadi suddenly looked at Rebba with that old twinkle in his eye.

"Okay then, let's go and see if we can get some joy out of another questioning session," Arkadi laughed and slapped Rebba on the shoulder.

Rebba walked along at his side, a smile on her face too. It was good to see Arkadi smile. Perhaps he was beginning to return to his old self again, though to be fair none of them would ever be the people they had once been only a month or so ago; too much had happened for that to happen...

Hidden above them, in the astral realm, Ry'Ana White Eyes watched the two humans go.

"Hence forth, let these few stand as an example of the valour of which all are capable. Let them stand for the difference that a few can make even to the fate of all."

Inscription on the Seven Heroes memorial erected in the new city square of Shandrilos, BY1347, a year after the Battle of Shandrilos. It represents all who died in the battle, but depicts the seven who went into the catacombs. Nathalia the Huntress and Garon the Monk are represented most prominently of all.

Appendix 1

CAST OF CHARACTERS

THE FRIENDS

* **Sir Darin of Kenarth** – a master swordsman and knight of the order of Saint Karodra (age 28).
* **Zara Halven** – a female mercenary and blademaster from Ostia who fights with two sabres (age 27).
* **Jon Madraig** – known as Bear, a warrior mage and tutor at the Magic Guild's school in Lauria (age 28).
* **Arkadi Talcost** – a master mage and senior tutor at the College of Magic in Shandrilos (age 29).
* **Rebba Korran**– a former student at the College of Magic and now a druid and healer in the vale of Aron (age 30).
* **Garon Vale** – a former student of the College of Magic and now a monk of the Sironacian brotherhood (age 31).
* **Natalie 'Nat' Bero** – former owner of a large inn outside of Ostia, a master tracker and hunter (age 28).

AT THE COLLEGE

* **Baden Erin** – Archmage of the College of Magic and son of the famed Melkor Erin founder of the College.
* **Eliantha Shamass** – Mage Master at the College of Magic, member of the ruling Conclave and head of the School of Magi.
* **Xameran Uth Altor** – Sorceror Supreme at the College of Magic, member of the ruling Conclave and head of the School of Sorcery.
* **Atholl Dorard** – aged High Enchanter at the College of Magic, member of the ruling Conclave and head of the School of Enchantment.
* **Zarina Agroda** – First Wizard at the College of Magic, member of the ruling Conclave and head of the School of Wizardry.
* **Marillia Aronis** – Chief Druid at the College of Magic, member of the ruling Conclave and head of the School of Druidry.
* **Jammu Quadai Pendi** – Magus General at the College of Magic, member of the ruling Conclave and head of the School of Warrior Magi.
* **Arimenes Corvindar** – Allseer at the College of Magic, member of the ruling Conclave and head of the School of Seery.
* **Izonda Tariadarmin** – Abbess at the College of Magic, member of the ruling Conclave and head of the School of Clerics.

TYPES OF MAGIC USER

* **Magi** – common term for magic user in general and for the school of magic relating to all aspects of magic and magical theory.
* **Sorceror** – magi of the school of magic relating to manipulation of space and reality, and the planes of existence
* **Enchanter** – magi of the school of magic relating to time and materials, to creating and using lasting magical affects contained by potions, objects, weapons, and other materials and items.
* **Wizard** – magi of the school of magic relating to the manipulation of energies and forces.

- * **Druid** – magi of the school of magic relating to the manipulation, control and understanding of living things and nature.
- * **Warrior Mage** – magi of the school of magic relating to use of magic in combat, allied to sword and war craft focusing on quick spells that enhance the wielder.
- * **Seer** – magi of the school of magic relating to visions, dreams and foretelling.
- * **Cleric** – magi of the school of magic relating to spiritual magic, the soul, good and evil.

THE WILDLAND PROVINCE RULERS

- * **Elgon the Golden** – Hereditary High Lord of the town and province of Ostia, a Nordic warrior mage, former student at the College of magic and veteran commander in battles against the goblins of the Dark Dales.
- * **Alinus Quan Sirona** – Founder and ruler of the monastic town and province of Sironac, Grand Abbot of the Sironacian order of monks and powerful prophet and healer.
- * **Raban Machaig** – Hereditary High Lord of the Nordic province and town of Dunegan, known as the 'Ironhand', he is a powerful warrior and commander of volatile temper.
- * **Tarik Ardan** – Hereditary High Lord of the Nordic province and town of Dunard, an acknowledged warrior and leader with a diplomatic temperament.
- * **Wolfstan Uth Tard** - Hereditary High Lord of the Nordic province and town of Arondar, he is a young, tall, brash warrior.
- * **Serales Kalizern** – Hereditary First Minister of the province and town of Kalizern, descendent of the founder of the town and youngest of the leaders of the provinces.
- * **Sir Arleas Di Mardul** – High Lord of the province and town of Karodracia and Grandmaster of the Holy Order of the Knights of Saint Karodra, he is a fine knight and swordsmen and an experienced commander.
- * **Zaras Ithill** – son of the High Lord of the town and province of Katurem, Adzem Ithill.

* **Aristos Ariventes Surtez** – First Minister of the Olmec town and province of Hadek, a well known and wealthy merchant and negotiator.
* **Korlin Di Vorseck** – First Minister of the Olmec town and province of Lauria, the oldest and largest of the Wildland towns, he is a renowned speaker, politician and leader and head of the powerful banking guild.
* **Boras Del Aro** – First Minister of the Olmec town and province of Torunsport, he is an obese man, formerly a sea trader who has made a vast fortune and looks only to himself and his provinces concerns.

ELF LORDS OF THE WILDS

* **Val'Ant Greycloak**– also known as the 'ghost prince' for his grey hair and eyes, he is an accomplished Lorewarden (Warrior Mage) amongst his people and the Gonhir or Clan lord of the most powerful group of elves in the Wildlands, the Suthantar Elves who live in the Aron Forest.
* **Dag'Nir Surestride** – a red haired, one eyed older elf, a veteran of many battles, he is the Gonhir or Clan lord of the second most powerful group of elves in the Wildlands, the Falorcatian Elves who live in the Dun Forest.
* **El'Caron Nightarrow** – he is the Gonhir or Clan lord of the Garcarost Elves who live in the hills and high forest around the Shandri and Ost vales.
* **Stor'Gan Greenheart** – oldest of the elven lords, he is Gonhir or Clan lord of the Daliari Elves who live in the southern stretches of the Karodran forests and the foot hills of the Barrier Mountains.
* **An'Tiara Treewalker** – the only female leader, she is the Gonhir or Clan lord of the Kurashandar Elves of the northern Karodran forests.
* **Suth'Lian Eaglebrow** – close friend of Val'Ant and scholar amongst his people, he is the Gonhir or Clan lord of the Salthurin Elves who live in the foothills of the eastern Druidhome mountains.
* **Car'Dolis Stormcrow** – close friend of Val'Ant and Loremaster (magi) amongst his people, he is the Gonhir or Clan lord of the Ulintari Elves who live in the high valleys of the western Kalizern hills.

DWARF LORDS OF THE WILDS

* **Afindor Ironcleaver** – scarred warlord and general, the most powerful of the dwarf lords and Clan chief of the Ironcleaver clan who live in the Bloodland Heights.
* **Saroth Darkaxe** – a craftsmaster and weaponsmith amongst his people, he is the Clan chief of the Darkaxe clan who live in the Druidhome Mountains.
* **Jarlis Hammerhand** – a young, but powerful warrior mage amongst his people, he is the second most powerful of the dwarflords and Clan chief of the Hammerhand dwarves who live in the central Darkheart hills.
* **Storlin Swiftaxe** – friend of the Archmage and a mage, he is the Clan chief of the Swiftaxe dwarves who live in the Ost and Shandri Hills.
* **Uldar Shatterstone** – a rich trader and merchant amongst his people, he is the Clan chief of the Shatterstone dwarves who live in the central Barrier Mountains and the Kalizern hills.

OTHER ELVES

* **Uh'Ram Bloodfire** – elven prince of the third house, grandson of the Ata'Gon, ruler of the province of Syth'Daargo, Kaldesar (warlord) and Lorewarden (warrior mage).
* **Ry'Ana White Eyes** – seer and daughter of the Ata'Gon, first princess of the first house, Lore Queen of her people, head and most powerful of the Lorewise and ruler of the Holy Province and City.
* **Dar'Elthon Ath Totheariss** – Hironsar of a War party and new head of House Totheariss. He is a Lorewarden (warrior mage) and accomplished swordsman.
* **Nar'Dolth** – Senior Parinsar of Prince Uh'Ram's forces, powerful warrior and general.

OTHERS

- **Roslyn Shanford** – local apothecary and healer in Shandrilos.
- **Master Gardon Rill** – Second Watchmaster of the college of magic in Shandrilos.
- **Master Sintharinus** –First Watchmaster of the college of magic in Shandrilos.
- **Master Bruenor Brae** – Elderly tutor at the college of magic in Shandrilos.
- **Master Abertha Tayvor** – Deputy Mage Master of the school of Magi at the college of magic in Shandrilos.
- **Sardyk Andar** – Halfling assassin.
- **Ivello** – former monk of the Karodracian order and convicted murderer saved from execution.

Appendix 2

CHRONOLOGY OF DARYLOR

Timeline for the College of Magic and the Wildlands of Darylor
(Based upon archive records from Lauria, Ostia and Shandrilos. - compiled BY1346 by Master Arkadi Talcost)

Blessed Year (BY):

* 1346 - Twelfth Grand Council of the Wildlands of Darylor held in Shandrilos (Present)
* 1344 - Arkadi Talcost becomes a Master Magi
* 1343 - The first Magic Users Guild School in an Olmec Province is set up in Lauria
* 1340 - Xameran Uth Altor becomes Sorceror Supreme
* 1337 - Guild schools for Magic Users are set up in Dunard, Arondar and Dunegan after the success of the first school in Ostia
* 1336 - Xameran Uth Altor becomes a Grandmaster of Sorcery
* 1333 - Elgon the Wise of Ostia dies and his son becomes High Lord Elgon II (the Golden)
* 1329 - The Eighth School of Magic, the School of Seers is created at the College of Magic.

* 1327 - A Magic Users Guild School is established in Ostia to find, educate and prepare children with talent to attend the College in Shandrilos
* 1326 - First Grand Council of the Wildlands of Darylor meets, pushed for by the new Archmage Baden Erin in response to the alliances formed to defeat the Goblin invasion. They agree to meet every two years to discuss trade and greater unity for protection
* 1325 - Death of Melkor Erin, first Archmage of the College of Magic in Shandrilos. Baden Erin elected as second Archmage of the College. In the wake of the Goblin invasion, Katurem sues for peace and signs treaties to secure itself as an independent province provided it destroys its links with the Thieves guild.
* 1324 - Goblin invasion of the Province of Ostia. The young fighter Mage, Elgon son of the High Lord earns the name 'The Golden' for his brash leadership, golden hair and armour. Laird Madraig of Redvale earns a name for himself in the battles against the Goblins, as does Sir Arleas Di Mardul and Raban Ironhand. The forces of all the provinces in the Wildlands are sent to aid Ostia. This is the first time provinces join forces
* 1323 - Elgon the Wise establishes his court as a centre for learning. Scholars and artists are invited to attend and establish themselves. Xameran Uth Altor becomes the youngest Master in the history of the College of Magic
* 1319 - Torunsport declares war on Katurem to curtail its growing power. The war lasts for the next five years
* 1317 - Arkadi Talcost born in Ostia
* 1314 - Xameran Uth Altor joins the College of Magic
* 1309 - Elgon, son of High Lord Elgon the Wise joins the College of Magic
* 1308 - Katurem begins to spread it influence and take control of isolated communities on the edges of the provinces of Karodracia and Torunsport. It also starts to set up those who serve the thieves guild from the wilds and from the empire with land increasing its population
* 1300 - Act of Dissemination - In an effort to spread the toleration and use of magic in the Wildlands, the College sends masters to establish small 'guildhalls' in other cities and provinces. These

are established in the Nordic provinces of Arondar, Ostia, Dunard and Dunegan.
* 1299 - Thieves guild has successfully set up small groups in the provinces and cities of Ostia, Torunsport, Kalizern and Lauria. In this year their actions bring about an organised response. The thieves are hunted and Katurem is attacked and sacked, but quickly rebuilds.
* 1297 - Xameran Uth Altor born in Varitia
* 1295 - Alinus Quan Sirona leaves the College of Magic to go north in pursuit of a vision. He takes most of the Sironacian Monks with him. He founds the settlement of Sironac and begins construction of a Grand Abbey and monastery in the northern wilds.
* 1293 - Sironacian Order establishes small chapter houses in Kalizern, Lauria, Ostia and Hadek Provinces to spread their order and gain new adherents
* 1291 - Elgon, son of High Lord Elgon the Wise is born in Ostia
* 1290 - Third Act of Governance - Shandrilos establishes itself as a province with formal treaties with Ostia and Lauria agreeing its northern and southern boundaries. The Shandrilosi Guard are established. The new leadership of the College is included in the governance laws
* 1289 - Act of Formation - The separate sections of the school are formed as seven separate schools in their own right with an elected leader and the schools are united into the College of Magic with its first Archmage, Melkor Erin elected.
* 1280 - Katur the Pirate sets up the hidden port and fort of Katurem and establishes his so-called Thieves guild
* 1279 - Baden Erin and Eliantha Shamass born in Shandrilos
* 1278 - Alinus Quan Sirona and a group of his followers flee the Empire and arrive in the Wildlands. They are welcomed in Shandrilos and form a sixth section of the school of magic, focusing on holy clerical magic. Sironacian Order of Monks founded. Missionaries are sent south to recruit more to the Sironacian cause.
* 1275 - High Lord Angar of Ostia dies. His son Elgon the Wise becomes High Lord
* 1267 - Act of Separation - School of Magic, due to expansion, creates five separate sections outside of the main school to focus on

specific areas of magic (sorcery, wizardry, enchantment, Druidic magic and combat magic)

* 1263 - Act of Mastery - formalisation of the rules of the school of magic users in relation to levels of mastery. The formal ranks of Adept, High Adept, Master and Grandmaster are created along with the development of initial trials and examinations for each.
* 1260 - Second Act of Governance - The council of magic users take control and responsibility for the administration and protection of all communities in the Shandri Valley with the agreement and support of Ostia
* 1255 - Act of Municipality - With the expansion of its size and population, Shandrilos is officially acknowledge as a city state
* 1253 - Angar, High Lord of Ostia, sends his son, Elgon to study at the school of magic with the Druids.
* 1246 - Atholl Dorard born in Shandrilos, grandson of Borric Dorrard, first leader of the community on Shand Island
* 1240 - Act of Governance - formal rules are established for the leadership and administration of the school of magic, the towns of Shandrilos and Port Shandri, and the smaller communities on the island of Shand. The council of magic users overseas the governance of these towns and communities
* 1239 - Elgon, son of High Lord Angar of Ostia is born
* 1237 - Town of Port Shandri founded. It is founded in the former main camp of the Ostian forces that blockaded the town. It becomes the second town controlled by the council of magic users and the first territory off the island of Shand
* 1236 - Act of Foundation - First formal school of magic established by Melkor Erin in the Elder ruins on the island of Shand
* 1232 - Melkor Erin brokers a deal with the Druids and the Ostians to end the blockade and allow Shandrilos to survive. He also gets the Druids to agree to them continuing to practise magic provided the Druids are allowed to supervise and have a presence on the island.
* 1228 - Shandrilos expansion draws the attention of the Druids from Ostia who convince the young High Lord of Ostia, Angar to attack the town. Shandrilos fights back and holds off the Ostians with a combination of magical force and its location on an island. Ostian forces set up a blockade of the island.

* 1225 - Alinus Quan Sirona is born in Carnacus in the Holy Alban Empire
* 1220 - Melkor Erin first meets the young dwarf, Storlin Swiftaxe and begins developing ties with the dwarven Swiftaxe clan
* 1215 - Town of Shandrilos established on the island of Shand as the magic users community expands and attracts river traders and artisans. It is led by a council of magic users.
* 1210 - Bruenor Brae is born
* 1201 - Melkor Erin born in the small community of magic users on the island of Shand
* 1199 - After the persecution of 'ungodly' magic users by the Nordic Druids a group of magic users flee the Nordic provinces and set up a secret refuge on the island of Shand led by Borric Dorrard
* 1194 - Nordic Druids, responding to the rise of practitioners of dark ungodly magic and the influence of Albanite Clerics, begin a persecution of magic users in Tutonia and Calonia
* 1144 - Trade Wars end with the Accords of Alleyn. The Olmecs agree to set up the merchant guilds in all cities to mediate trade and give a fair share to all and acknowledge each cities provincial territories. The guilds of bankers and moneylenders, traders, ship captains and rivermen, entertainers and artists, scribes and scholars, craftsmen (tailors, carpenters, wheel wrights, brewers, tanners, smiths, farriers, jewellers, bakers, apothecaries, barbers, builders, butchers, etc.), mercenaries and guards, and hunters and trappers are established.
* 1137 - Lauria begins to exert its influence and seeks to control Hadek and Karodracia. Torunsport and Kalizern oppose it. Trade Wars begin.
* 1134 - The Nordic provinces acknowledge each other's land rights and establish rough boundaries to their territories and to those of the neighbouring Olmec provinces. Ostia, Dunard, Arondar and Dunegan agree treaties with Lauria and Kalizern
* 1123 - The trade post of Hadek rises to prominence and takes control of the trade between the Wildlands and Kilimar
* 1111 - Death of Saint Karodra the Traveller
* 1095 - Traders under the leadership of Declan Di Torun, fleeing the religious wars in the empire, sail across the Great Lake and set

up a free port on the shores of the Wildlands. Fishing and trade allow Torunsport to grow quickly
* 1093 - Saint Karodra and his followers found a monastery in the Wildlands. The town of Karodracia develops around it
* 1091 - Settlers from the Nordic lands and the Empire begin to migrate into the Wildlands to avoid the Wars of Succession and the later persecution of the Witch Hunters.
* 1075 - Battles amongst the Lairds of Arondar and Dunard force many to flee. Ostia is settled by those fleeing the conflict
* 1034 - The town of Arondar is first settled by exiles from Tutonia who are shunned by the rulers of Dunard
* 992 - Cumbran and Tutonian settlers migrate east into the Wildlands. The fort of Dunard is built
* 960 - Explorers from Calonia begin settling in the north west of the Wildlands. The fort of Dunegan is built to defend the settlers against goblin attacks
* 951 - During the Second Varitian Wars, the Kilimarian General, Antonines Kalizern, mutinies and leads his army and its followers north from Kilimar into the Wildlands. He sets up a permanent camp. This will later become the city of Kalizern
* 923 - Founding of the settlement of Lauria by Olmec people fleeing the Varitian Wars of Independence

DARK HORDE RISING

A thousand years have passed since the Elder Kingdoms were lost. Once the Elder races ruled all the northern lands and their knowledge and power were legend. What calamity befell them, none now know.

Centuries on and the north is a land where fell beasts and evil creatures roam unchecked, save in one place, the Wildlands of Darylor. Here mankind has slowly begun to explore and settle where once the Elder ruled, and within those lands, built amidst the ruins of a lost Elder city, lies the College of Magic. Inside, mankind seeks to rediscover the lost magics of old, but in secret one man desires the power to rule all and will stop at nothing to achieve his dream.

Meanwhile, in the city of Shandrilos, in the shadow of the College of Magic, a group of friends come together. Jon 'Bear' Madraig, fighter and mage, and his best friend the roguish swordsman and knight, Darin of Kenarth come to meet old friends and relive past adventures. The master mage, Arkadi Talcost and the beautiful druid, Rebba Korran, seek only to relax and enjoy some time away from the demands of their work and the College. For these friends, this is merely a reunion. However, for Zara Halven, the notorious Whore of Ostia, and for the monk, Garon Vale, the visit to Shandrilos is more; for one it is a chance for redemption and for the other it is a test of faith. Yet for the last of the friends, the visit to Shandrilos is the most important of all. For the huntress, Nat Bero it is a chance for forgiveness... and for revenge.

These friends will be caught up in events that will change their lives forever, for the secret behind the destruction of the Elder is about to come to light...

"The fate of all can be decided by the actions of one who the gods guide to the right place at the right time. Do not underestimate the power of even the lowest to affect the paths of the mighty..."

The words of the seeress, Ry'Ana White Eyes

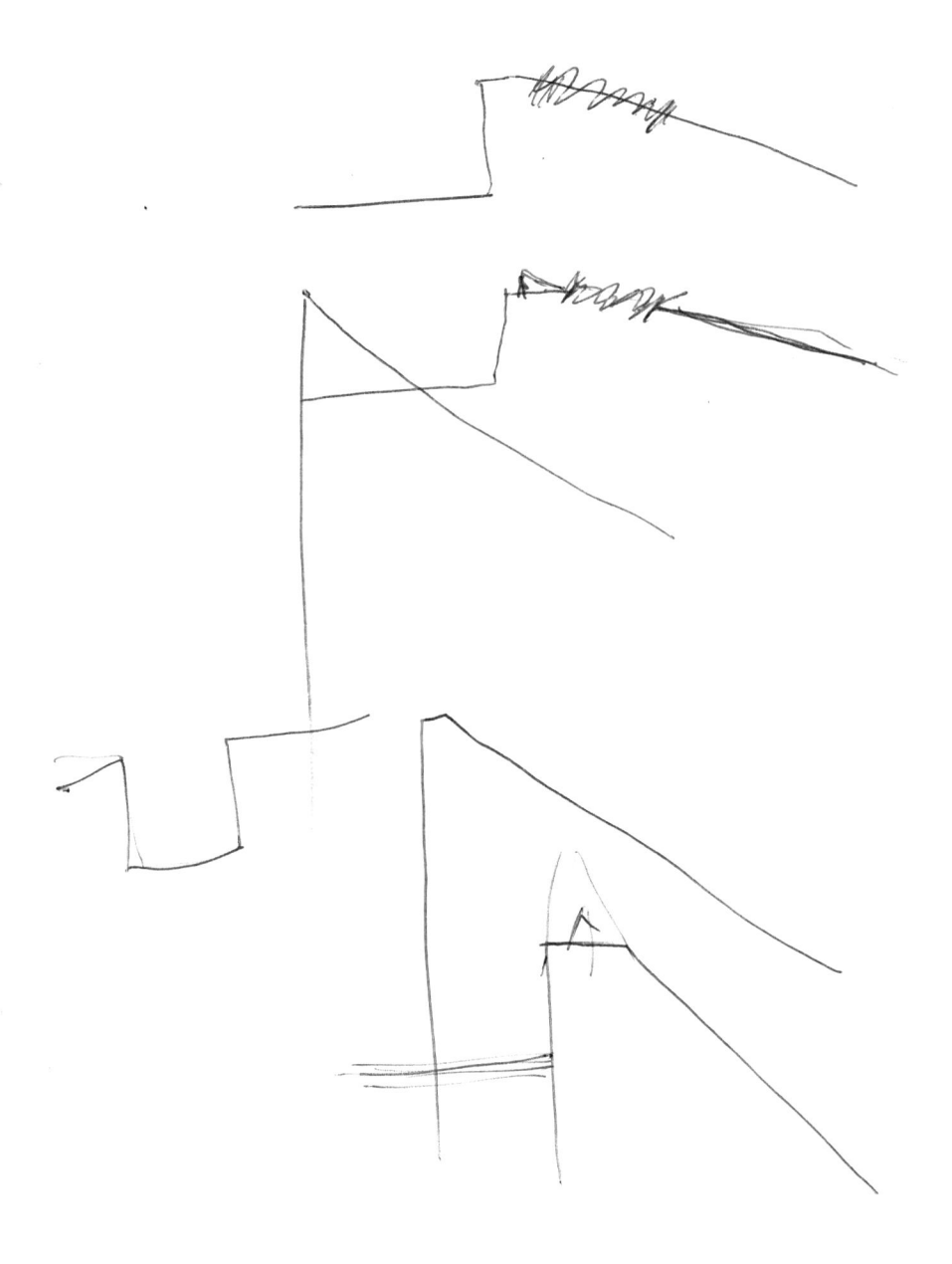

Printed in Great Britain
by Amazon